Ronald Frame

BLUETTE

The publisher acknowledges subsidy from the Scottish Arts Council towards the publication of this volume.

First published in Great Britain in 1990 by Hodder and Stoughton Ltd.

Sceptre edition 1991

Sceptre is an imprint of Hodder and Stoughton Paperbacks, a division of Hodder and Stoughton Ltd.

British Library C.I.P.

Frame, Ronald, *1953–*
Bluette.
I. Title
823.914[F]

ISBN 0-340-55109-7

Printed and bound in Great Britain for Hodder and Stoughton Paperbacks, a division of Hodder and Stoughton Ltd., Mill Road, Dunton Green, Sevenoaks, Kent TN13 2YA. (Editorial Office: 47 Bedford Square, London WC1B 3DP) by Clays Ltd., St Ives plc. Photoset by Rowland Phototypesetting Ltd., Bury St Edmunds, Suffolk.

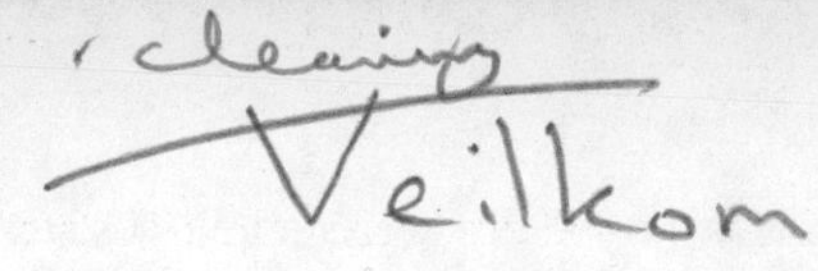

RONALD FRAME

Ronald Frame was born in Glasgow in 1953, and was educated there before going to Oxford. His first novel, WINTER JOURNEY, was joint winner of the first Betty Trask Award. He has since written several collections of stories and the widely acclaimed novels, SANDMOUTH PEOPLE and PENELOPE'S HAT. His plays for radio and television have received many critical plaudits; he won the Samuel Beckett Award for his first television play, *Paris*, and the Television Industries' panel judged him 'The Most Promising Writer New to Television'.

Also by Ronald Frame
and available from Sceptre Books:

A Long Weekend with Marcel Proust
Penelope's Hat
Sandmouth People
A Woman of Judah

For my mother and father

Contents

Part III Shooting Tigers

Part I

AQUAE-REGIS

'And have you seen the Bluebird,
Or heard the grass sing?'

M. Maeterlinck, *The Bluebird*

'. . . fading like the spine
Of an adventure novel behind
glass, behind the teacups.'

John Ashbery, *Houseboat Days*

1

Transport of Delights

'Hand in hand, lighter than birds, they vanished into the friendly dark, fragrant with flowers, lit with guiding stars.'

'The Tender Tale of Prince Jasmine and Princess Almond', in *Stories from The Arabian Nights*, retold by Naomi Lewis

FOLLOW the finger of Destiny.

Beyond Cairo and Basrah and Baghdad itself, City of Peace. Beyond the Green City, beyond the Magnetic Mountain and the Islands of Camphor and Crystal.

By the sacred seal of Suleiman, by the tombs of the ancestors! By Gog and Magog and the gyring stars!

Jasmine arbours; scented gardens of violet, myrtle, rose. Incense of nard, musk, ambergris. Feasts of lamb roasted with herbs; dishes of almonds and walnuts, baskets of fruit – grapes, peaches, figs, plums, dates, pomegranates, watermelons; spice cakes and pastries as light as air; jars of old mellow wine; sherbet drinks extracted from musk and snow and flavoured with amber. A lute plucked with a sharpened goose quill.

Emeralds, sapphires, amethysts, olivines, jacinths, coral, pearls, diamonds, rubies, turquoise, topaz.

Khalifahs and rope-makers. Wazirs, fakirs. Efreets, subterranean jinns and jinnees.

Benj, hashish, drugged potions. Bewitchment, imprisonment. Silken ladders, a raft of sandalwood. 'That all my cares should fly . . .'

'Esteem happiness before all else.'

'Evil doings produce an evil harvest, but the cultivator of good will glean the good he sows.'

'A beautiful virgin is more precious than diamonds; she is the soul's balm.'

Youth and beauty.

The ideals in both sexes are identical. Hair as dark as the hour of separation; skin of jasmine, of lily and narcissus, of pale magnolia, of silk; eyes black as plums, black as midnight pools; cheeks like full-blown roses, like two anemones; a nose like a sword; a mouth like a rose; hips like two full ripe melons; a waist like a bee, like a stalk, like a stem of wheat, like bamboo; a voice like a light west breeze soughing over a garden of flowers, sweeter than syrup of roses.

Beauty to disarm, to cause to swoon, like the silver moon among the stars.

'The old man brought forth a mirror, saying, "Here is the answer. Whenever you find a young girl of perfect beauty, with a reputation for purity, look in the mirror. If it clouds over, our search must still continue. But if the girl's likeness shines out clearly, your quest has come to an end." '

Locks and keys, hidden rooms.

The seventh door of the seventh palace, 'each with the taste of a dream'.

A slab of stone, and – beneath – a staircase of white marble, leading down to a brilliant hall of crystal and porcelain, pilastered with lapis lazuli; walls of shining green, like the core of an emerald. A marble slab, and – beneath – a cave, with twelve steps descending to a red copper door. A door in a rock, and – behind – a lucent lawn and a sparkling palace. A rock face splitting open, to reveal . . . the robbers' hall.

The sculptures of six beautiful girls, hewn from diamonds and raised on golden plinths. Woven gazelles, hung with chrysolites; tapestries of symbols that spell enchantment and desire.

The rukh bird so huge and strong that it can lift an elephant in its beak. A carpet that is carried in a fisherman's pocket: to a nail is tied a spindle-thread, and when he turns his back and walks away the carpet weaves itself of its own accord. A ring which can shoot a magic ray and send a man's head spinning from his neck. A boatman with an elephant's head. Necromancer's sand – the fine sand of knowledge, both light and dark. The fabulous sea rose of the Princess Brow of Lilies in China, which restores sight to the blind. A sugar cake which allows the eater to fly through the air. A camel which places its front feet in a bowl of water, rears its hind legs, dives fore-quarters first into the water, and disappears from sight.

For five years the Sultan of the Nile is turned out of himself. He becomes a tethered and blindfolded ass with a migraine, working a waterwheel and eating stale, musty beans.

A little alabaster pot transforms a poor flax-spinner into a princess who wants for nothing. A dull copper lamp is instrumental in finally metamorphosing Ala al-Din, an indigent tailor's son, into the Emperor of China. Enchanted pins transubstantiate a girl to a dove.

An ivory tube with a crystal disc at one end, through which you will see whatever you wish to see. An apple as large as a melon, of which a single inhalation will cure any known fever or disease, even death itself. A carpet of rare magic which will speed you as fast as you can think, which no structure of man or storm of nature can impede. A flying horse of black ebony, filigreed with gold and studded with gems, which will carry its rider further in a day than the swiftest steed could travel in a year, over cities and forests and deserts and oceans.

The life and the dream indistinguishable.

Living possibly to the end of one's days in happiness.

King of the centuries, sultan of the ages. The show and spectacle of kingly wealth, the profound fear of losing royal honour and power.

A prisoner bound inside a sack of quicklime and tossed into the sea, under the windows of the palace itself.

Angel of Death. The Certain-comer, the invisible Tomb-builder, whom there is no avoiding. That which concludes the existence of sovereign and pauper alike.

' "If you persist in desiring to know what you should not – " '

Sleepless, continuous melancholy. Kut al-Kulub, the Food of Heart, drugged and walled up inside a vault. Cages of singing birds.

Dervish robes. A garden of books, a library comprising coffers and shelves of scented wood.

Enchantment, desire. Silken ladders. An unknown princess, as fair as the moon, borne inside a magnificent palanquin. Love and transfiguration. Dog of wazirs but ah, Moon of Moons!

'Once in the days of long ago' . . . 'Legends tell' . . . 'In antique time'

. . . 'In ancient annals' . . . 'A curious and marvellous story' . . . 'This strangest of tales is told' . . .

*

They travelled there and back on a rug.

Not *any* rug would suffice, Catherine learned: it had to be a particular one, which happened – conveniently, but a little shockingly – to lie on the floorboards of her own bedroom.

Her mother called it a 'Turkey rug'. Village women had lost their eyesight working the stitches. Silk was woven into the wool on the loom, and as the women sewed their lives were woven into the design. While their eyes grew dimmer, they remembered and imagined on the points of their needles. Minarets, archways, the patterns of streets and gardens, the shapes of animals, large-headed or long-legged, depending on whether their chief attribute was guile or speed; skeins dyed in vats became the colours of blood or rubies, sky or lapis, of the gradations of light between dawn and nightfall; of water, of clouds, of the distance between cities, of sap in the leaf, of lost places, of the lovers' happy-ever-after, of Allah's heaven.

Her mother told her one evening, lying stretched out beside her on the narrow bed. Catherine was so close she could hear the liquid motions of her body, remembering them to understand later in her life: the blood, the milk, the saliva, the juices of her stomach, the waters in her womb. They lay together with the curtains left open and the sky darkening over Aquae-Regis, in the blue light of the gas fire. It was a rare and delicious proximity for Catherine, to have her mother to herself like this: and her mother, for once, seemed to have no concerns beyond here and now; she wasn't eyeing the condition of the room or attending to herself in a mirror or glancing at her watch or lapsing into one of her silences or turning her mouth in the fretful way she did when she was 'in company'. She was quite still and composed, the words were like featherweight secrets between the two of them, the watch – fastened to the wrist she'd placed beneath her head on the pillow – was silenced and forgotten.

'But why is it *here*?' Catherine felt herself obliged to ask, incredulous that it *was* here. 'The rug?'

'I suppose it has to be *somewhere*,' her mother said, reasonably enough.

'Is it the only one?'

'Like itself, yes.'

Then her mother told her about the fault always incorporated into the work, to signify the humility of humans before the all-seeing, perfect One.

'Have you found it?' Catherine asked.

'One of the borders sort of hiccups. The pattern, it repeats itself for an inch or two.' Her mother sighed, very softly. 'Your father told me that the shop he bought it from took five guineas off the price when he pointed it out to them.'

'*Father* bought it?'

There was the fleetest of hesitations.

'When we were furnishing the room for you, yes.'

'What if somebody else had bought it?'

'But they didn't. It was bought for *you*.'

'But what if they *had* bought it?'

'Then it would have been meant to happen. In that way. We have to judge from what *did* happen, though.'

Catherine lay considering.

'Can we choose what happens?'

Another hesitation followed the question.

'Well, in a way.'

'Good things?'

'Not always. Not even the right ones sometimes. But – but they're inevitable – '

'Because we choose them?'

Catherine heard her mother's head turning on the pillow, to look at her.

'Not "choose", really. It seems like that, but – something draws you: or *you*'re drawn. It's as if it's meant to happen: and you can't do anything else. If you try – not to let it happen – then it's all the surer to: it's as if, because you're deciding it isn't going to happen, then that must be part of the plan too. Do you see?'

But it was turning to double dutch for Catherine, and anyway she was starting to lose her interest in the subject. She lay looking up at the ceiling, where the gas flames threw long shadows. The wooden bars at the end of her bed suggested the spokes of a fan, then of a wheel, and gradually she was enticed into the motion of a waterwheel. A few moments later she was staring at the radial streets leading from a city: the silk road, the jade road, the gold road, the almond road, the oil road, the slave road.

'Don't you think so, Catherine – ?'

She had to say sorry, to ask her mother, think about what?

When her mother spoke, she had a laugh in her voice, but a kindly one.

'That the rug was meant for a dreamer like you?'

2

Aura

DANIEL Defoe, viewing the town on his approach from Seraphim Tor, called it 'the noblest prospect' not only in the West Country but in the whole of England, and one possessing 'the most subtile aura'.

Aquae-Regis is now twice the size, and the original prospect has been obscured and subtracted from (quite literally: too many boulders have swung from cranes), but the dignity and spectacle remain. Circuses, squares, malls, promenades, colonnades; the Abbey, the Roman Baths, the New Cross Baths, and King's Pump Room, the Assembly Rooms, the Nonagon Room, the Rotunda, the Pantile Walk; gardens, grottoes, river-groves, follies. Belvedere Hill, Beaulieu Hill, Paradise Hill, Vanbrugh Steet, Medlicote Street, Jamaica Street, Leycester Street, Potiphar Crescent, Clare Place West and East, Richmond Row, Prideaux Place, Kinges Dike, The Meads, Sion Buildings, Blue Walk, Virgil Grove.

This is the great *urbs occidentalis*. Ranged on its hills, it is raked like an amphitheatre. Strutting on its stage, men and women perform the stories of their lives. It's quite true: England offers nothing else quite like it for magnificence of prospect or aura. The waters have cured 'Lepre, Pokkes, Scabbes, & great Aches', and restored youth to the elderly; they have long had a reputation for inducing fertility in the childless, and have undoubtedly given generations of plain women faith in their beauty; over centuries they haven't made dull men wise or turned the loveless into whole persons but they have held death at bay awhile. All told, dreams have survived here with remarkable tenacity and acquired the grain of reality; memories have stirred and risen like revived blood, and anxieties have drained away to the body's extremities as when rest follows immersion and the blood ebbs.

Vivat Aquae-Regis! Fabled and fabulous. The town is dignity, courtliness and nobility, and wherever possible it proclaims the mathematical virtues of order and symmetry. Heat like a flannel poultice, breeze-wafted clouds of thistledown, green skies, forked blue lightning. Invalid carriages, colonial widows, feisty colonels, bounty-hunters. Visions and chimeras: sanguine expectation and hope forlorn. Joie de vivre, desideratum: madness, despair. Love, death.

3

Phantasmagoria

HER mother showed her the cunning of shadows, to conceal their identity: the personalities to be read on walls and ceilings – a hook-nosed face in profile, a grasping talon. With a light behind her, she used sleight-of-hand to release a flying owl from her fist, or a nervous twitching rabbit. When she asked Catherine to reach up with another of her letters to post, she told her that the slit in the pillar-box was a 'mouth' to feed, that without its diet of envelopes the postbox would lose its scarlet colouring and waste away. The tall, rake-thin lamplighter, she said, lived inside a lamp-post himself. Long canvas awnings above the upstairs windows in a certain house were heavily drooping eyelids; a particular hill they could see from the drawing-room window, almost into the next county, was an old woman lying on her side in bed, and the sunset was the glow of her candle; two birch trees in Marchmain Square which slouched together were 'up to no good'; a padlocked door in a garden wall, with scales of green paint hanging from the wood, was an entrance into the paradise their own hill was named after; the rushing of wind in the trees at night was the ghost of fire; it was the surly knife-grinder with his sparking wheel who kept the kitchen objects enchanted in a deep sleep – the dancing saffron-yellow saucers and cups, the jigging skip-legged ladles, the baritone clock with the wide grin, the pouting crocks, the vain and mutually admiring copper bains-marie, the conniving knives which would murder them all in their beds if they could.

When her mother taught her to write, every letter of the alphabet acquired an individual identity, as did each of the numerals: so that when she re-encountered them they all seemed to be acquaintances, even when her task was tedious, such as a thank-you note. Her mother told her of the travels which food had taken to reach their table, how every item of fruit and every single vegetable had a story, and all because they wanted Catherine Hammond to have the pleasure of tasting the flavour they'd kept fresh for her and for her alone. Her bed on the Turkey rug was a raft of dreams that took off in flight in the night but always brought her safely back, guided by the low flame in the gas bracket on the wall; anyway, it would never desert the other articles of furniture that were brothers and sisters to it, and painted the same shade of powder blue – the dressing-table, the wardrobe, the chest of drawers, the high-backed chair, all made from wood sawn from pine trees that grew together in the same corner of a Norwegian evergreen forest. If – so her mother once told her, being caught by chance in the very act – she tore up a letter and dropped the pieces into a coal fire, the eye of the moon alone read the secret message written there and divulged it to no one else: the same moon which when it was roundest and fullest turned people out of themselves, to live out their most private wishes, but afterwards would shrink to a cusp, a sliver, then a mere paring, while the seas recovered their tranquillity and the world seemed a more reasonable, bearable sort of place. And mirrors . . . When you had your back to one, how could you be sure that it showed anything at all then? – but turning round and looking straight at it again, you had to look very hard, to see that it really was the image of yourself and not a clever trick, because even flesh there was ice-cold to the touch, a mirror never but never felt warm.

'All of Aquae-Regis could be fitted into the kitchen ice-cellar.'

Catherine would stare after such a pronouncement but say nothing. The illogic could never be sustained for long, and yet those were the times when her mother seemed surest of herself, when she spoke to her as if she weren't a child but another woman.

'They lock up pears here, but they give you apples.'

'Everything belongs in the water. Forwards and backwards. To flow back, you see – '

'The stones in Tobago Street tell me. The voices.'

'Kabuki, Bunrahu. Hand-puppet-shadow. Marionettes in our pretty boxes.'

Her mother spent more and more time listening to the wind in the trees, until she interrupted a night-time story in her bedroom to tell Catherine that at last she could hear them all simultaneously: surging sea, raging fire (consuming driftwood), the screaming of beach shingle (the detritus of antediluvian sea mountains).

*

A scream.

Single, piercing.

When Catherine ran to the banister and looked over it, she saw her mother lying spread-eagled on her back, on the bottom steps of the staircase.

She started running downstairs, too shocked to think to call for help. But on the third or fourth tread above her head, she stopped.

Her mother was lying quite motionless. Her eyelids were closed.

Catherine could hardly breathe. She began swaying on her feet and reached out for the banister rail. Her mother was quite still, like stone. She listened to the silence, sifting down through the house, layer on layer on layer. A skewer of sunlight fell through the fanlight above the door, a long thin pointed spear resting on the wooden floor, stopping a few feet from her mother's knee.

The silence swirled, massed, came crowding down the staircase behind her. It nudged her in the small of the back. Do something, do *something* . . .

She moved down on to the step beneath, then on to the step beneath that one. She couldn't see any breath in her mother's body. She watched with her eyes wide: until they were filling with tears, the figure blurred, and she had to blink, blink again, so that she didn't lose these moments. They were on the point of being taken away from her, for ever.

A sob rose into her throat. She called out. She stared through tears, terrified for the loss.

Then, magically, her mother's eyes slowly opened. They looked up into the silence. Her dead mouth was transformed, gradually, into a smile.

Simultaneously a key was pushed into the lock of the front door, the handle turned, and the door swung open. Catherine watched the spectrum of expressions on her father's face as he ran forward – consternation, panic, terror, confusion, incredulity, anger.

Her mother, lying prostrate between them both, started to laugh. The sounds arose, spiralling, into the soaring forest of silence. Light and careless, quite inconsequential party laughter.

Catherine was frightened by it. Then by her father's reaction to it.

'Get up!' he said. 'Get up!'

But her mother only laughed more.

'Did you hear what I said, Marguerite? Get up, for God's sake.'

Her mother lay just as she was.

'What the *hell* do you think you're playing at?' The words imploded. 'Just *what* in God's name – '

He stared past her.'

'Catherine, go upstairs at once. Up to your room. And don't come out – '

She turned without a second bidding. The laughter continued, less partyish now, with a shriller ring. It accompanied her upstairs, to the gallery, where she stopped and turned and looked back.

Her father was tugging at her mother's arm, trying to get her to her feet, trying to bring her to her senses. But she lay on the stairs in the same state of abandonment as before, staring straight above her into space, laughing at the absurdity of it.

'Marguerite! Please – someone's going to see. For God's sake, Marguerite – snap out of it!'

But she was impervious to him, to the attitude of reason.

'Why are you doing this to me? Marguerite? What's happened? Why's it got to be like this?'

Catherine ran from the spectacle of them both. She climbed the second flight of stairs, but she couldn't get away from the laughter, which seemed to be twisting and gyring past her. The effect scared her, how it wouldn't stop, now nothing her father said and none of her own wishing could control it, it just unwound and unwound, longer and longer and looser and looser and too far now to be forgotten about as if it might never have happened, because it so unmistakably *had*, and she didn't honestly know how things could ever be again the way they used to, if this wasn't the day when all that past from yesterday backwards stopped belonging to them.

*

The cottage stood beside a wood, in its lee. A beaten path led along the edge of a corn field to a stile, to another path, and to a second stile. Beyond that a narrow lane meandered downhill between high hedges and lush verges. Where the flinty lane petered out, steps were cut into the gully between two cliff-faces. By turns and twists the sixty-six steps descended to a horseshoe-shaped cove of white sand and gently shelving shore, with the rusted skeletal wreck of a small tramp-steamer neatly lying against sheer cliff at one extreme end of the hideaway bay.

For two or three weeks they lived, mother and daughter, between the thickly green, fragrant copse and the turquoise salt sea. They made the journey to the cove and back a couple of dozen times at least, and the days in recollection were to be unfailingly blue and warm. As they walked they held hands and talked or sang, and they scarcely ever saw anyone else. It might have been at the world's end, or an island marooned in an ocean, not a particularly out-of-the-way corner of Devon chosen for its very remoteness and its countervailing cheapness. The latter may have been indisputable, but not finally the former, as her mother discovered on the washing-day their new domestic rituals were intruded upon so brusquely. Between the pistol reports as the white sheets bellied with wind on the line, they listened to the unwelcome sounds of a car's engine grinding in the lane. Her mother gathered her up and whisked her inside but already their fate was sealed. They hid in the airing cupboard at the top of the steep staircase, but their visitors had a key and something inside the black hole – perhaps a polleny residue garnered among the folded towels – caused Catherine to sneeze, and her mother wasn't quick enough to anticipate it and to hold her nose in the darkness. But the two men and one woman were professionals, and they did locate them; they lifted the latch on the door and out tumbled their secret, which hadn't been as secret as it needed to be. All this special time was immediately being undone, it worked free with gunshot clarity and floated off skywards like a great white windy sail, high above halcyon Devon and into the nameless, placeless ether.

The house was locked up behind them after her mother had made a rapid selection of the items they would need.

The car was hot and stifling inside, and her mother – placed in the front passenger seat – asked that the windows be opened please, which they were. From where she was sitting in the back, between the woman and one of the men, Catherine smelt for the last time the piney tang of the copse where at night they'd heard the gamebirds squawking and foxes barking and fallow deer (so it always seemed) crying. She tried to catch the flavour of the briny sea, but could only smell the car's exhaust, trapped like the heat in the tunnel of hedge and thicket.

Her mother sighed, as if it was all too silly but only to be expected. The man who sat behind her asked if she was feeling all right, and she didn't reply. A voice burbled from the speaker on the dashboard panel, relaying a coded message from police headquarters. The woman behind the driver said what a lovely day it was turning out to be, and – clearly visible to Catherine through the windscreen – the car's radiator grille pointed uphill into a cloudless, unforgettable azurine sky.

4

Davaar

IN the summer of 1937 they spent three weeks at a hydropathic hotel in a spa town in the Scottish Trossachs: 'they' being Catherine, her father, and her Aunt Dorothea, her father's only and unmarried sister. North they had come, while her mother elected to stay on in Aquae-Regis; she had been sorry to see Catherine go, but the prospect of the hydro clearly didn't appeal to her at all. Catherine's father must have known that very well, and taken it for a certainty that he would have his daughter to himself for these twenty days.

That wasn't quite the case, as events turned out, as he must also have understood before they set out on the long train journey to Glasgow and beyond. Because it just so happened that, living in the town in a modest rented house paid for by a group of modish-thinking Edinburgh medical alumni, was one of the Jewish refugees from the new and perplexing Germany, a pre-eminent child psychologist by the name of Doktor Elisalex Mandelbaum.

The first afternoon Catherine's father pretended they had lost their bearings on a walk through the town, along the grid formation of wide back roads. They stopped outside a red sandstone cottage with prickly sea-urchin shells by the front door, and a straight path bordered by white pebbles, and neat brown-painted palings and a trim gate. At their approach a figure moved behind the twitching net curtain, the front door was pulled open, and out from the vestibule with its mounted pair of stag's antlers stepped a small woman wearing, beneath a short collarless loden-cloth jacket, corduroy knickerbockers tucked into thick socks and Morschstiefel boots. Her grey hair was wound up into a bun and held in place with a criss-crossing, needle-and-fabric contrivance of Madam Butterfly complexity, giving – to the child, when the woman with her long, thin, possibly overbred face smiled at her – a skull-and-crossbones effect.

The introductions were made over the front gate, with only an approximate attempt at authenticity. Even Catherine could guess what she only established as a fact in her adulthood, that this meeting was scarcely a surprise, not even an accident: indeed it had been contrived by an exchange of letters and consultations with doctors extending over the previous eleven or twelve weeks. Doktor Mandelbaum hadn't met either of the parents, so the initial formalities were authentic to a degree: she spoke over Catherine's head for several minutes, very soon striking up a directness and immediacy which seemed to take her interlocutor father aback, before she turned her attention to her principal subject of interest, Catherine herself.

Her subsequent visits to the cottage called Davaar had been suggested ostensibly as a throwaway remark that first afternoon, but they too had been planned and paid for in advance: seven outings all told, at regular three-day intervals, 'sessions' in effect.

On the other side of the War that was coming, Catherine would read articles about Doktor Mandelbaum and her techniques – none of the pieces specialised, but only what appeared in daily newspapers and in magazines – and would realise that she had been one of two or three dozen research cases directed the doctor's way at a time when new subjects were crucial for her work, which had had so many stops and fitful starts imposed upon it by historical circumstances far beyond her own control or gainsaying. It was admitted that, occasionally, concerned parents – forward-thinking or merely desperate – were talked into submitting their children for 'examination', which customarily failed to bring about the desired changes and improvements in their behaviour. She was not a practical psychiatrist, delivering observable results, but a theoretician in the academic van. At that period, 1936–8, she had been especially interested in the child's use of fantasy in his or her imaginative life, the levels of belief and disbelief and the vital middle ground of partial belief. Before and afterwards she treated the compelling favourite among the topics she was surely making her own, the elements of violence in children's behavioural patterns, but *then* her studies had taken her along an intriguing by-road: neither a cul-de-sac nor a diversion, but the 'high' road to the 'low' or vice versa, a complementary route selected on the longer journey.

Catherine was always to wonder how much she had been able to provide the woman with in respect of raw material. Doktor Mandelbaum's subtlety was eximious, and expert. On each visit she served up a pot of tea and always had the brew far too strong, being a coffee drinker herself and uncertain just how tea *ought* to taste. When they drank it out of doors, Catherine sometimes slopped her cup (unseen, she imagined, although the magazine articles were to prove otherwise) into a flowerbed; but she did enjoy the accompanying slice of rather sickly and ungainly Swiss jam roll bought from the baker's on the main street, where the sturdy cakes competed for attention in the front window with the unappetising strips of sticky orange flypaper. Doktor Mandelbaum never ate herself, but seemed to take pleasure in the spectacle of her guest doing so. She apparently never tired of listening to her repeat the stories of her magic carpet excursions, and Catherine was happy to answer all the questions she was asked about her mother. Latterly, the only time she was conscious of themselves was when the grandfather clock interrupted with its quarter-chimes or the ponderous announcing of the hour: Doktor Mandelbaum would glance across at the case and pendulum with instant irritation, but only because she knew the noise might prove a distraction in the telling of some recollection she had already been several minutes preparing for.

And so their afternoons passed – for Catherine in contented ignorance of their eventual significance. It might have been that she could have gleaned a clue from her aunt's nervousness whenever she came to collect her at the house, the immediate outstretching of her hand to claim her, to lead her by the hand from the cottage of undercooked gingerbread, through the small garden of lollipop sunflowers and dahlias to the gate, and only letting her tension relax – transferred along her arm via her wrist to the hand that smoothed her hair – once the latch on the gate had rattled shut behind them. Back at the hydro, each time they returned, her aunt would present her with a postcard she'd bought – a black and white view of the turreted pile, or of the golf course, or of a deserted Sunday Main Street, or of Loch Katrine – and she would ask her to please write a few lines they could then post to her mother in Aquae-Regis. The tea in the hotel was weak enough to placate the feeblest constitution, but Catherine on consideration preferred the tar-black infusion which trickled into their cups through the leaf-clogged spout, because there in Davaar as she sipped from the fluted rim she was unloaded of that burden of being a child – Doktor Mandelbaum treated her as an equal, as her mother did, and she was able to say what she wanted, without having to watch her p's and q's (as her father, no longer on home ground, insisted – perhaps chastened by the example of those douce disciplinarian Scots parents in the hotel) and without her aunt's hapless but well-intentioned speaking down to her, as if she were only half thc age she really was.

On the last afternoon at Davaar Catherine looked through from the narrow hall into the kitchen-scullery at the back, but without being seen: Doktor Mandelbaum had thrown in a fourth heaped spoonful of tea-leaves 'for the pot' and was cutting a thick slice of Swiss roll. When she'd found a plate in the larder to put it on, she leaned forward to open the window, then she sank her fingers into the remaining log of yellow sponge and oozing plum jam, screwed her mouth up with distaste, and flung the object outside; calorie-laden, it thundered into the dustbin. Doktor Mandelbaum was smacking her hands together with satisfaction when she spotted the watching eyes in the little square of mirror nailed to the wall above the sink.

For several seconds, as each stared at the other, they were balanced in perfect equilibrium. Then Doktor Mandelbaum took a few steps forward; at the door of the kitchen her knees buckled and she stumbled. Catherine didn't know – she was never to know – what happened in the next few moments that they should have ended up as they did: Doktor Mandelbaum kneeling on the floor, howling out her tears, and Catherine crouched beside her on the runner of tartan carpet. She was unable to speak herself, her heart was thumping, she couldn't think what she was supposed to do. When she found Doktor Mandelbaum showing her how to wrap her arms about her, she tried to oblige, because she was too afraid not to. The woman, dressed like a boy, stayed hunched where she was, resting in her arms. Catherine felt the woman's shivering, and wanted to pacify her. The bun had come undone and the hair was unfurling, more and more of it, fine grey Rapunzel tresses lying along the curve of her back. Catherine lifted it and let it fall, lifted it and let it fall. The tears stopped at last; the woman's frame was no longer shaking. Her eyes closed. Her face was suddenly lined and very old. Catherine's face was close enough for her to feel the breath riffling her own hair on her temple.

Some words were being said. Catherine listened over the heaving behind her ribs; she tipped her head at an angle to let Doktor Mandelbaum know that she was attending, trying to hear.

'Scotland – ' the voice aimed for clarity ' – is a little like my own land, Catherine. But in Bavaria the forests are even larger, greener: and sometimes so darkly green that they seem to be black. Will you let me tell you about it?'

Catherine wasn't able to move, couldn't have run away if she'd chosen to.

'Yes,' she said, breathing in and out through her mouth.

'You will?'

'Yes.'

'Where do I begin? Where do I begin . . .'

Catherine waited, with her arms still wrapped in a caress as she'd been shown.

'For a while,' Doktor Mandelbaum began, 'we lived on the edge of a forest. When I was *your* age or just a very little older. It was quite frightening – the forest – but it also drew me. I felt – I felt I couldn't go in alone. But there was no one about whom I might have asked – to come with me. So, I did the only thing that I could – I invented a friend. Then I *was* able to go into the forest.

'We looked for treasure, Lotte and I. An old woman in the village had told me that there was a hoard of gold and jewels buried somewhere in that forest. Perhaps it was only a legend from very long ago. Or it might have been that there really was a fortune hidden there, from one of the times of war. But *then* I didn't know to ask these questions. The woman had told me there was treasure, and I hadn't yet learned to disbelieve what people told me.

'The forest is a separate world, Catherine. So very still, but – if you really listen hard – *not* quiet at all. It's full of birds and animals where you can't see them. Sometimes I'd glimpse a pair of eyes watching me out of the darkness, but I'd talk to my friend to keep up my courage, and we might start to sing.'

She sang a few words, under her breath, but in that kitchen in the Scottish Trossachs the tune seemed elusive, and the song tiptoed back into the shade of the trees . . .

'It doesn't matter – '

'No,' Catherine said, propping her spine against a straight surface behind her and swallowing more air through her mouth.

'So it went on. Thus and thus. *Und so weiter*.' Doktor Mandelbaum found a second wind of breath. 'Until one day, walking on the forest floor, beneath huge trees like pillars that held the sky in place, I looked ahead and saw – myself! It *was* me, how I appeared in the mirror, with hair the same common blonde colour and wearing clothes I had in my wardrobe at home.

'I turned and ran away, not so much because I was afraid but because I wanted to check at home, to be sure that my eyes hadn't deceived me. When I got to the house, I stared at the face in the mirror, the flushed cheeks and drawn features, and I couldn't be sure that it was me. Then I ran upstairs to my room and I rattled open the creaky wardrobe door and my heart stopped beating for several seconds! The wardrobe was half-empty! All I could think was that another girl wore my clothes as well as I, that my parents kept a child they had told me nothing about. When my mother found me, lying on the bed and crying my eyes out, she couldn't understand. I wouldn't talk to her. I said nothing. She shook me, very hard. I still said nothing, not even about the clothes. When my father came home, they had a quarrel about me, and their voices rose higher and higher. My mother said she hated this place, that I was impossible living here, and my father blamed her for the state I was in, and she blamed him for not caring and leaving me with her all day long. She told him a child had been *his* idea, and he shouted back it had been *her* body which must have wanted to conceive me, and on and on they went.

'I got up later, in the middle of the night. I hadn't eaten, I hadn't allowed myself to. When I reached the kitchen, I found the clothes that had been missing from my wardrobe, hanging on pegs on the wall, newly washed and starched. As if, I thought, as if another person's presence had just been cleaned out of them. And looking, it struck me as if they were about to take a journey, a long important trip to somewhere else entirely.'

Doktor Mandelbaum moved her head several inches closer to Catherine's heart.

'And that's when I decided to run away. In the middle of the kitchen, long after midnight, I threw off the clothes I was wearing and exchanged them for the washed ones. I found some food, wrapped it in a handkerchief, opened the door, and stepped outside. The sky was full of stars. I found the northern ones, and turned beneath them. And then I set out.'

Catherine started stroking the soft, silken grey hair.

'Every so often as I walked I would lift a sleeve and sniff the cloth. It smelt of the forest, not of the house, and I was comforted by the aroma of pine about me. I reached a station and got on a train, and hid beneath a seat when the guard came round. I changed trains, and already I felt very worldly, very grown-up. In two days I'd travelled the length of my homeland, from the south to Hamburg in the north. The city police found me, and I was taken into their care. I watched the stars from the window in the house I was taken to, by the harbour, and I seemed to be reading there a story – like one in a book – which I told the woman who sat with me: that I was the child of a high-born lady by a handsome adventurer, that I had been sent away from the castle on the Rhine with a wet-nurse and brought up by her in a cottage in a forest. I offered my sleeve for proof, but the woman didn't seem to smell anything. "Which forest?" she asked me. "The wolf-forest," I said, and when she brought me an atlas and opened it I pointed to the darkness of the Carpathian Mountains on the page. "Romania?" she said, and I nodded.

'The police never found my parents – they didn't know where to look – I made up some words which I pretended were Romanian, but I could see they had their doubts – and my parents never managed to find *me*. I was shown to various people, prospective parents keen to adopt. Eventually I was taken into the house of a university couple who seemed especially interested in me, and there I stayed. My "home" was now an elegant white house in a leafy street, the Rothenbaumchaussee. It was full of carved tribal masks and desert island shells: all sorts of exotica. They wanted to hear about my life, but I – politely – told them nothing. Nothing at all, and always politely. My silence on the past only seemed to intrigue them more. They continued to ask me, in the kindly way they had; they tried to coax, tease information out of me, but I wouldn't say, and they marvelled. My new father devoted to me an entire chapter in a book he was writing, and he referred to me by a pseudonym in his lectures. Then they seemed to realise I really wouldn't, ever, talk about what I wanted so much to forget. I had taken well to my Hamburg life, you see, better than anyone could have anticipated; I was determined to make a success of my fresh start, and I wiped out all that had gone before.

'My new parents wanted me, wanted to care for me, more than my old ones had ever done. Sometimes I dreamed of myself in a Moses basket, floating down the Elbe and bobbing about in the harbour, among the ships, and I'd wake up knowing I'd found my proper home at last, which was only where I ought to have been all the time. As time passed the edges were knocked off me, smoothed down, and I acquired manners. I was never very graceful, or pretty, but I was liked. Once a couple, colleagues of mutual acquaintances, they were meeting my new parents for the first time and told them I really resembled my "mother", and their eyes passed between us, and all three of us were amazed, and we were so delighted too that we laughed and laughed, and couldn't stop.

'A happy ending, you see. My story had a – a – happy – ending –'

Catherine stared as the woman started to sob again, into her shoulder. She felt the motions of grief pushing her back flat against the door jamb, pinning her left arm to the wood. With her other arm she plucked at the cloth of the woman's jacket sleeve. When her mother cried, she had seen her father smooth the hair back from her face and temples; with the tips of his fingers he would retrace in reverse the tracks of her tears.

She touched the hair on the woman's brow, very hesitantly, but she seemed to remain unaware of the contact. The sobbing didn't stop. Catherine was close enough to see the pores of her skin, the tiny red veins under her cheeks, the lines like crackle-glaze at the corners of her eyes. From this vantage-point the nose, curved along its length and thick and pudgy at the wings, was out of proportion to the rest of the face.

Embarrassed, Catherine looked away, to the window. Above them on the hill, the trees appeared to grow straight out of the rock. A burn flashed among the bracken. A bird clattered heavily out of the gloom among the trees, and rose haphazardly into flight, wings squeaking. The silence descended again, rolling down on them, and she realised that the sobs had grown quieter. Also, she discovered, the rôles were being reversed, and now the woman was attempting to hold *her*. She felt an arm wrapping itself around her waist; she smelt the loden-cloth – a thick, dusty, almost woody odour. The other arm drew so close to her, the wrist passed so near to her ear that she quite clearly heard the ticking of the watch. The woman was trying to settle her breathing. Catherine politely kept her eyes trained on the window, on the four squares of hillside visible through the slightly wrinkled glass.

'I knew I could tell *you*, Catherine. That you'd let me tell you.'

The woman's chest pressed against hers.

'You're pretty – and sweet – and you're an unhappy child – '

Catherine blinked at the window, with surprise. Outside, fickle sunshine rippled the hillside with light and shadows.

'People can call to one another across the years.'

A sudden movement in the corner of her eye caused Catherine to swivel her head round. Her father stood in the hall, with his hat and gloves in his hand. Behind him the vestibule was filled with purplish clouds.

He walked towards them, overdressed for the town in an office suit.

'What – what's going on here?'

The woman didn't move. She lay slouched against her patient, with her legs crossing the green linoleum floor like scissors.

'Please tell me, Doktor Mandelbaum – what is the explanation – for all this – ?'

Catherine didn't dare to speak.

'Are my eyes – deceiving me – ?'

The woman seemed to grow heavier on top of her. She felt a rush of cramp in her left arm, the one she couldn't move, and she winced.

'Catherine, tell me what's been going on.'

She contorted her face as she tried to twist her arm free.

'Do you hear me, Catherine? Tell me the meaning of this.'

Afterwards, when he had freed her and hurried her away from Davaar, away from Doktor Mandelbaum who was again in tears, she spoke only sparingly, only discreetly of the incident. The closer her father questioned her, the more reluctant she became to divulge all that she might.

It had something to do with the look of a stranger that had come over her father's face: he didn't look like himself, and she was confused. She also sensed that something very *private* had taken place, without her father or her aunt being involved, without her mother being here to tell. It was the first time she'd had an experience they couldn't share with her, and already she was able to understand its significance on that account.

Her mother would cry sometimes, but hardly making a sound, and a suffocating hush would settle on the rooms which Catherine would feel trapping the breath in her chest; the house would feel like a church, her father would look shocked and heartbroken and put his arms around her mother, and they would none of them discuss the happening in words, respecting her mother's sorrow. This seemed no different, even though it concerned another person's sorrow.

Her father didn't hide his displeasure, however. Her aunt hummed and hawed, and tried to ask the same questions in a different way, but the words – like the ones Doktor Mandelbaum had sung – trailed away on her tongue, and she looked helplessly over her head towards her brother.

On their subsequent walks they avoided the intersecting back roads.

*

'And you talked about *me* too?' her mother asked her again, for the third time perhaps, for reconfirmation. 'You and your friend?'

'Not really,' Catherine said cautiously, 'my *"friend"*.'

'But you knew her well enough to tell her these things?'

'There was nothing else to do.'

'You should have run away,' her mother said, and smiled very seriously as she pictured it.

'Father would have found me.'

'Yes – '

Catherine watched her mother's pained smile fade.

' – yes, I suppose he would.'

'She made me tea. And gave me Swiss roll.'

'Viennese torte it should have been.'

'What's that?' Catherine asked.

'Oh, poor Catherine, how they used and abused you – '

Catherine stared at her.

' – but you knew not what you did . . .'

Her mother turned away. She fanned her fingers flat against the glass of the window. Catherine stared down dismally at the Turkey rug, sensing that she had somehow contributed to this hurt of her mother's.

She looked up at a sound and adjusted her eyes against the light through the window. A hand was concealing her mother's face from view, hiding the tears that had at last proved uncontainable.

5

Héjira

HER mother left Aquae-Regis one afternoon when Mrs Ramage had been talked into taking Catherine for a long walk.

She didn't return.

Walking back home, they didn't know of course. Mrs Ramage told her it might be best if they didn't let on they'd been sitting in Jasper's Tea-Rooms instead of taking fresh air into their lungs. Catherine, only when Mrs Ramage had repeated herself, agreed. But afterwards Mrs Ramage seemed to forget all about the business: not surprisingly, finding that life in the house had been turned on its head.

*

At the time it was all that her father, red-eyed after a sleepless night and chain-smoking, was able to tell her.

'Your mother's had to go away for a while. I don't know when she'll be back.'

Mrs Ramage somehow semaphored the news to the other houses in the Crescent. For the rest of that day Catherine was haunted by the deceit of yesterday afternoon: not briskly stepping out for exercise and reviving air as her mother had requested but sitting behind the window of dripping condensation in the tea-rooms. At one point Mrs Ramage had leaned forward, corset creaking, and rubbed on the glass; when she saw what she saw outside she let out a throaty 'Well, I never!' as heels sounded on the opposite pavement and – Catherine just glimpsed them – a couple of figures hurried past. But Mrs Ramage had shaken her head, as if she couldn't trust her eyes to see aright through such a steamy window as Jasper's, and promptly upturned the teapot and poured them both a cup of the strong, tarry brew.

That night Catherine could hear from her bed the knocks at the garden gate and a delay until the bolts were pulled back and women's voices parleying and speculating down in the lane. Her father was in the drawing-room, too restless and fidgety to sit in the one place for longer than a few moments, waiting for the telephone to ring. She didn't hear it ring, but she was in another part of the house and maybe she lost consciousness sooner than she meant to.

In the morning the routine was altered. Her father normally rose early, breakfasted alone, and had left the house for work by the time she and her mother were up on their feet and washing and dressing. This particular morning – as on the ones that followed – he was sitting at the table waiting for her when she pushed the dining-room door open. Mrs Ramage served them with her eyes all over the place and her co-ordination gone to sixes and sevens. Catherine found herself raised too high on an additional cushion, and felt very much more prominent than she wanted to be. Her mother wasn't even referred to, but she knew her presence was as definite as when she had been here in the house with them: in a sense she was even *more* 'here', since her mother was all she could concentrate on all through breakfast, and because she guessed from the loud, busy silences that her father and Mrs Ramage couldn't dwell on any other subject either.

*

Then she was sent away, without an explanation, to stay with her Aunt Dorothea in a small, scrubbed market town in Cumberland. She spent several weeks there, where the fields were so damply, insistently green and the air so sharp and pure to the taste. Her aunt's white-painted house faced directly on to the market square, but Catherine came to prefer the dark rambling back corridors and dusty attics above the garden outbuildings to the tidiness and shininess of the front rooms, inches from the pavement and flooded with that searching northern light which flushed into every irreproachable nook and cranny.

When her aunt took her back to Aquae-Regis, it was to a false semblance of the life she'd known before. She was prepared for her arrival at the solemn and silent house, but only as they were being driven from the station in a taxi. Her aunt told her that her mother had 'gone to a better place': which Catherine presumed meant somewhere beside the sea, or Paris, which she sometimes talked about. Her aunt explained what she'd meant. Her mother, poor Marguerite, had suddenly become very unhappy and sad.

'Because of me?' Catherine asked her.

'What?'

'Because I went to stay with you?'

'Oh *no*,' her aunt exclaimed, seeming shocked at her own tactlessness. She clearly couldn't think what to say, confronted with all a child's naïvety. But it had to be spoken, the word: *that* word.

Catherine's response was a simple, confounding 'Why?'

Her aunt repeated her.

'"Why?"'

'Why is she dead?'

'Because . . .'

Her aunt's face turned grey, and stayed like that all afternoon. She frequently dabbed at tears. Catherine's father didn't cry, but he looked exhausted, and almost forgot to open his arms as she ran into the house; he kissed her vaguely, hurting her with his stubble. The curtains were half-closed even in daylight, and their drawing-room smelt strongly of the white lilies, which her aunt herself removed and carried to a windowsill on the gallery. Her mother was waiting for her in her bedroom, but only briefly, behind her back, and when she spun round to the spectral figure she was conscious was standing in the corner of the room . . . she had gone. But she *had* been there, Catherine was quite certain: come to wish her a proper goodbye, to see her for the last time, to let her final moments in the house be with her.

After crowding her chest, the guilt of causing the grave unhappiness which had taken her mother's life subsided. Catherine sat down on the edge of the mattress. She thought she ought to be crying, but while the tears pricked in the corners of her eyes they didn't appear. Instead she sat remembering her mother, all that she possibly could about her; raising her eyes from the Turkey rug to look into the angle of the room to check that she wasn't still there, and concentrating all the time on her thoughts, afraid to lose even a single memory of the life they had shared like a secret compact in the house.

*

'I can't be the same,' her Aunt Dorothea told her. 'I can't be the same as your poor mother –'

Her father took command of the conversation.

'But your aunt will be staying with us from now on. Here in the house. To help to look after you.'

Catherine stared at them both.

'What about *your* house?' she asked.

'This will be my home now,' Aunt Dorothea said, reaching out her hand and stroking Catherine's hair, seeming to depend on that sense of touch.

Catherine nodded at the announcement. She liked her aunt. But at the very moment when she was feeling the most content since her return, she started to cry: not because she wanted to, nor because her mother had taken overwhelming possession of her thoughts, but because everything was so calmly, surely being taken care of, the changes were being effected which meant nothing would be the same again. She wept – although she couldn't know it – because she was helpless to protect the old life, because it was everything and nothing, because the other Catherine she had left behind there was whispering to her that she might still have guessed her mother's sadness, that if they could have lived it over again they might have been able to keep all the past alive between them.

*

At night her aunt read to her from books: a chapter from a novel normally, and with only one exception they were the novels of Frances Hodgson Burnett. Catherine had lost the thread of the story by the third or fourth chapter but she didn't say so; she travelled on the voice and the words into a semi-conscious state where she seemed to be hovering between everything that was – so knowable and sure – and everything that was *not*, which was uncertain and guessable only. She floated on will-power alone between the two conditions, levitating between certainties and possibilities until she forgot which was which, until she entered into the happy confusion and was released into the blissful unthinkingness of first sleep.

Her aunt had to go back to Cumberland, and Catherine went with her.

They had no sooner arrived than the auctioneers called by appointment to arrange the sale of the house.

The front rooms lost their tidiness and shine. Furniture was emptied into the back corridors; tea-chests impeded Catherine's movements at every turn; the attics became dustier as objects were dragged from their furthest recesses and all the old hiding-places and lairs were surrendered. The house wasn't the same at all, and it was an unsatisfactory visit.

Aunt Dorothea was excitable, attention spread among the competing parties – the auctioneers, their workmen, her niece, her solicitous neighbours and the prying townsfolk, telephone calls from her brother in Aquae-Regis. Catherine only spoke to her father once in four weeks, and she wondered why she had been brought here, to only add to the mayhem.

*

She discovered on her return that it had gone.

The rug.

The Turkey rug in her room.

She ran to her aunt, who told her she would have another one. Well, not another *rug*, a piece of carpet rather.

'But why?'

Her aunt said the room would be warmer for it, cosier, more of a piece –

Catherine shook her head. She watched her aunt worry her bottom lip with her teeth. She wasn't saying what she really believed. There *wasn't* a reason why the rug should have been taken away.

She asked her aunt where the rug was now.

'In a poor person's house, probably.'

She asked when she would have her replacement.

'Very soon. Very, very soon, Catherine.'

But that didn't matter. There had only been one rug intended for her room, her mother had told her so. Since her mother's leaving them, it had lost its magic. Some days she had found herself standing on it and nearly forgetting its powers. But she'd been living in hope (when she remembered to do so) that the travels would begin again, following the course mapped out for her by the words of her mother's tales.

6

Aura II

FOR Catherine the house was their home; it was where she had been born, and the occasional sightseers and architectural students who passed in admiring reverence along the Crescent were eminently overlookable.

Some years later, at her second school, she would be required to apply a little thought in preparing a description of the exterior for a prep essay.

Five storeys, Doric columns at ground level – Ionic above – and Corinthian above those. With a frieze pediment on top. And on top of that several curious identical stone sculptures like elongated acorns in their cups.

But the stone was black with soot and weather, and Catherine felt it was all rather beside the point. She quite often heard their special, mutual 'heritage' spoken about, but even so it was only the town where they all lived, and Eveleigh Crescent just happened to be her address. She had to live *somewhere*, didn't she?

It hadn't occurred to her that the prevailing silence in the house had anything to do with its sheer size, with the fact that there was so much unused and unusable space. The people they knew also occupied houses built, like theirs, to accommodate dependants, general hangers-on, and a complete retinue of servants. Everyone of their acquaintance was living out of their proper time, but the mania for dividing and letting was still a couple of decades off. It was difficult nowadays to distinguish between indigence and eccentricity: for instance, the gallery of Lady Astell's house was famous for its puddles and on rainy days when one excused oneself it was necessary to travel to the bathroom carrying an umbrella; the Berridges in Havana Street still kept horses for transportation, and because they were so afraid of losing them they had moved them indoors from the draughty stables, and because they prized them more highly than their housekeeper they were given the run of the ground-floor rooms.

In Eveleigh Crescent some of the first-floor ironwork balconies were supposed to have lost the fastenings that held them to the stonework, and several of the columns leaned awry of their supports, and the flagstones on the long railed approaches over the deep areas were notoriously unsteady, and one of the giant sculpted acorns at the other end of the terrace had worked loose and crashed one hundred feet in a storm, and at the rear drainpipes hung from the walls and rattled on windy nights, and on the flanks a number of chimney pots had toppled and disappeared through roofs, nor were the railings at pavement level entirely dependable, but that was all part of life in the Crescent, in the Aquae-Regis of the 1930s, and without a long memory Catherine knew no differently, so the term 'heritage' left her feeling rather cold, as the weather had a tendency to do also.

They had more rooms than they could hope to use: six bedrooms in addition to their own three and Mrs Ramage's and the maid's, a billiard-room under the roof with two inglenook fireplaces, a tack-room, a dairy behind the laundry-room, an ice-cellar, and further servants' accommodation over the garages. They normally ate in the morning-room rather than the dining-room. Her aunt occupied her 'sewing-room' during the day, and they only tried to colonise the chilly drawing-room if her father suggested it of an evening; otherwise they confined themselves to the more compact, much cosier sitting-room on the ground floor, next door to her father's 'business-room'.

This was where they lived, and Catherine had no other concept of 'home'. A house of sombre quiet, where clocks partitioned out the day amongst themselves and chimes announced meals and retreats and bathtimes; a deep, opaque cave-silence in which the rumblings and splutterings of the water pipes were insignificant, in which voices turned to whispers and footsteps offered no clues to presences and whereabouts. They moved about its distances in earnest imitation of purpose: each in mutually vague embarrassment of catching the approach of another, which left them with time and space to find a ready detour but which required an expression to be fixed and held until the evasion or the moment of passage had been made. It was second nature to Catherine, however, and she wasn't specifically conscious that they were living in what was virtually an opera set: the house had a much more elementary function, being a cardinal circumstance of her existence. The rooms were lofty, shadowed, dusty, and perpetually cold at their higher levels; the three of them (excluding Mrs Ramage and the maid) occupied only corners and pockets, and words when they were spoken had to be projected with careful aim. Their surroundings overwhelmed them, and they strained to fit them, to be fitting and meritorious. All this was required to justify them, she later discovered, and somehow they were required to be equal to the responsibility of it; such fulsome and ponderous dignity.

Silence. Cold. Gilded, mottled pomp. Snuffy air. Ghostly footfalls. Words thinning, rising into the ether.

'Home'.

7

The Melancholy Zebra

THE only indications that the zoo was there – but proof enough – were supernatural shrieks and occult braying, and a frequent odour of rankness colouring the normally rarefied air of Belvedere Heights.

It lay behind high walls and railings screened by vegetation, within a triangle formed by three streets, Cholmondoley, Myrrh and Vespasian. The narrow entrance passage, open to the sky, was flanked by reliefs of Egyptian gods, copied in approximate fashion and comfortable proportions in the mellow local stone. Beyond that, paths of sparse gravel disappeared behind well-weathered stone obelisks and hewn miniatures of Greek temples afflicted with moss; topiary hedges losing their shape and resemblances added mass and greenness, and behind those – at the heart of the puzzle – were the roofed cages.

At the least their occupants were bored; some were comatose, others had acquired fiendish tempers, a few had disproved the naturalists' theories on animal mentality and gone stark staring mad. Tedium, however, was the primal condition whence the other hazards sprang. Several had preened and scratched themselves to premature baldness. Most held themselves conspicuously aloof from the few dozen humans who might walk round in a day, but when the browsers' backs were turned they sneaked looks. Their diet was a rough-and-ready mixture of what was to hand and what was guessed at as being 'suitable': as a result they were frequently constipated, and thus made unhappy to the point of general surliness, and scandalously undernourished into the bargain. Sometimes, and invariably in unison, they caught a whiff of savannah, or jungle, or desert, or tundra, wafted impossibly on a breeze, and they hooted and bellowed and whinnied loudly enough for their cries of longing to be carried to their very foreign homelands.

There was a modest but cosmopolitan collection: either one or two of dromedary, white lion, elk, chimpanzee, gazelle, sloth, racoon, zebra, lynx, rhinoceros, dingo, Madagascar lemur, Dartmoor pony,

Arctic fox, outback wallaby. In one cage, identical to the racoon's or the sloth's but called the 'aviary', a conversational brace of parrots cohabited with a wailing peahen, a French-talking mynah bird, a taciturn bantam, and a capercailzie which had taught itself to walk backwards. Feeding was not discouraged, and buns and wodges of fruit cake were pushed through the bars; sometimes chocolate couldn't be unwrapped from its foil before a paw snatched at it, and even edibles that weren't being proffered – a paper poke of boiled sweets, a lollipop, a toffee apple – were up for grabs. To the wearied, frequently depressed animals all and everything was fair game. They also collected walking canes and umbrellas, hats (ladies' and gents'), mittens on strings, teddy bears, handkerchiefs, newspapers, and occasional 'luxuries' such as a wrapped bunch of florist's flowers or a cashmere muffler or the slimmer sort of handbag.

The thinning, undisciplined topiary hedges couldn't finally conceal the ultimate confinement of the place. In toto the triangular space of zoo didn't exceed a couple of acres of ground. On summer days the atmosphere was fetid, and rather menacing. In late autumn and winter, when the cages were hung with heavy tarpaulin and braziers burned outside the bars, the ambience turned soberly wistful and reflective.

There was one beast to which all the seasons seemed equally dismal and unfortunate: the single and singular zebra. Its melancholy was as distinctively its own as its stripes. Mostly it was to be found standing with the length of its body parallel to the front of the cage and its head turned to face whoever was watching it. Its expression was uniquely, triumphantly sad: despondency had been refined to the perfect suffering and self-immolation of a martyr. The zebra was unpersuadable in its fine, righteous, noble, *pure* melancholy.

It was always to the zebra that Catherine was firstly and lastly drawn on her visits with her aunt. The creature seemed to have been 'designed', she once overheard a man saying. And it was quite true: while (she might have replied, if she'd had the words) everything else – even the rake-thin antelope – was functional to a fault, too naturally 'evolved'. The zebra (she might have said) didn't seem to truly belong to the milieu of steaming droppings and reeking emanations. Even its cage was cleaner, without the evidence of bowel disorders. If this was its home (or, properly, its prison), it gave the impression of leading a separate existence. The price of its separateness was its melancholy, but melancholy controlled and ordered into a noble *attitude*. The zebra didn't flinch when a human rattled on the cage bars or pushed through a carrot or flung a mint pan-drop at its hooves. 'Oh pitiable indeed, all ye who come to gawp at our condition, that ye should need to believe yourselves superior to *us*.' Standing in front of its cage,

Catherine would be aware for the only time on the circuit walk of the cages that she and her aunt were being looked at in their turn, *studied,* and with little mercy. But its unsparingness for them both was eclipsed by that abiding melancholy: all its other animal emotions were secondary to that compelling, enigmatic stance against the world, its very *other*worldliness.

From its homeland, across thousands of miles – over grass plains, and dune sand, and wide rolling seas – it had been brought to this manger of concrete and iron. The longer Catherine stood at the bars looking in at it, the more certain she became that it understood her own child's half-understanding of its chaste, mournful dignity. She might stand for ten or fifteen minutes at a time, until she heard her aunt calling her over the queer geometrics of the topiary hedges; she would have to shake herself out of her trance of attention, into the busy kind of inattention her aunt and everyone else took to be normal behaviour. Running backwards from the cage she would watch the zebra's cool unconcern, its gentlemanly ineffusiveness, its static moroseness reserved not just for itself but for the general condition of existence. And yet it did also seem self-aware, 'I am something eccentric, improbable, an exotic splendour, a dazzling but sad-eyed mystique, not quite (the worse pity) a chimera: I might almost be a horse, but (declared a woman once in a very loud voice) zebras are untameable and quite a different kettle of fish – so, try as you might in your teach-yourself, lending-library, provincial way, you'll never know more than a mite about me. You are captives of my mystery.'

So Catherine discerned later, of what had already been in her mind, but unformulated. And as the years passed she developed the habit of making for the zebra's cage not first but only at the very end of her visit, choosing in her adolescence to better savour the moment of her approach and its incurious, phlegmatic response, its Laodicean unwonderment.

But, like much else, it was done in remembrance of her mother.

The cage had stopped her in her tracks on the two occasions they'd visited the zoo together. Both times she had stood staring at the immobile zebra for several minutes; all her concentration had been fixed on it, as if it were a symbol of what only she, Mrs Hector Hammond, among the day's visitors could perceive.

It was to the same cage and the same zebra that Catherine in her turn was drawn. Maybe she did so to be brought closer still to the memory of her mother. But the strands of motivation didn't have to be separated in her own mind, and she merely went, presenting herself in front of the beast, to let it know that it wasn't forgotten when all about it clamoured for attention with their ceaseless histrionics.

*

'But there's nobody,' her aunt told her.

'There *was*.'

'Where?'

Catherine pointed to the patch of gravel walk in front of the zebra's cage, visible between clumps of shrubbery.

'Who did you think you saw?'

Catherine stared at the statuesque zebra, motionless in profile like the subject of a tableau vivant.

'Who, Catherine?'

She couldn't say.

'You told me you saw somebody.'

She had seen her momentarily. Standing the way she used to in front of that cage, transfixed by the animal's mournful aspect of sufferance. For a couple of seconds she had been there, until her aunt had called to her and distracted her; and then only a moment or two later, when her eyes had sped back to the spot, her mother had gone.

'Who was it you saw, Catherine? Somebody you knew?'

She turned away, as dolefully resisting as the zebra itself. She ground the toe of her shoe into the grass.

Her aunt took her hand.

'Now, what haven't we seen yet?' she asked in a more cheerful voice, signifying her relief that the unforeseen difficulty had been dispensed with for the moment. Anyway, Catherine knew very well, it wasn't a matter of *choosing* what to see: the zoo was set out in such a way that you walked around it in a circle and saw every exhibit in turn.

She turned back again and stared at the foreground vegetation on either side of the zebra's cage. The greenery was undisturbed, so her mother couldn't have made her escape *that* way.

'I think,' she said, 'I'd like to go home now.'

They could have stayed longer. But what, she was wondering, if they should both see her? They would have to decide if she was a ghost or not. However, she was more afraid of finding out what her mother might think of her now, seeing her being taken care of by another woman in the house and giving *her* her loyalty.

Catherine slipped her hand out of her aunt's. She didn't like it when people were told how well behaved she was now ('now' – always the qualification) and really no trouble, or very very little. She didn't set out to behave so that she would hear herself praised, but because you can keep your own thoughts not less but *more* private when you're quiet and it's assumed that you're all sorts of dull and decent things. No one knew where you might go to in your head: the world, as her mother used to say, leading her round the town's streets, is your oyster, and inside fleshy oysters – so she'd heard on the wireless since – are found the pearls that shine just as diamonds used to sparkle and gold dazzle in her mother's recollections of the tales of marvels Shahrazad told to her captor, King Shahryar.

8

In Jericho

FOUR months after their return south, when her aunt was settled into the house in Eveleigh Crescent with the few odds and ends she had brought with her, she and Catherine made a sortie by hired taxi one weekday afternoon, across the town to the lesser side, where life was conducted on the flat, where the terraces were of two storeys and gentility was a mere precarious commodity, where wisps of mist curled like shavings from a canal and food smells seeped out of front doors and the trees that grew in the small shabby squares of queerly named 'Jericho' had a shrinking, apprehensive deportment.

The cab stopped outside a church called St Botolph's and St Jude's. Beside it a graveyard ran back from the road for a couple of hundred yards, towards an area of vegetable allotments. The gravel paths near the church gradually lost their gravel covering and trimmed edges and became weedy tracks of earth encroached upon by the scythed grass.

Among the recent grave-mounds they reached a more substantial tombstone than its neighbours. Its polished marble distinguished it from the common-or-garden stone sort, but although it was thicker and broader and higher than any of the others round about it was perfectly plain and angular, without any angelic ornamentation or scrollwork or artful mason's handiwork. All it carried was a chiselled name and two dates beneath, 'MARGUERITE HAMMOND 1905–1937', and (Aunt Dodie translated) a somewhat ominous-sounding instruction, '*Requiescat in Pace*'.

To Catherine, how far away it seemed from everything: from the taxi waiting for them at the gates, from the Aquae-Regis she knew, from her memories of her mother.

'Why?' she asked.

' "Why?" ' her aunt repeated, with a little trepidation.

'Why here?'

'When people die, they need to have a resting-place.'

'But why here?'

'"Here"?' Her aunt clasped her handbag to her stomach and looked about her for inspiration.

On walks about the high-town Catherine had seen the shady churchyards laid behind railings and mossy walls, green corners of quiet tucked into the angles between streets and buildings. In the oldest of all, the Necropolis, there were obelisks and columned rotundas, even the mausoleum of a very rich man which was an exactly scaled miniature of the central portion of Les Invalides in Paris.

'Well, it's just a place,' her aunt said. 'Like any other.'

But Aunt Dodie had brought her here, across the town, to a quarter where they knew nobody, and the gravestones were smaller.

As they were leaving, a couple of women in long coats and felt hats watched them from beneath a tree. Catherine saw her aunt smile quite courteously as they walked past, but the women didn't smile back. Instead one whispered to her companion, and the other muttered a reply, and Catherine realised that they were being spoken about: and she must have been able to recognise at the time that it was done with little charity.

They were silent on the return journey in the taxi, and her aunt only spoke as they were turning from Tobago Street into Eveleigh Crescent.

'I do think it would be the best idea if we didn't tell your father where we've been.'

Catherine stared up at the soot-blackened frontages of the houses. At a couple of windows she saw a face looking down at them, following the taxi's progress along the street.

'Did you hear what I said, Catherine?'

Catherine nodded. She already sensed, even if she couldn't have formed specific thoughts out of an instinct and articulated them in words, that respectability weighed heavily on all the households in this street, that it was prized more dearly than in any other part of the town: the sanctity of appearance and repute, which far exceeded mere decency, was hugely significant. Regard and approbation were premises of these lives lived so mutedly and expensively, on hushed thoroughfares, along which a hired taxi's rattling chassis changing gear was sufficient to cause these ripples of consideration, a temporary disturbance of order and ritual, a frisson of unease even.

They did pass someone on the crossing with Jamaica Street, a housekeeper returning from an errand, carrying a basket. Catherine saw her aunt incline her head away as the woman lowered hers and leaned forward, as if determined to peer in at them. They proved too quick for her, and the woman was left tottering on her plump ankles. Aunt Dodie pulled at the fur tippet on her coat in readiness for their arrival at the house; she tugged at her kid gloves, pushing her fingers to the very tips and fastening the single buttons on the wrists.

'It's been our own little outing,' she said, speaking the words quite distinctly, so that there should be no mistaking their import.

She reached into her handbag and retrieved her bunch of house keys. Today, Catherine saw, they wouldn't be left standing on the top step while Mrs Ramage or Ethel were summoned from the basement laundry-room or their private eyries in the attic; today she and her aunt couldn't allow themselves to be left so vulnerable.

*

At times Catherine had been afraid for her mother, for what might have happened to her. The business had gone on for so long, and there had been such uncertainty, that she couldn't bring herself to believe the finality of the gravestone. However, nor could she believe that her mother would come back, not now.

Wherever she was, in whatever condition, Catherine couldn't envisage her as lonely. Her mother had never been at a loss to think up stories, stories that still continued to have an existence inside Catherine's head. She couldn't imagine a state of affairs where her mother's story-telling faculty might dry up, and she seriously wondered how stories could continue in existence while the original story-teller was denied that right.

So she was left – as she had been all along – in ignorance and muddle, which saved her from the shock of treating death. Instead she found herself being eased into the ways of her aunt, being asked questions in turn about how things were usually done, and her mother's name – when they were in one another's company – not being avoided. It was her aunt who told her that her mother's last wish had been that her father shouldn't be troubled with any mentions of her: if his mind was distracted from his work, he wouldn't be able to earn the pennies that kept them all living in comfort; which – Aunt Dodie assured her niece – would only have upset her dear mother deeply.

So her mother really *wasn't* coming back: but her wishes were commands, and she still held sway over them. Catherine couldn't associate the tombstone with her mother, because her mother would have been as much a stranger in Jericho as themselves. So she put it out of her thoughts and it didn't come back to haunt her dreams as it might otherwise have done, as her Aunt Dodie would surely have predicted.

The carpet rides to Arabia had become less frequent in her dreams latterly, but Catherine lived in hope. Her aunt's stories couldn't compare, but Catherine wasn't disappointed, because no one could have told tales better than her mother. She pictured her waiting there for her, at the eye of the needle or in a courtyard of plashing fountains or on the balcony of a steepled minaret. The child already perceived in her bones, to the marrow, beyond words, as her mother's daughter, that immediately and without a possibility of error they would recognise one another, as the romancer with a story to tell and the listener marked out by the secret confederacy to hear and remember.

9

Eveleigh Crescent

CATHERINE was troubled.

Where had all her mother's photographs gone?

Aunt Dodie told her that they had upset her father too much. She used to watch him lift them to the light when he thought no one was there to see. Sometimes visitors had said they didn't 'do Marguerite's looks justice', and sometimes she used to watch her mother lifting them to the light, when she thought no one was there to see her.

A second, third, and fourth time Aunt Dodie told her that they upset her father too much. So it must, Catherine felt, be true.

But she wished they could be brought back again.

'Could I have one of them? To keep in my room?'

Aunt Dodie said she didn't know where they were kept now, then that her father had put them under lock and key.

For a moment Catherine thought her aunt might be envious. Her curly black hair and round face, her dimpled chin and rouged cheeks gave her a resemblance to a dancer: a pretty dancer in a music-hall, but not a beautiful actress of the stage such as her mother – so her father confided to her once, only once, on the long journey south from Tullieweem – had been.

Catherine feigned loss of interest. Aunt Dodie responded by looking harassed, which didn't suit her kind of face. But she frequently looked harassed, and Catherine was slowly growing used to the spectacle of a face which was made to be pampered, to be coddled and crooned over, suddenly stunned and mesmerised, as if for that instant she completely lost the point because nothing was making an ounce of sense to her.

*

Several times – but only after her mother's death – her grandmother, Catherine Hammond, visited them from Malvern. She was as grand as a dowager, with yellow teeth and an ear-trumpet; she smelt of camphor, of an old dark wardrobe or press. She studied her only grandchild through lorgnettes, assuming the expression of a woman confronted by a riddle. She said little, but placed great emphasis on those few words she did speak. She only once spoke impulsively, and quite sharply, when she was asked by her son if she would like to be driven past the Hammond foundry. 'Certainly not. What makes you imagine I should ever want to see that place again?' Otherwise she gave the impression of hoarding her thoughts to herself.

Catherine was always on her best behaviour when those visits took place; Aunt Dodie was especially diligent about supervising the housework, and wielding a duster herself. Her father ran after their guest – sometimes literally – to ensure as much was to her liking as possible, and he talked more than he usually did, in a manner that suggested he was speaking only to cover their silences that were like chasms.

Catherine had no knowledge of her mother's parents, the Bradleys. She asked Aunt Dodie, who told her that her mother hadn't discussed 'that sort of thing'.

'Where do they live?' she asked a number of times. 'The Bradleys.'

But her aunt shook her head.

'That was how your mother preferred to leave matters,' she was told once, when her aunt's tongue was a little looser than usual. 'She put it all behind her. We must respect her wishes.'

*

The foundry stood only a stone's throw from the canal, in a part of the town Catherine and her aunt had no cause ordinarily to pass through. The name 'Edmund Hammond & Son', wrought in iron, arched over the front gates.

They had been given a guided tour, being kept at a ladylike distance from most of the operations. Catherine remembered the heat, and a crimson lava trail where the molten metal was poured into moulds, and the dustiness of the offices they climbed to up wooden stairs, and the wares proffered for inspection in her father's room – a brass-finished coal scuttle and a companion set of fire tongs, brush, poker and shovel; a brass hearth fender; a heavy-duty cast-iron bootscraper; an iron umbrella stand; a trestle table to support a sewing machine. Her father had seemed embarrassed by all her naïve attention for these accessories of the middle-class, suburban life. Her aunt had asked several polite questions, which had received rather blunt answers, as if her father found himself on the defensive, judging them both to be too patronising for comfort. The visit had been a token one only, so that it might never be claimed, subsequently, that he had failed to do the decent thing and show them. But since they were very seldom, if ever, to make mention of the foundry in one another's company again, it was to seem an unnecessary formality. Catherine never forgot her father's treatment of her aunt; his manner – becoming more and more brusque and reticent the closer anyone approached the subject of his work – most effectively precluded the possibility of their discussing his days 'at business', as the euphemism went.

Long days they were and, frequently, the early portions of the evening too, and every Saturday morning and every second Saturday afternoon. It was impossible to see the foundry from the house: from a little further uphill, and a little further downhill, one could – with considerable difficulty, because of the angle – locate it. Sometimes when night fell sparks were visible, and a flame-coloured tint lay on the stone of the streets behind, and the canal was streaked with the amber of autumn. But it was an out-of-the-way spot and inevitably Catherine wondered if she was seeing what was really there. Her father – and, more gently, her aunt – would warn her about over-indulging her fancy. 'You let your imagination run away with you,' her father would tell her: or, 'Your imagination's got the better of you this time, hasn't it?' Her aunt was less alarmist, yet tried her best to woo her away from figments and fictions, mental caprices. 'Tell me what you see,' she would ask her; 'there it is, in black and white, no two ways about it – but I want *you* to tell *me*.' Catherine would oblige, for her aunt's sake and because she'd been made to feel afraid of where imagination might lead her, if its sinister dark potential was to be submitted to. Their manner of living in Eveleigh Crescent derived from the hard graft undertaken in their name in Hammonds' Foundry, and what could be more stolid and matter-of-fact and unromantic than that? So what she *thought* she saw when the sun went down – the spluttering sparks, the russet flush on the stone, the torch drowning in the canal – she was ready at her own child's degree of understanding to believe, for simple domestic harmony's sake, was only a flight of the imagination, a poetic fancy, a maggot, and with a head-turn her attention would be directed somewhere else entirely – to the Meads, or Burlington Parade, or Salem's Glory, or Coldharbour.

*

On the first floor one of the rooms had been kept locked ever since her mother's death.

Her mother had used it as a small sitting-room cum study, where she might write a letter or two in the morning and take a short nap in the afternoon. When Aunt Dodie came to live with them, the room was emptied and Catherine thought she must be going to furnish it with whatever she had brought with her.

But that wasn't her father's intention at all. He ostentatiously turned the key in the lock before removing it, and ever afterwards the room's existence might have been forgotten.

Might have been.

But from the garden Catherine would stop in her play and look up at the room's narrow single sash window. Inside, a pair of shutters might be pulled across it, or one shutter would have been angled back to let in daylight, or both shutters would be folded back against the recessed panelling on the walls.

She asked her aunt about it, why the room was kept locked.

'We don't need it, Catherine, that's why.'

'But – '

'It's unnecessary.'

'But there's no key in the lock.'

'No,' her aunt told her on the several occasions when she repeated her questions. 'So it's all just locked up and left.'

At seven or eight years old she knew the answer's logic was false.

'Why, though?'

'Your father decided. So I shouldn't ask him about it.'

'Why not?'

Her aunt would dither. Once she had told her, 'It's not a very happy room,' but she never said it again.

'He doesn't think about the room. I should forget about the question too, Catherine, if I were you.'

Catherine failed to understand. All she could do now was ask her father. But for some reason – it must have coincided with one of his 'phases' as her aunt termed them, when his temper turned nettled and short ('Your father has too much to think about, Catherine. With his business and things') – she didn't ask the full question, although she had made a not-so-casual reference to the number of doors on the first floor. Her father just stared at her, but with the troubled, disorientated expression of someone surprised out of present time, in a seam between two tenses. She was never to be quite sure why, but she didn't pursue the matter that day: and, strange though it would seem to her that she should have behaved so, she resolved that she wouldn't ask again until her father made some reference to the locked room himself. She might have tried to trap her aunt into mentioning it, but it was a subject she was to prove singularly adept at avoiding. By the time she was nine and her father appeared to realise that she wasn't made after all in the image of her mother, she still hadn't asked him; and she didn't see how, suddenly, she could start to talk about the room when she had never done so before, as if she hadn't even perceived its existence.

She couldn't see through the keyhole. It had been plugged up on the other side, and not even a darning needle could budge whatever the impediment was.

She was intrigued, of course. One day she happened to be alone in the dining-room next door. She thought she heard a movement through the wall and ran out into the corridor. But she found the door was as it always was, locked. When she returned to the dining-room she placed each ear alternately to the connecting wall, the only one in the room unpanelled, and listened. What she heard this time was a snow-light fall of plaster behind the mirror. When she prised the mirror back she discovered a deep crack gouged in the wall. Taking her eye to the rift, she immediately saw through the thickness of wall into the room.

There in her sights was another plaster wall, the shadow of a shutter, bare floorboards.

She was enthralled, and afraid.

For a couple of years she saw no more than that whenever she looked. The room was unfurnished: all that was offered to her were the bare floorboards and a wall painted no recognisable colour – or, more properly, the colour of the wall changed somewhat in different lights, but was always a neutral shade, almost-white, or almost-grey, or almost-dun. A crack did appear in the plaster of the other wall, complementary to the one she stood spying through; it grew with time, although so slowly that she could only judge by comparing it in her memory. Yet by the time she was thirteen or fourteen the fissure ran the length of the portion of wall visible through her own, crossing it on a diagonal like a structural fault but – very oddly – showing no evidence of itself in the cloakroom on the other side. It made her think of a river plotted on a map, with many tributaries and sub-tributaries stemming from the mother-source.

10

Mise-en-Scène

IT was watching her aunt warm in the atmosphere of the theatre, seeing her face simultaneously relaxed and intent as the lights went down, that first convinced Catherine that this building was a special place.

The Panopticon was modestly sized but extravagantly decorated inside with burgundy plush upholstery and rich Lincoln-green carpets and drapes, swathes of gilt, copious plaster friezes. The tiers of balconies and boxes formed an intimate semi-circle, and from the domed ceiling hung a gilded chandelier fitted with a couple of dozen maroon silk shades matching those on the wall-brackets.

When the War came to complicate their pleasures, a few protective measures were thought advisable. The chandelier was unhooked from the ceiling and transported under cover of darkness to lie out the danger in an apple-loft above a cider press at the end of an exceedingly out-of-the-way farm track. In the theatre sandbags were distributed about the auditorium, and buckets of sand were placed at strategic points. The lights, as a concession to the grid, didn't burn so brightly under their maroon silk shades.

But Catherine's pleasantest memories were of a time before that, when the lights would be turned up full for the audience to view itself until the moment the orchestra struck up. Her aunt brought her twice a year: one visit coincided with the heart of the Christmas season, when they joined the restive, twittery throng at the pantomime; the other ritual visit took place in the third or fourth week of June, when discerning parents took their children to an orchestral concert of 'lollipops' selected to appeal to younger tastes. When she remembered those visits in later life she distinguished between the two kinds with her nose: the children's concert smelt of a contradiction – embarrassed perspiration and too much eau-de-Cologne – while the pantomime was a blend of odours, the mothballs that winter coats were stored in, minty humbugs, flannel poultices, damp squeaky shoe leather.

At the concert her attention wandered to the surroundings and to the other people and she could pretty much take the Thieving Magpie or the Queen of Sheba or leave them. The pantomime was easily her preference. Her memory stayed faithful to the noise, and the garish colours, and the heavy-handed make-up, all a little frightening in their way even with the sounds of laughter washing about the theatre: there were other smells to remember when she thought hard enough – the sulphur of the genie's smoke, and the overheated lamps in the orchestra pit, and the steaming deposits left behind by the ponies as they trod on- and off-stage preceding the same fragile spindly coach that was included in every production. The jokes fell thick and fast between the slapstick routines, which were interspersed between moments of stark and original terror when her eyes fixed and her stomach shrank and she felt her heart thudding against her ribs. Finally evil abased itself before good, as ever, but a chilling frisson of doubt was always left behind that such extraordinary powers *could* be curbed, even when the lid was slammed on the linen-basket with such determination or when the witch toppled head-over-heels down the wishing-well. Badness seemed to linger in the air afterwards, with the firework smell of the silver light and red smoke.

Her aunt too seemed to enjoy the spectacle of the pantomime. She always attended with her head cocked to the love interest at the centre, to the young couple in their innocence, a virginal girl with a clear falsetto and a principal boy with strong thighs and waistcoated bosom. She surprised Catherine by being able to hum along to the popular songs that were the pair's staple diet or duet, and had no qualms about singing aloud when the song-sheet was lowered from the proscenium. She viewed events on stage through her mother-of-pearl glasses as avidly as if she had been at grand opera. Even when the lights went up at the end she would still be that smiling and sentimental person, sharing the occasion with the other adults round about as they slipped their arms into coat sleeves and fumbled under seats for umbrellas and handbags and galoshes. The script would have included lines of purposely local appeal – about shops and private schools and posh addresses – and that lent the audience another temporary bond of community and commonality, that accompanied them up the aisles and along the corridors, allowing strangers to smile knowingly and self-contentedly at one another over their children's heads, dallying for several moments until they were outside, on the frosty pavement under the lit canopy, and cars and taxis drew up at the pavement to collect. It was lost after that, as the disappearing red tail lights and erect, orange-tipped indicator wands made their own model spectacle of display in the darkness, as home fires banked high with coal and late suppers kept hot and tasty under covers beckoned to make haste and tarry no more.

*

Catherine had asked the question before, but she couldn't remember the answer. She tried again, for what was to prove the last time, taking tea in the afternoon with her aunt as she always did in the school holidays.

'Doesn't Father like to go to the theatre?'

Her aunt nearly spluttered the contents of her mouth back into the cup.

'He doesn't talk about it,' Catherine said. 'Or about what's on.'

'I – I've never really thought –'

'He *doesn't* go, though. Does he? Ever?'

'He's very busy.'

'But not *always*.'

'Maybe – maybe there's nothing he wants to see.'

'Would he go then? If there was?'

'I really can't say.'

The smile that followed was too tight to convince Catherine, who by now knew better.

'*Did* he go?'

Her aunt pretended to have forgotten the subject they had just been discussing.

'Go where?'

'To the theatre?'

'Oh, I . . .' She lifted her spoon from the saucer to stir the tea in her cup, but saw that there was too little. ' . . . I can't rightly say.' She drew her mouth very straight indeed. 'For the time before I came here, I mean.'

Her eyes sped over the items on the tea-table.

'Have you had enough, Catherine? Are we finished, I wonder?'

She stood up and walked over to the bell by the fireplace. She tugged twice, three times, on the plaited velvet cord. The bell rang, very far away.

Tea-time was the closest, most cloistered interlude in the day they shared. Catherine knew from the stories at school that she had to expect *the* pep-talk soon, about the changes likely to occur any day now in her body. But the talk still hadn't happened: which must be because her aunt didn't recognise the physical symptoms which caused the subject to be broached. So they put off the fateful afternoon when their most intimate chat must take place, and meanwhile she fairly and squarely shouldered the burden of interim topic-finding with her aunt.

It seemed to Catherine that the matter of her father's liking for the theatre (or the lack of it) also belonged to the 'embarrassing' category. She felt an inexplicable and malicious urge to test her aunt's conversational squeamishness to its limits.

She pretended that she didn't understand anything.

'If we asked him to come with us . . .'

'No, I don't think so.'

The tone was as severe as her aunt could ever allow herself.

'Just once?'

'It's some people's taste,' her aunt said, shaking her head. 'And other people's it isn't.'

'Did you ask him?'

'No. I just knew.'

'How, though? How did you know?'

Her aunt looked towards the door for a timely interruption, but it didn't come. Ethel had left them and they were breaking in a new maid.

'If you didn't ask him – '

'It just came out.'

'When?' Catherine asked.

Her aunt turned to the door again.

'Talking about something else,' she replied, with theatrical reluctance.

'He *did* mention it?'

'Hardly at all, though. Just in passing.'

'What did he say?'

'Only – that he was giving all that up. The theatre, I mean.'

'Did he tell you why?'

'He didn't tell me why, no.'

'Did you know then?'

'I knew that he didn't – go in for it any more.'

Catherine suspected there was some point they were moving in circles round and round about, but she was starting to lose her focus. The feeling was like vertigo.

Her aunt seemed to suppose that the talking between them was done and breathed a stagy sigh of relief when the door opened at last and a head appeared.

'Thank you, Lily, we *have* finished now. Oh, Catherine,' she said, as if it had only slipped her mind, 'I'm going to stay with Miss Fontwell for a couple of days, did I tell you? After my visit to Bristol tomorrow. She's been poorly and she doesn't trust – '

Her eyes alighted on Lily's back, bent over the tea-table.

Their daily afternoon tea was now disposed of for the rest of the week. It couldn't have been accidental, but her aunt's pitying shakes of the head simulated so, as if Coronation Blend or Orange Pekoe were a gross indulgence, a thoughtless and selfish sacrilege against the unnerving, blistering, gnawing distress which shingles brings.

*

Catherine prised back the mirror on the dining-room wall a few inches and positioned herself to see through the deep crack in the plaster.

Inside the locked room was a wooden chair, turned away from her, and a person sitting at an angle, a woman, with one arm leaning on the chair-back and her hand supporting her jaw. Her face was hidden, but she had the bunched fair hair and outline of a woman in her twenties or thirties. Her hand was slender and fine. She seemed to be looking away into the corner of the room. There was something aloofly sad, or sadly aloof, about her bearing. She displayed great serenity, nobility even. She wasn't moving, she hardly breathed.

Catherine watched until she felt her neck starting to stiffen. She stood up slowly, and returned the mirror to its resting-place. She backed away, to the panelled surround of the fireplace. She scratched on the wood with her fingertips. She moaned very softly.

Later in the day she came back and looked again. The chair and its occupant had gone. All she could see were the bare boards, and some trails of dust.

No chair, no becalmed woman.

*

Gros point was Aunt Dodie's principal pastime, but it was hardly that, rather a fitful but consuming passion, which – when the mood was upon her – drew blood from her fingers.

She specialised in arabesques of flowers, convoluted patterns of entwining stems, tendrils, leaves, buds, blooms. Somehow, even when there were half a dozen species of flowers in an arrangement, she knew exactly where each portion of the whole wreath belonged, which leaf and head of petals issued from which stem. In the end, when the seat-cover or fire-screen was completed, one simply trusted the botanical veracity and sequential integrity of the handiwork.

It was the most fastidious labour, demanding on her eyes and concentration and time, and there were intervals when she desisted between projects. Normally there was an ulterior reason for her selecting a piece of canvas from the cupboard in her bedroom and tracing the outline of a roundel, and it was closely linked to domestic tension: her authority being questioned in the kitchen, her brother's temper 'lapsing' into one of its volatile phases, a visitor (usually northern) manifesting herself (the invariable gender) from the life before this one she was living now with her brother and niece. She judged the according tension of her canvas in the frame with the skill of a civil engineer, she threaded her needles in the blink of an eyelid, she could discern infinitesimal gradations in the colours of her strands of silk thread, she stabbed the needle with unfailing exactitude into the required point on the canvas and had completed the turn and pulled it back through in little more than a split second. Most frequently she sat stooped with her head angled over the canvas, out of conversational reach, and at last Catherine was to recognise the full significance of the activity, that its happening to coincide with a degree of turbulence in the house removed her aunt from the influence of that turbulence. At the same time she was satisfying the unsparing dictates of that puritan work ethic she'd had instilled into her in *her* childhood, so that she could disguise what was an act of self-preserving interest as something else entirely, in the truly duplicitous puritan manner.

Meanwhile the house was filling with the results of her endeavours. Perhaps the eye was growing used to those aureoles of perfect summer blooms, which – as her aunt invariably pointed out to new guests who enquired – she made sure were seasonally coincidental. Catherine didn't know what difference such dedicated authenticity made, except to prove that this 'hobby' (as it was claimed to be) was attended to with quite deadly earnestness. The beauty and formal elegance of the subject matter were, in a sense, deceptive: or rather they weren't true representations of the precursory artistic process. They were worked at in a state of inner turmoil, but reproduced a quite opposite effect. That was their proper achievement and triumph, outdoing even their fidelity to Dame Nature in her cycles.

*

Through the crack in the wall behind the mirror Catherine began to glimpse the room's past life.

She saw something thrown down on the floor, like white bunting when she first set eyes on it at dusk; then in daylight she made out that it was a long white scarf with the sheen of silk. Another time she saw a shoe, a woman's court shoe of a gooseberry-green colour, with a high thin heel, lying on the floorboards on its side. Next – when the shoe had disappeared, and after the room had yielded nothing more for several days – she saw something else: she disentangled from the shadows at the end of a summer's evening a coil of material too insubstantial to be a dress or underslip or another scarf, and she guessed that it was a dark-coloured stocking, dropped or abandoned and suitably composing itself into the shape of a question mark's stave.

She never heard any sounds coming from the room; she didn't surprise anyone going in or out, there were no clicks of the door in the middle of the night, although she had many chances to hear when she lay awake unable to get to sleep. She was still unable to ask any questions about the room: it was too late to enquire of her father, and her aunt would only look pained again and, as she had always done on the subject, retreat into a troubled, resolute silence. Conceivably she *could* have worked on her aunt, but she always felt rebuked by that distress she saw she caused: more and more her aunt seemed determined to dwell on what was 'pleasant' in life, and Catherine felt humbled and impaired by that determination on the point, even though she couldn't see the sense of it herself.

Later, she did start to recover the knack of sleep. The mystery of the locked room was still unexplained, but she was adjusting herself even to that.

11

Collegians

THEY dressed for the streets of the town in white gloves and maroon capes with hoods. Day-girls and boarders alike were allowed to visit only certain shops. Anywhere selling even the most innocuous beverages was out-of-bounds to them unless dispensation had been granted to join a parent, and they were reminded frequently to walk smartly and never to dally. The elderly and/or infirm and young mothers with children were always to be granted precedence to themselves: where that left the rest of womankind, Catherine was unclear, but she guessed that some of the teaching staff were not the most zealous admirers of their own sex.

Leaving the premises in school time on organised exeats to the town was directionless in effect – since their movements were restricted to the Promenade and a selection of main streets – but it was an escape. This part of the town had its own specific character, having been appendaged to the other and greater in Regency times: it had seen better days, and the ironwork of the little balconies and hoods was uncommonly rusty just as the plaster frontages of the houses were peeling and carbuncled. Clerics were thicker on the ground here, and doctors; in the Happy Valley gardens old colonials sat listening to the brass band and showed some fearsome complexions – jaundiced parchment-yellow, or dipsomaniac's berry-red, or nut-brown toughened to cracked boot leather. Present for seven days a week (even the non-boarders) in such a comparatively (for Aquae-Regis) louche ambience, they were nonetheless expected to acquit themselves elegantly, as wholesome, accomplished, optimistic ideals of young womanhood. School-bound for eleven and a half hours of the clock, from eight thirty a.m. until eight p.m., it wasn't easy to be hopeful on the frequent sultry days when rain-clouds hadn't the energy to drag themselves over the horseshoe of surrounding hills and emptied themselves then and there.

Confined in Aquae-Regis, Catherine wondered if life elsewhere in

England proved so tedious as this, and if other towns had nothing better than this hollowness to offer at their core. She heard it, the emptiness, as the striking of the town's clocks fell away or when the road outside the classroom was silent again after a car had driven past; blackbirds trilled unconcernedly in wet gardens, drainpipes dripped, a man's voice droned out of the speaker in her housemistress's wireless set, a girl doggedly practised 'The Green Hills o' Somerset' on a violin.

She wondered what it could all possibly be in aid of, to what end they were striving. She wondered quite often why she should be considering such a thing, why she couldn't jink the question as she supposed those other girls she lived alongside did. What was it that seemed to be making her different, which seemed to be marking her out?

*

'Yes, *but* . . .'

She had once overheard two ladies of the upper town, walking into the outer sanctum of the cloakroom of the Nonagon Room, in the interval during a charity recital.

'I have heard *he*'s quite pleasant.'

'Hammond?'

'Yes.'

'So he should be.'

'It's only his sister I've met.'

'But it's just as I said – '

Her friend nodded into one of the mirrors above the vanity-table.

' – after all, trade *is* trade.'

*

Her room was at the back of the house, but it had an open outlook, being higher than the stables and mews buildings on the lane.

'Open' in one sense, because she looked up to the crest of the hill, to the Great Circus which outdid their own Crescent for grandeur. To one side there was a slender colonnaded church tower in 'Greek' style, and the graceful high-Gothic spire of a second church, and a domed mausoleum on the Palladian model, so that at a fiery sunset she could begin to appreciate where her mother might have found some of the inspiration for her stories. But in another sense the view was restricting, too crowded, claustrophobic, without the possibility of change.

She sat at the window and stared out as if transfixed. In the glass she saw herself gradually emerging from the stonework, from the skeletal fretwork of trees, and the Victorian Corfu cypresses, and from the citrus flush of another slow dusk.

*

Her best friend at school was Audrey Stimpton.

Their bond was their neither of them having a surviving natural mother. While Catherine had become awkward with the fact, and sometimes even ashamed because of the difference it established between herself and others, Audrey – if she didn't exactly revel in her condition – saw it instead as a badge of distinction. She pitied the other girls, who would be induced to grow up into carbon copies of their mothers. Her own mother had died the day she was born.

Sprinting towards their mid-teens, they had an important heart-to-heart on the subject.

'You see, Catherine, it means we've been chosen.'

' "Chosen"?'

'That's what the vicar said to me. Once when I was being "difficult". He started off saying I should love my stepmother just as if she was my proper mother, but he didn't sound so sure in the end. Then he said, really I was "chosen", because my mother lived on in me. I carry her inside myself.'

'What happens to *us*, though?' Catherine felt bound to ask.

'What d'you mean? "Happen"?'

'If we just become our mothers?'

'He meant – ' Audrey hesitated ' – I think he really meant I was to behave myself, so I wouldn't bring my mother disgrace. But – ' she turned solemnly to Catherine ' – I think he meant too, our mothers want us to live out their lives for them, as well as our own.'

From the beginning of their friendship it was essentially what they had in common with one another: a loss that exceeded the measure of anyone else's. Audrey sometimes spoke of that absence as if they both must keep it a secret: apparently her stepmother had only referred once to any other 'Mrs Stimpton', and in unflattering terms. Whenever she visited the private quarter of the Duke of Buckingham Hotel, Catherine saw how Audrey would glower at the woman in a very unsparing way. Her own mother was rarely spoken of now at home: she had stopped asking questions, noticing how quickly her father's and aunt's expressions changed, to confusion or irritation or even anguish. It had become more and more difficult for her to articulate her own feelings, even with Audrey; she belonged to her mother as even her father didn't, she had experienced her life – the blood and the gut of her – as no one else had. She didn't know how she could have expressed her sensibilities in words. So surely, all told (or rather, *not* told), it was more apt that her mother should be acknowledged in the most meaningful and personal way, which meant in silence, in the echo of her own calm and consoling darkness.

*

The Duke of Buckingham Hotel occupied four houses in Cheveney Terrace, where it had been in existence since 1908, using the adopted name and traditions of a much older establishment.

It had earned its social laurels. The better class of guest was attracted to it – birds of passage as well as those who took six-month lets on the rooms – and nobody who lived in the immediate vicinity claimed to have any objections or complaints. The name itself was a token of its gentility.

The private quarters were on the first floor: a sitting-room and small dining-room at the front, and the other rooms at the rear. The back rooms looked down on to a long garden that was the Stimptons' own, but never wholly their own, since the guests in the back-facing bedrooms could also look down and see. An enormous cedar did provide a measure of privacy, but also too much shade in the first-floor rooms, and in summer and most of autumn the private lives of the Stimptons behind the baize door were conducted in a murky light, lacking proper clarity.

In the ground-floor public rooms the furnishings had altered little since the reincarnated hotel opened again for business. Audrey had grown up with them, and Catherine had had her introduction to them when she was eleven, as the girls' close friendship began. The décor became familiar and very nearly personal to her: the leather upholstery with the horsehair stuffing, the heavy velvet drapes, the green-painted panelling in the public rooms, the rugs like islands on the floors (reminding her of the sort unrolled in *The Arabian Nights*), the stained-glass lampshades that coloured the corridors oddly in the evenings, the framed prints on the walls showing street-scenes in Georgian Aquae-Regis.

The surroundings were tasteful in the moderate and unadventuresome English way. Life in this part of the town did not run to extremes. The gentility of the hotel was inescapable. It had composed itself into a particular odour, the smell of polish and the watered soil in the aspidistra pots and the old dust that couldn't be beaten out of rugs or curtains. Catherine would pick it up several seconds before she walked through the front door, and it followed her along the terrace every time she left, taking several yards to dilute into the air.

*

In the midst of Catherine's education the War occurred, which entailed certain precautions being taken. At home the curtains were double-lined and edged with sheeny black cotton, and a pile of sandbags was stored in the basement behind the kitchen-scullery. Iron railings disappeared from certain streets where their removal didn't constitute an added hazard to the public's safety. The school was evacuated into the country for a couple of years, but they still wore white gloves and maroon capes and woollen berets or straw boaters and remained largely ignorant of rusticity; they missed the shop windows and the wedges of walnut or cherry cake served in the Misses Fotheringham's Tea-Rooms, and they listened to the wireless bulletins with joy and fear.

On three separate occasions raiding parties did fly inland and bombs fell. Two sides of Launceston Square went down, and half of Fitzwilliam Place was left as rubble; the middle portion of Park Parade was blown away, and Melcott's Hotel received a direct hit. Notwithstanding those severe losses, the destruction mostly afflicted the less salubrious quarters closest to the centre, and there the toll of life was highest: the Baths and the Nonagon Room escaped damage, the stone emperors on their plinths stood proud of the swirling dust unsettled by the blasts, but there was grief and commiseration for the occupants of those humbler streets such as Catherine had the merest recollection of from the unnoticing years before.

When the school returned to its own buildings in Bethesda, the town smelt stale and sourish. The holes where buildings had fallen were already seeded with wild grass and buttercups. Several buildings seemed to have acquired slight tilts to port or starboard, and the pavements generally felt unstable. There was more dust now in the air, which sometimes furred people's throats and made them cough. Eveleigh Crescent and Paradise Hill were, structurally, unscathed, although Catherine found their neighbours fidgety and restless, watching from their windows (as if they couldn't quite credit their maverick good luck) and receiving what deliveries they could from the shops, to lay up emergency stocks.

As the War drew to an end, Catherine discovered the clandestine, sinful effects of make-up, applied with a shaky hand in the bedroom of her best friend, in the private quarters of the Duke of Buckingham Hotel, but when she came home with the handiwork still visible after a furious washing-off session her father shouted at her and, for the first time in her life, shook her by the shoulders, so that the word 'peace' suddenly acquired for her a false, deceitful ring. Her father stared at her – *through* her – as if he didn't recognise her, as if she was unconnected with the thoughts in his head, and she had to search out Aunt Dodie for an explanation: who wouldn't explain but didn't refer to her cosmetic experimentation either, and only said that the War had set *everyone* on edge, but now it was over, and nobody had to worry any more about air-raid sirens and whistles from the sky and homes and businesses going up in flames and smoke.

Catherine nodded. Of course her father must have been concerned for the foundry, and for his workers' livelihoods as for his own, for the dependent families like Aunt Dodie and herself. But now it *was* over, and they would no longer be jumping out of their skins whenever the siren wails whined, clawing at the house's outside walls; they were on the other side of all that, on the far bank – safe, cheerly and expectant.

*

During the War the trade of the Duke of Buckingham changed. Some of the residents lost their nerve and moved away from the cities, to quieter spas inland. Much less in evidence were the sightseeing tourists with their heavy guidebooks and heavier box cameras. The hotel still received the regulars, elderly colonels and majors and former colonials visiting relations or friends or consulting doctors. The few businessmen accommodated in the past became more infrequent. The hotel's new stock-in-trade were to be services officers on leave, accompanied by women referred to as their 'wives'.

Catherine, advised at first by Audrey, came to recognise for herself the true wives: slightly flummoxed- or disbelieving-looking women. Most services personnel went home on leave, she supposed, and they must have had particular reasons for not returning where they might have been expected to after so long away. The real wives never quite lost sight of the luxury of it, and inspected the items on their dining-room table as if checking on the cleaning and polishing skills of a maid. The 'wives' who probably weren't never noticed anything much, except the attention of the man they were with and the effect the two of them were having on other people. Wedding rings or the absence of them from fingers served as clues, and Audrey had become as adept as her stepmother at reading the situation at a glance.

When the War finished, circumstances changed again. A number of the resident guests stayed away, in the safety of their backwoods towns. Some of the regulars found the outlay necessary to keep up the old ways a greater strain on their finances, and they became less regular. The services officers returned in mufti, for sentimental reasons, and the women they brought with them very rarely wore gold on their fourth fingers. The sightseeing brigade were even more tight-fisted than they had been previously. Occasionally, when the other town hotels were busy, the Duke of Buckingham received more glamorous guests, who would drive up to the front door in a brand-new waxed Daimler or a sports convertible with sweeping, sculpted wheel arches. A number of times a more affluent type of commercial traveller made an overnight stop. A very few foreigners stayed and when they did they stared agog at the furnishings. Still the drawling lockjaw voices prevailed, and the conversation was much as it had ever been – about schools, and stocks and shares, and health matters, and the sorry falling-off in the quality of English life, and friends of friends – but the surroundings didn't fit quite so naturally into the auspicious epoch in which they all now found themselves.

12

An Incidental History

Mrs Moncrieff-King, Jennifer's mother, had been widowed shortly after her daughter was born. She was a woman with superior airs and a long pedigree but – it was generally believed – relatively little money to her name. Her husband had been a brigadier and Welsh Guards pietist, and consequently she was entitled to certain privileges, financial and social; she still had several decades of life ahead of her, however, so how – it was widely discussed – could she *not* allow herself to dwell on her 'prospects'? She veered between effervescence and melancholy, and neither was thought to have been her natural, God-given disposition: the reason for the former must have been that she had to be seen as optimistic and on top of the situation, the latter was induced by her recall of the past and consideration of the future, both tenses seeming to conspire against her.

Her daughter's behaviour was similarly inconstant. She was less pretty than striking, but from an early age she had known instinctively how to present herself to attract attention which more obviously well-favoured girls were unable to hold on themselves. She could be vivacious and sparky; being a creature of mood, however, she could also show her obverse side: her brow would darken and words would have to be pulled from her like teeth. During her sullen bouts of monosyllabism her scowls were alarming, and she gave the distinct impression that her secret knowledge of other people's characters and histories gave her an authority no one would challenge, and which no one did – anyone with common sense and an instinct for self-preservation taking care to steer a clear passage round about her. Then, overnight often, there would be another mercurial about-turn, and it would be a quite different face and personality she was presenting to Aquae-Regis, lively and talkative and wry.

All this at eight years old. By the time she was sixteen, her quicksilver temperament was a legend, and certain boys of her own age with whom she came into contact were intrigued by the discrepancies to the point of ignoring other, much more eligible objects for their regard. By now Brigadier Moncrieff-King's daughter had spent several years at a boarding school in Suffolk which catered for the educational and social needs of the daughters of officers and diplomatic gentlemen, and she returned to Aquae-Regis at the end of each term (when she wasn't visiting the homes of fellow pupils) with still more gloss and more hauteur. Catherine felt quite provincial by comparison: she knew that the school was located in the middle of rolling countryside, surrounded by farmland, but the vital factor of its geographical position was its proximity to London. Being so close – by a railway or no – the principles of fashion and etiquette must have blown there from the metropolis on a down wind and infected them all.

Catherine envied the girl the outer assurance – the easy way with rather glib words and her innate, unfaultable clothes sense – but not the inconstancy of her temperament, which the methods of her education could do nothing about. She could usually resist rage, but she didn't refrain from letting her irritation with people show; and always it was done with that dark imputation that *she* knew enough about *them* to be able to wipe smirks on to the other side of faces if she chose to.

She made Catherine uncomfortable. She always had done, since the days when they'd attended the same small preparatory school in Aquae-Regis. At first they'd had little to do with one another. Then, without any prior indication it might happen, Jennifer had suddenly become very much friendlier. Catherine was relieved to find herself no longer at the receiving end of those black looks the Brigadier's daughter would shoot across the room, but she had found it difficult to reciprocate in full. Anyway she had guessed for herself that there was more applied effort than contrition in Jennifer's advances, but she found herself feeling guilty that she might somehow betray her own knowledge that this was the case. So, she made a rather tepid and sickly show of friendliness in return, and was dissatisfied and a little ashamed with the result, and nervous about what it all might mean.

They continued on this same uneasy footing for a couple of years until they left the Treetops School and Jennifer departed for her boarding establishment in Suffolk. It was when she returned that Christmas and cut her dash at the annual children's party held in the Assembly Rooms that Catherine realised she had been correct from the beginning and the blood temporarily iced in her veins. She had been dragooned into a conversation, about parents. Jennifer said, without looking at her, 'I'd much rather have a mother than a father.' Catherine didn't reply, but someone else did on her behalf.

'If you've a father, he'll buy you things. He'll never leave you wanting.'

'Mothers are loving,' Jennifer replied loftily. '*Some* mothers are, anyway.'

In the course of the same evening Catherine heard that Mrs Moncrieff-King and her father had been observed together at a couple of soirées two months in succession. Catherine wondered if that was why Jennifer had been so disapproving. She found the girl who'd told her, who had blurted it out, recognising that something had been awry in the earlier conversation with Jennifer.

'How do you know?'

'My mother said.'

'Who to?'

'My father.'

'Said what?'

'That she'd seen him. And Mrs Moncrieff-King was . . .'

She stopped herself. Catherine prompted her.

'What *about* Mrs Moncrieff-King?'

'My mother was just talking – '

'What – ' Catherine had a disturbing premonition ' – what did she say?'

'Just that – she was tipping her cap. Something like that.'

'What did she mean?'

'That she'd had her eye on him.'

'On who?'

'Your father.'

Catherine paused to consider.

'Why? Why would she do that?'

'My mother said – '

Again the girl stopped herself.

'What?' Catherine felt impatient. '*What* did she say?'

'That that was her way.'

' "Her way"?'

'It was typical of her.'

'What was "typical"?'

'I wasn't really listening. They were just talking, my parents. They didn't know I was there.'

'But what was "typical"?'

'That she was always looking. On the look-out.'

'Why?' But she knew the answer of course.

'Because she's a widow.'

Catherine nodded.

'Then what? What else did they say?'

'Nothing much.'

'They said *something*?'

'Not really.'

'*What?*' Catherine asked with her voice raised. The girl looked round with fright.

'Just – that she was – barking up the wrong tree.'

Catherine didn't reply.

'He wasn't her "kind", really. But – that it was worth a try.'

Catherine gave the girl a long, menacing hypnotist's stare. Then she grabbed her right arm and squeezed the flesh just below the elbow as hard as she could. The girl gasped, wriggled, begged her to stop, please, *please*; she turned puce, she might have been going to squeal with the hurt of it.

'You – ' Catherine tried to think what she was ' – you little *baggage*! You bloody little *beast*!'

It was the swearword that finally took the girl's breath away and she was left heaving, like a landed fish. Before she let go, Catherine permitted herself a final twist of the flesh on the forearm; the girl let out a low, inconsolable wail and burst into tears.

Catherine walked off quickly. She made her way through the polite welter of children and adult supervisors, following the signs to the cloakrooms. Inside the ladies' Jennifer Moncrieff-King was standing alone in front of a vanity mirror, side-on in profile, one hand cupping an incipient breast. She was surprised in mid-movement and stared at Catherine open-mouthed. Then the colour rose from her neck: anger at the discovery.

Catherine marched past her, into the second room, and slammed the cubicle door shut behind her. She let down her knickers but was too upset to relieve herself. She adjusted her dress, flushed the cistern and threw the door open. Jennifer was still there, combing her hair, avoiding the velvet bows which were a new accessory.

Catherine walked through, and past her.

'Just a moment,' a voice said.

Catherine stopped.

'Haven't you forgotten something – ?'

'Forgotten what?' Catherine said, without looking round.

'To wash your hands. It's unhygienic not to. Hasn't anyone ever told you?' The delivery was caustic, a parade-ground put-down.

Catherine stood bunching her hands into fists.

'My mother has always told *me* so.'

'What does *she* know anyway?' Catherine snapped back.

'Quite a lot, as it happens.'

'Oh yes?'

'Yes, she tells me things she remembers.'

Catherine felt a metal band tightening around her head.

'She remembers *your* mother anyway.'

Catherine found the face in the mirror glass and glared at her, without mercy.

'What's *that* got to do with it?'

'I've heard her talking to her friends.'

'Why?' Catherine's voice was blunted, broken. 'What – what about?'

'Oh . . . nothing to interest –'

'What *about*?' Catherine couldn't control her ire.

'Why your father married her.'

Catherine put all the hate that she could into her eyes, searing Jennifer's face with them.

'You're talking about my mother.'

'Not your father?'

'My *mother*,' Catherine repeated, voice wavering. 'She's dead.'

'That's another thing.'

Catherine had to pump herself up with breath.

'What's another thing?'

'When your mother died.'

'What about it?'

Jennifer dropped her comb into her small, embroidered evening bag.

'I've not to talk about it, my mother said.'

'Your mother's a baggage.'

Jennifer only raised her eyebrows.

'A bloody baggage,' Catherine said.

The eyebrows drew together, but still wouldn't disclose more.

'Shall I tell her that?'

'You can tell her what you bally well like.'

Catherine turned away, too incensed and dispirited for more. Except one final observation.

'You haven't got any, anyway. Not *real* ones.'

'Got what?' Jennifer asked.

'Tits,' Catherine said, using the awful word she had never spoken before. 'That's what.'

In the next couple of seconds an object flew past her right ear: the hairbrush from the vanity set provided for general use. It hit the wall and fell to the floor.

Catherine stormed off, boiling over, nearly wrenching the door off its hinges in her haste to get away, but also – for these moments – elevated high in righteousness.

*

Despair flooded in afterwards, as she knew that it must. It lasted for days.

She watched her father, but saw him no different for Mrs Moncrieff-King's insidious influence. She looked into the crack behind the dining-room mirror, but saw no sign of her mother, only a photograph of a man's face she couldn't make out torn into several pieces and scattered on the floor. Her aunt was much as usual, taking care not to notice her sudden inwardness, busying them both in tacking holly along the picture rail in the drawing-room.

She flirted with the subject with her best friend. Audrey was more direct, and (finally) succinct.

'She's got grand tastes. But if she marries anyone else, then she won't be a brigadier's widow any more.'

'Is that important?'

'It means her husband has to be better than a brigadier.'

Catherine was humbled by her knowledge.

'But I'm not very interested,' Audrey told her. 'My father says she's very predictable.'

'*Is* she?'

'She needs more money and she resents people who have it. That's what he said. She once knew one of the guests here.'

'Who?'

'Sir Somebody Something-or-other. My mother didn't trust him much, which is usually recommendation. But for once she really was right about him. He was as poor as a church mouse, and he was using dud cheques to pay. Anyway, Mrs M-K came after him until she smelt a rotten fish.'

Audrey was always to speak so, with an awareness of such matters that exceeded her years. She saw people as complicated and simple at the same time: sometimes contradicting themselves, but in the end reducible to type. It was the lesson of life she had received as a hotelier's daughter.

Catherine didn't know how to dispute anything she said. Audrey only shrugged when she learned of the incident in the washroom.

'She's Mrs M-K's daughter, think what that must be like.'

Catherine mistook the reply for partisanship, sympathy for Jennifer. Audrey perceived the misunderstanding.

'She should see what she's going to turn into. Take a long hard look at herself.'

'That's what she *was* doing. In the mirror, in the lav. But I think she was quite pleased really.'

'Until *you* showed up?'

'What?'

'I expect you make her see things she doesn't want to.'

The adult reasoning was still beyond Catherine's reach.

'She won't admit about her mother. And she envies you.'

'What?'

'Because, darling – ' Audrey threw her arms around Catherine's neck with cod gush ' – because she can't stand how you look.'

' "Look"?'

Audrey led her inside, through the hotel's vestibule and hall, to the cheval-glass in the drawing-room.

'She hates it that you should be prettier than she is.'

Audrey's hands rested lightly beneath the hummocks of her best friend's breasts.

'It's really quite straightforward, Catherine.'

'That's how you make it sound – straightforward.'

'She will always envy you. Unless you grow plainer and she grows prettier.'

'Does it happen?'

'It can. But it won't.'

'How do you know that?'

'Hating someone is like taking poison.'

'Does she hate me?'

'Not just you. Dozens of people, I expect. But especially you.'

'But *I* might turn into – '

'Not if I'm always here to remind you – ' Audrey enfolded her waist with her arms. 'I shall never let you forget, Catherine.'

Audrey had mentioned her appearance to her before. The subject embarrassed Catherine. Audrey was the oldest-looking in their form: her nose was too big, and her shoulders too broad, but she had the determination to make people see 'possibilities' in her, for the time ahead. She was open-ended as Jennifer was already closing in on herself, diminishing her own range of potentialities.

Audrey could always console her and put her mind at ease, about whatever it was, and with such little difficulty or appearance of thought. Catherine felt she could tell her anything, and did tell her, and was to continue doing so, for as long as she was able, until circumstances were to take an outlandish – but perhaps, if she could only have read them, as Audrey must have been able to – predictable turn.

13

Un Homme et une Femme

In the first term of her final year it was a different Audrey who returned to school.

She was thinner; she had taken in her uniform by a full inch and a half and somehow the slimmer, straight fit made her look taller. Flouting her stepmother's wishes – as she took pride in pointing out – she'd had her hair styled in a salon. She'd had her fingers manicured and her nails painted with clear varnish. But it was her manner which chiefly disturbed Catherine: she seemed even more assured, in total command of herself, in a new, artificially seigneurial and languid way. She talked about London, where she'd visited family cousins in the summer, and about how exciting life was away from this 'hole'.

The expression was considered rather a shocking one, but Audrey needed to make her point forcefully. She announced, not quite out of earshot of some mistresses, 'I don't intend being stuck *here* till the end of my natural, thanks very much.' While she was more daring in front of people, Catherine saw that she was more thoughtful and also detached when there were just the two of them. In public, she noticed, Audrey wasn't giving away so much as she pretended with her more extravagant and extrovert behaviour. What she was imparting now seemed to have been rehearsed; when Catherine tried to question her further, to draw some more revelations out of her, she had relatively little success. Audrey shrugged, began two or three sentences she didn't finish, stared into the distance, knotted the fingers of her regulation white gloves. It might have been intentional – to make a deeper, more enticing mystery of the summer – but Catherine guessed that there were matters about which Audrey didn't feel confident to judge, which were confusing even her. Catherine was always hoping she might presume to be a confidante, but Audrey had a polite way of letting her see she didn't consider her as fully qualified for that function. She would return Catherine's looks of curiosity with looks of a different expression, shrewd and assessing and, so far as confidences went, as yet unconvinced.

Nearly a month into the new term, walking back home alone after prep, Catherine spotted Audrey's disciplined new outline passing under the portico of the Peregrine Hotel. Their form mistress had announced to the class that Audrey Stimpton was 'indisposed' and spending the day in bed. During prep Catherine had decided that, if she had time, she would call in at the Duke of Buckingham and ask one of the staff how the invalid was faring.

Opposite the town's smartest hotel she came to a dead stop. She might have been mistaken of course. But in fact she would have been more likely to be proved wrong if she'd seen Audrey wearing her uniform. The young woman she'd just glimpsed had been accoutred in sophisticated navy and black, not girlish bottle green and maroon, and the Look was brand New, à la mode de Dior. She couldn't be positive, but she had identified the gait as Audrey's, the half-run that always suggested to Catherine she was on her speedy way to somewhere much more exciting than any of *them* were bound for.

No. The longer she stood on the pavement looking across at the hotel, the more definite she became that she had surmised correctly: that Audrey wasn't languishing in her sick-bed, but hot-footing it into the foyer of the Peregrine, dressed up to the veritable nines in her wasp-waist jacket and mid-calf skirt, with the posture that was the latest rage in Paris and London – leaning backwards in her high pointed heels and rolling her hips.

Hotels and restaurants and tea-rooms were out-of-bounds, unless very special dispensation had been sought. Audrey might have been granted approval to visit, and made a fortuitous recovery from her indisposition. But Catherine's thoughts were differently inclined on the matter: Audrey was her own mistress this term, and gave the impression that she had made plans for herself, her immediate future was nicely mapped out and illness didn't come into the reckoning.

Dusk was coming down only slowly, and the evenings were light enough for the senior girls who walked home to go unchaperoned, but – as the rules stipulated – in pairs. Tonight Audrey was unavailable, but it had somehow slipped Miss Beveridge's mind that one of the girls would be returning home 'sola'. It didn't bother Catherine especially, although as she walked she was conscious of a lack – Audrey's running commentary on the townspeople, how they were dressed, how they wore their hair, their routines, what she had overheard her stepmother tell her father. But in the last few weeks that ready, steady flow of information, bubbling sotto voce and floating them home, up the hills and round the Circus and along crescents and terraces, such a plentiful source of gossip had dried up dramatically, and they had proceeded in relative silence, compared with the last days of the term before. It couldn't have been that Audrey didn't know, only that she didn't care as she had formerly; she hardly even seemed to notice their surroundings, neither the buildings nor what had always proved their human interest. Catherine's own comments – she spoke them to plug the gaps in the conversation – sounded more foolish and inconsequential and naïve than they ever had before.

There were several minutes of approximate daylight still left. The gaslights along the street gave off a pale, fitful blue glow. The cars that passed her were driving by sidelights only. She didn't feel herself to be in any measure of danger. She was only taking the night air, she believed, in tidy little ladylike sips. Her father was dining out tonight, and her aunt had arranged to make up a bridge-four at a house in Little Kelligan Street. So she had no reason to hasten back home; and Mrs Ramage's replacement kept herself too busy in her muddled way to be able to keep tabs on her movements, to remember if she had said she might be later home. It was quite natural behaviour, therefore, that she should be standing as she was, in the last of daylight before gloaming's onset, doing nothing so very extraordinary.

All the time, though – as she proceeded along the pavement, halted, turned back again, as if she was merely waiting to make a rendezvous – she continued to steal glances across the street, towards the Peregrine Hotel. She kept up her watch on the portico, insouciantly, and when she grew just a little weary of focusing on that and the shadows behind the revolving front doors she let her eyes stray across the façade of the building. It was in the course of one of her incidental sweeps that she spotted the figure again, at an upstairs window. She recognised Audrey's auburn hair, styled in the new 'draped' fashion, and her way of standing with her hands on her waist and twisting her hips as she turned her head. That was the indisputable truth, and the breath caught in Catherine's throat as she forgot all about the pretence of naturalness and just stood staring.

Audrey, scarlet-lipped, wasn't looking streetwards; if she was seeing anything, it was the prospect of Paradise Hill. At any rate she was turned in that direction, facing away from the stretch of pavement opposite the portico.

Catherine thought that, if she moved or as much as blinked, she could lose the figure. She wasn't expecting what happened next, the appearance of a second figure at the same window. He did appear, however, seeming to glide into position beside her best friend, standing so close to her in his shirt and braces that their bodies must have been touching, or all but. They both looked towards Paradise Hill, and then they both turned away; and in the next instant dematerialised among the furnishings of the room.

A bedroom, Catherine had to suppose: or the sitting-room of a small suite. She waited, in case they should reappear. When they didn't, she began walking, with her eyes trained downwards on the pavement straight ahead of her. On the corner of the street she paused and pulled at the white gloves of her uniform, quite ferociously, as if she meant to burst the tops of the fingers. She was thinking of the potential of pleasure which lay in the couple's deceit, and she was quite unnerved imagining it, she even felt her stomach squeamish; she stood at the kerbside and closed her eyes, tugging on the fingers of her gloves, experiencing just a little of what she hadn't ever dared to fully picture to herself before, and even that small portion was leaving her feeling yellow, bilious, broken-winded.

She opened her eyes to the falling dusk. Her whole body was rigid, as if she had been temporarily taken possession of, as if she had given away this that was her own to another, in submission or exchange. She looked forward, to the flank of Paradise Hill, realising something which Audrey already had some seasons before – what a terrible, enthralling kind of travel might lie in the passage between two consenting individuals.

*

His name was Reggie Billington.

It didn't immediately register with Catherine. Audrey rolled her eyes at her. She clearly hadn't wanted to say much, and yet – Catherine had been very surprised to find – she had been ready to acknowledge the fact.

'There *is* someone.'

'What?'

'Don't you mean who?'

'Who? "Someone"?'

'A man.'

Audrey, nearly smiling, prolonged the suspense.

'I see,' Catherine said.

'You *do* want to know who?'

Audrey read her stare as an affirmative response.

'His name . . .' she paused for full dramatic effect. ' . . . is Reggie Billington.'

Catherine didn't speak.'

'*The* Reggie Billington, that is. The racing driver.' Audrey couldn't suppress the smile of intense pride. 'There's only one.'

Catherine continued to stare.

'What is it they say? After Reggie, they broke the mould.'

Audrey smiled, in a relaxed but distant way.

'I know his name,' Catherine said. 'From the newspapers.'

'Oh, he's always in the papers. I've seen him in a newsreel too. He was winning something.'

They sat, less talking than whispering, in the farthest alcove of the school library.

Audrey leaned forward and hitched up her skirt. Catherine watched as she slipped two fingers under the top of her stocking. (The silk stockings in themselves were a small miracle. Audrey had told her that one of the regular men guests at the hotel was able to find her 'odds and ends' for the asking; and all it took was a few minutes spent chatting with him in the lounge when the other guests had drifted off to bed.) Catherine's eyes narrowed as the fingers drew out a piece of paper and unfolded it.

'I cut it out of a magazine. A guest's.'

The warm photograph showed a man's head and shoulders: a photogenic face with a cleft chin and handsomely broken nose and broad, sportsman's shoulders.

'I can never stop looking at him, Cath.'

Catherine felt her eyes narrowing again.

'He doesn't know I'm at school. He just thinks I'm something to do with the hotel.'

'He stays – at the hotel?'

'Good God, no. At the Peregrine. But I've told him about the Buck.'

Audrey refolded the magazine snipping and tenderly smoothed it flat on her thigh.

'How – how did you meet him?'

'You won't believe this – '

Catherine set her mouth straight in readiness for not believing.

'It was the night Rumpelstiltskin roped you into the Country Dancing. Remember?'

Catherine nodded.

'I was walking back. I had something in my shoe, so I stopped and took it off. Anyway, there I was leaning against this railing and straightening my stocking when a car draws up. And there he is – Reggie Billington! I recognised him at once.'

'Why – why did he stop?'

'To ask directions, of course.'

The photograph was replaced beneath the stocking and the suspender belt adjusted.

'He said he'd lost his way. He was looking for ... Oh, I can't remember where now. But it was a bit complicated, I remember that. So he said, well, if you know and it's going your way, why not jump in and I'll take you? I don't think it *was* my way – it might have been Jane Street, or Jeune – anyway we drove off.'

Audrey's eyes flitted across the spines of the books on the shelves.

'He went quite slowly, for a racing driver. He didn't seem surprised I knew. And I was prattling away – telling him Aquae Regis was a backwater sometimes, but at least it was a real town, and you got to meet some very unexpected people. I meant *him* of course, but then I mentioned the hotel, the Buck, so he asked me about that, and the ice got broken. Although it wasn't difficult with him, not at all. Very easy in fact. He kept smiling, and turning to hear what I was saying. I was pretty nervous, of course.'

Audrey leaned forward on one elbow and drew some shapes on the table-top with her fingers. At moments, Catherine had always felt, her best friend was capable of lapsing into this childlike state. It seemed to be abstracted, but – sitting in the library with her – she now supposed that it must be beguiling too, to those who were unused to it. At these same moments she would undergo a temporary sea-change, she would feel what she didn't at any other time in Audrey's company – older than her, more composed, more self-contained. But this composure didn't seem to bring her the special, covetable savoir-faire that Audrey's manner would customarily suggest. She continued to live in her mentor's wake, bobbing about in the backwash.

A number of times after that Catherine dropped a reference to the Peregrine Hotel, but it elicited only the most general sort of response. Once when they were walking past on their homeward journey from school, Catherine caught Audrey's eyes passing to the building's façade; but it was done in the lightest, most casual manner, and under cover of a smile.

Catherine was confused. For several days she wrestled with her puzzlement, until the realisation slowly dawned on her that Audrey felt no shame. Perhaps she was quite untroubled by the grubby gropings of conscience, as they would have afflicted one with a weaker constitution. She hadn't yet answered squarely about the Peregrine and all that the place might mean to her, but neither had she been intentionally deceitful in her replies. She must have been only too aware that her friend from childhood had failed to make full progress in all aspects of her education, and that allowances must be made.

*

Across the Abbey Yard she saw Audrey stepping through the small entrance in the Great West Door.

She delayed a couple of minutes or so – looking in shop windows, watching the reflections in the glass – before she followed.

She stood at the back of the nave and picked out Audrey in the middle of a row of rush chairs. Round about there were another half-dozen persons seated at strategic distances from one another.

It occurred to her that she must be filling in time before a rendezvous with Reggie: or possibly they had arranged to meet here. But, as Catherine watched, she noticed there were no backward looks to the entrance, no downward glances at the watch on her wrist. She was staring straight ahead of her.

After twenty minutes timed by her own watch, Catherine decided to join her. Audrey's face was bloodless, she saw at once. She only turned her head a few degrees to acknowledge her friend's presence, recognising her from her shoes. Catherine left a chair between them and sat down.

'I might have been wrong,' Audrey said in a voice pitched just loudly enough to travel that short distance. 'About Mother. I killed her, you know. Maybe it's what happens anyway, with daughters. Something makes us resentful, we go through life working little deaths on our mothers.'

Catherine held her breath.

'Because we envy them, our mothers, for having loved; or we think they're smothering us, competing against us maybe – '

'Why – what's brought this on? Audrey?'

'Well, I just killed her outright. Got it over and done with there and then. There wasn't time for all the rest.'

'I remember so little now,' Catherine began, but Audrey wasn't listening to her.

'I killed her good and proper. She must have known. Somehow – I don't know why – I felt that really she was hating me. What I was putting her through, after the happiest time of – It was such a terrible birth, you know – for me too – I think she might have been making me suffer as well.'

'No,' Catherine said, and she shook her head. 'No, Audrey. You're wrong, I'm sure you're – '

'She must've hated me so much. She knew she'd get her revenge, though: some day. That carried her – '

'You told me it was the opposite. Don't you remember?'

'That was just what people told *me*. What they wanted to tell me. It sounded quite convincing, at the time. But that was then, you see. Wasn't it?'

Figures moved in the side-aisles, in the half-light. Catherine saw them and didn't see them, not until afterwards when she thought back with a chill in her marrow to the place and the occasion.

'I think,' Audrey said, 'she's just been waiting for her moment, you see.'

Catherine was appalled. She wondered if she should just get to her feet and leave, to pretend between them that this conversation had never happened.

'So she's jinxed it with Reggie and me. She's really – ' Audrey cleared her throat and continued to stare ahead of her, at brass angels and blaring trumpets on top of the organ-case ' – really done what's for this time.'

Catherine shaped several words with her lips, but couldn't make any sound come out of her mouth. Audrey seemed to intuit the question, however.

'He was in a race. The car skidded on oil and it bounced off the track.'

Her hands had grabbed the back of the chair in front. Catherine didn't move.

'It somersaulted several times. Someone took photographs.'

'How – how is he?'

Audrey didn't seem to hear.

'What – what's happened?'

Audrey shook her head slowly. Ought she not to have been crying? – shouting the building down on top of them?

'Is – is he all right?'

Audrey's mouth formed a smile, or rather the ghost of one. She really had nothing to smile about, nothing at all.

'I wish he'd died,' she said.

Catherine clasped her hand to her mouth.

'If he'd died, I could just remember him. As he was.'

'How – what's – '

'They wouldn't tell me. When I telephoned the hospital. Only that he'd been – ' She cleared her throat again, and folded her hands on the back of the rail of the chair in front. From a distance she might have appeared to be praying. 'They said how bad it was, though. How he probably won't walk again.'

'Oh. Audrey – '

'And he might have brain damage, blood's been dripping on it.'

Tears welled in Catherine's eyes and she lost her focus entirely.

'I don't know if it's *him* or not. If it's Reggie – '

'Oh, Audrey – '

'I expect everyone feels so wise about it. "We told you so." Because it's so dangerous. But that's why he did it: the danger, the people telling him not to. He walked out of school when he was fifteen, you know: by mutual consent, though. Life was so deadly dull, he said, "*they* make it dull". That's why he raced.'

Audrey wiped her nose with the back of her hand. Her voice held steady, although it had become quieter.

'But "they" were really behind it all the time, I suppose. Like Romans and gladiators. You know? It made *their* lives a bit more exciting too – but *they* weren't taking the risks – '

Catherine leaned towards her and laid her hand on her arm.

'Please stop, Audrey – '

'He knew "the risks", of course. The famous "risks". But he didn't think there was an alternative. There wasn't really. He knew I understood that.'

Audrey leaned back in the chair.

'But there's some evil behind it. There has to be.'

'A terrible accident, Audrey.'

'He didn't deserve it, but maybe they'll say he did.'

'No. No, they wouldn't – '

Audrey lifted her shoulders and dropped them again.

'You – ' Catherine moved on to the next chair ' – you're so calm.'

'No.' The smile returned, grim and mirthless. 'No, not inside. Not inside at all.'

Catherine took her back to the Duke of Buckingham. The journey lasted three or four times as long as usual. There was no Parisian leaning backwards, no hip-rolling. Audrey talked and Catherine listened to all she was told, about the young man who had gone racing yesterday afternoon in his four-and-a-half-litre Talbot-Lagos.

As they were on the last stretch a car horn played a brief tattoo and drew up beside them at the kerb. The driver was a man of fifty or so, in a tweed windowpane check jacket and mustard waistcoat. He had a handlebar moustache, and he watched them both with furtive eyes that didn't seem to accompany his hearty, cocktail-bar voice.

'Hail, Fair Audrey! Got yourself a pretty young friend, I see?'

Audrey stared at him, quite blankly for four or five seconds. Then it registered with her who he was and she smiled, in a bold and knowing, wide-eyed way – until she remembered the circumstances, and the smile was abandoned.

'Back again, Audrey!'

She nodded. 'Yes.'

'Can't keep away!'

'No.'

'My wife's a wee bit poorly. But I've got some business to see to.'

'Yes.'

Mouth grinning under his topiary moustache, his eyes heliographed to Audrey. But she tightened her hold on Catherine's arm and turned them both away.

'Feeling okey-dokey, Audrey? Why don't you hop in?'

She looked back.

'I'm fine,' she said.

The driver's smile widened, showing his luteous tombstone teeth. He adjusted the chain of his fob watch, then slipped off the handbrake.

'See you later then?' he said.

Audrey nodded, and turned them both away again.

Catherine was curious to know who he was: if only to postpone the tragic subject of Reggie, delay it a few moments longer at least.

'Fred? Oh, he's – just a guest.'

No more was disclosed. Catherine watched the car as it climbed the hill and its driver smoothed down his hair, watching himself – or Audrey and her – in the windscreen mirror.

Later, upon the flat, walking along Cheveney Terrace, they approached the hotel from the pavement opposite. Catherine happened to look across and saw a windowpane check jacket, mustard waistcoat and handlebar moustache withdrawing from one of the first-floor windows.

She pointed him out.

'Oh, Fred? His wife likes that room.'

'But she's poorly.'

'Oh. Yes.'

They stopped. Audrey still clung to her arm. Catherine guessed that he was still watching, from further back in the room.

Standing with Audrey – who was clearly wanting to put off time – she felt that, the desperate fate of Reggie notwithstanding, she was beginning to see Audrey's participation in the life of the hotel in a new and troubling light. She had often wondered how she adjusted to it at the day's end: she knew she didn't care for her stepmother, that her father doted on the woman, so where did that leave Audrey? With time to kill, presumably, and a need to find more congenial, more amicable company to hand. Which was presumably the common instinct of men like the one who had sounded his horn so saucily at them, without or even *with* his wife in tow. Maybe it went no further than pecks on her cheek or a hand on her bottom. But the possibilities and permutations to Catherine's susceptible imagination were suddenly endless . . .

Audrey slipped her arm out of its hold. The temporary bond was undone, and with it the brief link of comprehension.

'Will – will you be all right?' Catherine asked her.

'Oh, *I*'ll be fine,' Audrey said, weighing the pronoun with the stress.

'I'm *so* sorry, Audrey.'

'Well . . .'

'I'll be thinking about – '

'Yes.'

Audrey nodded, stoically, as if such sore trials were only to be expected in the normal run. She was still tearless, and very nearly composed. Catherine couldn't fathom such decorum in the face of –

'I may be absent tomorrow,' Audrey said.

'Yes. Yes, you – '

'Probably I *will* be. My stomach or something – '

'Will – will you – '

'What?'

' – tell them? Your parents?'

Audrey stared at her.

'Catherine – '

'No. Of course not. I don't know what I – '

'I thought you understood – '

'I *do*. Really.'

About Reggie, about your parents, about tomorrow. About Fred too maybe, who'll be at a low ebb himself, who has found 'business' to occupy him while his wife is poorly.

She was forgetting Reggie again, who must be the significance behind everything now. Fred was incidental, and probably always had been, like his type.

'If there's anything – '

'I'm sorry?'

' – I don't know what I could do, but – '

'If you understand, Catherine, that's enough – '

'I do, Audrey. As much as I can. I've been trying very hard.'

Audrey smiled sadly. The next moment tears were coursing down her cheeks. She started sobbing, and instinctively Catherine put her arms round her and held her.

'I don't – I don't know – what I'm going to do.'

They stood side by side on the uneven flagstones of Cheveney Terrace, in full sight of the prying windows of the Duke of Buckingham Hotel, and Audrey cried her heart out. Catherine suffered an overload of remorse, a Sisyphus boulder of contrition, that she could ever have doubted the virtues of her friend's heart, for even a single moment.

Audrey clung to her. The sobs and shakes pulsed through Catherine's body too, the tears fell from Audrey's cheeks on to hers, grief lightning-jumped its passage and they mourned together in tandem for Reggie Billington.

She would have talked about Reggie if she had thought that it would have been welcome. But the impression she had was quite otherwise. Audrey didn't speak about him; after the first weeks of sorrowing, she emerged from that chrysalis with an appetite for the things in life that were most inconsequential and ephemeral. She bought fashion magazines and took care not to leave them lying about for hotel guests to filch; she learned to impersonate the comic characters she listened to on the radio; she became the repository of school tittle-tattle.

Catherine didn't allow herself to be too surprised. She supposed that it had been there all the time, her tendency to levity, and that now – lest she should remember – she was letting it flourish. Catherine had occasional doubts, however, when Audrey seemed to falter, or when she appeared to be reappraising her audience and went up or down a gear with her performance: but maybe she was looking to find these contrary indicators. She watched Audrey's gaze fix sometimes, and her features momentarily gel, as she gave a very convincing impersonation of someone suddenly finding herself in two places at the same time. And sometimes it happened that a performance of school gossip would be cancelled in the library or prep room because Audrey said she had a headache, or because she had worked out that the mechanics of placing a wicker waste-paper basket above Miss Anstruther's door wasn't going to work; she might fail to see where the rest of them were gathered when she walked out of school at the day's end, becoming confused afterwards – about who had said or done what – when she and Catherine discussed the day just past on their walk home each evening, up the steep streets and along the high-stepped pavements of Paradise Hill.

*

Reggie's brain was saved. But his body couldn't be rescued from the paralysis that claimed his left side.

He left hospital fourteen weeks after the accident, for a change of scene, with arrangements made for further physiotherapy on his return. The story appeared in several newspapers.

At the same time that Reggie was temporarily discharged, Audrey went missing. The pretext of absence from school through illness couldn't be maintained. The police were informed, but Catherine knew that their involvement was unnecessary.

They traced the couple to a hotel in palmy Paignton. The hotel was white and imposing and hardly anonymous: but the escapees didn't care.

Audrey had become Mrs Billington at a registry office ceremony: that much and little more was recorded in the press. They were photographed, however, leaving the municipal building in Paignton: cleft-chinned Reggie in his wheelchair, Audrey looking slimmer than ever in a pencil-line suit, holding either the dead hand or the living one.

Catherine was moved to tears, lots of them. But a photograph did not, so she felt, tell the whole story. She wished Audrey had been able to trust her sufficiently to confide more to her.

She realised that if Audrey hadn't had the measure of *her*, then *she* most certainly had misjudged Audrey. Maybe she had too easily subsumed into her calculations about her friend's behaviour the atmosphere of the disclosure of Reggie's accident, in the dark belly of that great echoing Abbey, and she had merely supposed that Audrey had gone there to deposit the matter in God's hands, to shed some of the appalling responsibility of deciding. The two of them had never quite confronted the topic of religion; they had attended school chapel and Abbey services on special occasions just as they were obliged to do, and Catherine distrusted God – if such He was – on account of the narrowness His Word had instilled in her more devout father. She didn't know how God manifested Himself at the Duke of Buckingham Hotel, but she had observed how Audrey sang hymns to the end even if her eyes were occupied by her fellow singers, how she might seem to be distracted during a sermon but would pull her eyes sharply back to the speaker whenever she caught a particular phrase or idea. She might whisper during an anthem or voluntary, but she would always interrupt herself to say the organist was taking the piece too fast or too slow or was only playing it 'in his sleep'. Automatic religion seemed to Catherine to be the whole point in Aquae-Regis, but something made her refrain from saying so to Audrey.

The marriage service had been of the secular sort, which still begged the question: it may have been Reggie's express choice, or *hers*, or a decision taken jointly. To Catherine, a church ceremony would have been sacrilege – blasphemy done to Reggie and his suffering – but she realised even better now that Audrey's opinions had been chiefly a closed book to her. Audrey had married the man – giving herself in the binding terms of law – while *she* hadn't calculated that such a formidable private morality might be quietly decreeing itself inside Audrey's alternative person, behind the façade of forgetful abstraction and anxious pleasure-taking.

14

Hesperus House

THE time after that was the loneliest of Catherine's life. She became quite despondent. She dwelled a lot on the new experiences Audrey must be undergoing without actually being certain what those might be. She saw Jennifer Moncrieff-King arriving home one holiday, with all the glory and panoply attaching to a princess, and with a face – she thought – grown quite vinegary with pride and misdoubt.

Home was no comfort to her, and she took to walking in the time left over from school and prep. She began to wonder who among the people she saw she might trust to be as they appeared. She had thought herself capable of knowing Audrey, but in the end she hadn't: perhaps not even in the third and fourth forms, in that sorry, self-pitying time of hot flushes and bloody leaks when their friendship had seemed easiest. Audrey had raced through her teens ahead of her, and that momentum had provided the velocity to propel her now into mature womanhood.

She didn't like to think of their love-making, which was why she had to, and could hardly take her mind off it. It grew to be an obsession with her. At night, in bed, she woke dreaming of the act, and couldn't get back to sleep again; lying in the bath she imagined the secrets of Audrey's body and inevitably her thoughts turned to Reggie's, not as it now was but as it must have been. Somehow, she knew, they were countering the physical impediments, just as they had overcome the other obstacles strewn in their way.

One Saturday afternoon she walked down into the town after peering through the crack in the dining-room plaster and seeing a naked woman sitting on a swing. She felt overheated and clammy, the 'curse' – as her aunt always referred to it – was upon her; her breasts felt slop-heavy, she didn't know which way she was headed, the streets cast a glare even off the grimy stone. She had to wipe the back of her neck with a handkerchief. She didn't want anyone to see and turned off the sapping pavements into the network of shadowed lanes. There she knew her way by touch and sound, directing herself with her fingertips on the green, lichened stone and by the sonar of her footfalls on the irregular slabs of paving or the old Georgian cobbles. She hurried along the echoing gussets between the towering flanks of buildings, past walled sunless yards, over the original conduits, beneath the branches of venerable trees which grew incongruously in the prevailing shade. Cats and rats darted at the merest sound of her, at the disturbance of shadows.

She felt her legs were trying to give her the slip. She didn't know where she was being taken. She looked up at one stage as she was running and saw blue sky like sea lapping beneath her and somehow – even with her perspective jumbled and her head spinning – she still kept running. Her soles clattered in the narrow passage between two house-sides like cliffs, then they grew very faint to her ear. Holding on to her glimpse of blue sky she thought she heard a liquid swill. For the briefest interlude of time she wondered as she ran full pelt if love-making between a woman and a man could cause sickness and delirium so complete as this.

The sea and the sky started to fall behind her, they tilted down and out of her range of vision, and she thought her head was going to snap off her neck and go rolling backwards. The buildings closed over her, perhaps she lost consciousness –

And then she fell into waiting arms and at the same instant she felt the tide she'd been carrying between her legs dambursting out of her . . .

The arms kept her upright. When she opened her eyes and could focus them to see, she realised blood was streaming down her thighs. They were a man's arms, she was suddenly aware, a complete stranger's, and she shook her head with grief and shame.

'That will do, thank you,' a woman's voice called out with clarion authority. 'Please hail a taxi, Sarah.'

When she looked Catherine saw an elderly face of great distinction, watching her with fascination from beneath the black leather hood of a wicker bath chair. The woman had pushed aside her wrap and her fingers played with the silver handle of a malacca cane. A car's brakes squealed, its tyres skidded on the road, and the maid came hurrying back to her mistress.

'A taxi cab, Mrs Larchmont. A taxi cab has stopped.'

'Excellent. Please instruct the driver to conduct this young lady to my house, Sarah. She can rest there and compose herself.'

The maid took Catherine's arm and directed her towards the taxi pulled up at the kerbside. She didn't know where to look, or at whom;

she was too intensely embarrassed to do anything except attempt walking in a straight line as she was being so gently bid, towards the taxi's open door and the privacy and concealment awaiting inside.

*

'Oh, I recognise profound distress when I see it. Profound distress, I think I can say.'

Catherine had no choice but to admit that the event – with all its bloody manifestations – had taken place.

'I'm so sorry to have troubled you.'

'It was providential timing. I am very happy I was able to be of some assistance to you, Miss – ?'

Catherine – unable to think of an alternative – explained who she was, who her father was, where they lived. Mrs Larchmont nodded at the information.

'Your poor mother died so young, did she not?'

'You knew her?'

'No. But I remember her. A very attractive, a very – ' she paused ' – a very *dramatic* woman.'

' "Dramatic"?'

'Some people are quite naturally the centre of attraction. They make things happen, round about them.'

'So few people remember her.'

'Maybe they have chosen to forget.'

'Why?'

'She was not at all what we were used to. Not at all.'

She didn't speak disapprovingly.

'Why not?' Catherine asked.

'I suppose she was – self-conscious. Of herself, of being a woman. You could tell by the way she walked, I think. Of course women were expected to – to tone themselves down in those days: to be shadows to their husbands. I did not know her, as I said, but I cannot believe that that would have been her way at all.'

'She married my father, though?'

'Oh, men are frequently attracted to such a sort. (Please excuse my talking generically, won't you?) If they think the woman in question can be won over and tamed. I am sure your father must have felt she was – well, a challenge to him. No one survives Aquae-Regis without adapting to it, as he knew. He must have believed that she would come to be admired: as only special women are, those who learn to exhibit their differences in a way that is a threat to nobody.'

'You really didn't meet her?'

'No. I have led a peripatetic life. She had died by the time I returned to Aquae-Regis. I was very sorry. But then I thought – '

She stopped herself, and seemed to consider the propriety of what she had been about to say. Catherine asked her to continue, please.

'Some people's destinies swamp them, I sometimes think. They overpower them. They are made not to quite fulfil themselves. But in the process they acquire an allure, a continuing presence – '

'You said, she'd been forgotten – ?'

'Purposely forgotten. Put out of their minds. That is different. *She* has never gone away, though, however much people will pretend that to be the case.'

They were sitting in a salon of vast proportions, on the first floor of one of the grandest residences in the upper town. A french window had been opened so that Catherine might find a constant supply of reviving fresh air to take into her lungs.

'Do you think – a séance might help me to find her?'

Mrs Larchmont shook her head.

'If you have a disposition to find her, you will. I don't think it needs that sort of performance. But my own experience has left me biased against the practice, you see.'

'You've been to a séance?'

'I have attended several, in fact.'

Catherine nodded, as if she had expected the answer. At school several of the girls had claimed the house was haunted, and that its enigmatic owner – who was only ever seen at a window, or occasionally being pushed in a bath chair like a three-wheeled miniature barouche – preyed on the spirits of virgins. She had accepted the myth as a vague truth, and had thought no more about it, until a friend of her aunt's chanced to recall one day that Mrs Larchmont had once been seen crying into her handkerchief on the Pullman express from Waterloo and that a male relation had once tried to intercept her correspondence in the post-office sorting-room: which information, for Catherine, redefined the woman's mysterious history as being more contingently and humanely melodramatic.

'But Madame de Conti – or howsoever she titled herself – told me that the subject I had enquired of was singing her a tune, which I knew he could *not* have done, because he was tone-deaf, but *she* claimed it was perfectly in key. She used some pieces of slang – about someone's nose being "put out of joint", and meaning to "show him what's for" – which he would never have allowed himself to. So, you see, I realised that she was in the pay of the pharisees.'

Catherine nodded. The house after all seemed merely gracious and delightfully airy. If Mrs Larchmont craved the blood of virgins, plenty of it had been spilled, quite painlessly, in the event – in an upstairs bathroom. It had taken two face-cloths and a hand-towel to staunch the flow, and a maid called Grace had very willingly taken over the job of clearing the evidence from the basin, bathtub, faucets and floor.

Catherine now felt pleasantly weakened. She had been made comfortable with cushions on a bergère chair. The slightly fusty-tasting blossom tea had helped to steady her stomach.

'Would you like to rest by yourself now, Miss Hammond? I am sure that a short sleep would aid your recovery.'

The housekeeper was delegated the responsibility and showed her to a bedroom on the floor above. She turned down the coverlet and top sheet. Standing on a table beside the bed was a vase of mixed lilies, Arum and Nile, with some sprigs of lilac, and Catherine fell asleep in seconds, almost as soon as her head touched the crisp linen pillowcase, breathing the sweet spiced fragrance.

She didn't wake until twilight. Shutters had been drawn across the two tall windows. A fire had been lit in the grate, and the colour of the flames lapped the walls and ceiling. She was dressing when there came a knock at the door, and the maid who had earlier cleaned the bathroom entered bearing crockery and a silver teapot on a tray. Catherine sat at a table drawn up in front of the fire and sipped at the thin, autumnal-tasting beverage.

For years she had listened to the girls at school speculating on the clandestine, cabbalistic rites performed in the house which nobody of anyone's acquaintance had visited for at least twenty years. The speculation had continued unabated, since the increasingly fanciful stories could never be disproved. Catherine had listened, but as if from a distance; as if, she now thought, she wasn't able to trade in their tittle-tattle because somewhere in them she heard the echo of her own destiny.

*

In that city of crescents and circuses and squares, Hesperus House stood alone, at the crux of two streets and belonging to neither. It was three storeys high, with an additional basement and cellarage and rooms in an attic at the back. On the street side the building rose to a dome topped by a cupola. The front rooms on the ground and first floors had direct access to stone balconies, a Regency addition to the façade; on either side of each balcony stood a stout and solemn caryatid, possibly survivors from another building.

Catherine's mother had been fascinated whenever she took them both that way. On the front and side windows deep awnings, of rather threadbare blue canvas, would be lowered on days of bright sunshine;

seen through the railings from Tobago or Chudleigh Streets, which met at the intersection, the house acquired eyelids heavy with tiredness.

To Catherine in turn as she grew up, it had been an enticing spot, its solitariness resonant with mystery and the undeclared. A secluded and shaded garden of unshaped rhododendron and azalea bushes and geometrical portions of infrequently and unevenly cut lawn between weedy gravel paths only compounded the arcane, indeed sinister ambience.

Alone of the properties in their immediate locale, Hesperus House had been painted – saffron yellow – but the deed had been done many years before, so that now much of the paint had flaked away to the honeystone beneath, and the variegated effect was much more Italian than English.

'Sienna gold,' Mrs Larchmont called the hue of the façade. Catherine thought it a romantic description. The more she was to see of the house, the more untypical it seemed of everything she was used to. It was furnished much more sparingly than was the prevailing Aquae-Regis taste, yet the objects themselves had greater grandeur and presence. Massive glass chandeliers hung from the ceilings, some covered with thin grey tulle and each a finer specimen than the Panopticon Theatre's; monumental oil paintings dimmed by time mapped their prodigious shadows on the walls; oversized chiffoniers and lacquer cabinets loomed in the rooms, and a child might have imagined them as immense, predatory rocks.

The house was kept tenebrous, aphotic; daylight was more or less excluded by the wooden panels pulled loosely across the windows and by heavy, moth-nibbled velvet drapes. However warm the day outside, Catherine always felt cool indoors; and when the weather was cold, in her first season of liberation from school, enormous log fires crackling in the hearths revived and cheered her and dappled the rooms with interestingly inconstant flickering shadows she felt luring her to stay by mesmerising her, like sea reflections in a cave.

'This is the House of the Constant Heart,' Mrs Larchmont told her the first day she returned. Catherine at first thought she'd said 'Hearth', but when she realised she had misheard she surmised that the woman was referring to her late husband and her affection for him.

'When did Mr Larchmont . . .' She paused with discretion at this point where she would have had to use the verb she was afraid to.

'Oh, long ago,' Mrs Larchmont told her. 'It seems like another age – another aeon – to me now.'

'Did he – did he grow very fond of this house?'

'Oh, but he never saw the place,' Mrs Larchmont assured her, her voice bright.

'He didn't?'

'Our home was in London. We had only been married three and a half years when he died. Our house there was much more commodious than this one . . .'

Catherine shook her head with disbelief.

' . . . I was looking for somewhere smaller. Away from the capital. This was the house I decided upon. I meant it to be a new beginning, but intentions of that sort . . .'

Her voice momentarily lost its buoyancy. Then she recovered.

'So, here I have been ever since.'

Catherine presumed that it had been for no little time. Hesperus House and its contents felt centuries old to her.

'At the outset I used to entertain. As I had done in London. Everyone whom I invited came. Then – I don't know why – I started to lose interest. The conversations were always the same, there were no surprises. The people here had rather fixed notions, about so many things.'

Catherine was aware of her own interest planing itself to the meaning behind the woman's words. She had merely supposed that Mrs Larchmont somehow represented the spirit of Aquae-Regis as it had been in the old days: not that she had actually been set at odds with it, obliquely distanced, a sceptic.

'When people know they have too much to lose,' Mrs Larchmont continued, 'maybe it *is* understandable they should not care to see further than the ends of their noses. But it fails to make for very stimulating evenings, I'm afraid.'

Catherine nodded.

'And I dare say I put myself beyond the pale eventually. Because I stopped pretending. They had heard stories about me probably: about how I had begun to work things out for myself, how I had learned to see through so much.'

*

The true circumstances were only revealed, in part at least, on a later visit.

First she had asked her aunt what she knew about Mrs Larchmont, and she had watched as the bland expression she tried to live out her days by was temporarily jolted out of kilter. Before she could recover her doe-eyed equipoise, Catherine recognised the indicator of unease in the temporarily pinched mouth – prurient curiosity unable to acknowledge itself, a little feminine envy.

'Why do you want to know?'

'Someone mentioned her once. At school.'

'What were they saying?'

'Only – that she keeps to herself.'

'Well, so far as the town goes.'

'Have you heard things? About her?'

'No more than anyone else.'

'But you've heard?'

'Mrs Larchmont – ' her aunt was taking care in her choice of words – she's something of a free thinker. So I believe.'

'How a free thinker?'

'It's not the sort of thing one really cares to discuss.'

Her aunt picked at a loose thread trailing from her cardigan.

'Why was she being spoken about, as a matter of interest? At school – '

'Oh,' Catherine replied airily, and too much so, 'someone just came up with her name, I can't remember why.'

'It *was* said,' her aunt told her, rather at a rush now that she had some courage up, 'she wasn't quite a decent woman.'

' "Decent"?' Catherine repeated. 'She's a widow. Mr Larchmont died.'

'I dare say he did. But it was a very long time ago.'

'Yes,' Catherine said. 'It was – ' But she stopped herself from saying more. Her visits to Hesperus House were still a secret.

'Not a *black* widow, of course,' her aunt continued. 'I don't mean that. But . . . I'm not sure she's always behaved in a very widowy sort of way.'

'She hasn't?'

For a few moments her aunt considered what a young woman still in her teens might be told.

'She had a gentleman friend, I believe. If I can use that term.'

' "Friend"?'

'No, "gentleman". You see – ' her aunt snapped off the offending thread ' – he was married.'

'When – when did it happen?'

'A while past. I don't know how long it went on for, of course. He's no longer with us, though.'

'Living here in the town?'

'Alive, I mean. But it's a long time ago,' her aunt repeated, 'and it's only what I heard.'

I have no distinguishing knowledge, she meant, this woman who may merit disparagement, calumny, she is protected by her mystery; and I can't expose myself further by discussing her with you.

It was with so tantalisingly little background that Catherine took up the parting words from her second visit and returned a third time to

Hesperus House. Mrs Larchmont seemed unsurprised when she was shown into the salon.

'You have not forgotten me,' she said, but not giving the words the intonation of an enquiry.

'No,' Catherine replied. 'Not at all.'

'Why *have* you come, do you think?'

Catherine was taken aback to be asked.

'I – I thought . . .'

'You feel sorry for me?'

'No. I . . .'

'You think I might be able to supply you with – I wonder what? You wish to learn something? Is that it?'

Catherine presumed she was referring to the town's gossip.

'I haven't heard – '

'But people talk?'

'Only – as they do anywhere, I suppose.'

'It has not dissuaded you?'

'I don't listen to it.'

'You don't quite fit into the town, I should guess?'

'I . . .' Again Catherine was taken aback. How could she have come to such a conclusion? Unless it was a fact.

'I'm not sure,' she replied.

'You lost your mother, of course.'

'Yes,' Catherine said.

'It's a frightful business.'

Catherine inferred she meant the loss.

'Why do we never quite trust them, our mothers? Do we imagine they've lived fuller lives than we have – only we shall never be privy? Or is it because mothers envy *us* our youth, and we come to imagine that we're rivals?'

Audrey had talked of her mother's resentment and wish for revenge, the bad seed of jealousy. How had it happened that seven or eight months later she was hearing the same sentiments repeated? Had Audrey sat in this very seat before her and memorised another woman's judgements?

'You have been spared that, then. *Your* mother did not die in childbirth, so you have no great stone weighing on your conscience. I'm quite convinced that guilt corrodes like nothing else.'

Mrs Larchmont spoke no more on the subject than that. She seemed alerted by the reaction she had caused. Catherine sat shifting in her chair, unable to prevent her eyes blurring. Her rescuer had seen to the heart of her, to matters she had been too fearful and inexperienced and self-deluding to acknowledge. It was the case that since Audrey's words to her in the Abbey, she had come to acknowledge her buried envy over the past couple of years for her mother's appearance, the awesome truth that she may have felt at times less sorry for her death than she ought to have been and harboured – involuntarily of course – feelings of relief that she and her mother would never have to undergo comparisons with one another.

'I shall now tell you the histories of some of the items in this house,' Mrs Larchmont said, letting the seriousness slip from her voice. 'Where I bought them, and why I bought them. Because their stories bewitched me, made music in my ears.'

That was how the rest of that visit, and the next, and the next, were taken up.

Each time Catherine noticed that Mrs Larchmont had visibly weakened since the previous occasion. The stories were told with less breath available for the accounts, but with more urgency. Catherine enquired – circumspectly – if the housekeeper was providing her with all that she required. Mrs Larchmont said 'yes'.

'It ends how it begins,' she said. 'Needing to be looked after. All that darkness just over your shoulder.'

' "Darkness"?'

'I suppose it is. What we come out of and return to. It's all very neat. Very logical.'

'The Egyptians believed we come back, didn't they?'

'It pays to be kind to animals in that case. Cats do often look so *knowing*, as if they have the measure of you only too well. As if they must have access to human knowledge, memory – '

Catherine thought it a very morbid subject, and she hadn't helped in the least by mentioning the ancient Egyptians.

'It's only a story anyway,' she said.

'Oh, more than that, I'm sure.'

Mrs Larchmont didn't seem inclined to give up the business just yet.

'I merely meant, I have a different interpretation; my own. Of the hereafter – and the heretofore. And this brief vale of tears.'

They were sitting, not in the starkly opulent salon, but in a room on the floor above. It was furnished as a small sitting-room but doubled as a dressing-room to the bedroom with which it was connected.

'I feel better able than I was,' Mrs Larchmont said, 'to understand.'

The words emerged from the deep interior of someone who seemed to be ageing as Catherine watched, spoken in another voice that belonged not to her but to a younger woman.

This was the spark of her, Catherine realised, brightening to its zenith. How could she now bring up that other subject of hypothesis,

Audrey's possible visits to the house, when she seemed intent on stating what was too vital to her not to be given the precious, diminishing breath of words.

'I fell in love, you see. After my husband passed away. Not suddenly, which happens when you are young and impressionable. I drifted into love, rather, but quite consciously so.'

Catherine sat very still.

'It was a divine sensation. I was taken out of myself. It hadn't happened like that the first time, with my husband. Every so often I lost my sense of gravity, I felt I was walking on air. I remember them as little acts of levitation, perhaps they were. I felt I could do anything to prove the strength of love.'

Catherine didn't move a muscle.

'It had to be secret at first, even from him. Then he realised, he understood. He had the proof of my mental and physical condition.'

Mrs Larchmont's spark flared.

'The two of us knew. It was bliss, it was rapture. Silly words now, I know, that are used where they shouldn't be, so they have become debased. But I knew my life was never going to be the same, whatever happened. That was quite impossible, because how was I ever going to be able to forget?'

'Who was he? Might I ask?'

'We met in London. I had gone – I was settled here by then – to visit. We were introduced at a soirée. Then – who knows how it happened – I met him in Aquae-Regis about four months later, at someone's "At Home". His wife had relations here.'

Catherine felt her eyes sharpening.

'That was rather ironical, I dare say: that she should have been the means of our becoming reacquainted. I presume she was unaware. Charles always assured me that she was, but I had my feminine intuition.

'If she *did* suspect, she probably imagined me incapable. I was a little frowsy, a little dusty – but true widows are invariably the opposite, have you noticed, they get a spring back into their step, they throw away their old clothes and buy new. She should have known that I was clad in an inappropriate disguise. Charles thankfully had seen right through that, but I did keep it for cover. It gave me greater satisfaction to think I might hoodwink the town, for a little while.'

Catherine felt compelled to ask the question.

'And did you?'

Mrs Larchmont smiled cryptically. In appearance she was *dis*appearing into the far distance, wrinkled and stooped, but her voice was that much younger woman's, bright and animated.

'I imagine they were on to me. I used to see Aquae-Regis faces in

London when I went up, when I would least expect to, on streets Charles and I happened to be walking along, or in theatre foyers when we arrived for a play. It was quite bizarre, but incidental to two people who are in love.'

Mrs Larchmont turned her back fully to the swatches of daylight.

'There is a point at which it even ceases to matter for the watchers, never mind the watched. The situation becomes – well, mythical, and *you* do too. They knew we were beyond their influence, and that it was of no concern to us at all what they might be thinking or saying. We had created our own world. And that is the point, you see.'

Catherine hardly breathed.

'A world within the world. Not a world apart. Fools we were not. We did trim our sails when we needed to, we followed the winds and we respected the elements. When you are in a world apart, you devise your own logic, and you can only survive if you never return. But I knew what I wanted our lives *not* to be – I had had my marriage to tell me, and he had his – and it could not be lived in fairyland, out of reach of conscience maybe but not of time. You need air to breathe, and if no air gets into these perfectly sealed little bubbles of unearthly paradise, they turn to vacuums.'

Mrs Larchmont paused while a horse and cart passed in front of the house.

'Anyway,' she continued, 'it was only – diplomatic, to be careful. Marianne would not have been permitted a divorce, not easily, not with the shire-Catholic background she had: I always knew that. I wanted as much as Charles would willingly give me of himself, and I could have asked for no more. I received all that his wife did not and he was a different man on that account. *She* was unable to take that man away from me. In fact – ' Mrs Larchmont hesitated ' – I have sometimes thought I was in her debt, because with me he was everything he was not and *could* not make himself with *her*. So – indirectly – it was a situation of *her* making. Whether or not he obtained a divorce, it mattered not to me. We were beyond all that, the littleness of the little men.'

*

The rest of the story was postponed until the next visit.

More of the spiced apple tea was served, of which Catherine took only very occasional, invalid's sips herself. Its fruity but bitter taste was oddly compelling.

'Charles worked in his wife's family business. Not that he had begun by doing so, but his father-in-law had been very persistent, and he proved to have an aptitude for mercantile life. His father-in-law's wife was American, and her family were in the same line, and they all joined forces at some point. After old Mr Westerberg died, the American side found themselves in difficulties of some sort and Charles was asked to go over there. He wanted to refuse, but it was I who persuaded him, that it would only be for a few years until he had got it back on its feet again, and over there he would see so much that was new to him. He told me I was being too unselfish, but in another sense it really *was* selfishness: I was afraid that if he stayed I should be racked by guilt that he was doing so on my account.'

Mrs Larchmont picked up a fan, unfolded it, and waved it gently against the heat.

'My arguments prevailed, and he did go, and I was more distraught than I could have imagined. But I ought not to have been surprised after the intensity of the time we had spent together. I read everything I could about New York, I pored over street maps. He wrote to me, long letters about his new way of life there, and I replied, with the duller news of my own life and all my questions about the city. He soon had to make journeys about the country and I followed those in my atlas, and he sent me postcards of all the cities and towns he went to, and I read up about them in gazetteers.'

She folded and unfolded the fan several times, and looked stiffly over her shoulder, towards the window and the fall of faded blue awning, dropping its dense, jagged shadow into the room.

She sighed, while Catherine swallowed her breath in anticipation.

'On his travels he had to go to the south-west, to Arizona. Phoenix. It was the year they had a ferociously hot summer there, and a fever got up, and he caught it: because he had no defence, because he was an Englishman, I suppose, and at the mercy of his own constitution. So it signified not how many doctors looked at him, there was only one outcome possible.'

Catherine shook her head, said how sorry she was . . .

'Poor Charles! It was all I could think: poor, poor Charles! Not just for what he suffered at the end, I pitied him that he had not been granted his span, I pitied him because he could know nothing more of the living world. And I wanted to die too. I took a quadruple dosage of sleeping powders, but it was not enough to do lasting damage, and I had to be spirited off somewhere so they could repair me – body and soul. I was sure my wish was not to live, but then – ' Mrs Larchmont sat considering the pattern on the web of the fan as she directed a little draught against her neck ' – then, it was very strange, a change came over me, I seemed to be viewing the situation quite differently. Why *should* it all be "over"? Was Charles not – in a sense – was he not saved from all that had kept him from me while he was alive? Now he had no wife, no family, and there were no more business responsibilities heaped upon him. He had been given his freedom, he had been liberated – '

Catherine watched the slow fluttering back and forth of the fan, the mandarin poise.

'Now I was reading up everything I could find about fevers, pyrexia, and always making that final journey with him too. Only of course I had not succeeded. One of those new-fangled Viennese doctors took a look at me, and he told me I had not *wanted* to die, not really. I boned up about illness generally, and certain people's predisposition to it, the mind-over-body theory. Immaterialism, I suppose. I wondered if it had really been Charles's means of escaping. While I had been left here, in the workaday world, for whatever end. To keep alive his memory perhaps: the *true* memory, that is, refined through love. He had died too suddenly, and if *I* had as well, we might have missed one another.'

' "Missed one another"?'

'Not met in the afterlife.'

Catherine was conscious of her eyes narrowing. Mrs Larchmont noticed, over the spokes of her fan. She smiled at her guest, with estimable charity.

'I went back over every letter and postcard he sent me. I drew maps of all his journeys. Then I traced the movements of his life before that, in England. I needed to complete my knowledge and see the whole picture. Because I knew it must be my duty to find him. Because – '

The fan continued to move, a little more quickly.

'They had shut up this house, you see, and they were keeping me in various places they took me to. Referred to as "clinics". As if they were covering over my footprints, so to speak.'

' "They"?'

'Two nephews. And a niece. The less said about *her* – '

'You didn't live here?'

'The house was being aired in my absence. I was supposed to be in Italy, for my health's sake. I was not, of course: far from it. They tried to have me sign papers so they could sell the house, but I refused, and I think my lawyer understood the situation well enough to defend me. He would surely have spotted a forgery. Anyway, when it became clear to them that they would get nothing from me, they lost interest.'

Catherine stared at her.

'What did they do? They left you?'

'I was in Cornwall for a few years. The Viennese doctor was conducting academic experiments, and receiving some sort of payment for his efforts, and it was too far to think of making a bolt for it – if you will pardon the expression. For a while I *was* a bit – well, operatic. I have to admit it. Howling on the moors, to the moon, that sort of thing. But Cornwall induced it.'

'And how did you come back here?'

'A discharge. In return for lending one of my nephews a not inconsiderable sum of money. Materialism triumphed after all. But I did return. Without an Italian complexion; without a sunny disposition But sure enough of myself to know I loved Charles beyond life.' She smiled to remember. 'He was the only comfort to me, his memory. But of course he could not come to rescue me, because he knew nothing about my being in Cornwall. And the disembodied become more dependent than ever on recall, on the knowledge of specifics. Just because they can pass through a wall: they have to be sure *which* wall.'

Catherine nodded. Of course the woman was mad. Only she would never have guessed from her gestures, even her appearance. It was mystifying. And now she might be in danger herself.

Mrs Larchmont closed her eyes.

'We shall meet,' she said. 'Very soon. I shall find him. He is waiting, I know. He loves me, so he knows I am on my way. I dread to think that he must have come when I was not here. He has gone back to his cities and railroads and highways because he imagines I am searching for him there.'

Mrs Larchmont opened her eyes and nodded, looking at nothing in particular.

'We do not have long to wait. I have put my affairs in order. My death will be honest to nature, and quite above-board. I shall depart this life for a better one knowing it is a graceful and legitimate transition.'

' "Transition"?' Catherine repeated in the silence.

'Yes. An elevation, if you like. To one state of eternal being. Our reward for enduring the slings and arrows of circumstance. Any last fears will fall away. Locks on doors will burst. We shall both be eternally free. Saved by each other, purified by love.' She closed her eyes again. 'Mortal love will become everlasting. Earthly passion will have turned divine.'

*

Catherine walked home in a daze, along streets she was oblivious to, past buildings and railings and steps and angles of walls that had been unconscious landmarks to her since her childhood.

She had never in all her days since her mother's time heard such a strange story. The poor woman was demented of course – as she had admitted being once, without actually using the word. Although – on second thoughts – it was her nephews and niece who had decided that on her behalf, committing her to what was called 'care'.

At school she'd heard the madmen in Shakespeare's plays referred to as 'wise fools'. They were said to see to the truth of things when others couldn't or wouldn't.

But what could the 'truth' of such a wild, fanciful tale as this one possibly be?

15

Mimesis

For hours at home she sat in front of mirrors: in her bedroom, or at the dressing-table that had been her mother's and now stood in the best guest bedroom, at any of the mirrors downstairs when there was no possibility of her being detected. She wore some of her mother's clothes; it hadn't been easy but she managed to get hold of the key with which her father kept the cavernous wardrobe in his bedroom locked, and to have a copy made from a cast.

Confronting a mirror, *any* of the mirrors, she wasn't looking for the attractiveness Audrey had told her was there, her ambiguous inheritance from her mother. Instead she learned to make a vessel of herself: on occasions she ceased to be Catherine Hammond and became instead transparent. She saw through herself, and she was transformed into the matter of her immediate surroundings. So, she guessed, if she were to concentrate just as hard on the metamorphosis in some place other – in London, or York, or Aberdeen, and among different sorts of people, at any of the levels of society – might she not hope to pass as one of them (whoever 'they' might be, in that place wherever 'there' was)?

The transformation exceeded mere dissimulation. It was a private magic, dedicated in a spirit of shrift to her mother, and she kept it to herself. After long practice she started to forget the hard work, the graft, and she came to think of it as a gift. In belonging nowhere or everywhere there would be nothing to hold her.

She stared long and intently into the depths of the mirror, through the layers of these rooms she was losing the capacity to focus on. She had lived in them too long, too long.

*

The car drew close to the kerb. Catherine kept walking, but more quickly. She had been aware of it tailing her for the past couple of minutes and had felt increasingly uncomfortable as she walked up Paradise Hill.

At last what she had been dreading finally happened: a man's voice spoke, only a few feet behind her.

'Can I give you a lift?'

She faltered before she continued on her way, with her eyes looking straight ahead of her.

She heard the car's engine straining as the handbrake was lifted and the driver followed her, at her own speed of motion.

She hurried across an intersecting street and jumped on to the pavement. Above the thumps of breath in her chest she could hear the car in pursuit.

A few seconds later the voice spoke again.

'Excuse me – '

Her feet performed a country-dance skip-step in their haste, but she managed to prevent them from running.

' – could I ask for your help, I wonder?'

Running away might be the only answer, of course.

'I'm looking for Miss Hammond.'

She stopped in her tracks.

'Miss Dorothea Hammond,' the voice said.

The car drew alongside. Catherine turned and looked. The driver was older than her aunt: he had silver hair, a small silver and grey moustache, and heavily tanned skin. His jacket was too light-coloured and lightweight for their own sort of climate.

He switched off the engine and pulled at the handbrake. Catherine took a couple of steps back.

'I passed the house yesterday. And I happened to see you come out.'

She didn't reply. Her father had gone to Manchester for a couple of days, about business, leaving them by themselves in the house.

'I was very much wanting to have a word with her, you see.'

Catherine didn't take her eyes from his face.

'I did take the liberty of trying the door. Your maid told me your aunt wasn't at home. That she had gone on holiday.'

Catherine continued to stare at him.

'I'm terribly disappointed, of course.'

'Why did you want to see her?' Catherine asked.

He smiled, not very easily.

'We once knew one another,' he said.

Catherine didn't allow herself to respond.

'Quite well, in fact. But it was a long time ago.'

She concentrated on keeping her eyes fixed on his.

'I've been overseas. For a good few years. It's difficult – keeping up contacts.'

'*When* did you know her?'

'Over twenty years ago it must have been. Twenty-two, twenty-three. Since our first meeting. We got well acquainted, for a few years.'

The man crossed his hands on the steering wheel.

'Then her brother got married. That is – ' he nodded at her ' – your father?'

She nodded back.

'Yes,' she said. 'My father.'

'And after that – ' she heard him sigh ' – I had to go off. Your aunt – she moved *here*. And – ' he shrugged ' – you know how it is, with one thing and another, we just rather lost touch afterwards.'

'I see,' Catherine said, sounding – she thought – not unlike her father for briskness.

'Now I've come back.'

Catherine didn't speak.

'I've been thinking of settling down. Tunbridge Wells, maybe. Or Hastings way, or Rye. But I thought I'd – strike up old friendships first. Get the lie of the land and all that.' He paused, to weigh the words with their full freight of implication. 'Weigh up all the prospects.'

She was aware of what charity she'd been feeling draining from her.

She stared at the pavement.

What if he did find her aunt? What if he could manage some rough magic with his words, even after all these years? What if her aunt heard, and was convinced, and he talked her into defying her brother? What if they didn't wait to defy him, but just decided to make their getaway? What if that left merely her father and herself, in the ruins of their house, and her aunt appreciated only after she'd bolted? What if . . .

She thought, I can persuade myself later: that Aunt Dodie truly doesn't want to see him. That I'm replying for the best reason. To save *her* from upset: to save *him* from disappointment. In her haste to find the words to speak to him, she scurried past the thought that she would also be saving her father and herself.

'She *has* gone away,' she said.

'Where to?' he asked. 'Do you know?'

'Didn't Lily say?'

'Only that her mistress was on holiday.'

'To Europe. With friends. To visit – the spa towns, I believe. In Switzerland. And Germany.'

'Do you know when she will be returning?'

'No,' Catherine said. 'She – she has acquaintances there. She may stay with them. Stay there for a while.'

'She writes to you, though? You would know where she was?'

'The post takes so long to travel,' she said. She steeled herself, for a worse untruth. 'But my father keeps what he can from me.'

'What?'

'Well, they had a quarrel.'

'She's run away?'

She had to think quickly, to elaborate the lie.

'She left him. In the lurch. She's very devoted to him. It's to teach him a lesson.' She paused. 'I expect she has already. But she wants to make quite sure about it.'

The man looked uneasy. He ran his fingers round the ribbed rim of the steering wheel.

'Oh well . . .' he said. 'I thought it was worth trying.'

He looked disheartened by this turn in events, and maybe by what she had revealed to him about her aunt's character.

'Should I try again?'

His voice didn't carry very much hope in it.

'As I said, I'm not sure when she'll be back.'

'I could write?'

'Yes,' she said. And added as an afterthought, 'But my father may . . .'

She let the suggestive silence do its work.

'Of course. Yes.'

They both looked up the gradient of Persimmon Street.

'And – ' she asked ' – and *you* are – ?'

'Oh, I'm sorry. My name's Pettigrew. Colin Pettigrew.'

He reached his hand out of the window. She offered hers.

'I've been very rude,' he said. 'Sitting here.'

'I have to go back now.'

'Might I give you a lift?'

'It's not so far,' she said.

'I have to go back the way I came?' he asked her.

She pointed to her left, down towards the town.

He performed a U-turn in the road, with one continuous movement of the wheel. Briefly she felt pity for the man. When he was on the other side of the road, facing now in the opposite direction, he lowered his head and waved across to her.

She hesitated before lifting her hand; she didn't wave, but held her hand in a kind of salute.

Then the car drove off, downhill; its red brake lights blinked on the corner, then in another couple of seconds it had disappeared.

When she returned home her aunt was red-eyed, but pretending that nothing had happened while she had been out of the house.

Catherine watched her, a little alarmed by the determined performance of normality. She also found herself confused, baffled by the possibilities of her aunt's life which she hadn't had cause to suspect before.

Her aunt had offered so many contradictions in her character: restrained, sociable, timid, canny in certain respects and naïve in others, self-sacrificing, observant or haplessly blind, self-conscious in her appearance and its effects.

Maybe she ought not to be surprised that she had uncovered another layer of her character: her vulnerability in the affection stakes.

It had surely been affection she had witnessed on the man's part. It took something exceptional to upset her aunt, who had conditioned herself by being so often on the receiving end of her brother's curt, laconic replies to questions. Above all else, her aunt 'coped'. She was coping now, just, but events must have come sweeping in on her at a wholly unexpected angle, and she was showing herself capable as people do in emergencies, before they succumb to after-shock and exhaustion.

She wondered if an oblique mention might be advisable, but decided against it. She stood trying to see her aunt as she must have been, before she had resolved that her life lay in keeping her brother's house. What had made up her mind? – fear of the other, fear of her brother's double disapproval, pity for a child who didn't have a mother?

Catherine had to open her mouth for breath, considering even the likelihood that her aunt might have refused marriage because she believed a child had needed her more. What if she had known she couldn't have a child herself, what if she'd wanted to be a mother even more than a wife, what if her brother had accused her of being uncaring, what if . . .

She caught Aunt Dodie watching her. The direct look exchanged between them lasted no more than a couple of seconds. But Catherine read its imploring message, that the matter wasn't to be discussed, it wasn't to be referred to even. All the water had flowed under that bridge that was going to, the current had carried all the traces with it and there was no point now, in the early evening of that day, to try to deny the results of what had only been a compulsive act of nature.

*

She went to Mrs Larchmont's funeral, but having told her father that she was going to call on her erstwhile housemistress, who had just returned from her Easter holiday.

She hurried up Ino Street. She heard the hearse before she saw it, being pulled by four black horses dressed in plumes. A number of figures wearing mourning trod a stately measure behind.

She followed them, last of ten or a dozen. At St Barnabas's Church she walked up the shallow steps past the watching eyes, her own eyes turned down to the shiny toes of her shoes. Inside she settled herself on a pew at the back.

The service was brief, without embellishments. No one wept. The organ played quietly as the polished oak and brass coffin was carried back down the nave on the shoulders of professional bearers, exactly matched for height and equally expressionless.

In the churchyard the housekeeper and the maids, Sarah and Grace, nodded to her. Catherine inclined her head in response, then she scanned the faces of the mourners by the grave. There were a couple of neighbours, elderly sisters from Tobago Street, and a few local notables. The others she supposed were professionals – advisers to the late Mrs Larchmont. She saw nobody who might have been a relative; so far as she was able to tell, there were no onlookers of the sort who infiltrate society funerals. She might have been presumed to be one herself, but she believed her curiosity had a purer purpose: it was also Mrs Larchmont's curiosity she was taking responsibility for with her own, to see how things would be done after her demise.

It was being done quite properly, by the book: a little mechanically, it was true, but she didn't judge that Mrs Larchmont would have set much store by a godly scheme of values. Dignity was attaching to the proceedings, and that was something at least in the absence of deep sorrow and tears.

The felt-shod horses had gone, and all the fancy creaking panoply, and the day was settling round about them: back to the reverberating silence that reigned on the flank of Paradise Hill, a massive dramatic inertia inherited from the generations of formal, regulated custom lived among the crescents and parades.

16

Salon Deluxe

THE Salon Deluxe cinema stood alone, in all its solitary gilt and stucco glory, on grassy waste ground near the river. By some fluke of war the night-bombs had destroyed almost all the buildings in the immediate vicinity (those not directly hit had had to be pulled down if they couldn't be buttressed); but the picture-house had been left standing.

Catherine went to see a film every second or third Saturday afternoon, when she had come home and changed out of her uniform and made the excuse – usually – of 'tea duty'. She had told her father that various mistresses held Saturday teas at their homes; they did it in rotation, she said, having decided that her story would be more believable if she opened it out. Her father had been very disapproving after he discovered about her first visit – *anyone*, he'd told her, anyone at all might have been sitting next to her. He hadn't forbidden her from going again, but merely presumed that she wouldn't. That being so, she decided it would be enough not to mention at home that she had been or had thought of going to spend a couple of hours in the overheated darkness. Aunt Dodie obligingly busied herself with gros point, or letters to Cumberland, or buried herself in the kitchen with Mrs Ginger, who had been taken on to replace Mrs Ramage. Afterwards the walk back uphill was usually adequate for the purpose of cooling herself down, removing the colour and letting the pupils shrink in her eyes.

*

When she'd left school, she continued to pay Saturday visits. The necessity was all the greater, with her future undecided – a domestic science course possibly, or conceivably a grounding in secretarial skills – and with not a word to anyone from Audrey. In the Salon Deluxe she found her cover, partaking in that ritual experience of insubstance, a track of white light beamed on to a screen and monochrome images thrown back, sculpting their fluid shadows across the audience's watching faces.

She always left with the throng.

But in less than a minute, away from the cinema steps, the crowd ceased to be so as everyone set off in the various directions of home. Bicycles were reclaimed from walls and lamp-posts, car doors were banged shut and engines growled to life. Among the lengthening shadows the spirit of community she had been sharing with them for the past couple of hours was pulled thinner and thinner, from the fabric to the bare threads.

The way she went, along Constantine Street, was one of the quietest: doubtless because the residents of the heights set above the streets were less given to the practice of democratic film-watching.

One evening she was aware of footsteps behind her on the high pavement: the steel tips on a pair of man's shoes.

Constantine Street was double-sided, narrow, and threw back echoes. She didn't look round, even when the footsteps followed her into Pink's Terrace.

She crossed on a wide diagonal to the opposite pavement, and heard the footsteps do the same. At least it was light, so late in May (as it was), and she didn't need to deviate from bona fide streets of houses and watching windows.

He caught up with her on Philomel Place.

She had stopped by some railings to remove a small stone from her shoe when he made his approach.

Her heart was beating quite steadily in her chest, and she wondered a little at her own nonchalance. She stood on one leg smoothing the stocking on her other ankle as he spoke, and she let him have his say without lifting her eyes to look at him.

'I hope you'll excuse me. But I believe – you must have left these behind you.'

While she replaced her right foot on the ground, he held out a pair of gloves. Robin's-egg-blue silk gloves, with little pearl buttons for fastenings.

She took them from him. They were too small for her hands; they belonged to an old woman, or a young convent girl, or a forgetful invalid.

'Thank you,' she said, laying them over her wrist. 'How stupid of me.'

She smoothed them flat with her fingers.

'But,' the well-spoken young man said, 'I'm sure it's quite easily done.'

She nodded. 'Oh yes.'

For some reason his appearance didn't surprise her. Not that she was meaning to judge him from his voice: but rather, he seemed not wholly unfamiliar, although she was quite certain she had never set eyes on him before. His colouring – fairish hair quite close to her own, blue eyes like hers, a clear complexion – her eyes adjusted to it immediately; and to his height, which she felt raised her eyes at an angle that was very comfortable to her, and more so than when she looked at her taller father. Inexplicably his physical presence – his proximity – wasn't alarming her. His manner was kindly, debonair.

And he didn't have the lean look she found as off-putting in men as the corpulent, which gave them a predatory air, or hunted, or haunted. She preferred that they should seem to have easy consciences and moderately, decently robust appetites. A moustache on such a man hinted at stability, at least when it wasn't clipped too closely. His hair was retreating from the crown, but instead of its signalling that the ageing process had begun in earnest (he was probably only a few years older than herself), it lent him – in her mind – a certain virile maturity. His tweeds and flannels looked newish and uncreased, and of good quality.

He accompanied her part of the way home. He looked about him, as an interested stranger, at the residences of imperturbable solidity. She glanced at none of the pedestrians they passed, and kept her eyes turned from any cars. In the course of their sparing conversation she told him that her father managed a business in the town, the family firm, but that disclosure caused her companion no disconcertment, seemingly no disenchantment either, and he nodded as if that was exactly how he had suspected the situation to be. Which caused her to look directly at him somewhere on South Nile Street, but he was already scrupulously attending to her, and she instantly blushed, like the schoolgirl she had only recently ceased being.

'Can I talk to you again?' he asked her.

'When?'

'Whenever you like.'

'It's difficult,' she said.

'Because of your father?'

'Yes,' she said. 'How do you know that?'

'Oh, I just guessed.'

'But that it was my father who – '

He smiled, as if it didn't matter. But to her it did.

'Actually,' he said, 'I *have* seen you. With your father.'

'When?'

She couldn't think of a day recently when it had happened.

'I've forgotten,' he said. 'But I saw you. I suppose he's rather possessive, is he?'

'Well . . .'

'You've no mother?'

'How do you know that?'

'I guessed.'

'But how?'

'He holds your arm, doesn't he?'

'Yes. Sometimes he does.'

'Maybe he's afraid he might lose you?'

'I don't know,' she said.

'Doesn't it hurt?'

'What?'

'The way he holds your arm.'

'Sometimes it does. A little.' She shook her head. 'You know so much.'

'*Can* I talk to you again?'

'There must be more interesting people in Aquae-Regis. Than me.'

'Am I being given the cold shoulder by any chance?'

'Oh, I didn't mean that – '

So she felt obliged to say when they *could* meet again, since he'd taken the inference, justifiably enough, that she was brushing him off.

*

It *had* to be the picture-house.

The film was *I Walked with a Zombie*, but she couldn't concentrate on the lush Caribbean atmosphere, nor on the plot – something to do with an elegant white woman, George Sanders' wife, laid under a spell of sleeping sickness, and spoken of by the natives as one of 'the living dead' – nor on the details of island voodoo. She jumped in her seat when the wind-blown sugar cane in a field parted to reveal a motionless, nearly naked black man, staring with eyes like white marbles. She shifted, causing the seat to creak, when the story returned to dapper, slightly sinister George Sanders confessing his love for the young Canadian nurse employed to care for his breathing but spiritless wife. She covered her eyes when the mad-eyed bald negro reappeared, in the garden of the house, walking stiff-limbed like a machine. She shifted again on the worn velvet when the husband told the nurse in his clipped accent what a wicked and unfaithful woman his wife had been; but she craned forward in her seat when the handsome alcoholic brother (or half-brother, she was uncertain) lifted the beautiful, lustful

Jessica from her bed and carried her off to their double-death by drowning in the surging, foaming, moonlit sea.

The lights went up. He sat with his arm resting against hers. She could feel the firmness of the muscles in the upper part.

'I don't understand what the mother had to do with it all,' he said. 'Do you?'

'The mother?'

'Was she a goody or a baddy?'

'I don't know,' she said, conceding her ignorance. 'It looked a pretty place, though. The bay at the end.'

'California, I expect.'

'It was the West Indies, though. Antigua – somewhere near there, wasn't it?'

'A studio lot and then a drive up the freeway, I expect!' He smiled. Then his face straightened as he realised that he was too sceptical for her, or merely too matter-of-fact.

'Not really?' she said.

'Oops, time to move,' he said.

'Oh . . .'

He nodded towards the over-officious clearer of seats approaching up the aisle.

'I suppose so,' she said, and sighed; and then wondered a couple of seconds too late just what interpretation he must be putting on the sigh.

At the doors he seemed to her quite uncertain how to proceed, unable to decide if there was any point even. In the future she was always to regard that moment as the crux. She was always to believe that at that point he could have said goodbye, charmingly enough of course, and left her, never to set eyes on her again. But her sigh disturbed her: she had intended it only to cover her own awkwardness as to what to do next, and to pass a judgement on the row-emptying tactics that didn't leave any time to savour the final moments of a film. He must have thought she was bored, unimpressed by his company, and quite uninhibited about saying so.

As he was on the very point of turning away she reached out her hand and touched the tweed sleeve of his jacket. There was a momentary hiatus, when they both froze but seemed not to react. Then, in the next instant, they unfroze. He smiled and she took an embarrassed step backwards, and thus all her life to come was set on course to its crazy haphazard end.

*

They continued to meet on weekday evenings at the picture-house, and afterwards to walk as dusk came down.

She told her father, who told her aunt, that she had been dragooned into going back to school to help out in Eastbury House: there was illness among the staff, and Miss Rowan was hard-pressed.

She thought it sounded a plausible alibi. Her 'future' was – for her – an embarrassing topic at home: they were postponing a decision for the meantime, so that she could 'look around'. She supposed that her father had marriage in the forefront of his mind for her, and that they were only awaiting a suitable candidate.

Wherever he had imagined interest to emanate from, it couldn't have been from a rooming-house in Juniper Street, in that quarter of town on the humble flat called from time immemorial 'Ægypt'.

So . . .

In the phase before he took her to Juniper Street they would rendezvous at the Salon, in the vestibule where she had to search for him in the soapy light.

They sat in the stalls. The films were held over for no more than three days at a time, which suited them very well. There was always the prospect of novelty just ahead. *Double Indemnity, The Wicked Lady, Night and the City, Gilda, Lady from Shanghai, Woman in the Window, Build My Gallows High, The Killers, The Third Man, Sunset Boulevard*, and – of course – *Mildred Pierce*. She liked the American ones best, with their sleek suspense and half-lit interiors which seemed to suit the temper of her mind at this time: night streets, flashing neon signs, the slow headlights of cars, venetian blinds, desk lamps, casually wafting cigarette smoke, bar counters. Jane Greer in a picture hat and low bodice, clutching her bag, striding into a Mexican cantena; a male silhouette in hat and overcoat limping on crutches; wearing a gold anklet in the Hispano-California villa, Barbara Stanwyck buttoning her dress, then coolly applying lipstick; the girl called Lola playing Chinese checkers; Googie Withers wearing ropes of pearls, Jane Greer swathed in mink, Ava Gardner in a black dress with a single strap, Margaret Lockwood showing cleavage. Gloria Swanson in dark glasses and leopardskin; Rita Hayworth and Joan Crawford aiming revolvers at multiple mirrors; Gilda tossing her hair back, fixing on her man, dancing alone in Buenos Aires; a gun wrapped in a chiffon scarf, a woman's hand placing it beneath a cushion; Rita Hayworth singing 'Put the Blame on Mame'.

The cinema was owned by a woman, Miss Ditchfield, which might have explained the selection of films, with their vapid inadequate male characters – Farley Granger, Dana Andrews, Fred MacMurray, brilliantined Glenn Ford – and enigmatic, elusive, seductive, amoral *femmes fatales*. The half-lit films dappled the darkness of the auditorium, exaggerating the menace in the stories but causing Catherine to feel safe in the hold of the chair with its well-worn plush, with Maurice's arm resting along the back.

To begin with, she was conscious of his watching her, and unsettled by it. However, her discomfort passed when she was able to look back at him, frankly, and to smile. His hand had sometimes brushed against her shoulder before she allowed him to rest it there. His finger slipped down to the tops of her arms, and it was then that she had to concentrate harder on what was happening in the film, in case she let go the tangled skein of threads. The afternoon he turned his head – to look backwards, she supposed – but in fact to plant a kiss on the back of her neck, her concentration was lost completely and she could only dwell on what had happened, the contact of his lips with her skin, the paralysis that followed, the reverberations of shock waves along her arm, down her spine to the small of her back. The film flickered on the screen, and she had scarcely any recollection afterwards of what she had been watching.

But by then the picture-house had probably outlived its usefulness to them both: or *they* had outgrown *it*, with its two-dimensional approximations to life that now – for her – lacked the impact, the brazen unpredictability, of the real thing.

17

Maurice

When she was to look back on those days, which happened often, she would remember them as the most exceptional of her life.

She relived them as she had seemed to live them, in black and white: moving in her memory between the darkness of the cinema auditorium and the lamplit streets, between her gloomy home and his cosy rooms at the top of the building in Juniper Street, between the secretive silences of one and the other's free-and-easy intimacy where they sat together over the gas fire. She moved between dark afternoons and the brilliance of early summer, between her first welter of unclear emotions to their impassioned fulfilment.

In her recollections she retraced every step of that journey between hypothesis and discovery, between hope and despair. She saw the two of them almost as figures in a film themselves, set against familiar backdrops he had turned into those of a dream. In front of her eyes, she was transformed from a reluctant innocent and ingenue to a woman of the world, spun on her axis but hardly chastened, and converted as zealously as any proselyte to the paramount, transcendent cause of Love.

*

Maurice was motherless, like her, and had only the faintest memories. His father was the youngest of three brothers of an old impoverished scion of ducal stock: one was a widower and childless, the other a bachelor, and he was the only representative of a final generation. In all probability the title would die with his younger, more robust Uncle Cedric. His own father had been disapproved of in his younger days, for preferring the fast London life; after his son's birth he had mellowed apparently, and they'd both left London for Herefordshire, where the family owned a small dairy farm in the vicinity of the big house, Curteys Court. The returns had been sufficient to educate the boy at an ancient public school before his National Service: to give an appearance of well-being, but 'appearances' was the sum of it.

'Father never married my mother, you see.'

'Oh.'

'All her other friends were theatrical types. Except Father. I think she acted once upon a time – before their paths crossed.'

'*My* mother did. Acted. It must be commoner than we thought.'

A bond seemed to be established between them.

'Not much doing in Herefordshire,' he told her. 'Ever been there?'

She said she hadn't.

'Okay for blood sports, but everyone's tucked up in bed by ten o'clock. Take my word for it.'

She said yes, she did.

'Would it have been different?' she asked him. 'If your mother hadn't died?'

'How different?'

'Then you might have stayed in London.'

'Maybe. But I think it was because Herefordshire was the opposite, my father could come to terms with it. Actually – ' he threw up the window in his room ' – she died later. She was dead by the time I could start asking questions about her. I remembered her a bit. But – ' he dug his hands deep into his trouser pockets ' – I think she knew it wasn't going to work out with Father. Or maybe they quarrelled. He regretted it later, of course, he saw his mistake.'

'I'm sorry,' she said. 'I just thought – in London you might have felt closer to her.'

'All I know is, what good fun she was. So Father said. But that it "couldn't have lasted". There was only one photograph, and eventually I got embarrassed asking him. Then when I went off to school, there didn't ever seem to be a right time to ask. And it got more awkward between us, anyway.'

It was one of the few occasions when he had allowed his face to show a wholly serious expression. His introspection was a little difficult for her to adjust to. She thought she might try to change the subject.

'Why – why have you come to Aquae-Regis?'

He smiled. 'Because I've always kept away from it, I suppose.'

She parried the point.

'Did you have a reason? Why you kept away?'

'We once came, my father and I. For some reason. I was two. Apparently I was left somewhere in my pram – a local girl was being paid to push me around, but her mind was on other things – and it seems I was whisked away by a stranger. Just for a few streets, but my father didn't know that of course, and it's more or less the first thing

I can remember, a woman looking down into my face and then over her shoulder, one move followed by the other, lots of times, and the noise of police whistles.'

'How awful!'

'And the speed of it must have contributed to my remembering so clearly. The sky must have been racing overhead. Only I'm not sure that part's really in my memory after all, about the sky, blue, with clouds.'

'Who was it took you? Did you find out?'

'Oh, she was too quick about it. I presume. Or my father didn't take it up and press charges. But anyway, he told me when I was six or seven that he'd nearly lost me once. And he'd tell me every so often after that, as if he wanted to remind me of what had *nearly* happened. Usually when he needed to remind *himself*, if I was proving a bit too much of a handful.'

She nodded.

'We never came back. Either my father or me.'

'Did he know people here?'

'I never asked about that. We were staying in a hotel. But I don't remember that. Only the high jinks.'

'They were anything but,' she said, and sounded almost reproving, so that he – and then she – had to smile.

'Some poor woman, so taken with the sight of me, I expect.'

'How old – '

'Why?'

'To think it was *here*. And we almost collided.'

'Were you born in Aquae-Regis?'

'Yes. When did it happen?'

'In broad daylight.'

'No, the year.'

' 'Twenty-nine.'

'I wasn't born until the next year.'

'Rub it in – '

'No, I didn't mean that – '

He grabbed her hands and planted ridiculously impassioned kisses on them. She turned and looked over her shoulder, to the view of Paradise Hill through the window, then she bent forward, laughing and telling him to stop, *please*.

He *did* stop, eventually, when the moments had yielded their maximum.

'You're dangerous!' she said, through more laughter. 'You're a menace!'

He affected to be dumbfounded.

'A *danger*?'

'Yes.'

'So why are you more relaxed than I've ever seen you before?'

She only slowly stopped laughing, but the remark had pulled her up. It was true, of course, perfectly true. She knew that he thought her restrained, stiff, uneasy with herself as with him. And now when she wasn't expecting it, when she had hardly even noticed the process was afoot, he was so adroitly splitting cracks in her ice.

*

Her aunt, she was sure, could see the truth written on her face. She must have known that her sudden dedication to school and Eastbury House life wasn't in her nature.

'I was talking to a young man . . .' she began. Of course he had to be someone she'd met through a girl who'd been in her form. 'Not a relation,' she said, 'no. A family acquaintance.' When she was asked *which* girl at school it had been, she picked a name her aunt hadn't been used to hearing.

She called him 'Maurice'. 'Maurice' had driven them in his car, on a day when it rained; 'Maurice' had walked them some of the way home.

Her aunt was grounded between attitudes: between a seemly prurience and middle-aged concern. Catherine caught the curiosity in her eyes every time, and was heartened by it; and all the more so when she felt it growing more complicitous. Her aunt began to use the name – 'this Maurice' – and she didn't ask why, when he was unused to Aquae-Regis and its ways, he happened to be staying on here so long.

*

He had taken her up to the roof of the house. The rooms were too hot, he said, up there they might just catch a breeze, if there was anything going.

They sat on cushions, right on top of the hot lead of the guttering. She almost scalded her right hand, reaching out to the slate tiles to keep her balance.

'It's still so close,' she said. 'So muggy.'

'Your aunt had the blinds down today.'

'What? Yes, she did. But how do you know that?'

'Surely that's what I *would* know?'

'You saw them?'

'Yes.'

'You walked along the Crescent?'

'Several times. My Sunday stroll.'

She looked at him. She bit her bottom lip. She rearranged her cushion, in part as a distraction.

'I went to the Abbey this morning,' he said.

'I didn't go.'

'I thought you might, though.'

'*You* don't go, do you? To church services?'

'I just thought you'd be there.'

'I only go sometimes.'

' "Sometimes"?'

'Does that surprise you?' she asked, staring at his mouth.

His answering smile was kindly.

'I just wasn't sure,' he said.

'My father's given up about me on that score. It doesn't seem to worry him now.'

'For how long hasn't it worried him?'

'Oh . . . A year or so. He told me I was old enough to be able to judge these things for myself.'

'That's quite enlightened of him.'

She didn't respond.

'Isn't it?' he asked, pursuing the point.

'He has these – these blanks with me,' she said. 'He doesn't worry about them. Well, he *didn't*. But it's not that really.'

'What do you mean?'

'I think it's – well, indifference. It doesn't bother him because he doesn't want to waste any more mental effort on it.'

'But he – he cares, doesn't he?'

She started at the word.

'Oh . . . About certain things.'

'What things?'

'Money, mainly.' She corrected herself. 'Our well-being, financially.' She pulled herself up straight on her arms, taking care not to touch the leading or the tiles.

'He's complicated, really,' she said, 'my father. More so than you might think. Than "one" might think, I should – '

'So he wouldn't be likely to be an admirer of *moi-même*, would he?'

She thought she must be truthful, so high up on the roof as they were. Maybe the altitude was affecting the working of her brain, could it be? – a rush of blood to her head?

'I'm not sure I know how to judge him,' she said. 'Not properly. Once I felt I was able to. But . . . It wasn't so bad until I was – fourteen or fifteen, I suppose. Before that I thought all fathers were like him. I didn't think about it. Then I got to notice his strictness: his stiffness. Partly through my aunt, seeing how she reacted.'

'She's his sister – but you get on fine with her?'

'That doesn't make sense either. But of course she had to help, how a mother would have done. Explain things – '

'Turning you into a woman?'

She took a deep breath of the warm air, but didn't feel herself blushing as she might have expected.

'Yes,' she said. 'So in a way I'm a different person. Although I see her faults.'

She glanced at him, at his moustache.

'She does have faults,' she said. 'But I've got used to them. More or less.'

He took his pipe from the breast pocket of his jacket, which was lying on the leads between them. From an inside pocket he removed a wallet of tobacco. She watched him fill the bowl of the pipe. His face was clear, it didn't show undue concern – if that was what he was feeling.

'Will you light it for me?'

She thought she hadn't heard him properly; then he handed her the box of matches. She opened it, selected a match, struck it, and took the flame – with her hand shaking slightly – to the tobacco. His head bent towards hers. He inhaled and exhaled, several times. She breathed the smoke into her nostrils; it smelt woody, bitter-sweet, she was reminded of garden bonfires in autumn wafting their grey mist about the hillside.

For those long and intense moments their faces were only a couple of inches apart. Briefly their eyes met. Then the tobacco caught alight. He adroitly directed the smoke away from her.

'He knows that I come out,' she said. 'My father.'

She watched him take the pipe from his mouth and hold it, considering it.

'Has he said?'

'No. Not in so many words.'

She shifted her cushion on the boiling leads.

'He doesn't know if he can trust me maybe.'

'You don't say where you're going?'

'I tell him – ' she swallowed ' – something else.' She watched him replace the pipe in the corner of his mouth. 'I *couldn't* say.'

'No,' he replied. 'No, of course not.'

'Not really explain,' she said, confirming the answer to herself.

'He wouldn't approve?'

'Maurice – '

'Have you discussed me with him?'

She shook her head. She looked away, across the rooftops of Ægypt and Jericho. It was always presumed that only the people on the heights had 'views': but from here, up on the roof, you could see too, for miles.

'Does he follow you?'

Her eyes gelled on the vista, on the strict geometric logic of life in the town, lined and ruled on squares and circles and hypoteneuses.

'What?'

'You allowed yourself to come here. Have you allowed him to discover where you go?'

'He doesn't realise, I'm sure. That I'm here. Only – only that I'm somewhere – '

' – where he wishes you weren't?'

She knew she was staring at him with the helplessness confessed on her face.

'Does it matter to you?' he asked her. 'What he says or thinks?'

She shook her head, looking away again, back to the panorama of sooty, forgotten honeystone.

He inhaled and exhaled on his pipe, several times.

'Does it – ' she swallowed ' – does it matter to *you*?'

She sensed that it did: more than the casual tone of his voice indicated.

'Only if it makes *you* unhappy.'

She smiled at him; it was the only response she felt she could give him.

She continued to smile as the minutes passed, sitting alone with him up beyond eye level, in the first pink glow of a summer dusk. She could smile with that enfolding forestry aroma of pipe smoke so pleasantly fugging the air, bringing such reassuring associations into her mind, of well-set-up men favourably disposed to the world, calmly ruminative and confident in their wisdom of experience.

*

He could tell her what she was thinking. Even when she wasn't concentrating wholly on him, he had the gift of knowing what was in her mind: the weather, a sound she was picking up, her Aunt Dodie sitting at home, something she'd looked at in a shop window, the colour of a woman's shoes she'd seen, the lines she'd heard spoken in a film at the Salon.

'I don't know how you know.'

'Could be luck.'

It might have been. But how did it happen that he was lucky so often?

'You don't think so?'

Sometimes she felt she didn't dare to think certain things, because he was bound to fathom them. She became unnerved when she imagined the sheer intensity it must take to trail another's thoughts.

'It's *not* coincidence?' he said, smiling at her.

She found it difficult to apply a smile to the subject.

'I don't know,' she said.

'There might be an alternative explanation ...'

She saw that he understood too well what she was thinking; she couldn't disguise from him the fact that her mind was filling with doubts. But maybe – she strained to convince herself – maybe all it indicated was that an attraction of this sort brings two people together in every respect.

'I don't know,' she repeated to him.

He smiled again, as if it was of no consequence anyway. But there was another reason why he was smiling, she knew, to obscure another fact, that this wasn't what he actually believed, that it was of some essential significance to them both, which she couldn't yet get the measure of.

She wrote his name on a piece of paper.

Maurice, Maurice, Maurice....

She formed her letters lovingly, to create a name that was unique, indistinguishable from the life of the man.

... Maurice, Maurice, Maurice ...

For these moments it was the closest she could get to him.

... Maurice, Maurice, Maurice, Maurice ...

And, strangely, she felt that in the quiet of her room she was corresponding directly with him, that he was aware, in his far room in Juniper Street.

The next afternoon she didn't mention her calligraphic exercise when he brought up, telepathically, the matter of their communicating. 'Can you keep a look-out Ægypt-way tonight?' he asked her. 'From a room at the front of the house?'

Eventually she distinguished a torchlight flashing, like a ship's beacon. She couldn't find a torch, and used a table lamp instead, passing it to and fro behind the opening between the curtains.

Together, she thought, they were conquering the taboo of darkness, stranding it with their own private method of parley: on Paradise Hill and the flats respectively, brief unacknowledged victors of time and space.

*

Her father mentioned the incident to her next morning. A neighbour had been walking uphill and seen; he'd mentioned the fact to his housekeeper, who mentioned it in turn to Mrs Ginger.

'What on earth were you doing?'

'I was looking for something,' she said.

'Like the Pharos, I was told.'

'I was holding the lamp. To see with.'

'What were you looking for?'

'Something I'd dropped.'

'What exactly?'

She coughed. 'The link from my bracelet. For the catch. It fell. On to the floor.'

'Weren't the curtains drawn?'

'Almost,' she said.

'How did it happen that it's become a matter for gossip?'

'I've no idea,' she told him. 'I can't say.'

She saw that he was sceptical. She wondered why he should be so concerned. She shrugged, to play the business down. But her gesture only appeared to confirm him in his suspicions.

'Can I presume that you'll take better care of your bracelet in future?'

She swallowed a little pride.

'Yes,' she said. 'Yes, I shall.'

'Then nobody will be tempted to confuse this property with a lighthouse.'

'No,' she said. She smiled, modestly and demurely.

He picked up his hat. She recognised the expression of riled weariness on his face.

'No,' she repeated.

He stood brushing dust from the crown with his fingers. His concern, she supposed, was social, on account of the embarrassment. But she knew him well enough to realise that when he wouldn't look at her, it was for more complex reasons that struck even deeper, into the smaller man inside forever liable to be ambushed by his past.

His eyes dimmed whenever he made the backward journey. He travelled there by a narrow rope. An insignificance, which wasn't really so because it spelled out the order of their life, would haul him back in an instant. In this case, the horn of the car sounding.

Mrs Ginger's husband regularly did chauffeuring duties on weekdays. Probably it was giving them all ideas above their station, but her father had long ago discerned the cardinal value of appearances, especially in a town where Trade, being such, might be excused if an enterprise was perceived to be a healthily thriving one. Thus the journey to and from the foundry was made every weekday morning and evening with Mr Ginger conspicuously at the wheel of the Daimler as became a successful businessman's dignity.

She watched the car leave. The wave of the hand she received was more cursory than usual.

She had an instinct that it would still be wrong to bring up the subject of Maurice with her father. He *must* have noticed the change in her. Perhaps Aunt Dodie had passed on to him that she knew, if only by accident, because she wasn't nearly foxy enough for him; but she knew very little, and between two women subtler notions prevailed.

The car turned the corner. She watched the brake lights blink, then automatically her eyes swung one hundred and eighty degrees, to scan the jostling, untidy rooftops of Ægypt where the other man in her life, the one she wanted for her lover, waited.

*

He taught her how to play cards: canasta, écarté, piquet, poker, pontoon. She watched how quickly his hands dealt the pack. He showed her how ombre differed from quadrille, bezique from pinocle, quinze from vingt-et-un and blackjack.

Accidentally – when he dropped his wallet – she discovered that he took his pastime seriously. He saw her looking at the name 'Rossignol' engraved on a business card.

'A nightingale?' she said.

He told her that, the law of gaming being as it was, the premises were a secret to those and such as those . . .

At school he'd picked up on how to win at advanced rummy, and that had been his introduction. Later a friend's friend had taken him along to the Rossignol. It was there, at the tables, that he'd mastered the rudiments of chemin de fer, baccarat, drag, faro, fan-tan.

'Don't you lose,' she asked him, 'more than you win? When you play?'

'But that isn't the way to play,' he said. 'Being an optimist is a profession.'

'You don't always win, though?'

'But I think that I might. And that's when I stop thinking, as soon as they deal the cards, the moment the wheel starts to spin.'

*

The next day he asked her, on a late afternoon walk through Jericho, 'Have you told your father about me yet?'

She shook her head.

'Are you going to?'

'I'm not sure,' she said.

'You're not sure what he'll say?'

'I suppose not.'

'Am I beyond the pale?' he asked her.

'It's just – ' she told him ' – maybe he's had other plans for me.'

'Such as?'

'Who I'd be suitable for.'

'Has he spoken to you about it?'

'Oh no,' she said, 'nothing like that.'

'But that's what he has in mind for you?'

'I expect so,' she said. She shrugged. 'It's just a feeling I have.'

'So I'm a fly in the ointment?'

'Well . . .'

'But it's *your* life.'

'It's only, if he finds out – '

'If you tell him?'

'He might hear,' she said.

'I see.'

She took a deep intake of breath. 'It's very awkward. I just know him, you see. What he's like. I know what to expect.'

'That's all right.'

'Is it?' She sounded doubtful.

'We'll cross that bridge when we come to it.'

She shrugged again. She couldn't think that far ahead. But even so, he gave her confidence. Already he understood her better than anyone, Aunt Dodie included. She was quietly amazed.

'Yes,' she said. She smiled. Then a question occurred to her.

'Does – does it bother you? What he might think?'

His quick smile was self-deprecatory, but she had the sense as his eyes tightened round the matter that he had given it a lot of thought during his time in Juniper Street.

She wanted to be positive. She brushed his moustache with the back of her hand. She felt that automatic constriction of her stomach he produced in her.

He took her hand. He kissed the fingers, electrifying her. She thought that, for this, everything else might go hurtling to perdition.

*

For form's sake she stayed at home until three or four o'clock in the afternoon. She would tell her aunt that she'd be eating again at Eastbury House. Instead she ate nothing, and walked and talked with Maurice until the Salon Deluxe opened its doors for business.

*

On the slow journey back to Eveleigh Crescent the first stars would be staking their pitch in the azurean.

'When your son or daughter is your age,' he told her after a second watching of *Mildred Pierce*, 'if light leaves one of those stars now, it still won't have travelled to earth.'

She didn't know if that was proven scientific truth or not, but she nodded. Perhaps the light she was seeing now had taken all her mother's life and the remainder to reach her. It was a dizzying thought.

'How funny,' she said, 'imagining a child.'

'Oh, well. Suddenly our lives fall into place, I expect.'

She nodded. But she was a little unsettled, that he should have spoken of 'her' son, 'her' daughter, while seeming to remove himself from the hypothesis.

She moved closer to him. His knuckles rubbed against hers, and she felt herself tense up.

A while later they stopped in front of one of the gaps in Burlington Parade where a house in the terrace had been blown away. In the future that spot – still a mound of rubble, with flowers and saplings growing in the dereliction – was always to be the most special to her in the town, so much so that she never returned to it. It was there that he spoke the words for the first time, that he loved her.

The shock and delight paralysed her.

He repeated himself.

'Yes,' she said. 'Yes.'

'Yes?'

She turned the words round, to refer to herself.

'Oh, *I* love *you*, Maurice,' she told him.

He smiled, a little hesitantly, seeing the paroxysm of joy he had caused: as if only now he realised the responsibility attaching to the words he had spoken.

They walked on, she in jubilant replete silence. She thought he must be able to hear the palpitations of her heart, almost doubling her in two.

In Mulberry Street, in the shadows from the gaslight, he placed his hand on top of her heart. The fingers reached up, over layers of clothing, fanning to cover her breast; his other hand spread over the other breast.

She had a most curious feeling between her legs, where suddenly a river of sensation seemed to run; a rush of heat, a boiling liquid wash. She was aware of her body temperature rising, as fast as mercury in a tube. When he leaned forward and kissed her cheek, she thought – in those few seconds – that her skin must be burning him.

But his lips had heat to counter heat, and she felt the impression branded on her. His hand stopped, his mouth made contact with her neck. She closed her eyes in panic. He didn't jump away from her fire, but – it seemed to her – he was somehow cooling the skin with the elastic length of his kiss.

He put his hands on the small of her back, to reassure her perhaps – she was shaking violently. He removed his hand. Opening her eyes she smiled wildly, past him towards the old yellow glow of the gas lamps. She could hardly breathe: not enough to speak.

'I'll walk you home,' he said.

She nodded. Couldn't think in which direction to turn. She heard his mouth smiling at her disorientation. She smiled with him, but not *at* him. Walking like this, it had never happened to her even in her dreams, feeling her feet might cease making contact with the ground at any second and hover above it, in joyous and ecstatic, miraculous levitation.

That night she dreamed about him with a bewildering lack of reason and shame.

At the day's end he was waiting for her, by the gate in the back wall, and while her father's house fell silent they made their escape. Formality had been dispensed with almost immediately, in a trice, as she had fallen into his waiting arms. She seemed to recognise his strength, just as his appearance had seemed familiar to her, setting eyes on him that first evening in Philomel Place. She gave herself to his purpose and was moved by it, to places that were confusingly near at hand – the Nonagon Room, Wymondham Bridge, the Lazurite Grotto: all much the same as before and yet not so, because why else was she revisiting them with him if not to prove the point that previously they had belonged to a lesser life, a shadowlife. In her condition of joy, they merely confirmed that she was a different person, no longer at the mercy of definitions but – paradoxically – by giving herself to another, become half (but she didn't know which half) of a new, elevating, enrapturing whole.

*

It was turning to a crazy time. Quite literally, she felt, since she knew she wasn't in her mind the person she had been before it. But she couldn't say she wasn't in her right mind, because this seemed to be living life in an extra dimension. She was more alive than she had ever been before; her senses were taut, super-receptive, and even the contact of objects with her skin was of an intensity she couldn't recall ever having experienced. Her days too were more intense than any previously, and yet they didn't leave her fatigued; it was only the clock that decided when she should take some rest and replenish her energies for the next day, otherwise she could surely have carried on indefinitely. She thought she must have spent the last few years of her life half-asleep: she didn't know how Audrey hadn't lost heart with her and given up on her. All that time she had seen and known nothing.

Now her father was watching her like a kestrel, as if he suspected. She didn't think she cared. From the dining-room mirror she understood that she wasn't the same person. Her aunt too couldn't find her usual focus on her, and rubbed at the lenses of her close-work spectacles. Catherine wanted to laugh about it, but her father made the subject so serious. It was a subject never directly referred to, of course. Sitting at her mother's dressing-table in the guest-room, she wondered how she could begin: positioning the side-wings of mirror at angles where she could study herself as virtually a stranger. But she knew she lacked the full courage for a confessional. So she experimented with her hair instead, sweeping up and letting down and asking Aunt Dodie what *her* opinion was. She answered her slowly and carefully.

'I – I like you best as you are, I think.'

'Oh *no*.'

'Maybe – you should give it some thought?'

'I *have*, though.'

'I'm glad that you should have asked me. I would like to be your – confidante.'

She wasn't, in all probability, talking about the styling of her hair.

'It's important,' her aunt continued, 'to feel you can turn to someone. If needs be.'

Catherine nodded, perhaps too energetically.

'*I* shall pay,' her aunt said.

'What?'

'If you want to have your hair changed. Restyled.'

'I . . .'

'But maybe you should consider it first. It takes some living with afterwards. So you should be as certain as you *can* be.'

'Yes,' Catherine said. 'I just thought I'd ask you – '

'But I should *like* you to ask me things.'

Catherine turned back to the mirror. Their eyes met on a diagonal.

Her aunt left the room and returned carrying a long, shallow cardboard box. She shook off the lid, removed some white tissue paper and handed Catherine the container. Inside was a silver and tortoiseshell hairbrush.

'It was your mother's.'

'I wondered if she'd left . . .'

'Your father didn't want to see her things – lying about – '

'Like – well, memorials?'
'I suppose so.'
'In case they upset him?'
'Yes. Something like that.'
'It's beautiful.'
'I think, Catherine, you should keep it in its box. In a drawer.'
'But he'd want me to have it?'
'I – I'm not sure.'
Catherine frowned. But only momentarily, because it was a very fine object, and now it was hers.
'So you can think about it and decide,' her aunt said.
'I'm sorry?'
'About your hair. Think about what you want to do with it.'
'Yes,' Catherine said. She pulled out one comb, then the other, and the hair started to fall down.
'Your mother used combs too, you know.'
Catherine turned round on the chair. She had no recollection of that, none at all.
'Combs?'
'Yes.'
Catherine smiled – for some reason – and wasn't able to stop.
'And then when *you* started to use them – '
No, she told herself, it wasn't a coincidence, not merely that. It meant more, it was a significance of a different order.
The years talking.
Blood stirring.
All which straight-thinking denied and said was impossible.
The tracks drawing together.
Their fates conspiring.

*

Sometimes she wondered how she could forget a face that meant so much to her.
She would close her eyes to remember him, but the face slipped from her. Was it because she knew each of the details too well, but singly and in isolation, and seldom allowed herself the physical distance and perspective to see the features en masse, in the round?
She felt guilty about it, deceitful, treacherous, when she cared for him so much.
But falling asleep, it happened again – she was in his arms, she was studying his eyes, his mouth, his nose, his chin, the pores of his skin, the bristles of his moustache – and she realised that she couldn't alter the dictates of her unconsciousness.

She loved him: –

for gratitude's sake,

to protect him, from she didn't know what,

because the nearness of him caused her heart to beat twice as fast as normal and made her breathing fitful,

because she felt a truth was *more* not less likely to be proven when it remained a secret,

because he took her out of herself,

because she wanted to be transformed, into another being, into oneness with him,

because he rendered everything else bearable in her life, and showed her what wasn't important to her, and also made her alive to the tips of her fingers so that she saw new splendour even in Aquae-Regis by viewing it through *his* eyes, everything considered afresh in the transforming glow of happiness, everything forgiven.

Her stomach churned running to meet him; eating and drinking were a matter of sublime indifference to her. She fell asleep thinking of him, and when she awoke he was the first thought of the day.

18

Oestrus

THEN, for the first time, they agreed to meet in a place where there would be a danger of their being seen together.

She ran downhill into the town. Her feet flew beneath her and she forgot all her aunt's warnings, about the perils for women's fashion shoes on the steps and cobbles. Instead she heard the clatter of her heels and was fleetingly conscious at street turnings and crossings of enquiring faces drawn to windows.

Past Launceston Square she took the shortest route, by way of the back lanes. She knew the gaps between buildings, and ran from hot August sunshine into dank green shadows, into gullies, along the curving side-walls where the builders had left the stone rough and untreated, with the marks of the quarrymen's tools still gouged into it two hundred years later. She touched the walls lightly, with her fingertips, to give herself a little confidence in those dark chasms with the honest blue sky so high above her. Her breath left echoes behind her; she knew from experience that that was how her breath sounded in those places, but – still – she didn't quite trust to look behind her. She was conscious at one of those sunless points of a shape passing in front of her: a cat maybe, or at the worst a large rat, and for several moments she closed her eyes, until she was past it, whatever it was, past and away. This was her secret town, and she prized it, notwithstanding all the small fears and panics it induced in her. She came because coming was in the manner of a dare to her courage. Here she could escape scrutiny, at any rate from those who thought they knew everything about her; she ran too fast for watchers to be sure who she might be.

But her secret town only lasted until Waterloo Street. Turning the last dog-leg between two buildings, she found herself facing the public world again: housewives, maids on errands, a businessman, a cleric, a nanny pushing a pram. In the open squares and broad streets, even walking behind the pillars of the arcades, she was her father's daughter, and she was always aware that the fact of her presence was being recorded. Today she felt especially uncomfortable but the feeling merged into others – skin-tingling anticipation, an easy seeping dampness in her own most private place, uncertainty about her appearance – and she covered the remaining distance to Benedict Row in a confused, unseeing daze.

She pushed open the door of Jasper's Tea-Rooms and in the next few seconds stumbled on the step down into the hall. She reached out for the wall and only just prevented herself from being sent sprawling.

Luckily no one had witnessed her acrobatics. She collected her breath but she could feel trembling behind her knees.

She leaned against the wall for several moments and happened to catch sight of herself in a mirror at the end of the corridor. Her face was glowing pink, and her shoulders heaved under her summer raincoat. Watching herself she untied the knot of scarf under her chin and pulled the covering – meant as a disguise of sorts – from her hair. She had spent the morning washing it and setting it and brushing it out, and now she doubted very much if he'd be able to guess: it looked like a nest which a very large bird had squashed very flat.

She used both hands to try to find the shape again. The result wasn't greatly convincing, she thought, but it must be an improvement.

She opened her bag and took out her compact for a closer inspection in the circle of mirror. It was her mouth, though, that caught her attention. She undid the top of her lipstick and drew the scarlet wedge, heavily, over her lips. She pursed them, how she remembered her mother confirming the evenness of lipstick to herself, and then she attempted a brisk smile that would show both rows of well-scrubbed teeth.

'What a big smile you have, Grandmama . . .'

She was so startled by the voice that she dropped the compact. When they both bent down to pick it up, she discovered that the mirror was broken. He took the compact from her, crouched down on his knees and picked up the splinters.

'That was *my* fault, Catherine.'

'No,' she said. 'No, I was – '

'I'll buy you another one, I promise you. At the very first opportunity.'

'It just fell – '

'You didn't see me?'

'What?'

'In the mirror?'

He opened his palm to show her the pieces of shattered glass.

'I expect a woman's lost without her compact?'

'It's just the mirror,' she said. 'The rest of it's all right.'

He returned the compact to her but kept the splinters of glass concealed in his hand.

'Thank you,' she said.

'For making you drop it?'

'No.' She shook her head, ashamed to raise her head any higher than the knot of his tie. 'It's all right, really.'

'But you wanted to look at yourself?'

She felt her face must be turning scarlet, vermilion, as she looked over his shoulder, towards the door and the street outside. She let him take her arm and turn her away from the tea-room chatter.

'I suggest we cut off out of here. Would you mind terribly?'

'But – can't we talk? Our tea – '

'We can manage something better, can't we? I thought we could get out of the town for a while.'

'What?'

He smiled as he reached for the handle of the door.

'In the car.'

'You've got a car? You didn't say.'

'I was waiting for my moment.'

'We're going driving?'

'Just for a spin. I'm not going to spirit you off somewhere.'

But it doesn't matter if you do, she wanted to tell him: it doesn't matter, only to be with you.

Somehow she must have remembered the step up to street-level. She blinked as they walked out into fierce sunlight.

She remembered later how birds were wheeling about the Abbey tower.

'You can show me what's what,' she heard him say.

'I don't really know,' she told him.

'No? Doesn't matter. We'll just drive off for a while, shall we?'

She let him guide her by the arm, towards the quiet passageway behind the south bluff of the Abbey. She concentrated on looking *dégagée* for the sake of the few passers-by.

On Studeley Street he indicated which car was his: a low sports model, a roadster, with a canvas roof.

He might have been reading her thoughts.

'I'll fold the roof down when we get away from here. Out of the town, I mean.'

He opened the passenger door and she lowered herself into the tub chair. The side-window wasn't glass but made of some clear fabric and she realised that she would be less visible behind it, against the distracting glare of the sun.

He turned the key in the ignition lock. The engine rumbled beneath the bonnet and the entire chassis shook.

'This is *real* driving,' he told her as they drew away from the pavement, revving. He nodded at the other cars on the street, squarish and upright and sensible.

She heard their exhaust puttering beneath them on to the road. Three or four heads swivelled round at the sound. She leaned her elbow on the sill and concealed the side of her face with her left hand, although she didn't believe that anyone would be able to offer a positive identification of her.

Three miles out of the city, with only greenery visible to her in the driving mirror, he stopped the car and lowered the hood. As he folded the canvas into its hold she laid the headscarf over her hair, carefully, and tied a knot under her chin. He smiled in a carefree way as he got back into the car beside her, turned the ignition key with a wrist-flick, and pressed his foot down on the accelerator pedal. They shot off, as if they were bound for the west, but they left the main road at the first turning.

A red side-road with a succession of gradients took them away from the possibility of observing eyes. It felt more like a lane, with high hedges and unruly banks of ragged robin, pheasant's eye, snapdragons, orchises and violets, and the heat of the day caught between them, stiff and unstirred and cloyingly, sweetly aromatic. The speed was lightly drugging her, so that she felt herself becoming insensitive to the danger, of another car or a tractor appearing over the next hilltop, but it didn't matter. In the state of mind she now found herself in, they were beyond hazard – the dangers were incidental, so unlikely and unthinkable – the two of them were quite unassailable. She laughed even, as *he* did, picking an insect from her lips, where the lipstick held it fast. On the flatter stretches, where he let the engine have full throttle, they seemed to go slicing through the afternoon, cutting swathes.

The hamlets they passed through belonged to the time before the First War. A sheep strolled out of an open cottage door, pigs snuffled in front gardens, an old woman wearing a long skirt squatted in a field. It was an unsettling discovery for her to make, that this existence was being lived out so close to their own in the city, only six or seven miles away. Women carried baskets on their backs and scrabbled with their hands for vegetables; children chased birds from the corn, or ran barefoot after the car; at a crossroads old men overdressed for the weather in hats and waistcoats sat on chairs and smoked clay pipes; washing was thrown over hedges, and in one garden a scalded pig carcass hung drying and bleaching from ropes; the corpses of other animals and birds, all hunters by instinct, were nailed in death to the branches of trees, like tattered bunting. It was dismaying, of course, and best taken at speed. What it meant was that the landscape watercolours at home in Eveleigh Crescent couldn't be looked into too closely, or at least not beyond the first plane of their prettiness: the prospect, in human terms, would have been too dispiriting to dwell on.

But to her companion it appeared novel, and insignificant, and rather a laugh, and maybe that was exactly the way to treat it. Rural life didn't accord with any of the principles by which their own was conducted. They might as well have been travellers in Morocco, or Siam.

*

It all happened much more quickly and more messily than she had ever envisaged.

She was hardly even ready for him when he was on top of her and sure-fingeredly preparing his entry. But she knew she didn't want to stop him, that desire inside her was like a hollow and a pain inextricably confused. She knew in another part of her brain that she couldn't afford it not to happen, because then she might lose this man who had turned her life on its head. She didn't speak in words but, letting him take charge, she moaned her encouragement to him in sounds he understood immediately. Then, as she was trying to lie flatter on the straw, the thing occurred.

She guessed afterwards that he hadn't been so much in control after all. His face contorted – with frustration, it must have been – and he tried to push deeper. At the same time her moaning involuntarily turned to a yelp of hurt. It was too late by then and he came into her just as they both were.

When he withdrew, maybe half a minute after that – as she still fought to steady her breath – she felt the viscous matter that sex was about starting to leak out of her. She rolled on to her side, away from him, and propped herself up on one elbow. The hair between her legs was wet and tangled; as she watched, his semen was already trickling on to the inside of her thigh. As if, not meaning to, she was rejecting him.

She turned and looked over her shoulder. He muzzled into her neck and followed the track her eyes had taken to her crotch. She watched as he leaned over her. Suddenly his face was curious.

'You're not bleeding,' he said.

'What?'

'There's no blood.'

She looked down.

'A little maybe,' she said.

'But not a flood of it.'

'Should there be?'

'Of course not. But – '

Their eyes were no further than three inches apart. As they continued to stare at one another, he pulled himself up on his knees.

' – I just supposed – '

' "Supposed"? Supposed what?'

' – that you were a virgin.'

'I *am*,' she said.

'I thought – there hadn't *been* anybody.'

'There hasn't been,' she told him. 'No one.'

He began to shake his head.

'Not until now,' she said. 'Until you – '

He closed his eyes, then opened them again.

He continued to watch her. His curiosity seemed to have become more rapt. The corners of his mouth flexed, there was the hint of a smile.

'Well, you *are* a complicated case.' His voice was intimate and confidential, but she couldn't decipher his tone. 'Aren't you now?'

She shook her head.

'No,' she said. 'No, I don't think so.'

He was still watching her, and with such intensity that she felt she had to look away. She reached her arm out, to where she'd dropped her skirt, but his hand was quicker and clasped her wrist.

'But you know what I mean?' he said. 'Don't you?'

'It doesn't *have* to be,' she told him. 'How you said.'

'How do you know that? Is that what your aunt told you?'

'Girls at school.'

'What did *they* say?'

'Sometimes it's like that and sometimes it isn't.'

'What does *that* mean?' He loosened his hold on her wrist. 'Do you know?'

'It can happen at another time. An accident.'

He took his hand away. She leaned forward for her skirt.

'You had an accident then?'

She didn't move.

'If you really loved me,' he said, 'you would tell me.'

She sat up straight, pulling her knees towards her.

'If *you* loved *me*,' she said, 'you wouldn't ask me such a question.' She wrapped her arms round her knees. 'You would trust me too much to need to – '

He pulled at some loose strands of her hair.

'I'm not sure I quite understand you, Catherine.'

'Really, you're wrong. I'm not "complicated". Not at all.'
'You promise me that?'
'Yes, yes, I promise you.'
He leaned back, on one elbow. He had already pulled on his underpants and shirt. She felt in a moment vulnerable as she didn't wish to be. But she had no means of concealing herself and had to stand up, only able to turn her back to him. She hadn't been wholly naked in front of anyone since she was a child. The thought of her nakedness hadn't occurred to her as she'd lain down in the straw with him and they'd hurried towards the moment that was compelling them, as if an event still to happen could be more certain than anything that currently was.

She heard him behind her, getting to his feet and shaking out his trousers. She started bending down to her bag, then remembered to crouch; inside she found a handkerchief and used it to dab at the stickiness in the gully between her legs and on her thigh. Then, standing up again after she'd rolled the handkerchief into a ball and returned it to her bag, she managed to get on with the business of dressing.

When she was finished, she found him waiting with his head courteously inclined away, looking much as he had when she'd first set eyes on him in Philomel Street. On the short walk from the barn back to the car he continued to spill out of her and she was stricken again with guilt, for her rejection of him. She wondered if it was possible that he was conscious of her thoughts: he was watching her with the same studious attention as before, with the same suggestion of a phantom smile playing on his lips.

He said it again, when they returned to Juniper Street.
'You didn't bleed.'
'What?'
'Afterwards.'
'I don't – '
'When we . . .'
He spoke calmly, without betraying emotion. He talked to her like a doctor.
'I've never loved a man before,' she told him.
'You didn't need to love him.'
'What do you mean?'
He didn't look at her.
'Don't you believe me?'
She asked him the question several times.
'Don't you believe me?'

*

She set off to walk home: alone, she told him.

Soon she was in tears.

He hadn't accused, she hadn't flared; there had been no raising of voices even.

But, by herself, she cried and cried at the words, at the thoughts behind them.

She turned at Quade Street and walked back to the house, the way she'd just come.

'You *must* believe me,' she told him.

'It's just – I can't understand.'

'How could I have said those things to you – said them if they weren't true?'

His stare was blank, uncomprehending.

He accompanied her back. They stopped to linger in the shadows of the Abbey.

'You *have* to believe me,' she said.

'I know. I know, I know.'

'Do you?'

'But shouldn't you have bled?'

'Were you a virgin too?'

He looked away at the question.

'It was love,' she said. 'To me. Not – not a butcher's slab.'

Maybe she hadn't said anything so biting in her life before. The anguish in the words set her rocking.

He moved closer to her in the shadows of the flying buttresses. She thought she should resist, to make her point, but she wasn't able to. She was too afraid of losing this new, transforming concord in her life.

Forgive me my sins, she called into her skull, but I do this for a greater good, in forgiveness of another . . .

Later she remembered, what she hadn't been able to connect with events as they were happening by the Abbey wall: a different age of her life altogether, suddenly as clear to her recall as that midsummer Kent daylight.

Of course. Of course.

One June weekend when she was eleven or twelve her father and aunt had been invited to a house in the country, and had taken her with them. Their hosts had also invited the husband's or wife's widowed sister and her daughter, and it must have been – so she realised before the visit was over – that there were ulterior purposes to the merely social.

The other girl was given charge of her for the afternoon, and they spent it in the wooded gardens. The beauty of the spot had left Aunt Dodie catching her breath several times on their arrival, but Catherine discovered from her guide that it was also the haunt of grass-snakes and toads and bloody-nosed beetles.

Tibbie – Aunt Dodie had gently forewarned her – was a 'tomboy'. She wasn't very clear about the significance of the term, but it was soon made plain. Tibbie had them crawling through brakes, stone-jumping across streams, spanning the two sides of a ditch with their legs as stiff and wide apart as a pair of compasses, and finally climbing trees.

It was there – up a tree – that she had her 'accident'. Not that she noticed immediately. Something rode into the gully between her legs as she swung them to straddle a branch; she felt a momentary stab of pain, but she had already been scratched by the briars and had grazed both knees when she fell on the path of stones in the stream.

Only when she was on the ground, knees shaking and shoulders and neck aching, did she notice: and it was Tibbie who saw first, pointing to her legs. She looked down; she lifted her skirt and stared at the mess of blood smearing her thighs. In the next few seconds she lost consciousness and tumbled past Tibbie's vaguely outstretched arms on to the soft mossy ground.

When she woke she was lying in bed. A doctor had been summoned and she heard him ask everyone to kindly leave the room before he investigated the patient.

It was an undemanding operation, with little effort required on her part. First, her nightdress was lifted up. He spent no little time prodding her with his thumbs and consulting the mirror in his right hand. Then he helped her pull down the nightdress until she was covered. She watched from the edge of the bed as he opened the door and spoke with her aunt, who appeared quite dismayed by his words.

Afterwards, when the doctor told her he thought it best if she rested in the house for another two or three days, she thought it must be the prospect of a prolonged stay as others' guests which so concerned Aunt Dodie. And indeed she seemed to be less and less at her ease over the next forty-eight hours, alternately sitting beside her and then rising to walk to the window, to watch whoever was down in the garden, her father presumably and their hosts and the widowed, blondely attractive Mrs Hodgkins. On the occasions when Catherine referred to her injury, 'cutting herself', Aunt Dodie went scarlet in the face, and Catherine felt the tropical heat must truly be excessive to cause it.

When she felt better and the doctor pronounced himself satisfied, her aunt accompanied her on a walk round the garden. Without intending to, Catherine found what must have been *the* tree, because the lowest branch now showed a dribble of red on the bark, the rusty colour like dried blood; but standing beneath, studying the branch from all angles, Catherine couldn't determine how her injury had been caused. There was no obtruding outgrowth, no malignant twig; and yet something, an object, had ridden into her when all her attention had been concentrated on negotiating the log-like branch and reaching the sloping trunk, to slither her way down to the ground.

Aunt Dodie asked her if that was the tree, and she answered yes, but told her why she was puzzled. Aunt Dodie pulled in her cheeks and surveyed the spot long and hard. The information must have been relayed to her father. Collecting her things to leave, Catherine watched him from the window of her sick-room as he lowered himself on to a deck chair beside Mrs Hodgkins. He was smiling, dressed for the journey back. Mrs Hodgkins was wearing another of the becoming outfits she had brought with her – this time a tangerine pleated skirt and a white bolero jacket – and she was toying with the handle of an antique parasol. But the conversation took a turn neither of them appeared to anticipate. Catherine watched as Tibbie's mother snapped the parasol shut and Looked Indignant – while her father turned his head, raised his arm and pointed towards the trees. Some heated talk followed. Her father got to his feet and walked round the chairs on the lawn a number of times; whenever he passed Mrs Hodgkins he looked in the opposite direction. She was holding the parasol so tightly that the shaft broke in her hands – with a sound like a pistol crack – and in frustration she hurled the contraption at her fellow guest, but it fell short, on to the grass. She pulled herself out of the chair and stormed off; Catherine stepped back from the window as her father stood watching the departure, doing nothing to stop her. Soon after, Aunt Dodie drifted into view across the lawn, feigning to peer for the last time at the house, eyes shaded by her hand against the sun and in all probability having missed nothing of the contretemps.

While the car was being got ready, Catherine escaped the mystified over-politeness of their hosts. She ran – feeling a little wobbly in her stomach – for the shade of the trees. She followed the stream, which burbled its own cool diversion from the sun's heat. She saw half a dozen stepping-stones breaking the surface, where they must have crossed and where she'd grazed and bruised her knees; but another forty or fifty yards further on she came to another set of stones very much like the other, and she wasn't sure *which* of the two must have been the actual fording place.

She left the course of the stream, keeping a weather-eye open for grass-snakes. And toads. And those black beetles with the queer name, 'bloody-nosed', which Tibbie had taken such undisguised delight in describing to her. She wondered why Mrs Hodgkins had reacted so angrily: unless her father had made a direct accusation of Tibbie's involvement and the woman had been caught off her guard.

Then she found the tree again. Only it wasn't: not the one she'd come upon earlier. The trunk of this one had an even more pronounced slope, to make sliding to the ground easier, but there was also a covering of moss which, now, she was able to remember. The lowest branch was round like a log, and projecting from the trunk she saw a stump of branch that had ceased to grow. Just above her head she found streaks of red on the green moss in the upper crevice between branch and trunk. Lowering her eyes again she noticed the two sets of footprints where they'd each dropped on to the yielding earth.

By then it was too late. As they took their leave, Mrs Hodgkins was another woman: no longer coy and with brown eyes glistening, but quite brittle and brusque. For the first time she wasn't smiling or looking duly sympathetic; she kept her mouth close-lipped, which drew all the features of her thin face very tight. She looked now a worrying, harried sort of woman, too used to having to fend for herself. Tibbie was close-lipped too, and the cast and features of her face resembled her mother's as hadn't been the case before. At one point, most awkwardly of all, Catherine found five pairs of eyes being trained on *her*, and the embarrassment set her coughing.

The invalid was escorted to the car and already the experience was starting to recede. When they passed between the gateposts and out on to the open road that wound downhill, Catherine started to breathe more easily. Aunt Dodie opened her handbag and rummaged for barley sugar. Her father's head was fixed, motionless, as he drove, and it took several seconds to realise that his eyes were all the time flitting between the road and the windscreen mirror, looking for a figure to appear running between the gates, to stand above them on the brow of the hill, to wave her arms wide to call him back to her.

She told Maurice, casually enough, what she remembered of the tree-climbing. And about the debouching on the street, in front of Mrs Larchmont.

He appeared to react casually enough, but she detected the relief just beneath the surface, under the skin. He didn't tell her that he hadn't meant anything by his remarks, and she didn't tell him that he'd nearly scuppered her for good: 'good' in the sense of 'bad'.

But they needed one another too much to waste any more breath on clumsy words of explanation.

He loosened the collar of her blouse and started exploring her neck with his fingers.

Never again, she told herself as his lips sent a shiver down her spine into the small of her back, never again shall we waste any of this, not even for the monstrous show of pride.

19

Cresc., Dim.

EVERY afternoon between half past three and quarter past four she ran up the stairs of the building in Juniper Street. On the top landing she started to undress; in his room she threw everything on to the floor and jumped into his bed.

Their love was ecstatic. One afternoon he took her twice in succession without withdrawing, and when she told him he cheered to make the window-frames rattle. From the pillow she could just see the spires on top of Paradise Hill. The bed bucked beneath them, they were on a flying ship, and the town was lost beneath them. He held her to the moulting feather mattress but she wasn't there, she wasn't geographically anywhere, she was travelling so far and so fast she never wanted to stop.

Blue diamond days, crystalline with possibilities, the streets awash with opaline light.

She had never approached this state of happiness before, never. Unmitigated, boundless happiness. To love, without doubting that the love received in return was unstinting and inexhaustible.

A city of flashing stones. Shafts of dancing dust, silver cobbles after rain, windowpanes burnishing bronze. Cupolas and spires, domes and minarets. Streets half as old as time, springwater alchemised from hot, solid rock.

La-la-la l – l – love! Audrey would know how she felt. Audrey was with her, she sensed, in spirit, returned to these pavements they had covered together scores and scores of times. One disembodied, the other unaware of who saw her or spoke to her. A sisterhood of *amoureuses*: a confederacy of angels.

A key had turned in a lock, a door was opening in a wall as high as a cliff. Beyond was the undying happiness of myth and legend, the ever-after. The jewel without flaw, the rarest fruit, the sorcerer's elixir, a prince's noble valour, a maiden's unblemished innocence!

Her life, she knew, would never – must never – be the same again.

*

Catherine was tired, and closed her magazine, and stood up to say goodnight

From his chair her father barred her way with his arm.

'Isn't there something we have to discuss first?'

She stopped in front of him; then took a couple of steps backwards.

'Sit down, please, Catherine.'

She complied; although in fact her knees gave way beneath her, and she dropped on to the sofa.

'I have it on good authority that you've been noticed in the company of a young man.'

She had to concentrate on keeping her eyes steady and her voice from stuttering.

'I telephoned the school some weeks ago,' her father said. 'They told me they hadn't seen you since you left.'

'Who did you speak to?'

'The new headmistress.'

'Oh, I see. Oh well . . .'

She held out her hands, palms upwards: a gesture of inevitable, unconditional surrender.

The tic appeared in her father's cheek.

'Is that all you've got to say about it?'

' "About" . . .?' She heard her voice trail away.

'Aren't you going to tell me what's been happening?'

She felt her heart dropping like a stone in her chest.

'I should be very interested to hear *your* account of the business. I have heard one side of the story, as it were: by hearsay. So it would be informative to hear the other. In your own words.'

Her tongue seemed to be stuck fast to the roof of her mouth; she had no saliva.

'Would it inconvenience you to provide me with an explanation?'

She shook her head, but she didn't speak.

'I am concerned, Catherine. Anything which begins its life as a rumour – '

'It's nothing really,' she said. 'We just met – '

He jumped on the words.

'You just met?'

She nodded.

'Are you in the habit of meeting many strangers?'

'No.'

'He's not a stranger to you now, though?'
'When we met,' she said, 'then, yes, he was.'
'How – how did your meeting with this stranger come about, might I enquire?'
She shrugged.
'Can't you remember?'
'It just happened.'
'In the street?'
'Well, sort of...'
'He must have proved himself a very interesting stranger to you.'
It was ridiculous having to face a grilling about it, at eighteen years of age and living in these modern times. She was irritated by the questions, but also by her own sullen defensiveness. He always had an instinct, her father, how he might get the better of her.
'You prefer to talk to him in the street?'
'No,' she said. 'Not prefer.'
'Have you introduced him to anyone else?'
'No. No, not yet.'
'Does he have friends or relations here?'
'I don't think so.'
'You're not sure?'
'I'm almost sure,' she said.
' "Almost sure"?' her father repeated.
She watched her fingers weaving together.
'You haven't yet told me the name of this gent.'
The term of course was unbecoming, as was intended.
'Encombe,' she said. 'Maurice Encombe.'
Her father nodded, as if only in confirmation of a fact already known to him. The facts in their fullness were what he wanted to be in possession of.
'It's only right,' he said, 'that I should be concerned – '
She sat quite still.
' – in a situation of this sort.'
As your father, because you are my daughter: so he meant, so he ought to have said but didn't. Wasn't it *his* reputation he was thinking about, and his own long-deceased father's?
'You will tell me when you're ready to, I expect.'
She stood up. No arm barred her departure now. She walked past him, towards the door, not speaking a word. She reached out for the handle.
'Remember, Catherine...'
She paused with the doorknob in her hand.
'... honour isn't to be traded. However high the price offered.'

She walked out into the hall and closed the door behind her. Words like 'honour' only left her breathless, foundering. Her father spoke as he did to intimidate her, only to assert his never-done power and command over her.

*

She didn't tell Maurice.

From Juniper Street she could imagine the hazard to be a lesser one. From the window she only saw steeples and chimneypots.

In the whole of Ægypt there were only themselves. They were the whole world to each other, its core and its circumference. She was able to believe that nothing mattered beyond themselves and this love they made.

*

'A gambler,' her father told her. 'A common-or-garden gambler.'

'No,' she said.

'Didn't you know?'

'He plays cards. But – '

' "But – "?'

' – it's for pleasure.'

Her father shook his head at her naïvety.

'For him,' he said, 'it's a business. That's how he survives. It's his living.'

She didn't speak.

'It suits him very well too, I expect. Rules of chance. No just desserts. No justice – '

'But isn't that . . .'

'Isn't that what?'

Rather admirable of him, she was going to say: submitting himself like that to hap, to Dame Fortune's wiles.

'You're not going to have anything to do with that kind of life. Or that sort. They're after some big catch. There's lots of them about now. Society adventurers. Trying to find themselves an eligible girl and clean up – '

'No!'

' – trying to clean up, and no shame about it. Up in the north they know what to call them – a pack of chancers.'

She turned her head away. It was so unfair, he was misreading the situation, just to suit himself. She knew Maurice better, much better, well enough to hear the spite and envy in her father's voice.

'Do you hear me, Catherine?'

'Yes,' she said, as flatly as she could. 'I hear you.'

A second or two later a pencil snapped between her father's fingers. She stared at the broken, jagged ends he held in either hand. Aunt Dodie would talk of the strength in his wrists, which allowed him to instantly twist off the tops of bottles that defeated her and Mrs Ginger and her husband; once when the car had broken down he and a boy from the garage had raised the front end between them while a mechanic looked beneath, at the underside of the chassis. But she wasn't going to let a shattered pencil influence her, or some couthy northern word from his nursery days, and she wasn't afraid that he should see so.

So much maleness, she thought, looking no higher than the stubble-line of blue beard on his cheeks. That straight mouth, for which 'firm' was only a euphemism. The cleft in his chin. Broad shoulders he had acquired river-swimming in his younger days. Those famous wrists. The sweep of black hairs on the back of his hand. The short, thick, blunt-ended spatula fingers. The harness of starched collar and cuffs, the shackle of tightly knotted tie, collar studs and cufflinks.

But she didn't pity him, for his maleness or for his responsibilities or for his constraints. He had never understood her, and moreover he had never even tried to. Sympathy has to be earned, which was an axiomatic truth he had quite failed to acknowledge.

'I needed to tell you this, Catherine.'

She wanted to shrug her shoulders at him, to rebuff him, but an absolute gesture of that sort might have signified a point of no return. Instead, keeping true to herself, she remained quite motionless. She gave nothing of her feelings away. She realised as she sat quite still that he must be judging her rockfastness for submission. But even by then it was too late, and one misapprehension was only compounding another.

*

'*Are* you a gambler?'

'Your father's been talking.'

She said yes, he had been.

'I thought he might.'

'You told me, though. About the "Nightingale".'

'I told you that I played the tables.'

'Yes,' she said. 'It's *that* word, though. How my father used it. He doesn't understand anything – '

'Oh, I don't know.'

He took her face in his hands.

'I doubt if I deserve you, Catherine.'

She was thinking of her father, hearing his words, knowing that

Maurice deserved all the moral recompense she could pay him, for the constant slighting he would have to suffer when he'd be unable to defend himself. She knew there must be no end to the atonement that was her own, happiest of obligations.

*

'What does he want from you?' her father asked her.

' "Want"?'

'Of all the girls he might have latched himself on to, he's picked *you*.'

'I think,' she said, smarting from the insult, 'you would have to ask *him* that.'

'He's a prospector, Catherine. A *chercheur d'or*.'

'No. No, he's not.'

'How do you know he's not? How can you be sure?'

'Can *you*? Can *you* be sure?'

'I believe so.'

'But I'm the one who *knows* him,' she said, ready again for tears.

'I wonder if you do.'

She felt herself blushing, the heat racing up from her neck and doing its wildfire damage across the top of her chest.

Her father seemed to take the full measure of satisfaction in her discomfiture. She was angry with him, too much so to trust herself to speak. But gradually his eyes were fixing in such a way that she knew he wasn't looking at *her* any more, but at some future potentiality or else a remembered time in his past. His eyes struggled for a focus.

She felt her heat subsiding. Momentarily an intensity of pain was concentrated on his face, and for those few seconds she was stirred to pity. But that too vaporised when he delivered the first of his parting salvoes.

'This is going to end badly,' he said, 'whatever happens.'

She started to shake her head.

'If he's after a sinecure for life, he can put it out of his mind. If he persists, I'll change the terms of my will and he'll realise he's out of luck.'

She opened her mouth to speak, but her father interrupted her as he strode towards the door, letting his bombshell explode behind him.

'Because I'll make damned certain that you have nothing to give him.'

He would actually conceive of leaving her nothing?

No event in her past, the life she'd shared with him in the house, had prepared her for this: this confession of vindictiveness.

They had never been close or especially affectionate, but that had always seemed to be chiefly a consequence of gender, as much as of natural disposition.

Could he actually be so calculating about it, so unapologetically practical, so brazenly open about his intentions?

Why was he *so* unchallengeably convinced that Maurice was wrong for her? Had he been making other plans for her future, which Maurice's presence and her affection for him completely cut across?

Her anger returned: but was eclipsed by her shock, her utter, dismaying failure to understand anything about the mind's workings of this man who was her father.

Her closest blood kin, but infinitely less than that, a hardly indifferent, coldly excluding, bloodily vengeful stranger.

*

One evening after dinner her father came into the drawing-room where she had found herself sitting alone. With neither warning nor preamble he had his final ineluctable say on the matter.

'I forbid you, Catherine.'

She could make no sense of the verb at first, and had to ask him to please repeat himself.

'I absolutely forbid you from seeing that fellow. From having anything to do with him.'

Spoken in the house it was a ridiculous word for the present day and age. Signs at railway stations and nailed to farm gates announced that it was FORBIDDEN to walk on the tracks or pass beyond this point.

She didn't know how to reply. She had surely said everything that there was to be said.

Aunt Dodie must have sensed the significance of the closed door; she kept a low profile for the rest of that evening and most of the next day. But it was she who came up to Catherine's bedroom when her place stayed unoccupied at the dinner table. Her face was filled with ruth and fellow suffering, and Catherine was able to cry as she hadn't been able to for twenty hours, on to one shoulder and then the other.

Her aunt's frame took the physical pressure very well; she didn't totter on her legs as Catherine thought she must, and at last she managed to seat them both.

'Why – ' Catherine's voice was angry and hopeless ' – why is he so against him?'

'It's what he thinks best,' her aunt told her, the answer sounding like rote.

'Do *you*, though? Do *you* think it's best?'

'I . . .' Her aunt lost her assurance. 'It – it's difficult – '

'But do you agree with him?'

'I – I don't know. It's not my place – '

'Yes, it is! *You* have to tell me, Aunt Dodie. Tell me what you think – '

Her aunt started to shake her head.

'I need you to help me – '

'But I don't see how I can.'

'I need an ally. Someone to think the best of *me*.'

Her aunt looked down at the carpeted floor where the Turkey rug had once lain. She made an air-funnel with her lips.

'I can't manage here on my own,' Catherine said.

Her aunt turned her face towards her; slowly and furtively she began to nod.

The gesture mattered, vitally, to Catherine.

20

Thief in the Night

HE had to leave, Maurice told her, to go up to London for a bit. Family business he had to have his say in. About his uncle's pile, Curteys Court.

'*I* could come too,' she said.

'It won't be for long, I hope.'

'Then you'll come back?'

'If I don't have to pop up to Hereford first.'

'Do you think you'll have to?'

'Well, maybe.'

'Are you *sure* I couldn't come up to London? I wouldn't get in the way, I promise.'

'How would you manage it, though?'

She stared at him.

'Anyway, it might quieten your father down a bit if you stay here. Wouldn't be a bad idea, you know.'

He was correct, of course. But she had felt she must offer, overrule caution and sagacity.

She accepted, with a heavy heart, what he was recommending.

'We can write, though,' he said.

'Oh *yes*.'

Immediately she saw how letter-penning would pace and discipline her days without him.

'But – ' Something had occurred to her.

' "But"?' he repeated.

'But there's Father.'

'I could write to your aunt.'

'He looks through the mail first.'

'So, what should I do?'

She considered for several seconds.

'The Duke of Buckingham Hotel.'

'What?'

'I had a friend there. She lived there.'
' "Had"?'
'Yes. She ran away. Sort of.'
Maurice's eyes narrowed slightly as he looked at her.
'I'll ask her father if I can collect them there.'
'What's the address?'
'Cheveney Terrace.'
'I'll remember.'
'And you *will* write?'
'Only if *you* will.'
'Oh yes,' she said, knowing there couldn't be a shadow of doubt. 'And I'll tell you *everything*. All my news.'

Already in her mind she was embarking on them, the nib of her pen was racing over the thickest, creamiest paper she would find to buy; out of the words – pages of them – she was braiding her redoubtable rope of passion and hope.

*

Her father announced he was leaving forthwith on business, to the north, and for a few days there was the stillness in the house which allowed her to concentrate on the only matter that was important to her.

She rationed herself to one letter a day, but put into it everything: sometimes she covered a dozen pages. The day ordered itself around the letter's writing. She wanted each one to be the affirmative, credal, ultimate expression of her love.

*

But no letters reached her.

She was mystified. She kept checking with Mr Stimpton.

She repeated what the arrangements were when she wrote to Maurice, and told him that she had received nothing from him, which she hoped didn't mean that he was under the weather.

She fell into a brown mood: the deepest hue of mahogany. She only had an address to write to, not a telephone number to call. She continued to write, as regularly as before, but was unable to prevent her disquietude from declaring itself on the page. She was anxious that she might be letting too much of her fearfulness show, but what else could she do? She lost the thread telling him what other news there was, her recollections of his time in Aquae-Regis trailed away, to accommodate some other solicitous probe. She reread her letters before posting them, and couldn't decide if they were too trivial or not. She wondered if they read more foolishly in London: worse, if it was conceivable that he was intentionally not replying, because he now saw her for some reason in an altered light?

There was nobody she could ask. Aunt Dodie knew about his absence in London but Catherine hadn't told her that she was writing or that she had agreed on a system for collection with Mr Stimpton. Her aunt might speculate, but these days her face seemed more relaxed, as if she was relieved that the strain and claustrophobia of the past weeks were temporarily in abeyance. She appeared more animated and less burdened. The transformation was causing Catherine to recognise the demands she'd been making of her, and inspired her to feel compassion and remorse for someone other than herself in this time of confusion. She saw the wisdom in one of them at least being allowed some respite – if only for ultimately selfish reasons, so that Aunt Dodie would have the stamina to lend her succour and support if all her own strength should finally fail her.

*

Her father dropped a pile of letters on to the dining-room table.

He handed her one of the envelopes. It had been posted in London and was addressed to her care of the Duke of Buckingham Hotel.

All the letters had been opened and, presumably, read. She counted eight in toto.

'How did you get hold of them?'

'I'm not sure that matters.'

'Oh,' she said, 'but I think it does.'

Her father winced to hear her.

'Mrs Stimpton thought . . .'

'*She* opened them?'

'She thought it was in everyone's best interests . . .'

'When did she tell you?'

'After the third or fourth.'

'Why didn't you tell *me*?'

'Well – I wished to see just what this young man's intentions might be towards you.'

'You read them? The letters?'

'I just – glanced inside them.'

'Mrs Stimpton must have read them.'

'Very possibly.'

For several seconds Catherine couldn't speak for anger.

'What right had you? Either of you?'

'We acted with the best intentions, the best will – '

'Don't tell me that.'

'Please don't forget yourself, Catherine – '

She swept up the envelopes into a pile and walked across the room with them. She opened her hands and tossed them into the fire in the grate. They crinkled in the heat. The flames lapped over them, singed them, then began to blacken and char the paper.

She watched her father's face: first astonished, then starting slowly to smile his pleasure.

'I didn't do it,' she told him, 'for *your* sake.'

The words stalemated his smile.

'It's for Maurice's,' she said. 'Because I'm ashamed, I'm disgusted – '

Her father's smile vanished.

'He doesn't deserve to have anything to do with you or this house. I'm burning them so I know I'll never have to share what they said with you. Or with that vicious woman who gave them to you.'

'Stop now, Catherine,' her father warned her. 'You're not thinking about what you're saying.'

'Oh yes, I am. He's not going to be *tainted* by you another second longer.'

She looked back at the grate. The only evidence left of the letters were some specks of paper dancing in the flames.

*

Her despair of the past few weeks was metamorphosed into mute rage over the next forty-eight hours.

When she thought she could control herself long enough, she sat down in her room and wrote another letter to Maurice. She told him what had happened, sparing neither Audrey's stepmother nor her own father. She told him, not that she herself had had to burn his letters, but merely that they had gone into the fire without her having read them. She told him that there were no means by which he could reply to her – not unless ('I pray that you will, Maurice') he could find a way to return in person to Aquae-Regis, as soon as he might, and 'rescue' her 'from this miserable, unspeakable place'.

She reread what she had written, with her skin still tingling all over from her excitation. She wasn't quite sure to what the words 'this miserable, unspeakable place' referred – the house or the town itself – but she took up her pen and underlined the phrase, twice.

She couldn't believe otherwise than that her life here was over. She couldn't undo time and retrace her steps, which was what it would have taken; and she was quite certain in her own mind that she didn't want to, that her methods of thinking and feeling now were fully an adult's, with quite different aspirations for herself.

She started again on a fresh page, telling him that she would go to the post-office sorting-room and try to persuade them to hold back any letter that came for her ('or a telegram' she added in parenthesis, hoping wildly). She asked him please not to be intimidated by what had happened whenever he chose to reply to her. Nobody would ever have an opportunity to read his letters again. (She suddenly remembered she had avoided letting him know that what he'd written had been read by others: she didn't want to score the sentence out, but put her trust in its seeming – merely – ambiguous.) She was, she wrote, so very, very sorry that she wouldn't now know what it was he'd written to her in his letters, but at least whatever it was had been – she took a risk with the spelling, and the poetic conceit – 'cauterised by fire'.

She finished as she had done in each of her dozen previous efforts, declaring her love and admiration for him (pairing the terms, as always). At least, she reminded him, *he* had *her* letters, and none of her opinions had changed since the very first: in fact, she wrote, she was more certain now than ever, and became so with every new day. Even though it lengthened the sum time of their parting from one another.

She concluded, 'With the Deepest Affection, Your Own', and signed her name with a stylish flourish and a purposeful, arching line added beneath. Four 'X's, she thought, were in order this time; no, five, she decided, one on each cheek and one for the part of his face closest to the lobe of his ear on each side, and the final lingering one for his lips.

She read the letter over again, several times, refrained from spoiling its neatness by arrowing in any additions, ran – as she always did – a fingertip of eau-de-Cologne along the fold, and sealed it inside an envelope.

As ever, after she had posted the letter she thought of what she *might* have said, which would have sounded better. As ever, she tried to record the emendations in her memory for next time: but knew that, as always happened, she would be bound to forget.

This time Aunt Dodie saw her leaving to catch the post and smiled at her when she noticed the letter in her hand. Maybe she had had the 'facts' presented to her by her brother, or maybe she had overheard some of their last exchange in the dining-room. Her aunt, beneath her spinsterish and sometimes vapid surface, was a more complex, less calculable woman than perhaps anybody except herself had grounds to suspect.

Then she waited for a reply. And waited.

She had no pride about asking the chief sorter in the post office – the matter was too important for that – and he appeared to take pity on her when she told him her letters had sometimes been opened at home by mistake, quite accidentally, 'with the best will in the world', but that the letters which she was now awaiting were of a very, very private nature, that she couldn't afford an accident to happen within the next few days . . .

The prospect of receiving Maurice's letter was her only solace in that dismal interlude. Aunt Dodie had tried to assist by making cryptic references to her father's fixed and habitual tracks of thought, the difference between a man's way of thinking and a woman's, the 'mish-mash' society seemed to be turning into at the moment with some people going up and others coming down and those who meant to stay just where they were being knocked all asquint . . .

She called in at the sorting-office every day and waited at the second door, where she was able to view the activity through the high porthole window. At first the chief sorter himself courteously presented himself, and would tell her that nothing had been received for her from London. Afterwards, it was left to one of his underlings to disclose the same information. Later still, in the third week, the subordinate would shake his head at her from where he stood sifting through handfuls of letters, piston arms despatching each to its proper pigeon-hole in a rack.

Her nervousness on each occasion didn't diminish. Her confidence was never done ebbing, the butterflies in her stomach became something more acute, whorls of pain that would stop her in mid-stride as she was crossing the post-office yard towards the sorting-room and leave her stooping to catch her breath. Always when she set out again on her return journey she felt light-headed, queasy, and bitterly disappointed, wobbling on her feet. For a while it occurred to her that the sorters might be intriguing with her father, as fellow conspirators; but she finally guessed that in that case they wouldn't have been so coolly disregarding, cavalier even, not if they'd had the suspense of a deception to maintain.

So she could only suppose that things were as they said (or *didn't* say, giving her only a perfunctory sideways shake of the head) – namely, that no letter from London in her name had been received.

Maybe, she thought, maybe she had alarmed Maurice unduly, so that he was unwilling to trust another reply to the post. It was possible that he would be deeply embarrassed to have any letter intercepted and the contents read. It was also possible – it quite upset her to imagine – that he had been shocked, even offended, to learn that his portion of the correspondence had been burnt, read or not; or the emotion they contained might have been unrepeatable, she tried to argue to herself, and perhaps he didn't know where to begin again.

It was a grievous, grieving time for her. She seriously considered opening her heart to her aunt, but she was deterred by the realisation that she would seem to be searching out sympathy. She didn't want to be seen to be hiding anything; but she felt her only duty was to be no less than completely honest and truthful, and if her aunt should ask her in roundabout fashion how far the relationship between the two of them had gone, she foresaw how deep her own anger would be with herself at not being able to disclose better than a partial truth to her. On balance, therefore – although it was a touch-and-go conclusion – she felt that it was neatest and tidiest to leave things as they were, for a spell longer, not to run the risk of turning Aunt Dodie away from her because she might happen to tell her too much.

*

The news didn't come from Aquae-Regis but travelled west on the down-line from Waterloo.

Jennifer Moncrieff-King had eloped with an adventurer or worse, and her mother – scouring London – was frantic. It had been a whirlwind affair, accomplished like the world in six days. And on the seventh they had bolted.

The desperado wasn't anonymous; in fact the pair had quite a number of acquaintances in common. His name was Encombe. His father was an Honourable, but rather down on his luck. Hardly surprising that the son should be on the look-out. In London that sort were rather encouraged; public-school rebels still kicking against the pricks; knowing their privileged place but with the little problem of equipping themselves with the wherewithal. His luck finds him an unspoken-for young woman, sound in limb and (probably) mind, who's supposed to have got into some well-off great-uncle's good books and suddenly has access to the 'necessary' but who lacks the social sureness-of-touch she needs to believe in her own gilded state. 'X' meets 'Y' and, before you can say 'God helps those . . .', Bingo!

Mrs Moncrieff-King departed from Aquae-Regis, leaving no one a forwarding address, bound for obscurity.

Catherine tried to make contact, but couldn't.

A small package was delivered to the house. It bore French stamps and had been franked with a Paris postmark.

Inside, wrapped in white tissue paper, she found a gleaming silver and blue lacquer compact. Engraved on the circular lid, in a classic face, was the single letter 'C'.

There was no sender's name, no message.

*

A view of Baden-Baden. Behind linden trees and a bandstand, the Casino swelled with self-importance. One morning a postcard awaited her on top of the dining-room sideboard.

> I may not be a wise man but I don't want to be a sinful one. It's impossible to explain, because I would have to break my oath on a secret. The town is distracting: so is the company, and I pray that we continue as we are. I think I'm more comfortable with the risks at 'the wheel'. But optimism is the best policy, and I hope you can see a way to forgive.
>
> M.

21

Quietus

It was another crazy time, only worse.

In the course of one week she didn't remember eating more than a couple of slices of bread and butter each day and tasting the tea Aunt Dodie would pour for her. She could sit, or lie, in the same position for hours. She dreaded sleeping because when she woke the knowledge of what had happened was already there, waiting for her, and then she started on the treadmill of thoughts all over again, until she stored up enough tiredness at long last for a fitful sleep.

All she wanted to do was to waste away. She couldn't find any bitterness in herself; she envied Jennifer Moncrieff-King more than she could have conceived possible, and she pitied Maurice for having been so misguided. She had no feelings at all left for her father, not even ruth for having none. Her aunt hovered about her, too fearful to make an acknowledgement but achieving more by her silence: her only link with present things, and her only reason for believing she might ever return to them.

She slid through a hole, out of the familiar and habitual, into an underworld of despair.

Weeks went by and she had no recollection of *how* they passed. At certain points Aunt Dodie, showing such ridiculous perturbation on her face but afraid to express it in words, linked her arm with hers and together they went walking for some air, but always by the partial camouflage of twilight and along the mews lanes behind the terraces. Only once did her aunt lose her composure. They were returning home, turning by the spiked area railings on the corner, when she said that this was like the past all over again. Maybe she didn't realise that she had spoken at all.

Catherine repeated her.

' "The past"?'

'What?'

'You said, "the past" – '

Her aunt shook her head. Catherine hadn't the strength of mind to pursue the matter, so she smiled, in that newly disconnected way that she now did. Her aunt only looked more distressed than ever.

She still didn't know if she ate or not. She still couldn't be sure that she slept, and for how long. Aunt Dodie ran baths for her, so that must have been how her personal hygiene was attended to. Her father came into her field of vision and moved out of it again, but she couldn't make sense of any of the exchanges the two of them might have had. Other faces that she encountered on her walks were blurs, no more, as she quickly turned away from them.

This was the nadir of experience, she felt sure: nothing could be *more* adverse, she couldn't feel any less than this. At least a physical injury would have given her that to focus on: brain damage would have minimised her own awareness of the fact. As it was, her frequent inability to recall was a version of oblivion, but it wasn't painless: her stomach was invariably tied in knots, in bed she curled up with cramps and aches, waiting always for the images that were baiting a trap for her, ready to flash into the forefront of her thoughts, memories – but far clearer and sharper than anything actual – of those last days with Maurice. She grew weary and heartsick with keeping watch for them and sometimes she dropped her guard and those were the moments when they would wreak their very worst.

She heard nothing about him, and nothing more *from* him. She thought some echoes might have been left behind, and she would have picked those up somehow, through what she overheard people say – or listening to the spaces between words, what it was that they weren't allowing themselves to say. But no echoes or murmurs reached her, and she was left with only that awesome silence she caused around her, which cut through Aunt Dodie's attempts at bonhomie and was really the raging of unanswerable questions inside her head, so incessant that one question caught another's tail and the result was perpetual motion like a propeller's blade, so that now and then she could almost confuse this whirring of her unspoken words for the stasis of her mind at rest.

Her aunt continued to cast her anxious looks.

Catherine didn't intend her additional distress. But she was incapable of intending *anything* in this state of somnolent despair. She managed, more or less, to get through the dumb-show of daily life, but aware – just – that she was convincing nobody. The first nights had been the worst, crawling round her bedroom on all fours, sobbing into the dusty carpet that wasn't a Turkey rug. Nothing could have been worse to endure than the sleeplessness, the momentary dozing and the sudden convulsive waking to all that colossal, calamitous knowledge.

Now everything was experienced on the mean, she merely suffered her life. *Pis aller, pis aller*. She had begun to stoop, her neck hung further forward of her shoulders, and it was gradually becoming a habit with her as the sum of days lengthened to weeks. She sloped from room to room without the compulsion to use her eyes for doing anything other than directing herself; she didn't raise or lower her voice from the monotone – punctuated by interludes of ungrammatical quiet and the frequent sighs she had got so into the way of. She wasn't impolite, but she made minimal contact with each situation, and her civility or discourtesy was properly immaterial. The small of her back started to hurt and the pain travelled between there and her neck; her headaches homed in on her eyes and when the blood thumped in her temples she saw momentary trails of sparks. She developed occasional twinges in her hips and knee joints which would suddenly force her to drop into a sitting position, onto a chair or the edge of her bed or a step on the staircase. Her skin was paler every time she swivelled her eyes towards a mirror. Her stomach had shrunk, her hair felt lifeless, her lips would stick together with under-use, she urinated irregularly and sometimes began to when she didn't mean to, her bowel movements were sluggish and stabbing, she thought she never wanted to read a book or newspaper again or go to see another film or listen to music on the radio or take walks or swallow one more mouthful of the hot milk Aunt Dodie personally boiled up for her or dare to perceive a single glimmer of hope in all the time banked like vast nemesis where this day eventually slow-drifted into the next, where today ran down into tomorrow.

*

And then, after the doctor's prognosis, Catherine had to leave Aquae-Regis.

Her father wouldn't discuss the reasons with her, although he was fully acquainted with them. Aunt Dodie told her brother that she had helped this far to bring up his child and she –

'Marguerite's child,' he attempted to correct her. 'If you don't – '

' – and I can't shirk my responsibilities now. When she needs me most.'

*

During the last weeks her father ate out, at hotels. He had left the house for the foundry by six o'clock in the morning; at night he let himself back in with a key some time after ten o'clock.

Aunt Dodie came into her own with the packing. She thought of everything that might be needed at the nursing home. She herself bought clothes for the baby, and tins of the mildest talcum powders she could find. Catherine was amazed by her energy and her fortitude. Her father could say nothing to deflect her. She heard him telling her he would cut her out of his will, but her aunt only humoured him as she might have done a child.

The child, made from love, whose right to a life both she and her aunt hadn't for a single moment doubted.

22

Envoi

HER father collapsed with a heart attack in South Nile Street one afternoon in May and died in the fitting-room of a gentlemen's tailor and outfitter to which he had been carried.

Catherine and her aunt returned from Eastbourne as soon as they received the news, too shocked to properly comprehend what had happened. They arrived back at Eveleigh Crescent wearing seaside clothes and with light esplanade tans on their faces and hands. The house was even more silent than formerly, because Mrs Ginger had stopped all the clocks.

The body had been prepared and laid out in the dining-room. The undertaker was still in the house; he had the coffin lid removed so that they might pay their last respects. It was too much for Aunt Dodie, who turned tail and fled from the room. Standing by the professional trestle table Catherine waited for tears to come, and only when she accepted they had no cause to did she manage to cry – difficult, stinging tears. She wept mutely on account of all that her relationship with her father had failed to be. She remembered his face in life as being no less stiff and inflexible than it was now.

She stayed in the room after the coffin had been closed up and the deferential undertaker's crêpe-soled feet had departed. There was one thing still remaining to be done, and she walked over to the mirror on the wall. She slid the frame upwards, as she had somehow found the strength to do as a girl, and placed her eye against the crack. From the room beyond she heard footsteps: heels sounding on the bare wooden floorboards, somewhere out of eyeshot.

She let the mirror bang against the wall and ran from the room, sprinting past an astonished Mrs Ginger and a shocked undertaker to find her aunt. She explained, breathlessly, that she had to get hold of the key of the locked room. At first Aunt Dodie pretended not to understand what she was referring to, but the simulation couldn't be kept up. She shook her head. 'No,' she said, 'don't, please.' Catherine fastened her hands to her aunt's elbows and tried leading her from the room.

'But I've got to see. I've got to see now.'

'No.'

'Oh please, please.'

'No, Catherine. You mustn't.'

Her aunt was unpersuadable. Mrs Ginger, when she was asked, said that she had never had a key to the room: but she would make them both a pot of tea so that they could try to settle, calm themselves down.

Over the tea Aunt Dodie told her what she knew. The room had been her mother's day-room, furnished by her, to have the look of the French about it. It had been her own private retreat.

'But . . .' Catherine prompted her.

' "But"?'

'You're not telling me everything, are you?'

'Your father wouldn't talk about it.'

'But you must have thought about it? Why he wouldn't say anything. You must have made guesses.'

Her aunt stared towards the sitting-room door, as if she was looking for a way of escape.

'*Please* tell me, Aunt Dodie. It doesn't matter to Father now. Does it?'

After several moments of deliberation her aunt nodded, very slowly.

'There was something – like a day-bed. A chaise-longue. I actually came across it afterwards, in a saleroom I was looking round. And I heard someone say it had once belonged to Hector Hammond's wife.'

Catherine waited for her to continue.

'I went to see Mrs Elmore once – before Mrs Ramage's time. A few years after she left us. I shouldn't have done, of course. I shouldn't have discussed family business with staff –'

'What did she say?'

'She was always fond of your mother. She thought she was very different from the other wives round about. Not just because she was prettier. She was proud of her. But she knew . . .'

'Knew what?'

'Your mother . . .' Aunt Dodie twisted herself round on the seat. '. . . Sometimes people came to the house. Through the day. Mostly the people your father knew too, their friends. But once or twice – I gathered – there'd be a stranger as well, a friend of the friends. A woman maybe – or maybe not a woman. Not many, but every once in a while. Your mother . . .'

Catherine didn't speak.

'. . . she'd send Mrs Ramage out for the afternoon. Once she'd got the tea things set out. Mrs Ramage didn't know anything more than that.'

'But she guessed?'

'It's *all* – all just guesswork. Maybe your mother just wanted to laugh. Or to play the wind-up gramophone loudly. She used to dance a lot.'

'Father never told me about her. Anything.'

'Nor did I.'

'*You* weren't meant to, though, were you?'

'She knew stage people. That was from the time before she met your father. They had rather gay times, I expect. Then she settled down here. Maybe too soon in her life. But it comes to us all, or most of us. And she'd had *you*, of course. Even so – sometimes she must have been set thinking of the old ways, don't you think?'

'I – I suppose so.'

'She *did* laugh a lot, at one time. People used to tell me that. Before she became much quieter and withdrawn and preferred not to go out. The life and soul. So it was probably just natural, that she should want to – to let down her hair occasionally.'

'That's what she was doing? In her day-room?'

'I don't know. It's what – I believe.'

'What you've taught yourself to believe?'

'Don't be hard on me, Catherine.'

'I'm not. I'm not, really – '

'I wish *I* could have been a more – a more humorous person for you. It wasn't the way I was brought up, though: I wish things could have "mattered" less. But I was here to do a job – help raise you – and your father kept me up to the mark.'

'You gave up your old life for me.'

'I wanted to.'

Catherine leaned forward and clasped her aunt's hands.

'You know I shall always be so grateful to you.'

Her aunt shook her head.

'That wasn't why, Catherine.'

'Something else – ?'

'It wasn't to make you grateful.'

'Another reason?'

Her aunt swallowed.

'I – I suspected your mother hadn't been so happy latterly. I hoped – there wasn't an atmosphere left in the house. I knew I had no choice, really. For *your* sake – Marguerite's child. I had to try to make it a different sort of house.'

'Did she fall ill?'

The question startled her aunt. Catherine felt her fingers stiffen inside the hold of her own.

'I mean,' Catherine said, 'I mean – because of her state of mind?'

She was remembering – she had never forgotten – the cottage on the edge of the copse, above the cove, in Devon.

'A decline – ?'

Her aunt nodded. 'A decline,' she said. 'Yes.'

'Did you know about it?'

Her aunt shook her head.

'Did Father not tell you?'

'I knew she wasn't keeping well. She took infections very easily.'

'About her state of mind, though?'

'We didn't discuss it. I was always his younger sister, right up to the end. Five years younger. It was how we were as children, there were things he thought I wouldn't understand. Ridiculous, of course. But that's just how it was between us.'

The fingers relaxed a little.

'Your mother was a forbidden subject. And I felt – it was rather treacherous, trying to find out, behind his back. I just wanted to think the best of Marguerite.'

'But there's so much – that's unclear. So much mystery left.'

'Well, people can be mysteries while they're alive. Very often to those who think they should know them best. Once they're dead, the mysteries continue, they grow and grow. It's just – the natural condition of – '

Aunt Dodie lifted her shoulders and then let them fall.

'Let's forget about the key,' Catherine said. 'I don't want to see inside the room. Ever.'

Her aunt nodded, and pushed her fingers between those that held her hands.

'I think it would be best, my dear. Honestly.'

Catherine attempted to smile.

'But – I had to ask.'

'Yes. Yes, of course you did. I realise that now.'

Catherine stooped forward and kissed her aunt on the cheek.

'Was it me?'

'What?'

'Who killed Father?'

'But how?'

'With Maurice. With the baby, with Felix. The disgrace – '

Her aunt looked truly grieved.

'Is that what you think, Catherine?'

'I can't help thinking it.'

'But his work was very taxing, you know.'
'Wasn't it more that...'
Catherine hesitated.
'Wasn't it what, my dear?'
'I don't know – just that maybe he couldn't – I couldn't make him care so much? In the end?'
'But that's not true. I'm sure it isn't. Of course he cared for you.'
'He cared that I didn't see Maurice again. All he wanted was for him to go away and never come back.'
'He thought it would be for your own good. That's what he believed.'
'It wasn't because he had someone else in mind for me?'
'Who?'
'I don't know. Did he never say?'
'He mentioned no names. Not to me.'
Catherine sighed.
'Well, now we shall never know – '
They both dropped their eyes to the teacups.
' – shall we?'
Her aunt cleared her throat.
'No. No, I suppose not.'
Catherine tightened the hold of her fingers on her aunt's hands.
'He was your *brother*. You knew him longer than anyone.'
'Yes. But – ' She cleared her throat again. 'But he also kept himself to himself. Always. As a boy as well. He had to be what his nature had made him. He – he couldn't change from that. Even if he'd wanted to.'
'*Did* he want to?'
'He was very used to being how he was. With his life organised just so. Everything in its place. Being his father's son.'
'But you left Aquae-Regis?'
'Our mother's – your grandmother's – family came from Cumberland. We used to go there for holidays. I got to like it.'
'Father didn't?'
'Oh, yes. I think he did. Even more than me probably. But there was the foundry waiting for him here.'
'He really couldn't do anything else?'
'So many people seemed to have expectations of him, in that line. He must have thought he couldn't say no. But it wasn't natural to him. As it was to your grandfather.'
' "Natural"?'
'He didn't have a gift for it. A "feel" for it, even. I used to get the impression – the business *embarrassed* him. Because of what they made. A bit "Pooterish", he once said, in the early days. And "*p'tit bourgeois*" another time. He never looked in the windows of Laidlaw's,

for instance, at the displays – did you notice that? Domestic hardware. It wasn't quite being an ironmaster, was it?'

'I – I don't suppose it was.'

Aunt Dodie smiled, wistfully.

'Not that he was quite – predictable either.'

'How was that?'

'Well – I'd have to say – marrying whom he did. I'm sure other young women had been selected for him, earmarked. Which is why, you know, I can't imagine he *would* have had eligible young men looked out for *you*, you know. His manner – it was a little deceptive. He wasn't quite how he appeared to be.'

'But you said he had to live with his nature.'

'Well, that's complex, isn't it? You can have two aspects, and they're continually contesting with one another. He *did* marry your mother, of course, but...'

She didn't finish the sentence.

'He regretted it?' Catherine suggested.

'Well, I mean – the other side of his nature took over. The severe side, which disapproved of the risks, which said "I told you so": *it* gained the upper hand, took control. The years passing, they just confirmed the victory. Do you see?'

Catherine nodded.

'It's never easy to judge. With your father, least of all.'

'Yes,' Catherine replied.

'The judgements will continue. They're only beginning, in a sense.'

'Yes,' Catherine said.

They each lifted a teacup and drank in silence, engulfed in the greater silence of the house. Time was standing still for these few days. And yet, as she drank and tactfully avoided her aunt's eyes, Catherine's thoughts were already elsewhere: in Eastbourne, with the baby they'd left behind in good care at the guest-house, whose coming into cognisant awareness coincided – more or less precisely – with the passing of his grandfather's life into the circumjacent community of the spirits.

*

Mr Bostock, her father's lawyer, offered to call at the house for the official business he seemed reluctant to put an actual name to; but she told him she would be happy enough to come to his rooms. In truth she wanted to escape the house for any time she could.

A little queasily, not feeling rightly balanced on her feet, she delivered herself at the offices of Merriweather, Bostock & Cleeve. She was seated, offered sherry which her stomach told her to decline, and then Mr Bostock – shifting his shoulders and fidgeting with his starched collar and tightly knotted tie – awkwardly began.

'What – what exactly did you know about your – about the subject of your father's business concerns, Miss Hammond?'

Catherine shook her head.

'Very little, I'm afraid.'

'No reason why it *should* interest a young woman like yourself, of course.'

'We just didn't talk about it much. In the house.'

'Your father didn't tell you?'

'No,' she said. 'But I didn't ask – '

He sat nodding at her replies.

'All perfectly understandable,' he told her.

She felt the matter must be more serious than he was suggesting.

Mr Bostock cleared his throat and leaned forward in his chair. He straightened the leather edges of the blotter.

'It falls to me,' he said, 'to inform you that – that your father's business affairs were – well, in a somewhat worse way than he might have wanted you to believe was the case.'

She didn't speak.

'If he *had* told you, that is – '

The lawyer cleared his throat again.

'It was a surprise to *me* to discover,' he said. 'Somewhat late in the day, I have to admit.'

'In what *sort* of way exactly? You said "worse" . . .'

'Everyone hereabouts knows of Hammond's, of course. Maybe everyone supposed that these – institutions, let's call them – that they're all naturally "going" concerns. But that needn't always be the case.'

'No?'

'Do you remember your grandfather, Miss Hammond?'

'Not at all, I'm afraid.'

'There's no reason – no earthly reason at all – why a son should inherit the skills of his father.'

Catherine lowered her eyes from Mr Bostock's face to the rounded tips of his stiff white collar.

'It doesn't follow by any logic – '

'You mean – ' she hesitated ' – you mean, he *didn't* have a business mind like his father's?'

'That would be a quite succinct summing up, I think.'

His eyes relaxed. But now he had his cue.

The hands crossed on top of the blotter; the man's face lengthened.

'It's a complicated matter,' he began, 'but suffice to say that the upshot is, because the business got into an unhealthy state, it's worth very much less than might have been the case.'

Catherine felt her neck and spine suddenly tense.

'Money had been borrowed, some equipment had been sold and re-leased, goods were used in part-payment for services and for security. The books are proving quite a headache.'

She wasn't qualified to offer an answer or even a comment, as her father's daughter. But Mr Bostock didn't appear to expect so either, and he continued.

'Your father did his best, I have no doubt about that. He was conscientious, so far as his abilities allowed. I have to stress that – both parts. He should have taken advice, of course. But I suppose he found that idea not much to his fancy.'

'No,' Catherine said slowly. 'I don't suppose so.'

'Your grandfather had a very strong personality. Dominant. More so than your father's. The son was bound to be in his father's shadow.'

Catherine shifted stiffly in her chair.

'Help, Miss Hammond, needn't have meant baling out. It would have prevented the situation drifting so far. It would have kept the worth in the company.'

She knew she was being compelled towards the inevitable question. But the lawyer did the decent thing as she moistened her lips with her tongue, and he anticipated her.

'I think what I'm attempting to say, Miss Hammond . . .'

She tried to look more encouraging in her turn.

' . . . well, I suppose the point is, you mustn't expect to receive too much. In respect of the business itself.'

She felt her shoulders tautening at the words, the nerves bunching in her back.

'It must have been occupying you of late. For all I know – ' Mr Bostock crossed his hands again, in a confidential manner ' – you may have been making certain calculations on the strength of it.'

Catherine concentrated on keeping her face impassive.

'That would be quite natural, of course. That's no more than I should expect. But sadly . . .'

Part II

METAMORPHOSES

'Wealth is not without its advantages and the case to the contrary, although it has often been made, has never proved widely persuasive. But, beyond doubt, wealth is the relentless enemy of understanding.'

J. K. Galbraith, *The Affluent Society*

'The reader will find here no high quests, no selfless endeavours, no mysterious distances ... Justice does not prevail; luck, sharp wits, abundant cash and a pretty face ... will serve a great deal better than goodness or goodwill.'

Jacket notes, *Stories from The Arabian Nights*,
retold by Naomi Lewis

23

Genesis and Exodus

I WAS born in the Marywood Nursing Home in Eastbourne, on the fourteenth day of April, 1950.

*

Despite my name, Felix, I couldn't bring joy with me. For my mother, however, I was the living proof that she had indeed loved. I was also the constant reminder that she had lost Maurice, but the inspiration too that she might – must – find him again, so that hope should triumph over all at last.

The house in Eveleigh Crescent was to be sold. Most of the furniture was to go into a saleroom.

Another house was found for my great-aunt and myself: in Bethesda, according to the land agent, but properly on the fringes of Ægypt.

*

One day, still in palmy Eastbourne, Catherine thought she saw Maurice driving past in a car along King Edward's Parade. She chased after it for three blocks, on her shaky spider's legs. It wasn't him, but instantly she understood where to go next.

*

My earliest recollection of Aquae-Regis is of skies speeding past.

My pram would be propelled along those pavements at a good lick. My great-aunt must have found a younger woman's power in her arms to negotiate those hazardous inclines, the ramps and the flights of steps. I could believe that she must have employed someone to push me on those expeditions if I didn't have the sure recollection of a plump, rouged face beneath a green felt hat's brim, craning forward and humouring me where I lay, a love-child, beneath the pram hood.

I seem to remember the high sooty façades of buildings – columns

– a cupola – stone women, caryatids, supporting the structure of a house of torn blue awnings. I believe I remember trees, and the silence of a park; and later (it must have been), a vertical view of iron bars and mysterious beasts moving behind them – the little zoo where I was taken to be entertained and instructed in the practical romance of other lands. I remember more of those looming flanks of buildings, streaked green, and elongated shadows and fleeting patches of sky: the horizontal view from my pram as I was hurried from one street to another by way of the network of lanes and alleyways which the town preferred to keep its own close, dank terra incognita. Those were days for moving like greased lightning, when other people's curiosity about my identity became too much and my Great-Aunt Dodie's bravery faltered.

Certainly in that city of smoky respectability – with its Abbey of flying buttresses we took the long, sunless way around, with its mossy stone emperors raised on pediments a hundred feet above the Roman Baths – the woman was taking an unconscionable gambler's risk with her own honour, which had already been having a hard enough time of it surely. She was slowly 'coming down in the world', as Aquae-Regis would have it, and she could ill-afford to hasten or aggravate that inexorable decline. She had elected to take the chance. I can only suppose that she did indeed suffer – quite unjustly – for her decision.

So it happened, for good or bad, that Aquae-Regis was my first home. Mere expedience had probably settled it: or desperation. My great-aunt hadn't expected to deal in her life with the rearing of one child, let alone two. I was a burden in every respect: to her peace of mind, to her social standing, to her physical stamina. My mother must have persuaded her with a silver tongue, or my great-aunt must have had too much pity left in her. Perhaps there was also a residue of pride inherited from her brother, to account for the fact that she persevered with me beyond the first weeks and months, that she 'settled' – in as far as she could – to the responsibilities of being my guardian. What then does it matter that occasionally I would see her looking at me so closely, from her (not always superior) vantage-point above the pram or the cot, because she couldn't be utterly, irrefutably sure about the final wisdom of what she was doing, and her capacity for carrying it off?

24

The Bayswater Muse

CATHERINE remembered that, living in London, was Morwenna Littig.

She had come to the school to teach English and been dismissed in her fourth term. She was the most unorthodox – and exciting – mistress the school had known in donkey's years. She had dressed just as the fancy took her – in knickerbockers, say, or a Thai sarong; on successive days she might be a maid of the Swiss mountains, then a *femme fatale* in a Hollywood suit and sheer nylons, then a black-clad peasant aristocrat. She was predictable only in her unpredictability, and she was both more popular and more disliked than any teacher in the school's remembered history. She was finally betrayed by a girl in the Lower Sixth whose father was a governor, but not before – as if she had a premonition – she had walked Catherine home one evening and given her her address in London.

'Audrey'll be all right,' she'd told her.

'How do you know?'

'She's found her man. It can happen early or happen late. It doesn't matter when, so long as it does.'

'But what if – ' it had been on the tip of her tongue to ask. But Miss Littig had just shaken her head at her.

'If you need a base in London for a while – probably it's the best place to look.'

'But why me – ?' Catherine had wanted to ask. Again Miss Littig had smiled away her doubt.

'Lesser than Macbeth, Catherine, and greater. Not so fortunate, yet much *more* fortunate.'

The house was in a very superior terrace off Bayswater Road, although the poor sister among its neighbours.

She hadn't expected to find Morwenna there, but she was, dressed as Flora MacDonald with a Rob Roy feather in her tartan beret.

Practically, the matter was solved in minutes. She would be their guest on the top floor, and if she – as Catherine insisted she must – took a job somewhere, then she could be their lodger.

The old staff rooms – bedroom, sitting-room, galley kitchen, bathroom – were dusty, rather airless, but quite comfortable. The décor was eccentric: icons, prayer mats, a plaster bust of Beethoven, Hebrew books, Hollywood fan magazines, an armchair designed with three legs, crossed scimitars on the wall, a stuffed otter, a cat's-whisker wireless set, a dressmaker's headless dummy.

It was ideal.

Morwenna's parents had been eaten by lions in Tanganyika, whither they had gone on safari, and with her working days now behind her she shared the house with her hugely dignified grandmother.

Mr Littig had been a banker, a Viennese posted to London. He had made many more sound investments in stocks than bad, and his mother and daughter still lived respectably. Their triumph above all else was simply to have held on to the house, which Morwenna filled with snatches of poetry and song and her grandmother with reminiscences of Hapsburg acquaintances and sojourns in the palast-hotels of middle-Europe.

In Lavinia Place the paintwork was dull, degs on doors and skirting boards had gone unretouched, and most fittings that should have shone had lost their sparkle. Fabrics had faded, mirror glass was tarnished, carpets had worn away in places to the cord. But the Littigs drank blends of China tea packaged to them from the importers in Boston, and once in a while a pot of this or that delicacy was despatched from Fauchon in Paris, and on days of traditional celebration in the house a cobwebby bottle of fine vintage would be unearthed. The Meissen was cracked, and the Venetian glass likewise scratched and lined when it was held to the light, and the hall-marked silver was the colour of brassy gold from neglect. Großmutter and Enkelin, they dined and drank in their own home, however, maintaining the customs, and there was honour and self-respect enough still to win what might have seemed to be a losing battle wiredrawn to a war.

Morwenna wrote poetry. Reams of it. Several collections had seen the light of day, privately printed at her grandmother's expense. These had been reviewed in journals, doubtfully, with hesitant approbation. Her next collection was to be published by an avant-garde concern sited on the fringes of Bloomsbury. An American poet called Abel Lord had, ambiguously, expressed interest in seeing her 'straddle the ocean'.

Most of the poetry was couched in symbol. They were monuments,

Morwenna informed her, to the potentiality of Image. Most of them were secretly sexual: 'dirty', Morwenna told her, if people had known how to read them.

Morwenna sought experience. She vaguely hoped for love, but she knew she was more likely to encounter passion, or mere brute sex. In the evenings she dressed like a Montmartre tart and went to join her friends in the watering-holes of old Fitzrovia. She returned sometimes at six in the morning, with another couple of poems written, then she would sleep all day, a full round of the clock.

'He's waiting for me somewhere, you know.'

'Who is?'

'The Man.'

That was all she ever called him.

'Are you sure?' Catherine would ask.

Morwenna always watched the cowboy films whenever they appeared on television. She sat with her legs wide apart at a hundred and ten degrees while her grandmother dozed and a man's ready hand hovered over the pistol sheathed in leather on his hip. Catherine heard her some nights moaning in her bedroom beneath her own; occasionally the bedside light flickered as a noise of furniture removal travelled upstairs and Morwenna took off in impassioned flight.

25

A Stranger in Soho

IN a public library Catherine found a set of telephone directories covering the whole of the United Kingdom. She looked for him in every one: but all trace was lost.

In reply to a letter she wrote, she received one from Curteys Court, signed 'Cedric Encombe'. He was very sorry to report that he wasn't in possession of any information that might conceivably assist her in her search for his nephew. Maurice's father had died earlier in the year; Maurice had seen the notice in the newspaper and come up to the funeral, alone. But he'd gone off again without telling anyone where.

Her eyes were always open when she made her way about London. The casinos were a secret twilight world, and she couldn't guess behind which reputable frontages they were concealed.

She lived in the sincere hope, the surest expectation, that their fates – crossed once – must draw together by dint of the tension collected in the lines. She couldn't doubt it for a second: although as to when it must happen, she had no idea whatsoever.

She only knew that time was compelling them both there.

*

She stopped beneath a neon sign bearing the motif of a bluebird, illustrated ingeniously and simply in a few sure, swirling lines of electric light.

She rang the bell and the door was opened by a woman wearing a white satin turban, a peacock-blue blouse and loosely cut, high-waisted black trousers.

Catherine watched the woman's eyes sweeping her, all in an instant, from her street shoes to her hair.

'Can I help you?'

Catherine reached into her bag.

'I'm sorry – I memorised the address, you see.'
She took out the business card Maurice had given her.
The woman – attractive in rather a hard way, with high cheekbones and a determined chin – held out her hand and took the card from her. Her silver-mascara'd eyes sharpened beneath their plucked brows.
Catherine pointed to the name.

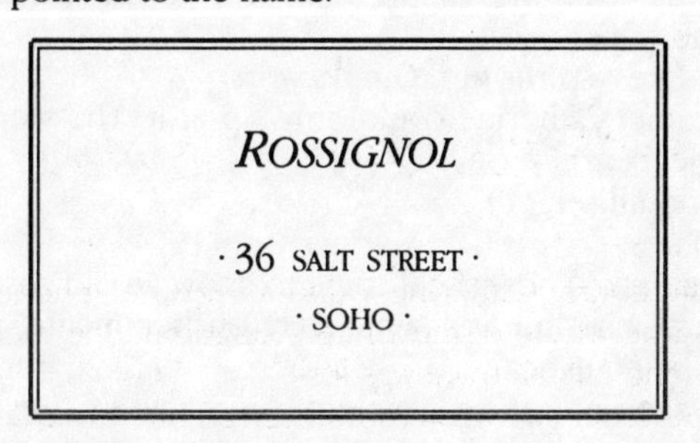

The woman stood staring at the card.
'It's French, I know,' Catherine volunteered, ' "Nightingale". A club, I think. A club – of some kind.'
The woman was still turning the card over: over and over.
'It is a genuine name?'
'Oh yes,' the woman said, with a Welsh lilt in the delivery. She returned the card. 'It was.'
' "It was"?'
'This used to be another club here. Called the Nightingale.'
'When? Can you tell me?'
'Five years ago. Four or five.'
'Is this club connected with it?'
The woman observed her more closely, more candidly, before replying.
'Only loosely,' she said.
'I was wondering . . .'
'How did you come by that?' The head and turban nodded at what she was holding in her hand.
'I knew someone, you see. Who came here, I believe. He had the card anyway.'
'Who? What was his name?'
Catherine swallowed. 'Encombe. Maurice Encombe.'
She caught a tic set off in the woman's cheek.
'Look,' she said, 'I think you'd better come in for a minute. No – ' She shook her head. 'No, not here. What about a drink somewhere?'

They went to a pub at the corner of the street. Sawdust blew out of one door; beyond the other, where they entered, were tiled walls, panels of frosted glass, angled mirrors showing the crowns of heads huddled together, lots of cold brass fittings.

Catherine had never been inside a public bar before; she was troubled by the noise, the dampness on every laying surface, the odour of bodies and hops.

'You look like a spirits girl. Gin do you?'

When it came, Catherine could only sip at it. The woman noticed her inexperience.

'Good tranquilliser, gin.'

'Oh. Oh, I see.'

The woman asked how she'd come to know an old customer of the 'Nightingale'. Catherine was sufficiently on her mettle, gin notwithstanding, to be equivocal.

'I haven't seen him for a couple of years myself,' the woman told her. 'That was the last time. It was *before* that I remember him from, though. After the War. Just out of school. He had some money to play about with. For a while. But it didn't last. He didn't come round for ages – maybe it wasn't more than a year, but it seemed longer. Good fun he was. High spirits. Larkish.'

Catherine nodded, but didn't trust herself to speak.

'I do remember faces. And names. Some people have a knack of forgetting, they seem to think it's – well, beneficial.'

The woman paused.

'I prefer to remember,' she said. 'Although my memory's not wonderful. I wish it was better.'

'But you remember his? His face?'

'Your Mr Encombe's?'

Catherine nodded.

'Yes. Well, he was young. First time out in the big city. He was looking for fun, excitement. A good sort, though. How – how come you know him?'

'Oh, it was in Aquae-Regis. He – he was staying there. For a while.'

'So *that's* where he got to. I presumed – '

Catherine waited for her to finish.

'You presumed – ?'

'He used to talk about a farm somewhere. I supposed somebody was forcing him to get his back into it. After he'd sown a few oats. You know?'

Catherine looked into her glass.

'I'm not quite sure *what* I know,' she said.

When she raised her eyes again the woman was watching her, quite intently. She had a worldly face, a London face, but there was no unkindness in it. She sat nodding at this stranger in Soho.

'What's brought you to London?' she asked.

'It's just to see it. Really.'

'Impressed?'

'I don't know. Yet.'

'Come up on your own?'

'Yes. Yes.'

'When are you going back?'

' "Back"?'

'To Aquae-Regis?'

'I don't think I will.'

'No?'

'No.'

'London spoiling you?'

'I've no wish to. Go back.'

Silence.

'Are you working?'

'I'll have to,' Catherine said. 'If I can find something.'

'So you've got an address?'

'For just now.'

The woman produced a small gilt-edged notepad and pencil from the back pocket of her trousers. Catherine gave her name – 'Catherine Stimpton' – the address and telephone number, noticing for the first time how many eyes in the room were attending to them both.

'Just in case,' the woman said.

Catherine nodded. She thanked the woman.

'But I haven't been able to help you.'

'You knew Maurice, though.'

The woman shrugged.

'Like you said, I'm not sure. What you ever get to know of someone. Really know – '

She sounded resigned to the fact. Catherine was intrigued, by the crack worked between the woman's hard-baked sophisticated appearance and the actual experience that lived behind it.

26

Leta

SHE received a telephone call before the week was out.

'There's a bit of an emergency on. I'm looking for a hostess, Miss Stimpton.'

' "A hostess"?'

'To look after the tables. See that customers are welcomed and seated, basically, then attended to. And to keep an eye on the waiters.'

'Are you sure you've got the right person? You mean *me*?'

'Oh yes. I thought you looked just right, the sort of girl I was looking for. So I thought I would ask.'

'I haven't done anything like that, though.'

'I didn't think you *had*. But I'll show you the ropes. There's nothing so much to it. But I'd like you to keep your mind on the job, please.'

When asked to, Catherine replied 'Yes', she *would* call in at the club.

'And we can discuss the matter then.'

Her caller sounded in no doubt that she had contacted the appropriate person for the job, that all that remained to do was a mere formality.

In fact there was very little to discuss, and they had shaken hands on the business after three minutes.

'Welcome aboard, Cath,' said Leta.

Her duties were explained to her in detail: how the customers were to be received, who paid what (chance trade as distinct from members), the cloakroom arrangements, which were the okay, better and best tables, who among the staff served which section of the room, the hierarchy among the waiters.

'You're always to be seen in charge. Make your presence felt but not obtrusive. Be in evidence, but don't be too visible: don't be *in*visible, because then people won't know they're being looked after.'

When Catherine showed her dismay, Leta reassured her.

'Sounds a lot, but you'll pick it up, really.'

'How do you know?'

'I've just got a nose for it, that's all.'

The Bluebird must have seen better days, Catherine decided as she looked round. The trappings were faded in places. Not badly so, in a Bayswater way: they were just a little weary.

The paper on the walls was oxblood velvet: here and there the pile had worn away with the contact of hands and shoulders. At certain points of social traffic the paintwork was chipped and scuffed. A spindly gilt chair at one of the tables rocked when she sat down on it. The wood on the grand piano had taken the unmistakable branding marks of a radiator. The carpet was quite threadbare where the demands on it had been, literally enough, heaviest.

In the evenings, she was to learn very soon, the place masked its condition, like many a canny *bonne vivante* stepping from the private into the public life. The soft rose du Barry illumination from the electric table lamps usefully veiled more than it shed light on, and flattered and dramatised the faces of the customers. The band's music was evocative and spirited the dancers back to their younger selves. The (purposely) moderate price of the liquor excused the failings of the club's disorganised, over-ambitious kitchen. Leta – dressed for an expensive night out in Tangier or Rio – moved elegantly among the tables with their carnation-pink top covers and white undercovers like petticoats, dropping a word behind her or aside, always smiling, suddenly and fleetingly accessible but only because she was otherwise so distant and aloof. She *was* the Bluebird, and a '*directrice*' at night, she had lost all trace of her provincial accent and bore more than a passing resemblance to Dorothy Lamour. Shedding years and looking no older than thirty she paraded herself, hand on hip, six or seven inches taller than nature had made her, thanks to block heels and a spangled satin turban; paste drop-earrings and bracelets sparkled wantonly, and she let no one – except Catherine – see the subliminal glances dropped at the face of her watch (alone in its genuineness), in this room notably without a timepiece. The men followed her with their eyes, and so did some of the women: she was unreal, but the septet's music was made for dreaming to, and the streets outside for escaping from, so how could they not desire her or envy her?

*

Leta's age could only be guessed at, since she didn't introduce the fact into any of their conversations. Forty-two or forty-three perhaps: in a certain light – Catherine didn't like to be seen scrutinising too closely – a fretwork of lines showed around her mouth and eyes and the skin on her neck slackened.

Quite often she caught the Welsh inflexion in the voice, but Leta volunteered just as little about her background. Now she belonged to London and her past life seemed to have been disowned. She didn't speak of places she'd known before London, or of people, relatives, friends – or of anything that had been in her mind except her own ambition to work in London's other 'clubland'.

She had a sweet singing voice, which she admitted had been her sesame. But Catherine realised what Leta maybe didn't, that the voice was too quiet. Professional singers *developed* quietness, cleverly muting sound to make it only *seem* intimate and personal. A personality like a voice needed to deftly and subtly swell to fill a room, and it might have been that Leta had left too much of hers behind in the past she never mentioned.

It was enough personality at least for a friendship between the two women. Catherine found Leta's considerations a little worldly: her constant preoccupation with her appearance, her inability to resist the temptation of a whisky or gin and the oft-repeated resolution that it would be fruit cocktails from now on, proving herself observant of the faces in the room but with a surprisingly poor memory for most customers' names, keeping herself remarkably well informed about modern songs and who sang what on which record, her ignorance of the other arts but the contradictory cultivation of a darting eye that could comb columns of print in the newspaper looking for what Catherine could never discover, an aficionado's fondness for dainty glass animals, a constant concern for her waistline but an inexplicable weakness for the chocolate cake stocked by the Viennese pâtisserie round the corner, a skill at stud poker, a sixth sense for adapting the fashions in the magazines to her own needs and an enviable talent for running up clever imitations on the trestle Singer upstairs (using as good materials as the couturiers if not better, courtesy of some of her contacts among the regulars in the audience). She swam at the Cheeney Gardens baths to undo any effects the thin wedges of chocolate cake might have, and walked a spaniel for an old woman who lived at the top of the building, and grew cress on wet blotting-paper for her sandwiches when she was being especially diligent about her waistline, and patched stockings so carefully that Catherine could never spot the mends; she smoked to keep her weight steady, and collected cigarette-holders (which now came her way as gifts); she had a habit of approaching a window slowly from the shadows behind and, when she had her vantage-point, quickly looking in all directions; she had eyes in the back of her head some days, she always knew what sort of cufflinks a customer had been wearing and how false and strained the women's smiles might be, she recognised certain customers by the contact the heels and soles of their shoes made and the speed and register of their steps. She referred to movements in the room according to a grid of mirrors so positioned on the walls that they allowed themselves to be 'read', and Catherine once saw her taking an impression of a key in a bar of soap.

'Maurice's friends – ?' Catherine said.

'He came to the Nightingale. But it was a big set. More hoity-toity than what we get now. Our sort are in business. His kind were Old Money – if they *had* any, that is. The only trade *they* did was in names. Names, names – like a foreign lingo.'

'He was one of them?'

'Oh yes. Why's it so important to you anyway? About Maurice Encombe?'

But Catherine didn't need to reply, and Leta didn't need to be told. Stealthy smiles were exchanged between them.

'I'd tell you if I knew, Cath.'

'If you can remember, *any*thing . . .'

'I would if I could. But it's gone.'

Like – Catherine thought later – like building sand-castles one afternoon and the next morning they've vanished: and you couldn't guess from the smoothness of the wet sand on the shore that there had ever been any at all.

*

Leta worked hard.

Catherine would find her at her desk at more or less any hour if it was necessary: head and neck inclined in the pool of light from the Anglepoise lamp. If she asked her 'Aren't you fagged?', Leta would reply '*Someone*'s got to do it' or 'The place won't run itself.'

'You wouldn't have to work any harder if you owned it.'

'One day,' Leta told her. 'That's what it's all for.'

'When? Have you got plans?'

'I'm biding my time.'

Leta had told her she was a partner in the Bluebird, but she wouldn't discuss the details of her share in the business, participation in decision-taking and percentages of profits and the like. Catherine saw that she was determined to succeed, to take over fully one day and to manage her own life for herself.

She was admiring and – for some reason – anxious for her, both at the same time. Maybe that was only one woman's reflexive instinct for another's well-being in the world that men carved up amongst themselves.

27

The Nightingale and the Bluebird

LATE one afternoon they were sitting in the back room of a café on Old Compton Street.

'You were going to tell me,' Catherine said, 'about the Bluebird.'

'Was I?'

'But you wouldn't tell me there.'

'No. Well, there's nowhere you can't be overheard.'

' "Overheard"? What about?'

'The Bluebird's not what it was. Surprise, surprise. It used to be the Nightingale, you know that. Wartime.'

'Yes.'

'It was going to be closed down.' Leta knocked ash from her cigarette into her saucer. 'But I managed to persuade the owner differently.'

'Who's the owner?'

She shook her head.

'I've to tell anyone who asks it's an old dame with a gammy leg and a parrot.'

'Who is it, though?'

Leta shook her head again.

'It doesn't matter.'

Blue smoke blew across the table.

'Why's it not what it was?' Catherine asked. 'How you said?'

'The Nightingale was quite a hot spot. We had smart people.'

'What happened?'

'To become like it is now, you mean?'

'No – ' Catherine shifted uncomfortably in her chair. 'No, I didn't mean that – '

Leta smiled.

'Fashions change. People have got more money now: certain sorts of people. They always did, but money begets more money. And they're not the sort of surroundings they go for any more.'

'Were you at the Nightingale?'

'Started as a ciggy girl.' She held her cigarette-holder aloft. 'Then I got other jobs about the place, this and that.'

'Then it became the Bluebird?'

'Eventually.'

'And you stayed on?'

'Well, I'd made myself fairly indispensable by then. I thought I could make it work. I asked for a chance to manage it.'

'And they gave you the job?'

'Oh, I made sure they did.'

She dropped more ash into the saucer.

'It does okay. Keeps eleven folks and the band in work. It turns over, as they say.'

'You're going to stay there, though?'

'It needs more spent on it. I got some plans drawn up. I want to use the mezzanine, make it look like an ocean liner. Get rid of that ruddy name, the image, it's too obvious. I want to move with the times too. Everyone's going to get rich – '

Her downbeat delivery of the words didn't match the optimistic sense. She sat staring at the silver-tipped ivory holder between her fingers.

'Are the alterations too expensive?'

'It *will* be expensive.'

'Is there room, though? For an ocean liner?'

'Oh yes,' Leta said. 'There's room all right.'

She nodded her head and seemed to be going to repeat herself as she looked past Catherine's head.

'Well,' Catherine said, 'I hope you – '

Leta suddenly raised her wrist and read her watch.

'Better be getting back now,' she said.

Something – a movement in a mirror – made Catherine turn round. A man in a fitted overcoat and brimmed hat was making his way quickly through the front room; he pulled the door open and passed out into the street.

Leta, she thought, was taking care not to notice as she made a show of looking in her purse for change.

'They should make purses with lots of different compartments. For what you need. Notes, all the silver, thrup'nies, coppers. It's hopeless finding anything. When you want it. Isn't it?'

She flashed a smile and Catherine nearly found herself taken in by it, nearly ready to believe it was the genuine article: nearly so, but not quite.

*

Maurice, Maurice, Maurice, Maurice . . .

She hadn't stopped thinking about him, wherever he was. In England, surely: in London very possibly. Their paths might cross: *must* cross. How could they not if she wished hard enough, to somehow mould thought waves out of her wanting, which would bend and reflect the atmospherics in which happenings and events were conceived, by a conspiracy of need and desire.

*

She had never seen Leta drink more than a couple of measures of spirits when she was working. Which was why, the night she broke her own strict rule, she was so surprised by the spectacle.

As usual she herself came off at half past midnight, but Leta motioned her to the bar and asked her what she would have. She couldn't think, and Leta asked Jimmie for two double scotches.

Leta seemed depressed. Catherine tried to say the right things: about the evening's crowd, how many, how well (comparatively) they'd been spending.

'Suddenly everyone's flush again,' she said, without quite knowing why she said it.

Leta lit a cheroot. The cigarette case was striped silver and gold.

'That's lovely,' Catherine said. 'Where – '

'I stole it.'

'What?'

'I didn't think the owner deserved it.'

'Oh.' Catherine pushed it away with her fingers.

'Shocked?'

'No,' Catherine said.

'*You*'ll go far.'

'Was it like Robin Hood?'

'Taking from the rich? Oh yes, it was that all right.'

Catherine swilled the whisky about in her glass. Really it was too much for her to drink. She didn't know how far she could afford to take the subject.

'Someone you know well?'

She presumed, of course, a lover.

'Too well. But I don't think I know anything about him at all.'

'Can you tell me?'

'That's more than my life's worth, Cath.'

She heard the seriousness in Leta's voice. It was a common enough turn of phrase: but it was said, Catherine was only to fully realise later, with a very literal emphasis.

'You can't tell me?'

'Well, he's got no money problems. No problems at all really. Having a conscience would be no use to *him*.'

Leta, still officially on duty, indicated that she wanted a refill for her glass. She tipped what was left into her mouth.

'The only problem he *does* have is how to keep the past neatly put away in its box.'

Catherine couldn't follow.

'A jack-in-the-box surprise would disturb his precious peace of mind, you see. Make him remember what he might choose to forget.'

Leta started on the second tumbler.

'Forget – ' Catherine ventured ' – forget what?'

Leta shook her head.

'Don't you want to talk about it?' Catherine asked her.

'Wanting doesn't come into it really.'

'Oh.'

'Not *my* wanting, I mean,' Leta said.

'No?'

The two of them were briefly silent.

'Wanting's what it's all about, of course. Really. In the big sense of it. But when does wanting turn to greed?'

Catherine shook her head, to indicate that she didn't know the answer – or the reasons for the question.

'Is it old? The cigarette case?'

'I don't expect it is.' Leta turned it over off-handedly: or affecting to be so. 'He's a Johnnie-come-lately. You know the sort of thing, don't sit down or you'll stick to his chair.'

Catherine didn't understand.

'Because the varnish is still wet, you see.'

'Oh.'

'It was the War, of course.'

Catherine looked into her glass.

'It was the making of some folks,' Leta said. 'Too grand to be called "folks" now.'

'They – they were heroes, you mean?'

Leta laughed, quite bitterly.

'No, dearie, that's *not* what I mean.'

Catherine rotated her tumbler on the counter-top. Leta swallowed another mouthful.

'You wouldn't think it now, to see him. You'd think he'd been born to it.'

' "It"?' Catherine prompted her.

'The Establishment.'

'Oh.'

Leta blew out smoke.

'He isn't?' Catherine risked.

'A man of the times, let's say.' Leta started on another harsh laugh, then abandoned it.

Catherine watched her, concerned at her condition, that she should be allowing herself to be seen like this, with her work still not over for the night.

'Well, you'd never think it originally had to do with silk stockings stashed under the counter. Or a lorryload of butter parked in a garage somewhere.'

'The black market?'

'That was the start of it. The humble origins. But you know how it is – '

' "How it is"?'

'One thing leads to another. And another. Whatever people *want*, they'll pay for. Pleasure is paramount.'

Catherine didn't speak, in case she interrupted the flow. But there wasn't much to follow that she could make sense of.

'So what society wants, it gets. It deserves all its little upstart gods, how can it complain?'

' "Gods"?'

'The high-and-mighty, the great-and-not-so-good. The connoisseurs of legs in silk stockings, as it happens. Pass the butter please, and all the past is – ' She held up her glass, in a mock toast. ' – poooff! It's forgotten!'

Catherine inched her own glass away from herself.

'This – you *could* say, Cath – this is the house that Jack built.'

Catherine studied the discontented, disenchanted movement of her eyes round the room.

'One of them anyway. The others are a world apart, so they like to think. They forget the low dives down among the dead men. Sipping champagne, listening to Mozart. "A little chemin de fer, m'sieur?" "Don't mind if I do." "Red or black, odds or evens?" Well, now . . .' Leta replaced her glass, noisily, on the counter-top. ' . . . it's not so different really.'

Catherine wondered how she was going to manage to sneak a glance at her watch. She looked at the restless eyes, still picking up on everything: checking the shelves behind the bar, straightening the tilting blue irises in a glass, having the dish of olives replenished, mopping at a wet circle on the wood, rubbing at a crease mark on the leather cushion of the next stool, trying to oversee an efficient house and insisting on standards. It was one continual, uphill slog.

Leta stubbed out her cigarette in the ashtray.

'Look, Cath. Forget what I've just said.'
'What?'
'Just forget I mentioned it. Please. I shouldn't have told you.'
Catherine watched her swallow what was left in her tumbler.
'If it ever got about – '
'It won't.'
'Oh no?'
'No. Honestly.'
'It *could*.'
'I don't know his name.'
'What?'
'You didn't tell me. The man's name – '
Leta seemed confused.
'Didn't I?'
Then she shook her head at herself. She picked up the cigarette case.
'I won't repeat anything,' Catherine told her. 'Promise.'
Leta swivelled off the stool.
'No rest,' she said, 'except for you. I've kept you back.'
'No, you haven't.'
'Take care how you go now, Cath.' The Welsh-woman in her resurfaced. 'Da doesn't like to hear stories – so mum's the word.'
And with that Leta walked off, soignée in a pencil-thin accordion-pleated white crêpe dress; but she was listing, a too slowly moving target perhaps.

28

News from Malvern

Aunt Dodie wrote regularly from Aquae-Regis. The letters contained little that didn't refer to her life there, and latterly Catherine had tended to skim through them. But one section in one letter brought her up short.

> I also heard from Sybil Canning. She's up in Malvern now, living with her sister, but she keeps up with the news. Anyway, I'm rather loath to bring the subject up, seeing as we haven't before. But nonetheless I decided I would, and I hope you won't think badly of me for doing so.
>
> It seems that, quite out of the blue, Jennifer Moncrieff-King came into an inheritance. A second cousin of her father, a farmer in Rhodesia, left her most of his fortune. Apparently he'd taken a terrible dislike to his side of the family, and got it into his head that he would spite them for some harm they'd done to him. Nobody was more surprised than JM-K evidently. It seems that Mrs M-K was livid, because her daughter was only prepared to give her a small annuity out of the whole. She told her that the rest was needed to support her husband and herself, that they were young and had their lives to make and that M. had been expecting money and 'counting' upon it, money which hadn't in the end come to him. So, there was pretty much of a falling-out there, I gather, between mother and daughter. Not surprisingly, Mrs M-K felt less than she ever had for her son-in-law, and isn't afraid to talk about him now, since she has lost most of what she had, including her daughter.

Her aunt had paused at that point in her narrative to change the ink in her pen and maybe to consider the desirability or otherwise of continuing with the subject of wayward dispositions in young, only children.

> With their fortune they've been swanning off hither and thither, I believe. About Europe. I don't know how long the money will hold out. Somehow

their marriage has lasted, though, which is a little surprising. It's evidently *very* stormy, and plates fly and hurtful things get said. Nobody knows where they are now, so all the hearsay gets dwelt upon, and there *was* plenty of that. J is supposed to control him with her money, and doesn't let him have any access to it. Sybil was told (which is the only reason I can put down the words) that he seems to satisfy some very strange and perverse compulsion in her to be – as the vulgar saying is – knocked about a bit. That makes their marriage very 'modern' apparently! It sounds a quite ghastly arrangement to me.

A spill on the page had been blotted. It suggested to Catherine inattention perhaps, and her aunt's unwillingness to conclude the matter just yet.

Even if she *is* well-to-do now, I doubt if she'd find anyone who'd put up with her ways as *he* does. And he, I think, must be fool enough to accept the challenge she presents him with. Maybe the money is enough to account for it, but he took her with comparatively less. (Apparently the old farmer coughed up something for them before he died, but I'm not sure even J *knew* about the inheritance in advance.) It might be that he'd feel much the same if she were a millionairess several times over. At any rate it strikes me as a very bizarre and quite sad 'set-up'.

Catherine was to reread this part of the letter a good many times, too many to remember *how* many, until she knew it virtually by heart.

When Sybil was writing to me last time she said that 'they deserve each other'. It may seem rather a hard and cruel verdict, but no less true for being so. *Mariage à la mode, n'est-ce pas?* Didn't I do rather well after all to keep myself so well out of it?

29

Rossignol

CATHERINE, meaning to see the dawn rise for once, found Leta drunk at three o'clock in the morning.

Her expression of astonishment must have been too apparent. Catherine found her arm grabbed, and she stopped and waited while Leta, office work completed or abandoned, manoeuvred herself off the barstool.

'If this was a ship – ' she swept a hand round the room ' – every night would be a fresh voyage. To who-knows-where.'

Catherine smiled at the hypothesis.

'Damn ruddy rations. Although – ' she had to use Catherine's arm and shoulder to steady herself ' – it's never troubled *some*. Has it?'

She steered them both – after a fashion – towards the staircase.

'There'll always be "haves". And "have-nots". Unfortunately – Cath – there's no future in the have-nots.' She shook her head. 'Sad conclusion. But there you have it, for the have-nots.'

She reached out her hand for the banister of the staircase. She knocked on the wood with her knuckles; the sound was dead, without resonance.

'This'll go, this – rubbish. It should be chrome. All this – ' She waved her hand at the midnight blue and burgundy. ' – all this clobber'll go. It'll be bright, streamlined. Everyone'll want to come, they'll want to be seen. A ship in Soho. "So, so clever, my dear – " ' – she spoke in the accent of a Belgravia dowager – ' "you have simply no ruddy idea what a perfectly whizzing wheeze that place is. No damn ruddy Bluebird, we're off on a liner, old sport, anchors aweigh!" '

She was climbing the staircase. Catherine tried to envisage the transformation. The staircase as it was had an elegant semi-circular sweep to it, and she saw very distinct possibilities.

Leta pointed to the corridor where the office was.

'Staterooms ahead!'

Catherine smiled.

They paused at the top of the staircase. The club lay beneath them, tables and chairs huddled in the gloom, pink lamps switched off. The only light visible from this angle came from the bar, where Jimmie and Leo were clearing up. The band's platform on the opposite side of the room was almost lost in darkness.

'Silver and white, Cath. And I was just thinking, what about – what about portholes in the walls? With fish tanks behind them. What d'you think of that?'

Catherine didn't know if she was being serious or not.

'It's an idea,' she said, judging it the safest and most innocuous response.

'Watch out, Cath, or I'll make *you* responsible for feeding the fish.'

Catherine followed her along the landing. Leta pressed a wall switch, lighting the bracket-lamps in the corridor that ran to the back of the building. The first time she had been admitted to the club, Catherine had been surprised by the sense of spaciousness, the disorientating loss of her bearings. Behind the club, and beneath this corridor, Leta had told her there was a warehouse, owned by a Jewish gentleman in the garment trade. She would make a joke of its being a 'quiet neighbourhood'. Catherine had always presumed that the warehouse occupied two floors of height, including the area behind the blank wall along one side of the corridor: that behind it was empty, muffled, unused space.

They were sitting in the office, on chairs drawn beneath the angled desk lamp, when Leta seemed to come to a decision. She stood up unsteadily, took several steps backwards out of the pool of light, and walked towards the bookcase, which with its calf-bound spines had always struck Catherine as lending the room a bizarrely donnish touch.

Leta paused for several seconds with her forehead resting on one of the shelves, as if she were compelling herself to reconsider. Then she reached up, pulled out several of the books, and activated a control switch.

The bookcase started to move, sliding out from the wall and creaking rustily. Catherine stood up in astonishment. Leta looked towards her, her face in shadow, and beckoned her forward.

Catherine did as she was bid. Behind the bookcase a door led into a large bare room: with a second beyond, Catherine saw, as Leta's hand found another switch and naked light bulbs hanging on their flexes revealed the extent of the secret.

They walked towards the second doorway, into a high, unfurnished room at least sixty feet long by thirty across.

Their heels clattered on the floorboards.

Catherine stared at Leta for an explanation. Leta's eyes were screwed up against the harsh glare from the light bulbs.

'It's hard to believe,' she said, swallowing hard, 'that this was once Aladdin's cave.'

She had brushed against dust trails at the door and tried, imprecisely, to remove them from her shoulder and hair.

'It quite left me gasping. The first time I saw it. Because it was so handsome.'

Catherine shook her head. She walked a few feet closer to one of the walls. The delicately patterned gold and black paper on the walls was rich slubbed silk. There were areas of shade where paintings had hung.

She walked back towards Leta. The sight – or her decision to show it at last – seemed to have sobered her up.

'Remember, Cath – once, the first time you came, you asked me about the name on the card you had – '

'The Rossignol – '

'I knew, of course. When you showed it to me. The Rossignol. This was it.'

'What?'

'The inner sanctum. They used the French for it. Not for our ordinary Nightingale customers.'

'Why not?'

'Where we're standing – right here – there was a huge roulette table. They had to saw it in two to get it in. And take it out again. By cover of night, needless to say.'

'There was gambling here?'

'Quite unofficially, of course. But "habitually". That was the term the law used. It couldn't be "habitual". But it went on every night. Quite a glamorous clientèle we had. Champagne crowd. It was beautiful, Cath. Furnished with antiques. Chinese screens, what's the word? – lacquer. Paintings. Good lamps, the sort made out of oriental vases. Sofas. Wing chairs. So it would seem like their homes. Champagne on the house some nights.'

'What about the other customers? Downstairs?'

'Oh, they didn't know. Had no idea, I don't suppose.'

'But how – '

'There used to be a back staircase up and down. They bricked it up when they closed the Nightingale. The fewer tales told, the better.'

'But – but *you're* telling me?'

'I've told you enough, I think.'

' "Enough"?'

'Enough,' Leta repeated. She seemed to be repenting her decision to show her. 'We should go now,' she said, and nodded towards the secret door.

Catherine followed her. Their heels left loud echoes behind.

'Never say, Cath, do you hear?'

' "Say"?'

'Tell anyone. About this place. What it was. Or that I brought you to look. Please.'

Catherine nodded.

'If anyone finds out . . .'

'Who?'

'No one should hear.'

'There'd be trouble?'

'You could put it like that.' She seemed to have shaken off the effects of her intoxication. 'Although it's an understatement, if ever there was.'

'Trouble to who? Has it to do with the man you took the cigarette case – '

'When – ' the voice was deeply cryptic ' – did I ever tell you about a cigarette case?' The smile was arcane. 'It must be your imagination, running away with you – '

Leta stood back, to allow Catherine to pass into the office first, and then she pushed against the bookcase. Catherine helped. The mechanism groaned.

When it was neat with the wall Leta reached up to the top shelf and Catherine heard the sound of some arrangement of locks. The books were returned to the shelf: dummy books, she saw, hollow inside and with the spines untitled.

Leta made her promise to keep her silence, in the solemn illumination of the desk lamp with the metal shade, standing beside her in the yellow splash of light. Leta didn't blink until she had received the assurance that seemed so important to her.

'Now please, Cath – '

Catherine nodded, and said the words. Leta blinked, several times, smiled her relief and told her they would never refer to it again, ever.

*

'Who are you looking for?'

The vigil had been kept up for most of the afternoon, from either side of the window.

'Leta?'

'What's that?'

Catherine smiled.

'You're rapt.'

'Am I?'

The smile seemed to go unnoticed.
'Are you watching for somebody?'
Leta turned round, looking for an ashtray where she could stub out her cigarette.
'It doesn't matter, Cath.'
'Is it somebody you can tell me about?'
'It's nobody.' Her thumb pressed on the cigarette butt. She hadn't been using her professional trademark, the holder. 'Really. Nobody.'
If she hadn't repeated herself, Catherine might have believed her. Maybe Leta didn't mean herself to be believed.
'I just wondered – '
'I think I need a change from Salt Street.'
'A change?'
'To get out.' Now the Welshness in her voice was undeniable. 'Today I've been thinking, I've seen this place just one day too many in my life.'

*

Then Leta was gone.
A man rang to say she had been taken ill, that she was being taken care of, but not at home. He rang off before giving his name or an address. He didn't ring back.

Three days passed.
After a telephone conversation which no one had an opportunity to overhear, Jimmie – the senior barman – took charge of the club's running. He showed a singular aptitude for his new responsibilities.
A week passed. Then another. There was neither sight nor sound of Leta. Her flat up in Town remained unoccupied.
Jimmie was forever looking towards the small foyer, but nobody appeared to take away from him his new-found self-consequence. Least of all the woman he had taken over from.

Catherine urged that they should go to the police and report Leta's absence. Her disappearance. Because if she had *really* meant to leave and not come back, she would have told them, told somebody.
Jimmie was all against it. He more or less – only pulling back from the word at the very last moment – forbade her.

*

Over a period of five months postcards reached Catherine from a wide scatter of sources: Copenhagen, Paris, Lisbon, Nice, Graz, Naples. They were written in large, featureless block capitals, said very little, and were signed simply 'L'.

Catherine was glad that Leta remembered her at least, that she found some time to buy a postcard and stamp and look for somewhere to post it. She wondered what hopes and new ambitions kept her in motion, why she had never been able to guess that it was foreign travel she'd had in mind for herself. What would be responsible for eventually bringing her to rest back here or wherever?

30

Rotherhithe

In Rotherhithe the tide is out and the river runs low. A barge sits stranded high and dry on the ramp of mud, on a long rusty chain.

The ramshackle pub teeters on rotten wooden stilts. A plume of smoke trails from a chimney. The brick walls are blackened by soot. The window sashes don't fit properly; the flawed glass is too grimy to see anything clearly through, except the travesty of congenial company inside – old beer-swilling women hunched in beaver tippets, painted tarts sitting like Morwenna with their legs apart, men in caps smoking cigarettes to the last fibres, a mongrel lying on top of the counter among the dirty glasses.

No place has ever depressed Catherine so much. Painted on the pitted and weathered signboard above the door is a ghostly angel turned on its head. Lettering appears out of the brickwork, and she stands back far enough to see. ALES. STOUT. EXTRA STOUT. And, like an exhortation, COOL CLEAR COURAGE.

While the carousing goes on inside uninterrupted and a harridan landlady with brass hair and too much lipstick continues to pull pints, a crowd has assembled in the street. They're disinterested, though, incurious: there is no after-frisson of excitement and menace remaining from the event itself. It might even be an unexceptional occurrence in these parts, at seven o'clock of a June evening with the air so oddly and persistently damp.

Catherine inhales the odours – stale beer, cat piss, the shrinking river and the black mud left behind. The spot is infinitely dispiriting to her, for what it is and on account of the tragedy that has taken place here. She might be reading about it in a book, or seeing it in a film, except that she would have given up on it long ago.

She feels cold to the marrow of her bones, she feels raw inside her flesh. She's not sure how she manages to keep upright and standing on the cobbles. They have a greasy shine to them, like every other surface. For a few moments she wandered off, to be by herself, but she made the mistake of looking down at the incline of mud and the traces of sewage, and had thought, This might be hell, this would drive a person to death.

Those willing to forsake the snug for the cold stand along the wall watching the activities of the police in their long rubber waders. Stooped, the searchers scan the mud for clues, sometimes directing a torch at a real or imagined object.

At last their colleagues, huddled about a couple of cars on the far side of the Seraph, call for her. With the length of the wait she has begun to forget that she arrived, courtesy of one of the drivers, still quite mystified by their summons. The mud might have been clogging her thinking, drawing her into sucking, sinking lethargy. She already feels as if the spot has trapped her, and she mightn't be able to unstick her limbs.

A hand on her arm makes her jump. She is conducted past the raucous Seraph to an unmarked police van. In the back, beneath a red blanket, lies a woman's drowned body, bloated and variegatedly green.

She has to be asked to look again before she is able to recognise the face, to catch any semblance in it to a forfeited life.

'Yes,' she replies at last. 'Yes, it's her. It's Leta.'

She wandered away, from the people, from their lazy, animal disinterest. She walked far enough away to hear the mud plopping beneath the wooden groynes and – further off – the river remorselessly slapping, gathering its strength and mass to rise again.

A gull called, and she watched it glide downstream on spread wings.

One mercy, the body was clothed.

She was wearing the one-shouldered black faille dress that was one of her club dependables; her right shoulder, well formed and athletically defined, was left bare, and covered now in gooseflesh a little greener than blue. Pinned to the front of her dress, above her left breast, was a replica of the club's motif crafted in white gold and blue semi-precious stones. Her other jewellery, which she had bought wholesale through one of the club's regular customers, was still in place: a silver charm bracelet, her gold watch, two rings, a thin gold-mesh anklet.

'How did she get here?'

'Who knows, miss.'

'Did she have anything to do with this place?'

'We hoped *you* might be able to tell us about that.'

'I can't, I'm afraid.'

'From the look of her, it doesn't seem likely she had much to do with hereabouts. Does it, miss?'

'Did she fall? From somewhere?'

'That's what you might imagine.'

'Or floated here, from further up?'

Apparently the body had been fished out several hours before. The police had been applying themselves to the likely circumstances.

She supposed that someone, by a fluke of memory, must have recognised the similarity of the brooch to the neon bluebird above the club entrance: against what odds of probability? But they were surprised when she mentioned it.

She asked again. 'You *didn't* recognise it?'

'No, miss. Not at all.'

'Isn't that why you called me? How you must – '

'We had your name.'

'From the Bluebird Club?'

'No, miss.'

'How then? How did you know to look?'

'For you, miss? Or for the deceased?'

'This is an accident, though.'

'We had a suspicion – '

'About what?'

' – that it might happen.'

'*How*, though?' She couldn't keep the frustration out of her voice.

'Some chap in Wales who'd taken a shine to her. Long ago. Before she left there. Did she tell you about him?'

'No. No, she didn't.'

'He came up to London after her. Kept an eye on her, off and on. He says he loved her.'

Catherine shrugged.

'I don't know,' she said.

'What *I* don't know,' the detective-inspector told her, 'is how he was so uneasy. Maybe he thought she wasn't in her right mind?'

'Do you know what happened?'

'You see, she *might* have fallen in – '

' "Might have"?' Catherine watched him.

'But we think we've found traces of rope, caught on her bracelet and watch strap. That puts quite a different interpretation on events.'

She fell silent.

'Now her boyfriend can't be found. That's the queer thing.'

'Oh.'

'He'd kept such a careful watch. Knew who *you* were. Now not a sign of him. We've been looking for hours. He's been moving about, it seems.'

'This is – beyond me.'

'I'm sorry about everything, miss.'

'It – it's Leta we have to be sorry for.'

'Miss Vaughan?'

'Well, don't we?'

Leta dragged to her death by the cold, dark currents. Dressed for a party she never got to. That ridiculous, gay, impossible bluebird.

Catherine leaned against one lop-sided wall of the Seraph and for the first time in months she gave in to tears. She cried; hardly moving her shoulders she cried violently, in angry mourning for them both.

31

Hungerford Bridge

LETA'S flat had been broken into and ransacked. Anything of any momentary value lay where it had fallen; twice, in two rooms, police found a roll of banknotes with its elastic band still intact.

They took Catherine to look, but there was nothing she could tell them. She had been to the flat several times, for quick snacks. She hadn't expected to find Leta settled in a solid, very respectable mansion block, even if it was one of the smaller accommodations facing the back, and she had been surprised by the décor's untheatricality and the scrupulous propensity for tidiness in evidence everywhere.

'We still can't find the boyfriend,' she was told. 'Boyfriend so-called.'

None of the neighbours had seen or heard anything out of the usual: although the flat above had been empty at the time, and the woman who lived below was deaf in one and a half ears.

'It's adding up to one pretty kettle of piranha fish, this one . . .'

The block of flats was on Marylebone Road, and from there it wasn't far to Regent's Park and the zoo.

Catherine followed her instincts. Inside, past the ticket counter and the turnstiles, she spent a couple of hours walking from exhibit to exhibit.

She spent longest sitting on a bench watching the more melancholy zebra of a pair. It stood apart, on top of a small grass knoll in its compound, almost motionless for several long minutes, in profile to her. Its ears twitched, it appeared to be listening, through the monkey screeches and the growling of the wild cats and the hyena laughter, for the evidence of something far beyond. After a while it started stomping its front hooves alternately, and – as she watched – the grass under each seemed to be worn away to its roots, then to soil, then to fine blown dust like sand.

*

Two days later a mailed envelope was waiting for her at the club. Inside she found a coloured postcard showing a zebra. It might have been either in its natural habitat or in enlightened captivity, telling was impossible.

She turned the card over and read what was written on the back.

> It's very important that I speak to you. About Leta. Could you meet me at Charing Cross Underground Station, the front exit? I'll be there waiting on Friday afternoon. Two o'clock. I know you don't start at the Bluebird until 7. I need to talk to somebody, and I'm sure I could talk to you if you would let me.

She was baffled. By the request, by the zebra. But the message mentioned Leta: and she found something about the last five words affecting, and quite desperate.

She kept the appointment, although on the way there she was only conscious of all her reservations. But she also knew that the journey from Marble Arch on the Central and Bakerloo lines was an obligation due to Leta, fished lifeless and nearly forgotten from the river.

She saw a man – apparently unexceptional, as ordinary as the other human traffic briskly walking past – standing by the wall on the far pavement, watching the barges on the river. She stood watching *him* until he turned round. He nodded to the flight of steps close by her. She hesitated, then turned to her right.

The stairs led up to a narrow public walkway which accompanied the railway lines across Hungerford Bridge. Mesh netting fenced off pedestrians from the tracks only a few feet away; a metal balustrade ran along the exposed river side. She could see down through the gridwork under the railway bridge, to the mournful grey water of the Thames. A wind blew from the balustrade side, and forty or fifty yards ahead of her a couple held on to their hats. Simultaneously, and much closer to her, a train rolled by, and the bridge was set rumbling, so that she wanted to cover her ears.

For a few moments she panicked, feeling unsteady, vertiginous. She knew nothing about why she was here. Except that it had to do with Leta. But Leta was dead now, she had lost her life after all the care she'd taken with it, she'd dropped into the cold muddy river, tied with rope perhaps.

'I'm glad you came.'

The words made her jump and she had to grab the balustrade with both hands.

'For Leta's sake.'

She shut her eyes against the drab river. She turned her head towards the voice and then opened them again.

He was older than herself, and younger than Leta, lean, bloodless, losing his hair. He had pale, distraught eyes. His suit was shapeless, his shirt collar was frayed, the unravelling woollen tie negligently knotted.

He placed his hands like her on the balustrade and talked into the wind.

His name was Eric Pembrey. He came from Swansea, as Leta had done, long ago, when she was called Mavis. They'd known each other when he was in his twenties, then they'd lost touch. It was six years since he'd met Mavis again – to briefly talk to – in Brewer Street in Soho. He was working on a building site in Hammersmith and, between the dust on him and the wear and tear of the years, she hadn't recognised him at first. But *he* had recognised her, even though so much about her was different, even though she had acquired sophistication.

And after that he'd pursued her.

'Maybe too much, I don't know now. She said no, but . . . Sometimes she'd know I was walking down the road behind her, and she'd look around, as if it was about nothing but really it was to acknowledge me, in a funny way. She'd sit on a bench somewhere – how you were, at the zoo – and even though she might've arranged to meet someone, a man, even when she was talking to him she'd look over her shoulder again, in my direction. Later, when she was at the Bluebird, I went in a couple of times, and she smiled at me and spoke a little, enough for me to see what the place meant to her, but *I* knew it wasn't her kind of life.'

He paused. Catherine narrowed her eyes to look at him. His last words were confusing her. She had always supposed that it *was* – more or less – the life Leta wanted for herself, what she'd chosen to do rather than any other job and (she had only presumed from that) preferable to an existence where she would have been married or kept (or both) and not have needed to work.

'I only suffered London for *her* sake, you see.'

Catherine nodded.

'I didn't go back to the nightclub: not then. She still met people, men. I'd see her sometimes, getting into taxis. Into the back of a big spanking-new Rolls-Royce once, with a chauffeur holding the door open for her. But even then she'd know I was there, and she'd look over her shoulder.'

Catherine concentrated on the threadbare collar of his shirt, the razor nick of dried blood on his chin.

'Maybe, you see, maybe I was her conscience. That's what I think now. That's what I tell myself. When it's too late. When she's dead . . .'

He started to cry and Catherine didn't know where to look. She might have placed a hand on his arm to comfort him but she didn't like to.

'It's all right, it's over for her,' she said. 'Look, let's walk. To the other side.'

Two trains were rolling past and the bridge quaked. He wiped his eyes with the sleeve of his jacket and they walked on. Catherine fixed her eyes on the great white gleaming flank of the Festival Hall, that veritable phoenix risen from the ashes and rubble of the bomb-blitzed South Bank.

'I chucked London. I wrote to her from Wales. Sometimes she sent me a line or two, never very much. But it was keeping in touch. I never changed how I felt, though.'

Catherine pulled her collar up against the wind; maybe also because she needed a little privacy, to think.

'I saw you, you see. With Mavis. You nearly stepped in front of a car once and she called out "Cath". That's all I knew to put on the envelope, you see.'

She nodded.

'Then – then it changed. Not about me. I mean, something about Mavis. She wasn't herself. I don't mean so smart as she'd got. I mean, how she looked in her eyes, how she was inside. I went back to the club again – the Bluebird – and she didn't even notice me. She was smoking, which she never used to, because her father had died from his lungs. It was her eyes; seeing and *not* seeing, at the same time. That's how I knew.'

' "Knew"?'

'That she was frightened. Really frightened about something.'

Catherine turned to look at him. Momentarily the panic returned – she was walking across a bridge like a plank with a stranger, and the other pedestrians were too far for them to catch her screams, they wouldn't hear above the din of the trains anyway – but very shortly it subsided, she felt herself calmer again, remembering Leta and the due of unselfishness owed to her.

'One afternoon I saw someone taking her arm in the street, a man. She was trying to walk away. I'd seen him before. A man in his fifties or so, in a business suit, prosperous-looking. People were starting to look and he stopped. Then he leaned forward to say something, and Mavis took an envelope from her bag and pushed it into the top of his waistcoat, and she ran off.'

'A man? In a business suit?'

'Did she sleep with blokes? Sell herself?'

'I . . .'

'You must know, Cath – '

'I don't think she did. Not – not professionally.'

'Are you sure?'

'She told me so,' Catherine said. 'Several times. Years ago she'd – tried, I suppose. Something in that line. Then someone she knew had got injured, beaten up, and that decided her, she'd be her own woman.'

'"Her own woman"?'

'It was one of her expressions.'

'Was it?'

'And I don't think she went back on it, the decision. She lived quietly. Given the life it is. She was a very good friend to me.'

'Maybe you didn't know her so well, though? As you wanted to?'

'No,' Catherine said. 'No, maybe I didn't.'

'It's a tragedy.'

Catherine allowed a silence to pass before speaking again.

'But the police,' she said. 'I don't understand. How they knew about you.'

'Because I went to them.'

She couldn't contain her surprise. '*You* went to *them*?'

'I tried to speak to Mavis. "Leta". I followed her for streets one day, in a taxi. She stopped hers in Chesham Place, then she got out, and so did I. She knew I was there, and she started walking, along Lyall Street, crossing over and back up again to put me off the scent. She wouldn't really talk to me that day, only to say I shouldn't follow her, she was all right, she could take care of her own business. She was got up so fancily, and I saw she was frightened about something, from her eyes, they had rings under them. Even then, when she was shaking me off, she was lighting up a cigarette.'

'Maybe – ' Catherine waited for a freight train to pass. 'Don't you think – she might have been nervous – because of *you*?'

'Not nervous, I don't think so. She'd lived so long with me being there. Years now. I think she knew *I* knew something: or I suspected.'

Catherine waited for him to finish that part of his story.

'Anyway, she got away. To where she was going – Eaton Square, I think. I didn't follow her any further. That was the last time I saw her. Alive, I mean. I wrote to her, with an address, but she didn't reply. I wrote again.'

'You said you went to the police, though?'

'I invented a story. I said the man in the street who'd taken her arm, he had a knife. That I was worried about Mavis's safety, that she wouldn't listen to me.'

'What did the police say?'

'Not much. Probably thought I wasn't the whole shilling. They just wanted shot of me. But after that someone on the beat noticed the Bluebird was being watched.'

' "Watched"? Who by?'

'Cars. Three different cars.'

'Did they do anything about it?'

'That's when Mavis left. Disappeared.'

'I thought she was abroad.'

'Why?' He stared at her.

'I got postcards.'

'From Mavis?'

'I thought they must have been. They had "L" at the end of them. "Leta".'

'But she never went anywhere. Jaunts or holidays.'

He sounded very certain about it, as he stood looking down into the cheerless grey water slapping against the arch-supports. The postcards seemed to offer him his sobering, conclusive evidence.

'No,' Catherine said, wishing she could distract him. 'No, perhaps she didn't send me the cards.'

'She just vanished.'

'She didn't tell me. That she was going away. I couldn't understand that.'

'I rang up the club. I asked to speak to her. They said she'd just gone.'

'It wasn't me,' Catherine said. 'Who answered – '

'No. No, I know that now.'

They both nodded.

' "A. W. O. L.", they told me. I thought it was the cold shoulder again, but it wasn't so long before I realised it was quite true. Then somehow I knew, in my gut, that she wasn't coming back, not ever again – '

Catherine winced at the prospect of instant death and oblivion, falling into the cold of the river, cold to shatter your heart.

'I just had a hunch. That she might've headed for Wales, to Swansea, so I went back. I knew she had an aunt in Rhyl, and I went up there next.'

All the Welshness welled out of him in his voice.

'I phoned the club, and put a handkerchief over the mouthpiece, but I always got the same story. I couldn't phone her flat because I didn't have the number, she wasn't in the book under her old name or the new one, and the exchange and the club couldn't – or they wouldn't – tell me. I came up to London for a few days – just footloose

– and I watched the flat, but it was never lit. I walked the streets where I'd seen her, but somehow I knew it wouldn't happen again.'

They hadn't reached the end of the bridge. When she looked, she realised there was no one in front of them or behind. Again the breath started to knot in her throat.

'The same feeling I'd had when we caught sight of one another in Brewer Street the first time. That it had been meant, somehow. I just felt an emptiness now, and I knew this wasn't the place. Not any more. Then I went back to Swansea – for good, I thought – and I got some work there, and I tried to think the best of her, that she was safe, that she was okay.'

A forlorn hope, and the lengthening silence between them confirmed it. At last she said what had to be said.

'The police, they think she – Leta – she was bound. Tied with rope.'

He didn't seem surprised to be told.

'I suppose she must've been.'

'Why? Why d'you say – '

'Because she was such a bloody good swimmer. All her instincts would have been against it. She'd have chosen some other way.'

'She went to the Cheeney Gardens – '

'Back in Swansea, in those days, she could always beat me in the water. Any distance. Good shoulders for it, you see.'

Catherine considered; remembered.

'Yes. Yes, they were.'

At the bridge's end they walked down the flights of steps, on to the promenade in front of the Festival Hall.

'I'm very glad you decided to come, Cath. I thought maybe you wouldn't.'

Back at ground level she smiled to hear the name Leta had used for her, which no one else except Audrey had ever done.

'You needed to talk about it?'

'I just wanted to tell someone. It had to be you. You knew Leta. It's funny, I used to think how she was doing all right, living quite grandish, but she didn't seem to have the *friends*. Those men apart. How I never saw her with anyone regularly except you.'

Catherine only nodded.

'It must've been an expensive flat. Being so posh.'

Catherine nodded again.

'Yes. Yes, that's what *I* thought.'

'Was it hers? Did she own it?'

'She told me she did. How she used to rent, but that was all behind her now, and she was relieved.'

'If she'd lived somewhere else – maybe it intimidated me – '

'It was so – ' Catherine puzzled on the choice of words to make ' – so, well – neutral. Impersonal even.'

'*Did* she strike it rich?'

'I don't know. She didn't want for things. There was a lot we didn't discuss.'

'About when she was "Mavis"?'

'Yes. And when "Mavis" turned into "Leta", I suppose.'

'There's too much we're in the dark about. But I'm going to try to find out, Cath.'

He offered his hand. She gave him hers. As they said goodbye she thought how sleepless and wasted he looked, but also how determined and resolute.

He telephoned her at the club a few weeks later. He sounded tired, but also anxious to speak.

'I didn't tell you everything. I meant to – '

'What about?'

'I've found out, she *knew* something. She discovered something.'

'What? About the Bluebird?'

'Connected to it. But before all that, she was in a set. Sort of "in" it – '

'What sort of set?'

'I should've told you. But I keep thinking about it. As if it has to mean something, it's all part and parcel – '

'A "set"?' Catherine repeated.

'Just a group of people. Twenty or so altogether. About six or seven at the centre, plus their hangers-on, their shadows. She was out on the edge – '

'When was this?'

'Just after the War finished. That's when "Mavis" – "Leta" as she was then – got in with them.'

'How?'

'It was just after that missing time. When she lost herself. You know?'

'Yes. Yes, I know what you mean.'

'The last year of the War someone had told me they saw her in Culross Street. Runs into Park Lane. That's where I first saw her, not to speak to, why I tried there before anywhere else when I came up. The fifth or sixth time I went, it happened, there she was.'

She waited for him to continue.

'Respectable street, to look at. I couldn't make much sense of it, what she had to do with the place. Then a bloke showed up one day. In a smart business suit, like the one I saw her with much later. They disappeared into a house. So I watched that house. Different world from the Bluebird later. Or that's what anyone who didn't know better was supposed to think, that it was a different set-up entirely, gung-ho part of town and all that.'

Catherine continued to keep silent, so that he wouldn't be interrupted.

'All sorts of people I noticed, at all sorts of times. Well dressed. For the period, that is, with the rations biting everyone else so hard. Women with jewellery at lunchtime, and fur stoles in the evenings. Men in suits, dark flannel, or dinner jackets. Then there'd be a younger one mixed in with them occasionally: a girl with a fancy hair-do, high heels, or a chap in sharper-cut clothes, quite casual clothes. The same people: acting so natural and discreet. Only not quite.'

'What?'

'It was a performance. Whatever time of the day or night. The same smiles, the same movements – touching their hair, moustaches, stoles – and always keeping a look-out although it all seemed to be so natural, so discreet.'

Catherine wondered if she could quite trust anything of what he was telling her. Why shouldn't they be as they appeared, going about their business? And what relevance could it have to the tragedy that had introduced the two of them? Why was he now imparting to her what he had failed to think important enough earlier?

'I think it's sinister,' he said.

She didn't reply.

'Are you still there, Cath?'

She mumbled into the mouthpiece.

'And there's always the Rolls-Royce.'

'A Rolls-Royce?' she repeated.

'A Phantom III. Two shades of grey. It's quite distinctive, but it only came at night. It never parked at the kerb, but at the street corner. The chauffeur stopped and *he* got out the back, then he walked to the house.'

'Who?' she asked. 'Who's "he"?'

'I don't know.'

Catherine sighed, but not loudly enough for him to hear.

'He wore a long dark overcoat. Fitted. And a homburg hat.'

'Maybe he wanted some air. In his lungs.'

'No.' He said it testily. 'No, that's not it. You don't understand.'

But do *you*? she wondered.

The line was beginning to crackle.

'Where are they now? Do you know?'

'Moved on. Somewhere. I have to find them.'

'Leta being there,' she said, 'it might just have been coincidence.'

'No, Cath. No.'

The line sizzled.

'I don't know,' she said.

Leta is gone, she wished she could tell him in plain enough terms. There is nothing we can do, even you with your manic resolution and willing imagination, nothing which is going to bring her back.

'I wish you luck,' she said, as brightly as she could.

He took the remark the wrong way.

'I don't need *luck*,' he said. 'I'll find out. I know I will. All it'll take is time.'

'Yes,' she said. 'Time. All I meant was – I wish you well. That you discover. What there is to know.'

'It's for Mavis's sake,' he told her. 'So she can rest in peace.'

When they'd said their goodbyes and she'd put the receiver down, she couldn't help thinking of Leta's fate with something like envy: not the terrible circumstances of her death, although it had taken a miserable death in low water to affirm the one sterling advantage Leta had over her – the continuing loyalty of one man to her memory, his endless dedication and undying trust, to whom she was still everything.

32

The Inclosure

CATHERINE sat watching from her place at the dining table.

He had hardly spoken to her, although he'd had a light morning's work and she had arranged flowers which she'd bought at the Women's Institute market in numerous receptacles about the public rooms.

She couldn't help but notice how slowly he was eating, only picking. Normally he had a very healthy appetite, and the food disappeared from his plate in half the time it took her to eat hers. Since her arrival, lunch had consistently been a highlight in his day.

'Is the sole all right?' she asked him at last.

' "The sole"?' he repeated.

'Yes.' She pointed to her own with her knife. 'Your fish.'

'Ah. Fish . . .'

She hesitated before she smiled.

'It's Wednesday,' she reminded him.

He nodded. 'And the Mothers' Union meeting at five,' he said.

'I just wondered – '

He inclined his head.

' – if you'd forgotten?'

He placed his cutlery on the plate.

'No,' he said, sounding sorrowful. 'No, I hadn't forgotten.'

'I shouldn't have said – '

'One day,' he said, 'is rather hard to disentangle from another. That's all I mean, Kate . . .'

On Wednesdays she cooks two fillets of sole for their lunch, because that is the day the fishman calls. He drives into the Close in his van, and she chooses the pieces of fish herself from a selection he lays out on broken ice. In addition to the sole she will buy some cheaper haddock for either a pie or the soup pot, and perhaps some smoked kipper fillets for breakfast or an early supper.

At luncheon, which is the main meal of the day in the Archdeaconry, she eats as he does, sitting at the same table. In the evenings he eats alone, but he chooses his own time, according to his 'fixtures diary' (as he calls it) for that day. The lunch hour is when they can discuss household matters, and whatever he chooses to divulge to her of cathedral business.

Apparently he respects her judgement: so he has told numerous colleagues and neighbours. His superiors, she is aware, view his openness to her on church matters with disapproval and, in some quarters, with alarm and hostility. But he is of an age – about Leta's, forty-two – not to be too trustingly ambitious (nor too dispassionate either), and he isn't tempted to be deliberately, *wilfully* injudicious.

Customarily it was on sole Wednesdays, she had noticed, that he grew more reflective. Perhaps it had to do with the simplicity of her culinary presentation, which he had told her appealed to him very well. As a rule she sat virtually silent at Wednesday lunch, waiting for him to speak. It had been so for most of the past eight months, ever since she had answered the newspaper advertisement, presented herself for interview, and been asked to take on the position of housekeeper. But her silences had acquired more and more weight over the thirty-two weeks. He had told her no more than one month ago that her silences possessed 'sanctity'.

'I don't think I quite understand,' she'd said. ' "Sanctity"?'

'A retributive silence,' he'd told her. 'A retributive silence. Silence with its great bat-wings stretched. To come calling with.'

She had shaken her head at him.

'You'll have to explain to me, Mr Haslam.'

'Please, Stephen – '

'Stephen.'

' "Explain"?'

'Yes.'

But he had only answered on the topic of silence with silence.

Methodically she had set about stacking the tray with their dishes and cutlery and glasses, suddenly feeling cow-heavy with exhaustion in the middle of her day, just as she had started to feel she was becoming permanently during those last brainsick days in the far town of crescents and parades, when she had seemed to be sinking into the ground that she tried to walk.

*

One night of moonlight he led her from the house and they walked across the Close to the cathedral's west porch. With an outsized key he opened the door within one of the doors. She stepped in front of him; he followed her, and closed the smaller door behind them both.

The interior was in darkness, except where moonlight fell through stained glass in coloured runs, squid-ink blue and deep gore red.

'Should we be here?' she whispered.

'That's what I want *you* to tell *me*,' he said, his voice no quieter than it usually was.

'How?'

'Just follow me – '

With his hand on her elbow he led her across the flagstones, between the sarcophagi. It was too dark for her to see more than outlines. She felt ready to chitter with cold and with the awesomeness of the place. The smells alarmed her: stone, dampness, pollen, wax, old wood, her guide's dried perspiration.

They stopped where the transepts crossed the nave, before the choir stalls. He let go her arm.

'Let there be light,' he said, and she watched as he reached into his pocket for a box of matches. He shook out a match, struck the head on the sulphur, and held the flame to a candle on a spiked metal rack. The wick took the flame and the two of them stood in a pool of fitful yellow light. Now she could see the wooden case of the organ pipes towering above them, and on top of it the carved figure of an apostle brandishing a sword.

He returned to her and stood close beside her.

'Now tell me,' he said. 'What do you hear?'

She was attending to his face in the dim yellow shine of the candle, to the unaccustomed shadows that fell across his features.

' "Hear"?' she repeated.

'Yes. Tell me, Kate. What is it you hear?'

She listened; she strained to hear. But whatever it was she was supposed to be acknowledging, she couldn't pick up.

'I'm afraid,' she said, 'I don't hear anything.'

'Are you being honest about that?'

She listened again. The building to her hearing was absolutely silent.

'What about this time?'

She shook her head.

'No?'

'I really can't,' she said.

'Nothing?'

'No,' she said. 'Not a thing.'

She thought he was going to put her right, that she was going to be embarrassed into a spiritual revelation.

He stood beside her, listening very intently.

'What is it?' she asked, letting her voice drop away. 'Maybe – I could hear it too – '

She looked at him.

'If you could tell me – ' she said.

But he didn't tell her. All he did was to place his hand on her elbow and, with gentle precision, steer her back the way they'd come.

'Should I have heard something?' she asked him.

'That's quite all right, Kate. You have answered my question.'

They retraced their steps to the West Door. He locked up behind them and they walked across the Close, back to the Archdeaconry. The only sounds were their footsteps on the cobbles. Even the trees where the rooks had built their nests, as high as the tops of ships' masts, offered less than a creaking branch, only their leafless silhouettes in the moonlight. A few windows were lit; she saw him considering them, with a mixture of incomprehension and pity.

It had occurred to her on several occasions that she now lived in surroundings every bit as stagy as that city in the west. What is more likely to be built for its effect than a cathedral? In certain lights, or half-lights, the Close made her think of a film set: the buildings lost some essential sense of mass and bulk, and existed in one dimension less, as if they were frontages only. It had also struck her that the effect might have been due to her expecting to see the life lived out according to a screenplay, because that was the only way it would be believable nowadays: updated and vulgarised Anthony Trollope crossed with, say, a bitchier Elizabeth Goudge. They were living in the 1950s, after a war and with many international skeletons still left clattering in the cupboards of ally and foe alike: even though – maybe *because* – the potential of events was so terrible, the political theatre had become more intimate and also more trivial, and God didn't deserve to live inside His soaring temples of faith. Stephen had told her how the cathedral had been built, about the companies of masons with their secret rites and the perils of sudden random death, artisans falling head over heels from scaffolding stilts. Longer ago than Christianity, the cathedral's had been the site of a pagan temple of sacrifice: and so the process continued, the common passage of life ritualised as grand and impersonal spectacle.

*

And so it was that he came to her room at the darkest point of the night. She woke to see the door closing.

He lay down on top of the coverlet, on her big bed. She turned over to face him but didn't speak. He lifted the strands of hair from her face, then drew his hand away. He smiled. Then he closed his eyes, and in less than a minute he was asleep.

He had gone by the morning, and she was left alone in the bed.

She watched him at breakfast. He was overfed by matrons who wanted not to appear ungenerous. He wore a size-17 collar. Too much going out in all weathers had roughened his skin. He had the sort of fine flyaway baby hair on his head that is the soonest gone. To judge from the backs of his hands he must have a surfeit of hair on his torso.

She pitied him, when she had begun of late to think herself incapable of emotion, except directed at herself.

He didn't mention the incident, then or afterwards. She supposed it must have been an aberration he regretted too deeply to be able to express his sorrow in words. So she was taken off her guard a second time when the door opened a couple of nights later – a little earlier by her wrist-watch this time – and exactly the same sequence of events ensued. He walked into the room, closed the door, crossed to the bed, climbed on to the mattress, stretched out beside her on the coverlet, smiled, tidied the hair back from her face, stared at her, and fell asleep.

She knew she could have kept him out with the simplest precautionary measure – she could have turned the key in the lock of the door – but she hadn't done so. She felt guilty. But, much more significantly, she felt her body was on fire. She marvelled that he wasn't aware of it, the heat unpeeling from her skin.

She closed her eyes and sensed that all the restraints and decorous sacrifices of the many past weeks were about to prove of no avail. When she was furthest in time from the affair that had changed her life, she also – most curiously – felt simultaneously as close to Maurice as she ever had since then. She was conscious of an unloosening between her legs, a quiet damburst as the months slopped out of her.

It soaked into the sheet and underblanket and into the mattress.

She reached out and opened the drawer of the cabinet. Inside was a white candle of the sort used in the cathedral, placed there with a pewter candlestick in case of emergency. This *was* an emergency, in a manner of speaking, and with a shepherd of the flock lying beside her, with the sound of his breathing in her ears, she took the candle to the source of her flood and staunched it, solaced it, in the only way she believed at this moment that she could.

33

Sawdust (Four Scenes)

I

SHE woke in Mickletwistle, to a sound she didn't recognise until she got up out of bed to look from the window. A phalanx of factory workers were streaming down the cobbled hill on rattling bicycles, whey faces grim beneath their flat cloth caps.

There was water standing in a ewer. She tipped the spout over the chipped bowl and, as she was washing, accidentally spilled some of the contents on to the crocheted cloth beneath. Eyes smarting, she reached out for the towel. She couldn't find it, and had to search the room until she did, dripping on to the carpet and the corner of the quilt on the bed where she sat down. The mattress groaned beneath her but the springs sang gaily. The towel smelt of allotment bonfires smoking in a dusk.

Breakfast was taken downstairs at a single sitting. Eight places were laid at the table in the large scullery. Between bouts of serving up, the landlady seated herself at one end, directly opposite the chief of their number, Adèle Adaire, who had been given a chair with arms.

After a plate of inert grey porridge ladled from a slurping cauldron, they each received a cooked course consisting of two slices of black pudding, a fried egg, one half of a fried potato, one half of a rasher of bacon, and one and a third sausages. Mrs Bunnidge supplied doorstep slabs of gritty bread for 'mopping up'. Adèle Adaire, holding her napkin flat against the front of her fluffy woollen coat-liner, looked mortified. The less fastidious of their number worked out a rota arrangement with their elbows and tucked in. 'Tea, Miss Astaire?' Mrs Bunnidge called down the table as she stood up to pour from the pot. The liquid was black and acquired an ominously oily sheen as the mismatched polka-dot cups and saucers were passed along from hand to hand.

'Let me guess, Earl Grey?' said the young man sitting on Miss Adaire's right hand, so to speak.

'It's tea for navvies,' she replied, not quite under her breath.
'Navvies? I missed them. Which room were *they* in?'
'Mr Pennicote?' Mrs Bunnidge called up.
'I'm sorry?'
'As it comes?'
He lanced the thin, wrinkled sausage on the tines of his fork and held it up for examination.
'Yes. Yes, pretty much, thanks.'
The spout was aimed at a cup. Black tea streamed in a dribbling arc.
'Story of your life, Guy, isn't it?' Miss Adaire said, hardly bothering to lower her voice.
'Well, it's *still* coming. Let's put it like that.'
He turned his fine profile towards her.
'Has anything come *your* way recently, Adèle?'
'Well, I certainly wouldn't tell *you*.'
'Just getting the lay of things, are we?'
Catherine watched both sets of eyes turn on her. She dropped hers to the bloody black pudding floating in its tepid fat.
'A taste, Mrs Bunnidge, if you please.' Adèle Adaire's voice projected at its ordinary pitch. 'A soupçon – '
'My tea,' Mrs Bunnidge said with the disapproval very evident in her voice, 'has always proved satisfactory before. I can't abide namby-pambies under my roof.'
'Is it just theatrics you take?' someone asked.
'More or less.' She slammed the teapot on top of the range. 'But *they*'re not what they were, any road.'
'Oh, you don't need to tell *me*,' Adèle Adaire announced, folding her napkin. 'These are cheap and tawdry days.'
Mrs Bunnidge misinterpreted (possibly) and glared down the length of the table so fiercely that Catherine couldn't force the food down her throat. She had thought the woman's appearance ferocious last night on their arrival, rouged and orange-haired, patrolling the dimly lit house in her flapping slippers and flighty nightgown, rampant breasts loosed from her unhitched brassiere and bouncing on her stomach.
'I mean – ' Miss Adaire qualified her remark ' – the spirit has gone out of it. The spunk.'
Guy turned his head.
'I hadn't noticed *that*,' he said, speaking slowly.
The others – except Adèle Adaire – were shocked into silence.
'Are there the plays, though? And that wee box standing in the corner of people's drawing-rooms – '
Catherine watched the former second female lead of several British

film features (*The Kennedys of Kensington, The Brighton Belle*) smile dismally at her social gaffe, as soon as she'd said it.

'So many people, you see, wanting to get on the television – '

'The theatre kept us going – ' Mrs Bunnidge said.

'Like the tea.' Guy spoke into his chest.

' – in the War.'

'They want realism now,' one of the other voices said.

Adèle Adaire stared, glared.

'Oh no,' she answered in all seriousness. She pulled her coat-liner tighter about her, with her slender, liver-spotted hands. 'What they need now is *glamour*.'

Another silence descended on the table. Eyes glanced down at the plates of food, setting in the cool, congealing fat.

'I suppose *you*'re really a hoofer,' Mrs Bunnidge spoke the words suspiciously like an accusation.

'I beg your pardon?'

'A dancer,' Mrs Bunnidge said, not mincing her words.

'Only very incidentally.'

'Very,' Guy said after her.

'Any road, so how come you're related to Fred Astaire?'

For several long seconds Adèle Adaire stared at the woman very, very hard.

'I am *not*,' she articulated, dropping the words like pointed icicles.

'This,' Guy said, 'is Adèle *Adaire*.'

Mrs Bunnidge bunched her lips, which was somehow confirmation of her further disappointment. With the side of her hand she swept some crumbs from the tablecloth.

'As once graced the silver screen,' Guy said.

'Quality British films,' the actress riposted.

'D'you know our Gracie anyhow?' Mrs Bunnidge asked.

'I know of her,' Adèle Adaire replied tentatively. '*Of* her, of course.'

'Thespian company is a little more Miss Adaire's line,' Guy explained. 'Stagecraft,' he mouthed.

'Gracie was one of us, you see.'

'Miss Adaire is one of *them*, though. Started at the Lilliput, don't you know, *way* back – '

The Thespian in question stood up abruptly.

'Work,' she said. 'I must get down to work. A little reading.'

'You haven't touched a bite, though. Or drunk your tea.'

'My concentration's better on an untroubled – I mean, an empty – stomach. A clear mind – '

'Will you be wanting your breakfast tomorrow?'

'I wonder, is there room service at all?'

An awful silence swilled round the scullery, washing into all its gloomy corners. Mrs Bunnidge's mouth gaped until it hung wide open like a trap-flap.

'I – I merely enquired,' said Miss Adaire, rising.

'Nobody's ever even suggested such a – '

'It's a while – since I toured, you see. One – gets out of the way.'

'Oh, *does* one?' Mrs Bunnidge sniffed. '*You* want to be in a hotel, that's what.'

'Very possibly,' the actress replied, and glided across the room in the most graceful, most wasted of exits.

II

'You've missed the point completely, Julia:
There were *no tigers.* That *was the point.'*
'Then what were you doing, up in a tree:
You and the Maharaja?'
'My dear Julia!
It's perfectly hopeless. You haven't been listening.'
'You'll have to tell us all over again, Alex.'
'I never tell the same story twice.'
'But I'm still waiting to know what happened.
I know it started as a story about tigers.'
'I said there were no tigers.'
'Oh do stop wrangling,
Both of you. It's your turn, Julia.
Do tell us that story you told the other day, about Lady Klootz and the wedding cake.'

They all looked up at the same moment.

Guy said, 'Is this prose or poetry? Either way, it's bloody difficult.'

'It's work,' Nancy Talbot said. 'Who'll be able to tell *what* it is?'

'But shouldn't we know?' Guy asked, pursuing the point.

'Why?'

'For our own good, of course.'

'God's teeth!' said Peter Aspinall.

'It looks like prose, but it is also lyrical,' Guy said. 'It – it swings.'

'Jazz swings, darling,' Adèle said. 'Poetry *rhymes*.'

'When *you* heard *The Cocktail Party*, you probably thought it was a musical. Like *The Boy Friend*.'

'Very droll, Guy dear. But I'd stick to the lines you're given.'

'I was after Edward, actually.'

'I *did* hear – ' Adèle lowered her voice, but didn't speak quietly ' – you'd struck lucky. With *someone*.'

'Edward. In the play. Top name in the programme, sweetheart.'

'Oh, a part's *never* big enough for you, darling, is it?

'But,' Guy said, untypically ignoring the innuendo, 'Alex gets more of the philosophy.'

'And is that a good or bad thing?'

'You do show a certain narrowness of view sometimes, Adèle. Not quite becoming a woman of your age.'

'Coming from someone with a one-track mind, that's rich, I must say. And bloody nerve.'

'*I* say,' Peter interrupted, 'we just get on with the damn play.'

'*Some* people,' Adèle countered, 'think they've actually got to understand it first.'

'Well,' Nancy responded, 'we know that's not a condition of the job. When *was* it, ever?'

Guy sighed. For the first time Catherine felt a little sorry for him. But Nancy had a point too.

'After all, who ever understands how they land up anywhere?' Nancy fanned her face with her script. 'It'd be a damn sight simpler if you could plan it, like some bloody Girl-Guide hike.'

Catherine turned to the point she'd reached reading her lines. In truth she found the play – not at all what it presented itself as being – infuriatingly slippery and elusive. One character was 'a man who finds himself incapable of loving' and his wife 'a woman who finds that no man can love her'. People, she herself had to declare at one point, 'make noises, and think they are talking to each other; they make faces, and think they understand each other.'

While the others lapsed into green-room memories of a typically scurrilous sort, she closed her eyes and spoke the words in her head, into that other darkened auditorium.

'. . . I suddenly discovered
That the dream was not enough; that I wanted something more,
And I waited, and wanted to run to tell you.
Perhaps the dream was better. It seemed the real reality,
And . . .'

She closed her eyes tighter against the outbidding of stories in the room.

'And if this is reality, it is very like a dream.
Perhaps it was I who betrayed my own dream
All the while; and to find I wanted
This world as well as that . . .'

III

'I used to get letters from women, you know. They went to the films not to envy me but because I would give them some sort of courage. Well, small hope at least. If I made people's lives more bearable – '

Adèle Adaire re-settled into the window seat of the compartment. 'Oh yes, what people want now is *glamour*. It is supposed to be old hat, of course – '

The others had drifted off to the train's restaurant car, to go dutch on lunch, leaving the two of them alone.

'But that's my mission in life, Catherine, to bring it to them.'

For the journey she was wearing a pre-War leopardskin and wool coat, a fuchsia velvet toque with an outsized hat-pin, a champagne jersey restaurant dress, salmon-pink leather gauntlets, black sling-back shoes.

'The fashions come and go. But classy glamour never grew out of style. Everything's up and down these days. Jack's as good as his master, Jill's as fine as her mistress. Well, I don't know about that. What too many people get their hands on loses its . . .'

She fished, but couldn't think of the word. She took a different tack.

'It seems to me that manners are slipping. Have you noticed? Of course everyone's had to put up with so much, but I've seen the greed in people's faces. There always *was* envy, but now it seems to imagine it's – well, *justified*.'

The door clattered open and Guy Pennicote re-entered from the corridor.

'Is this your League of Nations speech again, Adèle?'

'Pretty Miss Eveleigh and I are having a very pleasant *tête-à-tête*.'

'Suppose *that* means she won't get a word in edgeways.'

'*Be* flippant then, Guy. You'll be a lightweight all your life. See where that'll get you.'

'I'm young. I've got my future.'

'Reaching out in front of you?'

The two exchanged polar smiles, then turned their eyes on to their travelling companion.

'But Catherine's younger than *me*,' Guy said. 'Even.'

'How very gracious of you,' Adèle told him.

'She can do anything she likes.'

Adèle didn't respond.

'If,' Guy said, 'she puts her mind to it.'

'Well, that shows how little you know.'

'What?'

'About a woman's perspective.'

'A career, I meant.'

'That's what *I* meant.'

Guy raised an eyebrow.

'But *you* had a career, of sorts.'

'You make it sound as if I'm in Bridget Farley's Home. In Esher. For Retired Gentlefolk of the Stage.'

'I can't see that, Adèle. How'd we get on to talking about that, for Christ's – '

'Catherine's career.'

'And *you* said she couldn't have one.'

'No, I didn't. Well, not exactly. I meant, a woman is dependent. Made to *feel* dependent. She has to – has to – '

Adèle clammed up briefly, and avoided their watching eyes. She fussed with her fox collar, then with the pantomime pin in her hat.

'Naturally I had to – to be amenable. Placate egos. Go along with the . . .'

Adèle pulled her gloves tight over her fingers, so that her hands took on the semblance of claws.

'I thought we were supposed to be lending Catherine advice,' Guy said.

'Well, my advice is to . . .'

'Yes?'

Adèle straightened the toque on her head, and readjusted the pin with the giant, fake-pearl stud.

' . . . to go along with it. Things being as they are.'

'Given to the men?'

'Well, *you* should know that, darling. About giving to the men.'

'It's Catherine we're talking about.'

'But she should keep back the important part.'

'Which is? Her integrity? Her virtue?'

'Her independence of mind. Her privacy. The thoughts they can't get at.'

'What's the good of that?'

'So she won't *believe* them, of course. So she'll see through them for what they are. Users and abusers. If you don't keep your distance, you're lost.'

All three sat silently while the wheels rattled over the tracks, and the axles shrieked.

'And you're not lost?' Guy asked.

'What a little bitch you are, Guy Pennicote.'

'Not a user? And abuser?'

'Doubtless the latter. But I was talking about a man's world, and I excuse you, darling. Puts us in the same boat, sort of.'

'Oh no.' Guy smiled, but there was malice in his voice. 'You're in an old clapped-out tub. I'm in a speedboat, Adèle, just watch and see.'
She shook her head.
'You've been at sea too long, Guy. You're hallucinating. A rowing boat's more "you", I feel.' The malice evaporated, and they both started laughing. 'Giving those rowlocks all you've got – '

IV

Still wearing her Good Fairy outfit, Sylvia kicked the dressing-room door open and entered sideways, carrying a tray laden with pale ales and sherries.
They all lifted a tankard or schooner, as ordered.
Sylvia took Catherine's arm and guided her to the back wall. She flung her wand up on to the top of the wardrobe.
'These sodding pumps are killing me.'
She handed Catherine her tankard, seated herself, lifted the skirt of her gown and bent down to untie the laces.
'Have you been doing this long?' Catherine asked her.
'Man and boy.'
'Being the Good Fairy?'
'This is promotion. Although you may not think it.'
'Do – do you enjoy it?'
'Well, it's a challenge. Playing out of character, you might say.'
Sylvia opened her legs and reached her hand up under her skirt. Knicker elastic pinged and she retrieved two halves of a cigarette. She handed one to Catherine. It felt burning hot to the touch.
'I like a fag in the flies.'
A match was struck on one of the wardrobe's hinges and the cigarettes were lit.
'It isn't *your* game, that's for sure.'
'Can you tell?'
'Out there – ' Sylvia nodded towards the stage ' – everyone else goes about as if they're sleepwalking. You looked as if it was an opening night in the West End.'
She leaned forward and dropped ash into the basin.
'I'm the sort of person they warn you about, to steer clear of. Don't go talking to any of those greasepaint harridans, Catherine Eveleigh, they'll try to turn your head. They're contagious. Actually – ' she stood up and stubbed out her cigarette on the side of the wardrobe ' – we're just wise beyond our years.'
A voice, belonging to one of the Stepsisters, called across to her.
'Had you on the *Brains Trust,* have they?'
Her bad sister laughed over her head.

'More like, *she*'s "had" the *Brains Trust*.'

The principal boy snorted.

'Don't be disgusting, Deirdre.'

'*You're* a prude, Melissa,' the first sister said.

'Better than having a mind like Deirdre's anyhow.'

Sylvia cut in.

'There's nothing wrong with Deirdre's mind. Except, should it be between her legs?'

Again, to Catherine's ear, the off-stage talk had a weary, played-out feel to it. The hideously made-up faces showed only disinterest.

'I could snap your wings in two,' Deirdre said, without much vehemence.

Sylvia reached up to the top of the wardrobe.

'You'll get this wand where –'

'Do they allow fairies on the *Brains Trust*?' the first bad sister, Madge, enquired.

'That's where they live,' Allison (with two l's) said. 'At the BBC. Didn't you know?'

'Didn't Nigel go there?' Yvonne said, recalling one of their band who had seen the light. 'Into engineering?'

'That proves it then,' Allison said.

'He was just sensitive,' Melissa said, straightening the stockings on her long, slim boy's legs that had been the talk (and undeclared envy) of the troupe this season.

'He told me he wanted a "purpose",' Sylvia said. 'A "commitment".'

'He'd get it there all right,' Deirdre said. 'Some of the blokes in that place get very committed.'

'Nothing's ever happened to *me* there,' Allison said. Her occasional past broadcasts in radio drama were held up by her as evidence of a superior talent.

'No, well it wouldn't,' the first bad sister told her.

'What does *that* mean?' Allison enquired, with no little haughtiness.

'You'd have to be in trousers,' Deirdre told her, forgetting until she'd said it that that was Allison's "way", returned to civvies.

Even Catherine had picked up on the obvious, and she blushed. Allison noticed her.

'I suppose,' she sniffed at her, 'that's what *you*'ve got your sights on?'

'I – I'm sorry?'

'Speaking your lines out there like Fay Bloody Compton. Where do you think this is, for God's sake?'

Allison's remark, and her show of temper, caused a temporary silence in the room, broken only by Melissa announcing that *her* sherry was warm.

'Then get it yourself next time,' Sylvia snarled at her, enviously eyeing those long, slender pins. 'I'm so sorry the service fails to suit, sir.'

'I just said – my sherry was a shade on the warmed-up side.'

'And *I'm* saying,' Sylvia continued, 'you can hoof it across the street yourself and get your sherry poured to your satisfaction. *You'd* rather be in the films, I suppose, Miss Supple Thighs?'

The entire room adjusted their eyes and considered the suppleness or otherwise of Melissa Montford's shapely thighs sheathed in Parisian silk stockings.

'You only degrade yourself,' the principal boy informed Sylvia without looking at her. 'Speaking like that. *I* know what you mean.'

'Well, if you know what I mean,' Sylvia said, 'you're no better than me, are you? For all your pretending that you are.'

'Anyone would be better than *you*,' Melissa said.

A fight might have developed if the two bad sisters, Madge and Deirdre, hadn't intervened and struggled in turn to keep them apart. They were all saved by the first of the bells sounding which announced the close of the intermission.

Sylvia fluttered each of her wings separately, like a very practised fairy, and brushed cigarette ash from her white satin bodice.

'That's *me* ready,' she said.

'Looking after number one,' Deirdre called after her.

Sylvia held her wand aloft.

'If I don't crown you first with this, I'll turn you into something even nastier than you already are.'

'That's witches do that.'

'Goodness can disguise itself.'

A few moments' surprised silence followed.

'That's philosophy,' Melissa said.

'You're a boy, what would *you* know?' Allison said.

'Good can come from bad anyway,' the first bad sister said.

'I'll report you to management, then,' Sylvia said. 'Whatever I am – ' Then she must have realised she had left herself vulnerable.

'Oh, we all know what *you* are,' Deirdre said. 'It's got five letters and it gives birth to pups – '

The second and middlingly brief of the three bells sounded. The door of the room was thrown open. The expectant hysteria of children's voices crept upstairs.

'Sod the little buggers,' declared Allison.

'But they pay for treats,' said the first bad sister.

'What treats?' asked Deirdre.

'It's their parents,' said Yvonne, 'who pay.'

'The more fool them,' said Allison.

'It's a con,' said Deirdre.

'I agree with you there,' said Allison.

'They come to have their faith in magic revived,' said Sylvia. 'Good healing magic. They come to see *me*.'

The others stopped still and stared, quite astonished by such a degree of impudence.

'They come to worship at the feet of an angel,' she continued, stroking the white taffeta and gauze of her left wing. 'They come,' she said with memorable, very possibly rehearsed simplicity, 'they come to *believe*.'

34

Benefactors

She asked him if he cared for Eliot.

'Who?'

'T. S. He wrote the play.'

'Oh. Well . . .'

'Why *did* you come to see it, Mr Petherick?'

'I saw your photograph. In the foyer. When I was coming out of *Annie Get Your Gun*.'

She smiled. He smiled too and showed his crooked teeth.

They were in the dining-room of the best hotel in the town. Beef was carved at a trolley and served, gravy-soaked, with boiled potatoes and slices of carrot. She wasn't very hungry. She watched how he wielded the heavy cutlery, as a Chinaman might.

His suit, she guessed, hadn't come cheap, but it was an older man's cut. The starched collar of his white business shirt seemed to be causing him discomfort. The monogrammed cufflinks were of a very shrill gold that shouted their newness. His hair needed a barber who knew to shape and not to razor-cut a straight line at the back.

He saw her looking and she was embarrassed. She made a pretence of taking in the ambience, but she realised he read her better than that.

He explained that he was in business along the coast. 'In the building line.' His home was a Georgian rectory which he had restored from chimneypot to damp-coursed cellar, thus (said with a smile, but he might not have been joking) putting himself 'on the side of the angels'. He lived there with his mother. Near Bournemouth.

'We're Londoners, really.'

'Why did you leave?'

'Nobody knows about you. In the provinces.'

'Ah. I see.'

'I mean, don't know enough to judge. About your accent. Where you've come from.'

He spoke about himself quite freely. When he mentioned his father, however, his voice came from further back in his throat and carried a bitter flavour. His vowels became less placeless, and she heard the streets of London: Clerkenwell or Shoreditch.

'Dumped us. To all intents. And porpoises.'

'How? What happened?'

'You're not interested in that,' he said. 'Are you?'

She nodded. She saw how grateful he was, that she should want to hear. So she listened, to the saga of his father's philanderings. Jobbing for a clothier called Steingold and fooling about with one of the machinists after hours, knocking over a paraffin heater in a game of lusty tig and starting a fire that raged to a blaze and gutted the workrooms and warehouse. Being hounded the length and breadth of London by the Steingolds. Drinking. 'Boozing', 'getting a skinful'. Falling for the sort of women too stupid or forgetful to know better, until one day just before the War started he went out of circulation. Disappeared. Turned to empty air.

She sympathised. Then she told him about herself: not quite so freely, but he didn't seem to notice. She heard herself speaking like a shipfarer, of another land and time. Aquae-Regis fascinated him, and he asked her questions about the rituals of life there. The answers she gave him implied no fond affection for the place or its traditions, but he put his elbows on the table – her father would have been shocked – and concentrated hard. She was amused by his attentiveness.

'It's a very dull story I've got to tell,' she said. 'Honestly.'

'Not at all. Not at all.'

'I have to come from somewhere, I suppose.'

'But I *want* to hear.'

At some point she realised that her sitting talking like this wasn't unrelated to the effect she had been (inadvertently) working on him during the play: the experiences were similarly verbal. She didn't have any more of Eliot's lines to speak but she did have her own recollections, of a town that might have the lure of fable, which was undoubtedly unique in its architectural grandeur and watery utilities. An edificial folly rather than a community of souls, perhaps. But he was also keen to know about the people, their manner of life, the details of social behaviour among the crescents and circuses.

He was waiting again at the stage door the next night, and she discovered – because she asked – that he had put off his return westwards on her account. He suggested dinner, and when she hesitated he told her that there was another hotel a couple of miles out of town.

The food proved to be better there, and since they were sitting not so far from an amber-lit fish tank she explained to him the difference between langoustines and lobsters, which impressed him greatly. The glow from the tank was a little distracting to her, but not for him, as he fished among her memories and laid the bait that revived, sometimes disturbingly, this or that aspect of her past. She might have presumed she had forgotten, but he knew better, and bit by bit Aquae-Regis was resurrected, pieced together in his smilingly analytical way. (Those crooked, ivory-coloured teeth, she watched them with helpless curiosity, unable to bring to mind what it was they should be reminding her of...)

He made his shrewdest move on the third evening, in the vestibule of the Combe Edge Hotel, when she was a little tipsy and didn't understand at first that she was being steered towards the staircase. His rooms were on the first floor, a small suite, and probably the best accommodation in the building. She couldn't stop talking, even though it was about nothing, but he seemed perfectly content just to listen. Lines from the play became jumbled up with it, and she told him – frankly, very frankly – that she had drifted into acting, by default of being anything else.

'It's all – elegant acting. Life.'

'But you're good,' he was telling her. 'You're good.'

She started laughing in an actressy way.

'Really and truly – '

'I'm afraid I don't try very hard. I imagine, of course, the interior of the character. I go in a little way, until I get frightened off it – '

'It's very convincing.'

'I think it must be accidental.'

'Do you have to concentrate?'

'After a while the lines speak themselves. It isn't me *or* that character. I'm not there or anywhere. The thing just – happens.'

He was held by her voice, her voice.

'Nothing seems real to me then,' she heard herself tell him. 'When I start. At least I have the lines to speak. I don't always have to think, you see – '

She put her hands to her head, forgetting genuinely if she was acting now or not. Performing certainly, but did that mean 'acting falsely'? She was very disordered and closed her eyes.

'Oh God, oh God,' she was saying, but by then she was seated on the edge of the bed and so the rest was surely inevitable.

It was oddly unloving, oddly cruel sex. He said respectful things, whispered the words in her ear and let his stubbly jaw run along the line of her shoulder, but his actions were selfish, ungenerous, always demanding, taking and taking and never giving. His long, thin penis was sliding into her before she was ready for it. She cried out and he halted, then she cried again and pushed against his shoulders, but maybe – possibly – he thought she was afraid of losing him and that was why he thrust harder.

The experience left her, however, without any of the rancour she was expecting. Afterwards she felt nothing. As if she'd been upended and the contents tipped out. All that remained was a little pain, where the rubber had chafed her. He had come clean, clean as a cat.

She found her underwear, put on her petticoat.

She threw herself into one of the two chintz armchairs and lit the cigarette he handed her. He was staring at her, intrigued. She pulled her hair back, then she stretched the other arm, spread the hand that held the cigarette. He stood watching all the gestures, registering the sequence of movements.

'Come with me to London,' he said.

It was her turn to stare.

'What?'

'When the play's over. After the run. I'll buy us a flat.'

She almost dropped the cigarette and momentarily he was foxed by this lapse of poise. But she recovered, and placed her elbow on the high arm of the chair.

'What would be the point of that?'

'The point?' he repeated.

'Yes.'

'Does there have to be?' he asked.

'Usually – '

'I want to have you. With me.'

'To keep me?'

'Yes. Yes, of course.'

She sat considering the cigarette between her fingers. Her hand started to shake.

'Will you? Agree, Catherine?'

She cleared her throat. 'I have a career,' she said.

'You don't believe that, though,' he answered her back. 'Do you?'

She leaned her head against the back of the chair. Why *this* chair in *this* temporary room with prints of street-hawkers on the walls? The air smelt of under-use, but also of old time: a musty, lightless tunnel of years. A car whined past outside, and she was suddenly filled with despair, with a sense of complete purposelessness, to be here in this small stale room of faded chintz and dull copper, itchy horsehair and dusty velvet. She remembered the rooks wheeling at dusk above the Close, their raucous cries fretting at her nerves' ends, the dampness and greenness of England in its vast melancholy, the awesome stone structure of past time that sat so complacently lichened and lightning-scarred in their midst.

She turned her eyes towards him. At any rate he knew where *he* was going, whither bound. Which gave him an inestimable advantage over her, even with her start in life; for now she had no destination clearly in view, and what she had good cause to suspect was a disabling loss of nerve.

He had recounted his business prospects to her: interest serving itself certainly, but she was conscious of that redoubtable assurance as a power, a source of energy compelling her towards him, a subject to her master.

One advantage of London and the flat was that she couldn't see much greenness from George Street, which suited her quite well. The Edwardian block had been squeezed into its corner site; it was one room broad, and none of the rooms in the building had walls at other than sharply obtuse or acute angles.

She started off buying the theatrical newspapers, but quickly began to lose any inquisitiveness about that life which she'd had. They discussed her setting up a milliner's shop (high-class) in the area, but she didn't – at heart – want to be owing to him more than she already was. She convinced herself – but only by skittering through the argument at breakneck speed – that she would actually have more independence keeping her days to herself, even if it *was* his money she was spending on her shopping forays and diverting to Aquae-Regis. His abiding wish seemed to be that she should look at all times ladylike, which (she guessed) meant rested and untrammelled.

She was able to oblige, for a short while. He took her to cocktail parties where the other men were also in his 'line' and where she stuck out like a linted, swaddled thumb, but that was only as he intended. She called the Old Rectory one day to pass on a message and had to cheerfully parry the indignant, denying monosyllables of his cockney mother. Colleagues invited them to plays and concerts, paid for through their firms' books, and then they went on to supper-rooms with dancing, where sheer mutual relief caused the drink to flow and culture-bombarded heads to lighten and lubricated tongues to loosen. Contracts were talked over in the Gents. The wives simultaneously envied and pitied one another, while chatting animatedly – the overdressed and frumpish alike – about loose covers and pelmets, or high insteps and fallen arches, just like friends of a long time's standing: but with their telltale eyes semaphoring the desperate futility of it all.

Would a doctor be able to diagnose, she sometimes considered, just what is the matter with me? With ration books torn up and austerity all but gone and everything to live for now? She could keep a medical appointment secret, she was sure, and she would be back by the time his Jaguar was nudging its thick wheels into the pavement. No cathedral bells on the quarter either, and she counted her blessings for the location.

And no bloody rooks.

Sex, yes. She took it on sufferance, though. Deserving her humiliation. For what she had allowed to happen to her. But blaming nobody. Saying nothing when he was too rough, when he tore at the straps of the silk lingerie he bought her, when he rammed himself inside her, when he came too quickly. She fitted a cap, to give herself the onus; unsheathed he beat against it, and she leaked wildly on to the top sheet, having to mop with a handkerchief that she kept within her reach. She would think of Cleopatra, and Josephine, but the purple-sailed barges wafted past on their scented breezes, and an empire's fate didn't hang on a knife-edge balance because ecstasy might take flight into insanity. No empire quaked. She was no more than this, after all, the accidental Catherine Eveleigh and nearly beneath significance.

Almost beneath significance, that is.

She realised what her other purpose was, which was to provide Norman Albert Petherick with some instruction on etiquette and manners. A not so sentimental education in finesse, to equip him with the courage necessary for the social minefields ahead of him. *He* taught her how to drive his Jaguar, but there was infinitely more about the polite world's ways which she was able to impart to her only too willing student.

Nothing was too simple to be overlooked, especially table behaviour. How he held his soup spoon and placed it in his mouth, between which fingers the fork and knife were placed and the angle at which they were to be held, not to call pudding 'sweet', the precedence of cheese over pudding, not to fill a coffee cup too close to the brim, the prescribed method of passing a bottle of port. But she assisted in other departments of a gentleman's life, obeying what was only instinct in herself, but which seemed in his own case like some desirably devout, arcane wisdom. She helped him choose his clothes and taught him how to carry them – the type of cufflinks to be worn, the preferred cut of shirt collar and size of trouser cuff, the manner of rolling back a shirtsleeve and the lengths along the arm to which it was permissible, the favoured proportion of knot to show on a tie, how to fasten a sock (a very dark navy blue or black) to a suspender, steel tips on the heels of his town shoes, which tailor and which hatter for which purposes. Her dress sense had come through observation, she supposed – of her father, of the fathers of the girls at school, from studying Maurice so closely: he'd had an innate sense of sartorial correctness, which was why her father's protestations of his ungentlemanliness had carried so little weight with her.

She tidied up his vowels and glottal stops, those which the elocution teacher she found for him wasn't able to fine down during their weekly ninety-minute 'consultations'. She found him a barber, at an establishment on Jermyn Street with a royal warrant, from which she also re-equipped his bathroom cabinet. She removed the immature cursive excesses from his handwriting and 'italicised' it slightly, introducing him to oblique nibs. She wasn't very musical herself, but she knew which composers belonged on any self-respecting turntable – any Mozart, any Beethoven, some religious Handel, some patriotic Elgar, some moody Grieg, some clear-throated Kathleen Ferrier, some lightning-fingered Alfred Cortot. Being only an occasional reader, she allowed an assistant in a bookshop close to the barber's to decide which of the offerings displayed on the circular central table were the required reading of that season.

She attended to his education willingly enough, because she felt it was – in part – excusing the other elements in their relationship. She was *useful* in a way that went beyond mere physical lust (which was hardly the case) and steely-minded financial pragmatism (which surely was). There was also the spectacle of the changes she was effecting in him. In front of her she had the evidence of her worth to him, and it flattered her to perceive that her opinions should *matter* in this way. Her methods of instruction were a gloss on the tawdriness she didn't care to dwell on. She could convince herself that she was another person while she was attending to his social programming, that her mind could temporarily operate on another track. Further to that, he was genuinely grateful to her for what she achieved: if not on his behalf, at least (should there properly be a difference) in his name. His social 'value' was increasing, and he fully recognised the cause. They served one another, each by their own mercenary devising. The association was neat, symmetrical, quite (after a fashion) regular, and more and more without feeling.

*

Sex.

She told herself it didn't mean anything: no more to her than it did to him. In one sense it rid her of her guilt and frustrations, by proving that without the mind's co-operation the act signified nothing, all it was was animal gratification. Without a body *and soul* to be loved, it was no more worthy an endeavour than any of the other processes of mere survival – breathing, eating, drinking, excreting. Without heart, it was nothing.

She didn't care for this man. While with Maurice . . . every aspect of her life had been bound up with him and only him, with the person he was and the fact of his being disapproved of. Surrendering her body to him had been the full and uncompromising declaration of her loyalty, and she believed – then as now – that he understood that. She couldn't accept that she had been wrong. When she remembered him, she was seeing again the affection and concern as well as the desire in his eyes. Even what had happened subsequently hadn't altered her perceptions in that respect. Her faith at that time couldn't be unpicked now. She felt relieved, therefore, and safe with what she assumed to be her memories. Nothing could negate them, not even time.

She was thrilled and enthralled by such a vision of love, which – and not book learning – seemed a true measure of wisdom. Now, in George Street, West One, she only felt confident in her denigration. The more demeaned she was, the more assured she became – she who had been instructed to accept that she had no claims on certitude in her life. Love, once experienced, was thereafter invulnerable and indestructible.

Mysteries pertained, of course, but they were the fluid in which the yolk of the feeling formed, supporting it. They didn't reduce the conviction that *then* – with Maurice, the passion of her life – she had been loved in return. She couldn't argue otherwise to herself. Never, not once, had she entertained an angry or spiteful thought about him. The worst she had sunk to was an unfocused, gnarring, luxurious, epidemic envy for the woman who had snared him. She had been unable to persuade herself of any other explanation for the issue than that a misunderstanding had taken place, and thus he must be ruing the consequences. She didn't even look for his wife's suffering: it would be hard enough for her that events would show Catherine Hammond had been exonerated, proved blameless and beyond any reproach. She required no retribution or revenge against another. She demanded for herself only righteousness, probity, and then the actual, expedient business of her life could begin in earnest.

*

The clocks went back. Immediately the year was running down.

A wind blew one night and, gathering speed in the streets, it stripped the trees. In Aquae-Regis she had always disliked the fag-end of autumn, the dampness, the reek of smoking bonfires, the slimy pavements as hazardous to walk on as mud-slides. In London the sight of the car headlights on late afternoons depressed her, all going somewhere else – while she recognised in her worst moments that she was really going nowhere, not like this.

It was on one such afternoon that he called her on the telephone, to say he would be later back than he intended, he had a job down on the coast, maybe he'd get up by ten. All right, she told him, and wondered how she was going to get through the hours.

She lit the gas fire. She watched the rooms darken as shadows merged one into another. And when he *does* get here, it struck her . . . But she let the thought go.

She went out briefly, just to the end of the street, to the newsagent's. She bought the last copy of *The Times* on the counter and took it home, wondering what it was that was keeping him down there and why she was bothered now one way or the other. She kicked at the mush of leaves and felt the dankness seeping through her layers of clothing, to the skin and into the bones.

Back in the flat it took her twenty-five minutes or half an hour to reach the Social and Personal Columns. Then her eye was immediately caught, snagged. The breath caught in her throat as if her windpipe was jammed, but she was oblivious to the physical discomfort.

'The engagement is announced between Gloria Miriam, only daughter of Mr and Mrs Louis Barlow, Chesters, Branksome, Bournemouth, and Norman Albert Petherick of The Old Rectory, Sandmouth.'

At first, when she could unlock her brain, she believed it must be a hideous mistake: that his name had been meant to appear somewhere else on the page. Or that he had contacted the newspaper, to insert the notice on someone else's behalf. Or that it was some sort of practical joke.

But how could it have been?

It was true enough, though. Scarcely shamefaced, he told her it was 'only to make things official'.

'She'll be Mrs Pargiter?'

'Yes. But – '

'From Branksome?'

'Yes. But – '

'She's wealthy then, is she?'

'Her father – '

'Of course. "Her father" – '

'He's in the same line. As I am. More or less.'

'I see.'

'Jewish.'

' "Jewish",' she repeated.

'But it won't change things between *us*, Catherine – '

She had to laugh at that, and a caustic and cruel sound it made, naturally enough.

'Well, well, well,' she said.

He poured them both drinks. She threw hers in his face. He lifted his arm to hit her, she lifted hers to protect herself, and they froze like that. Then they pulled themselves apart, retreated.

'We have to talk. Catherine – '

'It's too late.'

' – sleep on it.'

'It's past the moment, I mean. Long gone past it. We couldn't talk about it.'

'Yes, we could.'

She shook her head.

'I should've known,' she said.

'It's a sort of front really.'

'I'm sure it *is* a convenience. But is she pretty?'

'Gloria? Yes. Yes, she is. But – '

'And young? What age?'

'Twenty.'

'My God.'

'*She* wants it.'

'I'll bet.'

'The engagement.'

'Have you slept with her?'

'No.'

'Of course not.'

'She knows. About these things too. Thought about them, anyway. She's in love.'

'With *you*?'

'I – I don't know. In love. With love maybe. I'm the first man she's – '

' – fallen for? Who's *made* her fall for him. Congratulations, then. That's what's in order on these occasions, is it not?'

'Catherine, listen to me.'

But she wouldn't.

'I'll stay at a hotel,' she said.

'What?'

'Edwarde's Hotel.'

She took the money from his wallet while he stared at her. Panic-stricken, she saw, to her surprise. Frightened that he might be losing her. Which he was. Because he surely hadn't counted on her pride.

'I want a couple of nights away,' she said. 'I'll phone you on Thursday. We can make the arrangements then.'

Downstairs, on the street, she slammed the taxi door shut behind her. She had carried the scene and made a clean, effective theatrical exit. But leaning back in the cold seat she started to cry. Not for the way of life she was giving up, or for him, but for her stupidity and weakness in having come so far. She bit her lip and dug her nails into her palms to stop herself. The tears still fell, but in silence. In the dismal streets autumn went unleashed and shameless.

35

At Edwarde's Hotel

'ORDER and system,' she told herself, letting the porter take her small suitcase from her, stepping after him – dry-eyed now – into the vestibule of the hotel.

In forty years Edwarde's had changed little in appearance, electric lighting and modern upholstery apart. There was still the same eccentric arrangement of panelled public rooms, a bamboozling warren to the uninitiated. The senior staff wore their own three-quarters version of tails. Dover Street was banished behind thick brown velvet curtains. Tea and coffee were served in ornate, wrist-straining plate-silver pots. Wood fires crackled in the hearths. Stalwart grandfather clocks most discreetly took the beat of time. The leather-bound books in the small library were the genuine article, not false fronts or trompe-l'œil; the flowers were supplied daily from a florist's, and were neither silk nor paper. Umbrellas were desposited in antique Chinese vases. All the Duke of Buckingham had aspired to be was achieved here.

She signed the register, and was escorted up to her room. When she was alone she ran some water into the basin, scenting it with the soap. She washed her face and then buried it in the softness of the towel. She unpacked her clothes and hung them on the rail in the wardrobe. 'Order and system,' she told herself, not daring to think beyond the immediate and practical.

She decided she couldn't yet brace herself for bed and what would surely be a sleepless night, that she would put off a little time downstairs. It was late, quarter past eleven, but there was still some life in the lounge. A few businessmen sat talking over coffee and brandy. A couple consulted travel books and maps, spread out on a table. Several lone guests occupied out-of-the-way corners.

A spry woman in her forties or early fifties, also alone, entered from the hall, throwing a clearly humorous remark over her shoulder to one of the management staff in morning-coat. A fur stole hung over the other shoulder of her cherry-red dress. Her eyes surveyed the company in the first panelled room before she selected a place to sit. She slid a magazine off the high table beside her and quickly glanced through it. She crossed her slim legs and Catherine noticed the businessmen's heads turn. If the woman was aware, she gave no sign and ignored them. Catherine looked for a wedding ring, or an engagement ring, but she couldn't see either.

Watching the woman, she was riven by envy: of her courageous manner of dressing and the scrupulous attention she'd paid to her hair and make-up, but also of her attitude, her thoroughly modern, independent air. It made her think of all the things *she* was not, and it was then – having breezed through her departure and survived (somehow) the taxi journey – that she started to cry again.

She managed to make an escape and reached the ladies' room downstairs. The attendant's chair was empty and the doors of the cubicles all stood open. She went into the nearest and snibbed the little bolt behind her. She continued to cry, quietly, flushing the cistern several times in case anyone should come in. She did hear footsteps at last, in the area of the basins, and after a couple more minutes and another pull of the handle in the wall like a bell-stop she unlocked the door and walked out.

There could have been no other red dress in the hotel like it, to be confused with it. The woman stood in front of a mirror, adjusting the line of the neck.

'At home I'm always late to bed. This hotel is better than lots of them. It's funny, even London's full of Marie Celestes.'

She had a warm, sympathetic voice. Home Counties vowels, but without ostentation or conceit.

Catherine stopped in front of the dressing-table units on the wall, leaving a mirror between them. She saw that no one could have mistaken her condition.

She opened her handbag and realised after a search that she'd left her powder and puff upstairs in the bedroom.

The woman had opened *her* handbag, as if she had somehow anticipated the loss. When Catherine looked up she was being offered the use of a mother-of-pearl compact.

'Or anything else? I'm stupid, I weigh myself down with this stuff. Go on, please. Do help yourself – '

Catherine couldn't speak. When tears – of gratitude – appeared, any restraints of formality remaining were overcome between them.

The woman pulled over a stool and sat down beside her in front of the mirror. Then, using the contents of the ostrich handbag, she started to work on her.

The result – twenty minutes in the making – was a transformation

Catherine couldn't have prepared herself for. She looked at her eyes streamlined and shining out of her face. Inexplicably her skin glowed. The very shape of her face seemed different: longer, more oval, with her cheekbones defined. All the features seemed more – more emphatic. But not strident. Except possibly her scarlet mouth, which even to herself was now thrillingly seductive.

'Does that make you feel a bit better?'

Catherine nodded.

The woman returned the implements to her bag: eyebrow liner, eyeshadow, mascara, foundation, powder, rouge, lipstick.

'That's my emergency pack,' she said. 'For a quick patch-up job.'

'Is there more?'

'For structural things. In-filling. You know?'

She was lost in admiration. And very slightly afraid, to have the responsibility of this other person reflected in front of her. A mask to mask art.

'It's midnight,' the woman said, reading her watch, 'but I think I should order some tea for us both. Not too strong. And we can talk, for a while, if you'd like to?'

Catherine nodded, smiled. The woman was persuasive, commanding in a very beguiling way. She wished her energy might be contagious. She let herself be directed upstairs, into the lounge, to a sofa against a lamplit wall, where no one would be able to eavesdrop on them.

The woman ordered tea and biscuits, then returned to introduce herself, as Claribel Cooper (no 'Miss' or 'Mrs' supplied).

At a certain point they reached the significant part of the conversation, when the waiter had withdrawn. The woman seemed to guess what might be the matter, and wasted no time in broaching the subject. The freedom with which she spoke of it was a revelation to Catherine.

' . . . I'm not sure I've ever liked men. Well, I don't think I've ever known much about them, as a gender. I grew up with two sisters, and we went to girls' schools. In purdah. My father was quite pleasant – by the standards of my friends' fathers – but he was forever away on business and so I didn't get to see him very often. His brother, my uncle, everyone called him "ineffectual" behind his back: *he* seemed quite reconciled to his wife making all the decisions. That was my "experience" of men, more or less, and it didn't add up to very much.

'It certainly didn't prepare me for the next stage. Finding a husband. Nobody pretended that a well-brought-up girl's ambition in life should be anything else. Frankly I don't suppose I was able to judge good from bad. In the end it happened, though. I became engaged. I can't say it was a choice as such. Or rather, it was a case of Basil being left when I had gradually eliminated the others.'

She picked up her teacup and drank from it. Catherine leaned forward in her chair, intrigued by the woman's candour.

'His mother had been keen on me, and he tried to see me as *she* always did, armed with my positive virtues. I was up on that famous pedestal without wanting to be, and he truly did idealise me, especially when his eye started to rove. To preserve *me*, I suppose, from his – his fleshly instincts. And after his mother died he seemed to associate me with that other time, and even "The Act" troubled him, I could see, and I became more tender with him, so of course without meaning to I only drove him into the arms of those other women. They roughened everything up, I dare say: which must have been what he felt he wanted. I do see that now. I only wish I could have sympathised with him then. But I fell into the trap, imagining I was slighted. Staying at home while he was out, how could I think any differently? I became resentful, and I tried to conceal it, and for both of us pretence became – a mutual requirement of life. The deftest skill of all. And how tiring it was – '

The woman paused to take breath. She poured more tea and water into the two cups.

'But then he became less discreet. People found out. I felt I had to react, for their benefit, when wives let things drop. I still didn't confront Basil about it. His past was altering too: his mother was safe, inviolate, but I was not. I had the feeling he thought I'd set out to bag him, to catch him in a man-trap. I could tell how constricting he felt the house was. I bought new clothes – with his money – to try to give myself a lift in his estimation, but – I don't know – in my gladrags did I then start to remind him of the women he associated with? He got jealous, absurdly so, and – even while we didn't talk openly about *his* infidelities – he dropped enough clues about what he thought *I* had in mind. Chasing after his colleagues, no less, which I just laughed off.

'But then, another time, he accused me of making eyes at a man, a married colleague, a friend. I wasn't aware I had; he rounded on me, though. The next week, quite by chance I met this man in the Strand, and he took me for lunch; another day we had another lunch, and on the way out of the restaurant he pulled me into a broom cupboard and showered me with kisses. I should say *I* was the first to make a move after the kisses, undoing the waistband of my skirt and letting it fall and stepping out of it. A harlot at last!'

The woman picked up her teacup, and so did Catherine.

'I must have wanted it. It had always been sinful. Until I actually did it. The "sin" element assisted. It was all quite matter-of-fact, though – and enjoyable, I'm glad to report. I thought, perhaps one could develop quite a liking for this. The duplicity.'

Catherine followed the movements of the woman, replacing *her* cup likewise in its saucer.

Two men walked past them, across the lounge, engaged in talk of business.

'I left Basil, although we were still married. I continued my affairs, with other colleagues, and then colleagues of theirs, until the men were social strangers to me. I took gifts, and then the gifts became cash, and the day came when I asked for money, a certain sum. There was no objection, relief in fact: as if I'd taken a load off the poor fellow's shoulders, and he could calculate the worth of the encounter, in time and pleasure. That became quite a good system, in fact. Nobody ever complained, or bartered. Giving *me* money, because they were businessmen they felt they need be less guilty about taking their pleasure: it was the language they liked to think they best understood. They could buy out their discomfort as well as assure themselves of my discretion. It was a business transaction, if you like. I was pleasant, polite, caring (I suppose): but never, *ever* loving. So that they were able to think what they liked – preferably, that I wasn't treading on the territory of their unfortunate wives. I was a kind of geisha, lofty and intimate at the same time, but not demeaning myself to whisper the sort of nonsense they expected to hear from their wives. Do you see, Catherine?'

The woman waited until she was certain of the reaction she required. Catherine did indeed see, and she nodded, with her eyes wide open.

'My father was a businessman,' the woman continued, 'and my mother's father and brother, and so was Basil. It was my "provenance" in life, my own area. To be trading in myself. Because I realised that I must have inherited some of my father's business acumen.'

Catherine nodded, already foreseeing the geography of the story ahead.

'Women really *are* the more rewarding sex, you know. Because of their introspection, I mean, because they're pushed back on their own mental resources, into their own silence. Men are territorial, they can only assess others and themselves in terms of status. Men are simpler; women can be sly and treacherous, but even so, they *are* more rewarding. If they're loyal to you, it's because they understand, they intuit, and they sympathise.

'I often used to wonder what a community of women would be like; like-minded women, of course, who could admit and exclude men whenever they wanted to. So, after thinking about it for a long time, I took the plunge. My women would have freedom, to earn and spend, and if they tired of the set-up they were quite at liberty to leave the house. I didn't want them dependent, or considering themselves as such, even though their trade demanded the participation of men. But it was the men who would beat a track to *their* door. *We* were just being – pragmatic. Not immorally – or amorally – calculating, I don't believe. We had come through fire, all of us, in some form or other, we were "worldly", none of us was going to be corrupted. We were "organising" ourselves, to prevent any of us making any more mistakes. That's all.'

Catherine smiled at the woman's facility with words, the easy and captivating cadence of her voice.

'The house is called The Paddock, and I'm going to give you its address. You are free to go and take a look, a good look, or else just to forget everything I've said to you. I believe it would interest you, though, because I think I can read minds, I can see fates written on faces.'

Catherine sat more upright. The woman reached forward and stroked the back of her hand.

'I cover my costs, that's all. I can afford *this* – ' she pointed to their surroundings ' – because my childless aunt left me her controlling stake in a factory that makes cough medicines and throat lozenges. If you can credit it –'

Catherine stared at her.

'At least – you'll notice – I don't have a cough, not so much as a tickle in my throat. So maybe I'm not such a bad advertisement.'

A male guest walking past with his room key projecting from his hand stared at them both. Catherine looked up anxiously, dreading the appearance of the man she'd left. Her companion smiled at the guest, with perfect civility but an explanatory chill. The man hurried away.

'I should be sorry, I suppose, for what you're going through. But what a drain on one's energies sorrowing is. And self-pity. Life, as they say, is too short. Too short not to know when to let a door bang behind you for the last time and never look back.'

'About Basil?' Catherine enquired in the lift, quietly, behind the boy's liveried back. 'What happened – ?'

'He was with one of his – friends.' The woman lowered her voice, although the boy must still have been able to hear. 'The string of pearls she was wearing burst and they flew around the room, everywhere. Some rolled under the wardrobe and – apparently – he was helping to retrieve them when his heart gave out. He'd had a shock before, but I think the circumstances finished him. His ardour, you see, and then the postponement, and then this strain. He'd grown quite – "sturdy" would be the polite word, "portly" – '

'I'm sorry,' Catherine said.

'That I had a tubby husband?'

'No. No, about – '

The lift gates were opened and the woman placed her powdery cheek against Catherine's.

'You've got the address?'

Catherine tapped her bag.

'Remember, when a door closes, some time has to be the last time – '

The two women exchanged smiles. The gilt gates were pulled shut. As soon as she was alone again with the boy in his bell-cap, in the humming silence of the lift shaft with the cables pulling, Catherine with her brave new face considered the question, how a solitude might most purposefully be endured.

36

The Paddock

IN the 1930s the house had arrived by road, on the backs of lorries, in its prefabricated parts. The design was one specifically intended for the Anglo-Indian market, which made the construction seem stranger still, to be found standing in a wooded two and three-quarter acres of garden in a small Surrey town.

The outer walls were extra-heavy-duty corrugated iron, now painted a fetching powder blue. There were two storeys, and on the upper as well as the lower the french windows of the rooms opened on to a narrow wrought-iron balcony running round the building's four sides and supported by elaborately welded iron tracery. No modifications had been made to accommodate the vagaries of the English climate, and the house conjured up an eccentric vision of heat and coolth, and the leisure that accompanied a manner of life enjoyed in the hill-stations, among the tea plantations. Interior specifications even included ceiling fans, but the mechanisms had rusted with lack of use and the propeller blades were furred with dust. The external appearance of the construction denoted a certain refinement in the manner of existence conducted within, but it had quickly become local knowledge that the private facilities were a brisk walk away from the house itself, in a wooden garage sited beneath the cedar trees and converted for that purpose. Townsfolk walking along the lane had grown used to hearing the clacking of heels from the other side of the high beech hedge as nature called and feet flew down the stepping-stones set into the lawn; in the rain the journey from the house would be made at an even faster pace, under cover of an umbrella. So much for the semblance of gentility.

Catherine's arrival at The Paddock coincided with a departure, and perhaps 'Miss' (as she was called) Cooper had anticipated as much. Being the bird of passage she was, the housekeeper had elected to take flight, to the South of France. The 'household' were left 'in a quandary'.

Telephoning Miss Cooper, Catherine suggested that she should take over the domestic duties. The woman instantly agreed; she was tactful enough not to question her on her experience of this sort of work, but must have had her intuitions to judge by.

Philosophically, Catherine accepted the premises on which the premises were run. But on the next two nights, back in London at Edwarde's Hotel, she had the same dream, that Maurice – hag-ridden – was driving his car down The Paddock's driveway and looked up to see her watching from the balcony.

The first night she woke in breathless panic, on the second in tears.

In the event she found herself charged with no less than the running of the establishment: overseeing the kitchen, the cleaning, laundry, structural repairs. It was also her responsibility to keep the books *and* the appointments book beside the telephone.

She was desperate enough to need to succeed, and threw herself into her tasks.

Her days and evenings were filled. Her managerial responsibilities got her off the hook morally, but – dressed as the girls did themselves, in perpetual undress – it nevertheless made her an accomplice in the business.

*

The town was all too predictably damp for two-thirds of the year. I grew used to seeing my great-aunt with a tartan travelling rug thrown over her shoulders, clutching a rubber hot-water bottle to her stomach or the small of her back or her neck. Colds and influenza and mouth sores were no more than was to be expected in Aquae-Regis. When the wind came up, it was a common practice to keep curtains closed the round of the clock, to guard against the ferocious draughts.

The wind was especially a curse up on the heights. But worse in lowlier Ægypt was that dampness, due to our proximity to the river and to the old meads, supposedly drained but slowly and surely reverting to nature. The houses had thinner walls and more meagre foundations, which meant a further weakening of our defences.

I became accustomed to my great-aunt's indispositions, and at the best of times she couldn't speak more than a couple of sentences without an accompanying cough into the back of her hand or delivering a sniff into her handkerchief. There was always a fire banked up high in one room, and sausages of rolled, unusable carpet were placed along the bottoms of doors. When she took to her bed twelve days after the turn into 1954, it wasn't such an exceptional event as to cause immediate concern. But when she didn't recover after a month, and the hacking coughs didn't stop, the alarm was raised among those she still counted her friends. I remember the embarrassment as much as anything else, knowing that our neighbours must be able to hear, and it was their sleeplessness that was leaving them red-eyed and looking not very well disposed towards myself or the house whenever they encountered me on Cadell Street. Some items of furniture disappeared – 'officially' – one afternoon, loaded into the back of a removal van, while a man carrying a sheaf of papers superintended; and the next day Aunt Dodie disappeared too, borne on a stretcher into the back of an ambulance, while a nurse in a grey belted raincoat supervised and our bleary-eyed neighbours disguised their relief as they mustered on the pavement.

I was taken care of – in their alternating homes – by a couple of my great-aunt's longest-standing friends but I knew the arrangement could be nothing more than temporary. (My suitcase was left with me in each of my two bedrooms, somewhere prominent, and I was 'lent' old ownerless toothbrushes, long-departed guests' face-flannels, and not given a ring for my napkin, which had to be folded while the others were rolled.) I was taken to visit my Aunt Dodie a couple of times, but she had difficulty recognising me, especially on the second afternoon when she was wearing a rubber breathing mask and I was put in mind of a photograph I'd seen of a wartime bomber pilot.

When she died, I have to confess I was less stricken on her account than rawly conscious (at four years old) of my own social awkwardness, my statelessness. For several days a dire silence prevailed wherever I happened to be, lasting until after the funeral, which I was judged too young to attend.

*

Catherine was there for the last days.

'I hope your mother believed I wanted to do all that was best.'

'Yes, of course she did,' Catherine said, stroking her aunt's wrist where it lay on the coverlet and not fully understanding.

'What was best at the time, I mean. Maybe that's two different things.'

'It's all right. Really.'

'I hope she trusted me.'

'Trusted you? Yes, of course she did.'

She watched her aunt shake her head.

'I didn't *know* that – '

'But why shouldn't she have trusted you?'

'Maybe she thought – I'd try to influence you.'
'Influence me how?'
'It's so long ago now.'
Catherine continued stroking her aunt's thin, cooling wrist.
'I *could* have done. If I'd set my mind to it. But I relied on Hector, for everything. If we'd fallen out – where would that have left me? That's the point, you see.'
'Yes,' Catherine said.
'Your mother, she was just misunderstood. Time and patience, it wouldn't have taken any more than that – '
Catherine didn't move, not wanting to disturb the flow and tempo of her aunt's recollections.
'Your mother was so smart, of course, so well turned out always. Hector was so impressed by her. Everyone was. She drew their eyes in a room. But not by choosing to, I'm sure. It just happened, quite naturally enough. It was very charming, and Hector thought so too at first, I know he did.'
Catherine measured a seemly silence.
' "At first"?' she repeated.
Her aunt shook her head.
'Something seemed to close his mind. I could never get to the bottom of it.'
' "Close his mind"? How?'
Aunt Dodie sucked in her cheeks.
'He always "knew his own mind", people said.' Her aunt lowered her voice still further. 'He liked to *think* he did. So, when he felt he might have been wrong, he didn't acknowledge it. With Hector, I really don't know if he was certain. The pity was, he let a distance come between them, your mother and himself, and he stood on his pride.'
Catherine bent over the wrists, straining to hear.
'You said, "not certain"?'
'There were always stories in Aquae-Regis. Going round and round. Gossip and rumours, tittle-tattle. It was just in the air. But some of it sticks. Like burrs. You know?'
Her aunt closed her eyes.
'It was so long ago. But it's as clear as . . .'
Catherine placed her aunt's left hand on top of the right.
'Another time,' she said, 'we can talk about it another time.'
She was intensely curious, but also deeply uneasy. She felt she wanted to down a stiff drink.
'I'll leave you in peace now,' she said.
But before she had reached the door Aunt Dodie rallied. She asked if she might see a hand-mirror, please, and when it was placed in her

hand she started fussing, quite urgently, with her hair. Catherine smiled to see it, reassured by an action too innocent to be vanity, too familiar for her to believe that she wouldn't always have the spectacle to behold.

Her aunt was buried, at her own request, in the Cumberland town she had left twenty years before.

In his brief address inside the church, the curate spoke of her being 'with the hosts of angels'; after her recent 'troubles', she was now 'crowned with glory'. The singing voices sounded feeble and half-hearted in that foxhole of cold, cheerless stone, with the window glass unstained and lozenge-leaded.

Cars had to be used to reach the secondary, auxiliary churchyard, and in the course of the uphill journey a lorry transporting sheep found its way into the middle of the four-vehicle cortège. At the graveside the curate adhered to the bald form of the funeral service, without any diversionary extolling of the deceased's particular merits as a human being. One of the bearers lost hold of his end of rope and with a couple of thuds and the macabre unsettling of the contents, the coffin lurched into its final resting-place.

Before leaving for Cumberland Catherine had organised afternoon tea in Cadell Street for a later date. But she was so distressed by the curate's conduct that on her return south she insisted the company present themselves at the Peregrine Hotel and damn the expense.

Chiefly what she was to remember of the afternoon in retrospect was her determination that Felix should have nothing more to do with Aquae-Regis. She hadn't returned since his birth, and she found it harder and harder to breathe as the afternoon wore on. She wished poor Aunt Dodie – she of all people – could have been here, to enjoy a 'treat'. She had sent her what money she could, and between them they had managed, but there had been less and less to sweeten time's passing in Ægypt. If her aunt was disappointed that she didn't come down to visit them, she hadn't reproached her. The many photographs and letters that regularly passed between them had had to substitute for a proper, meritorious relationship.

In the bathroom of the ground-floor bedroom which they were using as a cloakroom, Catherine wept bitter tears – and then she promptly made herself up using the cosmetics she'd brought stashed in her handbag in anticipation. It was done with an unsure hand, but it was better than nothing, maybe better than she thought, because outside in the corridor a man's head swivelled to watch her as his wife tugged on his arm.

She rang Miss Cooper from the telephone at the front desk, resolved that henceforth Felix's life should represent the etymological meaning of his name.

*

The winter and most of spring were behind me, as were those two dried, withered sticks, my minders, in Aquae-Regis. My mother had claimed me.

I imagined on my arrival in Surrey that we were now to be living – briefly – among family 'friends'. The house *felt* as if it must be a holiday. The french windows stood open, figures drifted in and out of the rooms, a lot of lemon barley water was poured from crystal jugs, knockabout tennis was played beneath the trees, an elderly spinster gardener sprayed the flowerbeds with a hosepipe and let me play beneath it.

When we were ourselves, late at night and in the mornings, we were – apart from me – a nest of womenfolk, seven in all plus the maid. Until lunchtime was over the only voices I heard were women's, unless one of the wireless sets had been turned on and a male announcer was speaking. The house smelt of women: talcum, shampoo, eau-de-Cologne, drying nail varnish, the leather of new shoes, wet stockings hanging from the kitchen pulley. Until we all sat down to eat lunch in the dining-room they swished past me (my mother too) in dressing-gowns or kimonos, in various stages of make-up, chatting or singing the choruses of songs or breaking in new shoes on the floorboards between the rugs or blowing on their nails; jewellery rattled lightly on their wrists, and just audible was the contact of one inner thigh on another.

I supposed they must be friends, because they were so at their ease, and always seemed to be involving themselves with my mother. My mother let herself be taken over, and I didn't see so very much of her. Everyone was kind to me, and considerate, and gave me little jobs and responsibilities, and made sure that I was in bed by the same time every evening, after somebody – the roster varied – had prepared my supper and set it for me at the kitchen table.

The customs were gentle, undemanding ones. I would be taken along (by whoever was available) to the grocer's or the baker's or the fruiterer's when the weekly supplies delivered in vans were running low on tea or Hovis loaves or mackintosh red apples, and en route we would pass Miss Spoak's Jersey cow grazing in its triangle of meadow, we would stop for a couple of minutes to play pooh-sticks over the wooden bridge that crossed the weedy rivulet we never learned the name of. When there were letters to be sent I would be lifted up to the level of the slit in the post-box set in a high mossy wall, and I always became a train engine in Church Lane with the gas lamps and stations to stop at and set off steaming from.

My time there lasted from the rhododendron season at the end of May to the chrysanthemums fading on their stalks in October. We had the advantage of a long, warm, blue summer and, afterwards, the bonus of a second little Indian one during our last days in that collapsible house intended for Indian climes. The french windows were only closed for rain, and never locked. My mother passed in and out with her friends and our life was as mannerly, urbane and piquant as any shown to a ripple of satisfied applause as the curtain rises on a stage.

*

The summer was an exceptional one, and she didn't feign to Miss Cooper that she regarded the position as any more than temporary. She herself acquired a summer disposition after the trauma of her recent manner of life. She breathed fresh Surrey air and even picked up from Miss Spoak who gardened for them a little skill in that practical art.

There were worse ways to bring up a child, and she wasn't ashamed on his behalf: he would remember of it (she hoped) what he chose to, and she'd have a hand in its making. The men who came – ironically their *raison d'être* – were, as a general rule, well turned out, well bred and courteous and not at all bad examples to set before a young boy. Sometimes they gave him a threepenny bit or a silver sixpence, which she would have preferred they didn't; but he showed no signs of being spoiled by indulgence, and politely mimicked surprise each time it happened.

Her hands were full with the house but not *so* full that she couldn't savour the summer. The girls all had their reasons for being here, stories to tell, which she respected whenever they wanted to tell her or *not* tell her. Miss Cooper had selected a congenial grouping – she clearly had a flair for it – and there were no major strains among them. No one seemed put out that *she* wasn't older and that she lived a celibate life herself.

There were temptations but she resisted them. She even enjoyed the self-discipline, the contradictions between the appearance of being one of the others and the actuality of her situation. The girls all knew that they could pack up and go any time, that they had money enough to cope, and realised too that Miss Cooper could probably have been persuaded to lend them some of the wherewithal to help set them up 'in business' on their own.

It was an enlightened community, Catherine believed. Everyone was in receipt of what they required; nobody was humiliated. The novelty wasn't to wear off for her. She was aware as she was living these days that she was collecting pleasant memories and associations for herself. She worked hard but she also drew strength from the peace of mind – a delicious kind of tiredness – at each day's end, resulting from that same concentration on the manual and mechanical, from this respite in dealing with the buffetings of real life, from this amicable truce in the sexual war.

*

The men never appeared before two o'clock of an afternoon. After lunch it would be my job to run to the top of the drive and undo the rope that held the five-bar gate to its post. If I stood on the first or second bar I had no difficulty, and the gate would swing back of its own accord. From a fork in a certain tree or from the upstairs balcony I would watch for the first car to turn in from the lane and send the thin gravel scattering. It might be a familiar car or one that was new to me, but the welcome downstairs seldom varied in its tone.

I would remember what I had to do, which was to keep myself to myself and not be seen. Indeed I had a reputation at that time for good behaviour. It didn't strike me that my conduct should be anything other than what was so politely requested of me. In the course of the eight months I very rarely had contact with other children, and when I passed any on our journeys to and from the shops we looked at each other with mutual suspicion. It didn't occur to me then that they were only responding as lesser versions of their parents, for whom the house of women in Parslow Lane must have been a frequent topic of surmise and speculation and worse.

So I, in my place, was considered 'good' and 'no trouble'. My mother occasionally had toys delivered for me, my 'rewards', but I don't remember making the mental connection that I ought to be well behaved on that account. Some of the women bought me clothes, or must have given my mother money to spend on kitting me out, so that I soon needed my own two drawers in the tallboy. All I had to do to be so popular was to remember to unhitch the gate every afternoon as the house's water pipes clattered, and to keep out of the way.

I *heard*, of course: it would have been impossible not to. Standards of soundproofing in the East must have been considered inferior to Western ones, and the house had been assembled with aural privacy clearly low among the practical priorities. From the linen cupboard on wet days I could hear a dialogue of voices through one wall or the other: voices rather than particular words, and laughter rather than the jokes which caused the mirth. Feet stomped on the floor despite a carpet and underlay, and I could pick up the force of impact whenever a heavy (male) body dropped into an armchair. It was quite in order, then, that I should also have been able to hear bedsprings squeaking and knuckles and palms accidentally making contact with the walls. Many small silences would be staked out with an irregular succession of throaty cries and bellows, sometimes a word spoken low or another laugh, stifled this time.

So it was that the friends we were among spent their afternoons. The latest a car ever left was seven o'clock. At suppertime, either making my way down the staircase or approaching the front steps from the garden, I would find my mother, head bent in conversation with one or two of our friends, maybe holding their hands or exchanging shoes with them or letting them pile up her hair before a mirror. She always had a single drink as the evening began, and she would make it last as she oversaw my supper in the kitchen or left me to someone else while she telephoned; occasionally she took the glass with her as she disappeared with the bathroom key and the back door swung behind her.

Upstairs, shower-distrusting and being got ready for bed, with my goodness on a looser rein, I sometimes clung to the handles on the window sashes and looked down into the garden. The friends were pursuing wooden balls through hoops with mallets, or patting soft underhand serves to one another on the grass with their tennis rackets. From my watch-post I could see occasional figures passing on the other side of the beech hedge, either dallying as they walked or slowing on their bicycles to peer through the greenery. On the warmest evenings my mother and our friends carried the kitchen table and chairs outside and made an impromptu *closerie* for themselves under Miss Cooper's rose pergola. Otherwise they ate in the dining-room beneath my narrow bedroom, and I would lie awake for as long as I could make myself, listening to the comfortable give-and-take, the easy ebb-and-flow of their voices. After supper on the alfresco evenings they would fetch cardigans or dressing-gowns and the basket chairs from the downstairs balcony and sit in their arbour talking or leafing through magazines. When the weather wasn't quite so temperate I would hear them clearing the dining-table, washing up (there were no indoors staff after lunchtime, and household duties alternated fairly among all, including myself) and then moving into the sitting-room; the wireless would be turned on if there was music, and the songs and tunes would weave themselves with an insidious, mesmeric grace into the stuff of my dreams.

The house still stands, not a great deal more than the sum of its prefabricated parts. The outer walls and the heavy-duty bolts have taken some rust in thirty years, and in places the blue paint has wholly peeled away, to the brazen metal beneath. The lawn has shrunk, less because memory has deceived than because most of the garden is now the 'wild' variety. A number of the cedars in the two and three-quarter acres seem to have grown together, and their knitted branches make cool green arcades of shade that surely would have been appreciated then.

But there's too much moss embedded in the grass, the trunks of the fruit trees are lichened and spotted, the hedges are shapeless, the weeds have appropriated the flowerbeds as their own, and thistles grow through the broken glass in the hot frames. The estate agent's notice by the (now depleted) three-bar front gate has been eaten by mildew.

Fecundity and decay.

Silence.

But someone still cuts a diminishing island of lawn, a little less each time, to save the house from total abandonment. A broom has recently swept a determined aisle through the dirt on the downstairs verandah. The windows show less dust on the panes than they might. All is not lost.

A modicum of respect persists for those who once lived here, and they fleetingly acknowledge it. There's a sound like rustling silk, or rayon, or cotton; a draught turns the dried twists of leaves on the bare boards behind me. The same gasp of wind sends the unhitched front gate creaking backwards. Somewhere an apple drops from a tree into grass and immediately I hear its true significance – the resemblance to a clever ball dropping dead off a tennis racket.

37

The Mink Coat

One evening she walked into the dining-room as Veronica was telling the others why one of her visitors, the tall red-haired Mr Whelan, had appeared that afternoon with a black eye, a real 'shiner'.

Two nights before, he'd been at the Two-O-Two Restaurant in Ludovick Street. He'd been sitting at his table with his fiancée, watching a young woman dancing with a partner on the floor. As one tune became the next in the medley she disposed of the man and reached out to grab the arm of a passing waiter to replace him. She was an able dancer, even half-cut, and most of the room was watching by this time.

Gradually the dancers round about left the floor. Another man was advancing towards the couple. He tried to speak, but the woman made a show of ignoring him. He pulled at her elbow, imploring her 'Jennifer, please!' She continued dancing, though, seemingly oblivious, with her eyes trained up at the ceiling. The waiter didn't know what to do. The man then began to shout. The woman was smiling, all the time drawing herself closer to the waiter. The man stepped towards them both and tried to separate them. He took hold of the waiter's lapels and shook him.

Mr Whelan's table was beside the dance floor, and perhaps to prove himself to his fiancée, he made a move. He hurried over to the brawling pair. The man who'd attacked the waiter was all the time hissing threats at the woman called 'Jennifer', and she was just laughing although her face was white with anger. As Mr Whelan reached them and put his hands on the two men's shoulders, meaning to pull them apart, he lost his balance and fell sideways; the woman stretched out her arm, presumably to help him, but by some misfortune – owing to the geometry of angles – her elbow reached his face before her hand could catch hold of him and her funny bone socked him smack in the eye.

Everyone in the dining-room of The Paddock laughed at the story,

Catherine included. But her mind was on overdrive. Her breath through the cheese course came to her in shorter and tighter bursts. When the clearing-up got under way, she managed to find a few moments alone in the larder with Veronica. She asked with forced naturalness if she knew any more about the couple in the restaurant. Veronica said she didn't, and she supposed that Mr Whelan wasn't any wiser than she: he hadn't put a name to them, and he hadn't said that he'd seen them before. Veronica started laughing again and leaned back against the wall. Catherine pretended that that's all it was to her too, an amusing and diverting anecdote, and she smiled, with a terrible effort of concentration.

She arranged with Miss Cooper a night off for herself. She booked a room at Edwarde's Hotel.

The head waiter at the Two-O-Two seemed uneasy that she was a woman alone. She concocted a tale, that her late husband and she had come here to celebrate a wedding anniversary, and that since she was returning home to – to Gibraltar tomorrow . . . The man nodded his head sombrely as if he *might* have believed her, but placed her nonetheless at the most remote table on the upper level, with a restricted view of proceedings on the dance floor.

She asked two waiters, the wine waiter and, later, the concierge, if they had heard of a couple called Encombe. They hadn't. That set her thinking. Most probably then Jennifer had come alone, and Maurice had trailed her. 'Mrs Moncrieff-King?' she asked one of the waiters again, but that name signified no more than the first. Or – or what if it wasn't *that* Jennifer at all, and *another* jealous or despairing husband?

The oval-shaped restaurant put her in mind of an ocean liner: 1930s elegance, recessed and muted lighting on the walls, handrails, alcoves of flowers. Leta would have been a little disappointed that they had held themselves back, all in the name of good taste: no portholes, and no aquarium tanks.

The evening passed, in expensive solitude in that well-patronised room. Nobody asked her to dance, because everyone was spoken for and earnestly asserting the fact. The music was resolutely romantic, and she found herself singing the words under her breath. She avoided the head waiter's eye, which reached even to her outermost point on the oval, furthest from the doors. She fumbled after the phrase from Latin classes at school – '*O me miserum*' – and she tried to smile in a mild and general way, not to spoil the evening of those into whose range of sight she fell.

*

In the ladies' cloakroom downstairs she gave the concierge her ticket and watched her scan the pegs. She returned holding a long fur coat.

'No, I – '

But the ticket pinned to the collar matched the one she'd given the woman.

The coat was placed on the counter, as if furs were nothing out of the ordinary in such an establishment. Catherine looked past the woman, but she couldn't see her own tweed coat. The woman smiled. Catherine undid the catch on her handbag, and pulled at the popper button on her purse; she removed two half-crowns and dropped them into the saucer.

'Thank you kindly, madam.'

The woman lifted the counter flap and came forward, holding the coat open. Catherine hesitated for several seconds before she slipped her arms into the sleeves. She shook out her hair and let the weight of mink fall on to her shoulders.

The transformation was immediate. The woman prattled away; upstairs the doorman jumped to attention and while he ran out into the rain for a taxi one of the management sped towards her. She panicked, that he recognised the coat and was going to apprehend her for the thief she was. But his unctuousness had no harmful intent, she soon realised, quite the contrary indeed; he couldn't have been more overweeningly trusting of her, fussing to find a good enough umbrella. In the taxi she was shocked also by the driver's *madams*, the stagy way he gave a half-nod of his head every time he directed a remark to her. When she reached Edwarde's Hotel, he charged her less than had registered on the meter, which seemed to her perverse: as if money, rather than being the life's blood to someone wearing such a coat, was a vulgar, disagreeably sordid matter beneath her consideration.

She saw in the wardrobe mirror in her room how the coat altered her appearance, gave her what the make-up did, grace and allure. She saw too how it not only socially removed her but dramatically isolated her face as well.

The right-hand pocket was empty but in the left she found a business card. 'Kilpatrick's Agency, Representatives for the Modelling Profession'. Beneath was an address in Upper Brook Street and a telephone number. On the back someone had written, 'Call Miss Montgomery. Say Two-O-Two, Mr Frankel. Back 4th November.'

She slept well, even with another woman's coat hanging inside the wardrobe, only four yards away from her. When she woke in the morning the first thing she saw was the business card, where she had left it, propped against the lamp on the table. She reached up for it and held it in front of her eyes. The room felt cold, she thought; last winter had been exceptionally mild, and she wondered what Surrey was going to be like in an unkind season for weather. Early November. She lay working out which day, counting on an imaginary calendar. The fourth. She stared again at the back of the card.

She telephoned. Said something about the Two-O-Two. Miss Montgomery spoke against a background of ringing telephones and urgent voices.

'This must be Miss Fairweather?'

'Yes,' Catherine replied. 'Yes, that's right.'

'Mr Frankel mentioned your name to me. He said he'd noticed you in the restaurant. He thought you might be just the sort we're looking for. Miss Fairweather, when can you come in?'

She considered the ambience to be one of controlled confusion.

'It's not usually like this,' a beautiful girl said to her *en passant*. 'Mr Kilpatrick's just back, you see.'

Miss Montgomery was too busy to see her at that moment and a young woman with chestnut hair tied under a turquoise bandana appeared. She quizzed her with her mismatched eyes from head to foot and back again.

'I don't know *you*,' she said.

'No. I – I've come to see – '

'Oh, I get it. Well, *you* should do well all right. You look as if you are, already.'

'I – I beg your pardon?'

'Doing all right. With a coat like that on your back.'

'Oh. This?'

'Better not enquire?'

'I'm sorry?'

'Never mind. *We*'ve got you now. Don't forget, you spoke to *me* first. When you're on the books you'll cover the cost of my jaunts for me, won't you? I'll get my father – '

The man in question entered the room; he seemed embarrassed. His daughter held his arm. He stood scrutinising her face, as if trying to calculate what she might have said.

The 'interview' was a very civilised procedure. Over Viennese coffee Mr Kilpatrick said that he had received a call about her: he gestured to his laden in-tray. He told her he was glad that *she* had done the getting in touch. He asked her how much experience she had of modelling, and when she confessed to none, he didn't appear put out. 'Well, you'll learn. Very quickly, Miss Fairweather, I'm sure.' He even smiled. 'I shall put Miss Montgomery on to it right away.'

She sat in the mink coat on a Florentine-embroidered Raeburn chair, in the man's panelled office, in the fall of light from a silk shade. Her surroundings bore no resemblance to the brash modelling agency she had conceived in her head. Twelve hours ago, she couldn't have had an inkling that anything remotely like this might be about to happen to her. She thought of a testing winter in Surrey and her son growing to an age when he must start to remember, always to remember.

An accountant in starched white collar and cuffs and half-moon spectacles handed her an envelope containing generous 'expenses'. A beanpole half his age in a white roll-necked jumper and with a deft line in banter whisked her into a room, seated her against a blue screen under a silver umbrella and arc-lights and took shots of her. To begin with she blinked straight into the flashlight, but then he told her where to look. The coat was kept on: the coat was removed. She didn't know what he wanted her to do, but he asked her just to 'be herself', and she was seriously puzzled. The photographs were taken with her own confusion registering on her face.

She returned to the hotel in a state of uncertainty. The coat became heavier and heavier as she walked. Every woman who looked at her she suspected of being the coat's rightful owner. It was in fine condition, must have been newish indeed, and she was intrigued by its mysterious impersonality, the absence of any marks of ownership. It carried the label of a Copenhagen furrier, but all that the pockets had contained was the business card. The coat *took* little of a person, but conferred – as she continued to notice – a good deal. And yet its weight and heat made her feel it was *she* who must become a servant of the thing. Contradiction and paradox, observable even from the very clothes she wore.

38

Mirror, Mirror

AFTER she left The Paddock – parting on good terms – Catherine returned to Bayswater, to Lavinia Place.

Morwenna had taken herself off somewhere – to Mexico possibly – and Mrs Littig lived alone. She said she would be very glad of the company, and immediately took to Felix. She also said that the sum Catherine was proposing as rent was twice as much as she needed, but her new lodger insisted.

The house was more run-down than Catherine remembered, and once she was settled upstairs – and with Mrs Littig's permission – she attended to the employment of a daily char. An additional room behind her own bedroom was requisitioned for Felix. Again with Mrs Littig's say-so she had the whole of the top floor repainted and repapered; curtains and light fittings were replaced.

For the moment, she felt, it was the perfect solution.

*

She was introduced to Miss Euphemia Montgomery, not quite the figure she had been expecting from the name. She was roughly of an age with Leta: wraith-thin, almost wasted, dressed not in muted tweeds but a black and white zigzag print shirt and tight raspberry corduroy pants, with dyed straw hair and a Peter Pan cut. Her handshake hurt. Her eyes narrowed on the new recruit, then switched between the pair of them, her and Mr Kilpatrick. While he offered a few polite formalities, Miss Montgomery continued to make an evaluation.

The agency's latest employee hazarded a smile, but she knew herself that it was done with too little confidence; and she saw that it had made very little impression on the person it was intended for, the redoubtable Miss Montgomery.

'I shall leave you two together,' Mr Kilpatrick said.

Catherine took a deferential step backwards, hands crossed in front of her. She happened to glance at Miss Montgomery at a certain moment when her eyes were full of her employer, and she recognised the look of a helot in glad bondage. The next moment the eyes turned back to *her*; they surveyed her quite immodestly.

A hand tapped her arm. She looked round. Mr Kilpatrick was smiling encouragement at her.

'Miss Montgomery will keep you right.'

The woman nodded.

'Another pair of hands on deck. I'll show her the ropes.'

'Miss Montgomery knows the ins-and-outs. *She* keeps the business in strict order.'

'Shipshape,' the woman said.

Mr Kilpatrick nodded.

When he'd gone and pulled the door shut behind him, Miss Montgomery played on the lengthening silence like an actress of accomplishment.

'I like to run a good tight ship.'

'Yes. I see – '

'I was in the Wrens.'

'Ah.'

'Mr Kilpatrick has told you quite a bit, I expect.'

'Not really.'

Miss Montgomery smiled at her guilelessness, and at the state of affairs indicated to her.

'He's a very busy man, of course, Miss Fairweather. People feel awkward about using up too much of his time.'

'Yes. Yes, I'm sure they do.'

The reasonableness of the observation prompted nods from both women.

'I can speak in his ear, naturally. He usually has time to listen to *me*.' The cat-grey eyes blinked just once. 'I'm his contact, you see. Between his office and the young women like yourself. He hears through me, that's how he knows.'

'I see. Yes.'

Miss Montgomery stood with her hands clasped behind her back, at buttock level. She wore very low heels on her shoes, no higher than services' regulation.

'I'm his link.'

Catherine inclined her head.

'I can read his mind,' Miss Montgomery concluded with emphasis, 'like a medium.'

Mr Kilpatrick referred to photographic sessions as 'commissions'. He called his models 'ladies', never 'Les Girls'. He made them feel they were engaged in a perfectly respectable, scrupulous, even edifying line of work, one which had an authentic artistic value. He clearly saw the rôle the most successful ones might have as the vehicles of other people's dreams, and quite shrewdly understood how their commercial value – not that such a vulgar term and concept was ever used in their hearing – could be assessed accordingly.

The agency offices were furnished as a plusher version of a barrister's office or a doctor's consulting rooms. They had the same professional dignity, but were softened by the comfortable feather armchairs and high-backed sofas. There were standard lamps and side-lamps instead of centre lights, and several good watercolours of English scenes hung on the pleasantly faded panelling. Fitted carpets and thick drapes and pelmets discreetly deadened sounds. Except in summer, fires were lit in the grates, and the coals or logs prodded with heavy brass-handled pokers. A French Empire white marble and ormolu clock occupied the centre of the mantelpiece in the main reception hall. The ladies' room was prettily wallpapered; the lavatories were very regularly disinfected, and a spray of flowers was always in place beside the basins. Every one of the other models responded as she was intended to, by thinking the best of herself. Catherine, too, started to feel quite reconciled to her new calling in life.

*

She returned the fur to the Two-O-Two Restaurant, wrapped in tissue paper and packed inside a cardboard box. She included with it an anonymous note of 'explanation', that she had 'confused coats' and was extremely sorry, she hoped they would be able to trace the coat's true owner.

She thought after she'd sent it, my conscience is clear, and for the first time in twenty-five years I am embarked upon a career.

*

The Kilpatricks, father and daughter, lived in a recently built mansion block on Kensington Road.

The entrance hall of Petra rose-pink marble was surely meant to humble arrivals, Catherine felt. The arrangements of waxy white flowers in alcoves of coloured mirror put her in mind of the sober, suffocating good taste of undertakers' establishments.

A carpeted lift with bronze doors transported her in seconds up to the third floor. She was greeted by a prospect of more pink marble – the building must have consumed a quarry – and a length of salmon-coloured carpet so thick that her progress along the corridor was eerily soundless. There were no voices, no evidence of lives being decorously conducted behind the coldly shining walls.

She stopped in front of the door of Number 34. Even the doorbell when she pressed the button sounded as if it was wadded in layers of discreet wrapping; she felt she was polluting this atmosphere of luxurious quiet.

She thought she might have to ring again as she stood waiting. As she lifted her hand to push on the button she was caught in mid-motion with the door being thrown open.

'Miss Fairweather, I presume?'

Catherine recognised the chestnut hair at once, from their previous encounter. But lustrous hair apart, Harriet Kilpatrick's appearance was less auspicious on reacquaintance: severely plucked eyebrows, a thin sharp nose, narrow lips on too straight a mouth, an ominously bony chin.

She shook Catherine's hand as a social penance it seemed, even managing a disapproving little scowl as she did so; but, Catherine noted, her father had his back to them as he took over the host's rôle and closed the door. She appeared relieved when the formalities were over, although it left them with the evening ranged unpropitiously ahead of them. In the event, however, the tight-featured Harriet with her complexion's blemishes disguised by a mash of foundation was able to direct most of her remarks straight towards the rest of the company.

At the table Harriet sat between her father and herself. She was oddly impassive, weighted with jewellery and exuding ramrod-backed regality. Each course that was served to them patently presented a test of ingenuity in the eating: undressed crab, bone-riddled turbot, a cream cheese speckled with gritty pine kernels and a scooped Stilton with rare qualities of internal suction when a spoon was applied, yellow quinces that rolled round and round on the plate. Catherine was thankful to reach coffee, even though it was poured into cups of such absurd fineness she thought she could quite easily leave a bite-mark in the porcelain.

While their host was most adeptly charming all evening, Harriet sat trying to possess him like a wife. She stared at him, but her covetous alarm seemed to go unread by him. She touched him at intervals, on his elbow, his wrist, the back of his hand. She inspected his food before her own, she could finish his sentences for him. Pointedly she refused to invite one particular guest into the conversation by any of her own contriving. Her father didn't seem to see what was happening in front of his eyes, and Catherine felt some trepidation – anxiety even – on his behalf. Harriet spoke of little that didn't refer to her father; Catherine guessed that her existence truly revolved around him. She was wearing her mother's jewellery and also bijoux (she let their unwelcome guest know) which he had bought for her, her dress was jade green because he collected Chinese jade figures, her touch on his arm and hand must have smeared a veneer of perfume; her own hand still carried a trace a couple of hours after her arrival – too much perfume, not unsubtle in small measure but vulgar in excess, intended as a suffusion of her spirit on her surroundings, most notably on the man who didn't look so very much like her except in the colouring of his eyes, one blue and one green.

It was only as she was leaving, as the maid handed back the coats, that Harriet spoke to her again, taking her to one side for the purpose.

'Isn't yours the mink?'

'No. I came in this jacket. Humble gaberdine. Thank you.'

'Well, you *have* got it all sewn up, haven't you, Miss Fairweather?'

For a couple of seconds Catherine thought she must be referring to the gaberdine jacket.

'Oh. My work?'

'I expect everyone imagines it's a holiday.'

'I – I don't know. Is that what they think?'

'My father really seems to have organised things for you, hasn't he?'

'He – he's been very – helpful.'

'He overdoes it, of course. He's had a couple of scares with his heart already, did you know that?'

'No. No, I didn't.'

'He doesn't like people to know about it. So don't tell him I told you.'

'No. No, I won't.'

'He has to be careful. All the doctors said the same. Of course he isn't young.'

Catherine replied too quickly.

'But he's not – old – '

'And you're an expert about that sort of thing?'

Harriet turned away, to dispense some very blatant charm to their two guests with the highest social profiles. Catherine felt she had been put in her place. She stopped in front of a mirror to check her appearance in the jacket, and to wait for her host to come through to say his farewells. Looking behind her she caught Harriet's eyes moving off her and noticed the momentary after-effect, her mouth – those mulberry lips – bunching with undisguisable displeasure and irritation.

*

'She has a melancholy streak.'

'I'm sorry? Who has?'

'My daughter Harriet.'

'Oh.'

'You don't know what to make of her, I suppose?'

'Not really,' Catherine confessed. 'No.'

'I'm sorry. She *can* be – well, awkward.'

'I *did* try.'

'I know you did. And I'm very grateful to you.'

'But I didn't do it for that reason.'

'Your paths wouldn't have had to cross if it wasn't for me.'

'Exactly. That's the whole point. So I was very happy to come.'

'But it wasn't quite what you were expecting?'

'I don't know *what* I was expecting really.'

'What did you honestly think about her?'

'I – '

'Tell me, please – '

'Well, she *seemed* to be ignoring me. But – I'm not so sure that she was.'

'I don't expect she was. Ignoring you, that is.'

'Oh, well – '

'She – she's concerned for me, that's all.'

'That – that's good,' she said.

He didn't reply.

'Isn't it?'

'She lost her mother too young, you see.'

And I, she could have told him, and I also . . . She should have been offering Harriet her pity. But she was prevented by a sense of the vital difference in their situations. While there hadn't been an over-abundance of love between her father and herself, the currents of affection which Harriet coursed were deep and probably fast and perhaps furious.

*

My mother was always looking in mirrors. I think the action was done too critically, and sometimes too uncertainly, for mere base pride to be behind it.

In the street she would open her handbag, take out her silver and blue lacquer compact and tip back the lid to look. Walking past shop windows she inclined her head at a due angle. In the backs of cars she found the driving mirror, and in the front seat she kept watch in the side-mirror on the bonnet. She lingered in ladies' rooms. In the Bayswater flat she always consulted the dressing-table mirror before leaving the bedroom, and passing the bathroom she could look straight in from the hall and see herself reflected in the mirror over the basin.

Sometimes it seemed to me that she regarded herself with curt approval, with cautious satisfaction: but it was on account of the effect alone, for the exterior's sake, and I don't think it extended to include the full self. Her expression showed too much concern otherwise, frequently nervousness. Her little victories were never more than fleeting – mirror, mirror – and then it would be back to square one, she had to rebuild her confidence all over again from scratch.

39

Pierrette

SHE was unaware of it starting.

Then one day she noticed two of the girls exchanging nearly subliminal, very knowing looks as she was called through into Mr Kilpatrick's room.

He took pains with her, he was helpful and considerate, he never forgot to ask her how she was fitting in and settling down. It didn't occur to her there might be more to it than that until a photographer told her that, for the first time he could remember, The Big Man himself had phoned him about this job.

'I'm always afraid,' she said, 'that I'm going to make a mistake.'

'About your men?'

'What?'

'It happened once before, I think.'

'What did?'

He stared at her; then backtracked.

'That – he took such an interest in a girl's career.'

'It's because I'm new,' she said.

But she felt she was blushing under her make-up. As the photographer fussed with his equipment and the props she tried to fix her eyes on something that wouldn't move: a corner of the plaster frieze around the ceiling, gambolling Roman nymphs and shepherds in Arcadia.

She couldn't help noticing after that.

She thought it must explain Miss Montgomery's Jack Frost sharpness with her. She saw how the woman admired him, humoured him, protected him, nothing could be too much trouble.

She now felt herself more self-conscious with him than before. Simultaneously she was aware that he was changing his tack. He joked about himself, cut himself down to size; he demystified his trade, and – without any unkindness – divulged to her the human aspects of its little gods and potentates.

*

A 'Rex' above all must be dependable, she was sure. The contraction had had to be assumed with confidence in the first place, meaning to inspire as much in others.

Opportunely he put her in mind of a slightly less louche, tauter, more battered Rex Harrison. The folds over the eyes, perhaps, the corrugations on his brow, the height, even something of the famous voice – its enveloping confidentiality, that rather worldly, rather world-weary grain.

One eye blue and one green.

The faint odour of musk, like a signal. To top it all, a chemical reason – if she needed one – to convince herself that she had no possibility of holding out against him.

She was late back one evening, and he invited her out for a drink.

Another day in the office, standing near a telephone in the middle of the morning, she heard his lunch appointment being cancelled. At midday he made his move, where no one could overhear, and she found herself accepting. The restaurant was in a large hotel and apartment building near Regent's Park; their table was positioned behind glass and looked down on an indoor swimming-pool. She was charmed by the watery place, by the meal, by his company.

The following week he again invited her to lunch, this time at the weekend, and he drove her out to a hotel near Windsor and delivered her back to Bayswater.

Dinner was next. Because it was the first, he selected for them a restaurant in Hampstead, on the borderland, but gradually – with the weeks and months – they moved further into the West End, until one evening she was following the maître across the dining-room of the Ritz, to a window table with a view of the garden.

It was there that they were spotted, but Rex insisted on introductions all round, and he joked that these were the only surroundings in which to conduct business. She didn't blush; she happened to have a large buff envelope of instructions with her, placed beneath the chair, and she offered no grounds for the couple's disbelief. Unless rumours were in general circulation, and she couldn't doubt that there must be some in the process of manufacture: but in the office only Miss Montgomery was brisk, with time always pressing, while the girls seemed just as friendly as before, sharing their problems with her and spilling the beans, or telling her the chit-chat, 'this'll make you hoot, honestly, what a scream!'

*

He was about the age her father was when he died.

She couldn't think why that fact should have struck her. He didn't have her father's darkness of colouring and demeanour: but he did have an intensity in his mien – she had also seen it, carried on to another generation, in Harriet – and it must have been that which was the origin of the resemblance. There was a similar focus of concentration on her, only now its purpose wasn't to criticise and find fault, but instead to find reasons for praise and admiration, however ridiculous it sounded to her ear.

Like negative and positive, she told herself: the Aquae-Regis part of her life, with all its sacred acknowledgements to the past crowding in on their lives, and the London, which floated only on the buoyant surface of this present tense.

She knew which of them she wanted to give herself to.

As her career took off, she was unable to dissociate her good fortune from the stability of her personal life, the quiet and decorous happiness she had discovered in a city where she had once imagined it couldn't have happened.

Rex's considerateness became affection, and that strengthened to something else, uncommonly like 'love', although she had lived for so long in trepidation of the word.

The feeling was stirred in herself, but gently and not immoderately, given the events of her recent history.

She overcame her caution finally. She conquered the fear and trembling, and submitted herself to the experiment, to this assay of emotional alchemy.

*

At first she couldn't accept that anything had happened to her, even when it was suggested.

' "Happened"?'

'Having your face seen.'

She had never quite believed that it *was* her face. Beneath make-up and wearing another woman's clothes, temporarily blinded by spotlights and flashbulbs, she had always felt that what resulted bore no particular resemblance to herself. Clever make-up could restructure a face: in some shots her face was lengthened to an oval and she acquired a narrower chin than she knew she had in fact. Her hair could be lightened or darkened; it might be permed, or the perm would grow out and combs used, or in other situations she was conspicuously bouffant. She wore gloves, or her nails were painted. So long as her image was – in Mr Kilpatrick's words – as 'the sophisticate', she could be kept that person in a Fath gown or a Dior suit, or Audrey Hepburn blouse and pants. She accepted a man's gift of orchids as she coolly looked the camera directly in the lens with her hands on her hips and a bemused wry smile of self-assurance making her point. Her height and balance altered, depending on whether she was wearing heels or pumps; stockings gave her a city feel, and without them she sometimes took on an unpredictable, tomboy look which the photographers seemed equally keen on.

She was quickly gaining – so she heard from various sources – a reputation for 'professionalism'. What she guessed *that* meant was that she had the amenable, compliant, raw appearance that let the eye behind the lens impress any image upon her, and – on a minimum of directions – she would take it. Acting on the stage had involved much less conscious effort than she had imagined must be the case; in the event it hadn't been so very different from 'life', except that you spoke wholly from memory and in performance you let your face show and articulate more than you hid. Even more so in modelling, there wasn't really any deliberate skill involved, she was quite sure of that; and no 'art' either, not in the high-minded sense. It just 'happened', quite naturally to her way of thinking: if any effect achieved in a photographic studio, in the heat of lights and with a walk-around background, could be imagined as being quite 'natural'. She persuaded herself it was the life she was equipped for best, and that she hadn't the experience or the intellectual confidence or maybe just the sheer gall for anything else. She didn't think very hard about any aspect of the business, except to concentrate on holding her pose, but that was a relief to her. She didn't even consider the end product, or rather, only in an exactly factual way: was her head being held high enough or low enough not to show the hat-pin, if she were to lean an inch further forward would the shoulder line sag and give away that she was being held in by safety pins behind? But at least on these points she could ask for advice and an answer would be given her: she was never alone, nor finally 'responsible'.

She was told she had 'the fingers for gloves', which turned out to be a compliment. Her long neck 'balanced' the sweep of a broad-brimmed hat and – it transpired – was apparently the best kind to lend sparkle to drop-earrings. She accepted what she was told, that her shoulders were seen to best effect in collarless dresses, that she flattered their cut and vice versa. Her narrow waist was deemed perfect for nipped-in cocktail and evening wear and the 'H' line, and – a little later – the hooped day and beach skirts. Evidently her slim ankles helped the look of any pair of shoes she put on, heels or 'flatties'.

*

She liked to think she was socially prepared for the photographers. A few were well connected and patrician; they either liked or loathed the job, but manners and courtesy were the common ground between them and her. The others were gentlemen, for the most part, and manners again was a shared currency: she didn't suspect any mischievous intent, and since there was nothing very much about her to send up or cut down to size, it didn't happen.

One young photographer called Danny Hepple had come into 'the game' (as he called it) in a different way, by roundabout routes not referred to, and she learned to admire him for his persistence and determination when his background – or what she could guess about it – must initially have proved an obstacle. Her father would have called him a 'rough diamond' (at best) and definitely 'tradesman's entrance', but he cleaned up his language when she appeared, and she came to the conclusion that he was in private awe of her, even though he made a running joke of complaining she was 'fussy' and too good for *his* joint.

'Why do you bother with me, then? There are others. Other agencies.'

'Kilpatrick wouldn't like to hear you say that, I bet.'

'He knows the situation, I'm sure.'

'Like *you* do, you mean?'

He had the unsettling habit of saying things that would cause her to blush: because she couldn't quite be certain what he was probing to discover. Maybe he was too personable to be taking such risks with. He was good-looking in the lean, unrefined, rather pushy way she recognised from the streets, men who didn't drop their eyes when you passed them.

'I just try to get on with my job, Mr Hepple.'

He would laugh at her formality, but not in an unkind way.

'*You* shouldn't have a job.'

'Then what should I be doing?'

'Getting yourself fixed up with a proper husband. A cushy billet somewhere.'

'Then you'd need to find yourself a replacement.'

'But you said there's lots of people.'

'Quite true. And they wouldn't be as fussy as me, would they?'

'Well, sometimes a fuss is about nothing. And sometimes it isn't.'

'Ah, I see.'

'*Do* you?'

Since she'd known him his body beneath his neck had grown a little portly on success. Some days he had a red drinker's tinge to his complexion, which hadn't lost its boyishness even though his hair was prematurely flecked with grey.

She might have been bothered that his assistants tended to disappear in the later stages of a session. But he had cultivated a quite absurd (she thought) degree of respect for her. When there were just themselves, he spoke in an ungainly accent that porported to be neutral and classless; he must have heard its ineffectualness in the silences with which she frequently responded. However, she never betrayed her own knowledge of what he was about. She wanted him to believe she took him at his face value, but also had her own reserves of savvy from her past which she wouldn't discuss with him, only hint at.

They continued in the same vein, enjoying a gently ironic, strictly secondary relationship which seemed not to be leading anywhere. It was one which, in the next few years, she was to look back on with some fondness, for its meekness and a blithe innocence, remembering it (despite her best intentions not to) from a time, the jangling first years of the 1960s, when such behaviour seemed very old hat indeed.

*

The room gradually emptied, until only the two of them were left, Miss Montgomery and herself.

'Well, you *are* the apple of our eye, aren't you?'

Catherine smiled, but only with a great effort of will.

'Aren't you?'

'Am I?'

'You don't need *me* to tell you that, surely?'

'I just try to do my job.'

Miss Montgomery's habit of staring at her disconcerted Catherine every time it happened. She judged that she must rate a very low placing in the woman's popularity league. Did she think she was stealing work from the much longer-established names?

'It's a helter-skelter life, Miss Fairweather. Up and down.'

'I don't think – it'll go to my head.'

'You wouldn't be the first.'

'No. I appreciate that.'

'Do you indeed?'

Even the woman's smiles seemed sour.

'I've a lot to learn, I dare say.'

'Yes, I dare say you do.'

Anything she said to her was turned inside out and then tossed back at her.

'Patience, I suppose,' Catherine began. But she got no further.

'Oh, that's what we need, is it?'

Catherine contrived another smile, but diffidently.

'By trial and error – '

'*You* don't seem to have made many errors, not *so* far. Do you?'

'Mr Kilpatrick – '

'Oh yes, of course.' Miss Montgomery snatched a pile of papers from the top of her desk. 'Well, if you have *him* on your side – '

'But . . .'

'But what, Miss Fairweather?'

'Isn't he – on everyone's side?'

'Oh yes. Generally, that is. In *that* sense.'

Catherine started at the words.

'I – I'm sorry?'

'The knack is to do better than "generally", though. Isn't it?'

' "Better"?'

'Get the knack of – well, winding him round your little finger. Isn't that it? The trick?'

'I – I don't know.'

The pages were lined up on the desk and noisily mustered into rank.

'What's that expression? *I*'ll believe you – but dozens wouldn't.'

Which wasn't what she meant at all. She patently did *not* believe her.

Catherine realised she was reddening. She watched as Miss Montgomery opened a metal filing cabinet, deposited the papers and sent the drawer thundering shut. The key was removed from the lock and she folded her fingers over her palm, very tightly. Her smile was frugal, impenetrable.

'What lovely roses,' Catherine said, pointing to an arrangement. 'Yellow too, they're – '

No reply was forthcoming.

*

He took out a lease – renewable annually – on a small maisonette in a modern complex in Gloucester Place, only round the corner from George Street and six or seven blocks from where Leta had set herself up. It was there, not in Kensington or Knightsbridge, that they were alone together.

I am coming to know London, she thought: the real map, with its web spun of genteel deceits, infidelities, infamies.

No one knew about the flat, he told her: except his own accountant, and he hadn't an idea where it was.

'I enjoy the secrecy. Being able to disappear. Through a crack in the day. Like magic.'

She smiled, and said that she understood very well: only too well.

'Do you think less of me?' he was anxious to learn. He asked her the question several times.

' "Think less"?'

'Think I might have taken advantage of you?'

She *could* only smile her response.

'Why should I think that?'

'You told me you were an actress once.'

'Not a very good one. I needed to do something. But it's behind me.'

'For ever?'

'Don't you believe me?'

'I suppose modelling's a kind of acting – '

'Oh, *everything*'s acting,' she said, surprising herself by her own assurance. 'But – it's purer acting than most of real life.'

He nodded. Then he repeated that he loved her.

'So soon, so soon? Can you be sure?'

'I want . . .'

'You want – ?'

' . . . to protect you.'

'No one's ever said that to me before.'

She smiled again.

'Protect me from what, though?'

'London's a minefield.'

'Yes,' she said. 'Yes, it is.'

Still, after everything, she was smiling. Somehow. Don't let him ask too much, she wished: don't let me need to evade him, lie to him.

But he didn't enquire in any more detail than he had at her interview, or since.

She enjoyed the release from the past. One afternoon, though, she recognised a Surrey face from The Paddock emerging from a gentleman's club in St James's Square and she was set remembering. For days she dwelled on them, those polite but purposely impersonal encounters in the blue house, and she was at a loss to know why she couldn't put them out of her mind at this remove of months.

Watching how couples carried themselves in public convinced her more than ever that acting was an essential component of social behaviour. Away from the spotlights she and Rex didn't need to act, there were no performances, no equivalent of histrionics in the wings. Even though they didn't admit the past, or very unwillingly, nonetheless she believed they acknowledged a degree of naturalness with one another that too much theoretical posturing killed the appetite for.

Even with the fact of her son unacknowledged and even holding to the surname Fairweather, she saw that she lived more honestly with him and he with her in their retreat, and she deeply regretted any initial suspicions she may have had about his faith in her.

In the flat he didn't unwind: he kept in a state of tension, but – she tried to work it out for herself – his momentum of energy with her derived, not from the urgency of work that occupied his daylight hours, but from the dynamism set up by the antitheses in his existence: there and here, then and now, a public life and a private, the rush of others and her repose, the office's hubbub and the quiet of their rooms, the flow of life in Gloucester Place and (only yards away) their discreet elevation above it, Harriet's perpetual watchfulness and the aura of tranquillity she tried to make her own unique contribution to the 'arrangement'.

'Doesn't Harriet notice – ?'

' "Notice"?'

' – that you don't come home some nights?'

'I tell her I have business trips. And sometimes she goes away. With her friends. She'll have to settle down, but I suppose there'll be time for that.'

'She trusts you?'

'I don't really know.'

'Could she find out?'

'She's too busy being social.'

'With her friends?'

'Maybe I was too – too wishy-washy with her. I should have sent her to a convent school.'

'That might have made her *more* social, not less.'

'It keeps her occupied. For just now.'

'Won't you have to wean her off it? Later?'

'We'll see.'

'What are her friends like?'

'I've just had glimpses of them. A few anyway. A sports car with its engine turning over can make a hell of a lot of noise.'

He sighed.

Let's not talk about her now, he meant. She had sniggled him into the conversation. But Harriet weighed on her mind some days, and she didn't know why. Waiting for him in the flat, it was his daughter's presence and not his own which stalked the silence, causing her once in a while to turn sharply round as if she'd caught a well-shod foot's inopportune fall.

*

But . . .

But for all her best intentions, she found her body unwilling to yield itself. She could see the puzzlement it was causing Rex. Every time he brought her to that brink she felt herself go rigid, all her muscles tautened. It didn't owe to any lack of attraction for his body, which had aroused her curiosity from the beginning. It owed nothing, she was sure, to other people's perceptions of the relationship, as having a commercial basis. He tried all the tactics he knew of to put her at her ease, but she would not – could not – relax.

Intimacy between them was, literally, painful. She had wanted it from the outset, when it was clear that their feelings were mutual. He had courteously, diplomatically, held off, and it was she who had contrived the early occasions when they were able to draw nearer to a physical expression: not that final consummation, but closer and closer to it. When the moment did come, finally and unstoppably, it proved oddly dissatisfying to her, as much flustered and pothery as intense.

Perhaps she was too afraid of failing him. He gallantly affected not to notice: neither then nor on the next few opportunities they snatched from circumstances. Later, he was obliged to acknowledge what she felt she had no option but to confess to him – that she wasn't reciprocating as she wished to. He may have thought it was due to inexperience, but she suggested – as vaguely as she needed to – that in the past her body had functioned as she had wanted it to.

She clung closer to him after that, she shaped her body to his at every turn of their love-making. She was never done touching him in the car, even in the office when no eyes were watching she rubbed against him and made every gesture she could tactile, and always it was done to reassure him, to show him that there was no earthly reason why she should be a victim of her body's reluctance.

She was thrown back on her own mental resources to deal with this one critical, inescapable matter that was causing her such distress.

The answer (if it was) only occurred to her gradually, clearing the fog of her thoughts: but it ought to have been the obvious conclusion. That she now cared for him more than she had ever supposed she would care for anyone other than Maurice. It hadn't seemed a possibility to her that she would have to cope with. And now that it was happening, she *couldn't* cope.

She survived her days because she had a professional reputation, because it was understood that there were personal and agency 'standards' and because she needed the space of time not to have to think too hard. But when she was reduced to her own mental devices, to that predictable loop of thought, she lost her air of certitude and self-confidence which the camera lens – so Danny had conceded in his very nearly sarcastic way – always recognises and loves. She wondered if there was anything at all lovable about her or deserving love. She had a child to prove that it had happened once, but she paid Morwenna's cousin to come in and look after him on the too many occasions when she wasn't there herself. When she had left Aquae-Regis under its green thunder skies and shrouded in miasmatic dampness, it was with the sole desideratum that gave her life any significance and unity at all – her unmitigable resolve to find Maurice. But the years were washing over her, and now that she had won herself this first unlikely success of her life he seemed furthest from her. He would never become any easier to find and win back than he'd been when she rounded the corner into Salt Street and read the name 'Bluebird', illuminated in mid-air, like a finger-post leading her into a place of lucky and dangerous enchantment.

40

Miss Mayfair and the Spirit

SHE was best known as 'Miss Mayfair'.

A couturier in Grafton Street called Helmsley launched a perfume. It had been blended in a Parisian laboratory and was manufactured in a still in Lyons, but it was called 'Miss Mayfair' and promoted by the advertising agency under the banner 'The Fragrance of . . .'

'The Fragrance of . . . Arden'
'The Fragrance of . . . Spring in Park Lane'
'The Fragrance of . . . Paradise Garden'
'The Fragrance of . . . London Dawn'
'The Fragrance of . . . Lost Time'

Catherine was selected as the sole and exclusive model for the product, and photographed in various locations: Glyndebourne, Park Lane, Sissinghurst Castle's garden, Flask Lane in Hampstead, Grantchester, Ann Hathaway's Cottage.

The advertising agency took occasional risks with the image: in one advertisement during the blitz campaign Catherine was photographed in the familiar garb of a silk day-dress and fancy hat, standing on a deserted corner of the Portobello Road early one Sunday morning. The copy-lines became limper: 'The Fragrance of . . . Albion' featured 'Miss Mayfair' dressed as she always was, walking along one of the grass ramparts of an Iron Age fortress at first light, with mist curling off the fields of Dorset beneath her. 'The Fragrance of . . . Modern Woman' had her seated at a table in a restaurant with her eyes turned away from the man she was (presumably) with and looking towards the window and a parasol light. The last of the series dropped the tired slogan and quoted Wordsworth as she stood in the prow of a Thames barge in full sail –

'This City now doth like a garment wear
The beauty of the morning.'

The photograph which they used was taken at the very moment the wind lifted the hat from her head, scooping it up as if it were a flying saucer.

In addition to the advertisement work, she was involved in making promotional appearances, on Helmsley business. She 'introduced' the fragrance in a number of department-store perfumeries, in London and elsewhere. 'Miss Mayfair' was referred to in several Christmas pantomimes in 1957.

*

Miss Montgomery was typing a letter, or pretending to.

'Next thing you'll be moving to a swanky new address – '

Her voice was knife-sharp.

'I will?'

'If they turn you into a – personality.' She spoke the word with evident distaste.

'I hadn't thought – '

'Accommodation all right as it is?'

Catherine's eyes were entoiled by her. What did she know?

'They say two can live as cheaply as one.'

'Do they?'

'But of course when you're buying somewhere, that doesn't come into it. Unless you're buying together, splitting down the middle.'

Catherine edged away from her desk.

'I have no definite plans,' she said. 'About moving. Just yet. From Bayswater.'

'Some of our younger girls share. They make up couples.'

'I'm – all right.'

'You look the sort of female – ' the term was altered, not so subtly, from 'girl' ' – who can cope by herself. *Are* you?'

'I – sometimes it's a little – tiresome, I suppose.'

'I suppose *so*.'

'Do you . . .'

Miss Montgomery stopped hammering the keys and clenched the ends of the machine's roller. Her grey eyes pinked.

' – advise on those things? Recommend who . . .'

Anyone who crossed Miss Montgomery lived to regret it. From her first day Catherine had been on her toes, fearful of inadvertently causing offence.

'*Me?*' Miss Montgomery sounded incredulous, or just mocking.

'I just – wondered – '

A smile spread across the woman's face, and Catherine was mystified.

The roller was slammed back to the beginning of a new line and a bell rang.

'I mustn't keep you,' Miss Montgomery said.

The voice as it dismissed was accommodating, softly courteous. The grey eyes were attending to the sheet of paper in the machine; the ringless fingers hovered above the keys but didn't type.

Catherine picked up her bag.

'Goodnight,' she said and walked towards the door, catching a momentary glimpse in the glass of a picture frame, of Miss Montgomery's head following her from the room even as the keys rattled.

*

The Helmsley triumvirate turned their attention next to their new range of *prêt-à-porter* wear. 'Miss Mayfair' took a back seat while a second campaign was launched. Now the mottoes read 'The Spirit of . . .', specifying an abstract quality: Modernity, Tranquillity, Endeavour, Serenity, even Prosperity.

The company wanted an exclusive contract with their model, which would have precluded the possibility of Catherine Fairweather engaging in any other work. But when the agency resisted, they gave in with good grace.

As before, the photographs made use of notable locations as their backdrops. Black and white prints were ingeniously hand-tinted afterwards in an art studio. Briefly the Spirit became more famous than Mrs Exeter in her heyday.

Catherine was kept so busy in fact that she was hardly able to keep track of all the wheres and whens. The location work for the advertisements and magazines occupied days at a stretch. She was seldom left alone with her thoughts. The photographer often had a personal assistant, a magazine would send a fashion editor, she would bring her secretary, and a dresser and a make-up girl and/or hairdresser; there would also be a studio hand or two intent on engaging her in conversation.

Following Rex's and the agency accountant's advice, she put her money into bricks and mortar: the middle-floor flat of a large white house in a well-considered Kensington street. An arty Parisian décorateur-ensemblier from Heals furnished it for her. It seemed to her that she only slept there, and stored her clothes in the wardrobes, and saw Felix and the help in passing, and – she felt – that was all. The magazines piled up without her being long enough awake to read them, and sometimes she would give them to the help to take away without having opened them.

She didn't know why she worked so hard when she scarcely cared some days. It was success, but even so she believed it was chiefly owing to the others – *they* made it possible. She was the least conscious of those involved in the process. She could have gone on to *What's My Line?* and, if they hadn't recognised her face, foxed them all. But someone *would* have recognised her, that was the point, the whole bloody ridiculous point.

*

Then celebrity came upon her.

The word was used by others, Rex among them, and she had to accept that it was the correct term. But only in a very minor way, she told herself.

Her so-called 'celebrity' really had to do with the frequency with which she appeared in advertisements in magazines and (less often the case) in newspapers: it operated on a kind of arithmetical principle. Its purely functional, pragmatic, more or less scientific basis was the element she chose to regard: she no longer had any fascination to see herself – if it *was* 'her' – and she hadn't the faith left to trust in what the advertisements were saying, since the products – a hand lotion, bottled spa mineral water, a hair-drier – were often added to a shot after her own part in it was over. The advertisements were essentially the space-fillers between the articles, and their subsidisers. It was only out of that that any little renown had come to her, and she didn't think she could afford to take it too seriously.

But it did seem to alter the way in which people behaved towards 'her'. She found herself being treated with undue caution, or else being flattered. People in the business took her up at social gatherings, as if to reflect a little of what they must have imagined was her shine on to themselves; or they took her up in pursuit of some ideal 'her' which – she guessed – they didn't really want to learn the whole truth about. It was exhausting, she found, constantly having to question motives and to smile brightly at the same time.

So, in spite of all, it had come to this, in the space of not years but seasons: that, by everyone's reckoning (even her rivals'), she was the Kilpatrick Agency's star turn. She had received the technical explanation at soirées, from those who were presumed to know: she had the social confidence, even the hauteur, of the generation of models now being superseded, and she also had a mysterious quality, an evasiveness that was alloyed with a certain very discreet sensuality ('sexiness', quote), which placed her in the van of the best of the new, younger brigade.

She felt it must be best not to reflect on it, in case she were to lose the knack. But she continued to study her face in mirrors, with and without make-up: she tried to surprise the separate selves in herself.

The social confidence was a quality that didn't show when no one else was there to observe, and she certainly hadn't been conscious of 'hauteur', so she looked instead for her mystery, her evasiveness, and only saw features that were too familiar to her, fallen into impassivity and even vacuity, as if they wanted to return to what was now their natural condition, the flatness of a page in a magazine.

And 'sexiness'? '*Discreet* sexiness'? That was something else she could have no way of identifying. She hadn't intended it, but if that was how other people interpreted her, there was little she could do to counter the impression. Perhaps it had its origin in a tale, a rumour, and the story had just passed on and on in wider and wider circles, like a game of Chinese whispers. Or maybe people's reactions to attractiveness – since that was what they said she had – was to render themselves its victims? – and that, credible or not, was how they came to terms with it?

41

Night City

We moved from Lavinia Place.

The new flat was in a leafy cul-de-sac behind Kensington High Street, between Warwick and Earl's Court Roads. Very little went on in that neck of the woods, or so I could believe, and the location seemed to suit my mother very well.

We arrived at the start of a summer. We slept late and she rustled up meals from largely bare cupboards, which we ate at the kitchen table. We went for walks in Holland Park, and we looked into the windows of the shops, and we played snakes and ladders, and the time passed much, much too quickly.

Once – after I'd started at the Willow School – she took me to a pantomime, in the latter days of its run in mid-February, when some of the spirit had gone from the enterprise.

The visit was to be memorable to me because it was the first pantomime I had ever seen and the last I was to be taken to until my middle teens.

The story was 'Cinderella', more or less. My mother sat throughout paying diligent attention to the production, applauding the changes of scene and leaning forward in her seat to listen to the scripted and ad-libbed lines through the chirruping of children and the rustling of sweet papers around us.

Then something happened on our way out of the theatre. My mother was enthusing – about the costumes probably, or on some more technical point, such as the chorus's timing – when her mood instantly changed. It coincided with our preparing to step out of the vanishing warmth into a piercing easterly wind. Through the corridor windows cars were driving by their headlights and, picked up in their tracks, sleet was blowing across the street.

The spell was undone.

My mother's hand gripped mine very tightly. I looked up and saw her staring over her shoulder with her mouth and eyes suddenly tight.

After that I lost her, for maybe a minute all told. I turned in all directions before I was swept up in the movement of bodies passing through the exit doors. I couldn't make my way back in. I called out for her but my voice wouldn't carry. I found myself outside in the cold night. I was at panic point and already crying when a hand clasped my shoulder, she said something, and I was borne off towards a rank of taxis.

I remember a fuss, that we weren't waiting our turn. She bundled me into the first taxi while a musquash mother with children complained; but the woman was brushed aside with an imperious sweep of a gloved hand while the other hand rapped on the partition glass for the driver to start. As we drove off I watched her looking backwards, out of the rear window.

'Is she angry?'

She didn't hear, and I had to repeat myself.

'Is she angry?'

'Is who angry?'

'The woman.'

'Which – '

Then she remembered, the commotion at the very last moment. But that's not what had been on her mind.

She turned back round and settled on the seat. She pulled up the collar of her llama coat at the back and half her head disappeared from view.

I asked her who she had been looking at.

'Nobody,' she said, her voice almost lost.

'Or at what?'

'Nothing, Felix. Nothing.'

She didn't say it impatiently, but abstractedly. She didn't even try to stage-manage a smile. Instead she rubbed at the window glass, with the hand that had just been so dismissive. She looked out, into one wet street after another as we quickly crossed over them, the silent bisecting laterals of a mysterious night city.

*

The brothers Helmsley and their sister invited her to dinner at Wilton Crescent. Perhaps the champagne went to her head to cause her joie de vivre that evening. Someone mentioned Aquae-Regis, and she forgot herself long enough to say that that was where she had been brought up. Everything she proceeded to tell them about the town had sparkle and wit, or so she guessed from the delighted reactions of those sitting round the table. Even her voice confused her, sounding unrecognisably vivacious, with a gleeful humour in it.

Afterwards, in the drawing-room, Millicent Helmsley congratulated her on her form. She said she wished every dinner party could swing along with the same verve. (Catherine smiled through more confusion.) She told her she reminded her of one of those sparky virtuoso pieces of music that used to captivate salons in the days when those things were done.

'A bluette,' her brother Victor said from the fireplace.

'Isn't that some kind of film?' his twin Antony enquired from the sideboard of bottles.

'I think it's both,' Millicent Helmsley said. 'But Catherine *could* be in the movies, couldn't she?'

Everyone within hearing range agreed.

'But it's a splendid idea,' one of the siblings' ex-debutante friends called across from the sofa. 'A professional name for Miss Fairweather.'

'Which name?' someone else asked.

' "Bluette"?' said Millicent Helmsley, immediately assessing the potential of the sound, the 'concept'.

Her brothers each repeated the word several times. For the remainder of the evening the subject recurred. Meanwhile Catherine's luck continued to hold, and the champagne continued to do its work, and a quite serious man with Jewish features quietly told her that what was needed now was a model 'with a modern attitude'.

'All those mouthfuls of names. It isn't Debrett country: you're in a glamour profession.'

The next day the Helmsleys telephoned the agency. Rex took her off to the Dorchester for supper and brought up the matter as soon as they'd given their orders. For Catherine it was another disguise and she had no objection at all. In the ladies' room, repeating the name under her breath, she thought it did sound modern, modish, chic. And abstract: as she had realised for several years past that she was surely becoming, not by choice but by a necessity imposed on her by others. Now it was her social *raison d'être*, to be somehow a little less than herself, and an object of desire.

She tidied up her face as Claribel Cooper had instructed her and practised the word, balancing it on her tongue. She saw the letters set down in magazine newsprint. She nodded at the face in the mirror. 'Bluette. Bluette, Bluette. *Mais pourquoi pas?*'

*

And lo, it came to pass.

Beneath the photographs that appeared every so often in the society magazines, the caption would usually refer to her as '*Miss Catherine Fairweather, alias "Bluette"*'. In the newspaper gossip columns, where she merited an occasional mention, her fate was to be called, simply, '*The model Bluette*'.

She received a regular supply of invitations, and Miss Montgomery – who heard through the grapevine – would advise her which to accept, and almost always on the principle of what might be 'good for business'. Three times she watched horses thunder down a course in a spray of hoof-churned turf; twice sculls flashed past on a scintillating river and her head ached for shade. She attended one catwalk fashion show, one charity ball, and a few evenings hosted by Helmsley friends and friends of those friends who wanted a 'lively mix' of guests and whom she invariably believed herself to be secretly disappointing.

She always received solo invitations and she always arrived alone. She and Rex gave no indication to others that they had become more than, say, polite confederates in the inevitable cause of business. He had told her it was the 'safest' way for herself, to protect her career. For a short while she suspected that he lacked confidence in her social abilities, or that he was uncertain of their future. But in time she evolved another, preferable theory: that more than anything else it was the deep, covert privacy of their relationship that he appreciated, the preservation of an enigma in circles very well versed in gossip and innuendo. (Even when they were together by themselves and discussing other people it was noticeable to her that he didn't dig too deep; he maintained a reticence in respect of people's reputations which she could only hope – not too sanguinely – was reciprocated by others regarding *them*.) She offered no clues to the girls in the agency, and Rex's own sense of fair play as their employer – his declared unwillingness to espouse 'favourites', the care he took to select the most suitable of them for each assignment – didn't give anyone cause for suspicion, she was (ninety per cent) sure.

So she explained the situation to herself. The double-guise of her name – 'Catherine Hammond' alias 'Catherine Fairweather' alias 'Bluette' – confirmed to her that distancing was precisely the purpose. She still hadn't told Rex the surname she'd been born with, nor the substance of her history, but it was because of that that she felt safest with him, and truest to the person he wanted and needed her to be. He had discussed little of his past with *her*, and she didn't ask him to. It hadn't to do with lack of trust, but with the hope that, together, they might each make a new beginning, they could also define *themselves* as they wished to be and as only the other, of all their acquaintances, had an opportunity of perceiving – through affection, tenderness, kindness, devotion. Secrecy was the pledge, and she understood without the need for words.

In George Street the secrecy had been shame on her part and sexual stimulus for her demon lover, and added up to no more than a lie. In Gloucester Place, some half a mile away, their silence and shared withdrawal from the world was a strength, not a faint-hearted evasion. They were convenably courteous to one another at parties and not a good deal more, each of them fully confident in the tact of the other. The collisions and criss-crossings that occurred were always the high-points to her, like the crackle and spark of pylon wires, but subsumed by both of them into merely a startled smile, a resettling hand-touch on the other's elbow, some civil and mannerly word of apology that trailed away in a codified, expertly casual suspension . . .

*

Once she sent me to answer the front door when the bell chimes wouldn't stop ringing. I had my instructions, and repeated them to the man in the long overcoat and brown felt hat.

– She's not here.

– Where is she?

– She's gone out.

– Are you sure?

– She isn't here.

– And she's left you alone?

– What?

– You're sure you don't know where she is?

– She isn't here.

He stood deliberating for some moments: long enough for me to come close to banging the door shut on him and running to the corner of the flat furthest away from him. But he took a step or two back before I was ready for the culminating act of panic. He told me it didn't matter anyway, another time would do. Then he turned his back on me and began to walk downstairs.

I stood watching until the crown of his hat disappeared from view and all that remained of his intimidating presence was the scraping of the steel tips of his heels on the steps outside.

I suddenly felt a hand on my shoulder and nearly jumped out of my skin. I was steered back into the flat with my heart pounding in my chest. My mother closed the door, very quietly, but projecting all her weight against it. We walked back into her bedroom. She sat down at the dressing-table. 'Oh là là,' she said, and I thought they must be the words of a song. She picked up a hairbrush and started pulling it through her hair. She avoided the image of herself in the mirror; rather, her eyes flitted over the mossy green sward of carpet. At last she looked up and saw me standing in the doorway, watching her. She hesitated momentarily before she smiled.

'Thank you, Felix.'

She laid down the brush and shook out her hair. She stood up.

'Lunch,' she said, 'we must have lunch now. Do you have any ideas?'

She walked towards the door. I moved back against the wall to let her pass and didn't see until a couple of seconds too late and with that small, awkward distance between us that she had held out her hand to touch my shoulder or my arm.

She dropped the hand to her side.

'Have you any ideas? What we could have?'

I didn't. I had very little appetite.

In the kitchen I caught her glancing once through the window, to the cars down on the street. I guessed as she turned the taps on full and busied about with pots and bowls from the refrigerator and lit the gas in preparation that she was now conveniently occupied, that she didn't intend mentioning the incident which had just taken place on the landing let alone offering me an explanation for it. She didn't look again from the window but her show of busyness in the kitchen couldn't deceive me, I saw how frugal the portion of scrambled eggs she served herself was compared with mine and – affect indifference as she might – just how much water she drank to help the food's passage down her throat to her stomach.

*

When she looked back on her life, sometimes all she saw were accidents, a welter of them. At other times she perceived the accidents as belonging in a sequence, a particular order, and lying in bed at night she would find sleep at last in threading them together.

By day, travelling by taxi in the cold, factual, grainy light of drab, grimy London, she asked herself – why am I 'Bluette'? She could have been anyone, anywhere – a lawyer's wife in Norwich, a farmer's wife in Devon, a Jewish businessman's mistress in Brighton, the divorced mother of four children in Edinburgh, or a colonial widow in Nairobi. But here she was, being sped across the centre of London from the agency to an assignment and back again. Couldn't she have had some foreknowledge? Danny had told her of three months he'd spent in South America: coming upon an Andean village where an old man seated in front of his house would exactly foretell the events of the next five or six hours, to the very article. In that case, she'd puzzled, could you avoid a disaster by cancelling your plans – or would you be *drawn* to it in the effort to disprove it: if the disaster didn't happen, how could the man be said to have been correct?

Despite its melancholy, Britain – grey where it wasn't green, and damp – wasn't made for such prognostications. Those needed mountains and thunder and flash-floods and the dry, blazing heat of the sun. Here the business was only hocus-pocus, and given its place, under flimsy canvas in tatty fairground tents. But what if her country's ways were wholly misinformed?

She could have been anyone, anywhere, and here she was. She had the photograph in the newspaper on her lap for evidence – '*The model, Bluette, seen* . . .' All possibilities had been present in her from the moment of her conception, and also one especial end: everything had conspired to *this*, and the other lives had failed to happen, because – she could only hope and trust – they hadn't been allowed to. A fated bias in herself and in subsequent events, a weighting, had decreed this way and not another. In which case she couldn't help her situation being so, and the 'accidents' had to be understood as necessary elements in her story. Far from her being a piece of flotsam on history's scummy tide, she could claim that everybody with whom she had come into contact had *had* to be there: objects and situations had only been awaiting her involvement with them to be granted their own *causa causans*. Far from being engulfed by circumstances, she was in a position to reinterpret the world according to a giant, ego-centred blueprint.

There were days – and more notably nights, trying to sleep in the flat she'd bought on the proceeds of becoming a 'Spirit' – when she felt whatever was the mental equivalent of being disembodied from the past. Still her physical appearance, when she saw it in advertisements and features, seemed a different person's, when the little tricks of the trade had been applied which removed the blemishes.

A word spoken in a moment, 'Bluette', a flashy, sparkling, soonest-done piece of music: what more suitable for someone wedded in the public's eye to the present moment? Such fashions pass, the past devours them for revenge, and she couldn't be in any doubt what her future held – only forgetfulness.

Her current life was the single choice she had, until whatever would happen next happened. She could have turned her job into a joke, yet – understanding that her life was sequential but not understandable beyond that – she was aware that it merited as much seriousness devoted to it as any other aspect of her existence.

Her modest fame was pooh-poohed by the other parents at Felix's school because of its source. But it also gave her a spurious social worth in respect of what they weren't privy to – her income, how she spent her evenings, the opportunities her shoulders might have to rub up against those of the truly and deservedly famous. She knew that she couldn't let 'Bluette' go, not now: too much heft was loaded on her. 'Bluette' would eventually begin to falter under the burden, but by then events would be developing to another end. She would have the theoretical capacity of determining, road A or B or C: but where she didn't care to look, the part of her beneath the level of consciousness – the amalgam of her past and heredity in which she couldn't quite believe – was deciding. Even if she were to choose road A and then change her mind to C at the very last moment, out of sheer wilfulness, couldn't it be argued that that caprice was a profound element of her mental disposition?

So, what could she do? The answer was, absolutely nothing that would be contrary to that character. The chances were that its elements had been there from a very early age, in prime childhood. So what oh what could she do?

And invariably at that point she would fall asleep, neither Catherine nor Bluette but a mind relapsed into winged flight: as her mother had instructed her, on those ancient evenings when they'd boarded the Turkey rug and embarked on their travels, out of place and time, a journey on which they lost even the mindfulness of themselves.

42

Rumours

THE Willow School was snobbish and rudimentary. We wore blue corduroy knickerbockers and grey blazers. We were twice asked to work on a drawing of 'My Father'. I was invariably bottom of the class. I would pick on someone and find my moment to land a punch on him, or – if it was a girl – pull her hair until she screamed at me to stop. The headmistress told me I was an ungrateful little boy with much to be thankful for, but even then I could see that she didn't believe the latter words as she spoke them.

I remember my tantrums at home: luxuriating in my anger, filling the flat with howls, refusing to acknowledge reason, refusing every attempt to bribe me into good behaviour. On the evenings when my mother went out, I was left with a succession of female Argus-eyes from a domestic help agency; in the afternoons a woman called Mrs Nancy Letts would be waiting in the house to make my tea and, as happened more and more often, to get me ready for bed in my mother's absence. I would hear the taxi dropping off my mother outside half an hour or so after my official bedtime, and I knew that it was deliberate timing, because she didn't know how to handle me.

I was proud of my recently evinced devilry, and at the same time I was already bored with it. It was becoming much too much of an obligation.

*

In the morning's mail one day she received a postcard of the small clapboard-fronted town in Surrey. On one half of the obverse side was written the name – 'Miss Catherine Hammond' – and her address; on the other half appeared the single word, 'Remember', followed by a question mark.

It couldn't have been from any of the girls at The Paddock because the evening she'd arrived at Edwarde's Hotel she had signed the register using her mother's maiden name, Bradley. That was how she had introduced herself to Miss Cooper, and how she had continued during her time at the house.

She remained in the hall turning the card over and over in her hand. She forgot about breakfast, and discovered Felix standing beside her, teeth brushed and satchel packed, ready to go off to school.

She walked downstairs with him and opened the door. As usual he offered his cheek for a kiss, and as usual – as if he was tempting her to what ought not to be done – he slipped away at the first contact of her lips with his skin. She waited on the top step as the crocodile line stopped. She caught the woman leader's sly sideways glance over the top of the hedge and the quick jerk of her head backwards, to supervise the file.

She lifted her hand to wave. Felix half-raised his, as he usually did, so that it would seem neither a full acceptance nor a total rejection of *her* gesture. Then they were gone, and she was left listening to the tramp of their feet on the pavement.

When she returned upstairs she found that the postcard, which she had taken care to place picture-side up on the hall table, was now picture-side down. He must have looked, and seen the message and her name, '*Miss* Hammond', on the other side.

Aunt Dodie had instructed him in the basics, as she had insisted – that he had no grandparents and that his father was dead: a father (although Felix wasn't told) who had left not a single photograph behind him, spurned by a late grandfather in Aquae-Regis whom his own daughter found it more and more difficult to be charitable about.

He had once asked his great-aunt why she was 'Mrs Hammond' to their neighbours and teachers at school. She had taken fright and told him the reason was 'legal', then confused him by saying she had wanted to keep her old name, and doubly confused the issue by adding that his grandfather had made retaining the surname a stipulation of his will.

'Aunt Dodie said I should really be Felix Morris – '

She started. When could they have decided such a thing? She only remembered hoping for anonymity, that the question of the surname wouldn't occur to him. Wrong again.

'Yes, well . . . Don't you prefer the name you have? "Hammond"?'

'Not really.'

Forgive me; forgive me, Felix, for giving you so little when I thought the gift of life was enough. But even that, she now couldn't deny, had been selfishly done, for no one else's sake but her own, to keep the memory of a lost love from fading and so leaving her with nothing, with her innocence unreturnable.

*

She had tried to humour him when he came home that afternoon to find her in the house. But she saw it was wasted effort, done too late. She wasn't to be forgiven. And the worst of it was, she didn't feel in her heart, in all truth and honesty, that she of all people had the right and privilege to blame him.

*

Then things started disappearing: little things, but always of a very personal nature. Two pairs of cami-knickers. An underslip. An unused pair of stockings.

Millie, the cleaner, was in the last weeks of pregnancy, and she wasn't coming in. So she watched Mrs Letts until she realised that the disappearance occurred whenever the woman had a plausible alibi.

She turned her attention, with worse misgivings, to Felix. The possibility of *his* being responsible was a much more disturbing interpretation of events. He was seven, almost eight years old: a very difficult child, but only that – a child.

Other minor thefts followed, equally inexplicable to her, and all from her bedroom. A lipstick. A lace handkerchief. A pot of red nail varnish she only used very occasionally. A phial of eau-de-Cologne which one of the other girls had passed on to her. A pair of oyster-grey silk gloves.

Always from the bedroom. No money ever went missing, and no object of greater value than the gloves was removed – no harm came to her mother's silver dressing-table set or her aunt's tortoiseshell brushes or the silver and blue lacquer compact, the Sèvres plates on the sitting-room wall or the Bristol silver candlesticks on the mantelpiece, the carriage-clock in the hall. She lost a cheap bracelet of threaded coral, given to her by one of the Helmsley location crew, but all her good jewellery remained.

She watched Felix. Wouldn't he be bound to have left some evidence of his foraging? But the business was immaculately done, and she only discovered when she went to look for this or that. She asked herself every time if it was possible she had mislaid the thing. But she was orderly in her routine of putting away, and took care that she knew where items were stored, so that she could put her hands on them at a moment's notice. Absent-mindedness wasn't to blame, and she had been certain of that since the second pair of cami-knickers vanished.

The news circulated at the agency that she had been involved in a contretemps with the doorman outside Helmsley's new salon in Bruton Street; that there had been a fracas with a policeman over parking; that she had left a taxi with its meter running outside Harrods and never returned, but having foolishly told the driver all about who she was on the journey to the store.

None of it was true. Miss Montgomery nodded her head when she told her, and she saw she was willing herself to believe that no such things had happened. When she told Rex, in his office, he questioned her closely; but she knew from the moment she walked into the room that he hadn't a single doubt in his head, that the ridges on his brow were only for the idiocy of a situation that strictly wasn't one.

Some of the girls weren't so certain: three cases of wrongful supposition in a row? For others the bringers of the news were themselves deserving of suspicion, and an air of unease hung over the general office and waiting-rooms for several days.

Catherine felt knocked askew by the stories. The most dangerous phase supervened when it occurred to her that she might be cheating herself, that the tales were essentially true and she *had* been there on each occasion; only, she had wiped the recollections from her memory.

But it was Rex who shook his head at her when she voiced the fear to him in Gloucester Place, who told her she should just try to forget.

'But maybe – it might all have been too much for me, mightn't it? Maybe it's been waiting to happen – '

Again he shook his head, and told her no, it wasn't like that at all.

'What about Miss Montgomery?'

'I hear she has great faith in you.'

'She does?'

'Things will blow over. They always do.'

'But I'm innocent,' she said. 'Worse, though, I'm ignorant, I can't understand – '

But it was the crisis – as she saw it – that served to bring them even closer together, which made the feelings between them incontrovertible. She accepted his belief in her, and he insisted on hearing her say so. From Gloucester Place the situation lost its immediate menace if not its incomprehensibility; it organised itself to more manageable proportions.

'Why were you so worried?'

'For my career, I suppose.'

She knew it wasn't a wholly honest answer, but no less to herself than to him.

'*I*'m in charge of that, Catherine.'

She had him unequivocally and categorically on her side, he was telling her, and that was all she needed to know. For only the second time in her life she had won someone over to herself, evangelised them to the faith. Even poor Aunt Dodie, she'd felt of her social compromise at the time, was fulfilling family obligations rather than wholly understanding.

Now she ceased to question the conditions, in the sequestered calm of the flat in Gloucester Place; now she was ready to receive, to *accept*, and this plumb trust she found herself capable of in turn was a lesson to her. Once before she had trusted, too well maybe, but it had happened before she was twenty years old, in the feverish tinder-dry abandonment of first love; it had happened in a town where her mother had shown her how to conjure fantastic possibilities out of common-or-garden shadows on walls but had forgotten how to prepare her for the anti-climax of the shadows running greyly into dawn, the curtains having to be pulled open on a new day in the same staid, unchanging, grave town.

*

Another item of news reached the agency: that she had been seen in an amorous lunchtime clinch with a stranger outside a restaurant in Frith Street.

Rex only laughed. Catherine was dismayed.

'But – aren't you tempted to believe it – even a little bit – ?'

His laughter had a wearied edge to it, she felt. But that, she came to realise, hadn't anything to do with herself, except very accidentally.

'Not in the least.'

'Why did it happen, though?' she asked him. '*How?*'

'Mistaken identity.'

'Every time?'

'Don't turn devil's advocate on me, Catherine.'

'I'm not. But I can't understand how the confusion's come about. So often, I mean.'

'No idea at all?'

'None. Please – '

'I'm on *your* side, Catherine. Remember?'

'Unless – it's one of the others?'

'Well, it's possible. But just forget it, it'll pass.'

'Will it?'

She didn't sound hopeful on the point.

'Did you really think,' he asked, 'I could picture you necking someone before or after lunch, in the middle of Frith Street?'

'Can you be sure?'

'*Yes.*'

'It could be a double-bluff, though, couldn't it?'

'But I think not,' he said.

She sighed. But the sound was too emphatic and ungrateful sounding.

'There must be *something* in it, though. To explain – '

'Confusion,' he said. 'If someone *wants* to see you, then they will.'

She nodded. She watched him place his hand across his brow and hold it there.

'Are you all right? Rex?'

'Yes, yes.' He smiled, nodded. But when he took his hand away, he seemed paler, more harried.

'A headache,' he said. 'It was coming on this afternoon.'

'And this was probably the last thing you wanted to listen to. I'm sorry.'

'Well, we had to talk about it. And now we have.'

'And now we have to help your headache go away – '

She enjoyed how domestic their behaviour became sometimes: but not because he should be suffering any kind of pain.

She seated herself beside him on the sofa. She thought, I am older now than I have ever been in my life. I ought to be my wisest too.

She smiled, to let him know that her vulnerability had only been temporary, that when they were together no just cause or impediment on earth should be allowed to interpose between them both.

*

I told my mother that I'd seen a man.

'A man? Where?'

'Coming out of the gate. When Mrs Letts brought me back from school.'

'*Our* gate?'

I nodded my head.

'Maybe he was delivering something.'

'But he was running.'

'*This* gate?'

'Yes.'

'It must have been for upstairs.'

'Maybe.'

But the Whytes had been in Malaya for the last six months.

'What did he look like?'

Just a man in a suit, I said. Like the other men who walked along the street to go to their work. Holding his hat in his hand.

'Why was he running? Do you think?'

It was an impossible question to answer.

'Did he see you?'

'No.'

'Did Mrs Letts see him?'

I shrugged, then I shook my head.

'Oh well,' she said.

She returned to the room a couple of minutes later.

'And he was carrying a hat?'

But I was starting to lose interest.

'Where did he go, do you know?'

Pause.

'Do you know, Felix?'

She had lost me, and she saw as much. She walked over to the window. I had seemed quite sure. She couldn't explain it. Perhaps it didn't matter, but why then should I have mentioned the sighting to her?

She knew that if she were to pursue the matter, I would start to deny it. She was finding me more and more difficult to fathom. She would learn no more, except that our side-entrance of the house received mid-afternoon visitors, hatless men who made their exits on to a scrupulously respectable street at a run.

*

The telephone rang late one evening.

'You've outstayed your welcome.'

'I beg your pardon – '

'I think you heard me.'

The voice was a woman's: youngish, speaking into something, a handkerchief perhaps.

'You must have the wrong – '

'Oh no, I don't.'

Who? One of the other girls presumably.

'It's time you packed this in.'

' "Packed it in"?'

'If you know what's good for you.'

'I'm sorry – ?'

'I'm sorry for you too.'

'But I don't understand – '

'You should bow out when you're on top. Before you fall. It's a long way down.'

'But it's my living.'

'Living – dying. What's the difference?'

Which girl? A depressive?

'But – '

'Just take my advice. While that's what it is, before I have to show you. Just get the hell out – *now*.'

'Who – ?'

'This is the only warning I'm giving you.'

Catherine reached her hand out for the wall. She was cold, her stomach had shrivelled, her mouth was too dry to speak with.

The receiver went down at the other end. Catherine stared at the earpiece of hers.

How could anyone be so envious of her? It was luck, she had never believed otherwise: everybody in the business knew that, that it could desert you tomorrow. It had always seemed to her that her colleagues were very enlightened on that score; it was a knowledge that bound them – even though a moderate degree of fame and reputation had come to some and not to others.

It *had* been a living, an unexpected one. She was most afraid of disillusionment, because it was only what she had suspected all along must happen. She pictured the rooms of the agency offices, and tried to see herself behaving as before, as if nothing had happened: meeting any eyes that engaged with her own, offering no concealments in return.

She replaced the receiver on the cradle. She turned round and caught the perplexity of the figure turning round in the mirror, as if the other had very nearly lost her cue.

She glanced away, to the right, and saw Maurice's child watching her from the door of his bedroom. It took several moments to think how she should be looking for his benefit, and how to effect it. He appeared unconvinced. Worse than any bloody enigmatic mirror, she thought. Showing her nothing of what she wanted to see of Maurice: but – rather – the features of her own father, his darkness, a hint of his dourness.

She closed her eyes to shut him out, the father and grandson, Our Father, everything except the memory of Maurice, in a time when she knew she'd found love and when her life had been crop-full, bough-dipping with promise like the sweetest fruit.

A number of the girls started to see her in places where she knew, was almost certain, that she hadn't been.

'But it must've been you.'

'No.'

'I was *sure* it was.' And they would tell her what she'd been wearing.

'It really wasn't me,' she would assure them, without – she could hear for herself – sounding very positive about it.

'Oh well . . .'

But the sightings persisted, and she sensed there was a presumption that she was trying to keep some of her movements a secret to herself.

*

'I don't think London's right for me,' she told Rex at the flat. 'Or rather, I'm not right for it.'

He stared at her.

'It's getting very confusing,' she said.

'What's brought this on?'

'Nothing. In particular – '

'It – it's not because of us?' he asked her

She shook her head.

'Why then? For God's sake, Catherine – '

He sounded quite incredulous.

'I know it must sound stupid – '

'Has something happened?'

She looked away.

'Has something happened, Catherine? That I don't know about? You've got to tell me.'

'Somewhere quieter,' she said, 'might be better for me.'

He lit a cigarette.

'Brighton?' he suggested, in all seriousness. 'We'll go down there. There's the Brighton Belle, that'll – '

'I don't know.'

'Just say where, Catherine. Anywhere. Best if it's convenient for – '

'This way of life, I mean.'

'What?'

'Modelling.'

'But, Catherine – '

'I've been thinking – '

'Give it up, you mean?'

'I suppose so.'

'We have to discuss this, Catherine. Seriously – '

They did discuss it. By mutual consent the business was left in the air for a while. Nothing was being solved, she knew. But at least she had told him, and she was glad on that account.

The sightings stopped for a while. She spent more time with Rex, because his trips away were fewer and Harriet had gone off somewhere with a posse of her smart friends, the ones who skied and drove speedboats. So temporarily she became almost reconciled, London didn't seem so bad, and there was the equivalent of a St Luke's little summer of good behaviour at home, and no more hat-carrying visitors were spotted in Caerphilly Gardens.

Then she started to see herself.

The first time was in Liberty's, when she turned round sharply, remembering something she'd forgotten, and found she was looking at herself running ahead up the stairs. The camel coat was belted like the one she'd decided not to wear today, and the headscarf was a Hermès pattern of barouches which Rex had given her on her birthday. She was sufficiently aware of the resemblance to stop on the staircase between treads and to almost trip forward on to her hands and knees. She did steady herself, in very ungainly fashion, and she caught the expressions on other shoppers' faces, imputing her of being tipsy in the middle of an afternoon.

The second time she was in the viewing rooms of the Royal Academy, at an exhibition titled 'The Romans in Britain'.

In fact, it had started to rain as she walked back from the Mayfair Hotel, where she had gone to meet a shoe manufacturer who thought she might have 'the right image' for his company's products; one of the agency chaperones had been in attendance, and when she'd said goodbye to the pair at the doors after the official eyeing over she had felt the attention of the northern cordwainer's eyes like a tangible caress as they followed her departure up Berkeley Street.

On Piccadilly a photograph of the emperors at Aquae-Regis had lured her under the Academy arches, and she had been walking round the glassed exhibits somewhat desultorily, her mind half on the slightly dated (if expensive) lines of shoes that the factory produced up in Halifax and half on her not very placid, not very consoling memories of the Romans' Aquae-Regis.

She stopped at a case containing an incomplete square of mosaic work, showing the head and shoulders of a rather unconvincing 'mountain tiger' in a snowy Alpine landscape. The accompanying card postulated that this might be one of the very first instances of landscape art in human history, but her mind was already wandering off at a tangent.

She looked up and saw a pair of oyster-grey silk gloves like the ones she'd lost from her bedroom, moving off the glass on the opposite side of the case. Her own reflection obscured her view as she tried to follow the woman's getaway. She pushed past the people crowded round the next case. She raised herself on tiptoe to see better and in an instant recognised the Helmsley silk duster coat from the 'Spirit of Edwardiana' shot where she'd been walking between a dog-cart with venerable driver and an early Rolls-Royce with handsome chauffeur, vanward of a Lutyens house occupying centre-stage of the sylvan prospect. The coat billowed behind the woman, as hers had done – thanks to a propeller fan – in the advertisements. The arms were held out to avoid collisions as the woman fled from the room.

The coincidental fabric of the coat plus the precise greyness of the grey gloves (the Paddock girls had presented her with them among their leaving presents) aroused saturnine suspicions in her which she later found herself afraid to consider, because no explanation – none whatsoever – had occurred to her.

The third time she was in the lower-ground-floor restaurant of Simpson's, famished.

She had just been shown to her table when she looked across the room and saw the disappearing back of a luxurious mink coat. What reminded her of the coat she'd worn to the interview were the accessories – the olive-green velvet artist's beret just like her own, and the thin clutch-bag of black kid so similar to one she'd bought on the Petherick account at Derry and Toms as a little revenge for some slight, not telling him and (to her surprise) hearing nothing about it when the itemised bill arrived in the post. A customer entering held the door open and the woman made a swift, unimpeded exit.

Catherine rose halfway from her chair, as if impelled to set off in pursuit but lacking the courage. She dropped back on to the seat. She felt her appetite deserting her. It *couldn't* be coincidence, she told herself, not again: another sighting just long enough to stagger her, to take the wind out of her sails, to give her more troubled nights. It was the insomnia that finished her, as the searchlight of memory shone into the darkest corners to prove that they too were unforgotten and nothing in her life was lived beyond.

*

When she needed calm to think, I gave her none. With her old assurances gone, I offered none in their place.

Those were my hooligan, hoodlum days. At seven years old I was the self-proclaimed terror of my class at the Willow School. The crocodile line in the morning turned anxious eyes towards the house; I knew they hoped I might take ill, so that was the reason why I never did. I had no friends among the children in the houses round about, and they were too timid, or too nicely brought up, to gang up against me, as I deserved. I was cock o' the walk, the scourge of our photogenic, pleasant-mannered corner of Kensington, and nobody dared come too close to me. I must have sent my mother to her wits' ends, to think what she might do with me.

*

Then the sightings ceased.

She thought that she must have been mistaken, or at any rate confused: because at some level of her consciousness she had been thinking of the clothes, she had willed them into apparent existence. Also, there was Felix's behaviour at home, the guilt she still suffered at not revealing to Rex all about herself that she could . . .

She managed to forget the previous coincidences long enough not to demand further resemblances in whichever corner of London she found herself. She negotiated staircases and sat down to light lunches with no more than the minimal attention required by the act.

Until, that is, the fourth – and most daring – sighting occurred.

As before it occurred in a public place.

She had gone to a hotel in Knightsbridge for tea with Victor Helmsley. From there she might have thrown a stone – with Samson strength admittedly – and it would have plummeted down on Wilton Street, which made her suspect he had reasons for not inviting her to the family home: the most significant being, she supposed without vanity, that he found himself attracted to her.

The old-fashioned hotel – reminiscent of the Duke of Buckingham of long ago – was a popular place of rendezvous of an afternoon. Two lounges were in operation: upstairs, an airy L-shaped one of citrus lime and lemon fabrics, and a darker, eccentrically melodramatic one on the ground floor, hung with tapestries and furnished with massive, scroll-ended sofas and wing chairs of Gothic proportions. Not surprisingly she found him in the latter, among the coral-shaded lamps and Constance Spry flower arrangements.

They were served tea – she had politely begged to differ, choosing Lapsang when he suggested Orange Pekoe for them both – and a selection of dainty comestibles. She wasn't in the least hungry, and when he lifted the stand and offered it to her she picked the most meagre-looking of the doll's-house-bite sandwiches. He protested, of course, but she charmed him with a smile that would have cleared the trees of the birds in Cadogan Gardens.

She was sipping her second cup of tea – she didn't much care for its smokiness, but she had selected on a principle of choosing differently from him – when her eye was caught by a figure twenty or thirty yards away on the staircase. She recognised the wide, fondant green straw hat which she'd been photographed wearing last season for the first *Vogue* cover of her career. She also recognised – immediately, from the belt and the sleeves – the spotted chiffon dress from an earlier year: the photograph of herself in the dress had appeared in a Susan Small promotion.

She replaced her cup in the saucer and rose from her chair.

Victor Helmsley got to his feet beside her.

'You've seen someone you know?'

The woman, taken by surprise, saw them both; caught between steps, she reached out for the banister. Catherine stepped forward. She dropped her napkin on to the sofa and, as the woman turned on the staircase to return the way she'd come, set off in pursuit.

Running was taboo, but she was damned if she was going to lose her prey this time. Guilt had been written all over her, in (expensive) basket-weave and polka dots.

She flew after her, up to the mezzanine, and then up a curving flight of stairs to the second lounge. She couldn't catch her. She called after her twice, 'Stop!', in vain.

Guests and staff alike looked startled as one and then the other ran across the room, dodging the tables and trolleys, and out into a corridor. Two sets of heels stabbed into the parquet. Catherine nearly slithered at the corner, and in the few seconds it took her to recover her balance, holding on to the wall, the woman had pushed open the door marked 'Ladies' and disappeared from view.

Catherine dashed in after her. One of the three cubicle doors was closed. She stood in front of it for several moments before she lifted her arm and rapped with her knuckles. There was no reply. She knocked a second time. Again no voice answered. She listened for any sounds behind the door but couldn't hear anything. She stared at the plate indicating 'Engaged'. There was no space above or beneath the close-fitting door to try to see over or under.

Several women came in at various points; she had to busy herself at the basins, but didn't take her eyes off the cubicle door's reflection in the mirror. After quarter of an hour a member of staff entered. Catherine invented an explanation. The woman knocked, shouted several questions: 'Are you all right, madam?' 'Do you need help?' There were no replies.

A handyman was summoned; he removed the handle, undid some further screws, and working with simple pliers and wire succeeded in holding open the lock.

The manager's secretary, as she had introduced herself, took responsibility for pushing the door back and looking in first. Catherine looked past her. The cubicle was empty. Behind and above the cistern a window of frosted glass gaped open. Outside was a fire-escape. Even in the deep well of the building the traffic of Knightsbridge blared and stunned, raising Cain.

*

She took it out on Felix, and – sometimes – on Mrs Letts or any help they had in the house.

She heard herself and she hated herself for it, but she couldn't cope with domestic crises on top of the persistent mental shocks. With Rex away, her insomnia was back with a vengeance.

She would look into Felix's bedroom when he was asleep – or pretending to be asleep – and wonder how he was bound to remember her. The command of memory, greater than a person's will, frightened her, and she recognised its inscrutable workings in the intensity his eyes often showed. She hoped for charity, although she didn't believe she deserved it: he was Maurice's child and her own, conceived in passion and gestated with love and gratitude and then fear and foreboding.

43

Champagne and Roses

At the agency party Miss Montgomery refilled their two glasses from the champagne bottle.

'I'm no oil painting,' she said. 'With the girls around, it couldn't be more obvious.'

Catherine looked down at her glass.

'Well, Miss Fairweather, that's just how it is.'

'You – you mustn't think – '

'I'm not fishing, honestly.'

Catherine smiled again, but tentatively.

'I've never pulled the wool over anyone's eyes. Least of all my own.'

To Catherine she sounded quite far gone, well into her cups.

'I don't think one should beat about the bush. Do you?'

Catherine responded with a mumbled 'no', and watched the lip of the bottle deliver into both their glasses.

'In private, I mean. In business there's appearances to be kept up. I hope I can talk to you like this – Catherine, may I call you?'

'Oh – yes. Yes.'

'Helps to put everything on a more intimate footing.'

'Yes,' Catherine repeated.

'I felt things had gone on long enough in the old way. Didn't you think so too?'

Miss Montgomery lowered herself on to the chair next to Catherine's and drew it a few inches closer. Now their knees were almost touching.

The older woman leaned forward, with a smile hung from cheek to cheek.

'Haven't you guessed, Catherine?'

' "Guessed"?'

'Yes.'

'I'm sorry. Guessed what?'

'That you're the reason I put up with it.'

'I – I beg your pardon.'

The woman was in earnest mid-flow. Her cheeks were burning red.

'I couldn't stand it otherwise. The indignity. I hate the job. I was all ready to hand in my notice – I'd written it out in my head – when the door opened that day and in you walked.'

Catherine stared at her.

'*Me?*'

'Yes. Yes, of course. I've tried to involve myself in everything you've done.'

Catherine continued to stare at her.

'I've wanted to share in it, have a part. Even if – ' the woman's brow furrowed with a terrible possibility ' – even if *you* haven't seen, quite – '

Catherine still stared.

' – why – why I should want to.'

The deepest furrows faded on Miss Montgomery's brow, the skin eased.

'But you *must* have guessed?'

Catherine was grappling with a Gordian knot of recollected moments.

'*Didn't* you?'

'Not – not especially.'

Miss Montgomery's face was poised between reactions; the frowns reappeared on her brow. For a second or two her mouth hesitated, pulling on air. Then the corners were stretched back, far into her cheeks, and her lips opened wide to show two rows of unrealistically regular, porcelain-white teeth. Laughter rumbled up from the pit of her stomach. Catherine noticed the bluish tint on the back of her tongue and looked away, lowering her eyes to her hands crossed on her lap.

'Maybe – ' Catherine swallowed ' – maybe I should be getting back now.'

'Oh my God – ' now Miss Montgomery sounded in abject distress ' – you really *didn't* know, did you?'

' "Know"?' Catherine repeated, simulating casualness.

'What I was thinking. How I was feeling.'

Catherine didn't raise her eyes higher than the woman's neck. She heard a determined intake of breath.

'When you walked into the office, you see – I presumed – '

Catherine shook her head.

'Of course,' Miss Montgomery said, 'I had my job to perform. But – you must've seen through all that?'

In the silence Catherine sat listening to the voices in the other rooms, the ebb and flow of cocktail-party talk and the bright, shiny, trilling laughter. That was where she ought to have been, with the company.

She looked again. The eyes – curiously sad and scavenging at the same time – settled on her shoulder, the sleeve of her dress, then inched towards her breasts.

'Only another woman understands, Catherine. Understanding should mean nothing is ever hidden – '

Catherine stood up. She realised that her wrist was about to be taken hold of and she snatched her arm away as she stepped back.

'I think – I should be mixing,' she said. She heard her breathlessness. She nodded across the room to the door. She felt immobilised.

'Most people have no insight – no poetry in their souls.'

Miss Montgomery jumped to her feet. Catherine couldn't turn away quickly enough and felt two hands on her waist.

The contact electrified her. With her own hands she pushed down on the woman's forearms.

'Please – '

Miss Montgomery seemed not to be expecting the reaction, or the full force of it, and she was knocked off-balance. Catherine jumped back. Her assailant fell against the high wing of the chair.

'I – I *have* to go now – '

'*No!*'

The flank of the chair should have prevented Miss Montgomery from falling further. But she went down, with a crash of joints, on to her knees and the flats of her hands, and Catherine felt the floorboards shudder beneath the carpet.

For a few seconds the woman's face steeled itself to the physical pain. Still on all fours, she looked up and bared her teeth in a smile.

Catherine was aghast. She saw the distance still left before she could reach the door and she shook her head.

'Tell me – what else do you want, Catherine – ?'

'No. No, please – '

'Do you want me to beg?'

Catherine shook her head with her eyes closed.

'No,' she said, but more quietly. 'No.'

She felt the pressure shifting on the floorboards. She opened her eyes again and saw Miss Montgomery crawling towards her. Her skirt was rucked up and a shoe had fallen off.

'This is best, Catherine – '

But she didn't stay to hear the rest, words that floated behind her as she ducked round the other side of the chair and ran for the door, past an outstretched arm and deviant hand. Words like '*pure*', '*blessing*', and – very worst of all – '*love*'.

*

The next week she was at home when a giant bouquet of roses was delivered to the front door. Yellow roses; she counted fifty of them.

She was delighted, enchanted.

Felix seemed decidedly unimpressed when he saw them on his return from school.

'But they're beautiful, Felix!'

She couldn't understand his reaction, or the lack of one.

'Don't you think they are?'

He didn't speak. He stared at them as if they came unbidden into the house as intruders, stealth meriting hostility.

She came back in the evening to find the roses decapitated. Every single one of them.

The carnage of blossoms covered the carpet, a deep drift of petals.

Mrs Letts was wringing her hands. She'd talked to the au pair downstairs after they'd come back from school. Felix had gone ahead and discovered the mess.

'"Discovered" it? Don't be ridiculous – '

Felix was hauled out of his bed and dragged through to the sitting-room.

'Explain this! *Explain* this to me!'

He told her that he'd just walked into the sitting-room and seen – he pointed to the floor –

She slapped his cheek, even with Mrs Letts watching.

'Don't lie to me!'

'I didn't do it,' he said. 'I didn't – '

'That means you *did*.'

He was crying. She took her hand to the top of his head.

He started to scream, but even then she didn't stop. Mrs Letts had to intervene. She wanted to strike her too, she wanted to lash out at everything in sight.

She ended up on the floor beside the outlandish and pitiful froth of yellow, in tears. Her sobs drowned those of her son and any words of comfort Mrs Letts could find to speak to her.

She had to put a brave face on it and conceal the horror from him.

'I loved the roses,' she said gaily.

Rex looked puzzled.

'Did you think,' she asked him, 'I was never going to say?'

'"The roses"?' he repeated.

'Yes, the yellow roses.'

She was smiling when she realised he really didn't know what she was talking about.

'I wish I had,' he said. 'Sent them.'

'They weren't from you?'

'You must have another admirer, Catherine. Does this mean I have to be jealous?'

When she awoke the next morning she had a picture in her mind's eye of Euphemia Montgomery telephoning the florists's when she couldn't contain her romantic flight of fancy any longer.

'No,' she said when he rang her. 'You don't need to be jealous.'

'So you *do* know who they were from?'

'An unsuitable admirer,' she said.

'I'm very glad to hear it.'

Another fifty roses arrived in the late afternoon as she was packing for a Helmsley shoot. This time they were all red. The message on the card that accompanied them read, 'I should have thought. Please forgive me, Rex.'

She was frightened for their safety in a house where none of the room doors had keys. She explained to Felix that the roses had to do with her work, and no harm must come to these ones. He responded with predictable sullenness, but she spoke in an urgent tone of voice.

'If anything happens to these,' she said, 'I'll be out of a job.'

Afterwards she failed to explain to him why they didn't leave the house but stayed there, for more than a fortnight. He didn't mention them; she never saw him look at them, not once. A calm, she thought, a truce; but only achieved by violence and by deceit.

44

Gloucester Place

ONE afternoon she went to the flat in Gloucester Place to wait. It grew dark. After seven o'clock she glanced at her watch every few minutes. He didn't telephone her.

The office would be closed. Had he forgotten to tell her he was meeting someone, a colleague? – but nothing like that ever slipped his mind.

She stared at the window, to watch for a taxi. It was as she kept guard that she noticed the Austin Healey sports car parked on the other side of the street, directly opposite the entrance to the building. A young woman sat behind the wheel looking straight across.

Taking a step back into the unlit room Catherine watched, until the face was somehow detached from the reflections of light and traffic on the glass. The features slowly collected themselves, and she stared – starting on her feet – when she recognised who they belonged to.

'It *was* Harriet?' she asked him.

'Yes. Yes, it was Harriet.'

'How did she find out?'

'I don't know,' he said. 'I just don't know.'

'How long was she out there?'

'The taxi got me here at ten to seven. I just happened to spot her. I couldn't believe it.'

'Where did you go?'

'The pub at the corner. But there was no phone to call you from, and the one in the box I *did* try wasn't working. Anyway, if you hadn't found out – '

'You wouldn't have told me?'

'We could have arranged somewhere else. A hotel.'

'No,' she said.

'It's only giving you worry. A headache – '

'But I *need* to know.'

'She – she's always been – jealous, I suppose. When she was seven or eight, I was going to marry again. But she got so jealous of Judith, and frightened her off in the end. I thought she must have disliked her because of her loyalty to her mother, but it was quite the opposite. I found out she'd made all these drawings – of Judith – and that's what she'd rechristened her doll. But when I learned that, it was too late to do anything. And it just went on, with her jealousy getting worse for any woman she thought I might be interested in. Oh, she *pretends* it's for her mother's sake, but she can't really remember her. She found out she never really got better after her birth – it was traumatic, and Louisa wasn't very strong even before it – and maybe she has some guilt notion about it. It's possible, do you think?'

'About her mother?'

'Assisting in her death. Because she gave her all those hours of pain.'

'It could be, yes. "Poor Harriet," I suppose I should say.'

'But you can't?'

'We mustn't,' she heard herself say, 'let ourselves be – pressurised. Dictated to.'

'No. No, you're right.'

But Harriet was on their minds, she knew, even as they refused to mention her, pretending to one another that she was confined to the shadows cast by the white sodium of Gloucester Place through their windows.

After that the sex became better and better.

She started to consider if it might not be the case that he loved her in inverse proportion to his daughter's disapproval of her. Which wasn't to say that his love wasn't wholly true and unselfish: but perhaps its major impetus came from the history of his life with Harriet, which was akin to the Dark Ages for all that she could know about it. And she felt determined to prove to herself and to Rex that what she provided him with greatly exceeded Harriet's limited comprehension of it.

In the night they belonged to each other and the phone calls that had already disturbed them four or five times, and which had gone unanswered, couldn't and wouldn't unmake the trust of lovers between them. Harriet might be eating her heart out, but she would never find them both in the places they reached to.

*

They had gone to bed just after eleven o'clock. By half past one or so they were ready for sleep.

He turned over on his side while she lay on her back listening to the breath swelling his body.

Knowing he was drifting off, or possibly asleep already, didn't stop her speaking softly. His brain, she thought, would somehow *know*: the words would penetrate however they would. She told him that she loved him, that it had been a perfect place to come to, that she hadn't been so happy for a very long time. She only wished she was able to offer back to him in equal part. But maybe she would learn, she might be taught how . . .

She woke much later with stirring beside her, words in her head, her name repeated several times, a gasp. It seemed to be time repeating itself, the interval between going to bed and feeling sleep trickling into her like sand, filling her limbs where they'd lain sapped between the sheets. She probably didn't wake for several minutes, not fully, hearing the vague disturbance but only sensing the comfort of his presence beside her.

What stirred her to consciousness was the touch of his hand on her left breast. She murmured softly, presuming, and expanding her mouth to a wide, mellow smile of welcome. She remembered the final words spoken before sleep. She murmured again, then opened her eyes as breath exploded out of him with a pistol crack. His face was over hers. For a split second she saw a helpless confusion and a terrible rage to live battling on it, distorting his features. It passed in almost no time at all and the full weight of him landed on top of her. The rest of the breath left in him oozed out on to her shoulder and into her ear. After that she knew – knew incontrovertibly, from the earlier passing over of her aunt – that no breath remained.

She lay beneath him, pinned to the mattress, but her panic subsided. She was merely alone with a dead man.

She *knew* that he was dead. She knew that there was nothing to be done.

It took her several minutes of straining but finally she did extricate herself. She slid off the mattress and let her own weight drop on to the floor, on to her bottom.

When she got to her feet, she walked through to the bathroom, but struggling a little with her balance. She perched on the cold edge of the bath.

She didn't think she would, *could* cry. Not that she hadn't felt the deepest affection for him; 'loved' him indeed, which was the most difficult achievement of all. But she had never foreseen a future, a possible and specific life for her or for him or for both of them. She had never imagined that far ahead in their two and a half years together.

She hadn't (she supposed) any expectations of grieving for their loss. So she didn't believe she could really be anything very much other than dry-eyed. And of course she now had to be practical, to think straight.

Think straight, think straight. She stood up. She walked back through to the sitting-room, switched on a couple of lamps. She paused at the entrance to the bedroom. She decided she wouldn't look at him, lying face-down with his back and shoulders bare.

She dressed, not too quickly and taking care with all the hooks and buttons. She took care also that she didn't tread too heavily, and opened and closed the drawers and wardrobe doors as quietly as she could while she repacked her suitcase.

She collected what she'd brought with her and placed everything that was hers on the little sofa in the sitting-room. It didn't amount to so much.

She looked at her watch. In a couple of minutes it would be half past three. Too early for the alpenglow.

She picked up her hat and tried various angles on her head. She settled on turning down the brim and then gave the whole thing a decided tilt to starboard, so that the right side of her face was partially obscured.

She tarried in front of the mirror in the vestibule. She delayed again as she turned away and looked down at her feet in her shoes, caught in mid-stride.

It was now or never: she could do the thing which was the most daring possible.

She opened the door, and let it shut behind her, pausing with her back turned to it until she'd heard the lock bite. She walked along the corridor to the lift and pressed the button. She watched through the bars as the cables jumped, then pulled on the wheels and pulleys.

When she reached home and had – very quietly – shut the door behind her, she was shaking uncontrollably.

She took off her shoes. Keeping a check that Mrs Letts' and Felix's doors stayed shut she paced the rooms in her stocking soles for a couple of hours, holding her hands to her cheeks or combing her fingers back through her hair.

She didn't disentangle from the fact of his death her own involvement with it. Her panic, her cowardice, her disavowal of the situation. Countless times she shamed herself to think how she hadn't been able to behave better than an instinct in the crucial moments had caused her to. And with such clear-thinking casualness. She continually relived the death and her flight, until she was left blinking through tears, trying to remember where she was now. Here, home, but it was nowhere.

In the middle of the morning, when Mrs Letts had gone, she telephoned the caretaker at Gloucester Place. She explained that she'd called Mr Kilpatrick's number a dozen times, but couldn't get an answer. The man was aware of their intimacy, she was sure, but his flat was at the back of the building and he wasn't able to keep a watch on nocturnal movements.

He rang back, to tell her he couldn't get a reply either.

'He's definitely there,' she said. 'Please – could you use a key?'

'But – '

'*Please* . . .' she said.

He did use the key, but – what he didn't tell her at the time – his conscientiousness compelled him to summon the constable who walked that portion of Gloucester Place on his beat. Together they discovered the body.

He rang back with the tragic news, that Mr Kilpatrick was lying dead in his bed, cold to the world.

She listened, and she really did cry at the simplicity and finality of the man's words, and tried to speak herself but couldn't.

The police called in on her, but only after they'd been to Knightsbridge and the agency, some time in the late afternoon. They found her collected and coherent – and, she could only hope, plausible – in her half-truths and evasions. She had to say that she knew the flat (a little), and was – had been – an occasional visitor there. She was handed a leather pocket address book with the name 'Catherine Fairweather' and her address written inside the front cover; she felt herself reddening dangerously as she took it from them. She divined what was on their minds – that she'd gone round there a few times for a bit of malarkey and how's-your-father – and she left them with their complacently sexist thesis intact.

Her mind dwelled more and more on Harriet hysterical in Knightsbridge, that day and the next.

Only *she* would have been capable of guessing; she couldn't have known positively, but she bore her father's mistress enough accumulated resentment to draw the most stigmatising of conclusions.

Over the next forty-eight hours Catherine was on tenterhooks waiting for the telephone to ring. But only Miss Montgomery called. They discussed Rex as if he were still alive, and she told his right-hand help that she had once supposed her to be infatuated with him.

'That's really what you thought?'

'Yes. Yes, I did.'

'If I'd known that then . . .'

With silence restored to the flat she started to think again of Harriet. She must have spent a total of several solid hours in deliberation before deciding she wouldn't ring, that she simply hadn't the pluck, the guts it would take, to hear her sympathy being returned with another sterner sort of silence or the first cryptic criminations.

*

In her dreams he is still inside her, she holds him anchored, she doesn't let him go. But he is only a mote on the horizon, she stares into his eyes and she cannot find him. He has fallen on top of her and she lies just so, looking past his shoulder up to the ceiling, but there is nothing. He is still inside her, swollen and wet; a few seconds later she feels the last delayed spasm of life trickling into her womb. Infecting her, she knows, with its subterfuge and paradoxical purpose, with the simultaneous seed of death.

45

Despatches

On the evening before the funeral, needing something to do, she found the small valise with her aunt's papers. A South African bank and a firm of brokers had each written to her three times over the year requiring information.

She found the letters just beneath the top surface, tied into a little sheaf with a length of discoloured wool. She had forgotten the appearance of her mother's handwriting and was puzzled for several seconds until she recognised it with a shudder over her heart.

She laid the letters, five of them, flat and smooth on top of the table in the dining-room of the flat which her mother's daughter's modern and flibbertigibbet success had brought her.

4-v-30

My Dear Dodie,

What if *you* were to talk to Hector? Maybe you could dissuade him and he wouldn't have to really know the reason. If you were to say you had suspicions, that you weren't sure, and he should give himself some more time. If he had time to think about it, then the situation could just drift for a while . . .

12-v-30

My Dear Dodie,

I asked you just because I thought it *would* be for the best. I'm positive it would be. If it gave us a little more time, which is what I was hoping. You wouldn't need to speak untruths as such – just to tell Hector he should take a while longer to make up his mind, and he should think everything through very very carefully. He would listen to you, I'm certain of it. Sisters and brothers can say these things to each other. And it would be doing exactly what I hoped you might be able to, so everyone would be best pleased, in the end. Do you see that?

27-v-30

My Dear Dodie,

Well, I'm very grateful that you tried. I'm sure it had to be done. I didn't believe that Hector really *was* so certain as you tell me. Or maybe he likes to believe his mind can't be changed? Some men are very proud about that, I think.

I don't know what to do now. *You've* done what you felt you could – I quite understand that, Dodie . . .

21-vii-30

Dearest Dodie,

I think I've made a mistake, a terrible mistake, but I don't know how to tell Hector. I don't know who to talk to, and maybe it shouldn't be to his closest relation – *you*, Dodie. I think you know I'm wrong, don't you? – to have gone ahead and tied this impossible knot. I haven't led Hector on, I truly don't think so, not at all. Perhaps it will seem that way to him and that is what he will believe. I want to save him from everything that will hurt him . . .

5-viii-30

My Dearest Dodie,

It's not that I *didn't* care for him – I do, very much. It's because I care for him that I think he has to be told, or warned off me in some way, and must be made to care for *me* less.

At any rate he *is* attracted to me, I know that. It frightens me a little to think he might not be thinking as clearly as he should. You told me once that he doesn't let his feelings run away with him, but I wonder if they haven't this time.

Is this really not a case of the head being ruled by the wayward heart?

You even smiled when I talked about his 'heart', but it's true enough surely, for him just as much as it would be for anyone else. (I'm not flattering *myself*, am I, giving myself grander airs than I should? Oh good God forbid –)

She couldn't decide, but in the end she did go to the funeral, arriving late.

She noticed the agency girls, guarded by Miss Montgomery, seated in two pews beneath a particularly dramatic fall of green and golden light through stained glass. Heads were turning in the congregation to view them, these wares on display, who now found themselves on the open commercial market, since it was inevitable – unless Harriet rallied herself and showed an interest – that the company would be taken over.

She was far enough away from the lectern to be unable to hear most of what was said, so the service was less affecting than it might have been, and she remained composed. Heads kept turning to look at *her* too, to gauge a professional price, but she remained – appearance-wise – oblivious. As the voices sang, pitching hesitantly at the unfamiliar hymn tunes a second or two after the organist, she tried to persuade herself that she had been a positive element in Rex's life, a benefit, and that he had been a happier man for having met her.

When the service was over, they waited in their places for the principal mourners to pass down the aisle. She stared in shock as Harriet approached. *En grande tenue*, she was enveloped by a mink coat like the one presented into her arms at the cloakroom counter in the Two-O-Two: it had the same high ruff collar at the back and reached to just below mid-calf. On her head she wore an imitation – if it was – of the stark black and white cartwheel straw hat with the veil held by a scarf tied and knotted at the neck: how she had appeared in the Helmsley shot taken on the Clifton Suspension Bridge as the 'Spirit of Invention'.

The heavily made-up eyes swivelled towards her beneath the hat's crown, behind the veil; the mouth – those mulberry lips – bunched. She swept past, but the eyes returned to Catherine later outside, while she was standing on the steps to receive the sympathies of the august among the congregation.

Catherine had given them a wide berth, in some haste to avoid Miss Montgomery, but when she turned round she noticed Harriet watching her with her veil raised while the silver-haired heads of a respectful couple inclined towards her. The eyes stared quite brazenly, as if she were anxious on this day of all days to identify the reason for Catherine's hold on her father. She seemed mesmerised, as if she were a rabbit fixed by a snake.

Catherine felt perturbed, rattled, by the effect she was having on the woman. She nearly stumbled on the steps. Someone held an arm out to catch her, and she said 'thank you' without looking. For some moments all she could see, casting round the knots of mourners, were the mascara-ringed eyes singling her out, beneath the luxurious folds of that designer's pastiche of a widow's veil.

'We don't know one another,' he said in a voice quite in fitting with his appearance. 'Officially.'

He moved closer. His hand took her arm again, gently but purposefully.

'Would you think me most terribly forward if I were to offer you a lift back into town?'

'I – '

'You *have* come from town, haven't you?'

'I – Yes. Yes, I have.'

He smiled at her, in a very solicitous way. He drew apart from her to let others pass between them and she took advantage of those few seconds to look at him.

He was forty or so, with very English, patrician features, and neatly cut fair hair which had thinned to a widow's peak on his high brow and was long enough at the sides to be swept back over his ears. There was a touch of the dandy in the cut of the black wool or cashmere coat with its velvet collar: and the gold tie-pin on, not regimental or club colours, but what might have been a Hermès tie.

'You *did* come here by yourself?' he asked her.

'I did,' she said. 'Yes.'

'So you won't object – '

'I don't *see* any taxis.'

Laughter lines appeared about his eyes.

'That's splendid,' he said.

She was ready to believe he really did mean it.

'Maybe we could even have a bite of lunch – '

They were hardly out of the chapel, she felt, and here they were discussing social arrangements for the day. And she shouldn't have smiled, she thought, she shouldn't have been lured into it, that was the very last thing – She was ashamed again, for the sake of the man they had come to mourn.

She allowed herself to be led down the steps, towards a Bristol coupé parked importantly on a part of the driveway which carried the instruction put down on the tarmacadam in white paint, NO PARKING. The stranger unlocked and opened the passenger door. She smelt the new leather of the interior, saw the pile carpet and walnut trim. As she stood hesitating she looked behind her and caught the eyes of the woman who might almost have been herself in the Helmsley advertisement. She was with several of her father's business advisers, but her eyes were trained most assiduously on *her*.

She turned her face away and lowered her head beneath the car's roof. Her companion glanced momentarily in the driving mirror as he settled into his seat beside her.

'We haven't – ' he said, starting the engine, 'we haven't been introduced.'

The engine's turning over was scarcely audible as he steered them along the driveway's serpentines.

'I'm Hugh Denbigh.'

In the chrome side-mirror on the car's front wing Rex's friends and colleagues were reduced to clusters of figures, like a scrabble of cocktail-party stalwarts.

'I'm Catherine Fairweather.'

'Well, of course I know who *you* are.'

The corners of his eyes crinkled and he smiled. His lips opened to show very white, very perfect teeth.

'You do?' she said.

'Have you thought that people must dream about you?'

'*Dream* about me?'

'Don't you think they do?'

'I – Why should – '

They reached the gates and turned out into the street of traffic.

She was confused. She felt she sounded as if she was angling for his compliments.

'You knew Rex Kilpatrick?' she asked him.

'Yes. Yes. I did.'

'Knew him well?'

'We used to meet. Socially.'

'You – you're in the same line? The same business?'

He smiled.

'Not exactly.'

'Oh.'

'What *is* my line? Can you guess?'

'I don't know.'

'Not even a guess?'

'I might guess terribly wrong – '

'I'm an oculist.'

'Oh.'

She had presumed something to do with the theatre.

'You expected something more exciting?'

'You weren't *his* oculist were you?'

'Oh no.'

Perhaps he'd had dealings with some of the girls. But then she remembered he'd said it had been a 'social' relationship. She was getting muddled. She knew, though, that she didn't want her thoughts to stray from the man they had come to bury.

'I've watched your progress,' he said.

'You have?'

'You sound surprised.'

'Well . . . "Progress". Is that what you mean?'

'You seem very detached. From your career.'

She shrugged.

'Maybe,' she said.

'Kilpatrick was very proud of you.'

'He was very good to me.'

'I bet he worshipped you.'

'"Worshipped"?' She smiled, although she felt painfully sad.
'I should think so.'
'No.'
'Were you with him?'
'What?'
'With him, when he died?'
She stared ahead.
'Yes?'
She continued to stare.
'Well, Catherine?'
She replied with a coolness she wasn't expecting to hear.
'Was I?'
'Unless I'm very much mistaken.'
'How on earth – '
' – do I know that?'
She nodded.
'I saw you walking down Gloucester Place. At quarter to four in the morning.'
She sat staring a second or two too long at the sky above Mortlake, and sunspots danced in front of her eyes, like microscope life.
'I was driving back from Dover. To Portman Square. I thought I'd have a few hours' sleep so I could get some work done in the morning. My consulting-rooms are in Queen Anne Street.'
She closed her eyes, opened them again, closed and opened them. She felt a straitjacket tightening on her rib cage.
'You're not going to the bash, let me guess.'
'"The bash"?'
'The lunch.'
'No,' she said. 'No, I'm not.'
'Nor I. Maybe – maybe you would do me the kindness? The great honour?'
'I'm sorry?'
'And have lunch with me?'
'Lunch?'
'Please. And turn it into a special day for me.'
'But – '
'Special in a different way.'
He didn't give her the opportunity to say no. They drove up into the West End, to the Berkeley Hotel, where she found the table was already booked. They sat prominently displayed, and she realised he wanted them to be seen together. One phase of her life was over.
She felt worn out, shipwrecked, cast high and dry, and she hardly

cared. The sadness had taken away her appetite and she stared at the menu without making sense of it.

'Your photographs don't do you justice.'

She pretended not to hear.

'Excellent as they are.'

He gave an order for her to the head waiter and she nodded her head. The waiter seemed familiar with his ways.

'I thought,' he said, 'it was going to be one of those gloomy days when you wonder why *you're* left. In the world. Why *you've* been let off the hook, *this* time – '

She nodded again, staring at the weave of the tablecloth.

'But I was wrong, you see. Quite wrong, Catherine. I couldn't be more pleased now that I *am*. Alive. And having lunch with *you*.'

*

She didn't go back to the agency. She had several conversations with Miss Montgomery, who seemed to suspect that a rival was bidding for her. She told her that she didn't feel it 'appropriate' to return at the moment, and supposed Miss Montgomery knew enough by now about her relationship with her employer to appreciate why.

In the morning post one day she received a letter on Kilpatrick Agency notepaper.

Dear Miss Hammond,

I have taken over management of the agency's affairs and have decided that, with effect from today, we shall cease to represent you.

You can hardly be surprised about that. I have every certainty that my father would be here today and sitting in this office were it not for your irresponsible meddling with his affections. Naturally I am dissatisfied with the doctor's verdict on the circumstances of his death, and I have notified the coroner accordingly.

No doubt you will be tempted to take yourself to another agency, but perhaps you should accept the situation with some grace and realise that your modelling days – not to beat about the bush – are now behind you. Your face is too well known for the wrong reason – advertising one product – and our clients tend to appreciate novelty. It would be worse to be well known for notorious reasons, but I'm sure you'll take that into your calculations too. I believe openings will present themselves to you in other spheres, where you can put your past experience to profitable use. I hesitate to speculate what these might be.

Faithfully,
Harriet Kilpatrick

It was a ridiculous step for her to have taken, of course: the letter would have been construed by anyone she might show it to as a clumsy attempt at blackmail.

But then she must have known when she sent it that the chances were most emphatically amassed against the possibility of the recipient's showing it to any other person. This was a matter between themselves alone, and it would proceed only so far as Harriet Kilpatrick dictated that it would.

What did she expect of her? Nothing, it seemed. Or rather, her silence: and the ignominy of losing her career: and the disrepute that might come to attach to another being hinted at with sledgehammer subtlety.

Catherine folded the letter in half, then folded it again. She hadn't had any clear idea anyway of what she might do. The accident, and then her meeting with Hugh Denbigh, had both put it to the back of her mind. Trying to have the decision reversed was naturally quite out of the question. Doubtless her lover's daughter would contrive to have her, quite unofficially, blacklisted in the modelling community – by a gradual dissemination of calumny. So her hands were well and truly tied.

She consulted her watch. She didn't feel up to breakfast. The arrangement stood that the Bristol would pick her up at midday. Lunch was to be somewhere elegant. Could she recover her appetite, as well as her equipoise, in time?

'Spirit of resolution,' she said to encourage herself, turning to look in a mirror. She scrutinised herself, hair piled up on top of her head, which all the photographers had told her was *her* 'look'. She started to undo the plait, letting her hair fall down. She glanced at her watch again and suddenly, quite seriously, wondered if she could make an appointment or land a cancellation for this morning at Leonard's or Raphael's or Raymond's, at the masters' hands preferably but a sorcerer's apprentice would do, to have her mane lopped off.

When the Bristol drew up outside the house at midday she was ready for him, just about.

Denbigh, standing on the pavement with the passenger door open, did a double-take when she walked down the steps in her gamine look: Eton crop, à la Zizi Jeanmaire, tight black cigarette pants, bare ankles, flat black kid loafers, her geranium-red beehive coat unbuttoned. It took him several seconds to adjust. She produced a pair of sunglasses from her pocket and put them on.

'Spirit of a New Age!' she said.

He nodded, unbuttoning his camelhair coat.

'You don't approve?' she asked him, immediately sensing that he might not.

'Oh yes,' he said.

He seemed to be making a very rapid assessment of the situation and its implications.

'I'm not who you thought I was?'

'I didn't think I knew you anyway.' The words were benignly intended. 'Not *yet* anyway – '

'You're not going to drop me now?'

He closed the door after her and spoke through the window.

'Quite the contrary, I assure you.'

As they drove he took his fill of sideways glances.

'It's done now,' she said. 'A *fait accompli*.'

He was smiling, as if he had merely needed a little time to become comfortable with the transformation.

'Now you won't be able to introduce me to anybody.'

'Different people, Catherine, *different* people.'

'Will I really fit in with them, do you think?'

'Very well.'

'With who exactly?' she asked.

'My smarter friends.'

'When's this going to be?'

'You sound very anxious about it!'

'Oh, not really,' she said. 'I just think – my life needs shaking up.'

'The modelling?'

'I'm not sure about that any more.'

'I'm glad to hear it.'

'What?' She stared at him.

'Maybe your situation is going to change soon.'

'How?'

'Well . . . marriage for one thing.'

She couldn't help smiling. This was taking anticipation far too far. But it was a pleasant, flattering, whimsical joke – perhaps.

He picked up speed. She was starting to forget about the letter, her mind was shedding its gloom. She had her new acquaintance to thank for that.

She pushed her fingers into her hair and felt the closeness of her scalp. She enjoyed the new sensation. She was suddenly buoyant, as if she had lost ballast. It was exactly the lift she needed, the exhilarating irresponsible fillip for *now*.

46

The Emigré

PERHAPS it was the hair that tipped me over the edge: or standing at the window watching the Bristol drive off, believing that she didn't care for me.

Simply, I went haywire.

My mother started to consult gazetteers and spent a lot of time watching me while she pretended to be doing other things. She brought home a very sedate grey flannel suit for herself from Helmsley's, which she wore several times on taxi journeys that clearly weren't assignments and thus 'on expenses' and that left her, on her return home, pallid and swollen-nosed.

She took me with her one day, although the taxi driver had to help, lifting me down the front steps to the cab when I wouldn't move, telling them my feet were buried in the concrete. We were deposited at a cheerless building with glass bricks on the landings and long linoleum corridors, and we had to wait our turn – for what, I was far too stubborn to ask – in an open hall, sitting on hard wooden benches while people, not of our sort, came and went. In a green-painted room which we were finally shown into, my mother produced photographs she'd cut out of the *National Geographic Magazine*, informing the man that they'd been taken by a friend. The man took me to a stern woman in a white coat who measured my height and weight and examined my chest and back with a stethoscope. When she asked me questions I didn't reply; 'Say Aaah!' she barked out when she wanted to look into my mouth, but I wouldn't part my lips for her. 'I see what your mother means,' she told me, and she grabbed my hand and marched me back to the green-painted room. On opposite sides of the desk my mother and the man had their heads lowered and were examining typed papers. When I reappeared, the man swept the papers up into a pile and said, Well that was decided then . . .

*

'For a while, Felix,' she said, 'for a change of scene.'
'Where to?' I asked her.
'A long way.'
'And I won't have to go back to school?'
'Not *that* school,' she said.
'I hate it.'
'I know,' she said. 'I know you do.'

Earlier the headmistress had called on us, presumably to inspect for herself the house and the 'set-up'.

My mother was charming but wary, and I scowled insolently before going into the kitchen and playing the radio loudly enough for her to hear and (I hoped) take offence. But in my absence she told my mother quite bluntly that the school couldn't cope with me, and my mother must have been reduced then to tears, because when the woman left and we were alone she was red-eyed.

She hit me on the side of the head and I fell against the kitchen table, on the corner, and broke a front tooth. Blood flowed, and she flew to the telephone to call the dentist. I wasn't reacting at all, which upset her still more. Waiting for the taxi she couldn't help herself and she shook me by the shoulders, very hard. She took her hands away and stared at them, sheathed in their fashionably mauve suede gloves. 'Jesus Christ,' she said, and I quite failed to see how He was involved.

The driver 'accidentally' touched her leg as she was getting into the taxi. She froze for a couple of seconds, then carried on as if nothing had happened. En route for the dentist the driver winked at her in his mirror and when I started kicking the tip-up seat she started to cry again, and maybe she thought she was slowly losing her mind in this graceless, endlessly conspiring man's world.

Even the agency which supplied the girls to look after me lost patience, and only Mrs Letts was left.

She had the saving capacity of being able to ignore me when it suited her. It was she who packed the suitcase (and bought the suitcase for me, on my mother's Barker's account), and an aptly unsentimental job she made of it. Would I be wanting this? she asked briskly – or that? I enquired where I was being sent and she said it was up in the air. Why? I asked her.

'Nobody wants to have you, I expect. Unless you learn to show some decent manners.'
'Who to?'
'*Me* for a start.'

I must have looked sceptical. She muttered 'Hmmph,' and turned her attention to the underwear drawer.

'You'll need long-johns more like,' she said, but I didn't do as she wanted me to and enquire further, so the remark went uncommented upon but nonetheless lodged in my mind and echoed there, in the privacy of that forbidding and excluding space.

I flung a shoe across the sitting-room and it broke the mirror on the wall.

My mother appeared in the shattered glass. She didn't shout at me when she spoke; she declared herself with exemplary calmness, addressed the point in measured phrases.

'I think,' she said, 'we must find you another home. For a while.'

'Where are we going?'

'*I* have to stay here in London,' she said. 'But how would *you* like to go on a journey? A long journey on a ship, a voyage?'

I thought she was only expressing a wish, her own, so of course – for perversity's sake – I agreed.

'Yes,' I said. 'When?'

'Oh, some time.'

How soon, how soon can I leave?

There were more tears. Silences of a solemnity unlike any others in the past. Some days she scarcely looked at me, on others she was unable to do much else *except* look.

She had second, third, fourth thoughts. I found her searching through my toy boxes, another time just sitting on my bed staring at nothing. I heard her up through the night, pacing the rooms.

I became even more untidy than I'd been. I dropped my clothes, scattered my toys, let books fall like heavy birds with their covers spread. I broke a window in the flat upstairs with my catapult. I barked at a woman on a bike and she tottered off it, into a holly hedge. I tossed a lit match into a rubbish bin on a lamp-post.

My mother came with me to the station. We had tea in the hotel, but she ate nothing from the cake-stand and didn't check me for shedding crumbs on the chair, the carpet, my trousers and legs. She screwed her lips into some very peculiar shapes, as if they were made of rubber. Where she couldn't see – she had her back to them – businessmen with briefcases singled her out for their attention. I tried building an igloo out of sugar cubes, on the snowy white cloth, and when the structure caved in and I set the table rocking trying to save it, she still said nothing.

A woman approached our table. My mother stood up, but I didn't.

'This lady is going to look after you, Felix.'

All three of us walked down on to the concourse. One or other of my mother's hands never left my head but she wasn't fussing with the hair or smoothing it down. She started to cry at the last minute, after she'd bent down to kiss me and I'd deftly sidled away and put the woman's sturdy torso between us.

'Please don't, Mrs Hammond – '

I looked back when I was on the other side of the ticket barrier. She raised her arm; her hand must have been too tense to open. I thought she didn't really care. I half-raised my arm, managed an accidental sweep of the hand, turned round and let myself be led away by the woman. I looked back again when we reached the second or third carriage of the train. She still stood in the same spot, but she was half the size; perhaps she didn't see us because she wasn't waving, and in the next seconds – still looking behind me as I continued walking along – a man in a camel coat appeared at her side. She stepped back, as if she was startled. He placed her arm through his and rotated her one hundred and eighty degrees in the direction of the station entrance. She glanced back over her shoulder, towards the platform, but he must have said something because she nodded and turned her head to look at him and that was the very last either of us was ever in our lives to see of the other.

I travelled down on the train with the stranger with the fuzzy face. She held open a bag of mixed caramels and treacle toffee squares for the two of us to dip into as we felt the urge. She wore a dark blue serge suit with epaulets, which was in effect a uniform: completed by black seamed stockings and flat black lacing shoes. Her lipstick was a too brightly frivolous shade of vermilion, which might have been her one concession towards assuming a civilian appearance but which she had wildly misjudged. She took advantage of there being only ourselves in the compartment to tell me that I would be staying in Canada, not with some far-flung outcast from my great-aunt's Aquae-Regis circle, but with people who would be quite new to me. Whoever they might turn out to be, they would be my 'parents'.

'For how long?' I asked.

Miss Turnbull said, 'Come again?'

I repeated my question.

She might have suspected a leg-pull, if that was what she was used to. But since she knew we would have no more than three hours of one another's company, she must have willed herself to presume the best of me.

'For quite a long time.'

'Oh.'

'It's not a visit, you see. Your old "mother" will be staying here. Canada will be *your* home.'

'Till when?'

'From now on.'

'For *ever?*'

'Yes.'

'Oh.'

She shook the bag of sweets and thrust it towards me.

'You'll like it,' she said, in a voice that sounded more ominous than encouraging.

'Will I have to go to school?' I asked her.

'Of course you will,' she said.

She proceeded to grill me (while feigning not to) about my educational history. I sensed that she set little store by establishments such as the Willow, where I'd been a pupil for five terms, because she believed them to be élitist and not what in fact they frequently proved to be – sloppy, amateurish, and basic in the extreme. Doubtless she imagined privilege to be breeding greater privilege from one generation unto the next, and she was creating from it her own private monster.

'I'll have a new mother?'

'And father. A mother *and* father. In Canada.'

'Why?'

'So you can begin your life all over again.'

The journey was tasting of caramel, and went down so badly that I started to choke and she had to thump my back. That put tears into my eyes and she must have had me then just where she wanted me, doubled-up in gawky acquiescence.

The train, snaking south and west, took us to Southampton. The town and sea, the docks and terminals, the ships and cranes, the sky and smoke trails, everything was approximately grey.

I was delivered to a hangar, where I found a crowd of children of my own age, in a readier state of anticipation than I was capable of. Names were recorded in a register, details checked (including height and, for some reason, shoe size), birth certificates surrendered; a couple of photographs were taken behind a curtain. The contents of my suitcase were gone through; more forms were provided, which Miss Turnbull attended to. I was given a number, and a tab on a length of string was tied to my arm. Miss Turnbull waited with some colleagues until my time came as the numbers were called through a tannoy hailer. She straightened my collar and tie, told me that when my hair was cut into a crew at the other end I'd look like a Canadian good and proper, and maybe – if I forgot my past – I'd grow up to wear the Mountie uniform. I turned round, and there on a poster on a wall an uncannily handsome young Royal Canadian Mounted Policeman sat astride his mount, speaking down to a leather-faced Indian chief who stood tall but not so proud in his feather headdress.

On the ship we were each allocated a berth in a single-sex cabin that slept six. The five others I found myself with came from different parts of the country. Three of them competed with their hearsay stories of this land to which we were bound – with its mountains, wheat plains and tundra, the totem poles, the lumberjacks felling redwoods, the rivers running gold, the herds of rampaging elk.

As we steamed out of Southampton, hooters bellowing, our minds were filled with these preternatural wonders. Round about us families clung to the railings, and we tried to bond ourselves as they did, although we must have guessed we had very little in common with one another. But it seemed to be necessary, becoming more embroiled as we were in the all-pervasive greyness, and finding ourselves already pitching in a sick-making swell.

England existed on our right-hand side for several hours, the perfect greyness of grey, but towns and forests and cliffs were too far to distinguish. The sea rolled under us, sounding like the slapping of whales' tails on the keel of the ship. Everyone around us alternated between relief at what was slipping behind them and fearfulness for what might be to come. We were all, as it were, in the one boat. Even the gulls dropped away eventually and headed back for that land we were so soon beginning to forget.

47

Silken Web

At Denbigh's invitation Catherine became a regular at Whistlefield, his country home in Sussex, beneath the Downs.

The oldest part of the house was Jacobean. In Georgian times it had been a dower-house; a Regency prebendary had extended it with a side-wing; a second wing had been added in the 1920s, and twenty-five years later Denbigh had built himself a garage for this three cars. A once modest building now contained seven bedrooms; the public rooms interconnected, in the tradition of grander living. She liked the irregular exterior, and the informality of its knapped flint, limestone, and red tile walls. The two stables and the tack-room still smelt of their past. There were five acres of privacy: lawn, a paddock, a wild garden, a small kitchen-garden with crumbling walls, a slow millstream, and a tennis court.

'I wanted a tennis court,' he told her. 'So I had to buy a house *with* one.'

'*This* tennis court in particular?'

'I had a few games with the chap who was selling. I actually played not too badly. Or he was allowing me to get a few points. Anyway, I thought it was bound to improve me, and it was the only court I'd seen and been on which did me any good.'

'Are you so keen? On tennis?'

'So-so. But it gives people something to *do* when they come.'

'So it was for them, not for yourself?'

'I wanted to entertain, you see. The court would be the distraction, the big draw.'

'You had it very carefully worked out?'

'Well, to a point. I wanted to get out of London occasionally. Any self-respecting medic should encourage exercise, shouldn't he?'

'Yes,' she said. 'Yes, he should.'

They played a little tennis themselves. At the beginning it was still possible to play, because there were only themselves, plus Mrs Collis in the kitchen. After that they were never so alone again.

Some of his guests were patients, or had formerly been so. He had a distinguished clientèle. She half-recognised names and faces from the newspapers. Most of the men wore their importance lightly, and the women dressed down for the country, but all of them were high-powered socialites and the conversation very seldom flagged.

While Denbigh appeared happy just to sit back and let them take over, she noticed it was he who orchestrated them.

She pitched in, feeling bound to, and hoped she wasn't being remembered as a model who'd had her moment's glory. There seemed to be no confusion in anyone's mind that she was there as Denbigh's guest, the only woman on those first few visits not attached to a husband or fiancé. She was embarrassed by the identification, and would snatch looks at Denbigh, who gave her no clues in return, and she would feel herself becoming more disconcerted as a result.

She became still more so when they'd all gone and Mrs Collis had hung up her apron and squelched on to the saddle of her bicycle and pedalled off home. The intense awkwardness had to do with the perplexing fact that nothing ever 'happened'. She waited – but he made no advances to her. He invited her to the house, and she accepted because he had chosen to do so. But that was as far as it went.

She hadn't ventured into his study – the door was usually shut – and she realised there were areas where she didn't have the confidence to enquire. It was possible that there was a romantically linked young man in the wings, but none of the guests seemed the sort. She combed the gallery of framed photographs in the public rooms but saw no likely specimen there either. There were a number of camera portraits of younger women propped up in prominent places, and she vaguely asked him about some of them. They were either attractive or well born, and all he told her was that this one or that had been a friend. 'Had been', she noticed: and how much should be read into the word 'friend'?

He would drive her down and drive her back in the Bristol or his AC. They sat low, close to the road, and the miles vanished into the radiator grille. Often the journeys back were done at night, in darkness. She was never invited to stay at Whistlefield. In London he took her back to her flat, slowing as he turned the corner from Cromwell Road so that the engine was no louder than a taxi's and neighbours' suspicions wouldn't be aroused. She had been to his flat in Portman Square, but again there had been no possibility of her staying beyond nine or ten o'clock. Was there another 'arrangement' she didn't know about? Perhaps he assumed that if she had strong reservations about his fidelity, even the platonic sort, she would refuse the next invitation? Why did he continue to invite her, though, and why did he choose *her* company for the opera or a party? Occasionally they had dinner together, but she realised that those *tête-à-têtes* were becoming fewer: mostly other people were present whenever they met, and they continually made demands on his attention, which of course she was unable to do anything about.

He would drop her off at her front door. He always made a point of kissing her, twice, once on each cheek. He didn't linger over the deed, but nor were they the approximate kisses of people who know one another only too well after too long, where the lips hardly made contact with the skin. She distinctly felt his lips imprinting themselves on her cheeks and the intimacy of the gesture intrigued and tantalised her with its chasteness, causing a little thrill low down in the small of her back.

*

The Helmsleys had taken their account to a different advertising agency. They in their wisdom decided that the Fiona Campbell-Walters and Barbara Goalens had had their day. Instead they used an artist's silhouette. Ironically enough, from Catherine's point of view, the sketches showed a gamine-like girl with a Peter Pan haircut, of the sort Jean Seberg was shortly to make the latest vogue. Forget the business of long necks and superior airs and the arty photographers' shots, this was life as it was lived now: fast, breezy, informal, chic, not quite but almost innocent, and ever oh ever in the gift of Youth.

*

Denbigh took her to parties, swanky evenings in Mayfair flats and riverside houses in Chelsea and mansions on Highgate Hill.

So many people attended them that she could lose herself in the activity, talking just a few words to a great number of guests and being passed round the room like a rumour or a reputation or a betting tip or the name of the newest, most fashionable restaurant to be seen at. She was introduced to politicians and actors and peers and brokers and couturiers. The faces of some of them were already familiar to her from the pages of magazines she'd read in the early days at Kilpatrick's before she became too busy to have time to spare.

There were people they regularly encountered whom Denbigh steered her about, most noticeably a woman with a rather cheap, brittle face and a falsely superior accent. She was called Mrs Russell, and the most surprising doors had been opened to her. It struck Catherine that she was always present whenever some especially beautiful woman was to be seen at a party, and that the older would attempt to keep the younger in her sights even when there was a crowd of people between them. Those beautiful women would sometimes seem almost too much so: each of them would be dressed in nothing but the very best, and their behaviour with whomsoever they were accompanying, as companion or wife, was always very apt, very seemly: as if they had received some common instruction in such matters. Mrs Russell with her strawberry-pink bouffant might receive a covert nod or a quiet smile as a reward for her attention, but she wouldn't involve herself in any spoken exchange.

Denbigh, Catherine realised, was as much aware of the woman's ubiquity as she was and doubtless guessed at the reasons rather better than she was able to. She was puzzled why he was so particular that they shouldn't meet. She asked him, and he was (courteously, charmingly) evasive.

'*Was* I avoiding her?'

'Weren't you?'

'She's a bit of a bloodsucker, I expect. Wouldn't you say?'

'I don't know.'

'They're just a social hazard.'

'A frequent hazard, though.'

'Paying them attention just flatters them.'

But wasn't there a difference between paying them no attention and taking pains to make sure that tracks never crossed, that eyes never engaged?

Even though Mrs Russell's eyes were always too quick for her to catch, Catherine had sensed the woman's attention for *her* as well. She often felt that the younger women had been educated to ignore her as Denbigh's companion, being too involved with their own performance, angelically smiling but intent like high-wire walkers. It occurred to her that Denbigh was cagey of them too, these archetypal wives and the most discreet of mistresses, who for very suitability might have been the products off an assembly line; and he conspicuously didn't care to solicit an introduction or – as many of the other men did – to presume on an acquaintanceship, true or not.

So, Catherine came to appreciate, the lush-life evenings were actually more tense than they were conceded to be. She saw past their smiling surfaces. She perceived how careful was the choreography of these intimate strangers, who directly approached or stepped near to or circumnavigated whom. An ocular and crural extravaganza was staged each time, with a roomful of eyes and limbs in synchronised motion. There was no one who could not be flushed out.

*

She asked him in the car, being driven home one night.

'Don't you get rather tired, Hugh?'

'Of what?'

'Of – of squiring me.'

'Tired of it?' He laughed. 'Not in the slightest.'

'Oh. Well – well, why are we *doing* this?'

'This? I don't underst[illegible]'

'The parties.'

The headlights swung into The Vale.

'Going places,' she said. 'All the flying about.'

'Because I thought it would be fun for you.'

She didn't speak.

Of course she felt uneasy even asking, when their last serious conversation had followed the discovery that he'd paid four sizeable cheques into her bank account which he then refused to have paid back. The money had been a 'pledge' and why – he'd asked her – shouldn't he be at liberty to offer such a practical consideration?

He changed gear.

'You know who I am, what my job is.'

'Yes, but – '

'You know I like you. That I care for you.'

She knew none of these things at all. That was the point. Or was the point that he thought she was a fool? But he'd told her he respected her 'intelligence', her 'powers of discernment'.

She sighed. But maybe he didn't hear, because the engine then revved on the corner into the Old Brompton Road. She was no closer to an explanation for these speedy drives home before the goodnight kisses at her door. A few journeys ago a police car had stopped them, a couple of hundred yards from a police station. He had been requested to go inside please, but he had asked that an officer come out to *him*. In the end, after papers had been produced and taken into the police station, a sergeant did present himself. Denbigh got out of the car and a discussion ensued on the police station steps. It ended in a mutual show of good spirits with the sergeant holding the car door open for him and closing it and wishing him a very good night through the window. She hadn't been able to ask him what *that* might all have been about and he hadn't offered her any clues to the situation.

She had nothing to go on, she felt. Her place was in the passenger's seat and more and more she saw London by night, while her afternoons were reserved for the ritualistic preparations. She spent those after-dark hours in brilliantly lit rooms, with too much chatter confusing her hearing and sometimes upsetting her sense of balance and so much cigar and cigarette smoke that her eyes smarted and her throat roughened to sandpaper. She was still 'Bluette', but she arrived on the arm of Dr Hugh Denbigh, and the best she could expect was, not sociable interest, but bemused looks of curiosity and (no less frequently) wary, speculating side-glances, as if everyone was in on some shared secret report which she was not.

*

A tramp was walking in her direction. He continued walking towards her. The traffic along the Embankment was too fast for her to step out on to the road and she realised that she had no means of avoiding him. The Savoy, where Denbigh would join the party after work, was still a hundred yards off.

She set her face so that she would be quite unaffected by him. His clothes were spattered with stains and frayed at their edges, his jacket lining was slashed and in tatters, his shirt front was open. He came very close to her and she couldn't escape the heat and stink of his breath. Drink, but also neglect over too long a time – abscesses possibly.

He started to speak. She wasn't listening to the sense of what he was saying, but to its lilting, lyrical rhythm and tone (a tale told too often) and to his accent: not London at all, but Welsh.

It was then that she turned to look at him. She found he was fixing her with his eyes. Their pale fawn colouring had almost been washed out. He was lean, bloodless, and had lost his hair. His gestures were helpless, distraught.

'I don't know,' she said, and shook her head. 'I don't know you.'

Which wasn't the case, of course. But she couldn't admit the possibility to him. And the possibility of acknowledging it to herself was making her unsteady on her feet, until she felt she was starting to reel.

There was no adjacent iron mesh this time, although she thought she could hear – distantly, from behind her – the sound of trains.

In her amethyst gown from the Norman Hartnell salon she might have considered herself – been considered – invulnerable. She hesitated, waiting for him to touch her arm, or to offer her his hand in the way drunken men do, blessing a stranger with the clasp of the hand of God.

But he backed away from her. His eyes careened past her, they fixed woozily on whomsoever else was visible to him behind her on the pavement. He hadn't been assessing her at all except abstractly, as a woman in fancy clothes who might have a bob or two on her to spare.

She had less than that, though, and even less than she realised. She had only slightly delayed recall, but she didn't have the will to apply her memory to her current mode of life, to extract a lesson from the past which might also be an action-alert warning to her.

*

'This is where it happens, Catherine.'

She turned her head and looked at him. She smiled, in the stalling way smiles were useful for.

'I don't think you believe me, do you?'

'I – I'm not sure.'

'There has to be *some*where. Actually, there are several somewheres.'

She looked ahead, towards the tennis court. Two corpulent men (politicians), a younger slimmer man (future Whitehall mandarin) and an elegant woman (American diplomat's wife), all in pristine whites, were playing strenuous tennis. At the same time they were managing to engage in a four-part conversation.

'For the decisions to be taken, you see.'

'"Decisions"?'

'The sort that decide. Which determine people's lives for them.'

She smiled again, as charmingly uncertain as before.

'People who need – and expect – the decisions to be made for them.'

'Oh.'

'It has to be done. It has to be done *some*where. And wherever that is, there probably has to be a host.'

'Yes.'

'And if, as I suspect, the decisions are being taken out *there*' – he pointed to the tennis court – 'then in all probability *I* am the host on this occasion. So that's how *I* fit into this divine little pattern. Do you see?'

It was Denbigh's turn to smile. She was aware of the combined condescension and gentleness with which he treated her.

While Mrs Collis's country-plain but efficient daughter spoke to him about a telephone call of the morning, Catherine leaned back in the canvas chair and wondered, as she often did, about her own part in this exclusive ritual. It was like a fabulous web, and her companion was at its centre, the controlling intelligence and maker. He shouldered his own significance quite lightly, considering, with those precise and meticulous manners of his, with his ready smiles and unruffled good cheer.

'What are you thinking about?' he asked her, but he already knew.

She shook her head and adjusted her sunglasses on the bridge of her nose.

'This,' he said, 'is the historical process at work.'

She wasn't sure if it was a cue to smile. Instead she focused on the game on the court. The ball was returned from one side to the other, backwards and forwards, while the talk continued. On and on, plung-plung and the dinner-party voices. When was the rhythm going to be broken, with a disguised shot or a lob or a backhand slice?

'We're so close to it,' he said.

'But – ' She spoke the word and hesitated. She looked at him through her smoked lenses.

'But – ?' he repeated.

'You're the host. Didn't you say?'

'That's only to make myself sound important.'

'*Aren't* you?'

'Not in the final totting up. I have my uses, and I'm worth knowing. But I always realised my capacities – and their limits. I just – accentuate my positive.'

'You're hiding your light under – '

'Not under anything,' he interrupted, but genially. 'I do mean just what I say. I facilitate. I help to make whatever *does* happen happen. But I don't cause it. I don't even precipitate it.'

'Why do they come then?'

'They're all acquainted. I like to think they're relaxed here as they wouldn't be in certain other places. It lowers their guard, maybe.'

'Why do you want to do that?'

'I put things into a fresh perspective for them.'

'Is that all?'

'Not for altruistic purposes, you're right.'

She held her breath. It hadn't been in her mind to suggest such a thing.

'The decisions they make are the outcomes of previous decisions. And so on and so forth. I'm *watching* history, if you like. That's my privilege – rather dull, monotonous history, I have to say. Sitting at the same tea-table, more or less.'

He smoothed the silk of his cravat and adjusted the tips of his shirt collar.

'I wonder, though,' he said, 'why it is that *you* bother to come.'

'Oh.' She shrugged, still smiling. 'It's very nice to be asked. To come down here.'

'Isn't it boring for you?'

She perceived a flaw.

'Why – why do you invite me then?'

'Well,' he said. 'To be frank, you *are* in the way of a decoy. To alleviate the boredom – the possible boredom – of the others.'

'That's why I'm here?'

'It's *one* of the reasons.'

'What are the others?' She turned round to look at him, feeling a surge of courage in herself. '*Are* there others?'

'I enjoy having you here.'

'But you think I'm being bored.'

'I do hope not.'

From behind his sunglasses she just caught his eyes sharpening as she turned her head and looked away. Then, on the tennis court, she saw a deceptive ball leave the two men wrong-footed and batting at empty air. There was another moment's pause, a double-take, then the four players started to laugh in unison.

Beside her Catherine noticed their facilitator lean forward to brush an insect from the turn-up of his trousers. How was it that he had such an air of self-assurance about him, even when he denied having any influence in these matters he helped to cause?

'I really don't care to interrupt them,' he said, 'but sometimes needs must. I've arranged tea for four o'clock.'

'So you *do* have some say?'

'*Some* say, yes. Heads don't ignore stomachs, even if they're trained not to be ruled by them. I just have to make the temptations tempting enough, you see.'

In loco Catherine heard the tinkling sounds of a tea trolley. She looked across the terrace and watched the slow, formal approach of the laden paraphernalia from the house. A wood pigeon chortled, a breeze riffled the skirt of her dress; *oh*, she thought, *oh to be in England now*.

*

Away from Whistlefield they were always, she noticed, drinks parties or stand-up move-around buffets: not sit-down-and-talk-or-be-spoken-to dinners. She was kept in continuous circulation. It was as if she were on general public display (except, that is, for the benefit of Mrs Russell).

Later, as the coteries they mixed with became noticeably less egalitarian, she was conscious that one particular pair of male eyes was being trained on her.

Denbigh, she had realised, was in the habit of positioning her in rooms so that she was always being seen – quite literally – in the most favourable light. The rooms were now in South Kensington, St James's, and St John's Wood; the company was essentially political, both government and Whitehall. People were somehow impersonal and grand, even bombastic, at the same time. They tended to dress more alike, according to a sober fashion, and that made them appear to be a herd when she first walked into a room. But it also caused her to concentrate almost exclusively on their faces as Denbigh piloted her, his hand on her arm, and as her eyes did the inevitable preliminary surveillance work.

He was a white-haired man in his mid-sixties, of an aristocratic mien and with a domineering look about him. He smiled most affably when at last they were introduced, after a little counterfeit shot of surprise, as if he had never chanced to cast eyes on her before. But those eyes were brilliantly blue, and stiletto-sharp. They were missing nothing, she noticed, as he and she stood on that evening of their introduction and talked.

She had recognised the name, Lord Marlott, at once. The aristocratic appearance was merely fortuitous, since rank had come to him in the Honours Lists. A self-made businessman, he had been placed in charge of a number of reconstruction schemes after the War and had chaired official committees researching the redistribution of population. The New Towns had been one particular development he was closely associated with. Labour and Conservative governments had both valued his services. The newspapers had carried generously effusive editorials on his recent 'retirement' and challenged the term, since his business interests – primarily Marlott Construction – as well as his various commitments to charitable organisations continued to present him with a much younger man's workload.

They spoke, Lord Marlott and she. He asked her questions. She thought he was listening to her, or maybe he wasn't really, but at least he was making a pretence of doing so, and she felt indebted for that reason alone, even if the cunning in his eyes had put her on her guard. He had a quiet manner: but he addressed her with such precision of accent and meaning that she knew he must be a man who was listened to with respect and possessed a great weight of authority. He had thin lips and a Roman nose and a high princely forehead. He might have intimidated her; but she believed she had nothing to lose, he could have no high expectations of her that she might disappoint.

She was quite in the dark as to why he was continuing to converse with her, when everyone else in the room must have him targeted. But he didn't indicate that he was tired of her, and even when she paused and shrugged self-deprecatingly with embarrassment he found another strand to extract from the strand of talk before, and in this way the conversation was effortlessly directed.

Afterwards, on the drive home, she had difficulty remembering just what they'd been discussing. Denbigh was very interested to discover.

'Are you terribly jealous?' she asked him, smiling through the windscreen.

'I *could* be.'

'You are or you aren't?'

'Not *terribly* jealous. After all, I've been trying to get it to happen for – '

'What?'

In the next breath he sounded apologetic.

'Didn't you guess that?'

'No,' she said. 'No, I didn't.'

'Not really?'

'No. Not at all.'

'I knew he was wanting to meet you.'

'How did you know that?'

'Oh, I just have an eye – and an ear – for these things. But anyone could have guessed, I suppose.'

'How?'

'Because of the way he was looking at you.'

'How was that?'

'With an appreciative connoisseur's eye.'

'So – so you were looking for some way to make it happen?'

'A meeting? Yes.'

'*I* see.'

'That was harmless enough.'

'Oh, was it really?'

'Yes. Yes, *I* think so.'

At their journey's end she got out of the car, said a curt goodnight, banged the door shut, and walked off without looking back.

In the flat she couldn't settle. It was the first time they'd had words. She had brought them to it, but she couldn't accept that it was her fault.

He telephoned, and she knew she sounded obdurate. She felt acted against. Why should Denbigh have taken her anywhere, everywhere, only to engineer meetings with a man who couldn't take his eyes off her?

She realised she might be over-reacting. Perhaps there *had* been less harm in it than she was concluding. But why had she been left on her own, why hadn't he stuck with her? He had implied that he was continually on the look-out – in a defensive way – for whoever might be watching her; yet he hadn't mentioned to her that she was in the sights of anyone so notable.

His lordship had told her that *he* recognised her, from her photographs, but she'd slid past the subject. It was old hat to her, and she hadn't engaged in the business for vanity's sake, but because it had given her a living and might have allowed her her independence (or so she'd deluded herself) and because it had supplied her with a modicum of self-belief at a juncture when all those things were so desperately required. It hadn't occurred to her at the party that it was anything other than an accident, his happening to remember where he'd seen her before. Later she read the situation differently, and couldn't credit her own naïvety.

48

Aubade

THEY continued to meet.

One evening she happened to see Lord Marlott arriving in his long, fitted overcoat and the homburg hat that was his sartorial signature. He was having words with a young male guest in the hallway: they were delivered through a smile, but – she could tell – they were harsh words. The young man flinched, and wrapped one hand tight into a fist behind his back.

Half an hour later Lord Marlott introduced him to her. He was none other than his son, Lawrence, and she must have gawped on receiving the information.

Lord Marlott laughed.

Even his son smiled.

They were left together. The son didn't have his father's high features. He was dressed as a bespoke London professional but from the physical details she might have thought him half-Italian, or half-Armenian even: olive-skinned, brown-eyed, swarthy. He told her he worked in Whitehall, at the Home Office.

'That sounds grand,' she said.

'It gets pretty mundane. My father pulled a few strings. I'm safe for life, I suppose.'

He was conspicuously well mannered, even in that gathering: like a text-book example of good behaviour, in fact. He didn't leave her side, and showed no signs of wanting to. Lord Marlott appeared too busy to return to them. Similarly Denbigh was otherwise engaged. Forty-five minutes passed in one another's company, but it was only when their hostess came to separate them that Catherine looked at her watch. She couldn't believe the time had gone; it hadn't felt longer than quarter of an hour. Lawrence beamed at the woman.

'Haven't you said everything you've got to say to one another, my dears?'

'But I'm having a great time,' he assured her. 'Enjoying myself to the hilt.'

'How long have you known Lord Marlott?' she asked on the drive back.

'Not "*known*",' Denbigh said.

'But if you talk to him – '

'We've just found ourselves at the same parties. For years now. He came on the scene at the end of the War. The *serious* party scene, I mean.'

'What about *before* the War?'

'I can't say. He only became so grand about eleven, twelve years ago.'

'And that's all? You don't know him any better?'

'Am I a terrible disappointment?'

'What?'

'After Jack Marlott? Can you afford to be seen with me any more?'

He laughed. She smiled, not very cheerfully. *She* was being serious. But by treating it as a joke maybe he was being no less so.

*

On a couple of later occasions she encountered the wrathful eye of Mrs Russell.

The woman stood in corners of the respective rooms staring at her; her hostility was almost tactile, and Catherine was conscious of losing the pace of each of the evenings. Both times she had arrived with Denbigh but had been taken up by Lawrence Marlott. She would have thought herself protected, 'accounted for', if it hadn't been for the withering scepticism of that crisp-chinned, peroxide blonde on the other side of the room.

She noticed Denbigh now watching the unbeliever too, and she felt more confident that if she was going to be approached he would step in. It had become very clear to her that, while Denbigh had always pleaded utter indifference, there was no love lost between them.

*

Thirty-odd, she guessed Lawrence Marlott's age to be. Thirty-two or -three possibly.

He was tall, and held himself very erect. His physique defined his clothes. He had broad shoulders, and firm biceps and forearm muscles, and sturdy, strong legs. There was even a hint of awkwardness as he walked, which might have had to do with muscle fatigue after too much strenuous exercise: he did circuit training every morning at a gymnasium, and swam thirty lengths of the RAC pool before he came home. He had a moustache, a darker shade of brown than his hair. His face, she had to admit to herself, on occasions had something of the inanimate solidity of a statue about it: as if he intentionally curbed his feelings from straying into the features of his face, to betray him. He had a thick, powerful neck, but not a fold or tuck of fat about his person. (She discovered that the very first afternoon she slept with him, when they drove down to Cuckfield to wait for his father to join them for dinner and found the house empty. They made their love on a chaise in a summer-house on a knoll, with the doors open and Sussex spread out before them and sunshine warming the bare soles and toes of her feet. His shoulders and back had a light scattering of hair, which by choice she would have done without, but his love-making was brisk, rapid-fire even, and he didn't linger in the undressed state.)

She was conscious of his masculinity – dressed in charcoal suits with the neatly tapered waists and a little extra material provided in the trouser thighs – as she hadn't been with Maurice, or Rex Kilpatrick, or even with Norman Pargiter. Lawrence had drawn her not by his bodily attractiveness (she wasn't sure she was a very able judge of that) but through his maleness, by his physical strength, by what seemed to offer an explicit contrast to his compliancy with his father.

*

Lawrence's father saw her from the other side of Piccadilly and sounded his horn at her. He wound down his window and waved.

She waited for a break in the traffic and ran across to the car.

'Where do you want to go?' He picked his homburg up off the seat beside his. 'Just say, I'll take you.'

'I couldn't ask – '

'Tell me. You were heading somewhere?'

'Just to Albemarle Street.'

'It's still a trek. Come on, jump in.'

So she was driven to Albemarle Street in fine style, the finest, occupying the front passenger seat of a Bentley.

'Is your car a recent purchase?' she asked.

'*Fairly* recent.'

'I haven't seen it before.'

'I've got a weakness – '

She smiled.

'It's a Park Ward.'

'I see.'

'Continental.'

'Ah.'

Lord Marlott smiled.

'Boring information. Doesn't mean much to that pretty head of yours, does it?'

'Not an awful lot, I'm afraid.'

He asked her what she meant to do in Albemarle Street. She told him she was buying a painting for Lawrence's birthday.

'From a gallery?'

'It's only a little painting. A watercolour.'

'Look, Catherine, I have an idea. When you've finished we'll go and have lunch. Is that all right with you?'

She protested of course, but he seemed determined that he would have this opportunity to see her alone. At last she accepted his invitation, with a nod of consent and a smile that grew and grew.

When she had attended to her own business (assiduous service in abundance, she realised, with the car parked at the kerb outside), they drove to Mount Street, to La Coquille. She was in the ladies' room when she remembered the comb that used to lie on Leta's dressing-table at the nightclub, with the restaurant's name embossed in gilt in the tortoiseshell. Leta had seen her eyes alighting on it the first time.

'Background will out,' she'd said. 'Is that what you're thinking? Light fingers?'

She'd been embarrassed that Leta should have been so observant.

'Background *will*, anyway. I was taken there, for a sort of business talk. Not a treat really.'

Leta had sat casting through her lipsticks for the one she wanted.

'I went to "powder my nose". I wasn't thinking; I'd forgotten my own comb, and put it into my evening bag. I didn't notice until I got home. I thought, should I take it back, tell the attendant I wasn't concentrating? I could just see her scowling when I handed it over. I didn't *want* it, honestly. I don't know why I used it even, something that had been through half a dozen heads already. But I couldn't concentrate, I wasn't myself.'

'It must have been a very posh night out.'

'It was meant to put me in my place. It was meant to show me I didn't belong there, that I didn't have a clue.'

'Why *were* you there?'

'As I said – a business talk. Well, I thought *I* would be doing the talking. But as usual it got turned the other way about. I was talked to. Made to feel small. All done very charmingly, of course. But ruthlessly too. On a table on a raised platform, so it was like being in a theatre and everyone could see.'

Several years later they had replaced one tortoiseshell comb with another. She wondered about the table, though, if it could be a coincidence; they were shown to one set apart, at the top of three shallow steps with a little balcony rail in front of it. Maybe it was meant to be secluded from the rest of the room, but it only made her feel they were especially obvious to the other diners seated at tables on the flat.

Her host knew the menu without having to be shown one, and asked if he might order for her? She told him, yes, certainly, and he gave his instructions to the maître d' in French.

Seafood was the speciality of the house, and the murals on the walls, alternating with panels of elaborately gilded mirror, showed scenes of seashore and subterranean life. In the background was a harbour, complete with lobster pots and baskets of shellfish. Beneath their table, under the balustrade, actual wooden boxes of flatfish, crab and langoustines were set out, the wares displayed on white ice and garnished with cut lemons and ribbons of seaweed.

They began with lobster bisque, followed by brill poached in fennel. It was during the second course that the purpose of the visit was suddenly revealed to her. She mistook the remark at first for levity, for humorous party banter.

'I think you should marry very soon, Catherine.'

She thought she might pretend not to have heard, but he had spoken the words very clearly. She merely smiled a response. But, as she was to discover after that, he spoke in all seriousness.

He told her that she and Lawrence were very well suited for one another, that she showed she had the makings of an excellent professional wife, that she had great gifts of poise and intelligence and something he called 'adaptability'. All of which had her looking at the crockery on the table, unable quite to believe that it was herself they were talking about.

'I really am in favour of it, Catherine. You do understand that.'

'Oh yes,' she said.

After all, it was none other than the leonine Lord Marlott talking.

'Oh yes,' she repeated.

'I wanted you to be quite sure how I think. How I feel. For things to be expressed between the two of us.'

He patted her hand where it lay on the table-top.

'Not,' he said, 'not that I think we need tell Lawrence.'

She nodded. Once, twice.

'Of what has passed between us.'

He covered her fingers with his.

In London Lawrence took her walking, after making his formal proposal of marriage.

Once they stopped to look over Chelsea Bridge, and she was almost certain that it was her life running in eddies and ripples beneath the arches and away from herself. He lifted her hand from the parapet and kissed her wrist, her fingers. He didn't tell her that he loved her, but she didn't mind. She did ask him a question – 'Are you sure that I'm right for you?' He smiled the question away, though, and turned them back for the Embankment without saying another word.

She didn't love Lawrence.

No, it wasn't love.

He wanted her. Perhaps he needed her. Her own career was in suspense, or at an end.

When he wasn't there, she could still feel the strength in his body. When he *was* with her, his maleness made her dizzy – all that muscle, leanness, stubborn facial and body hair – it drew her.

He didn't love *her*, not 'love'.

But he was becoming a predictable presence she was quite comfortable with.

Each of them knew little about the other. That didn't make them exceptional. For what could be worse than two people knowing more about themselves than they needed to? She had seen that staleness impressed on too many faces.

*

They were married in a service at Lord Marlott's home, Lambdown House.

She had considered whom she might invite – the Helmsleys? Euphemia Montgomery? the Littigs? – but she hadn't been able to decide how best to justify the marriage to them. In the event she didn't know who most of the wedding guests were, and she felt strangely alone.

A marquee had been set up in the garden, and there everyone mingled. She was wearing a Helmsley wedding gown of shantung silk and Honiton lace.

At the breakfast she was spoken to by someone who had known Rex Kilpatrick. She felt herself turning very hot as the man and his wife meshed her in conversation. She guessed that they weren't unacquainted with the true state of affairs on that front. She saw Lord Marlott noticing their interest in her and doubtless recognising her prickly unease. She hastened away from the couple, leaving them standing and only making her own embarrassment worse.

She moved round the room, accepting the congratulations of strangers, and all the time she was looking for Denbigh. She *had* invited him, not with a printed card but with a couple of letters, letting him know – as playfully as she could – that she *expected* him to be there. When she did find him, he was talking to an arresting young woman she'd happened to spot arriving, arm in arm with an older, dyspeptic-looking man whose face had been rigid with ineffable boredom. Her companion had deserted her; Denbigh finished scribbling some lines on the back of a business card and handed it to her. The girl read what was written and nodded her head. She was tall, and attractive in a decorative way, and something in her manner suggested to Catherine that she had determination, ambition. She spoke a few words, smiled winningly, and walked off. Denbigh stood watching her for a few moments.

'A new tennis partner?' Catherine asked him.

He turned round and smiled, but with a fraction less self-possession than she was used to seeing.

'Why not a consultation?'

'Why not?' she said. 'A bad case of double vision perhaps?'

'That's all behind you now, Catherine.'

'Really? And what happens to me next? No physical exercise at all?'

'You'll get some, I'm sure.'

'What about *you*, though? That's what bothers me.'

'Nervous energy. I use up bags of the stuff. Didn't you notice?'

She noted the tense.

'Have I lost my chance, then? Aren't we going to stay friends?'

'I hope so. If you'll still remember me – '

'Why ever shouldn't I?'

'You're a married woman, Catherine.'

'You'll have – compensations. Won't you?'

'Will I?'

'At Whistlefield,' she said. 'Your tennis parties. Watching history make itself. Over the tea trolley.'

'Is that a subtle side-swipe?'

'No one ever told me I was subtle at anything in my life.'

Circumstances determined that she wasn't able to speak to him again that afternoon. She did excuse herself and go looking for him as the first guests took their departure, and she finally caught a glimpse of him. He was standing talking side-on to Lawrence's father. Lord Marlott's hand was on his elbow, as if he'd apprehended him. Denbigh was speaking, with his eyes ranged on the older man's mouth or chin. Whatever the subject was, it seemed to be fully occupying both men's attention. Denbigh smiled when he'd stopped speaking, a too neat smile. Lord Marlott soberly and unsmilingly shook his head; Denbigh shrugged his shoulders and walked away from the hand that had held him, without a backward look.

49

Catawpa

'YOU'RE lucky, Felix,' Mr Matheson said in his un-Canadian accent, removing some sheets of typed paper from a filing cabinet. 'It seems we've got you fixed up already.'

I stared at him, then at the few pages of paper.

'The honest-looking ones go first. Then the pretty boys. And the rest – ' He shrugged. 'We do what we can, of course.'

I had hoped we might have gone on a train, but – setting out at seven o'clock in the morning – we drove there, all the four hundred and fifty miles from Toronto to the badlands of North Ontario beyond Timmins and Cochrane. Off the highway, every time we passed through a town I noticed how Mr Matheson's eyes scoured the streets for the signs of children. I watched them with not a little envy, even though the boys had shorn hair and wore cheap, fairground colours. There was a radio in the dashboard, turned down low, but after a while I became numbed to the music and the voices – an anodyne wash of sounds – and I was only conscious of them when we drove under pylons and the speaker sizzled or when we passed into a vertical interference zone, between band marks on the channel-finder.

We reached Catawpa Narrows about four o'clock in the afternoon. Already the street lights were on: those of them that worked. I saw a plain and regular, right-angled small town. The sidewalks were clean of litter, but the buildings looked scruffy and tired and in need of a good lick of paint.

Mr Matheson first drove us to the motel where he was to spend the night. He checked in and carried his overnight bag, with me following in his wake, along the covered walkway to his room. It smelt a little of disinfectant. The walls were laid with Formica strips of imitation wood. The fabrics in the room were purple and chestnut. The basin in the shower-room was cracked from side to side. Mr Matheson looked round and said to me, everything was quite satisfactory.

We returned to the car and then drove to the McLuskeys' house. It was a compact prefabricated bungalow raised on bricks, set on a square of damp grass sprouting toadstools. The houses on either side of it were exactly the same, without any hedges or fences to separate and distinguish neighbour from neighbour.

They were standing on the stoep waiting for us, Mr and Mrs McLuskey. They immediately looked past Mr Matheson for a first sight of me.

They were older than I was expecting, and smaller of stature. They both had rather floury, sunless complexions. *She* was swamped by a bottle-green cardigan, and her inexpertly cut, straggling hair gave an instant impression of untidiness; her face must have been pretty once, but it had grown fleshy and shapeless. My eyes were also drawn to *his* hair: thick, and Brylcreemed back from his broad, narrow brow, and too evenly black. His upper lip was very neatly moustached: on another man the effect might have been to suggest a Services past of some sort, a disciplined attitude, but he too wore a cardigan – in pale blue – several sizes too big for him, and chocolate-brown trousers that were very full and baggy at the top but stopped about an inch short of his shoes, curious braided green moccasins.

I kept smiling, but it wasn't such a simple business. I glanced round the living-room, which we had walked into straight off the top step. It must have been the centre light in its blueberry shade which made the room seem so busy, so clamouring. The wallpaper was heavily patterned; the pictures were brightly coloured views of Canada, aquamarine lakes and fiery mountains at sunset; there was a lot of lickety-split yellow brass – a barometer, fire tongs, a wall clock, some horse brasses, a lucky horseshoe fixed the wrong way up above the fireplace, a coal scuttle, models of moose in three different sizes ranged along the mantelpiece; the fitted carpet was indigo blue, and the tweed three-piece suite donkey brown.

Mr Matheson and I were invited to sit down on the two oversized armchairs on either side of the half-moon-shaped orange brick fireplace. The McLuskeys seated themselves on the settee. From the vantage-point of my chair there didn't seem to be an inch of unoccupied space in the room. Our knees appeared to be drawing closer together, to almost meet and touch, as we all sank into the cushions. I watched Mr Matheson peering over the two peaks of his knees as he began his official spiel on the purpose of our visit.

Almost his first words as we'd edged past the McLuskeys had been, 'Those are your new parents, Felix.' But at some point during that first afternoon my adopters gave up the pretence. They were both to leave the room on the excuse of making tea, and they were gone no little time.

'We reckon,' Mr McLuskey said on their return, as the scalloped teacups were handed round rattling in their saucers, 'it'd be better if we were Felix's uncle and aunt.'

'Why so?' Mr Matheson asked.

'It strikes me, sir, it'd be a deal more natural. In the circumstances.'

'In the circumstances,' Mrs McLuskey repeated.

Mr Matheson coughed into his fist as he considered.

'We usually recommend it as you know. But since Felix isn't used to our ways here in Canada – '

I glanced away.

' – *he* might not feel it quite, well, natural either. The English are a more formal race, of course – '

'We just thought,' Mr McLuskey cut in, 'the other way, "ma" and "pa", it might sound too . . .' he paused ' . . . presumptuous maybe.'

'Presumptuous,' Mrs McLuskey repeated.

Mr Matheson watched them both and was thoughtful.

We ate supper in the dinette, as they called the small room, not much bigger than an alcove, off the kitchen. We crowded round the table, and I could feel Mrs McLuskey's breath, hot and troubled, on the side of my face as she scraped the best pieces of meat in the stew from the sides of the pot to give to Mr Matheson and myself.

'I've gone left this on the range too long,' she said, hair falling into her eyes and her handkerchief escaping from the long sleeve of her cardigan.

'Vi is a cook and a half,' her husband said, sounding proud as punch.

I followed Mr Matheson's lead in nodding approvingly.

'My mind was wandering, I guess.'

'We were discussing important business,' Mr Matheson reassured her.

'That's why,' Mr McLuskey said, looking at his wife with more concern as the serving ladle screeched into the corners of the stewpot. Her face was as red as one of those Canadian sunsets and her frilly handkerchief was dragging in the gravy on her plate. As daintily as I could I reached out and eased the handkerchief from the sleeve. Her serving arm stopped in mid-motion; I felt everyone's eyes upon me. I laid the handkerchief as respectfully as I could on her side-plate.

'Oh,' she said, 'thanks, son. Thanks.'

Hearing the word spoken threw me into confusion. And now it was my turn to turn puce in the face.

50

Holy Matrimony

SHE guessed that Lawrence wasn't an instinctive lover. He was looking for a wife first and foremost, but the rest – the loving part – might follow. The advice columns in the magazines made that very point, that it was a duty of couples to be loving.

They hadn't discussed their previous existences in any great detail, and she had her reasons to doubt that they should. There would be too much to talk *about*, and since Lawrence hadn't so far volunteered she felt she should reciprocate his reticence or his prudence (surely it wasn't shyness?). So well placed as they were in a house in Thurloe Walk, they were starting their lives over again, from 1958, and such memories as she might give him would be of the lighter sort – uncomplicated and unthreatening – about her modelling days, for instance. She would extract some from him, inevitably, but she wouldn't make it seem like prying. All their dealings would be quite open and above-board. They would prove to one another the fact of their maturity.

Lawrence was in spiritual obeisance to his father as she believed she had never been to *her* father, not even in her teenage years.

Whenever she saw them together and could compare them, she was conscious that Lawrence was his father's walking shadow. In their talks, which were effectively monologues, he would defer to him in single syllables, and she could hardly accept that this was the same man of strong opinions who would articulate himself so forcefully and volubly when guests were seated at their own dinner table. The discrepancy between the two versions of Lawrence Marlott reminded her of the limits to her own knowledge of character (as if she of all people needed reminding).

Lord Marlott occupied their patch of sky like God. She was nervous of causing him some affront – more nervous than she'd been in her unmarried days – so she made a performance of her pleasantness and only embarrassed herself. But he excused her; he singled her out in company for a compliment or the benefit of one of his observations. Lawrence told her she'd made quite an impression, that his father had very few favourites.

'Why *me*? Who does he think I am? I can't think – '

'Father likes pretty women.'

She thought it very likely that he did. But he'd settled on *her* out of a crowded field. As with Lawrence, she couldn't believe they had a great deal in common. That first evening at the party he had told her he could remember her from her magazine days (even though little more on the matter had been said), and she felt that that must have been her principal recommendation: because she had seemed to be a person honed to an image – 'Miss Mayfair' in an extravagant garden-party hat and elbow-length gloves – while *she* knew that it had just been another exercise in masterly posing by the photographer and of dumb patience by herself. Hers was a dream life – that, she felt, was her justification – no less for those housewives in Pinner and Macclesfield she used to imagine than for certain redoubtable peers of the realm: all those women of England inexplicably reduced to daydreaming or boredom or some more complex want in their lives.

*

'Who is Denbigh?' she asked Lawrence. 'Do you know?'

' "Who is he?" '

'What do you know about him?'

'Nothing I can think of. Why?'

'He brought us together. Indirectly.'

'He's fond of attractive women. That's all I need to concern myself about.'

'Aren't you – '

'Aren't I what?'

'Well . . . jealous? Just a bit?'

'Of what?'

'Because I knew him?'

'You're not with him now, though?'

'No,' she felt obliged to answer.

'And you told me you hadn't seen him anywhere.'

'No, not since the wedding.'

'And you haven't *gone* to see him.'

(Was he quizzing her, by any chance?)

'So – I presume – you must have wanted something better. End of subject surely?'

She placed her elbow on the table and cupped her chin with her palm. She'd had to ask him to have her own question explained. He knew her – perhaps – just as well as she was capable of knowing herself.

*

A room was always available for them at Lambdown House. 'If you should want to come.' Catherine had to smile at the use of the conditional.

A very attractive bedroom it was too, at the back of the house, next to Lord Marlott's own quarters, and with the finest views. When they did go down to Sussex, a welcoming fire was lit in the hearth on dark days and, in the spring and early summer, bulbs sprouted in bowls and vases were filled with flowers. The sheets and pillowcases on the bed were always crisp and smelling of the wash, the surfaces of the room were dustless, the shelf above the basin carried a selection of fresh soaps and fragrances, towels might be replaced twice in a day. No room in her experience had ever been more enticing. She told Lawrence so, but of course to him none of this could have any novelty: she couldn't expect him to respond to it in the same way as herself, and – sure enough – he didn't. But *she* was flattered, unreservedly delighted in fact, and she felt it would have been very impolite of her not to say. Lord Marlott waved the palm of his hand and shook his head when she spoke about it, dismissing her gratitude as quite unnecessary. The pleasure, he was letting her know, was as much his: Lambdown was *her* home too, she inferred, as it would one day be Lawrence's inheritance.

'If my father had just kept on his flat – '

'In London?'

'Where else?'

'In Kensington?'

'Belgravia.'

'Whereabouts?'

'Eaton Square. Then we *would* have been set up. We really would have been laughing, wouldn't we – ?'

*

On a couple of occasions she caught Lord Marlott losing patience with Lawrence. It happened in a split second. The anger was transmitted through his eyes as much as it declared itself, *sotto voce*, in words. She wasn't sure that anyone else saw or heard, apart from Lawrence and herself.

The anger frightened her. Its expression was instantaneous, but she sensed – she couldn't quite think why – that it had been long-brewed, that it was showing itself merely as a reflex to some word spoken, some old taboo between them. There wasn't time on either occasion for foreplanning or judgement, the anger flared instinctively.

Lord Marlott didn't apologise, and Lawrence was left ruing the moment, ears burning to the tips and his eyes fixing on some object of no significance. A story went untold, she guessed, and so she was intrigued. But she didn't see how she could confess to having seen without hurting Lawrence's pride still further. She said nothing therefore, even though she came to suspect that Lawrence suspected her of knowing: and thus inadvertently, acting with what were the best intentions, she may only have given him an excuse for, not gratitude, but resentment.

'I believe you lived in Eaton Square,' she remarked to her father-in-law over coffee.

'Ah, Lawrence has been talking – '

She already heard a critical tone in his voice.

'Did he tell you it was a lost investment?'

'Not – not really,' she said.

'I felt London wasn't the same any more. For me it was a ghost-town.'

Later she mentioned the cars, the garage of Rolls-Royces she'd read about.

'I picked one of them up for next-to-nothing. They were beautiful machines. But somebody wrote about them in an evening newspaper, and suddenly – everybody's eyes were peeled for them – they weren't mine any more. They were public property.'

The tone of his voice changed subtly. She heard his contempt for the incident and its originators in Fleet Street.

'It *is* a pity,' he said, 'we could have taken a spin in them. Worked our way along the line of them.'

She shrugged, sympathetically.

'But I *still* insist on having two. A Rolls-Royce and a Bentley. So you can take your pick, Catherine. Whenever you like – '

He held his arms open wide, in a gesture of unbounded generosity. His eyes had a certain shine in them which she found herself turning from in embarrassment.

*

The essence of Lambdown House, Catherine felt, was experienced best on frosty mornings with the mist slowly lifting from the fields. Inside, fires would be crackling in the grates; betwixt inside and out-of-doors, standing on the top step of the flight at the front of the house, she was able to smell the woodsmoke trailing in almost stationary ribbons from the chimneys. It seemed that as soon as you even *thought* of a want, the staff ran and fetched: hot-water bottles, mufflers, travelling rugs, hip flasks, walking sticks and shepherds' crooks.

It was in similar conditions that the hunt met. Saddled horses stamping in the cobbled yard, the hounds wraithed in scuds of their own hot, steamy breath, the functional creak of leather, the genteel rattle of silver on silver as quaffing-dishes were returned to out-stretched salvers, the hearty party guffaws and tinkly female chatter. Then the swathed sounding of a brass gong and the mustering of the dogs and the rather unathletic final mounting into stirrups.

Lawrence and his father both rode to hounds and repeatedly enjoined her to do the same. A farmer friend of Aunt Dodie's in Cumberland had taught her to ride a pony when she went to stay, but it was too long ago now for her to remember how. She finally had to invent a wild story about a grandfather killed when his horse threw him at a hedge, and even that – she saw – only set Lord Marlott thinking of ways to overcome such a phobia.

When they were all out of watching range, enveloped in layers of mist, she would stand listening to the fading rumble of horses, the dogs' distant baying and the unmusical blasts on the horn. She didn't care to dwell on what happened after that, when the fox or deer was cornered and held at bay. Otherwise well-bred, mild-mannered people called it sport, 'great fun', they excused it as 'exercise', and she felt it was *she* who must be out of social alignment. To them nothing seemed especially out of place about a barbaric death in the English morning. Tourists took photographs, and children jumped on one another's backs and blew into their rolled fists, and the slash of colour – huntsmen's scarlet on the rural dun – graced calendars up and down the land, hanging on counting-house walls and in grandmothers' front parlours and cold north-facing bedrooms in brick terraces and pebbledash semis alike.

51

My Lucky Day

ONE morning the post brought a package addressed to me, under my old name. I saw my Aunt Vi weighing the parcel and scrutinising the handwriting.

She put it into my hands. It wasn't heavy. The stamps were American. I tried to read the postmark, but couldn't.

My aunt followed me into the dinette. I placed the package on top of the table.

I unpicked the sellotape, then began to unwrap the brown paper, but slowly, to prolong the unprecedented pleasure in my life.

'This *is* a surprise,' my aunt said, and sounded none too thrilled about it.

'Yes,' I nodded.

'Your lucky day.'

The wrapping covered a cardboard box. I pulled all the brown paper off first. My aunt picked it up, folded it neatly – for future use presumably – and nodded at me to continue.

I unstuck the sellotape holding the flaps fast and went into the box. I had to pull out some tissue paper before I could see what was inside.

'What is it, Felix?'

'It' turned out to be clothes. Three self-coloured boy's shirts with Brooks Brothers labels, a woollen tie like a club tie (grey stripes on maroon), from the same source, and a leaf-green roll-necked pullover in Shetland wool.

My aunt looked at the Pringle label on the jumper.

'I guess it'll do,' she said. 'You can grow into it.'

Underneath the pullover was an envelope. It carried my aunt's name.

She took it from me and flicked her thumb under the gummed flap. With her fingertips she picked out a folded sheet of notepaper. Inside that was a money order for one hundred and fifty Canadian dollars. My aunt followed the lines of print on the accompanying note; her lips moved, but I couldn't follow the sense.

'It's from someone who doesn't say,' she told me. 'Who they are. Only – ' She saw that I had read the total on the money order ' – that I'm to buy you a pair of trousers – ' She pinched her mouth. ' – I guess that means pants – '

I nodded.

' – and a sports coat. I understand *that*.'

She closed the sheet of paper over on itself. She took on that faraway look which indicated she was thinking about something she couldn't get to the bottom of.

'Better than a birthday,' she said.

It was a loaded remark – I'd had my birthday three weeks before – and I knew to avoid a direct response.

'Do you know who sent it?' I asked, although I was aware she didn't. Another diversionary question occurred to me. 'Do I have to write a thank-you note?'

My aunt kept a battered paperback of etiquette tips among her meagre library on the living-room bracket-shelf zoned for books. She hesitated briefly, then she smiled.

'There's no address,' she said. 'So I guess that means not.'

I nodded.

'It really *is* your lucky day,' she told me, putting that slicing ironic edge to her voice she could always surprise me with.

'Yes,' I said, relieved not to have to write a reply.

I saw her looking again at the money order, at the figures for one hundred and fifty dollars. She looked almost regretful for several seconds. She had been talking to my uncle about needing to buy new curtains for the living-room and bathroom. The money could have come in very useful. But she was a good woman, I'm ready to testify, virtuous in the rather flinty-faced, self-denying presbyterian fashion which was as much as I knew intimately of Canadian morality.

52

Thurloe Walk

SET up in the house in Thurloe Walk, they should have been set up for life. Among the Piranesi prints and Colefax and Fowler fabrics, she should have discovered fulfilment, even felicity: at any rate, she ought to have been able to appreciate comfort and security. But the gloomy prints of elaborate ruins left her cold, and while the printed fabrics might have been of the highest quality she had never been a woman for all that material *fuss*, long-legged kutani cranes and pouting amaryllis heads reaching for her legs with their greedy, rampant, erect, leaves.

The possibility of happiness, like a tide, started to recede. She didn't know how it happened; the process was imperceptible, as subtle as atmospherics. A creeping chill entered the house and it took her a long time to recognise that a change of temperature had occurred. Only an involuntary shudder at last awakened her to the fact as Lawrence snapped at her for the first time and, another evening, didn't attempt to offer her his customary explanation why he had been delayed yet again at the office. She began to notice that he wasn't finishing the food on his plate, that at weekends they ate with the radio turned on, that he didn't tidy up after himself in the bathroom in the mornings, that most nights in the week he would fall asleep within a couple of minutes of his head dropping on to the pillow.

*

Did sex matter? Ought it to be mattering?

Technically she thought she understood what was required of her. After George Street nothing much could have surprised her. Lawrence appeared conventional enough. Quite why it was called the missionary position she had never comprehended – was the man prostrating himself like a native, or was he asserting his power over the subject beneath him, and how did God – by distinct implication – come into the reckoning?

Sometimes she felt that her body caused Lawrence distress: the sexual organs, rather. His nostrils had a certain way of twitching when he could smell her, his mouth would flex uncomfortably, apprehensively, at the corners. Twice she had taken his hand in hers and gently placed it on her mons pubis. The first time it was inert and lay like a damp poultice; the second time, clammy in her hand, it resisted and got away.

She was conscious of a lack. Some days it clawed up into her, a painful absence, and she found herself in its grip. It ranged about in the emptiness of her womb for a while, until its point had been inescapably made, then gradually it retreated and left her to the dullness and monotony of no sensation at all.

Did sex matter? Ought it to be mattering?

Rather than disappointment she sensed conspicuous relief on Lawrence's part. Maybe it wasn't the swimming and circuit-training which were to blame, exhausting him. It might have been an appetite which his body rated low among its priorities. But why then should she also guess that their mutual failure was contributing in some measure to his irritation, to the tetchiness she not infrequently saw on his face?

Such a toned body, such a virile presence. Yet his eyes didn't stray to other women, except in the way of social politeness (always polite, always a smiler). She couldn't identify that particular glazing of the eyes which betokens covetousness. She had intercepted nothing, and that was precisely why she found herself perturbed, weighted with misgivings.

*

He could still smile for strangers. She still saw the envy on other women's faces for the life she had and its location.

Either they were too stupid to bother with, or else she and Lawrence put on a more convincing display of harmony than she was sometimes inclined to believe.

Smiles. And it's how, she thought, we shall go to our graves.

The Helmsley advertisements had now dispensed with representational figures altogether. Trick photography rendered human movement to a dress without the wearer being visible. The dresses ran across the colour pages like wraiths.

Every so often she would catch sight of his face, momentarily, in a crowd – Maurice's. But when the moment had passed, and the person, it was never him.

Only once – on an afternoon when she must have had a brainstorm, escaping from the prancing kutani cranes and the writhing orchids – did she climb the steps of a club, a house in Carlos Place which Lawrence had told her was a gambling den. In the foyer, greeted (but it was hardly that) by a beefy Latin in a tuxedo, she was reduced to mumbling inanities. Behind the man, beneath a chandelier, she saw a member being handed a grey herringbone coat, bowler hat and umbrella, and recognised in the saving seconds before he turned round that he'd been one of Monica's clients at The Paddock, a burly, bearded dead ringer for James Robertson-Justice.

But as he turned from the cloakroom attendant, she had already pirouetted on her ankles and was flying down the steps on her squawking heels and away.

53

Tendrils

Once she was standing in the conservatory of Lambdown House, breathing a little heavily and perspiring inside her dress but simply relieved to have some spare time to herself. She was fingering the leaves and tendrils of the hothouse plants in their pots when a sudden presence by her side shocked her like a charge. Her knees and ankles snapped, her arms shook in their sockets, her heart jumped into her neck.

'Has someone stepped on your grave?'

Lord Marlott placed his hand on her shoulder. She could feel herself shuddering, almost in spasm, like a thief caught red-handed.

She stared down at his shoes, which she had noticed before made not a sound as he walked.

'Camellia japonica.'

'I – I'm sorry.'

'These are camellias. Japonica Adolphe Audusson.'

'Ah.'

He must have noticed her flinch. His hand lifted and settled on her further shoulder, so that his forearm was left lying across the other. She stared at the plants without seeing them. When she was able to turn her head sufficiently on her neck, she found him watching her with his eyes open wide. He was engrossed by her. The obsessive quality of his attention had been there at the beginning, a little disguised for caution's sake in those rooms Denbigh had taken her to, where his eyes would always track her and where she was under his constant surveillance.

The pressure of his hand on her shoulder increased momentarily before he removed it. As he took it away, she shook a little on her feet. That was her only acknowledgement that his hand and his arm had been where they ought not. But following him out of the conservatory, she couldn't be sure that he wasn't viewing her in quite a new light.

*

Anderson, the new assistant, was too good to be true: deferential, smartly dressed, never a hair on his head out of place, smiling with white film-star teeth. She didn't trust him an inch.

'I'm sorry, Mr Anderson, I'm very sorry,' she would tell him, brushing past. 'I can't tell you *when* my husband will be back.'

She wasn't fooled by Lawrence's late arrivals home, which meant Anderson would be left waiting with her. The other departments of Whitehall must have been exhaustively scoured to unearth this treasure. She actually enquired of the young man what his credentials for the job were, and his blue eyes gelled and he stammered. It was the only major fault she'd been able to detect in him, his inability to account for himself.

'Don't you get enough of him in the office?' she asked Lawrence.

'He has to bring me reports, if I've been away.'

'Doesn't he trust me?'

'What?'

'To give them to me to give to you?'

It was a ridiculous situation: waiting for the ring of the doorbell every third or fourth evening, and opening the front door to admit this wholly characterless young man into their home. She had to offer him a drink, of course, and several times Lawrence suggested that he stay on and join them for something to eat. So they would seat themselves in the dining-room, she the least comfortable of the three of them, although realising that neither of the others was much at his ease either.

Everyone spoke of Lawrence's charm, but it came to seem like cold sunlight to her. 'Charm' was a word people used when they couldn't get to the inside of a person, when the outside was all they were offered, and the offering was done with smiles. At gatherings – which were the staple of their life – he appeared interested and confidential, but she knew it was a ruse. His purpose was to draw you out, by a sociable trick, and if you could be drawn as straightforwardly as that he realised you weren't worth persevering with. Your only worth lay in holding out against him, in which case the charm became secondary and his eyes brightened as he tried to work out your reason for resisting.

At stand-up evenings she incidentally served to warn him whom he should avoid: anyone who took up too easily with her was to be walked round about and given a very wide berth. He seldom introduced her to those people who clearly did interest him. She was aware that he took careful note of where she was and with whom, and how often certain individuals engaged her in conversation. His indifference to her movements on such occasions only went so far.

There was another type of social event which operated on different principles: the dinner party. At these she was required to conceal her intellectual failings (of course) but also to talk to whomsoever was expendable to him: usually the other wives. Sometimes there were fewer wives present, or they turned out to be blue stockings, in which case he involved her rather more, by watching the effect she had on this or that man, by locking them both in conversation and claiming that his wife enjoyed opera or gardening, by letting the men do most of the talking.

They had both become opera-attenders. In Denbigh's company, Verdi and Bizet had been a novelty for her but now she hadn't the patience for long long evenings of stage histrionics. She suspected that Lawrence's enthusiasm was less than he pretended, that he was quite lukewarm to the experience: but that it was also professionally expedient for them to be seen in the Covent Garden stalls. They attended the theatre less often, but she much preferred those visits: in the course of the two and a half hours she *forgot* more – about herself, and about Lawrence and herself. The taxi journeys back home at eleven o'clock passed in silence for the most part, and she saw the drivers' curiosity as they studied them in their mirrors.

Except during the ten or twelve weeks of the British summer, their house always felt cold in the hour or so before midnight. Some nights she couldn't stop shivering and Lawrence would look irritated with her. At the same time he seemed to prefer that she keep her dress and jewellery on until the last possible moment. She walked about the house finding the excuse of something needing to be done and all the time felt as Cinderella must have felt after the ball, with a massive depression and a screaming headache pending, although that part of the fairy-tale was never told.

In the second year of their marriage Lawrence had trouble with a stomach ulcer, which dated back to his early twenties, and that must have been his excuse to move into another bedroom, nearer the bathroom. He didn't move back.

She presumed the big bedroom was hers now, and she requisitioned the laying surfaces, claiming them with the 'lighter' sort of novel that got her to sleep, with posies of real or dried flowers, a few pot plants, a careful clutter of hairbrushes, combs, tubs of talcum powder. Lawrence still considered himself free to walk in and out of the room to talk to her or to search in the drawers for cufflinks or a shoehorn. On the other hand she felt a trespasser knocking on the door of his, and she only went in when he was out of the house – he must have known that she did, to keep the daily in check – but the bareness and orderliness would put her back into low spirits and she took no furtive pleasure at all in her access.

The house itself sank her spirits some days, and she took to spending mornings and afternoons away. All she had to do was to fill her time. She walked round shops, and visited galleries; she swam at the Lansdowne Club, and compounded her ignorance of gardening and horticulture by visiting Kew; she even mixed with school parties at the Regent's Park Zoo; she lunched – frugally and economically – in pleasant restaurants with (where she could find them) airy, romantic décors.

*

Despite all her attempts at off-handedness, Anderson continued to call of an evening, at least twice a week.

She watched for the glint in Lawrence's eye. He never seemed surprised that he should find Anderson here.

Ho-ho, she told herself, so this is your little game. Do I fall so far beneath your respect? But I must be worth something to you still if you need to view me like a voyeur. Is this how the jaded palate is to be titillated, by some intra-marital sexual perversity?

She wouldn't speak when they were seated in the dining-room. She watched the young man flounder, and she shut off when Lawrence mentioned cricket or squash.

I cannot be worked on, she meant to inform by her silence, I cannot be tempted and induced, not by such a hollow man, an empty vessel if ever there was. Nature, don't you know, abhors a vacuum –

'It's nothing much,' was all she would say, serving up, and knowing that it far outclassed anything Anderson would have been feeding himself wherever it was he lived (she didn't even ask where). She wasn't drawn by any of their questions, their conversational man-traps, she simply concentrated on the plates on the Welsh dresser and on reaching the end of the meal. *Yes, he probably thinks we're matched well enough, me and this callow youth. He thinks I have no more taste, that I would not be fastidious. He knows as little about me as that. So, what have the thirteen months and three weeks been in aid of?*

*

A photograph appeared in *Tatler*. It showed Lawrence and herself being escorted by their evening's hosts.

She was actually smiling, although she couldn't remember what it had been at. She looked – by some distortion of the flashbulb – *dégagée*, but in a good humour, blithe, even gay, which was quite unbelievable to her. She saw herself as she never did, and it was a shock to her, the contrast between the outside and what she knew must have been her proper feelings. It was no wonder that Lawrence hadn't wholly given up his confidence in her.

54

Rencounter, Re-encounter

At a mandarin's 'At Home' she became conscious that a pair of eyes were cutting across hers, wherever she looked. For several seconds she was uncertain, but the stare confirmed it, and the involuntary tightening of her body was like the jolt of a tripwire, instantly hauling her back into the past.

His manners were now faultless. His hair was greying, he had a moustache. His teeth, or the visible ones, had been capped. He smoked Havana cigars. Gold tie-pin, like Denbigh's, and gold cufflinks, and gold signet ring. A Mediterranean, or possibly Caribbean, suntan.

'Mrs Marlott?'

'Didn't you know?'

'Of course. But I was awaiting my moment.'

'Your wife isn't here?'

'Gloria doesn't come to things.'

'Don't people expect to meet a Mrs Petherick?'

'Mrs Collingbourne-St John.'

'What?'

'I bought an estate in Wiltshire, with a title. We decided we preferred Norman Collingbourne-St John to what we don't mention now.'

'I see.'

It sounded rather less than likely.

'I don't use the *title*, of course. But the surname has been ... convenient.'

'Oh well – '

'About Mrs Collingbourne-St John. My constituency team wish she *would* put in an appearance.'

'What?'

'Just now and then.'

'No. What you said. About "constituency".'

'I'm an MP. Didn't you know?'

She shook her head.

'Up north. Cheshire neck of the woods.'

'Why there?'

'Carpetbagger.'

'Tory?'

'Most certainly.'

'And your business?'

'I keep an eye on it. Discreetly, of course. At a remove.'

She stood shaking her head.

'What does that mean? Incredulity? Or admiration?'

'Well, I did recognise you. At least.'

'Little suspecting – '

'Should I have done?'

'No point in just being a common-or-garden *Member*. A little responsibility wouldn't go amiss.'

'I'm sorry, then. But I don't keep up with all that sort of thing.'

'You married to a Marlott, too?'

'Lawrence married *me* as well.'

'It really *was* you in the ads, wasn't it? "Miss Mayfair"? I could never believe it. I thought she just looked like you.'

'I was a miracle, technically.'

'I really am – thrilled. To meet you again.'

She closed her eyes and shook her head, and was somehow able to manage to smile at the same time. Remembering momentarily the transformation that had taken place in the ladies' room of Edwarde's Hotel.

'Well, well, well,' he said.

'Indeed.'

They walked around one another for the whole evening. She knew he was watching her all the time; even when she had her back to him, she felt his gaze on her neck, her shoulders, the backs of her arms. She realised he was mentally undressing her, and later in the evening she had proof positive when he brushed against her and the knot inside his trousers grazed her thigh.

He telephoned her during the week, as she had guessed that he would. An invitation to a party, she supposed, but it turned out that he had been applying himself to circumstances rather more urgently. They would engineer a collision, he said, in the foyer of the Savoy Hotel one lunchtime.

She shouldn't have gone, but Lawrence had put a gloom on her day with one of his moods, and she was at their rendezvous when he'd asked her to be. *He* was not, however, and it occurred to her that he had planned some such humiliation to get his own back: this was his revenge for her having put him, as it must have seemed, out of her mind for half a dozen years. But while she was buttoning up her coat to leave he hurried through the doors, out of breath.

'Toadying,' he said. 'Some awful old fart who pulls the strings.'

She didn't respond to the word. Did its use mean he was trying to be at his ease with her?

'Looks hopefulish, though,' he said. 'But I'm very sorry I'm late.'

'For our collision?'

'What's that?'

'For our accident.'

'Oh. Yes.' He remembered. And he smiled with his capped teeth.

This is folly, she told herself, all through drinks and all through lunch, and then as she travelled upstairs with him in the lift to the room with the river view he'd had the foresight – or the arrogance – to book. This is ludicrous, this is demeaning, she told herself as she undressed for him. This is utter stupidity, she knew, as she took her place in the bed: and also the measure of my desperation, that I have to do this for want of anything like love, and for the lack of any compensating carnal satisfaction in my life. Sex and loneliness can drag you *this* low, this is the terrible end of it all.

As he leaned over her, she closed her eyes.

His fingers explored her ravenously, immediately homing in, and she was ashamed by the sensation of moistness between her legs. How could he do any differently when she was giving him the signs he wanted? His knee pushed between her thighs, with brusqueness and strength, and she let them part. It was weeks since Lawrence had covered her at night, and she had persuaded herself that it didn't matter, it was a relief to her. She had hoped to believe it maybe, all the time knowing quite well the vassalage in which her own body kept her.

It was the first of a string of days.

Days, never nights.

Sultry late-summer afternoons, in the shadow – as it were – of Cleopatra's Needle. Lunchless usually, but invariably cheered along with a couple of drinks inside them both. Sometimes they had tea afterwards downstairs, but with time he became a slave of the Division Bell. Taxis drove him at speed to the hotel and back, and most often the love-making – no, she preferred the term 'sex' – was hasty, forceful, messy, with spillage. They spoke little, and there was hardly any pretence of tenderness. The sex was functional for her, and for him in a rather different way, since he liked her to wear jewellery and expensive perfume and to parade herself (briefly, since time was so restricted) in the fine silk lingerie he bought her. They knew what they had to achieve every time, and they did so, without fail. She took pride in that. And of course she also hated herself for the duration of those regular Wednesday afternoons, but even her revulsion became less incommoding, it placed itself further back in her thoughts, as she merely disciplined herself to routine and went into mental 'neutral', really to save her sanity and soul.

They encountered one another on the social circuit on a couple of occasions. She found the sham of unconcerned acknowledgement provocative and exhilarating, and she worked herself up to a heat before and after.

On the second of those evenings, after their nods of recognition for the company's benefit, he took her off to the back of a basement cloakroom, behind a rack of coats, and hitched up her dress. He raised her on to an upended laundry basket and she kicked off her shoes and wrapped her legs around his waist. He shuddered into her like – like a power drill, she imagined it, biting on the sleeve of a stranger's fur coat, so intense was her wish to scream out. Afterwards some of his semen spurted on to the fur and a gent's topcoat, and they smiled at each other, not warm smiles but complicitous.

When the parliamentary session was over, their Wednesday afternoons were longer (and darker) but less brutally satisfying to her. Once he went walking with her, before they had tea, on the Embankment: to the Needle with its hieroglyphic scratchings in one direction, and in the other up the steps on to Waterloo Bridge. They stood watching the late sun silver the Thames, then they continued walking: apart all the while, he in a double-breasted Savile Row suit and she in the softest alpaca coat with the luxurious silk lingerie so soft and lightweight beneath the razor-cut pleats of her jersey-wool dress. Layers of concealment . . .

No one, she knew, could have confused them for lovers. But as a married couple? – yes, perhaps, seven or eight years on, with their past talked out or not spoken of at all, in mutual limbo, in the unclaimed corridor of convenience that runs between one country's border and the other's.

55

To Damascus

By the time they visited Switzerland for a conference, Lawrence and she were already well and truly started on the rocky road. In retrospect she thought certain events must only have been waiting to happen. All that had been needed was the location. And where better, where more given to the presentation of a dapper outer show – not a petticoat flounce out of place, not a crease or a smudge to be seen – than spruce Geneva on her lake, offering such a dubiously bland, scrubbed face to the world?

*

'What did you do?'

'Do?'

'This afternoon.'

'Oh.' She shrugged.

'I rang you,' Lawrence said.

'I was looking around.'

'What did you see?'

'Oh. Just the streets. Some buildings.'

'Aren't you hot?'

'I'd better have a bath,' she said.

'Farrer's coming over at quarter to seven. For a drink. With his wife.'

'Here?'

'Yes, of course.'

She saw her panic in a mirror.

'Are you feeling all right?'

'Yes. I've never felt better.'

'So, you'll feel up to some socialising?'

Sighing, she walked across to the french windows. They had a view of the lake and the giant spout of spray and the far Vaud mountains. She saw him watching her in the glass.

'You can't live in bloody bathrooms all your life, Catherine.'

*

'You were Rex Kilpatrick's mistress?'

They were sitting on a private terrace in Lugano, with unobstructed views of Lake Maggiore beneath.

'What?'

'You didn't hear me?'

She stared at him.

'I *said* – you were Rex Kilpatrick's mistress, weren't you?'

'I – '

'Yes or no.'

'But – '

'Yes or no, Catherine.'

She circled the word for several moments. She spoke at last.

'Yes.'

'A-ha.'

Lawrence folded his napkin; halved it, halved it again, halved it a third time.

'I see – '

'Didn't you know?'

'I heard rumours.'

'Or did you enquire?'

'Perhaps.'

'Why?'

'Because *you* didn't tell me, Catherine. That's bloody why.'

'It – it didn't come up. We didn't discuss him.'

'Kilpatrick? Well, naturally I presumed it was a professional relationship.'

She didn't believe he'd presumed any such thing.

'But is that what a professional relationship *is* in that line?'

'It's perfectly respectable,' she said.

'You sound defensive.'

'I'm not being defensive. I'm telling you the *truth* – '

She threw her napkin down on the table and stood up.

'Where are you going?'

'I'm not staying here – '

'You're walking away from it? Just like that?'

'You're *trying* to make me angry. Make me feel . . .'

'Feel what?'

He was making himself sound so reasonable. He was trying to make himself unassailable in his sensibleness and good humour and that air of –

'Bloody self-righteous rectitude,' she said, but not quite loudly enough for him to hear.

'What's that?'

'Never you damn well mind.'

'Well, this is a new Catherine I'm seeing. Catherine Fairweather that was, do you prefer that?'

She closed her eyes.

When she opened them, she saw the housekeeper approaching up the steps. An acquaintance of Lord Marlott's had lent them the waterside villa and she was learning to hate it for its grandeur and its privacy that made the garden feel like a prison yard.

And it was still only the sixteenth month of their marriage.

'I'm going out,' she said.

'Where?'

Wherever there might be left that he wouldn't be able to find her.

'To do what, might I – '

'Do nothing. Walk about – Do damn bloody all.'

*

On her subversive, sexual Savoy afternoons she refused to let her dislike show, or her physical fear, or her private pleasure at the chicanery, while he spun her nipples between his fingers and dipped his head between her thighs. She wore the lingerie he bought her and he frayed the silk with his afternoon stubble, he pressed the jewellery so hard in his embraces that her ear lobes and wrists hurt and bore the imprints for long minutes afterwards. He didn't warn her when he was on the verge of orgasm, and sometimes didn't enter her at all but soaked her stomach and midriff. Even Lawrence had more consideration, but he was the coldest fish in the sea, while this man branded her with his heat. She opened her legs wider and wider to take him, and all he would request of her was to speak to him, in that Aquae-Regis version of lockjaw he remembered from the last time, which seemed enough in itself to swell him to another erection. So she recited the names of the streets, that geometric puzzle of squares and half-circles – Potiphar, Vanbrugh, Prideaux, Medlicote, Tobago, Belvedere – and he was carried on her voice to the point where his semen flew, he no longer cared where. As he rolled off her, she was left craving a response that never came in herself.

They dressed on opposite sides of the room, as the strangers to one another that they had always been.

*

When they were at Lambdown, she sometimes went off by herself and walked round the vegetable garden.

But where she went in the middle of these empty afternoons didn't remain her own secret, and her refuge was infiltrated. The means of assault were hardly subtle, but perpetrated in such a way as to wholly confuse and overwhelm her. She was standing by a hot frame, leaning forward to look beneath the streaked glass at the globe artichokes, when one hand pulled the blouse from her waistband and another reached up to manhandle a breast. A body was pressing on hers and she couldn't straighten herself. Both hands worked on a breast apiece. She was quite dazed at first, and several moments passed before she thought to struggle. She tried to speak, to protest – 'Lawr – ' – but the words wouldn't form themselves, and all that came out of her mouth was wheezing hot air. She realised enough to be struck by the ridiculousness of what was happening, this comically formal distortion of their two bodies, upended over the forcing frame.

'Please!' she was able to blurt out at last, as a concession to decency, wifely shame. But when he said nothing in response, she heard all the equivocalness in the word, as if she was teasing him further, not to stop.

The palms cupped her breasts, fingers pulled at the nipples. She felt the weight of groin pushing against her buttocks.

The hands pressed flat on her breasts, squashing them. She felt all the breath was being squeezed out of her and she opened her mouth to gulp down some air. She should have guessed that this was how it would finally be, a furtive possession even in daylight.

Suddenly she turned, wrenching her head round. She looked over her shoulder and found herself staring into eyes only three or four inches from her own, not her husband's – or even her unloving lover's – but those precision-boring instruments of the venerable Lord Marlott of Rittenham.

56

Sleaves . . .

'MAYBE we should talk, Catherine?'

The simplicity of the request had meant that she couldn't refuse, and Lord Marlott had shown her – with consummate politeness – into his study. She had seated herself on the chair closest to the door, imagining his intentions must again be carnal.

'A cigarette?'

She shook her head.

'Awful habit,' he said. 'But I was glad to see it's one of your – occasional – vices too.'

He took one from his case and lit it. Then he closed the case.

She stared at it as he held it in his hand. He was concentrating on the cigarette.

'My doctor thinks I should give them up. What would Denbigh's opinion be, do you think?'

She couldn't take her eyes off the cigarette case.

'Maybe you could have a word in his ear for me? I've heard how able he is. Knows his way round the whole body. Got a gift for it.'

'How far back did you look?'

'What's that?'

'To find out about me.'

'Oh . . . There were rather too many blanks. I suspect you've changed name several times. Aren't I right?'

She was still watching the cigarette case.

'How far back did you trace me?'

'Not so far. I didn't know who I was looking for, you see. Catherine Somebody-or-Other. In fact I didn't fare too well. Nothing before our year of grace, nineteen fifty-five.'

He flicked some ash from his cigarette into the ashtray. 'That was the rather curious summer you spent in – Surrey, wasn't it? A quaint little house. With some girlfriends?'

She stared at his evading eyes.

'And your little appendage in tow, of course. But you don't talk about *him* now, I dare say.'

She didn't speak.

'That, I'm afraid, is more or less that. But I expect there's quite a story to be told. Maybe you would care to divulge it some time. I assure you, I'd make a very appreciative audience.'

He smiled as he did on the venerable guests he entertained at his table.

'Did you tell your friend Denbigh, I wonder?'

Her eyes dropped back to the cigarette case. It might have been bluff, claiming he knew as much, and no more – he was wily enough for it. But in Leta's time she'd called herself Cath Stimpton, and in the Archdeaconry she was Kate Vaughan; she had acted as Catherine Eveleigh, which was also how she'd given her name using the Petherick accounts.

'This seems to have caught your eye?'

He held up the cigarette case.

'It's very unusual,' she said.

'It was a birthday present. My fortieth, I think. From a colleague and his wife.'

He turned it over. The exterior comprised alternating diagonal bands of gold and silver.

'I lost the original. I had another made. I never said that I'd lost it. It was the sentimental value. Not *quite* vulgar, although maybe it comes close.'

She watched him as he opened his hand and held out the case.

'Please,' he said. 'Take it.'

'What?'

'Take it. My present to *you* – '

'I couldn't – '

'A seal on our – our understanding.'

'You had to have it made especially?'

'Yes.'

'It wasn't stock?'

'That would have been easy.'

'Was the original made for you too?'

'My colleague's wife did the design; she had copies of it. I took the drawings back to Asprey's and they obliged again.'

'I see. I see.'

'Do – do you collect cigarette cases?'

There was a caustic note sunk low in the remark.

'No,' she said.

'Keep it, Catherine.'

She took it from him. He smiled at the care with which she handled it. But not care, of course: a superstitious fear. She closed her eyes and smelt the quagmire of mud down at Rotherhithe.

'I've got another case, it's silver. I'm giving you this one as a present.'

'How did you lose the first one?'

His eyes betrayed only a single second of unease.

'I didn't take enough care of it. I mislaid it.'

She wrapped her hands round it.

Outside, a car's wheels churned the gravel.

'The return of the prodigal son, I presume.'

But she didn't move.

A car door banged shut, almost directly outside, muffled by the heavy velvet drapes. Her eyes were momentarily held by his, by a degree of ferine, malign coldness she had never encountered before, lower than zero.

*

At last she rang Whistlefield. Mrs Collis answered, and presumed she was someone called 'Miss Gregory'.

'It's Catherine Marlott,' she corrected her.

After profuse apologies had been offered, she learned that Denbigh was in Morocco.

'Oh, I see.'

She couldn't remember him ever taking a holiday.

'When will he be back, do you know?'

'He has some people to look up. But his appointments don't resume for another three weeks. He has made arrangements to – '

But she had learned what she needed to: that he wasn't there, and that she'd let two years go by incommunicado that she ought not. She had known where he was all this time, and done nothing about it: while *he* might have been apprehensive about intruding into a marriage. Twice their social tracks had crossed; but on the first occasion they weren't able to speak, and on the second he arrived directly on the heels of a young woman and she didn't feel inclined.

Now she had learned what she needed to. He wasn't there, and she'd let all that time go.

*

Her Wednesday afternoon rendezvous three weeks hence – not at the Savoy but at the Grosvenor House – would now have to be cancelled.

'You'll never guess – '

'What?'

'I've been invited down to Lambdown House.'

'*What?*'
'To lunch.'
'Why?'
'He has a Members' lunch every year. I never thought I'd get to go.'
'When is it?'
'The twenty-fourth.'
'He's asked *us* then. But Lawrence can't go.'
'Please be there, Catherine.'
'Oh God.'
'Will you?'
'I don't want to go back to that place, really.'
'I'll drive you. There and back.'
'He's invited you?'
'It's an annual do. Bright hopefuls get their names put forward and he has the bother and glory of hosting it.'
'We weren't here for it last year.'
'You will come?'
'Perhaps,' she said. 'I'd have to gird my loins.'
'It's quite a coup – '
She didn't enthuse.
' – isn't it?'
It was too simple, too easy, didn't he see that?
'Catherine . . .?'
'I thought the doorbell rang,' she said.
'I'll cancel the room.'
'What?'
'At the Grosvenor House.'
Why did she allow herself to care? Every Wednesday was a humiliation to her, but one she thought she couldn't do without. They had no affection for one another, yet they went through the travesty of love: as if, she felt, he was trying to prove to her that 'love' is a lie, unbelievable, and she was still trying to prove to herself that it comes only once truly in a life, and that its callous re-enactments are hollower and hollower echoes, evanescing into silence.

57

. . . *Skeins*

A HAND seized her arm as she was turning the corner into Hans Crescent. Even before she could cry out, the woman's other scented hand had reached up and clamped itself to her mouth.

'Highly unorthodox, my dear – '

Catherine struggled to see who her assailant was.

' – but needs must . . .'

The hand was removed as the other guided her along the pavement. She found herself on the cobbles of Pavilion Road, which served the back entrances of Sloane Street.

'What about some reviving morning coffee, Mrs Marlott? Fortifying too.'

'Mrs Russell? What on *earth* – '

'Now, now. This isn't the time to become moral and superior.'

'How did – '

'Your maid told me where you were.'

'Floy?'

'Is that the name? I don't think I'd trust her one hundred per cent if I were you. Probably Mr Marlott twists her arm now and then, figuratively speaking of course.'

Catherine stared grimly at the cobbles in front of her.

'Somewhere genteel for coffee, I thought.' This morning she was managing to maintain her elocution-class accent. 'The Lambert, perhaps?'

Catherine still didn't speak.

'I give it the English pronunciation – my antecedents being somewhat common. You favour the French, I expect.'

When they reached the hotel, they walked up two floors to the lemon and lime lounge. A table had been reserved in a corner, out of hearing reach of the other tables. They lowered themselves into two wing-sided chairs. Mrs Russell smiled to suggest that this was the most harmless and fortuitous of occasions.

Tea was ordered and brought to them.

'Shall I be mother, Mrs Marlott – ?'

Catherine hadn't spoken more than the minimum since they'd arrived. Mrs Russell sighed.

'We really *must* try – '

'I don't know why I'm here.'

'Just for a little talk.'

'What have we got to talk about?'

'Oh, I think there's plenty.'

'You're just going to run down Hugh Denbigh, I suppose. Find out what you can, worm it out of me – '

Mrs Russell reacted with mock shock.

'Mrs Marlott!'

'I'll have you know, I'm very grateful to him.'

'Very touching. Now do have some tea, Mrs Marlott. Wet your whistle.'

The brew was poured.

'But what, might I enquire, have you now got to thank Denbigh *for*?'

'We were friends – '

Mrs Russell smiled, shaking her head.

'He doesn't *have* friends. Acquaintances, yes, and people he can use.'

'You don't know – '

'What do *you* know about him?'

Catherine was too indignant to answer straight away.

'He's a mixer and shaker, is that it? All jolly cocktail stuff? You'd get a surprise if you really knew.'

'Knew what?' Catherine asked.

'He's fairly subtle, he covers his tracks. But he's not what he seems.'

'I don't want to hear what – '

'If I said – ' Mrs Russell's shoulders rose as she scanned the nearly empty room and swallowed breath – 'if I told you there's currently some Czech infiltration of the British establishment afoot you'd probably think it was spy-story stuff, wouldn't you? Out of a book?'

' "Infiltration"?'

'It's not *quite* like the yarns in the books. The goodies, let's call them, they're desperate types like *me*' – she pointed to herself – 'and the baddies for our purposes, they're the charmers, smooth-talkers, with everything going for them, nice cars, tennis courts.'

'I really – don't know what you're talking about.'

'You've nothing to thank Denbigh for, I can assure you of that.'

'But – '

'What *do* you know about him, Mrs Marlott?'

'What everyone else does – about his career. And what he wanted to tell me. He *is* charming. He made me very welcome at Whistlefield – '

'What did he tell you about your husband, for instance?'

' "Tell" me? What I wanted to know.'

'About his – peccadilloes too?'

Catherine stared at her.

'No story is complete without a little sexual – "duplicity", let us say.'

Catherine shook her head.

'I don't expect the intimate side of your marriage is altogether satisfactory, is it?'

'That – that is none of your business.'

'*You* know a little more about such matters, of course, don't you? You must have learned quite a bit – during that summer of 'fifty-five.'

Catherine's eyes fixed.

'Well, you could hardly have kept *that* a secret, could you? Not from me. Even with the change of name. All it took was one photo: not very good, just an old box camera, and Rosemary was no expert, but the face was unmistakable.'

Catherine didn't speak.

'You're under no obligation to *believe* me, Mrs Marlott.'

Catherine sniffed, loudly.

'Certainly,' Mrs Russell continued, taking note of a trolley's movements across the lounge, 'I *could* furnish you with evidence if needs be. Of your husband's – ' she paused ' – misadventures.'

'*What* "misadventures"?'

'With some of his young men friends.'

'No – ' Catherine shook her head.

'Hardly men at all in fact, so young are they.'

'No,' Catherine repeated. 'No.' The shakes of her head became more forceful.

'Why do you think there was such urgency to get the two of you married? You weren't exactly the *ideal* wife, if you don't mind my saying so, Catherine. A little too obvious – with your model's face, how you hold yourself – and, frankly, not well enough connected. *N'est-ce pas?* Not for his lordship anyway. First generation title, you see. I rather wonder what dark secrets are hidden in *his* past, that *would* be interesting to – '

' "Secrets"?'

'Well, he's the most elusive man *I* have ever come across. Which is saying something. He makes Denbigh look positively forthcoming, quite garrulous by comparison.'

'He – he's in the public eye. Isn't he?'

'Oh, he's everywhere. In the newspapers, the social columns. But no one really *knows*, do they? It's camouflage. For what, though? All the time the "real" man is incognito.'

Catherine didn't let herself respond.

'*You* are in a privileged position, of course. Jack Marlott will set you up very comfortably, to ensure you stay married to your better half. He's sort of obliged in that respect, anyway: with the police so interested in his son's predilections.'

'Why – why should I believe you?'

'If you consider carefully, I trust you'll see I speak sense, Mrs Marlott. Catherine – '

'I don't want to hear – '

'Certainly I should have preferred one of my own brood to be in your position, that's true. The *Virginia* Fairweather I had on my books, for instance. Why should Denbigh have had the luck, that's what I'd like to know.'

'Ask him then.'

'Lawrence *needed* to marry, of course. It's all been romantically whirlwind. Does his father really not have an inkling about Denbigh, that he'll begin to sneak his way into his affairs, through your delightful self?'

Catherine shook her head.

'This is fantastic – '

Mrs Russell ignored the remark.

'Lord Marlott does intrigue me very much. Our self-made pillar of the establishment. With Swiss bank accounts, are you aware? You appreciate the arrangement, I'm sure – the investor pays the *bank* interest, and no questions are asked. Why should he have chosen to do business – because such you are, Mrs Marlott – with your friend Hugh Denbigh?'

'He's an oculist, he has a wide circle – '

'If only it were so simple, my dear. But it really isn't, I must tell you. It's a frightful maze. A wonderful opportunity for someone like *me*, though.'

Mrs Russell smiled coldly.

'I'm from nowhere. But I'm not the only one. You learn how to preserve yourself. Now Jack Marlott seems to have left himself a little vulnerable. Vis-à-vis Denbigh. Of course his son has done that to him already, so he's been obliged to patch up the damage, as best he can, with a marriage – '

'No.' Catherine shook her head again, but less categorically.

'What does Denbigh *know* about Marlott? Supposing Marlott doesn't have access to my information about Denbigh? Your friend is in the pay of our Intelligence people, of course, but the Czechs pay him more, a lot more.'

Catherine's head shakes slowed.

'This wretched business about Lawrence, you see. Being so indiscreet. It might all have seemed worthwhile to Marlott *père*, just to clear it up. Sex is at the root of everything – unwise sex – although we try to brush it under the carpet.'

Mrs Russell smiled again, just as chillingly.

'But Denbigh, I dare say, knows something about his eminent lordship. Not sexual this time, but similarly unfortunate. Or he's hinted that he knows a little. For Marlott maybe it'll just be a temporary inconvenience: after the damned sex business with Lawrence, those hints of blackmail in the air. Undoubtedly he'll extricate himself from Denbigh's – as yet – veiled threats too. A hoity-toity eye consultant's past professional life must be fertile grounds for discovery as well, wouldn't you say? Can he *actually* be celibate?'

'This – this is ridiculous. Preposterous. I don't believe *any* of it – '

'Wilder than fiction, certainly. It would be blue-lined out of any halfway decent novel.'

'Why are you telling me this?'

'It's a calculated risk. But – I ask myself – who would believe you if you were tempted to spill some beans? *I* can lay my hands on evidence about your own fair self, name names and all that – '

'You're bluffing me.'

'If you think that – ' Mrs Russell's voice was ice, her accent lapsed to Lancashire ' – you've understood nothing.'

'I don't know anything about it.'

'If you concentrate on the matter – take a fresh look – '

'No – '

'Are you still seeing Denbigh?'

Catherine shook her head.

'He'll be in touch with you soonish, I'm quite sure.'

Tiredly Catherine got to her feet.

'This is nonsensical-sounding, I know, Mrs Marlott. Like a fairy-tale.'

'I believed in those,' Catherine told her.

'It presupposes – ' Mrs Russell seemed struck by a thought ' – that the premises don't alter. That the dramatis personae remain as they are, that this play will run and run. A little chamber piece, rather, all to do with cryptic themes, with submerged motives. We're not taking into account the wholly unforeseeable. Bolts from the blue irrupting on this little country-house entertainment.'

'I have to go now.'

'I think I *can* rely on your not speaking to anyone – '

'You must have known that?'

'I must confess that, yes, I did allow myself to presume.'

'I told you that I think the whole thing's quite absurd, mad – '

'You listened, but you don't believe me, I know. Well, I'm not certain I can honestly blame you. You think I'm taking some kind of revenge on you. I'm not. If you could just focus on what I've told you, please, give it your most *serious* consideration – '

Catherine could only sigh as she picked up her bag.

'I just don't see why – '

'Because I'm sure *you* are the clue to it all, Catherine, to its unravelling. *You* are at the centre, *you* will have a vital part to play.'

But with that Catherine blundered from the room, feeling that her life was on the point of slithering out of her only haphazard handhold on it.

*

The following day was a Wednesday, assignation day, a week before the luncheon was due to take place.

She was in the taxi before she found she had forgotten her diary and she had to work out the hotel she was bound for from the rota, counting back over the weeks. The Ritz, she deduced.

She was correct, but she was also late arriving. She hadn't slept the previous night and she sensed how obvious that fact must be.

He asked her what was wrong. She burst into tears. While he lay on the bed, on the side nearer the telephone, she told him: meaning at first only to hint, to suggest, but finding herself drawn more and more into an explanation, as if to help herself reason things out. She discovered she had told him so much, she couldn't omit the final piece of information which the Russell woman had imparted – the key to the whole sordid tale, her husband's amatory predilections.

Afterwards he lay back on the pillows staring up at the ceiling and saying nothing. She thought he must be reflecting on her stupidity, her naïvety: but then that could be no surprise to him, since he'd known she'd given up her Wednesday afternoons for him. He started to whistle very softly. She stood staring at him, desperate for a response she could make sense of.

'Well, well, well,' he said at last.

She waited for him to sound sceptical, or sneering, or angry on her account: nauseated at least. She didn't need his sorrow, but she wanted him to say something that she could react to in turn: to make her shout or weep tears, to do anything except defend her husband. What she wanted most of all was not to feel alone with her knowledge.

But she was to be disappointed.

'Well, well, well,' he repeated.

She wrapped her hands tight into fists.

'Who would have thought it, eh?'
She tried staring him into the padded board behind his head.
'Is that all you can think of to say?'
He turned his head and looked over at her.
'Well, it's something and a half to take in.'
'Don't you believe me?'
'Of course I do.'
'I didn't make it up.'
'I know you didn't.'
'If that woman is right and wasn't saying it to – '
'Lawrence Marlott. And his poor father.'
'Oh, sod his father.'
'He'd probably draw the line at that, wouldn't he?'
'What?'
'Doesn't that make you want to convert your husband? Or has the horse – the stallion – already bolted through its stable door?'

*

She watched Lawrence so carefully, how he moved, behaved, every gesture. He saw her watching.

She stared at his swimming trunks hanging to dry from a tap on the bath. She found a trail of tiny black hairs he'd emptied into the basin from his razor. She smelt his foreign maleness on a towel. She imagined the soap in the shower dish being used to lather his armpits, his biceps, his thighs, his groin, between his legs. So much virility made her feel like retching. She couldn't get away from it in the bathroom they shared. It was smeared on every surface. Sweat, muscle, hair, urine, his ivory sperm that came more and more spasmodically, with too much straining, with his eyes tight, tight closed and the sinews on his neck standing out like whipcord.

She watched how he balanced himself when he was standing up, how considerately he moved his body with reference to its fulcrum, his crotch. She watched how he sat sometimes, seemingly unaware, with his hand draped over his groin and lying along his thigh. His penis was the centre of his being, protected and worshipped (he had shied away on the occasions when she'd tried to touch it), inspiring whatever was gentle in him and also what was most assertively, peremptorily violent.

*

After the parliamentarians' luncheon Lord Marlott said he had to excuse himself, he was driving up to town: the BBC had arranged a round table discussion for the Third Programme. He begged their pardons, but they should depart only when they felt they wanted to: the staff were there for their convenience. With a saintly smile he took his leave of the company assembled in the drawing-room, managing – Catherine didn't know how he was able – to make those solid Oxford shoes soundless, squeakless.

Ninety minutes later all the others had drifted off, and only the two of them remained. It had been in her mind all through the meal, the only thing that was keeping her animated. She took him upstairs to the bedroom she and Lawrence used when they came down. She locked the door and, without her needing to ask him, she unzipped her dress. He pulled off her brassiere and buried his face between her breasts. His hands pushed under her slip and clawed her buttocks through silk. She gasped, panted, spluttered, like a cliché harlot. His fingers kneaded the buttocks and pulled them apart while she wrenched off his tie and undid the buttons of his shirt. No kisses, and nothing to say. His tongue curled round a nipple and she would have given him suck if he'd wanted it. Instead his teeth grazed the flesh and pinched it, but she didn't complain, she didn't speak.

On the bed they abandoned themselves, with a strange detachment each from the other, to their bodily pleasures. For the first time with him and with only the second man in her life she experienced a multiple orgasm and she screamed out, with uncontainable joy and a terrible agony of guilt. She felt the sheets rapidly dampening with sweat, blood, semen, excrement perhaps, her juices. He sallied into the gully between her breasts and soaked her neck and chin. It's nothing, a voice was shouting in her head all the while, it's nothing, it's worthless –

She started to laugh – laughed and laughed – and only now, to stop the sound, did his mouth close on hers. She was considering how she could wash the evidence from the sheets, how and where, while his mouth sucked and sucked, as if she really had a soul left to be suction-spirited out of her.

*

A postcard lay on top of the morning's mail.

'It's for you,' Lawrence said.

She took it from him. He must have read it, of course. The view was of a Himalayan village.

> Came up here from Kashmir. You wouldn't believe it. But can a Leica lie? It's as if I've never breathed oxygen before. This really is living! An Italian is teaching me Zen: the importance of the 'not', what isn't there. So much hasn't been there, I fear, for too many years. Too late to cross

that one, I suppose. Anyway, I shall live to be 300 – well, since I'm a reprobate, 150. But a reclaimed one now.

All love, Danny H.

The telephone rang, and Catherine answered it.

'Mrs Marlott, I think it's time we met again, don't you?'

Catherine held her breath.

'I don't have to announce myself, do I? One or two intriguing matters have come to my attention. I think you would be interested to hear about them, too. I suggest we meet at the same place as before. Let us say, on Thursday at three o'clock. I believe Wednesday afternoons have been difficult for you of late. Does Thursday suit?'

'I – Why do – '

'Does it *suit* you, Mrs Marlott? Please tell me, yes or no.'

Catherine inhaled.

'Yes,' she said.

'Very good. Until then.'

The line went dead.

So she knew, about the Wednesday afternoons.

Catherine lowered her arm and let the receiver drop on to the telephone's cradle.

'Progress,' Mrs Russell declared with a satisfied beam. 'At long last.'

Catherine seated herself. She removed her gloves and crossed them on the table in front of her. She lifted her eyes very slowly.

The woman was having difficulty containing herself. She reached into her handbag and produced a photograph. She placed it on top of the gloves.

'Look at it if you will, Mrs Marlott.'

She did look.

A croquet lawn, cypress or yew trees, a restrainedly Gothic country house behind. Four figures: one in a robust tweed suit, one in blazer, white flannels and cravat, a woman in matching striped wool suit, cloche and scarf, and a third man in a three-piece flannel business suit.

A second photograph was quickly laid on top of the first.

'This is later.'

Three men and two women on a terrace, standing or perching on the balustrade. She recognised a younger Jack Marlott, and turned back to the first photograph where, in his flannel business suit, he swung a wooden croquet mallet.

'There's twelve years between them.'

'Why are you showing me these?'

'You see a familiar face?'

'Yes.'

'It's the same place. A charmed group. A *corps d'élite*. First in nineteen twenty-nine. Then in 'forty-one.'

'Who are they?'

'Kindred souls. Birds of a feather.'

She was about to return the photographs when Mrs Russell leaned her elbows on the table and inclined herself forward.

'By 'forty they were political, although they were getting so in the mid-thirties. The word is "collaborators". For who they became, once the War got under way.'

'What? Lord Marlott?'

'Try to talk a *little* more quietly, Mrs Marlott. If you don't mind.'

'Lawrence's father?'

'I knew there was something along these lines. I only had to keep searching. Of course, it's history now.'

'He – he wanted a German victory, you mean?'

'He was banking on it. I don't know if he wanted it, but he'd picked *them* as the victors. A dire misjudgement, but maybe he thought he knew what others didn't. And maybe it was more touch-and-go than we remember it.'

'The other people – ?'

'I'm not sure if they'd interest you. It all happened long ago.'

'Where?'

'Herefordshire.'

She picked up the earlier photograph. The young woman was shielding her eyes against the sun.

'She was a model or actress, I forget. Found herself a boyfriend – he's in the tweeds, it's his family's pile – and she fell in with his crowd.'

Catherine handed the photographs back. When she raised her eyes she saw how intensely she was being watched. Then she was disarmed by a disconnected smile.

'Is – is that why you wanted to see me?'

'Doesn't it interest you? Even if it doesn't shock you – ?'

The voice was nippily nannyish, although the smile remained in place.

'I think it disturbs me.'

'I think it disturbs *him*. Having the memory of it. Or rather, *others* having the memory of it – '

'Yes. Well . . .'

Catherine picked up her gloves.

'Your father-in-law's been trying to protect himself for years. By hook or by crook, I expect. Most of his fellow travellers are dead now.

It must have amazed them, to see how he traded his causes so easily. Do you know how he made his money afterwards?'

'Business, I suppose. Stocks, shares? – that sort of – '

'He's always had a construction company. He married early, a woman who betrayed him with a rival. I don't think he ever got over that. He landed some government rebuilding contracts after the War – currying favour, or maybe through blackmail – and he became something of an ideas man too, but his talent was for the swindles he could pull off. All the while keeping a soaped and flannelled face to the world. He worked for some charities – he got lots of publicity for that – but at the same time, unbeknown, he had a hand in some gambling outfits.'

'"Gambling"?'

'A profitable sideline.'

'I used to see his name, in the newspapers.'

'Of course you did. Good friend of some of the proprietors. He was elevated to the Lords. To the surprise of us all. God knows how he pulled *that* one off.'

Catherine pushed back her chair. Mrs Russell grabbed her wrist, freeze-framing her.

'I haven't finished yet, Mrs Marlott.'

'I don't think – I want to hear any more.'

'About your esteemed father-in-law?'

Catherine shook her head.

'Let me be generous then. I'll call it a split personality. The good – which we all know about, thanks to his publicists – and the bad, which we don't. Maybe it's not so difficult to understand, though: people's psychologies seldom are in the end. His wife was high-caste, but the family had fallen on hard times. He was fascinated by her sort, and after she left him he learned to hate them. I suspect he hates England – '

'I think I have to – '

'Just a minute, Mrs Marlott – '

Catherine tried to wrest her hand away, but she couldn't, it was held fast.

'There's a rumour – that he met some Romanians in Paris – in the build-up to Suez. They made a certain proposition to him, after some business talk they were having. We don't know what happened. But that's when he discovered about Denbigh. That he was someone to be avoided. Only now he's considerably more dangerous, your friend and mentor, since he seems to have a fuller hand of cards. Wouldn't you say?'

'I think,' Catherine said, as the woman released her hand, 'you're talking nonsense. Only – '

'Only it's not.'
'So you tell me.'
'Don't you believe me?'
'I can't tell.'
'You'll need time.' The smile returned. 'I realise that.'
'I have to go now.'
'Back to home-sweet-home?'
'No,' she said. 'No, it's hardly that.'
'Stick it out, Mrs Marlott. For as long as you can.'
Catherine shrugged.
'Are you sure your Svengali Dr Denbigh hasn't been trying to get in touch with you?'
She shook her head.
'He's landed you in it.'
'He's not – what you say.'
'And you can be certain about that too?'
'He said it was a crazy world.'
'That's one term for it. What a nice line in understatement – and cliché – your old friend has.'
Catherine walked away from the table, but Mrs Russell followed her – all the way to the empty ladies' room.
'I think something's going to happen.' The accent was hybrid Mayfair and Lancashire. 'Denbigh could expose Marlott – '
'If what you say is true, *he* could expose Denbigh.'
'Who'll be first?'
'*You* could expose Marlott,' Catherine said. 'And Denbigh. Both of them. Why don't you?'
'If Denbigh can frame Marlott, bring him over, what wonderful deceits there might be. Marlott will be owing to Denbigh *and* to us. Somehow we have to maintain a fruitful tension without Denbigh knowing.'
'How could he *not* know?'
'If we feed you information, Catherine, and you pass it on, and it tells Denbigh what he wants to know about Marlott. And if Marlott is fed false information – '
Catherine covered her ears.
'But this isn't how people live!' she said. 'This has nothing to do with people's lives!'
'Oh yes, it does. It has everything – '
'No. You've all invented this – shenanigan. You've no shame. A pack of terriers – '
'Oh, poor Mrs Marlott. You've got hold of *quite* the wrong end of the stick – '

'How dare you talk to me like that.'

'Like how?'

Catherine opened the cubicle door and slammed and locked it behind her. She flushed the cistern and reached forward for the window handle.

The woman was still speaking, mouth close to the wood of the door. No, no, no, no, no, no.

She lowered the toilet's seat cover over the bowl, stepped up on to it, crouched on her knees on top of the cistern, and manoeuvred herself through the window, out on to the step of the cast-iron fire-escape.

From the white-tiled well of the building, covered by stretched net to repel pigeons, she heard the traffic of Knightsbridge, blaring and stunning, raising Cain.

*

A castellated house, dark stone, bearded with red virginia creeper. A Victorian garden of Irish yews and Lebanons, orderly rose beds. Dapper lawns on several levels. A terrace, edged with a stone balustrade and urns. Voices, the cultivated and the aspirant; a rich mulch of opinion; some laughter.

The Honourable Herefordshire farmer leads the party on to the croquet lawn. He dresses as an older man, in tweeds that are too heavy for the weather, because tradition has a weighty significance in the shires. With all his advantages in life, he has never been a London man, and he feels easiest in his sartorial backwater. Blazers and white flannels and silk cravats are all very fine, but he leaves that to those who can carry them off with some panache. Another of his guests is wearing a sober business suit, as if critically uncertain of the modes on such an occasion; he is dressed 'up', in Sunday best, to a manner of life he is unaccustomed to. Only the one woman in this purported 'quartet' (there are at least five, because one holds the camera: there may be six – or more – but not all are so willing to have a record taken of their visit) seems wholly at her ease, but then she is an actress and the behaviour of stage folk is notoriously chameleon-like. She looks more at home than anybody, although it is no mere performance on her part. For several months this *has* been her home, alternating with London, and she is now more of a chatelaine than she could ever have believed possible of herself at the beginning. She helps to concoct the social cocktails, she is a born 'mixer'; she also adds a piquant touch of sparkly, *Tatler*-ish innocence to gatherings that – already, at this stage in their chronology – have a much more serious purpose than first appears to be the case.

The tweed suit is a disguise, camouflage, to a personality that has been rebellious since its troubled schooldays. The blazers and whites are no more than might be expected and so the eye passes over them: 1929 to a tee. But the charcoal flannel suit confirms that there's a latent degree of awkwardness about this seemingly unremarkable scene, that this may be the first time they have all met in these surroundings and that it is a country-house assemblage of a particular ordering.

No one, as they come and go, talks of Michelangelo. The conversation, soft-spoken except where an intermittent comment is passed on the progress of the croquet, is submerged beneath the sylvan chortling of wood pigeons and the singing of blackbirds. Privilege at play: but in this theatre of understated social ostentation, not all is as it purports to be. The battlemented house looms out of the past, the trees are melancholy, the birds are wholly indifferent, and each of the foreground players has some reason for, at the least, discontentment, and at the most extreme, hatred and spite. They have been crossed, or they have cause to resent the demands made on them by lives prior to their own, and more than anything what they share is an ambition to assert themselves, to see revenge done. Even the woman, who seems the least concerned: she is an actress because of some lack in herself, an inability to believe in what others do – marriage, profession, a future. She doesn't mention her past to anyone, she lives only in the present, but that makes her an ideal hostess on such occasions, when she concentrates on the food and the weather and not on the darker undercurrents of their talk on the state of the realm.

This is England fair and green: a quiet corner of its temperate garden. Only the woman appears to be aware that the photograph is being taken, and she shades her eyes, incidentally concealing the topmost half of her face. What happens in the next few seconds, after the shutter has done its work, can only be speculated on: astonishment, irritation, or perhaps they have all trusted one another too well to suspect that there might be any future incriminating danger in the deed.

This is England green and fair and hateful, and it offers the most discreet refuge of all, a northern oubliette. With the rolling swards of Herefordshire on every side of them, their mission – as it will shape itself – is safe and cryptic in the interim. While the Depression bares its fangs to bite elsewhere, they are still optimists, and – by the most benevolent interpretation possible – they are naïves. The political charade ahead will have been made for them, with promises not worth the paper they're written on. But, equally, the medicinal cure-all – like a quack's spiel – will prove as potent as coloured water, madman's piss corked and abstrusely labelled in a green-glass *bocksbeutel*.

58

Imbroglio

SHE was leaving the Ritz by its main Arlington Street entrance. A car was parked at the kerb. The back door opened as she descended the steps.

She recognised instantly Lawrence's father's voice from inside.

'Catherine, my dear . . .'

She stood transfixed. She went cold from head to foot, then hot.

'I rang Thurloe Walk – '

Whorls of pain drilled through her stomach.

'Although Wednesday afternoons you set aside for shopping, do you not? Didn't you tell me that? How could I forget my own daughter-in-law's movements – ?'

She took a step backwards on the pavement, then another. The window was fully lowered, to allow the face to lean further forward, so that none of the words would be lost to her.

'Just noticed that MP chap who was talking to you at Lambdown – '

Her heart lurched in her chest.

'The Members' luncheon, remember – ?'

She thought she might be going to dip forward, unbalancing herself completely.

'All of us congregated here, in this one spot.'

His voice was poison-sugar.

'On this one street corner. More or less altogether – '

Hadn't they decided to use different doors of the hotel, as they did at the Savoy and Grosvenor House?

'Funny yarn of a name he has – '

Was it a bluff? Or had something been said over the lunch, drawn out of him, which she hadn't been quick enough to hear?

' – Norman Collingbourne-St John. Isn't it?'

He was staring at her.

'I *am* right, aren't I – ?'

He was trying to mesmerise her with that scavenger's jackal smile.

'I expect *he's* got his future all sized up. Frequenting swanky hotels like this one – '

Her tongue was stuck fast to the roof of her mouth.

'That sort think they know exactly where they're going, where and who with – '

'I've left something – ' She croaked the words out, pointing behind her. 'In the cloakroom – '

'Can't I give you a lift? Back home? You *are* going home?'

'I'll have to get it – '

'Then I can take you to Kensington?'

'No.' She shook her head. 'Oh *no*. I've errands – things to buy – '

'So you *are* going shopping after all?'

The smile stuck on a long yellow tooth.

'If you tell my driver where – '

She ran away, up the flight of steps, back into the hotel. She reached the ladies' room and found a cubicle and then she was sick.

While the mess was being swabbed with a mop, she attempted to make herself up at the table. Damage-containment. But her hand shook too badly for her to continue.

She stood up and had to lean against the wall – lean hard – or else she would have fallen down. At one point she tried prising back the gilt-framed mirror but found it was secured, screwed into position.

She started to cry now – oh how she cried – cried for her mother, for herself, for Maurice, for Felix – lost souls for whom she couldn't do more than weep her salt tears and lament.

That night, in London, she dreamed of Leta, fixing her with a death's-head grin. Her one-strap dress was dripping bladder-wrack, and she was casually picking little silver fish from her hair.

In one hand she held out the cigarette case.

'Don't let on to anyone I told you, Cath. It's more than my life is worth.'

The cigarette case was mesmerising her.

'Quaint, isn't it? Asprey's. I didn't think the owner deserved it. It was only taking from the rich. He could buy himself another one. Another dozen.'

Leta put her head back to laugh. Wriggling through the open 'O' of her mouth and bearing the stink of bodily corruption an eel slithered out of her gullet and Mrs Marlott woke in her bed screaming to wake the length of Thurloe Walk.

59

Coups de Grâce

At Whistlefield she parked Lawrence's car on the gravel at the side. She reached for a small notepad and pencil that were kept in the glove compartment, opened the door, swung her legs out and stood up.

It had turned sunny and warm. She stood with the notepad open on the car bonnet and the pencil held above it. What could she say?

She noticed the french windows were ajar at the back of the house, facing the tennis court. A cup and saucer rested on the arm of a slatted wooden bench, and a magazine's pages fluttered on the seat. Someone was at home.

She closed the notebook. What could she have said anyway, to let him know that by tomorrow she would have disappeared but offering him no clue how.

She picked the panama hat off the back seat. She'd spotted it on her way out of the house and grabbed it off its hook. Denbigh had bought it for her: it was a proper gent's panama from a hatter's, and the assistant in the shop had looked at her askance when Denbigh had explained it wasn't for him but his friend –

She put it on. There had been no occasions lately to wear it. Lawrence had told her it was 'mannish', people would think she was 'a rum sort'. By that he'd meant 'lesbian', and she'd said as much but he'd flinched at the word.

She walked across the gravel to the back of the house. She hadn't been expecting the sunshine, the heat. There now seemed to have been a lot of days just like this one when she'd sat watching the players on the court. But perhaps there hadn't been more than half a dozen when she was able to sit outside without Denbigh solicitously asking her and re-asking her if she didn't feel a chill. All the men in her life had learned manners: even if the last one pretended she didn't deserve them –

She looked up at the windows, sclaffing her feet on the gravel and allowing him to see *her* first if he was inside. She whistled a few bars of an Irving Berlin song they'd driven to, 'I say it's spinach' – the hell with it . . .

She took the shallow steps up to the crazy-paving terrace.

She whistled again. She measured out several long paces, backwards and forwards, listening all the while for sounds of activity indoors.

Then she noticed shards of glass and saw that a pane in one of the doors was broken. She walked closer. She stepped forward into the room that had been her favourite in the old dower-house, the sitting-room with its lattice-patterned walls and, over the mantelpiece, the Rex Whistler oil she knew so well, of a nonpareil of country houses in its consummate park, glowing in the rays of a blood-orange sun.

She stared at the sight that greeted her.

Tables and chairs were overturned and objects strewn everywhere. A vase had been thrown at the wall – there was a damp map of Africa on the paper where the water had run – and flowers lay in that corner of the room like a garden. A feather cushion had been disembowelled. Even the curtains had been torn from their rails, and the sagging pelmets hung loose.

The destruction made her want to cry as she picked her way over the debris, but she couldn't. She clasped her head as she negotiated the mess on the floor, porcelain limbs and icicle shards of glass that crackled under her feet.

She reached the connecting door into the study. His workroom retreat had suffered the same fate. A bottle of black ink had been emptied over a rug. A painting had had a knee or a foot butted through it. Cigarettes had been tossed out of a silver box. Photograph frames had been hurled to the floor or into the fireplace. The workings of the Leroy mantel clock had been ground underfoot.

She didn't call out from the hall. But she heard nothing, nobody.

She went upstairs, as if drawn.

A trail of blood led along the landing to one of the bedrooms. The door was open and there was the bloody mark of a hand on the white-painted wood.

She suddenly felt so weak she had to reach out her own hand for the door pillar. She closed her eyes, then opened them and looked forward into the room.

A man's two bare legs protruded from the far side of the bed. Their nakedness momentarily shocked her more than the scribbles of blood beneath them on the white carpet.

It took her several seconds to find the courage to enter the room. She took slow, unsteady steps towards the bed.

The body was lying on its front. She was certain it was Denbigh's although she had only ever seen him clothed, a few times in tennis whites.

She couldn't have recognised him from the pulped head. A kitchen knife stuck out of his neck. She covered her face with her hands. She almost fell stepping backwards: it was only the corner of the bed she came into contact with, but she screamed nonetheless. She tottered, still moving backwards. On the near side of the bed, where she hadn't looked, a bloody silk dressing-gown lay on the carpet, slashed to shreds. She backed away from it, clutching the edge of the door. Her hand fumbled for the knob and touched not the coldness of brass but the stickiness of blood. She held her fingers in front of her face before seeing the wall and smearing her hand on the slubbed paper he'd searched London to find.

She made a second vandal's mark. She looked at her hand: it was left almost clean, which she couldn't understand. It couldn't be so easy to rid yourself of a murdered man's blood, it couldn't *mean* so grotesquely little –

She stepped out of the room backwards. She stared in different directions before remembering her bearings. She let the wall take her weight.

Suddenly she had the sensation of death ensconced in another room.

She stood paralysed, rooted to the spot. She felt its presence slowly, slowly stirring to an awareness of hers. She had interrupted it about its task and she couldn't be allowed to bear witness to the fact, to live to tell the tale. It might move as effortlessly as wind, but it was able to do what wind or light could not – pass through walls, snatch at rogue life in an instant –

It was blind terror that *un*stuck her. She ran from the bedroom, along the gallery and down the staircase. Making for the front door she saw the open french windows in the sitting-room and changed direction. She blundered past the overturned chairs and tables and lamps, nearly slithering on the carpet mulch but racing like a sprinter for daylight.

She ran across the terrace and down the steps. She pulled the car door open and threw herself into the front seat. She slammed her foot on the clutch pedal, turned the key in the ignition lock and trod hard on the accelerator. Gravel ricocheted beneath the chassis and the back of the car dragged at an angle in her panic to get away. She steadied it, though, leaning forward, pressing herself against the steering wheel. She reached the tarmacadam driveway and the engine revved. A rabbit disappeared beneath the grille and the bulge on the bonnet and she didn't know or care if she'd hit it. *Jesus, Jesus, Jesus* . . . The trees flew overhead, the sun striped migraine shadows.

At the gates she turned into the main road. Fifty yards or so further on, as the engine growled between gear changes, she caught sight of

Mrs Collis riding her bicycle towards her, on the other side of the white lines. The woman appeared to recognise her; she took her hand off the handlebar and lifted an arm as if she was going to wave –

But Catherine pushed her foot hard down on the accelerator pedal and roared past her. She would never have seen the car before, and she wouldn't know a Rover from anything else. But why had the arm been raised if it wasn't to offer her a greeting? Mrs Collis was a country woman and *they* always remember, catching the resemblance to the life, even after the toll of such an impossible marriage.

After that she drove and drove. She wasn't really thinking about what she'd just seen, she made sure that too much was happening through the windscreen. She would have time to think about it later, as much time as she needed. She might even cry, but she doubted it. All she had on her mind at the moment was losing Sussex; not having to see it again, not ever.

She found a wood, beside the Tenterden road. She stopped, got out, undid a rusted padlock that was hanging loose, and pushed open the gate of rotting wooden spars; she climbed into the car again, and drove forward. She halted, got out a second time, closed the gate behind her, then climbed back into the car and restarted the engine.

The track led into a copse. The trees grew taller and darker on all sides of her. Momentarily she thought of Doktor Mandelbaum's enchanted forest.

She stopped the car and switched off the engine. She wound down her window. At first the silence was deathly. Then she started to hear – slowly – all the noise that was there, the sinister din of a woodland's unseen life: objects dropping through the trees, creatures slithering through long grass, twigs cracking and snapping, birdsong, piping alarms, sounds like intimate breath, far bleats, canorous croaks, solitary screeches.

She looked over her shoulder several times. She felt her lower arms trembling, then her upper arms, almost to her shoulders.

She started the engine again. The carburettor rattled; she heard the whines as the engine turned over echoing for miles. She lifted the handbrake, lowered her foot very slowly on to the accelerator, and let the car creep forward.

Her sickness had left her: as incredibly to her as the thing had been incredible. There was simply no believing at all what she had seen. Now, in a moment, she realised far too late that she didn't have the panama hat with her. As the car rolled she put a hand to her forehead and only passed in and out of the next few seconds.

Then she raised her eyes. The track began to climb up the back of a ridge. She applied some more pressure to the accelerator pedal and followed the twenty or thirty yards of tractor tyre furrows to the top of the incline. She stopped the engine. Beneath her, on her right-hand side, the ground fell away sharply. Above her the trees were like cathedral columns. Leaves and feathers floated where sunlight slanted to oblique shafts. She thought she must be about to receive a vision, to the quick of her soul.

She got out. She opened the boot and took out her suitcase and carry-all. In the middle of a private forest staked by 'Keep Out' signs, which was a closed book to the cars that drove past it, she fitted her fingers round the leather handles and lifted her burden.

She was walking away from the car – she'd left the front door open and the boot lid up – when she heard the crunching of leaves. She turned round and saw that the car was starting to roll forward, away from her, towards the fall of earth on its right-hand side. Beneath was a steep escarpment and a ditch covered by vegetation at the bottom.

She must have forgotten to secure the handbrake. She realised she could have dropped everything and run after it, but the car was Lawrence's, without – for once – the dubious privilege of joint ownership attaching. She stood and watched as the wheels gathered more speed.

There was only one possible end, of course. It happened within twenty seconds of her turning round to look. The wheels were drawn to the edge of the bank and the car's mass very logically tipped it over. It gathered more and more speed as the back wheels followed the front ones and the grille and bonnet bulge nosedived. There was a flurry of leaves and twigs and stones, a creaking of axles and the chassis frame, then the briefest of ominous silences when the wood seemed to hold its breath before the Rover tore through the disguising undergrowth and hit solid ground.

It was a tinny sound, considering the make of the car: a demeaning thump as the front half of the shell crumpled in concertina folds and the bumper chrome buckled and lacerated the bodywork.

She saw the car's rear end sticking up nearly vertically out of a thorn bush, with its boot lid now perversely clamped shut. As a kind of afterthought, glass shattered somewhere – falling out of the headlamps and quarterlights probably – with an almost light-hearted tinkle.

While the wood chattered over the sounds, she turned round and tucked the luggage handles into the curled palms of her hands. She lifted the suitcase and carry-all carefully – all that she was taking out of this world – and calmly, collectedly, began to walk down the leafy mud track as hastily as she could in her going-away heels.

Part III

SHOOTING TIGERS

'Harness my zebras, gift of the Nubian king.'

Silent film caption from *The Hollywood History of the World*
by George MacDonald Fraser

'The deeps have music soft and low
When winds awake the airy spry,
It lures me, lures me on to go
And see the land where corals lie.'

Richard Garnett

60

The Alexandria

THE Hotel Alexandria still stands, in the swirl of traffic between Fifth and Park Avenues, but it is judged only a matter of time before a realty developer makes an offer the owner will be unable to refuse.

In 1960 Art Deco is not in fashion, so that the cream-tiled façade seems especially old-fashioned and beside-the-point among the thrusting steel and glass blocks. But the discerning East Coast out-of-towners who know a good thing when the price is sensible enough make it their base when they hit Manhattan.

For Catherine, however, it is too modestly sized as mid-town hotels go to become her own regular base of operations. The senior hall porter, George, misses nothing, and even though the Levantine Lounge is just out of sight of the clerks at the check-in desk, she hasn't been able to work out just how much they *can* see in the wall mirrors: it may be that the mirrors' distribution isn't so haphazard, but subtly clever. Nevertheless no one on the staff has yet approached her – as distinct from those worldly-wise unescorted men in town on business, who have studied life in hotel lobbies across the country and know just who is not so innocent as she or he seems to be.

She may come in for a cocktail at six thirty of an evening, but her favourite professional pastime – because so self-consciously quaint and un-American – is to partake of afternoon tea. The Alexandria is (quietly) famous for its teas: triangular bite-size sandwiches, muffins, diced butter and strawberry preserve, fruit cake, a pot of Hu-Kwa, milk and lemon – cake-stand, fine crockery and monogrammed cutlery served at your table on a crisply laundered pink linen cloth.

It is an eminently civilised business. Anglophiles appreciate it, and it is they who cock an ear whenever she addresses a waiter in her cut-glass, purebred English accent. When she tries for a waiter's attention – 'Excuse me . . . I wonder . . .' 'Would you mind very much if . . .'

– she always gets it: and although she speaks softly, she realises the other tables are listening in.

Conveniently for her purposes the ladies' rest-room is on the storey above: in fact it's on the mezzanine level and can be reached by its own staircase, but she prefers to take the elevator to '2' and walk back down a flight. There are a couple of telephone boxes on the same level, so that even though the elevator cage comes equipped with a bell-boy operating the brass levers, any man who gets into the lift with her knows to rattle the small change in the trouser pockets of his business suit, to make nothing seem so natural as that he should be getting out on her heels at '2' to put through a call from one of the wood-panelled telephone booths. She has often thought to thank the Alexandria's architect for his eccentricities of layout.

Sometimes the men are shy, or take cold feet, or are upon her in the corridor too suddenly, or become briefly and dumbly uncertain that she is in fact the sort of woman they've suspected her to be. But these and the other sorts she can instinctively soothe and assure, with just the minimal gestures at which she has become so adept. With only a couple of exceptions in ten months her customers here have all been guests staying at the hotel: her 'Alexandrians' as she cryptically refers to them when she is jotting down the financial details afterwards in her spiral-bound account book. At the Alexandria she charges her mid-town rates, which are only slightly less than her Park and Upper East tariff, and only slightly more than she requests for her Murray Hill or Gramercy Park one-offs.

For the pleasantness and refinement of the surroundings and the cleanliness of the clientèle, the Alexandria ought to have been in the top category, even though some of the mattresses were a little soft and the supply of hot water from the shower faucets somewhat erratic about 7 p.m. Despite her occasional resolutions to give herself to the bland high-rises, she was drawn to the place because of its old-world atmosphere and the informed good taste of the décor that drew its other guests, as if it were a club for those of like minds and values: fumed-oak panelling, English and Irish furniture, log fires, brass fenders, Chinese prints, Tiffany shades, Turkey rugs. It is all very familiar.

Several of her regulars paid psychiatrists for their services. Perhaps her own job was in the same line of country. With whomsoever she went, she disclosed about herself as much or as little as seemed appropriate: each of her temporary lives ebbed and flowed, the details came and went and didn't hold their definition too well, but who cared, and she gave multiple versions of the woman who stalked the woodblock-and-Bukhara rug corridors of the Alexandria Hotel, on any of its eleven storeys of suites, studios and more humble, pantryless bedrooms.

Her name was Corinne Lacey. Her parents were dead: her father had been an English diplomat and her mother an actress from Wisconsin. She had been educated in the shires, at Cheltenham Ladies' College, and at a finishing school in Lucerne, Switzerland. For a while she'd worked in a couturier's salon on the Avenue Montaigne in Paris, then she'd been a photographer's assistant in Rome, then she'd been companion to a Hapsburg princess in Munich.

Her history silenced even the agnostics. Europe required specialised knowledge and experience, and thankfully even the guests of the Alexandria were too inwardly American to ask questions that were other than polite. Seeing a copy of the *National Geographic* lying around in a bedroom could give her heart and system a nervous jolt, but she was as adept at side-stepping as a nightclub shimmier. Her Englishness induced a respect in most men, and intimidated some; professionally it was her chief expedience.

She became the intimate confidante of some forty men during that first American chapter of her afterlife.

A majority of them wanted to tell her about their childhoods, and did so without her asking. For some of them it had been the happiest of times, for others the opposite was the case, but for them all childhood was similarly unforgettable. She became – as requested – mother, sister, girlfriend, sister's friend, fiancée, the unattainable girl, stepmother, mother-in-law, the forbidden temptress. She learned of the havoc that might be wreaked by a word spoken casually or by a word refused, by a single glance or by the refusal of eyes to see and acknowledge. She learned too how easily love can chill, and she discovered how close hatred may come to fear or shame. It was an unexpected education she received in those Manhattan bolt-holes, dispensing pity and cheer along with the afternoon Hu-Kwa, or brewing some of her own 'Russian Caravan' in the little private pantries that are a civilised touch of hotel life which the Americans have beaten the British to.

Childhood: the alpha and the omega. She time-travelled, with her Wall Street brokers and her out-of-towners alike. She wondered if they heard a nanny's no-nonsense admonitions in her Englishness, or a soothing calm instead.

At any rate her services were much in demand, and as one acquaintance would recommend her to another she seemed more and more to move with ghost-like ease through their past, in their mind country.

*

Mostly she could forget, but not always.
She dreaded those razzias and night raids.

Sic itur ad astra.
She had remembered the words on the corner of East 57th and Second, waiting for the lights to change. She had remembered from Miss Whittingham's Latin class, the thick primer with the red covers that resembled a bible, which she devoured so devoutly at morning prayers, because her Latin prep could never stay overnight in her head and because Miss Whittingham was a staunch believer in her girls learning reams of vocabulary parrot-fashion.
Sic itur ad astra wrote Virgil, age advising youth to take courage and aim high, for the skies. In English it lost its urgency and pith. *'Tis thus one journeys to the stars.*
Then the lights had changed and the motion of the crowd carried her forward, on to the road and towards the opposite kerb and sidewalk. Her father had dropped down dead in a hot street because he had lost the will to live. Of late her own will-power had been on the wane, sputtering like a candle in a draught: an inherited potential for tragedy, depressed on days when the smog lifted and she could see clearly, but even worse when night fell on the city and the blinking tallow threw up a spider's nest of vengeful shadows – those were the times when she lost her mind to blind terror.

*

Did she think she was betraying Maurice? Or did she believe rather that there was a certain measure of safety, a preserving sanity, in numbers? The more men she acquainted herself with, the more exceptional Maurice became. By satisfying her body, she left her mind free to pursue its search unimpeded, and in a state of virtual purity. In the middle of the act itself, her imagination behind her closed eyes was brought closest to the man she had most truly loved.

61

Washington Square

LIKE angels on the heads of pins, they balance hundreds of feet in the air. She has been taken dancing to a supper club, to the Starlight Room on the top floor of the Kramer Building. The late, late lights of Manhattan scintillate and it is all, at this remove from gravity, rather incredible to her.

His name is Eustace A. A. Weissmann II. All his life doors have opened to him, without his having to lift a lily-skinned, long-fingered hand to bid them. In the Starlight Room he aspires to youthfulness, holding on to the precipice edge by his nicely cuticuled and regularly buffed fingernails.

He lays his fingers flat on her back and leads her not too forcibly about the floor.

Astaire and Rogers would have been in their element here, dancing up the peach-pink walls and across the ivory ceiling. Wherever they can be hung, ruched hyacinth-coloured drapes of some sheeny material fall to the sea-silver floor. This is a film set in its completed third dimension, too nearly too-too to be quite true. The music carries them, and they float like sylphs, like spirits of the air.

*

Baby-blond Mr Weissmann was still in his early forties – she discovered – but he dressed as an older man, and had assumed another generation's mannerisms: holding himself with a slight stoop, placing a supporting hand on banister rails, folding his hand over the fly flap of his overcoat to protect himself from cold. He had no wife, so he'd told her, and she supposed it really must be the case, to account for such an appearance of bachelorhood. He was, nonetheless, a physical man, in a curiously dispassionate way, given to silences and interludes of watching her: never merely 'watching', because it was then that he seemed most intensely alive, when the pupils of his eyes grew darkest in the iris.

A refined man, she supposed, cultured. The twelfth-storey apartment on Washington Square was furnished in muted good taste, of the sort called 'informed'. (He told her – quite emphatically – that he had not employed a decorator.) A small Klee hung on one wall, next to a Braque; the wooden mask on another wall hailed from the Upper Amazon, where it had been used in ritual. The colours aspired to neutrality, and were very nearly anaemic instead: but, again, his powers of judgement had been in the right.

It marked an advancement for her, from the Alexandria Hotel, although she didn't doubt that she would be back there, eventually.

He had inherited the family's papermills, and she might have thought it a gentlemanly occupation, as trades go. But on the telephone, when office calls were transferred, he sounded on edge.

In roundabout fashion she had asked him how business was. He told her he had rivals for contracts, and explained how the unions operated. One frequent caller was 'Mr Jones', a private detective who had half his salary paid by Weissmann's. 'I need to know more than I'm supposed to know. It's bad enough – ' he held up his hand ' – keeping the left and the right in order. But I need to have eyes in the back of my head too.'

She asked him what the private detective 'did' for him, but he was evasive. The man did what he had to, she gathered. His loyalty wasn't wholly to be trusted, but if money talked, then it would . . . that was as much as one could hope for.

The few disclosures about business life failed to accord with the Washington Square ambience. Or maybe the former required the latter, so that troubles could be made lighter of and conscience appeased. Here they had the best of it: a modern apartment looking out to the north side, with its sedate frontages, its Greek porticos and uninterrupted formality of gates and railings, a very picture of orderliness.

'My mother had an English governess,' he said. 'She spoke more *your* Hampshire than ours.'

'Is that why?'

He repeated her question. ' "Is that why" . . .?'

'Is that why you just let me talk?'

'Do I?'

'Do I sound like her?'

'I guess you do,' he told her.

'Is that important to you?'

'What's "important", really?'

'In the Alexandria I saw you looking over. When I was talking. It had to be my voice, I knew then.'

'You talk, Corinne. And I'll listen.'
'Talk? What about?'
'Anything. The weather. Lunch. The furniture. Your shoes.'
'Or the view,' she said, walking towards the balcony doors. 'Washington Square. Living like the birds.' She stretched out her arms. 'Daedalus was it, who fell? In melting wax. Or the other one, Icarus?'

*

At last he steeled himself, he got up his courage.
'I want to show you something, Corinne – '
In the second bedroom he pulled open the doors of the walk-in wardrobe she had already discovered to be locked. Inside were rails of women's clothes, in the styles of twenty and thirty years before, all of very fine quality. He lifted out some hangers to let her examine them: a box jacket suit by Mainbocher, a painted chiffon party dress, a diagonally striped black and white dress by Lelong, a white silk piqué Biarritz dress.
They were all the same size, which was also – to her surprise, but apparently not to his – her own. He said she should try something on, did anything catch her eye? She picked out a pansy-purple crepe dress with a blue fox boa, and he left her while she exchanged outfits.
When she walked through to the sitting-room, towards her reflections in the balcony doors, the effect was even more startling to him than to her. He spun round, cigarette in hand, his wide eyes opening wider as he stared and his mouth dropping in astonishment. She smiled, embarrassed. He wouldn't stop staring at her. She didn't know where to look. She vaguely pirouetted in front of him. Cigarette ash dropped on to the virgin beige carpet and he didn't notice. She thought he must be regretting having let her put the dress on. She was stepping backwards, retreating to the door, when he held out his hand.
'No, no,' he said.
Even now, in the thirty-first year and after so much, she wasn't able to add two to two.

It became a diverting pantomime, dressing for him from the wardrobe. She obliged, since it seemed to her a city of riddles and secret symmetries. She would look down on the pedestrians and traffic and try to detect patterns in the chaos, but they always eluded her. In Washington Square, she thought, it must be possible to perceive sequence and rhythms on the serpentining paths beneath the trees. It never happened, however – that unending flow of human activity failed to offer her any means for its interpretation.
She persuaded herself that by dressing for him she *was* – she must

be – serving some purpose, however obscure. At least the ensembles weren't exotic, or demeaning, or (for the most part) gaudy – the very contrary in fact – and the transformation was unexacting, perfectly painless, indeed illuminating for her. Clothes of the late twenties and thirties had a swing to them, and a generosity of cut that had gone quite out of vogue. She didn't have an appropriate hairstyle and her make-up was modern, but he seemed to be imagining the rest.

He made no stipulation about what she should wear, he only asked that she pick out whatever she thought 'suitable'. Some were an easier fit than others, but she could only judge from a reflection in a mirror or lit window. She enjoyed best the view of herself afloat over Waverley Place or MacDougal Street, arms spread like wings to give shelter to Broadway, dervishing all the while against an East River sunset. She put on for him whatever happened to engage her fancy that particular day: a tiered dress by Chanel in black crepe, a pale blue taffeta picture frock with chiffon bodice and surplice, a white organdie party dress, a Schiaparelli tweed jacket and corduroy trousers in lettuce-green, a beige angora travelling dress with lynx collar and cuffs, a pink satin tied blouse from Lanvin that wrapped round a black satin skirt.

It paid for her late mornings shopping in her own clothes at Fifth Avenue and Fifty-seventh Street, it subsidised her dainty lunches at the Russian Tea-Room and Dunbarr's and even Gloucester House, also the occasional films she took in at a matinée, and the taxi trips up Broadway or Fifth or Park. She walked out now in soft kid shoes, because mostly she was on carpet or in the process of being transported, and when she thought of taking some air or exercise she wasn't sure how a woman *could* walk alone in Central Park. A couple of times she spotted faces from the Alexandria, but had turned away before *they* could pick out *her*.

A city of riddles, she told herself, of secret symmetries, and one can never be careful enough.

*

'What do you know about me?' she asked him.

'Well . . .'

'Really *know*?'

'But it doesn't matter,' he said.

'We never talk about my past or my future.'

'You never tell me.'

She fanned her fingers on the window glass and pressed hard. When she took her hand away its impression was left, like an X-ray: but fading, second by second, as if its fleeting purpose was merely to supply proof of her own insubstantiality.

She turned round and saw him looking at the print, watching the moisture evaporate. She wondered why he should be so intrigued when the only thing that seemed to keep him interested was her vagueness.

Perhaps it was time to go back to her old routine, her missionary work in the more sedate, older-fashioned hotels of Upper Manhattan. But when she imagined it now, she was hearing her own silence as she selected the areas of deepest pile carpet to walk on in those meandering pink-lit upstairs corridors, taking care not to disturb or raise suspicion. The silence was ghostly, and the glow of the light somehow sepulchral, and she wasn't sure that she was ready yet to return to that nunnish life of devotion, caring for the souls and bodies of her rich derelicts of Broad Street.

In Mrs Weissmann's clothes her insubstantiality was – paradoxically – compounded.

Transubstantiation.

She laughed at the term when it came to her, lying in the tub in the marble bathroom. The apartment was too high in the air to risk blaspheming with an easy conscience, but she felt she had to laugh, laugh and laugh.

*

She had seen that he'd been wanting to talk about the other presence in the apartment for days.

'Mother started to lose her memory.'

'Yes?' she said sympathetically. 'How was that?'

'Not at first so you'd notice, since it would be with things she'd put down somewhere and couldn't find again. She had some problems with words. But then she started to get confused about her friends, and places she'd been, and then she couldn't remember who it was she'd seen and where she'd gone to meet them. And after that she started to lose her hold on the past, the nearest things first and the longest-ago part last of all. Then there was a strange development: she began to remember the things she'd managed all her life to forget. Because – because it had suited her best not to think about them. And – and since she couldn't distinguish any more, and since she couldn't remember having wiped out this or that, it all just floated up to the surface, and out it would come, usually in company. Everyone would be staring at her, and no one would understand.'

'But *you* did?' Catherine asked him.

'Sometimes. Sometimes, yes. I tried to direct her away. Because – because it was confusing *her*, you see.'

Even as he told her, he was looking – she thought – flustered and uncomfortable. She hadn't intended to lead him into any disclosure, but now that she had, she saw that the relationship between this mother and her son had been an unusually complex one.

She had to wait a couple of days until he would speak about it again. The sight of her in a floor-length Grecian white jersey dress had driven him to the bourbon bottles.

'You've never mentioned your father,' she said.

He refilled his tumbler for the second time.

'The revered Mr Weissmann died twenty years ago. He's history now.'

'But – he was your father . . .'

'He hardly noticed me. It was Mother who obsessed him. He was the most jealous man I've ever come across.'

He swallowed noisily from the tumbler.

'He sent me to Deerfield and I had my own Best's account. I got all that a son of his should have got. We vacationed in Europe, he was quite definite about that. But that's what finished him too.'

'What do you mean?'

'One year we went to Switzerland, then on to Rome. And I saw this man on the Via Condotti, I knew he was the same one who'd been in Gstaad, he'd sat near us on a mountain train and gone skiing in the afternoons when my mother did. He had a scar on his chin, and I knew it was him. The next year he was in the Prado in Madrid the very same day we trekked round the galleries, and he was getting out of a taxi when my mother walked off to have a dress fitted in a shop by the Gran Via. I don't think my father saw – any of it – but I guess he must have known, in his gut. The man had blond hair, I kept looking at it. I'd never understood where I got mine from, because my mother had brown hair and my father was very dark, *his* hair was black. Before it suddenly went to an old man's white.'

He swilled the drink around in his glass.

'So, you see, we had all this first-class life – people trying to educate me, the right crowd of friends, ocean liners and wagons-lits, swish hotels, our American voices and everyone kowtowing to our money – and it really didn't mean a damn thing.'

He put his head back and swallowed.

'The man – ?' Catherine said. 'With the blond hair – ?'

'The year after Madrid something happened – I knew that my mother was going all to pieces. We were staying in Maine with people my parents both knew. I was fifteen, I guess, or sixteen. My father was still in New York. Suddenly Mother just let go – tears, doors banging, she wouldn't come out of her room, she wouldn't eat. The people phoned my father, but he'd had to go off somewhere. Mother opened the door of her bedroom to me but she wouldn't speak. She ran a bath. She forgot to close the bathroom door quite shut, and ... I tried to clear up, what I could, and I found a newspaper under a cushion, with the print starting to wear off the page. There was a photograph of the man I'd seen in Europe, he'd been killed riding in a race in Kentucky, he'd fallen from his mount and the other horses had trampled over him.'

Catherine closed her eyes.

'I put the newspaper back. *Then* of course I hadn't made the connection. About his blond hair and mine, why it was the same colour. But I knew from school that two other boys' mothers had had love affairs that got hushed up. The man was quite handsome, and my father wasn't, and that seems to me now justification enough.'

'What – what happened with your mother?'

Immediately he seemed evasive. He half-turned away from her.

'It was hard, you know. Getting her – readjusted. My father would beg her to show herself on social occasions, and sometimes she did. Looking glamorous but not really engaging with anyone or anything that was said.'

'I'm sorry,' Catherine told him.

'And I started to get difficult too, for a while. I straightened up a bit when Father heard about his lungs. Then when it turned out it was going to be terminal – '

'I'm sorry,' Catherine said again.

'Well, I'm not sure *I* was. But it was over by then.'

'What about your mother?'

For a second time she thought he was reluctant to answer her on the point. His eyes swivelled round the room; the skin at their corners tightened, and his mouth drew very straight.

'It must have been a very great shock to her,' she said.

'A shock,' he repeated. 'Yes.'

'Now there were just yourselves,' she prompted him. 'The two of you.'

Again his eyes slid past her, to flit around the room, and again they found nothing to hold them.

'It was a crazy time,' he said. 'Best forgotten.'

She remembered how the conversation had begun.

'We – we never talked about it. For years afterwards.'

'At the end, though?'

He stared into his empty tumbler.

'We didn't always share an apartment,' he said. 'Later I felt I had to. Although I'd always visited her, most days. It was a kind of opera set she lived in. Crimson velvet, little tinkling chandeliers, baroque furniture from Sicily, Spain. Verdi on the gramophone. A lapdog, like a duchess's. Anna Karenina clothes for winter. I thought – well, I had to simplify it.'

'I'm sure – you were right.'

'Right or wrong, I had to do something.'

'I'm sure she was grateful.'

'I didn't do it for gratitude.' He sounded almost petulant. 'That wasn't the reason.'

Why then? But she didn't like to ask. Because he'd known what would happen, that she would turn forgetful and become a social liability?

'It's over,' he said, 'and done with.'

He smiled, past her, towards his own reflection in the wall mirror. A cagey, defensive smile.

'Water under the Queensboro Bridge.'

She appeared the next evening with her hands in a black mink muff she'd unwrapped from tissue paper, and wearing a matching Davy Crockett hat.

He walked round and round her, smoking his cigarette to a stub.

'I shouldn't have brought her here,' he said.

'It was for her own good.'

'No, I was afraid. Of the past, and what she'd say. And I ended up living with it every day. She – she couldn't just forget: all those things we'd never mentioned. She'd start talking about them, even though we never had. She – she'd open her mouth – and I'd have to pretend – '

'It's all right,' she said, only meaning to sound bright.

Then she saw that he was crying.

'Why . . .'

' "Why"?' she repeated him.

' . . . when I loved her . . . how could she – how could she make me *hate* her so . . .?'

'When did your mother . . .' she paused, but he gave no indication of wanting to interrupt her ' . . . decease?' she said, using the lamest word.

'Four years ago.'

'Here?' she asked him. 'In the flat?'

'Not here,' he said. 'In the country. She was staying with people.'

'*You* were here?'

'I was here, yes.'

'It must have been a terrible shock. Getting the news.'

'Getting the news,' he said. 'Yes. Yes, of course.'

'Had she gone for a break?'

'What's that?'

'To the country – '

'Yes. Yes, for a break. For a change of scene.'

'What a time – for you.'

He stood up and walked over to the balcony doors. He seemed quite unable to settle.

A few moments later she got to her feet, without making a sound, and crossed the room on tiptoe to where he still stood looking down on the square. When she stretched out her hand and laid it on his shoulder he jumped as if he'd touched current, jumped right out of his bag of skin.

*

She took a taxi all the way up Fifth, to Eighty-second Street, to the Metropolitan Museum. The Egyptian Wing wasn't quite what she was looking for, but it was close to the Great Hall and wasn't likely to wear out her kid shoes.

She looked into the sepulchre of Lord Chamberlain Per-nedbi, walked past the sarcophagi and mummies in the corridors, and soon realised that nearly everything exhibited here pertained to death – sculptures, figurines, reliefs, tomb paintings, papyri from the Book of the Dead. Thirty dynasties of transmigrating souls.

She bought a cup of coffee in the cafeteria. She consulted a map and realised she should have been on the second floor where the Arabian silk carpets and hangings were on show.

She was beginning to tire, though, the stone and marble were sapping her energy through her ankles, and she thought, I shall return another day. But she didn't care to plan ahead; she had started trying to live in this pulsing, quivering city only on the surface of the day, not meaning to backtrack more than even a few moments in case she looked down and caught vertigo. It had never happened when she flew on rugs, but then she'd had her mother and now she had no one except herself.

After too strong a cup of coffee she picked up her handbag, assiduously bypassed the predatory eyes of a lone male doughnut-eater, and headed as fast as dignity allowed – on winged feet – for the doors on to Fifth and daylight.

Outside, waiting for a cab, she looked over her shoulder. The doughnut-eater stood reading a newspaper. Behind him towered the shaft of a stone obelisk carved with hieroglyphs, another Cleopatra's Needle, and she was temporarily confused, stranded between places and times – until a cab at the rank blared its horn, and she jumped, and the driver's cracked voice of some remote Third World extraction called out to her, 'Jump in, lady, it's now or never!'

62

Story of a Fall

SHE was sitting on a bench in Washington Square, looking up at the apartment block, counting up to the twelfth storey. A petite woman she recognised, from one of the lower floors, was walking past when her spaniel on its leash spotted a bird and made a lurch for it. She was pulled forward, all four-foot-whatever of her, and she went over on the side of her shoe. She hauled on the leash and hobbled over to the bench.

Which was how they started talking. About life in the building: life and death. Catherine said how fortunate they were to have balconies and the elfin woman – who had a gravelly, cynical voice, and to whom she must have been only one face out of many – shrugged and told her they were a mixed blessing, what with the birds and the threat of intruders, cat-burglars, and with kids it would have been hopeless.

'But the sunshine,' Catherine said, 'they must be suntraps. Aren't they?'

'I can't take the sun,' the woman told her, and sucked in her cheeks. 'Because of how my pigment reacts. Blue blotches and I vomit.'

'Oh, I'm sorry.'

'Yes. So am I.'

Catherine decided it might be best to take her leave but the woman, diminutive in her neatly tailored slacks and fitted reefer jacket, was pointing to the façade of the building.

'Up on the twelfth there was an accident.'

Catherine turned to look at her.

'An accident?' she repeated.

'Mrs Weissmann.'

'Why? What happened?'

'She fell over the balustrade. Right down on to the street.'

'*Mrs* Weissmann?'

'Mr Weissmann's mother. Have you met him?'

The question, she was sure, wasn't loaded.

'I've met him, yes.'

'The papermill people.'

'But Mrs Weissmann died in the country.'

'Oh *no*, she died right here,' the woman said, tugging on the dog's leash. 'Smashed her neck, her back. Every bone in her body, I wouldn't be surprised. Such an elegant woman too. She made you think of Old New York. But she was getting a bit muddled towards the end, her mind was wandering. Still, it was a terrible way to go to your Maker.'

With her other hand the woman crossed herself, across the lapels of her reefer jacket.

'And her son to see it all. That must have broken his heart into a thousand pieces.'

'How – how did it happen?'

'Leaned out too far, lost her balance.'

'Was she compos mentis?'

'She should have known she was in danger. She was frail, of course. But you see, the front supports – ' she pointed again ' – they're a little raised, like they've tried to protect you. So it's not so easy just to tip over the edge. She might have been standing up on her toes, I dare say.'

'Could she have jumped? Wanted to jump?'

'I guess she *might* have wanted to.'

'You don't sound sure.'

'Well, she was still quite sociable. She liked to have people over, or to go out to *them*, but her son wasn't so happy about that. She had just been phoning friends, I heard, to arrange they come to visit her. That doesn't sound like she had dark thoughts on her mind. Does it to you?'

'Not really,' Catherine said.

The woman called to the dog to sit still.

Catherine sat staring up at the balcony, trying to imagine the incident, how it must have happened. Walking back to the block with the woman and her dog she was stopped in her tracks when she looked over her shoulder and chanced to see, projecting through an open car window, the telescopic lens of a camera being pointed in their direction.

She stared, until the lens was withdrawn. The window was quickly wound up and the driver, camouflaged by shadows on the glass, drove off.

She was astonished. The woman was still talking to the dog and clearly hadn't noticed.

A blue car with a white flash on its side. She immediately felt her privacy had been invaded, even at the centre of such a jam-packed city.

'Have you seen a ghost?'

Catherine turned round.

'You looked as if you were somewhere miles away. On a desert island maybe?'

The woman was smiling. Catherine smiled down at her, or attempted to. One of the tiny shoulders twitched at the leash. She'd had all her life to learn what not to see in this absolute metropolis.

*

A cinema on Broadway was showing *I Walked with a Zombie* in a double feature, and she went to see it one afternoon.

Afterwards she didn't go straight back to Washington Square. Leaving the cinema after the first film and walking along Bleecker Street she had been aware of a man's shape out of the corner of her eye, following her at ten or fifteen yards' distance.

The deli was a timely refuge; she was known there. She sat down at a table in the back room and took out Maurice's silver and blue lacquer compact. In the mirror she saw a man behind the glass of the front door, looking inside. Her hand started to shake and she couldn't hold the compact steady. She snapped the lid shut and called over to the counter in the New York fashion for a coffee, brown please.

When she left the premises he'd gone: or at any rate he was nowhere that she could see. He had been dressed in a businessman's rather formal casual wear – navy blazer and light chinos – and she wondered if he could have been a client from the Alexandria.

She walked back smartly. Where more likely to find yourself being accompanied by a spirit of the undead than in New York City – stock-pot of witch's brew. At the Judson Church she turned and looked back, but there was no sign of him. She breathed a little more freely after that, opening her bag to find her key, grateful for the first time for that beady, prurient stare from the desk-clerk.

63

Atlantic City

TODAY she has picked up another woman's perfume on him. She recognises it: Chanel No. 19.

'Who is she?' she asks.

He laughs, immoderately.

'Who is who?'

'Whoever she is.'

'I don't know what – '

'I can *smell* her.'

'Smell who? Where?'

'On your shirt.'

When he was in the bathroom she found his trousers and sniffed the cloth. The perfume was there too, on both thighs, where her head had rested, poised at the fork.

When he came back he was all smiles – such amiable but opaque smiles – and then she knew positively that he was lying.

Lying, lying, lying.

On and off she tailed him for two weeks. It wasn't until he told her he was flying to Chicago that she knew she had her chance.

On the day in question the streamlined white Lincoln coupé left Washington Square but it didn't head for North Queens and La Guardia. Instead it travelled one hundred and twenty miles down the Jersey shore. She had employed a car and driver for herself and they sped, discreetly, in the Lincoln's wake: on to the New Jersey Turnpike and the Garden State Parkway, off at the exit arrow, and then turned left on to the Atlantic City Expressway.

The Lincoln's journey finished as downtown as Atlantic City got, at the entrance portico of the ritziest address in the place, the Chalfonte-Haddon Hall Hotel. She waited for a while watching, then paid off the driver the remainder of his charge when she'd asked him to drop her a few blocks away at her own hotel, the Claridge.

She telephoned the Chalfonte from her room and discovered there was no guest staying with the name Weissmann. She walked over and found the Chalfonte's garage valet. She said something admiringly complimentary about the Lincoln, a brand-new Continental Mark 4, and he let slip that the owner's name was Adams. When she'd returned to the Claridge, she telephoned back to the reception desk and enquired how long Mr Adams would be staying at the hotel. Three or four nights, she was told.

The only practical thing she could think to do next was to keep a vigil at the Chalfonte. So she walked back once more, along the breezy Boardwalk, and entered where he had done and seated herself in the lobby, surprisingly cramped given the building's palatial proportions. It was a far from ideal location for spectating, but voices did carry so she listened.

She didn't have to hear the name Adams mentioned, however. She recognised the chauffeur as he emerged from an elevator and crossed the lobby, turning the car's keys on his fingers. He stopped at the hospitality desk and she heard the words 'dinner', 'suite', 'delayed'. Wrist-watches were consulted, the clerk at the desk lifted the telephone and presumably altered the order that had been given to the restaurant or the kitchens.

The chauffeur left the hotel and she waited, sitting upright and alert on her chair and with a magazine in her hands, for the purpose of hiding behind whenever Mr Adams himself should come down. But he didn't either step out of the lift or descend the staircase, although she kept a very sharp look-out.

The chauffeur reappeared half an hour after he'd left, and he didn't return alone. He was accompanied by a woman.

She was of her own age, approximately. She walked quickly, but without a hint of awkwardness, and with her head held high. The moment she walked through the doors and a liveried flunkey tipped her a bow, something was familiar to Catherine. The effortless hauteur, perhaps, the angularity of the features which were so quintessentially English, the paleness of her skin. She didn't recognise *exactly* for nine or ten seconds, and it seemed an interminable delay appertaining to some essential, verifiable past truth as she ransacked her memory.

Then it came to her. After the resemblance, the actuality – the fact that it was *her*, and couldn't be anyone else. The tracks of their lives must have held an incontrovertible force of attraction since once crossing, and the tension had reverberated for years afterwards – a compulsive destructive energy.

Most curiously, Catherine was scarcely surprised at all. The further she travelled from the past, the more insistent its echoes became: and, when they should have been confined to her imagination only at this distance, they were at their most formidably literal.

It was Jennifer Moncrieff-King.

She had grown a little stouter, a little coarser too, despite her famous education and that streak of financial good fortune. She was expensively dressed, but not in the way she and her contemporaries at her Suffolk school must have been advised to rig themselves out: she was wearing wide white trousers and a short dark navy or black tunic top with gilt buttons, over a champagne-coloured roll-necked jumper and a knotted rope of pearls. A few stones sparkled on her fingers. A not-so-subtle fragrance of Chanel No. 19 – too much of it – was just perceptible over the protective shield of the magazine cover after she had passed.

The whole effect – Catherine decided – was jazzy and really rather vulgar. She doubted if Aquae-Regis would have approved, but Aquae-Regis should have been history now. She wasn't sure what *this* was, as the chauffeur led the way to the elevator and Mrs Moncrieff-King's daughter eyed his buttocks in a professionally appraising way.

When she'd gone, Catherine had several drinks at the bar, whisky-chasers.

Events ought to have been unreal, by the proper rules, but they weren't. And since they weren't, she had to confront the significant truth of what was happening. Which was that she had been ousted for the second time in the affection stakes by the same sly, conniving, gloating bitch.

A partial judgement, of course, solidly weighted, but how else might she have been expected to react?

She had to wait until after midnight, obliged to drink small measures of soft drinks she ordered from the bar waiter. First the elevator doors opened and the chauffeur hurried through the lobby turning the car keys on his fingers. Ten minutes later the doors of another elevator opened and out stepped the pair of them.

Catherine pulled herself out of the armchair and followed them cautiously, in the wake of the reapplied Chanel No. 19. It had been an outside chance that she would see either of them again before the morning. But they were saying their demonstrative farewells at the door – the bitch with her arms thrown round the Weissmann shoulders and one foot off the ground, he with his arm round her waist and both of them kissing in the empty vestibule. Behind them the ridiculous car with its high shark fins and chrome fenders was framed against a curdled, late fall sky, the moon playing hard to get among the feather-bed clouds.

She spotted a side-entrance marked, and sidled across the hall undetected by them. Outside she saw a taxi parked at the opposite kerb; she waited for a couple of cars to pass, then she ran across the street. She climbed into the cab and explained to the driver that he was to follow the white car getting ready to leave the portico of the hotel. He seemed quite unperturbed by the request: maybe he thought the woman sitting alone in the back of the car behind the chauffeur was a friend of hers, or maybe he was only too used to requests from jilted spouses or amours.

When the Lincoln pulled out they set off after it. The journey was short, only six or seven blocks, a kind of courtesy trip.

Perhaps.

But outside the apartment building, the Lincoln's sole passenger seemed unwilling to lose the company of the chauffeur who stood holding the door open. He wasn't especially good-looking but he was well built, rugged, manly as these things are judged.

Jennifer took his hand and led him twenty or thirty yards along the street, away from the entrance to the block with its striped marquee. They turned into an alleyway, which was when Catherine threw open her door, dropped some money – too much – into the driver's hand, and sprinted off after the pair.

They were in a service doorway, on the building's flank, where the glare of the street light didn't quite reach to. But Catherine could see and hear what she needed to: Jennifer, wearing her white trousers, kneeling on the stone step, and the uniformed chauffeur, standing against the door, with his trousers open and his moans of manly pleasure uncontainable.

*

After that, of course, she couldn't sleep at the Claridge.

She got up and watched the dawn breaking: not rosy-fingered but grey and cold.

The same questions repeated and repeated themselves. Was she still Mrs Encombe? Was Maurice still with her, or abandoned somewhere along the way? Did he know, had he known the sort of woman he'd married?

But in giving your body where was the thin line between respectability and whoring? When was a woman 'kept' and when did she keep herself? What cause had the pot to call the kettle so black?

One thing she needed to find out, and she would have to wait until the Boardwalk showed signs of life: insomniacs taking air, early dog-walkers, the garbage trucks.

She dressed and walked north eight or nine blocks. She came to the street, Maryland Avenue. In the lobby of the apartment building a porter was sorting the first delivery of mail. She asked him, 'Can you tell me, is Mrs Encombe staying alone?'

It was too early in the day for suspicions to be aroused.

'No, miss. She's here with Mr Encombe. They're leasing awhile.'

Catherine hesitated, lips suddenly dry.

'Can – can I come back later and leave a message?'

'Sure, miss. Just hand it over this counter when you're ready.'

'Or if I leave it in the box? At the front door?'

'Apartment five twelve, miss. In case *I*'m not here – '

'Thank you.'

She left the building and walked back, past Madison and Gramercy and all those fine, displaced States of the Union, Virginia, Pennsylvania, Tennessee, Illinois. There were six and a half miles of them, if she'd wanted. But her only purpose was to get back to the Claridge and start making her plans.

*

Catherine met 'Mr Jones's' colleague on Caspian Avenue. He gave her his handiwork inside a plain manila envelope. She handed him cash inside a sealed white envelope.

'Check it if you'd like,' she said.

'I'm sure it's okay.'

'That's very trusting.'

'I know where to find you anyway. Washington Square – '

'Don't be so sure of that,' she said.

Whereupon he opened the envelope, took out the bills, and counted.

'Exactly right,' he said.

'I want us to be quite certain about everything.'

'Businesslike?'

'Above-board,' she said.

She saw him raise an eyebrow.

'Have you ever tried to get into movies?' she asked him.

'D'you think I should?'

'You've got the "look".'

'But I got a good life here. Lots of love-birds, weekenders. It falls right off the tree, into my lap.'

'Strange fruit,' she said.

'What's that?'

'Billie Holliday,' she said.

'Billie Holliday,' he repeated.

'Have you got the other item?'

'Certainly,' he said.

She took out another, fatter envelope. He produced a parcel from his coat pocket: a hand-sized object wrapped in brown paper.

They made their exchanges.

'Do you want to check?' she asked.

He hesitated.

'No, that's all right.'

'Should *I* check?'

'Here's the receipt,' he said, taking it from the breast pocket of his jacket.

'Thanks,' she said.

'For – for self-defence, is it?' he asked, nodding at the parcel. 'Or sport?'

'That's outside our little business arrangement. For you to ask or me to tell.'

'Sorry, ma'am,' he said.

'Forget it.'

She offered him her hand, and they shook.

'Ain't Nobody's Business If I Do,' she said.

'Begging your pardon?'

'Billie Holliday,' she told him, dropping the name behind her.

'Billie Holliday,' he repeated.

Then she was gone.

*

There was no one on duty in the lobby when she walked in. On the porter's desk she noticed a partially drunk cup of coffee, still letting off a little steam.

She travelled up in the elevator. When the doors opened she saw a long corridor with a runner of blue carpet.

Their apartment, five hundred and twelve, was halfway along. She rang the bell.

His wife answered the door.

'Yes? What is it?'

'Don't you recognise me?'

'What? Should I?'

'My voice?'

'What do you want?'

'Back at the beginning.'

' "Beginning"?'

'The town – '

'But I – '

'Aquae-Regis.'

The eyes skewered her to the wall of the corridor behind.

Then her mouth fell open.

'It's not – Catherine Hammond? Are you?'

'Can you believe it is?'

Immediately Catherine smelt the Chanel No. 19.

'Not Hammond now.'

'But it *is* you?'

'*I* married too,' Catherine replied. 'But that's neither here nor there.'

She pushed past.

'What're you doing in Atlantic City?'

The front door closed. Catherine walked into the lounge.

'This is fancy,' she said.

'How are you, Catherine?'

'Expensive place?'

'Oh. So-so.'

'I'm not sure if I'm impressed or not.'

'How – how have things been with you, Catherine?'

'You didn't used to ask me questions like that.'

'No?'

'No,' Catherine said, stating the negative very positively.

'Heavens, it's a long time ago now.'

'But *you* cling on to the past.'

'"Cling"? How's that?'

'That husband of yours.'

Catherine thought she saw a reflex stiffening of the back and neck.

'Maurice?'

'Yes. Where is he?'

'Something's wrong with the car. The porter rang the garage – '

'You're immobilised? Both of you?'

'I realise – that – you knew each other once.'

'Rather well, actually.'

The response came instantly. 'Really?'

'Yes, indeed.'

Jennifer gave her a brilliant smile of quite dazzling insincerity.

'It *is* a long time ago – '

'He took my virginity,' Catherine said.

The brazen smile wavered.

'All that,' Catherine added, 'pre-dates your own interest in him.'

'My – ' Jennifer's voice shook, with trepidation or indignation ' – my "interest"?'

'Well, that's what it must have been. For you to grab him the way you did.'

The smile was abandoned.

'I – I didn't "grab" him.'
'Snared him, then.'
'Catherine, please – '
'You must have told him a few good whoppers to lead him on.'
'*He* came after *me*, though. He pursued me.'
'So, what *did* you tell him?'
'He was the first man – '
'And were you so afraid to lose him?'
'I *liked* him.'
'Enough to lie to him? While lying *with* him – '
'He was so charming. *You* must remember that – '
'Yes,' Catherine said. 'Yes, I remember.'
'They weren't lies in the end – '
'At the time they were, though, I'll bet. And you hooked him with them.'
'That sounds so crude.'
'Is that how you land your Don Juans?'
'What – what do you mean?'
'They never taught you the art of that, did they?'
'Who?'
'At your fancy, toffee-nosed school.'
'I don't know what . . .'
Catherine quickly unbuckled her raincoat. She took out the manila envelope and ran her thumb under the seal.
'Your extra-marital sorties – '
She shook out the photographs and handed them to Jennifer, who glanced at them with cold, contained fury.
'You don't deny them?'
'What do you want from me?'
Catherine stared at her. She felt her brain slipping gear, losing some momentum.
'I – '
'What do you want? Money?'
'They're copies,' Catherine said.
'Of course they are. You're wily enough to – '
They both turned round at the same moment. Maurice was standing in the doorway. Catherine recognised the moustache, although he was greyer, his hair had thinned, his face was a little fuller. She blinked at him; she felt her knees ready to buckle.
'How long have you been standing there?' his wife barked at him.
'Maurice – '
'You rotten little tramp.'
He might have been going to strike her but Jennifer stepped back.

She pointed at Catherine, who was swaying on her feet, seeming to hear the words before they were spoken.

'You're not going to listen to *her*, are you?'

'Why not?'

'It's all absolute nonsense. A misunderstanding. Fiddlesticks!'

Here all three of them were, in Atlantic City, talking the Queen's implausibly English English.

'You're a bloody fool,' Jennifer said.

'So it appears.'

He tried to take hold of the photographs. Jennifer wouldn't let them go, and they ripped.

'She's got copies.'

'I heard that.'

'What were you doing listening? No man behaves like that.'

'You've said enough.'

'I haven't started yet.'

'Melodrama gives me a headache.'

'Too bloody bad.'

Catherine had to lean out to grab the mantelpiece.

'I needed to come,' she heard herself saying. 'To put everything straight. Straightish. More or less.'

They were both staring at her: as if she wasn't quite believable.

'Santa Monica,' she said, 'it should have been. In the film.'

'What the *hell* are you talking about?' that woman's voice yelled at her.

'You sound like a fishwife, Jennifer.'

'Shut up, Maurice.'

'Santa Monica,' Catherine repeated. 'In *Mildred Pierce*.'

She thought she caught Maurice's eyes tightening; she was almost certain of it.

'She's mad, Maurice.'

'No.'

'Like her mother.'

'What – ' Catherine tightened her fingers on the edge of the mantelpiece ' – what about her? What about my mother – ?'

'Don't you know? You *must* – '

Catherine shook her head.

'Well, *I* knew. *I* found out all right.'

'What?'

'She went off her rocker. Stark staring.'

'No.' Catherine shook her head. 'No – '

'Right out of her mind.'

'No – '

'She didn't know *what* she wanted.'

Catherine couldn't speak. Nobody had ever told her, and yet somehow – all along – she had understood it.

'You can only be in one place at the one time.'

'I don't – '

'She couldn't tell. Couldn't remember. Which home, which bed – '

Maurice reached out his hand to stop her but she shook him off, violently.

'She doesn't want to hear, Jennifer.'

'She's going to – '

'No.'

'Piss off. No one's going to stop me.' She stood between them both. 'My mother told me what she was. Some actress who thought she'd found a rich man and couldn't keep her legs closed. Anyone could see – '

Catherine stared at the pointing finger.

' – *she* didn't look anything *like* her father. So-called father – '

'My father – ?'

'Your guess is as good as mine. Who *he* was. Probably your mother couldn't even remember – '

'I said, shut *up*, Jennifer – ' Maurice grabbed her arm. 'A whoring little bitch like *you*.'

'Don't tell me you've just discovered *that*!'

'I didn't want to know.'

'Liar!'

'Why, Jennifer? For Christ's sake – '

'Because you're so bloody rotten at it, that's why. So bloody predictable.'

Maurice went white with anger.

'I started on the gardener's boy at school. At home I had the baker's boy in the basement, three times a week.'

'But – ' Catherine tried to aim the words across the room ' – you said he was the first man. Who'd – '

'The first *man*. Adult. The first one above stairs. The first one I could be seen with. But he wasn't worth – '

'Why did you stick with me then? All this time?'

'Because I stop getting the bloody money if I leave you.'

'What?'

'That old codger on his farm, Great-Uncle-Bloody-Godfrey. He was soft in the head, he thought we looked a perfect couple. Some girl had ditched him once, so this was to make up for it. But I had to get married and *stay* married. He was even more of a fool than I thought.'

'And that's why?'

'And that's why I put up with a pisspot like you, yes.'
Catherine called out.
'I loved Maurice!'
'But he didn't love *you*, did he?'
'That's not true,' Maurice said.
'You dropped her.'
'I – I had a reason.'
'I'm not interested in your bloody *reasons*. You're useless. Worse than useless.'
'You said – ' Catherine gasped for the words ' – he had charm – '
'You scared me, showing up – '
'What you said about her mother – ' Maurice interrupted her. 'You're no better – '
'*She* did it for money,' Jennifer snarled back. 'Tuppeny-ha'penny acting jobs. She wanted a cushy life. She just sold herself. *I* took on a hard-luck bastard like you. I deserved sex, I deserve it *and* I get it. But no one's ever paid *me* a brass farthing. I go out and I get just whatever *I* want. *Her* mother – ' the terrible finger pointed again ' – she'd have lain on her back in the gutter for a shilling.'
Still wearing a glove on her right hand, Catherine reached into her raincoat pocket and drew out the gun. She directed the muzzle across the room at the woman's chest. She felt beneath the barrel with her index finger for the trigger.
Mrs Moncrieff-King's daughter was staring at her: not with fear, but with that haughtiness and condescension which Catherine remembered from the painful evenings of social put-downs in Aquae-Regis.
She flexed her finger on the trigger. Then her eye was caught by a stretched skin hanging on the wall. It was a zebra pelt. Suddenly the zigzags were distracting her, disorientating her. In the same second her arm was knocked upwards and Maurice snatched the gun.
'No, Catherine!'
She tried to hold it in her grip but she lost it. Suddenly Jennifer was laughing: hoarse, cruel, hyena laughter.
'Christ Almighty, my saviour! Look at him! Good for something, after all – '
'I loved him,' Catherine shouted at her.
'I've had a better time with geriatrics.'
'No, no – '
Catherine shook her head, over and over.
'No,' she shouted. 'I loved him.'
Jennifer only laughed at her, at the pair of them, at their myth of love.

In the middle of the laughter he fired the gun.
First the crack. Then a tidy after-puff of smoke.
The Brigadier's daughter only held her stomach, as if she were playing at being injured, as if the gun couldn't really have fired. She continued talking.
'You're pathetic, Maurice – '
'But I had a child by him! A boy – '
The gun went off a second time.
Jennifer's eyes grew wider and wider. She opened her mouth. Then she crumpled, folded at the waist and collapsed on to the rug, arms flung out to her sides.
Neither Catherine nor Maurice spoke at first. Simultaneously they took a few steps forward, but hesitantly, towards the body. They stared at it, then at each other, then at the body again, at the seeping blood.
Maurice knelt down and felt the pulse. He listened for breath in the chest.
'She – she's dead.'
He stood up.
'You must get away from here, Catherine.'
She shook her head.
'No,' she said. 'No, I can't.'
'Jesus, I need a drink.'
He lifted the stopper from a crystal decanter. The top rolled on to the floor. Whisky slopped into two tumblers. He handed her one.
She stood, still shaking her head. Then her legs gave way under her. She slumped down into a chair. The glass of whisky fell out of her hand; an amber stain grew and grew on the blue carpet, and she looked back towards the body, to the other stain, scarlet, over Jennifer's heart.
'I should have done it long ago,' Maurice was saying.
Catherine stayed mute. Despite everything else that was happening she felt the voice thrilling her, from her scalp to her toes.
'Long, long ago.'
He avoided looking at anything except the crystal tumbler in his shaking hand. Catherine couldn't believe they were really and truly sitting here: the two of them, as they'd done in that flat in Juniper Street, in the happiest few weeks of her life.
'Your father came to see me in London.'
'What?'
'When I left Aquae-Regis.'
'To warn you? To warn you off me?'
'Yes.'

Suddenly, breathing the fumes of Johnnie Walker Scotch beside a corpse in unseasonal Atlantic City in 1960, she was full of spite for her father, the man she had struggled to find affection for.

'He had good reason, Catherine.'

'What?'

'He knew things.'

'Knew what?'

He lifted his eyes. He looked straight into hers.

'He knew he wasn't your father.'

'What?'

'She was right.' He pointed at the body. 'You didn't look like him anyway.'

'But – '

'It wasn't just that, though. Not resembling you.'

'How – *how* did he know?'

'He didn't say exactly. Except that he'd made investigations. He didn't want to talk about it.'

'He never really loved me, as a father.'

'I'm sorry, Catherine.'

It was beginning to make a terrible and furious sense to her.

'Why did he tell you?'

'Because – there was worse.'

'Worse? Worse than that?'

'He'd discovered everything was repeating itself. That your mother had lived with someone else before him. When she'd been acting. Someone near the Welsh border, who'd been bowled over by her. He kept telling her he would marry her, but there wasn't much hope of that.'

Catherine covered her mouth with her hand.

'She lived with him for a while. As if she *was* his wife. In the expectation. Chalk and cheese. An actress and a farmer. But they were quite close apparently. What *she* said – ' he nodded across the room ' – she *wasn't* a whore. She gave love. Something *she* could never have done.' He nodded again. 'Only your mother didn't pick the right man maybe. Men. It might have *looked* as if she was trying to do the best for herself. But I think – I think she meant to convince herself that she *could* settle down. Make a match. But it was so – so improbable, unlikely. It only happened in plays and films.'

Catherine was willing herself to digest this information.

'Why,' she asked in the gentlest tone of voice she could manage, 'why is it so important to you?'

'When she lived up in Herefordshire she was called Bradley.'

'That was my grandparents' name – '

'Margaret Bradley. Not "Marguerite". But that would have been a simple change to make. For an actress.'

An appalling possibility was gathering in Catherine's mind when he spoke across her thoughts.

'I was their son.'

She stared at him.

'Their son?'

'Margaret Bradley's son.'

'But – '

'Which means – '

'No – '

' – we're half-sister and half-brother.'

'*No* – '

'Your father knew.'

'It *can't* be – '

'He'd been asking around. Lots of enquiries, he told me.'

'No. No, he was making it up.'

'That's what *I* thought. I told him to sling his hook. But – '

'Oh no, oh no . . .'

She let the lids close over her eyes.

'I went back up to Curteys, the farm. To ask my father. He didn't want to tell me. But on the fourth day, when I was ready just to give up – to defy your father – your legal father, that is – '

She held her head in her hands. She watched the amber lake glisten on the carpet.

'It can't be true,' she said. 'Jesus, Christ Jesus, it can't be true – '

'Please, Catherine – '

She was shouting, sobbing, pushing him off with her hands all at once. But it was such a shock to her system she exhausted herself in seconds. He crouched in front of her, clasping her hands tight.

She tried to speak.

'We didn't know,' he said. 'We didn't know.'

'Why Aquae-Regis, though? Why did you come? Why did you ever – '

'My father had gone looking for her once. He'd taken me along. It was the first place I could remember. For that reason it had always been – well, special to me. I wanted to see it again. I had gambling debts in London, things were getting a little – hot – '

She freed her hands and covered her eyes.

'Jennifer was a mistake,' he said. 'I wasn't in my right mind. I came down on the train but I lost my courage and got off at Salisbury and went back. I wanted to see you, Catherine. So much. How my father wanted to see your mother. *Our* mother.'

She moaned, into her chest.

'At least *he* had the courage. *I* didn't. Jennifer was all over me. I found she'd paid off the debts behind my back. It was a terrible mistake, the worst thing – '

He stopped himself.

'And – *my* father – my real . . .'

'I don't know who he was. And *he* didn't know, your father: who you called that, I mean. He never found out. Someone she met after she left mine. That's all I . . . Please, Catherine – '

He folded both her hands with his, but she suddenly drew hers away, with a strength that seemed to surprise him as much as herself.

'But why – why on earth did you say we'd had a child?'

' "Why"?'

'You said it – '

'Because – ' she swallowed a mouthful of breath ' – because – we did.'

His mouth made the shape of a smile. She looked away, but saw the stiffening spread-eagled body instead.

'Don't joke, Catherine – '

She almost shrieked.

'I'm *not* . . .'

'But it's impossible.'

'It happened. It happened, a boy – '

'*What* happened? You were carrying him, a foetus?'

'A boy – '

'He died?'

'No,' she said.

'No?'

'A boy. Our son.'

'Where – where is he?'

'I don't know.'

'You don't know?'

'Not now. I couldn't cope. It wasn't a life for him.'

'You had an abortion?'

'Christ, *no*!' Tears poured from her eyes. 'A boy, a real boy – '

'But where is he?'

'New Zealand. I saw photos they said they could send – '

'Speak sense, Catherine.'

'I couldn't keep him. I had him adopted.'

'Our son?'

'Of course,' she cried. '*Our* son.'

'Jesus Christ! Oh, Jesus *Christ* – '

'I'm sorry, Maurice.'

She wept in front of him, wept uncontrollably without stopping.

'My son. Where – ?'
She shook her head.
'Where, Catherine? Whereabouts in New Zealand?'
'Leave him – '
'But – '
' – where he is. Leave him be, *please*.'
'But we've – '
'He's suffered enough. Too much – '
'Why didn't you tell me?'
'I couldn't.'
'Why not? Couldn't you find me?'
'I – I went off the rails. A bit. For a while. When I got back on them again . . .'
He was sitting on the floor, hunched forward with his head held in his hands.
'Go, Catherine.'
'What?'
'Please go.' He raised his eyes. The torment and despair in them took her breath away. 'Get out of here.'
She couldn't look at the body.
'But she – '
'It's all right.'
'How will you – '
'It's okay. Everything'll be okay.'
'Please, Maurice – '
'I promise you. Just go now. Everything'll be all right.'
'The Claridge. I'm at the Claridge.'
He nodded, but she realised it wasn't registering with him.
She stood up. Somehow she made an exit from the room. She needed cold fresh air, open space about her, so she could think, just think.
Without knowing how, she reached the lobby. She hurried out of the elevator, mumbled an apology to a woman she almost knocked down. She ran through the empty hallway, pushed on a glass door and stepped out on to the sidewalk.
She took a few steps, then stopped. She could smell the sea.
She looked up at the façade of the building. She counted five storeys up. She saw lit windows and a verandah. The french doors stood open and curtains blew.
Then, as the wind abated, she heard a sound like a gunshot. Followed by another.
In the two or three seconds between them she perceived their significance: that there and then he took the love left in her heart with him, that they died together, Maurice and she.

64

Christina

IN Atlantic City on this October night in 1960 the wind was whipping the sea to foam and slicing in on the Boardwalk. It pummelled the canvas awnings above the shop fronts. Sand blew along the streets as if this was a frontier town.

It was after midnight, and the front was deserted except for herself. The street lights flickered with the fluctuations in current. Lit windows in hotels and apartment buildings seemed to be on the blink.

The wind rumbled between the blocks of condominiums and the gaming parlours, the salt spray flew. She had come a long way to find all this, waiting for her on the New Jersey shore.

A single automobile coasted by, a long white car with high shark fins and tail lights like two great fiery round eyes. But she couldn't hear it with the wind cracking in her ears.

She continued walking along the pedestrians' Boardwalk, in possession now of her bearings. Earlier, in the lobby of the Claridge Hotel, she'd stood looking at a map of the town and she'd been intimidated by its exactly regular grid pattern of streets, named in one direction after the States of the Union and in the other after the world's seas and oceans. But there was a grim, po-faced reasonableness to it all.

Central Pier was behind her on her right-hand side and so on her left were Illinois Avenue, Kentucky Avenue, Tennessee Avenue, South Carolina Avenue. At North Carolina Avenue she turned off on to Steeplechase Pier; past the closed cafés and diners and the boarded-up hot-dog stands. One dive was open, and she heard an out-of-tune piano through the dim, salty glass of the windows. She halted momentarily – as if she was trying to remember a place or a time it reminded her of – then she passed on again.

Her heels echoed forlornly on the pier floor. She pulled the knot of her headscarf tighter.

In the spaces between the planks the sea writhed and foamed. The toes of her shoes encountered papers stuck to the wood, sodden Dixie cups. Her soles, she chanced to see, left prints impressed in the sandy grime.

A few lights on standards glimmered along the pier and lit her way. For a while, as the wind blew stronger and flapped the edges of the scarf across her face, she lost the sound of her own footsteps.

Then the wind dropped and she could hear her heels stabbing into the wood. Her skin hurt where the wind had flayed it and when she lifted her hand to soothe her cheek she found the evidence of, not sea spray, but tears.

She took a handkerchief from her pocket and dabbed at her eyes. She stopped at a railing and fastened her other hand on to it as she stared down into the blustering black sea. She gripped the bar tighter.

Suddenly the iron roared and she felt something like a shock pass through her hand. She jumped back. She looked to her left and saw a policeman holding a truncheon or night-stick walking towards her, soundlessly on his soft crepe soles.

She stared at him as he approached. Three or four feet from her he stopped and, very purposefully, he leaned back against the railing.

'I'd guess there's something bothering you?'

Catherine didn't respond. She turned towards the sea that came bellowing for the shore.

'Yes, lady?'

She felt his truncheon lightly touch the collar of her raincoat, as if that way he might see her better.

'Fancy having a dip? Is that what you've been thinking?'

Catherine stepped back.

'I want to be by myself,' she said.

'Just supposing you *did* take a dip – then *I'd* have to take a dip too. Does that make much sense to you, lady?'

She stood listening to him, but didn't speak.

'So maybe you do feel like ending it all, but does that mean I've gotta get laid up with pleurisy?'

He was speaking very clearly and deliberately, but calmly, without any hint of provocation.

'Now, I'm ready to bet you didn't look at it quite like that. Did you now?'

Catherine turned away. She replied by repeating, three times, a sideways motion of her head.

No. No. No.

'So I guess you oughta take another think about things. Don't you reckon?'

She looked at him, a long careful querying gaze that lasted several seconds. She lifted her hand to her cheek as she had earlier, but now her tears had dried. She pulled at the edges of her scarf before turning her head away.

She walked off without addressing another word to him, following the line of lights shining hesitantly overhead. From here the absurd façades of once great hotels all along the Boardwalk, *folies de grandeur*, had the substance of cut-outs. A Barnum and Bailey world. Further off, on Virginia or Maryland Avenues, the two round tail lights of the finned Lincoln Continental Mark 4 watched her like ogre's eyes in an enchanted wood.

*

Back in New York she took a train to the East Tremont Avenue stop and walked from there to the zoo.

Inside the vast park moats replaced iron bars. The animals appeared to have had their freedom returned to them, here between Fordham Road and Bronx River Parkway.

She headed for the African Veldt.

Elephants lumbered past, trailing dust behind them. Two or three hundred yards away five ostriches gathered in a cabal. The ochre plain stretched for acres, only defined by a few trees and some areas of low green scrub.

She followed the track until she came to a refreshment kiosk. She bought a coffee and sat down at a table in the mild sun. She felt unslept and listless, but she'd told herself she had to get out of the apartment, away from Washington Square.

She sipped at the tepid coffee. She closed her eyes, and must have dozed for some moments. When she opened her eyes again the table closest to hers was occupied.

The man gave her a smile and, with her reflexes so slow, she looked at him a little longer than she realised was advisable. He was in his late fifties, at a guess, but well preserved and modernly dressed in expensive casual wear: a navy blazer, light beige chino slacks, black penny loafers. His black hair had thinned only slowly, which always helped a man to look youthful.

She watched him as he tracked his eyes on to the roan perspective of Africa. But when she turned her head to look in the same direction, she caught the movement of *his* head – towards her – out of the corner of her eyes.

She sipped at her coffee. She didn't want the added stimulation of caffeine – anything but – yet she was tired and thirsty after the journey up and she couldn't remember when she had last drunk or eaten. Also, the prospect of Africa made her thirst seem like dehydration.

She sensed that her neighbour wanted to talk. She decided that she wasn't going to make it easy for him, so she continued to ignore him. He coughed a couple of times, but she didn't look round. She sat stirring her coffee, and somehow forgot her resolution when he crossed his legs, caught the tin table with his knee and sent his own cup slithering out of the saucer.

She looked up at the commotion before she realised it must be a ruse for her attention. He smiled in a well mannered way and said it was a very pleasant day.

She nodded her head non-committally. She didn't feel up to smiling. Several days of closed windows and darkness weren't equipping her for so much sudden light and she felt her eyes prickly with sunshine.

She blinked a number of times, afraid for a moment that her eyes were going to ooze what might seem like tears.

He opened the newspaper on his lap.

'I've just been looking through this.'

'Oh?' she said.

'Do you ever read the New York papers?'

'I did at first. I've sort of – lost interest.'

'I think they're always worth a *look* at least.'

'I don't know,' she said.

He opened the newspaper and shook out the pages. He hadn't commented as people always did on her English accent.

'You might be missing something, you never can tell.'

He spoke in a light manner she might have taken for bantering.

'I doubt it,' she said.

She found she was being offered the newspaper. Her impulse was to smile and say 'no thank you' but he was nodding at the right-hand page; his thumb seemed to be indicating a news story he thought she should read.

She took the newspaper from him. She started to read and felt her heart juddering in her chest.

POLICE SEEK MYSTERY ENGLISHWOMAN

New Jersey police investigating the deaths of English couple Maurice and Jennifer Encombe are seeking information from any members of the public who were in the vicinity of Maryland Avenue in central Atlantic City last Thursday.

A neighbour of the deceased couple claims to have seen a woman making a hurried exit from the elevator on the night of the slayings. She describes her as being about thirty years old, five feet seven or eight inches in height, attractive appearance, smartly dressed in a raincoat. Her hair colouring was probably dark brown; she was wearing a headsquare at the time. The witness judged her to be in an excitable state as she ran out through the main lobby of the apartment building. The mystery woman is said to speak with a pronounced English accent.

Police investigating the deaths now believe that Mr Encombe first shot his wife dead and then turned the gun on himself. They would like to contact the woman seen running out on to Atlantic Avenue at Maryland so that they can eliminate her from their enquiries. She may also be able to lend them evidence which will help to shed some further light on the tragedy of Apartment No. 512.

She handed back the newspaper.

She realised too late that she must have been betrayed by her arms shaking as she read it.

So, who was he? A policeman? An amateur sleuth? A blackmailer?

She untied the knot of her headscarf and pulled it from her hair. The silk smoothly and effortlessly slithered round her neck.

She tucked the scarf into the right-hand pocket of her raincoat.

'I don't blame you for not reading them,' she heard him say. 'Some rum goings-on in the world.'

She turned to look at him.

'That's not an American thing to say.'

'What isn't?'

' "Rum goings-on" – ' she said.

'I spent quite a lot of time in England. Once I did, anyway. A few years, on and off.'

'Doing what?' she asked, to steer them away, to postpone –

'I talent-spotted for the movies.'

'What sort of talent?'

'Actors, actresses. Writers. I was writing part of one myself. Well, *re*-writing what the studio gave me: to tidy up.'

'What do you do now?'

'I shoot them.'

Momentarily she hesitated.

'Films?'

'Films.'

Was it bluff? Another bluff?

'I'm sorry. Should I recognise you?'

'You're under no obligation.'

It was an idiotic conversation. An idiotic afternoon. Sitting here in a zoo, in the Bronx.

She stood up. He stood up too, folding the newspaper and pushing it under his arm.

'*I*'m Paul Lenkoff.'

The name wasn't quite a surprise to her; she had encountered it somewhere before.

'And you're – ?'

The question of course was a trap.

'Margaret.'

The word – one single word – jerked him fully upright.

'Margaret?' he repeated.

'Yes.'

A smile slowly appeared.

'I can't believe it,' he said.

'What? Why not?'

'Of all names – '

'Why not?'

'Your ring says "C".'

'What?'

He took hold of her left hand, gently, and lifted the fifth finger with the signet ring.

'It was a present.'

'Very nice too.'

'From my aunt.'

'The initial – '

'I'm Christina,' she said. 'I changed it.'

'Not Margaret?'

'Christina – '

'I like "Christina" very much.'

'Christina Moncrieff-King.'

She turned to look at the exhibits, the zebras in the semblance of their freedom. Then she turned away again: they were disturbing her.

'Do you mind if I walk with you?'

'That's the sort of old-fashioned question my father might have asked my mother.' She faltered. 'My father – '

'*Do* you mind?'

'I don't know who you are.'

'Paul Lenkoff.'

'Why, I mean. Why you're here. Beside me.'

'Professional reasons, let's say.'

The words 'New Jersey Police' leaped out at her again from the remembered print on the page.

'Professional?'

'I've never stopped talent-spotting. Except now I put the talent into my own movies.'

'I don't understand,' Catherine said, and put a hand tiredly to the side of her head.

'Like Zanzibar.'

'"Zanzibar"?' she repeated. 'What's that?'

'I'm sorry – didn't you read that bit of the article?'

'The article?'

He took the newspaper from under his arm and opened it up again. Oh God no, she thought, don't let it happen like this –

He shook out the newspaper, at the page he'd handed to her earlier. He nodded, and again his thumb showed the place: an inch or two to the right of last time, where a couple of Arts columns ran down the whole length of the page. It was a review of a film called *Another Road to Zanzibar*. She read his name in the first sentence, 'Paul Lenkoff'.

'That's *your* film?'

He smiled as she stood considering him. Maybe he just thought she was timid, taken aback by the circumstances? Or else that she was backward and couldn't make connections in her mind?

'I'm sorry,' he said.

'What for?'

'You – you're dyslexic?'

She paused before breathing out again.

'Reading difficulty?'

'Yes,' she said, hurrying into the lie. 'Yes. Yes, I am.'

'I *am* sorry, really. But they've great treatments for it now – '

'I need time,' she said, 'that's all. To make full sense. Of anything.'

'I see.'

'To get by. You know?'

'It must make life one hell of a performance.'

(Had he really not seen the news story?)

'How's that?'

(A raincoated Englishwoman on the loose: not black hair, or blonde, or fiery, but dark brown: awaiting elimination from the police enquiries.)

'Having to simulate.'

She stared at him.

'I've seen your face before,' he said.

'What?'

'Does that surprise you so much?'

She continued to stare at him.

'I . . .'

The neighbour in the block had been a woman, the story said. Or had she misread it, taken it in too quickly?

'That's my job, after all. *Was* my job, rather.'

'What was?'

'To see and remember.'

'Oh.'

'I've seen you in an advertisement. I knew that. I couldn't think. Since then I've been turning it over and over.'

'When?'

'Following you about.'

'About where?'

'Manhattan.'

'What?' She stopped still.

'And then you went off somewhere.'

'I'd like to be alone – '

'I'm sorry,' he said. 'Don't be alarmed, please – '

'But – '

'I know, I know. I've no right. I quite understand that. You ought to have your privacy.'

She didn't know what to say.

'Didn't you guess?'

'"Guess"?'

'That I was watching you?'

'How?'

'Discreetly, I meant it to be. I tried to make it discreet.'

She clutched the buckle and belt of her coat and turned away.

'Please, just hear me out. I know I've no right. But I'd be so grateful – '

She looked over her shoulder, to the zebras scratching at the dust with their hooves.

'Then it clicked. God knows how. But that's how my mind works. Spirit of Something.'

She froze.

'Of Invention?'

She stared at him. It *was* a trap. Strangers didn't just happen to remember, from the maze of memory, from that hash.

'Or was it Freedom?'

She could have shaken her head at him, and flatly denied it. But he was too intelligent, he already realised from her reaction. The smile was returning to his face.

'I *am* right, amn't I?'

He sounded so desperate to know, to be proved correct.

'Or I *should* say – "aren't I?" '

She nodded.

'English English,' he said.

'Why do you remember so much?'

He laughed.

'I forget the really major things. Anything financial, the legal ins-and-outs.'

She started walking again, but she didn't know if she would be able to keep her balance or manage to follow a straight line.

'It's your face,' he said.

'I was the Spirit of Endeavour. *And* Modernity. *And* Prosperity.'

'Oh yes,' he said. 'But you reminded me of someone I knew once. When I saw it in the ads I thought, that's why they've picked her, she's going to make guys like me think of their past.'

'I didn't *really* remind you of someone then? An actual person?'

'Oh yes,' he said. 'Oh yes, you did.'

'Who?' she asked.

'An English actress. She was young, like you. I helped to get her started. We – lost touch.'

She nodded, blockishly.

'How you said that name – '

'The name?'

'Mar-gar-ette. When I heard it – '

Her actressy delivery of the third syllable, she supposed he meant.

'Marg'r't, then.'

'But you're darker,' he told her.

Dark brown. As the article said, beneath the headsquare.

'It was your nose and chin, though, the colour of your eyes. It really spooked me, seeing it. You made me think – '

She nodded again.

'You made me happy. And sad. I cut out the advertisements and kept them. I've worked with so few English actresses.'

She tied the two ends of her belt together, knotting them.

'Have *you* ever acted, Christina?'

Hearing a novel Christian name had a pacifying effect on her, she felt mildly tranquillised. She smiled a little woozily in all this late October sunshine.

'Before I modelled,' she said, 'I did a little. But it was just something to do. Trying my luck.'

'Please. Take this, Christina.'

He handed her a business card, with a Los Angeles address.

'I've got plans. A new script I'm working on. I realised yesterday, you'd been in my mind. That image of you, standing on the bridge, Westminster Bridge, and the Wordsworth quote. I found the poem last night, I read it. "Dull would he be of soul who could pass by A sight so touching in its majesty".'

She shrugged.

'Everything's so muddled up,' she said.

'How d'you mean?'

'Everything crossing like this, coinciding. Wishes. Memories.'

'Have you got an address? Where I could find you?'
'I rent an apartment. I might be moving.'
'You'll be going back to England?'
'Oh no,' she said.
'Whereabouts are you at present?'
'I've got this,' she said, and placed his card in the left-hand pocket of her raincoat.
'Reverse the charges when you call.'
'I – I don't see how,' she said.
'I could test you.'
(That was the oldest line in the book, wasn't it? First Wordsworth, then the infamous audition.)
'I mean,' she said, 'I'm not an actress now. I never really knew how.'
He smiled, disbelievingly.
'Everyone acts anyway,' he told her.
'You too?' she asked him. The question couldn't be helped.
'Movies are about significant moments. Losing time, time changing, how time connects. I make movies because I don't understand so much about my life.'
She couldn't really follow him.
'That's just what *used* to happen,' he said.
'What did?'
'When I spoke to *her*. The woman you reminded me of. I always talked too much.'
'You were fond of her?'
'I loved her, yes. I didn't know that properly till later. The real thing, and I only understood in Tinseltown.'
'She came here?'
'No. No, she never left England.'
She spotted the sign to one of the buggy pick-up points.
'You won't forget?' he said. 'To get in touch with me? Call, and reverse charges?'
He sounded as if it was actually important to him. When she looked at him, she saw something very much like fright in his eyes: alarm that he might indeed lose contact with her. For the first time the initiative was with her.
'Maybe,' she said. 'But I have to go now.'
He touched her arm as she turned away, but she didn't allow herself to respond. She walked off, along the shale path, to make the first connection on her journey back to Greenwich Village, a return by feasibly logical means to a city of concrete and glass improbability and harum-scarum vertigo life and nothing to break a fall.

65

Aristeid

SHE took her drink out on to Mr Weissmann's balcony.

It was on cloudless nights just like this one – but warmer, presumably – that Fred and Ginger had danced in penthouse supper-rooms, and transported them all out of themselves where they sat in the blue darkness of the Salon Deluxe.

Sic itur ad astra. And then she remembered something else from the Latin class, a passage in Ovid where the spirit of Julius Caesar, after his death, ascended to heaven and was turned to a star.

She looked above her into the skies, into the sweep of stars.

Somewhere was a particular avenue of stars where she must be familiar with the soul of each.

Somewhere in the apartment he was drinking.

For the first time – she had always slept nude – she had worn one of his mother's flimsy nightdresses to bed, and she couldn't have predicted the consequences. As soon as he'd seen her, he'd struck her a blow on the cheek and left her crying. Then he'd cried himself, for what he had done. He'd wandered a while through the flat, then he'd come back into the bedroom and pulled the nightgown off her where she lay, ripping the silk and lace. He'd gone wandering through the rooms again, until she fell asleep, and then he'd returned to the bedroom and made love to her like never before, but without once mentioning her name, and then later having her sit astride him.

Somewhere in the apartment he was drinking. Bourbon. Jack Beam, which he'd told her had been his father's poison. He'd been walking about for what felt to her now like hours, with his mind unfettered.

She couldn't hear him and she turned back to the view, over Chelsea and up to the Empire State Building and the towers beyond Murray Hill. Seen from the Salon, it had been the epitome of glamour, a rich harbour of dreams.

She took a couple of steps forward, to the high balustrade of the balcony, and rested her glass. Beneath her in the square the lights were lost in the partially leafed branches of the trees. A couple sat on one of the benches, and – indistinguishable from a child – the woman in the reefer jacket who had spoken to her walked her dog on one of the winding paths. The situation, she thought, was only as it ordinarily was.

But in the next second the ground was taken from under her feet. Her heart lurched. Washington Square tilted, it ran away from her, and the tumbler took flight. She screamed and she saw her hands waving like a diver's in front of her. She opened her mouth and screamed again. Her knees were held, pinned together. She tried kicking out with her feet but that was only tipping her further forward. She managed to fasten both hands to the balustrade and she pushed back with all the force she could. She gasped for breath, and pushed again. He let go her knees and grabbed her right leg. She lashed out with her left foot but started tipping forward again on the tiles and almost lost her hold on the balustrade. She tried to wriggle on to her side. He folded his arms round her leg and lifted it higher. She took one hand off the balustrade and pushed it into his face. He reeled back without letting go of her leg. Her own face was grazed by the concrete but her hands found a tighter grip on the balustrade. With her right foot she aimed the stiletto heel of her shoe at his leg and kicked back. He let out an agonised bellow. He gripped her calf and ankle and again tried to hoist her higher and forward. Her hands clawed at the balustrade, she knew she couldn't let her other foot slip on the tiles. The square swung back into view. She corkscrewed her torso into a position where, pushing herself as flat as she could against the front of the balustrade, she could take aim with her right shoe. She kicked behind her. The heel met soft flesh and, yelling fury and vengeance over her shoulder, she stabbed the sharp point deeper. He screamed with the pain and let go of her.

She almost lost her balance with astonishment.

When she turned round he was lying on the balcony floor clutching his crotch, doubled over it. She stood where she was without moving, but fighting to get her breath back. He had forgotten that she would have the strength of a woman half his mother's age, with the primed, primal instincts of her anonymity.

He howled, a banshee wail, and that did force her to move. She put her hands to her ears and stepped a wide semi-circle around him. She saw blood on the tiled floor. When she'd passed through the balcony doors, she started to run. Into the bedroom where she snatched her bag and tried to think. She might pack a small suitcase, but she was terrified to give him a chance. She opened the wardrobe door and grabbed her mackintosh and his mother's ankle-length musquash coat. She reached back in and pulled one of her own dresses off its hanger. She opened the drawer where he kept ready cash and stuffed the envelope into her bag.

She ran out of the bedroom into the corridor. She stopped outside the sitting-room. She saw herself afloat in the plate glass of one of the balcony doors and was drawn forward by the reflection. Then through it she made out that he was trying to get to his feet, lurching at the glass panel and daubing it with bloody hand-prints. She thought of what had almost happened, how he'd meant to murder again as he had before, and walking forward she unflinchingly lifted the heavy bronze figure from the desk – a naked youth, with some impressive saleroom pedigree which had meant nothing to her – and, taking precise aim and then closing her eyes, she hurled it for all she was worth at the man behind the glass.

*

Fleeing across town in a cab, she saw women of whom any one might have been his mother, walking on every block, stars fallen to earth. They stood watching the plaster mannequins in lighted shop windows, and they seemed to be viewing their elegant, erotic selves when young.

Because sex drove the whole damnable, combustible machine, its heat blew as steam out of the sidewalk pumps and wall ducts. She closed her eyes. She looked back to that afternoon when he'd gone into his mother's bedroom and found the newspaper, when she'd run the bath and the door into the bathroom had stood open and through it he'd watched her dropping her clothes, transformed by a few gestures into any of those women they pored over in magazines in the school dormitory. Almost naked, she had glanced up and seen the observing eyes. Through a combination of grief and the vagaries of the coastal light, her teenage son was transfigured too, into the ghost of her Kentucky lover. He had inherited the build of his natural father, his stance, the shock of fair hair falling over one eye.

She was nude by the time she reached him. Her breath reminded him of how his Manhattan father's smelt, after a bout of bourbon. She pulled her hair out of its combs and it tumbled down her back. Her breasts rose, the nipples hardened. She closed her eyes and pulled him towards her, inhaling his youth, letting it appetise her.

He offered her no resistance. Both were metamorphosed: she into her lover's arms, he into the most desirable of conditions, manhood. Maine was transmuted into legend and myth, the realm of unlocked secrets and airborne magic . . .

Headlights tracking, the taxi cab sped her through Little Italy and Chinatown and across the Manhattan Bridge to Brooklyn Heights. 'Just keep going,' she told the driver every time he asked. On a clement fall night she sat with fur on her lap like a tsarina. On Ocean Parkway, straight as any Roman road in the Old World, she read the names on the illuminated signs as they flashed past – Coney, Jamaica Bay, Rockaway.

Neighbouring planets, she supposed, while through the windshield the sodium lights were transubstantiated into an avenue of stars, and she was spirited through them, a time-traveller among the unforgotten dead.

*

She spotted the name written on the side of the aircraft, 'Spirit of Valiance', and her resolution almost gave way. But she persevered, climbing the steps to the door, doughty when so many of the others about her were white-knuckled and green about the gills.

The hostesses smiled as they patrolled their cigar-shaped capsule. The engines started up, the propellers spun, faster and faster until she couldn't distinguish them from the motion.

The man in the aisle seat beside her started to talk. She smelt the spirits on his breath, which she had presumed at first to be Dutch courage. He told her he had been east visiting his brother and his wife: she'd taken very ill after they'd come back from an excursion to the Amazon.

'The Amazon? You're sure?'

'I'm sure sure.'

They'd returned bearing carved heads and native gee-gaws – illegally smuggled out, he didn't doubt, knowing his brother – and they'd also brought back home with them this disabling nerve-sickness that had rendered his sister-in-law immobile and speechless.

'She *looks* okay, that's the weird thing, when she's lying quite still. She's beautiful, you see. But my brother has never appreciated her, not as he ought to. He didn't deserve her, and *she* deserved something he couldn't give her, joy and happiness –'

But Catherine shut off as the plane taxied along the runway. She felt she had heard this zombie story before, only the old Caribbean setting had become New York. She closed her eyes as the engines thrummed in readiness for build-up and take-off. Ahead of them was their tarnished El Dorado, all that they had left to them now, the stake-all: the syncopated, seductive swing lullaby of Lala land.

66

Weekend in Alberta

THE next spring Mr Matheson took me on a short trip to the Rockies. We travelled to rapids country, to the legendary Kicking Horse, carried down from a glacier, and up the Bow Valley, between the Spray and Bow Rivers, to Sulfur Mountain.

The highlight was staying at the Banff Springs Hotel, that huge brownstone château. I swam in the Olympic-length pool. After I'd changed, Mr Matheson had a drink in the Alhambra Room, then we dined by a window in the Rob Roy Room, watching a Rockies sunset. Afterwards Mr Matheson gave me a tour of the hotel's public rooms.

Naturally the thought of the expense had occurred to me, and I knew it had nothing to do with any Aunt Vi and Uncle Don. It mattered less and less with so much else to occupy my attention, waking to the views of snow-crested mountain and fir forest and fast white water from my bedroom window. It could only have been *her* doing, of course, my mother's, and somehow I could subsume that fact, I could contain it, and feel neither beholden to her for it nor hard-done-by on account of the condition of things the rest of the time. I was wearing clothes and shoes provided by her, but then I was her son, catching frequent resemblances to her in mirrors, turning over my memories sometimes and presuming that at least *she* knew what all this was in aid of. Mr Matheson said nothing about it, and merely seemed thoughtful as he settled the bill next morning and we packed our bags to leave. He had watched me all through dinner when he must have thought I didn't see, but I had been able to study his reflection in the windows against the sunset. Well, it's okay, I wanted to tell him, if there are going to be days like this ahead too. I can put up with home. Another time I can pick up a golf club, and there'll be the excursions to go riding the ice rapids at Shotgun on rafts, and no boy can grow up a Canadian and not learn to paddle his own kayak.

We loaded our bags into the trunk of the battered Oldsmobile and Mr Matheson read the signs for the valley road. The snow had thawed very early this year, and was only in evidence beneath trees, where the hot sun didn't reach. Steam rose from the fir plantations. A scatter of white clouds blew briskly across the vaulting blue sky like Indian smoke signals. Jack Benny passed us, being chauffeured in the back of a big black Imperial; contrary to his reputation he was counting a thick gratuity of banknotes from a bulging wallet.

67

Twister

(High heels walking on a wooden floor in an empty-sounding room. A hint of silks, and a schoolgirl's French voice reciting, perhaps singing.)
Establish, then cross to:
SCENE *1: Paul Lenkoff's house, Beverly Hills: Catherine is meeting the press.*

Bromfeld	And tell me, Christina. How did you come to meet Mr Lenkoff? Or how did *he* come to meet *you*?
Catherine	I *used* to be an actress. In England.
Bromfeld	'Used to be'?
Catherine	He knows – about that. My experience . . .
Bromfeld	I'm sure he does. Did he tell you he was making a movie?
Catherine	Yes. He's told me . . . how much this one . . . means to him.
Bromfeld	You *knew* about him, of course?
Catherine	I – Yes.
Bromfeld	Everyone's heard of Paul Lenkoff, haven't they? And he . . . brought you out here?
Paul Lenkoff	(*interrupting*) After a little persuasion! I hope Mr Bromfeld isn't prying, Christina. You told me this was for the 'New Faces' column, Art.
Bromfeld	Tip of the iceberg. (*More slyly*) Wouldn't you trust me with anything longer?
Lenkoff	You must have enough.
Bromfeld	I just wondered how much 'persuasion' it took. To come out here. Has Hollywood always been your ambition, Christina?
Catherine	Well, it's only been theatre I've done. In England, of course.
Bromfeld	What d'you think of California?

Catherine I've hardly seen it.
Lenkoff She only got in Tuesday night.
Bromfeld Quite an introduction you've got, Christina: Mr Lenkoff. This house. Beverly Hills.

Then the journalists left. Her new Svengali had fed them bait about the film he had in mind. But they hadn't risen to it as he must have intended. Instead they'd stood around looking at her, trying to get an angle, making their own suppositions.

Lenkoff Just wait till we get to San Alfonso.
Catherine Why there?
Lenkoff I've got a lease on a house. It'll be ideal. For the movie.
Catherine You're not making it in a studio?
Lenkoff Have you seen *À Bout de Souffle*?
Catherine No.
Lenkoff Godard. He's French. I want something – I don't know – jerky like that. And try something new, shoot it on location.
Catherine *In* the house?
Lenkoff I thought we could stay there. Move in. Live on the set. When it *is* the set.
Catherine All of us? Everyone?
Lenkoff (*Laughs*) No. Just the two of us. In our own quarters. (*Pause*) You'll sleep then, Christina.
Catherine Will I?
Lenkoff It's got orange groves on three sides of it. You get wafts of the aroma. Sweet and delicate, like a perfume. And so soothing, all you'll want to do is sleep . . .

Cut to:
SCENE 2: Lenkoff's car, a Ferrari, interior. Car in motion. Music from car dashboard radio: Sinatra singing 'Lonesome Road'.

Catherine Tell me about the film.
Lenkoff *Twister?* It's difficult –
Catherine The film is?
Lenkoff Everything about it is. I'm not proving such a genius persuading people to part with their money. It's too European. Too 'existentialist', although that's not

the word they use. Anyway, they don't like auteur-directors out here. Tough luck –

Catherine It's got a story?

Lenkoff Girl in a lonely, rambling house – pretty house, very pretty girl – she gets to think the house is haunted, it's not but she starts to haunt herself – she remembers all the murder stories she's read, seen in the movies – the phone rings but it's only a faulty line – the fear comes out of *herself*, guilt . . .

Cut to:
SCENE *3: On aural tape*

Hello? Hello? Is someone there? Hello? There's someone there, who is it? Look, I *know* someone's there. Who are you? D'you hear me? Who's there? Okay, so you think this is some kind of fun. It's *your* kind of fun – Look, it's not mine. Who's there? Cat-and-mouse, is that it? Yes, cat-and-mouse. You're the cat, right? I get it. No, I don't get it. You think it's going to be so easy. You just come out here and get your fun. (*Shouts*) Who's there? Look, I *know* I'm not alone. (*Smashes something*) I'll find you – I will – I'll track you down. Yes, I will. (*Smashes something else*) I'll track you down. I'll find you. This house isn't haunted, it's not . . .

He took some shots, what he called 'crucial' ones, with his own ciné-camera.

Cut to:
SCENE *4: San Alfonso villa, interior: night*

Lenkoff Look, Christina, I like this. I'll play it back.
Catherine Which bit is it?
Lenkoff After the telephone call. You've got it just right.
Catherine Who's supposed to have called her?
Lenkoff (*shrugs*) Oh . . .
Catherine Well, shouldn't I know?
Lenkoff Time will reveal all.
Catherine Can't you tell me?
Lenkoff If you were working on TV, if this was a soap – God help you, my darling – you wouldn't know then. You

wouldn't know anything about what was coming to you. Depends on your popularity what happens to you. In a couple of shows' time, you could be written out. Dead, even.

Catherine I thought you said, in the film I might be dead. *Might* be. I'm my own ghost, come back – to haunt the house.

Lenkoff You *might* be dead, yes.

Catherine I think – I really think –

Lenkoff What? You think what?

Catherine – I'm getting out of my depth

Lenkoff Just look.

Catherine I *can't* watch myself.

Lenkoff You'll just have to learn, then.

Catherine No.

Lenkoff Jesus, Christina, a movie actress who can't look at herself?

Catherine (*manages to laugh*) I'm hopeless. Absolutely. I know I am. (*Walks off: her feet echo on the floorboards*)

Catherine Want a drink?

Lenkoff I'm going to run this again. (*Resets the projector and runs the scene again*)

Catherine (*loudly, as if for effect*) I read an article about California somewhere. Its diseases. Loneliness, violence. The war of the sexes. The money psychiatrists make. Therapy centres, people standing howling and shrieking at each other as if they're banishing demons. 'Relaxation' institutes for the laying on of hands. Here . . . (*handing over drink*) It called it 'The Death of the Heart' here.

Lenkoff You don't like it? (*Pause*) But you like the house?

Catherine Is it real?

Lenkoff What? Why shouldn't it be real?

Catherine I don't know. It sounds hollow. The columns. What do you know about it?

Lenkoff Some industrialist or businessman built it. A German. In the eighteen-nineties. He had a new wife, she was half-French. She was really a child.

Catherine What d'you mean?

Lenkoff His wife. When he married her, she was under legal age. Maybe he wanted to hide her here. And he built it to make her think – I don't know – she was on some Caribbean island maybe.

Catherine What happened to her?
(*Pause. Ice tinkles in glasses*)

Lenkoff Went mad. The story goes. Out of her box.

Catherine Poor girl. Perhaps she's here, and I'll hear her silks rustling? (*Pause*) Perhaps not. You need a half-light for ghosts. (*Again loudly, as if for effect: against the dailies*) There's nothing here between daylight and pitch darkness, I read.

Lenkoff You've been doing a lot of reading up.

Catherine I've had time for it in my life. Magazine knowledge anyway.

Lenkoff That's enough knowledge.

Catherine Scott Fitzgerald said there's no twilight in California: the dark just comes down, like a curtain. Someone else said there aren't any shadows in Los Angeles. I think they meant there's no history. Not in the sun, in the heat; the place, time, they melt: there's no past, no resistance. No drag. Or maybe they meant there's no complication in your character: no . . . conscience . . .
Fade

The San Alfonso house reminded her of New Orleans, although she had never been there: or even of *Gone with the Wind*.

The outer walls were wood-panelled, and two balustraded verandahs enclosed both floors. The house had been designed for heat and crinolines and desultory conversation.

In the evenings before bed they would sit side by side on a swing-chaise. He would stroke the arm next to him, her thigh, her knee, and she would also be aware of him watching her, in a cautious and considering manner that didn't seem to accord with the physical closeness, their intimacy.

Sometimes he would show her what he had written.

Cut to:
SCENE 5: *San Alfonso Villa, interior (verandah): night*

Catherine (*reading aloud*) 'I can't go on living there. It's just a feeling I get, as soon as I walk into it, the house, every time I go in. Like I don't know how I'm going to get out again. I know it's crazy, I *know* it is, I'm telling you it is.'

He called it his 'treatment'. But it was always changing. When she learned lines, they were superseded by others, and perhaps those by others. Things became less and less clear to her: about the plot and about the money talk; she was losing the thread of this story.

68

Home Thoughts

HE repeated the name.

'Aquae-Regis?'

'Yes,' she said. 'It's just a town.'

'I've been there.'

She wished she hadn't mentioned it. She hadn't meant to.

'When I was working in England,' he said. ''Twenty-eight, 'twenty-nine. I went a couple of times.'

'Tinseltown it isn't.'

'I didn't go back. I lost touch with my contact there.'

'I doubt if you missed much.'

'Were you brought up there?'

'So to speak.'

'You lived there, though?'

'I mean, my mother died.'

'I'm sorry – '

'It wasn't the same after that.'

'I guess not.'

'But I didn't go back. I told myself I wouldn't. And I never did. That was something – '

'You felt so bad about it?'

She shook her head.

'Because I knew perfect happiness there. Too perfect to find again. First with my mother, only I didn't know. And at the end with my lover; then I *did* know, that nothing could be better than it. I lost him, though. But so long as I wasn't there, so long as I was just remembering, I could hope – he'd find me again – and for years it was like the air I breathed, it was how I survived.'

*

They'd come back to the city, for reasons of 'business'. A table had been booked for lunch at the Ambassador Hotel. But first she had a consultation with a dental surgeon, who was famous for his skill at capping teeth and making smiles. As she was leaving his surgery, she was handed a message. 'From Mr Lenkoff'. He told her he was sorry but a meeting had been fixed up at the last minute and, if she could make the hotel on her own, he would be over just as soon as he could get away.

The eye turning in the restaurant embarrassed her, especially when she felt she was failing all those expectations of her. The table she was shown to was one of the most prominent and she was fearing the worst of solitudes when, out of the corner of her eye, she caught a shape moving towards her. She thought it must be him and as she looked up from her lap she smiled with those teeth she could only think of now as crooked.

But it wasn't him at all. It was a 'her'. Not any 'her'. It was Mrs Larchmont, who had been laid to rest beneath a headstone in 1948.

Catherine's heart leaped forward in her chest and she lurched after it, nearly tipping the table over.

Mrs Larchmont was wearing her grey shantung silk afternoon dress. She advanced with that quiet social confidence of long, long experience. She looked not a day older.

Catherine tried to control her palpitations. Mrs Larchmont lowered herself into the vacant chair.

'My dear, what a *splendid* surprise!'

Catherine couldn't speak.

'You know, I've been hoping to get you to myself for a few moments – '

Her manner of speech had lost its Aquae-Regis formality, it had loosened up to the town. She was smiling, with more of that understated assurance.

'But you're dead.'

'Technically. My heart stopped beating. But my spirit had its own ideas. It was never very keen on the body part of me anyway. So there we left it, beneath the sod on Paradise Hill.'

'Why – why are – are you here?'

'On my eternal quest,' Mrs Larchmont replied. 'For my dear Charles.'

'No. No, in Los Angeles?'

'Somehow I never picked up on the information – but apparently (the after life is simply *full* of gossip) Charles met his mortal end in a car accident. Or, as they insist on saying here, an *automobile* accident.'

'He was killed?'

'He was on holiday, it seems. On vacation. And the fever overtook him, but he was out here, not in Phoenix. So *voilà*, I have travelled west, in pursuit of the facts.'

'But – but how can that help you?'

'Oh, it makes all the difference in the world. This is where I should have been focusing my thoughts all that long time. I was barking up quite the wrong tree – when there are really so few trees in New York City. Or Phoenix, or Tucson, or San Diego. That is, if you catch my drift, my dear.'

Catherine jerked her head forward.

'This is the proper neck of the woods. So lo and behold, Catherine!'

Mrs Larchmont was flaunting the joyfulness of her mood.

'Don't tell me *you* were in any of those places?'

'In New York. Actually.'

'And I missed you? Oh, *isn't* that vexing?'

'But . . .'

A thought occurred to Catherine, not of the most respectful kind.

' – but *shouldn't* you have known? About Los Angeles?'

'How, though?'

'He could have sent you a message. Somehow. After he – '

' – died? But he had no idea that I lived in Aquae-Regis, you see. And the angelic gossips had their eye on his wife all the time. So *there* is the glorious good sense of the situation, in a nutshell.'

Catherine still wasn't convinced however.

'Do you feel – that you belong here?' she asked.

'In California?' (She pronounced it 'Cali-foar-nya'.) 'I suppose one could say it is immaterial now. One could adjust to the weather, I think, to the sky's vivid colours. It's always a question of attitude, I believe, of mind.'

'Aren't you hot?' Catherine asked her. The new situation could have done with a change of clothes, she honestly felt.

'Mind over matter, my dear. In truth I have been too preoccupied to notice.'

She might have asked Mrs Larchmont where she was staying but she feared the question might be superfluous.

'Somehow it seemed appropriate that it *should* be a new place to me. Do you see?'

'Oh yes.'

'I heard someone call the climate here "heavenly", which is truer than they may have meant.'

'More than a turn of phrase?'

'Oh good, you *do* understand what I'm talking about, my dear.'

Catherine smiled, crookedly, but said nothing, placing her elbows on the table – which had never been the 'done' thing – and holding her head in her hands.

When the wine waiter bent down to speak to her she jumped at least three or four inches. Once she'd recovered, she discovered – with a pang of loss over her much-exercised heart – that the visitor had gone and now she was sitting quite alone in her expensive conspicuousness.

*

'I don't think I'm in the Anglo-US market any more,' Catherine said, in response to his memories of London at the tail end of the twenties. 'I've given up Englishness. Too high-risk.'

'But that's your charm.'

'I need elocution lessons. To learn to pass as a native.'

'It's not just your voice, though. The skin tone too, something about living without extremes of weather. English faces always have time imprinted on them, they're the mirrors of the past.'

She looked at him.

'Are you an aficionado?'

'I guess I was once. Years ago. But I go about with my eyes open, I'm always on the look-out.'

'And you just spotted me, huh?'

'Yes, I guess that's how it must have been.'

She laughed with disbelief. She laughed out the window, at all those smart, new glass houses on stilts, stretching in an arc from here to Pacific Palisades. She smiled down on the sea piers she couldn't pick out through the smog, whose names she'd read off the maps: Santa Monica, Huntington Beach, Malibu, Pacific Ocean Park, Redondo, Long Beach, Seal Beach, Balbao, Newport, Venice. Beach cities, Surf-land.

'I don't know what I'm doing here,' she said.

'It's just where you happen to be.'

'That's what I mean.'

'And that's what *I* mean, Christina.'

'But it's too hot to think,' she said, 'too hot to think.'

He kept himself trim, he was firmly in control of his appearance. A handsome man, still, and unbelievably in his early sixties. He had a good head of hair, naturally sun-bleached from mid-brown to fair, and that aided the impression. The skin of his body was hardly creased at all, and clear, without a hint or tint of age's greyness.

He spoke East Coast. She might even have thought him of British origin, if she hadn't known better: or Bermudan perhaps. Few American men had his neatness, that narrow-waisted look which the twin vents of his blazers emphasised. He eschewed cravats, with no stringiness to disguise at the neck, and in his open-necked shirts might have passed for a man in his late forties.

*

He proved himself kind, and gentle, and considerate – he made no passes at her, and she was relieved after all her expectations – but it was also true (the thing he'd said) that she repaid him with indifference. It should have been easier to respond to him, not more difficult, with the event only just behind her that she hadn't been able to think of for more than a very few seconds at a time – Maurice's death. She ought to have been seeking consolation, an enveloping sympathy. If only she hadn't seen him *there*, in the Maryland Avenue apartment she couldn't remember the details of, with the wife he'd spent ten years of his life with. He had turned the gun on himself because *that* woman was dead: for love or hate, in wrath or fear, he had sacrificed to her all of himself that he could. Now Jennifer would always possess him.

She drank to stop herself remembering. Sometimes she heard gun-cracks in the bushes outside. It never rained, or she would have imagined Atlantic City drizzle, but there were always cars streamlined like rockets, and liveried chauffeurs, and sidewalk marquees, and her mind was constantly ducking and bobbing in the course of a day.

She was free and easy with her choice from the cocktail cabinet. She didn't mix drinks, but she was oblivious to which bottle she served herself from. Occasionally she realised that now she was living on the other, false side of hope, where there was nothing. In her past, she felt, it was as if she had let herself be drawn as low as she needed to go to believe that her love for Maurice was the truer, because it could elevate and excuse *anything*, the worst that could happen to her. Perhaps she hadn't had to visualise Maurice to herself, but her love had been there as an instinct, pure and absolute inside her and beyond desecration by anybody, even by her parliamentary lover or her misogynist husband. She had been challenging them, throwing down the gauntlet to do their very damnedest, because she knew that in her heart she could outdo them. She'd had a child to prove it, and Maurice would be waiting for her somewhere, some day.

But the child had gone: because, she tried to tell herself, if she'd had to give all of herself to him, there would have been too little left for Maurice. If he'd been a ruly child, she wouldn't have had to make the choice, but she hadn't had the stamina to cope, and the choice was no choice. Maurice would have understood, she felt, in time, only needing to believe the best of herself.

She drank to forget that too, and to forget New Zealand. She drank cheerlessly, without imaginary healths or toasts, for something to do on those long days when telephone calls took Paul down to the studios, into the city. There was no one else to take her out of herself, and letter-writing (except for contractual purposes) was less than a secondary art in a mechanical city like this one, a vapid and misty way of communicating when your eyes or voice could tell a different story in the game of social confrontation. Anyway, who was left to write to? The only method that would have helped her now – and too unreliable to trust to, with the currents of the Pacific Ocean leading in the wrong direction – was as old as glass (as old as papyrus probably), a message she might have thrown to the insouciant sea in an empty Coca-Cola bottle.

*

Sometimes she took the VW and drove herself about the canyons, but never very far: up to Mulholland Drive sometimes or down to Brentwood. She knew all these houses already from the Salon Deluxe, and nightfall was the best time to see them, when she watched again out of the darkness. Their style was 'Spanish Colonial Revival', the guidebooks told her, and she recognised at once the studded wooden doors, the ornamental wrought-iron work, the fluted roof tiles, the archways and buttresses, the Moorish windows and fake bell-towers, the fountains dripping in paseos and the feather palms and laurel bushes.

She was glad she wasn't returning to any of them. She preferred the glass walls and flat roof of her temporary home, the split-level rooms and open staircase. These carried no associations she was aware of. There was little furniture: some Eames chairs, a boxy sofa and a couple of low tables in the lounge, and more cupboards and sliding walls than she had ever set eyes on before.

This was spare, functional modern living. All the furniture had been brought new into the house; there were no inherited pieces, no investment paintings. The architect's design was of clear, sharp right angles. The decoration was provided by pots of rubber plants and ferns, placed in rattan baskets. The rooms were painted white, or the walls were panels of fine, polished wood. The rugs on the floor were woven in geometric patterns, of squares and rectangles and triangles of bold primary colours. The room where she slept, her own room, contained the minimum of clutter, and she was grateful. There seemed, she thought, to be no lurking spaces for hangdog shadows when night dropped on them, without the need for that infuriating English habit of dusk and twilight. Here they lived between the complementary extremes of day and night, sunlight and dark: a definitive either/or existence (she believed), which must leave no room for ambiguity or doubt.

*

'Do you think of Aquae-Regis often?' he asked her.

'Not so often,' she said. 'Now and then.'

'Do you ever want to go back?'

'Not any more,' she told him.

'Why not?'

'This is where I am. Isn't it?'

'Maybe we never leave places.'

'But here I am,' she persisted.

'It's a replica, Christina. You're a duplicate.'

She considered the possibility as she swilled the very dry martini in her glass.

'How many of me are there then?'

'Oh . . . dozens, I expect.'

'I see.'

Anything went, she felt, in Hollywood conversations, where the future was considered a knowable, definable quantity. Concepts and potentialities had overtaken them all.

A possibility did occur to her.

'Does that mean, it might happen that I encounter myself?'

She could tell that he was quite taken by the hypothesis.

'Can you be certain you'd recognise yourself in that case?'

She thought for a few moments before shaking her head.

'Perhaps not,' she said.

But if it did ever happen it would be here, she knew, in this place, in this gimcrack city wonderland raised on its seismographically authenticated faults and fissures.

69

A Pursuivant Player

THEY returned to the villa in the San Alfonso Valley, to her new life-style and their two bedrooms on opposite sides of the building.

The film was no nearer a starting date. The financial talk was endlessly complex. He commuted back and forth to Los Angeles.

She didn't mind being left in the house. The furniture was ancient, but there was enough cane-work and stripped 'bamboo' for it not to seem gloomy. A woman came in to clean. A homosexual couple, San Francisco escapees, had rented the old estate-manager's house five or six hundred yards away, and intentionally left an electric imitation of a paraffin lamp in a window, so she only had to look out and see the illuminated shade of hyacinth glass.

She would open the windows and catch the aroma of orange blossom, pungent even at the darkest hour of the night. He had told her it would calm her, and she supposed that if anything could it would be the blossom.

She listened to the stillness, the breathing inside her, and again she caught the faintest evidence of a disturbance, like the manufacture of thunder somewhere hugely remote from them. The sound in her head faded to almost nothing, to the infinitesimal, to the merest expansion and contraction of magnetic fields over the globe.

*

Paul was busy in the city, talking business apparently, and it gave her an opportunity to get out of the house. She called a cab and headed for a bar, any bar, on Sunset.

The one she went into resembled an Edward Hopper painting: night in the streets, low lights inside, excluding glass and chrome and solitude.

She ordered a bourbon on ice and drank it too quickly. She ordered a second. The bar was almost deserted, although it was only ten o'clock and warm and on the Strip there was money to burn in spirits.

She was conscious of a figure sitting on the bar stool two along from her. When she turned her head to look, she saw the paradoxical presence of Mrs Larchmont. She was smiling at her.

Catherine's heart jumped in her chest, but not so wildly as last time.

The barman was somewhere else, so they were just themselves, the two of them.

'I'm having so many new experiences,' Mrs Larchmont said more naturally than if they had been seated in her salon in Hesperus House. 'I don't know why I'm not more tired, but I keep going, my stamina's okay. Hasn't flagged, I mean.'

Catherine watched her very, very carefully.

'I don't know where you sleep, Mrs Larchmont. Or where you're staying.'

'Oh, that's all a bit up in the air,' the woman said lightly, tossing the words like juggler's balls. 'But I do appreciate your concern.'

Catherine shifted uncomfortably on her stool.

'It isn't what you think it is,' Mrs Larchmont said.

' "It"?'

'This condition I inhabit.'

'Isn't it the end of everything?'

'Oh no, it's just the beginning.'

Catherine looked doubtful.

'You're a special person, Catherine. It was meant to happen that you should come to Hesperus House and share those afternoons with me. With the days running down into winter.'

Catherine still must have appeared doubtful.

'I received a telegram from Charles today.'

'What?'

'Composed with his usual lightness of touch.'

'How?'

'I always hoped it would be a telegram, so dramatic. We shall meet one another in a few days' time. At an hotel.'

Catherine stared at her.

'I'm so excited, like a girl again, you can't imagine.' She paused, and rethought. 'Oh, but of *course* you must, my dear!'

Please don't involve *me*, Catherine wanted to tell her.

'It's all that I hoped for, you know – '

'I'm glad,' Catherine replied, just a little curtly to her own ear.

Momentarily the shadow of a frown passed across Mrs Larchmont's brow, qualifying her exultation. Immediately afterwards her expression was restored, to joy and optimism.

'It's quite a coincidence, though, isn't it?' Catherine felt impelled to remark.

'I never let a word stand in my way,' Mrs Larchmont said. 'However many syllables it has. Coincidences will happen and they do, so why impede them? It would be churlish to, don't you feel? It's a silly way of behaving we're encouraged into only because people have lost all their capacity to *think*.'

*

They stayed on in Beverly Hills.

He continued to go out in the evenings, leaving her, and not coming back until after midnight. As a child might, she would lie awake in bed in her room until she heard the approach of the car, the familiar tread of footsteps on the gravel.

She didn't know where he went, but this was his city, and he must know every hideaway that it offered. Maybe he had appointments to discuss business, in the cocktail bars of the Hollywood and Bel-Air hotels, when the money-men tried to unwind at the day's end and he could catch the Europeans en route to their night flights from the airport.

It was the least reposeful part of the day to her. She felt jumpy and couldn't settle. There was too much glass about the house; she felt exposed. Sometimes she could shock herself, catching her reflection where she wasn't expecting to see it.

One evening she walked into his study. The filing-cabinet was locked, but when she sat down behind the desk she found the key still in the controlling lock. She looked through each of the drawers. She glanced into diaries, and the first words of some business letters, leafed through blue-marked synopses and treatments, without reading them. Lying on top of the contents in the bottom drawer she found a faded cardboard wallet of papers and pulled it out.

Inside were cuttings, photographs, postcards, theatre programmes. They all appeared to be English in origin, dating from the time shortly before she was born. He had told her of his English visits, his involvement with the script of a film that hadn't got off the ground through some misfortune. She supposed the folder might contain its quota of memorabilia, souvenirs.

First she picked up a programme for a play staged at the Gaiety Theatre in Brighton, on a March evening in 1927.

THE PURSUIVANT PLAYERS

PRESENT
'THE IMPORTANCE OF BEING EARNEST'
A CLASSIC OF THE THEATRICAL REPERTOIRE
BY OSCAR WILDE

She turned to the cast list and ran her eyes down the two columns of print.

THE PERSONS OF THE PLAY

John Worthing, J. P.	Torquil Carstairs
Algernon Moncrieff	Stephen Strand
Rev. Canon Chasuble, D.D.	Edmund Shadwell
Merriman, *Butler*	Jonathan Hayden-Clarck
Lane, *Manservant*	Graeme Goffaux
Lady Bracknell	Lavinia Gillespie
Hon. Gwendolen Fairfax	Caroline ffinch
Miss Prism, *Governess*	Gladys Saunders
Cecily Cardew	Marguerite Curteys

She stared at the last line for several seconds before laying the programme aside and picking out a newspaper cutting from a sheaf of others. It was a review for a production of *Hay Fever*, performed the year after *The Importance of Being Earnest* at a theatre in Bristol. Her reading slowed when she reached the third paragraph; she read it through once before she took her eyes back to the beginning and read it a second time.

> In the rôle of Myra Arundel, Miss Marguerite Curteys gamely attempted to bring out the character's social self-possession. Her voice strained a little to project itself in an auditorium which is notoriously difficult to 'travel', and inevitably her delivery lost something in clarity of diction. But her physical mannerisms were fully convincing, and the changes of expression on her face – whose attractiveness is quite sufficient to render it compelling and memorable – proved a particular delight for this reviewer.

Clipped on to the notice was a cutting from a magazine. It referred to the making of a film at a British studio. Catherine read through it quickly until, for the third time, she encountered that name. Then her eyes returned to the first sentence, and she started again.

> Attention is focused on the Lilliput Studios at Haywards Heath, where work is shortly to begin on a filmed production of *Roxana*, for cinematic presentation in the summer of 1930. This most exciting project is the fulfilment of a long-held ambition by the distinguished English director Philip Colley Reeves to adapt for the silver screen Defoe's novel *The Fortunate Mistress*, the tragedy of a woman who rejects the honourable institution of marriage to make her own way in what she imagines to be a glamorous world, as a courtesan.
>
> Mr Colley Reeves' most recent productions are *Jason's Fleece* and *Afternoon of a Faun*, but on its completion *Roxana* should most certainly prove to be his finest and outstanding achievement.
>
> To the title rôle Lorinda Blair will assuredly bring her considerable powers of dramatic persuasion, founded on a sensitive reading of the character as delineated by Mr Colley Reeves in his adaptation of the novel. Playing opposite Miss Blair will be another highly respected practitioner of the art, Mr Paul Winstanley, who has of late liberally bestowed his fine thespian talents in the cinematic medium.
>
> Additional interest has been excited by the participation of several actors and actresses of lesser experience but undoubted gifts, who will each be gracing the screen for the first time. These include the debonaire Miss Myfanwy Rogan, Miss Eileen Mitchell (whose recent Viola has received much critical approval), and a comparative newcomer, Miss Marguerite Curteys, speedily gaining a reputation about the country for her professional versatility and fetching presence on stage.

Catherine reclipped the cuttings together, and returned to the programme for the production of *The Importance of Being Earnest*. A brief synopsis of the plot followed the dramatis personae, and then sandwiched between two double-pages of advertisements were to be found six pages of photographs showing the cast in costume.

One of the faces, accompanied by the caption 'Introducing Miss Marguerite Curteys', was only vaguely familiar to her for several seconds. Then – it was an inexplicably delayed reaction – she realised who it was: a younger, more self-assured version of the woman who had occupied the silver frames in the sitting-room at home, in the days before the photographs were put away and her aunt had to confect her excuses.

In the roundel of light from the desk lamp, in the Californian silence of heaving jungle vegetation and ghostly aircraft rising and descending, in the Hollywood Hills of her tangled dreams, she watched her hands shake. The theatre programme fell on to the desk-top.

Later . . .

. . . Later she remembered what was left.

Among the other press notices there was no mention of Marguerite Curteys that she could find. There were no more photographs to shock her.

But there was an item of news that surely had some relevance to the rest. The cutting had been torn out of a newspaper. The paper itself was yellowed and curled.

Accompanying the story was a photograph of the event.

BLAZE PUTS PAID TO BIG SCHEMES
OF 'THE LITTLE STUDIO'

In the early hours of yesterday morning fire destroyed the premises of the renowned Lilliput Film-Making Studios at Haywards Heath, Sussex, and in the process added a concluding 'Finis' to the short history of one of the country's most enterprising co-operative ventures in the Arts.

Witnesses reported that the fire appeared out of control within minutes of the first flames being seen. Firemen battled for three and a half hours to regain the upper hand.

It is believed that the conflagration started in the vicinity of the joinery department, where work was being undertaken on the set of Lilliput's newest production, a filmed version of the eighteenth-century literary masterpiece, *The Famous Roxana*. A good deal of space has been accorded in newspaper columns in recent months on the subject of this latest exercise by the 'little studio' with Goliath aspirations. One cannot but reflect now on whose reputations might have stood to be enhanced by their appearance in the intended film. Such must now remain idle and vain conjecture. By eleven o'clock yesterday morning this modest home of worthy industry and valiant ambition had been reduced to an ignominious waste of smouldering timbers and dying ashes.

Catherine sat down and again she sifted through everything the file contained, every single item.

She came across one further integrand in the chronological sequence. A whole page had been removed from the local Aquae-Regis newspaper, an edition for a day in spring, 1929. A repertory company had been performing a country farce at the Panopticon Theatre, and the photograph showed a moment of frozen stage embarrassment:

several members of the cast in tennis whites looked aghast as an astounding revelation was divulged by a stooped gardener wearing a baize apron and a beekeeper's hat with a gauze veil drawn up on to the crown. Catherine recognised one of the young women holding her racket close to her midriff. The critic approved of her performance.

> Marguerite Curteys adds to her professional laurels by her competence in the rôle of Phoebe Lonsdale. She displays a conviction and elegance that may well excel the call of duty in this occasionally wayward *pièce de théâtre*. The part, it must be said, doesn't tax her, and one hopes to see her (before too long) equipped with one which will do her abilities full justice. One can only trust that time and providence will reward well the patience and resolution of such a delightful stage presence.

70

Tsunami

It was impossible for her to settle in the house after that. She thought she must be twisting events to secure the evidence that she had a past, lived so far away from here. Just the sight of the name 'Aquae-Regis' had jolted everything else out of its alignment. A coincidence was causing her to constrain innocent matter into fulfilling some more sinister function. This was the paranoia of distance and loss. She was cramming everything into the Ali-Baba jar, in the expectation of some magical, transporting discovery: when all that had happened was that she had alighted on some papers in a drawer, which she should never have opened anyway.

She searched for a crack on any of the walls, but there was none. She tried to hear her mother's voice and couldn't, not over the swell of the garden and the breath caught in her own throat.

She ran into the kitchen, ransacked the cabinets, and returned to the dining-room with an arsenal of sharp knives. She threw them down on to the table. Armed with several, she walked through to the study, to the locked filing cabinet. The blade of the first knife she used, a carver, slashed the drawer front and bent in the lock, but it didn't break. She took up another smaller knife, for vegetables, and tried again. After a minute or so of graft and perseverance, the lock gave.

The contents mainly consisted of accounting documentation inside buff envelopes, and cardboard rack folders containing business correspondence. She moved on to the second drawer, and the third. Everything she found – filed inside more cardboard folders – related to films: treatments, scripts, detailed shooting plans, letters despatched, some magazine and newspaper notices, letters received on film company notepaper. At first she bundled them back into their folders, then she lost patience and let them fall to the floor.

In the fourth drawer she struck lucky – or unlucky. It took the blades of three knives to break into it. Everything was inside loose cardboard or plastic folders, three armfuls of files which she transported to the desk. She switched on the swivel lamp and began at the beginning, with the first file on the pile, tipping the folder up and shaking out the contents.

He had let go of nothing, she realised after she had worked her way through the top half. Postcards, folding maps, hotel bills, bar tabs, train and airline timetables, magazine travel articles, address cards from offices and shops, more addresses scribbled down in fading ink or pencil on scraps of paper.

She realised she was getting closer when she opened an envelope of photographs, square and bordered by white edges. They showed a family on the stoep of a modest clapboard house, taking up attitudes in the garden, gathered in a beach dune, walking on a long straight country road, looking green and lost in the streets of a big city. She felt sympathy for this family – for the mother with the sensitive face and restless hands, for the balding father with his compensatory moustache, for the two sisters who always found a reason to smile, for the two brothers who didn't seem to belong to one another, one with the forced air of a pugilist and the other in his shadow, with his mother's face. She came across a shot of the mother taken from behind, sitting on a porch swing; half her arm stretched along the seat back, the forearm was raised to support her chin and jawline – in the hot, dusty light from the desk lamp the photograph and its subject exuded great stillness and grace.

And then she found it, inside a large creased white manila envelope – what she had been looking for without realising that she was.

Sheets of blue notepaper, once folded but smoothed flat over years; ink once black but now discoloured and with a rusty, coppery tint she might have scratched off with the edges of her fingernails.

9 Eveleigh Crescent,
Aquae-Regis
2.v.36

My Dear Paul,

Maybe this will never reach you, but I have to write it, and I'm sending it to the last address you sent me.

I can't go on being the only one who knows. There's nothing to be done about it now, and you can't help me, because I have my life here, with Hector. There are two things you do not know. I am not as you must see me: a woman who fell for you but who took a husband and had his child. For one thing I already *had* a child. Hector knows about some time I spent in Herefordshire, but only half the story. I was, as they say, 'delivered of a boy' there. His father was pleased, and I'm grateful to him for that. He'd taken me off to Switzerland at the beginning, and we conceived our son – without meaning to – in St Moritz. Which is German for 'Maurice', so that is what we called him. Anyway, that now seems so long ago, although not a day goes by but I try to imagine their lives.

You saw Hector, you were able to watch him and judge. He was proud of me, intrigued, fascinated – at the start. I told you I was tired of the acting life I'd gone back to, briefly, and he was heaven-sent. When you reappeared, I wasn't so sure, but I was married by then. He was showing me off, because really – at heart – I felt there was something of the rebel about him, a rebel against Aquae-Regis. I think it was true, but it might have been a late adolescence in his case, because now I see less and less of that independence of spirit in him. He's starting to bob and truckle to opinion again, and that does depress me – you can't think how much. He has started to care more than he should – more than anyone should – about What People Say.

But they don't know all that they might, and it frightens me to imagine how he would respond to that knowledge, because at times he seems to me a man disposed – if he should be provoked sufficiently – to violence. I think it would be quite possible.

Maybe he suspects, but I doubt if he *can* know about it himself, not positively. You see, my darling – I can't believe that you do either (know positively, that is), altho' I have times of doubt even about that, as I do about everything else – little Catherine, whom he named after his mother, is not his own.

I understand that very well in my blood, altho' I also worked it out from a calendar, comparing the dates when he had his business trips to the north and to the Low Countries with the dates when you were here.

Sweet, pretty Catherine is yours.

I don't think I like the name, but – you see – I had to comply. Whatever he might have said, my conscience would have compelled me to agree. Altho' I have not one regret, and I'm not afflicted by conscience like the rest of Aquae-Regis, which chooses to think itself so moral, so smugly virtuous.

You couldn't have cared less about Aquae-Regis, I suppose, and neither do I. When I read this page again, I see I drop the information into a paragraph – about our daughter – which is not how I meant to tell you. I didn't know *how* exactly to tell you. All I was sure of was that I wanted to tell you, by some means or another.

I want nothing done, and I'm sure you understand why. You have to forgive me, please, for not telling you *then*. But it would have ruined everything, and not only for me, but for you too, because I realised you wouldn't stay here, that this place was incidental to you, it had nothing to do with your ambitions. I took fright maybe, another sort of stage-fright, paralysis, when I thought of the future away from here – even with you, my dearest Paul. You had ambitions, in plenty, but no most sure and certain plans, and I didn't think I was ready for that, the unsureness. I couldn't have left my daughter here, and if I'd told Hector the truth, he would have disputed it and kept her.

Sometimes I can hardly keep my head in one piece, my brain seems to be bursting. I'm appalled, I get very afraid, I feel such loneliness – an intensity of solitude in the house, with all there is around us, and eyes everywhere.

Of course they don't know my true feelings, because I deploy any stage skills I had for a different purpose now. Their ignorance of me makes me feel no better, though. Share my knowledge with me, Paul, please, *all* my knowledge, because there is nobody else. I'm afraid, and I'm worn out, and I can't stop thinking that I've ruined the only chance I get at a life. It's a failure, a mess, and I've made it so myself, because I lost my nerve and hadn't the heart that it took. You had *your* life, but *I* had the chance too: I should have hazarded I-don't-know-what, because there is nothing without it. Nothing.

With all my love to you,
~~Marguer~~
Margaret

Catherine lashed out with her arm and sent the lamp crashing to the floor. Her skin hurt where it had touched the burning-hot metal of the hood, but she only noticed for an instant. She scooped up the papers on the desk, blue letter included, gathered them all between her hands, and tossed them up into the air. She sent everything else flying – pens, appointment diary, clock, ashtray. She pulled at the trailing flex and then hurled the telephone to the other side of the room. It hit a picture, the glass smashed and the frame slithered down the wall.

For several seconds she lost her balance. The room was running from her, it seemed to tilt and dip. She covered her face with her hands. She was trying not to think, not to think.

Her thoughts were massing against her, though.

But if she gave in to them, she knew, then she didn't stand a chance, as sure as fate.

She took her hands away from her face. The room was a wreck. The books had tumbled from the shelves; a crack had appeared on one wall. She walked over to it, and placed her finger into the scissure of soft plaster. She laid her ear against it and heard the hoarse grinding of rock on rock. The crumbs of plaster were warm on the tips of her fingers.

She turned away, stepping over books, over a welter of covers and titles and authors. *Tales of the One Thousand and One Nights, A Tour Thro' the Whole Island of Great Britain, Mildred Pierce, The Cocktail Party, Great Expectations*, Kerouac, Maeterlinck, Ovid.

71

Sheng Fui

HE didn't come back, and she raged about the house.

For hours she stormed through the rooms. At last she ran outside, got into the VW and raced away from the house. She drove all the way up to San Alfonso, on the switchback ocean road. With the window down she smelt the orange groves before she saw them.

Inside she wandered through the rooms, for one hour, two hours. She waited for dawn. She didn't sit, she kept walking, always in motion, upstairs and down, along the colonnades and from room to room, until at last – in one of the ground-floor corridors – she faltered, fatigue overcame her.

With sheer exhaustion she stopped where she was and leaned her back against the panelling. She made two fists of her hands and punched them backwards into the wood.

In the next instant the wall started to spin vertically. She couldn't gather her senses together before the panelling's momentum was turning her out of darkness into a coral-pink glow. She looked down at her feet and saw she was standing on a ledge; in the next few moments the wall had completed a 180-degree rotation and she heard the locking into place of mechanical parts. There was no going back now, and she started to panic. But almost simultaneously she began to smell a sweet, soothing, warm balm wafting from somewhere; as her eyes adjusted to the primal pink colouring, a sharper source of light was visible to her from further off and lower down, and she realised that she was standing close to the top of a flight of steps.

She looked at the walls leading down, at an arcane motif pattern chiselled in the stone, a more elaborate version of Greek-key. She was staring and didn't see or hear a figure approaching until his head appeared above the gradient of the stairs.

She couldn't move for terror.

He was an aged Chinaman, dressed in a loose scarlet gown with trailing sleeves. He wore an embroidered gold cap; from beneath it a long plaited pigtail curled over his left shoulder. His skin, the colour and texture of museum vellum, was stretched very tightly over the bones of his face. His eyes scrutinised her inscrutably.

Catherine spread her hands behind her and clawed at the wall. The Chinaman stopped on the second top step. He considered her again before, with consummate elegance, bowing; then he raised his right arm and indicated the ramp of stairs he had just climbed.

She shook her head but he motioned again. She continued to shake her head.

He spoke, in heavily accented English.

'You are expected.'

She prised her mouth open.

'What?'

'Please follow me.'

He stepped back on to the tread of staircase beneath, turning his body away. When she didn't move or respond, he looked round at her and gesticulated with his arm for a third time.

'If you follow me,' he said, 'all will be explained to you. Please follow me – '

His delivery was gracious, his gestures quite exquisite. Her panic started to abate. She might have screamed and pummelled her fists on the wall, but – her mind nicely re-argued the point to itself – the wall's locking into place had sounded final and indisputable, so what else *could* she do?

Another upward draught of the clinging, alluring balm reached her, in a little pufflet of steam cloud, and she felt herself yielding. She took several steps forward, to the top of the staircase.

'Please follow me, miss.'

She fixed on the Chinaman's pigtail, resting on the left shoulder of his gown. The scarlet material was stitched along its seams with gold-coloured thread. His hands were ancient and horny. He continued to climb down and she began her own descent. The perfume rose to enfold her, and she was aware of it lulling her, smothering her resistance, tempting her to stillness and placidity, so that acceptance seemed the easiest, most painless, unthinking course for her . . .

At the foot of the staircase she was introduced to the first corridor in what came to seem like a labyrinth. She followed the Chinaman, he and she instinctively keeping the same exact, formal distance from one another.

To left and right an occasional door – every ten or fifteen yards, and each painted a different colour – would suggest further perspectives and specific (but unimaginable) functions. The soft coral light guided them, not always steadily. When she looked closer she saw that naked flames burned behind the pink glass shades on the wall-brackets.

One corridor would tail off, turning a corner or making a dog-leg, and a new one would begin. They were each of the same width, no more than six feet across, with walls indented with the same motif as the staircase walls. The ceilings were taller than a very tall man, about seven foot high, muted maize-coloured stone like the walls and inset at regular intervals with simple geometrical symbols, like coded hieroglyphics: a blue triangle, a green square, a red hexagon, a brown star. Beneath her feet the same symbols were reproduced on an endless runner of purple carpet.

'Please . . .' the Chinaman would say when she slowed or stopped, always aware when they weren't advancing at the same speed and distance from each other.

She spotted ducts in the walls, just below ceiling level, and noticed that the perfume always smelt sweetest and most compelling at those points. It reminded her of no fragrance she had ever worn against her skin, although it didn't alarm her with any intimations of its strangeness.

The final stretch of corridor widened by degrees; the walls with their running motif drew apart, and she saw the level floor give way to a further flight of steps ahead of her. The wall in front curved and as she descended the six or seven steps of carpet she saw the old Chinaman looking through the gilded bars of a pair of gates.

He received whichever signal he was waiting to receive and pushed the two gates open.

She stared at the prospect beyond: a huge circular room with a ceiling that rose upwards like a funnel. The walls were screened by tapestries, or – from this distance – it was possible she was mistaken, that they were elaborate lacquer panels. Three-foot-high naked flames burned without covers or shades, in brass pots supported on squat legs. In the middle of the room, sunk into the floor, was a round pond eight or ten feet in diameter, stocked with lilies.

At that very moment the walls started to move. There was an ear-splitting cosmic roar.

'It's happening!' the Chinaman cried out. 'The moment – '

'What is it?'

An area of the ceiling was caving in, rubble cascaded down in a deafening maelstrom of dust.

She knew it was an earthquake, that the screams were terrestrial, the impact of rock grinding upon rock. The room was crumbling in on itself. She saw the gates buckling. Dust blew so densely that after only seconds she could scarcely see in front of her, and she had to shut her eyes against it.

She ran for the doorway. She opened her eyes momentarily and glimpsed her pigtailed Chinaman crawling up the staircase, which was sinking beneath him.

A portion of the ceiling whistling close to her ear knocked her off balance. Another smaller piece of debris grazed her arm. She protected her eyes with the other arm and ran in the direction of the doorway and the corridor beyond it. The staircase had fallen in and she jumped over the shattered flagstones. The corridor floor hadn't subsided, but she guessed from the shudders behind her that boulders were heaving beneath the round room.

The smooth-faced corridor walls were tilting inwards, as if the rock behind was straining to burst the stones apart. The dust had partially cleared and she was able to see better by the sputtering braziers. But she had lost sight of the fleeing Chinaman and the corridor forked in two directions.

On her right-hand side a door stood open. For a moment she thought it must be lit by a window, because she could see daylight. If there was a source of natural light, there must be a way of escaping.

She looked over her shoulder. Flames swept through the swirling dust, and the boulders continued grinding and wailing.

She turned her head round. Now black smoke was swallowing one of the corridors. In the other the floor began to split apart before her eyes. She had no alternative left but to enter the room.

She hesitated at the door. There was no window, the room was a false room, an unfurnished space hewn out of the bare rock and with its surfaces left untreated. She heard a wrenching above her head and looked up. The heavy slab of wooden lintel was straining against vast pressures. She stood staring for several moments until the ends simultaneously ricocheted out of the supports in the rock.

The beam simply snapped in two. One half reared up and hovered for a second or two in mid-air until gravity pulled it tumbling down.

Transfixed by the violence performed like ballet, she must have been standing directly in the beam's path. She was fleetingly aware before it happened that her head was going to be struck, but she couldn't think how to remove herself quickly enough. By then it was too late, and yet perhaps – in the final analysis – it was the timely accident of concussion that saved her.

72

Symbiosis

When she came to, lying on her left side, it was as if she was waking from a dream. There was no groping towards consciousness. She remembered nothing, and was mystified by the crimson blood, still sticky, on her hands and clothes.

She pulled herself up from the horizontal, then pushed on her hands and clumsily scrambled on aching legs to her feet. Her knees trembled as she straightened. She waited until her giddiness had passed and she had her balance back.

She opened and closed her eyes several times, trying to get her focus.

She coughed until her throat was clear and her breathing unimpeded.

High above her she saw daylight, as if she was looking up from the bottom of a well to a bright, pellucid disc of blue sky.

In fact the shaft of well wasn't vertical, but a drop of fifty degrees or so from ground level. Once she started climbing – finding finger- and footholds in the still warm rock – she discovered that the effort was less than she'd dreaded it must be. The quake had already drained much of the strength from her arms and legs, but she was able to lie on the rocks at certain moments to recover breath and energy. Several times there was a fall of smaller stones and she had to cover her head with her hands as the scree showered over her. Then she would begin again, taking as much care as she could not to set off a worse landslide, fitting her fingers and toes into the rocks and pitching herself forward with all the spirit of purpose that was in her.

The eye of blue grew brighter, it expanded, and she felt the direct touch of sunlight on her hands and arms, then on her face. She was filled then with radiant, unquenchable hope. Physical might came from she didn't know where, she felt it pulsing down her neck and into her chest, then into her limbs. She took slower, deeper breaths.

At last – with a final heart-splitting push upwards – she fell through the opening, the tunnel's end, into heat and silence. She lay flat on the flinty ground, reaching for the shade of a scrub bush. She cried, simply for the solace of hearing herself. She didn't know if she wanted to be alive or not.

Perhaps she passed out. When she was aware of herself again, the bush's shadow covered her arms and stopped just a couple of inches short of her forehead. She felt the stern glare of the sun and screwed her eyes up tightly. She remembered, vaguely, the view towards sky and the steep climb, and a grinding of rocks. But she couldn't think of what must have happened before that to leave her like this, exhausted after being pitched like a fury out of the earth.

The second thing she was conscious of was the sun, through the trees. And at the same time the heat, like an oven with the door left open, in a witch's kitchen, in a fairy-tale.

But all that was then and this was now and when she put her fingers to the side of her head, her temples, she felt stickiness, and when she held them in front of her eyes she saw blood.

'Lie still.'

She opened her mouth.

'Who – '

'I'm a doctor. I'll help you.'

'How did – '

'You've had an accident.'

'You – '

'I was passing. In my car.'

'But – '

There was a question she wanted to ask, but she couldn't quite grasp it.

'It was coincidence. That's all.'

Later.

'Like in a film,' she said. 'A movie.'

'What's that?'

'This – this happening.'

'Don't speak.'

'But – '

'Please. Just lie still and don't speak. There's an ambulance coming. It'll be here very soon.'

She lay back.

'It's the best I can do for shade, I'm afraid.'

'It's fine.'

Everything was fine. Was going to be fine.

*

From the back of the ambulance, before they closed the door, she saw him standing by the roadside explaining to the police. He looked over at one point: he saw her watching him and he smiled. A true and genuine smile it might have been worth crossing an ocean for.

He was her only visitor in hospital, but a frequent one.

'You're a doctor? You said?'

'Yes.'

'You've – restored my faith.'

'What's that?'

'In your – what's it called – '

'Don't tire yourself out – '

' – your profession. That's right. Your noble profession.'

'Is it?'

'It *should* be. Isn't it?'

'Yes. But I'm making you talk too much.'

'Who am I?'

'You really don't remember that?'

'I'm not sure.'

'Oh, well . . .'

'You stare at me, do you know that?'

'Do I? I'm sorry.'

'You don't have to be.'

'I'm intruding – '

'No. Have you seen me before? Is that why you look?'

'I just – like to look.'

'Professional interest?'

'No. Not quite that.'

'Ah.'

'I should go now.'

'No, don't. Don't go.'

'What happened, though?'

'I don't know. I don't remember.'

'Nothing?'

'Nothing about how it happened.'

'It will come back.'

'Maybe I don't want it to.'

'Ah . . .'

She recovered, slowly but steadily. He came to see her as often as he could. He sat quietly, rapt in her condition.

He was a widower. Learning that, she felt much less awkward with the certainty that she was falling for him.

She had told him, willingly enough, that she was called Clothilde; also that she was a widow. Her Venezuelan husband had died not so long ago, but in truth it hadn't been a happy marriage. She told him that she'd been married once before that, to a man called Maurice she'd cared for very much, who had died in a shooting-party incident.

He accepted the very little that she said, and didn't ask for anything more. She offered him her hand and he took it, held it. Once he lifted the hand to his lips and kissed it; the next time he kissed the knuckles of each of her fingers. The third time he leaned forward in his chair, clutching her hand, and kissed her on the mouth with a sweetness and tenderness she had almost forgotten.

*

They were married in Acapulco, where he had taken her to recuperate. They were photographed in their hotel suite, grouped with his three children, Nadine, Tom and Ricky. Pride shone in Tom's face, and Nadine asked for a special photograph of just the two of them; Ricky was too young to know how to cope with social embarrassment, but placed his hand inside the security of his new mother's.

She wasn't sure that this was really happening to her. She had accepted that she must have forfeited her right to anything like contentment.

Later, all Alan's colleagues and their wives and families came to the reception in Washington State. She felt quite at her ease with them. There were no one's eyes she was trying to avoid. She gave herself to them as the person she wanted to be, and it seemed a very much simpler business that way.

*

At forty-two years old Alan had healthy, robust good looks, and a skier's weathered tan. At first she kept fixing on those white teeth, and conceded to herself that it was all too good to be true. His hair contained more grey than black: a distinguished but youthful combination. She admired the strength in his wrists and hands, and enjoyed the contrast to the thinness and fineness of those deft fingers, such a godsend in his job of work.

Not really that, of course: the surgeon's art was a vocation, rather. He had a private consultancy in Seattle and a share in a clinic, and he performed operations wherever he was required to fly to. He'd begun his professional life in general hospitals; he had quickly attracted favourable notice for his skills both practical and theoretical, and had been invited to serve on government health committees.

Someone, a former colleague, once let slip to her, 'He was the best son-of-a-bitch that ever got away.'

She was puzzled.

'We never got over it really. Alan jacking the system.'

She was still in the dark.

'We did our training together. Alan was always brilliant at everything. He was brilliant in the hospitals, and they were the best days of our lives, everyone's, the medics', the patients'.'

'Isn't he still brilliant?'

'Yes. But it's not the same.'

She just came out and asked him, why not?

'I don't think he did it for money,' the man told her. 'Just to be rich. But he lost something. He was an idealist when we all began. He had ambitions: and he had principles, scruples, and he was going to leave the world a better place.'

'He does make it better, though, doesn't he? I mean, he improves it.'

'It just wouldn't have occurred to him to be one of those doctors with the big Caddies or Mercs. He didn't think it was bad or waving the white flag or anything else. It just didn't enter his reasoning. He was too busy, with his head down.'

'But he *does* work very hard.'

'That's just business. But it's "clients" now, with his patients, and *then* it was – '

She nodded at the floor.

'He's a good man,' their guest said, 'who . . .'

' "Who"?'

'I'm not sure – that I should say, I mean – '

'Tell me. Please.'

'He's a good man, who could have been a great one.'

*

She learned how to care for his children. She heard people comment that Alan had never looked better or more at his ease.

He proved a perfectly accommodating and appreciative husband, with a mature steadfastness. Mystery was still present as an element in their marriage – chiefly concerning their previous lives – but that was by their unspoken mutual consent. He couldn't tell her too much about his day-to-day work because he was obliged to respect the confidence of his patients, and *she* respected him for doing so. She could think of nothing to fault him for, and she took every pain to ensure that *he* would have no reason to find fault with her. They didn't quarrel: she guessed that he had experience of some marital disharmony, as did she, which kept him – as herself – on action alert. Now they were determined not to fritter and squander time that could never be found again.

She had never informed Alan that she was *not* a Venezuelan's widow. She only said she didn't want to talk about it please, that time in her life, and allowed him to suppose that it had been especially unhappy. She made it seem that she was being pointedly discreet in not making mention of his wife. Thus they skimmed over the past, and it was no great ordeal or tribulation to either of them.

Seattle was only a base. He travelled two or three times a month to undertake operations elsewhere, and a certain percentage of his fee was paid into a research fund administered by the clinic.

Sometimes she travelled with him on his commissions – to Denver, Minneapolis-Saint Paul, Oklahoma City, Houston, Atlanta, Miami, St Louis – without exception to cities, which felt somehow natural to her: cities without proper histories, erected on the grid plan, forever dynamiting and demolishing to root out the dark hiding-holes, so that everything might gleam and glitter in high-rise innocence.

So it seemed to her, but she saw these cities from a false angle, from the backs of taxi cabs on the days she ventured downtown from their hotels. Nervous but grateful patients invited them out to ghettoes of affluence, arrow-straight verged avenues of white plantation mansions on immaculate lawns.

Otherwise – he wanted her to have interests and amusements of her own and maybe she did, with the supposedly best of both worlds: tennis and swimming and golf to hand, and the concert halls and cinemas and art galleries only a short drive away. She struggled a bit with the medical company, but she told herself she would have had to labour with any group of professionals. She became quite adept in the domestic virtues, and cooking and gardening became wantonly luxurious practices when she always had another pair of hands to tidy up after her, leaving her free to experiment and take whatever risks she might – on a whim – decide to.

*

And sometimes she remembered this or that about her English life, and very often she didn't.

She might have done if she had tried harder, but she wasn't disposed to. She surely stood to lose too much.

Six months after Los Angeles it started to come back to her: occasionally in alarming detail, so that she could remember the touch of plush in the Panopticon Theatre and the feel of taffeta against her skin posing for the camera on Cadbury Hill. Alan had begun by asking her what she could recall: after the first four or five months he seemed to lose interest – certainly not his interest in her as the woman he married, but in the necessity of remembering. Perhaps he thought she was happier without memory, that she was deliberately failing to remember, and that if she did recall then they might accidentally provoke some imbalance in this very meticulous domestic harmony which seemed so special to him, which seemed to be benefiting him in his work with the peace of mind he had gained from their marriage.

Anyway, when London was swinging and the Mersey generation sang, it was no England she recognised, rather a pantomime land. So she tried to let it go, and came to imagine that it was starting to let *her* go too.

73

Schooldays

THE school was the essential life and purpose of the small town – in reality an overgrown village with pompous pretensions – in a backwater corner of a southern English shire. Marshalled pinnacles thrust above the cluttered, mossy roofs where the out-masters and shopkeepers had their homes.

It was reckoned to be a 'good school', as those things are judged, but perhaps there was very little competition in the land. A number of old boys happened at that time to hold prominent positions in Whitehall officialdom, the Services, and industry, and since they favoured their own kind the school was thought to assure a proper start in life.

*

The only letters I received were from Catawpa Narrows.

I swapped the Canadian postage stamps for, first, fine stringed conkers and then for lengths of cigarette. Blood relations in Canada were permissible, but in other boys' cases they turned out to be eccentric, misfit bachelor uncles who swam in cold water and hunted elk or else a father's or mother's colourless sister married quietly to an engineer or something like. Canada, I was too shrewdly aware, was less a land of new beginnings and opportunities than Britain's convenient back-room where issues and persons could be swept under the proverbial carpet. It was a topic in geography classes for several weeks of one term and I jolted in my seat every time the name 'Ontario' was mentioned.

I briefly remembered the year's extremes of weather, the blizzard cold and the mosquito heat, and the swings in my aunt and uncle between their faith that they were in charge of their lives and their sudden, total, incapacitating failures of confidence. It had been a shapeless time; I might have been sleepwalking my Canadian life as I'd lived it, and my recollection of it was as insubstantial and fragmentary as if I'd been attempting to recall the progress of a dream on waking.

*

The understanding was that during the school holidays I would stay with Mr Scrimgeour's family; and that when they left on their holiday, another housemaster would take me in for that interim.

It worked out after the second term that my friends' parents took pity on me, and that while I did spend some time with the Scrimgeours in Faine House, essentially it was a formality. I had three regular bases, in Suffolk, Wiltshire and Gloucestershire (one always spoke of counties in that proprietorial way: I quickly learned the knack). I sailed a number of times, mainly from Plockton on Loch Carron over to Skye and down as far as the Crinan Canal beside the awesome Moine Mhor; I saw some European cities and resorts, and crossed from Gibraltar to Morocco on a two-day trip.

I had nothing to complain about. It was a lush life. Except, of course, that however welcome I was made I remained a guest in the house of friends, only pretending my ease with their rituals.

I believed that I was popular enough, that my wishing not to cause problems made me an amenable guest: and also one who might be invited again. I had to take a hard-eyed market judgement on my 'social worth' of course, and in addition to getting my clothes sense exactly right I developed a personality through conversation: through my verbal felicity and the quickness of my wit, my adeptness at punning, my memory for jokes.

74

Head

THE realisation came to her in the middle of a Sunday afternoon. I could get up out of this chair, walk to the door and leave this house and not come back and nothing would be so very different afterwards. After six years I have eliminated the necessity for my presence. I have organised everything so efficiently that there is hardly even the possibility of a hitch. I really have been very clever, but far too clever for my own good.

For several long seconds she had difficulty with her breathing. She even thought she might be about to pass out.

When Alan asked her a question she had to concentrate her mind to answer. 'We saw them in October, I think, or it might have been November. More likely November.'

She picked up the magazine on her lap. She ought to have been mending, from her work basket, but in this house clothes were just thrown out when they were ripped and frayed, and replacements for them were promptly bought. She had no excuse to knit: Seattle had never seemed to her to be a sewing city, which explained why the departments in the stores were usually so disappointing.

And, she wondered, how long would the loss of me register? Alan has been through it once before, and the children were brought up to cope. They have their own lives now; Alan has taught them more than *I* could ever have done for them.

She turned the pages of the magazine. Images of desire passed in front of her eyes. Provocative faces, airbrushed flesh, beauty preparations, hair conditioners, leisure centres, vacation clothes, party shoes, hotels in Barbados and the Orient, voluptuously photographed luggage.

The models had updated versions of the faces *they* had presented to the camera in the fifties. Their expressions were detached, in their own way: a little haughtier, oddly so considering these were egalitarian times, but with the same faraway stare either over the photographer's shoulder or offside, out of camera range. They also seemed more flagrantly sensual: but she didn't believe that they offered any more by their poses, the promises were just as false as their own had been and more cynical perhaps, for being so shameless, and tinged now with what suspiciously resembled greed.

She looked up and saw Alan watching her from the sofa, from the soft abandon of the feather cushions. She smiled over at him, then dropped her eyes and skimmed through the remaining pages.

What was on his mind? What was he watching her *for*? And why was her face so prickly hot?

As she fanned the edges of the pages, desire – so much of it – rushed in front of her: all that unassuaged wanting. Too much for it to remain a secret any longer, among all the innumerable other secrets that preserve a life, which buoy it and keep it afloat.

*

'*But I didn't think I was ready for that, the unsureness. I couldn't have left my daughter here* . . .'

She woke in the bus, with sunshine in her eyes and her mother's words confused with the straining of the engine. She turned round in the seat and looked out at the scrub bushes that fringed the highway, and then beyond them the incontrovertible desert.

But now she was gone, she'd got away.

' . . . *and I can't stop thinking that I've ruined the only chance I get to a life* . . .'

Six and a half out of ten, she would have given herself for the last phase, although it had largely been going through the motions. She was hardly natural mothering material. But she must have convinced them for most of the time. And their affection for her was genuine and heartfelt.

Only she had known, far inside her head, that it came too late in Seattle, Washington State.

Desert streaked past the window. She laid her head back in the seat. She saw a blue cactus tree with a splayed hand of bright red fingers on top.

'It's a failure, a mess, and I've made it so myself . . . because I lost my nerve and hadn't the heart that it took.'

*

Her last hitch, on the second day, was in a two-tone cream and brown Plymouth; it had seen better days, about a decade before. It stopped for her where she had positioned herself, fifty yards or so beyond the motel. The driver was young and sloppily dressed and full of slightly crazy good cheer.

'I don't have a radio,' he said as he drove, and then he started to sing, 'He's a real nowhere man, living in his nowhere land . . .' When he'd finished and she'd applauded, he pointed to the back seat and, strewn across it, sheafs of pages covered with minuscule handwriting.

'That's my novel,' he told her.

'It is?' she said, leaning her arm along the back of the bench seat and looking at all that work.

'Kerouac wrote on long rolls of paper, wrote and wrote. Well, I'm no J. K. maybe, but beat ain't dead.'

He clicked a rhythm with his fingers, remembering another song which he started to sing under his breath.

'That's wonderful,' she said. 'A whole novel.'

'Oh, it's not done yet. It gets written every day. Another bit gets added to, you see. It's not on a roll, Jack's was – '

'You should take great care of it,' she said.

'Why's that?'

'Do you use carbons?'

'Never.'

'What if you lose it? Or it gets stolen?'

'Then I guess that's part of the story too.'

She turned round, frowning.

'Where to?' he asked her.

'I'm not sure,' she said.

'Can I ask you where you've come from?'

'Somewhere I stayed too long, I guess.'

'You're glad to get away?'

'I've no regrets,' she heard herself reply. 'But I've no hard feelings either. It just wasn't right for me, that's all.'

'I get you.'

'You do?'

'Sure.'

He started to sing another song, 'Subterranean Homesick Blues', and she joined in for a few bars.

In the glove compartment she found a collection of poems called *Cowboy Soup* by Morwenna Littig. The publisher's name was Alfred A. Knopf.

'Jesus Christ,' she said.

'She's just a gas,' her driver told her.

She leafed through them. Some were shaped on the page, they fell into the patterns of a leaf or a house or a whorled shell.

'Well, I never!'

'Maybe you're going back to England?'

She stared at him. The possibility had occurred to her a few times, but she had convinced herself that all her life had been tending to a certain end, and that must be America, since here she was.

'I don't know,' she said. 'And that's the truth.'

They had lunch in a roadside diner called the Sugar Shack. Indeed it was a shack, with a jukebox and checked gingham curtains and tablecloths. For some reason she thought of the flying clapboard house in *The Wizard of Oz*, sucked up in the tornado's vortex and sent spinning into space.

After the break, he filled the Plymouth with gas, used his foot to kick shut the faulty flap that was supposed to fold flush over the tank cap, and off they set again.

The afternoon turned hot. Occasionally they came to areas of more greenery and shade. Between them the distances shimmered and the straight highway appeared to buckle and lift. She felt empty-minded; in a different way from how she had as a wife, when her head-vacuum had given her palpitations, so hard had she latterly found even fastening on a thought and pinning it down. Not thinking like this was a gentle relief, and she had no angst either for her safety or for her eventual destination. This was freedom after all the suffocating affection that had preceded it, even sitting alone with a stranger in his car, travelling an almost deserted highway.

She leaned her elbow on the sill of the door and every so often she smiled into the palm of her hand.

'*You* look happy,' he told her.

'Do I?'

'Hey, we'll make this a happiness trip.'

'All right,' she said. 'Al-*right*!'

She found him pleasant-mannered, and she didn't believe she had any cause for anxiety. Somehow the sight of the novel – if that's what it actually was – had given her some assurance. He was a man questing for patterns in an illogical world, clues to purpose wherever they might reside – in science, in mathematics, in repetition, in memory, or in the transmogrifications of first love.

Later in the afternoon he stopped the car in the shelter of trees and they got out.

'Do you want to carry on with your novel?' she asked him.

He rolled up his sleeves.

'I guess not.'

'I don't want to keep you from it.'

'It'll get done.'

They reached an oasis of grass shaded by some tamarisk bushes in pink flower. He lay down, and she did likewise, unafraid, three or four feet from him. She lifted her arm to shield her eyes against the sun slanting down on them through the layers of branches.

Possibly she slept, for a brief time. When she took her arm away from her face, he was sitting up cross-legged, in the merest suggestion of a blue haze.

She noticed the thin, crooked cigarette in his hand.

She lifted herself on to her elbows, then pulled herself like him to a cross-legged position.

'Hey, wanna try this?'

He took it from between his lips and handed it to her. The cigarette. Only of course it wasn't, not the tobacco sort she had been used to.

'If I could,' she said, taking it from him, 'if I had the means, I would give you a case. To keep them in.'

'A *case*?'

'Gold and silver stripes, diagonals. Made by Asprey's workrooms. In London.'

'Are you sure you *need* that?' he asked her, laughing. 'I don't think *you* need anything. You're on your own trip!'

It smelt and tasted sweet. And a little woody: vegetarian.

She joined in the levity, laughing too.

'Oh, it's been a long, long trip,' she told him, 'this one.'

She obviously intrigued him. It was difficult to guess why.

The cigarette passed to and fro between them.

' "Joint" ', he corrected her.

'All right then,' she said with good spirit. 'Would you pass the "joint", please?'

A mellow sort of sunburst afternoon followed. She *was* happy, in a careless but cared-for way she hadn't experienced for – for oh so long. Too long. She had been *dulled*, before, into a condition of not worrying, driving on automatic, on cruise-control. That hadn't been happiness, though, nothing like.

He was speaking to her.

'I get kinda – Huck Finnish on all this. Know what I mean – ?'

'Oh yes,' she said.

' – where I'm coming from?'

'Oh yes,' she repeated.

'That's good.'

'This,' she said, 'is a real – ' she sang the words of the song title ' – la-a-zy after-noon – '

'Best kind,' he told her.

'Oh yes,' she said, in perfect agreement with him. 'Oh yes.'

'Strong stuff, this.' He lay back, with his head propped up on his arm. 'Venezuelan, you know.' He waved the cigarette in front of his eyes, scripting something across the sky.

'My husband – my second husband – he was on those committees at the end. You know? The great and the good shaking their heads and not at all approving. "What are we to do, Clothilde? About those poor kids?" '

'What did you tell him?'

'Legalise it. Nobody'll care a tuppeny farthing then. But I only said it to him once. He blamed it on someone we'd had to the house, he must have brainwashed me. "Very likely," I said, passing the buck. And after that I just nodded my head at everything he told me, every single word of it.'

'Why did you leave him?'

'He was too good for me.'

'Say it again – '

She shook her head.

'I'm not sure I was ever there to begin with.'

'So where were you?'

'I don't know. That's why I've come looking, I guess.'

'Do you think you're gonna find what you're looking for?'

She leaned her back against the tree and pulled her knees up to her chin.

'Oh, anything's possible,' she said.

From there they passed to headier matters, and she found herself fumbling a little with the sequence of his story, about a medieval saint called Anthony – and a blaze – and rotting wheat-fungus – ergo, wasn't it wonderful (she heard this part more clearly) that the US Army chemical warfare chiefs and those psychiatry experts could get this thing going between them, that they wanted to bequest lysergic acid diethylamide to the world. Dr Hoffman in Switzerland had got to it first, and she tripped over the word 'Switzerland', seeing in her eye as it widened mountains of milk chocolate and weather-house people in cuckoo-clock chalets, forgetting Lugano meanwhile, and shading herself from the sun by placing her arm across her face. Her eye was widening and widening, and every direction she looked in she was seeing further, not of any object in particular but of her own potential. Now she was gifted and blessed in quite exceeding measure, she was sure, her mind could bend to turn any corner, it could weave its way between tenses, crinkle like silver foil and empty itself like glass. It flowed, a molten melt, and she only had to let herself be carried with it, through substance and its opposite, by the real paths and the not so real, and it was all much the same, you ended up wherever you had never truly left, people in one and many places, and nothing was impossible, which was only what she had known at the beginning – in her mother's time, maybe in her womb too, knowing all the world beforehand so crystal-clear in its details and then having the burden of unlearning it. Everything already belonged in the head, it evolved and perpetuated itself there, and shocks and surprises were hardly so but features of the organism. There were no limitations, the borders were down, the sphere held a world and the system in which it moved and she might have believed just now that she could know the intricate intimate secrets of that suspenseful universe, because they must already be established within the context of her own life and she should only have to flow with the flow – the flowing floe of her thought experiences – to locate them . . .

She smiled. Laughed maybe. Under the sun. Hot, chafing sun. Smiled certainly, feeling her mouth stretch and stretch. Until she could have taken a big bite out of the day, swallowed it. But rested a bit first, leaning her spine against a tree, just conscious of when he closed her fingers and opened them again. Becoming less and less so, though, and losing the feel of her limbs, *her* limbs, which might have been hers but might rather have been somebody else's. With her eyes shut she was ready to go passing into and out of this and that, to prove the point, that nothing could hold her, *nothing held her*, and she might be devoured by another life, St Anthony's perhaps, who drew such fine fire, all across the festering wheatfields of the Middle Ages. Headwise, it was certain. Oh yes. Oh yeah, as they said now. Headwise, she had no doubts, it was as transparent as it could be.

And then she leaned back on her elbows and slowly lowered herself on to the grass. She crossed her arms to shield her all-seeing eyes against the tree-sifted sunlight. Possibly she lost consciousness and drifted briefly into sleep: into a dream, and into a crack of sensibility, or might it have been that nothing was so very different from how it had always been.

When she opened her eyes again and pulled herself upright, she had forgotten where she was. She had lost the memory of the young man, his uncompleted novel, the rusting Plymouth sedan. Out of the dappled glade in front of her appeared what she thought at first sight was a horse: pristine, a thoroughbred. But when she'd blinked, blinked twice and looked again, she saw it was a zebra.

It made its ambling way towards her and stopped five or six yards off. She got to her feet – quite easily, without cramp – and started walking forward. She reached out her hand and, against all probability, the animal didn't bridle or spit when she placed her hands on its striped neck and mane.

She hadn't ridden since those very few times at Lord Marlott's express behest: equipped by Swaine, Adeney and Brigg of Piccadilly and certainly not bareback. But this wasn't then, and those former rules of equestrian etiquette did not apply to her now.

She grasped the mane and jumped up. The zebra only lightly stamped its hooves, which made her job simpler as she positioned herself so that she sat exactly and evenly astride it, her legs overhanging its flanks.

The zebra waited until she was ready and then, at her command, it moved off at a sedate walking pace. They reached the longer shadows of the trees and passed among them, the substance and their reproductions, until she couldn't tell which was which.

Then the zebra, with consummate care, began to trot, then to canter, but so gently and considerately that she scarcely noticed the gathering speed at first, nor that the wind was streaking past her face. They cut a swathe between the trees and their shadows and vice versa, curving like the air, and thereupon her perspective changed and she realised that they had left the ground. She clung on tighter as the zebra's barrel body tilted away from the trees and shadows ranged beneath them, as they went skimming over the confusion and rose higher and higher. They ventured through rapidly cooling vapour, through stray fleece, into the chill collusion of nimbus, then upwards and out again, into a vision of diaphanous blue where the heavens spread.

The zebra broke into a gallop, so hard and furious that she could feel its hot, savannah breath on her brow. She entwined her fingers with the hairs on its mane and put her head back and imagined that the pellucid blue light above her was the shallowness of summer sea running over sand, and that the zebra was pounding along a beach's shoreline, not through the thin ether. Faster and faster, and her heart was swelling in her chest, with joy and excitement and the harmonious assertion of *life*, faster and faster, eastwards across the firmament, under the arc of the welkin, towards the beginning and an end, towards alpha and omega, towards home.

It was London she found herself in, with only a few US dollar bills in her pockets, but the city had become the focus of her English life latterly, and anyway the zoo in Aquae-Regis had been defunct for at least ten or a dozen years and so the zebra's waiting soulmate was the one she had gone to Regent's Park to watch, on afternoons when she tired of waiting in the flat in George Street.

They had ridden into a spectacular blazing sunset of rippling pinks and yellows, magenta to orpiment, and then into gradual seeping darkness, which had amassed about them but caused her no fear. Their markers, the lodestar lights of London, directed them, and they made their descent on to an abandoned Regent Street in the middle of the night. Following the broken white line on the tarmacadam, the zebra galloped its length, up to Portland Place and across Marylebone Road. It had slowed to a trot when she lost her balance, when her fingers could no longer maintain their grip on its mane, and she toppled off, on to the soft springiness of mown grass. It was a midsummer's night, the heat still lapped around her, and the earth gave off no hint of dampness. She lay there for a minute or an hour or several hours until the night sky cracked and the maiden dawn came creeping up on the somnolent, silent city. Trees and spires manifested themselves first, then slowly a plethora of rooftops, chimneypots, television aerials, gable ends and weathervanes, as darkness ran off them like inky water, like old blood.

Her zebra was indistinguishable from the others when she could decipher their outlines through the mesh. They weren't lying down but standing, in detached, aloof postures. She watched their muzzles declare themselves, then the tips of their ears, then their gleaming horn hooves, and only after that did she descry the shininess of their jet eyes. Had they been sleeping where they were standing? She pushed closer to the grille-work and thought she felt again the veldt heat of their breath on her skin. Which one had transported her here? But it was being kept from her, a confidential matter among the zebras, and maybe it was best so, in case it should ever happen that – in an aberrant state of her mind – she should start to doubt that the journey had ever taken place, riding bareback above the cirrus, above the stratus.

*

London, she discovered, was definitely swinging. Skirts had lost inches; heels were higher, cars were lower, music was louder. With her dollars, she was smiled upon, but also mistaken for being American, which suddenly wasn't the thing to own to with England now on the upbeat.

Naturally she was uneasy that her path might cross her previous husband's or his father's, and she thought it wasn't really the place to be. She noticed that some of the smartest-dressed young people who were walking about didn't appear, to judge from their eyes, to know where they were: inside their heads they were on liberating trips that emptied them out of themselves, that allowed them to be whoever and wherever: fantasy excursions in magicland, floating along Carnaby Street in their tasselled sheepskin jackets in the middle of summer, striding out to be streets ahead in patent kinky boots, making geometric black and white puzzles of themselves and vanishing into the swirling mathematics of their pop art which was the newest fad. Joy and salvation? She wondered. Well, very maybe, baby.

75

More Sawdust

ABOVE a theatre on Shaftesbury Avenue she saw the name 'Adèle Adaire' in letters four or five foot tall, surrounded by flashing lights.

She was starring in a play called *We Close on Saturday*. The reviews blown up by the doors were raves. The storyline concerned a once moderately well-known actress serving out her time in a touring rep company: these were her last days, as she sometimes understood and sometimes appeared not to.

The matinée and second performance were sold out. But a shifty-looking man in a shiny blue suit offered her a ticket. When she informed him she could only pay him in dollars, he seemed about to glide past her into the crowd – but he quickly thought again, did his advantageous conversion work from sterling into American and came up with a figure. She paid him from the roll of Alan's money in her deep pocket, asked no questions and was told no lies.

Catherine thought the play was merciless and cruel. Her heart bled for its principal, having to play an actress whose best days are far behind her. One of the newspapers had called it 'the part of a lifetime', and another claimed Adèle Adaire's was 'a performance and a half': but she had serious doubts about the latter judgement and a ghastly sense of the literal truth of the former. She simply couldn't be certain if the slurred lines were deliberately botched or not. It seemed to Catherine that there was a very distinct possibility that in this greatest success of her professional life Adèle was only playing . . . herself.

The audience's laughter made her wince and, later, twist with discomfort in her seat. Some of the lines completely went, and a prompter was heard from the wings, and the audience merely presumed it was in the script. At the interval she heard a couple say that the prompts came at different points every evening, that that was the beauty of such a witty production: the only inference from the remarks being that the performance was a matter of ab-libbing, spontaneously done, and that this was Adèle Adaire's triumph, to remake the play every time.

Catherine's brow furrowed as she listened. She rather thought not: indeed the very contrary. But why were there no sceptics, no vultures sniffing corpse meat? Because, she realised, nothing succeeds like success: it begets itself over again, over and over, and thus it acquires its specious glamour, and also its undeniable invulnerability.

She remembered, though, from their time in the north: the hashed lines, the retakes, the panic that would grip Adèle so that her eyes gelled, like a rabbit's in a butcher's window. It wasn't conceivable that she had improved to the extent that now she was playing herself as she *had* been ten and fifteen years before. This was 'realism' in quite a different sense, and the author and director must both have had a very shrewd and callous idea of it. Why else should she have been plucked from her obscurity, and put through this? – for several hundred pounds a week, no doubt, but also because it was intended as a ritual humiliation of a class of thespian and a generation of their audiences, a gloriously subversive black joke on one entire and sacred British tradition.

Catherine longed to get up and leave, but there was a terrible fascination about the play and its lead, which also kept everyone else riveted. Anyway, she couldn't have allowed the tipping of her seat in the auditorium's darkness to have upset Adèle – for poor Adèle's sake.

She found she was sitting with her hands tightly gripping the arms of the chair. She was ashamed of her own complicity. Adèle deserved better of her, even in these thoroughly modern times when probably no one questioned the provenance of the surname, when 'Astaire' never received a mention. She wasn't at all sure that *this* had deserved a zebra flight of four thousand miles.

Afterwards, in the ladies' room, she had to struggle to hold back her tears. Not tears for sentimental reasons, she told herself, because she wasn't that sort of person: and equally, her life hadn't been the sort made for sentiment. This angry sorrow she was feeling was for all of them, not just for Adèle, and for what they were being subjected to at the hands of the satirists, the knockers-down. *The Cocktail Party* had been beyond them all, and they'd been touring the Ridings to pay the gas bills and the off-licence's chits, and even then the past had been better than their present, but – viewing it dispassionately – they had survived on expectation, they had worked through it shored up by their common hopes: that the past would come back if in a slightly different form, that the opportunities ahead would be the making of all of them. Listening to the author's muddled, scamped, camped words, she had caught their vindictiveness ringing round the theatre and she'd hated it, a nasty indiscriminate slashing at the past with no hint of a reason or purpose; there wasn't even the pretence of something being aspired *towards*. The performance was frightening, the writing deadly in its accuracy, yet the whole was empty, barren, hollow self-echoing. A halfway clever idea had well and truly played itself out, Catherine felt, and been exposed after a meagre, short-measure eighty-five minutes as threadbare. Here was the dismal confirmation of moral bankruptcy, at top-rate West End prices: every house a sell-out, 'returns' only. Nothing was offered at the conclusion except the spectacle of Adèle's too evident exhaustion, her unsteadiness on her feet, the unrelenting bleakness of the follow-spot, the chasm of silence before the curtain started to fall and the self-satisfied applause broke out, cracking like gunshot fire in the tarted-up, over-gilded, over-plushed belly of the theatre.

*

'Darling! How *wonderful* – '

It was obvious to Catherine that Adèle couldn't think who she was, at least for the first twenty-five or thirty seconds. Then muffled bells seemed to ring, and she sank down into a chair.

The woman was haggard with tiredness, fagged out, but smiling. Catherine was relieved to discover that she was largely oblivious to her humiliation.

'Isn't it a divine play? Everyone tells me so. I'm no judge, of course – '

'It – it's been very successful.'

'We're transferring. This is our last night here. It's reopening in a couple of weeks. Oh darling, why don't you come to the party – wouldn't that be a scrummy idea – ?'

'I – I've nothing to wear, I'm afraid.'

'But how *fab* you look in that!'

'This?'

'Yes, your gear.'

Catherine stared at her Seattle outfit in the mirror: black leather jerkin and white cotton shirt, and sawn-off black-and-white-striped cotton stretch pants, a little crumpled from sitting on a zebra overnight.

'Has life been good to you?' Adèle asked.

'Goodish and baddish, I'd say.'

'Didn't I see your photograph?'

'Very probably.'

'How exciting for you!'

'Hmm.'

Adèle looked confused before Catherine remembered to smile.

Tonight it was the triumphant survival of Adèle Adaire that was being celebrated.

'You *will* come?'

'To the party? Are you sure – ?'

'But darling – ' Adèle seized her hand ' – of *course* I'm sure. Absolutely positive!'

She laughed, in a throaty, very theatrical way Catherine didn't recall from the past. While the chortles continued, she noticed the clutch of telegrams pinned to a wall, signatures angled for the observing eye – Evelyn Laye, Athene Seyler, Danny La Rue, Ralph R., Diana Dors, Dickie A., Ken Russell, David Frost.

'You *will* come, Caroline?'

'If you would like me to.'

'I should like nothing better in the whole world.'

None of the telegram signatories was at the party, but maybe she arrived too early or too late. She *did* spot (because she heard the names being singled out) a cherubic Ned Sherrin, bespectacled Caryl Brahms, regal and billowing Ann Shelton, and – left holding two glasses – one Kenneth Tynan. She also saw the great author and artificer himself, Lionel Quynn. He was dressed entirely in Juliette Greco black: a black corduroy suit with a black roll-neck jumper, and black zipped Chelsea boots. His brushed-back and Brylcreemed hair was uniformly black, as was his trimmed Left-Bank moustache and goatee. He wore a signet ring inset with a sloe-black stone, and Catherine considered that – with those very intense, very dark eyes – he might have been the Devil incarnate.

He looked over some of the young, shapely girls with lowly functions in the production – *she* was at least a decade too old to come into the reckoning – and he moved in on them with hellishly lascivious intent written all over his face. They gave themselves like too earnest novitiates, and she was puzzled. But of course these were liberated and experimental times, and she was conspicuously out of step, however 'fab' Adèle had said she looked on the outside.

There was much ambitious, optimistic talk in the room: of a new satirical magazine to be put together, of a snook-cocking stage review, of a film to co-star Hermione Gingold and Anthony Newley, of an arty restaurant in Curzon Street which would only admit as diners those who were members, of a fast-moving social set which made Denbigh's sound like feet-draggers and shufflers. She became quite dizzy with so much remorselessly aspiring conversation.

Mental vertigo seemed to have affected Adèle as well. Eventually she was obliged to excuse herself, but reminding everyone this parting was just au revoir and not goodbye.

'I must love you now and leave you,' she said, fortified by Beefeater gin, raising her hand in a blessing. Catherine (treacherously) spotted a wide circle of dampness under the arm dispensing the benison.

'Until we meet again – '

In a fortnight, she meant, when the play transferred to the new theatre a couple of streets away.

Her eyes were bloodshot. She was wearing white lace gloves, because Catherine had seen the evidence in her dressing-room that she had tried, unsuccessfully, to have the liver-marks on her hands removed: blow-torched, to judge from the damage of scorch burns. She looked quite anorexic, as if worry about every performance must have whittled her appetite away to nothing.

'God bless you all!'

There was an outburst of applause, led by Lionel Quynn, who blew her kisses on the palm of his hairy-backed hand. Even though Adèle was now enjoying the good life – newly mortgaged with a mews cottage in Knightsbridge among the Mini-Coopers and Afghan hounds, taxis everywhere if need be, party invitations for most nights of the week – physically she didn't give the impression of benefiting. At moments during the evening she had seemed to be up to high-doh, delivering those manufactured whoops of laughter, eyes widening and widening with simulated excitement as a story was told (or retold) to her, passing with fluttering fingers and a shaky hand from drinks tray to drinks tray, missing her aim twice with a glass and hearing it crash to the floor, mistaking the distance and gradient to her mouth with a vol-au-vent case and a caviar-topped cracker and stupidly, direly, watching them crumble and shed their soggy detritus on to her dress and her shoes. She was, Catherine was certain, already a walking liability, an animated cliché. Could *she* perceive it? – was that the reason why she seemed perilously close to collapsing in on herself, like the structurally unsound pastry shells and two-bite-sized meringues supplied by the caterers?

Adèle took her with her. She was badly needing an arm to support her, and to guide her into the sleeves of her brand-new seven-eighths-length stranded blue fox coat.

'I have to look the part, darling,' she explained, smiling serenely at all and sundry.

'It's a *splendid* coat.'

'Some people are getting so frightfully sensitive about fur, aren't they? Dreadful spoilsports, killjoys – '

The coat was apposite: if the animals had suffered and paid the ultimate price for human vanity, so was the coat's owner now paying her own terrible dues. The collar was hitched up.

'The cost of it would have kept a village in India going in rice for ten years, I expect. Or twenty. But then – ' she sank her thin, gloved fingers into the luxurious pile ' – they don't have to put up with the cold as we do. And I have to make sure I don't catch a chill. For the company's sake – '

It was the middle of an English summer; London – by its standards – was sweltering. But the coat to Adèle was as the shell of a snail, a sort of movable home and her literal *raison d'être*, her identity, so she was obliged to wear it, with a combination of pride and perfunctoriness.

Tonight she had brought her own transport. The Jensen was three weeks old; the garage had been tightening the handbrake, testing the brake discs, checking lubricant levels, and fitting a radio. A driver had brought the car to the theatre, washed and waxed and vacuumed.

'Avaunt!'

'Where to?' Catherine asked.

'Home, of course. How are you placed?'

' "Placed"?'

'For accommodation?'

'I – '

'I could give you a kipper. If you need one for the night – '

Miss Montgomery's shadow passed and was gone.

'Really?'

In truth she wasn't tired. She couldn't believe it; she had last slept properly on the Greyhound bus to Boulder City.

'Of *course* I could.'

'I haven't got anywhere – '

'So that's settled, my dear.'

'I'm very grate – '

'Phooey! Lay on, Macduff, and home!'

*

The house had charm (lots of it), chic (ditto), and as a concept-of-living was bang up-to-the-minute. The other frontages matched the exemplary Dulux-ad whiteness, and the cobbles – notwithstanding the Mini-Coopers and Mini-Mokes – had a scrubbed appearance; flowering leaf-trailers glissaded from hanging baskets, and every window had a cultivated box on its outside sill. It was a pretty setting, and very definitely bijou.

The interior was on three levels, each 'gallery' demarcated by a stained wood balustrade. The furnishings were uniformly reproduction, the fabric colours were shop-coordinated olives and chestnuts: rather too much on the dark side, Catherine felt sure, and looking round she quickly realised that there was no material evidence in these semi-rooms of their owner's having had a life before this one, excepting three portraits in frames, of Adèle with Gladys Cooper, Adèle with Cecil Parker, and Adèle with Googie Withers. And excepting too, she supposed, a collection of dolls in national costume, which *might* have come from London shops, since Adèle had never mentioned any treading of foreign boards. Two teddy bears with new, burnished fur occupied the two cocoa-brown leather swivel chairs; when Catherine was invited to sit down, the bear growled as she turned it over and she smelt the behind-the-scenes storerooms of the shop.

There were few other accessories: no books (only a few colour supplements in a pile), a couple of paintings in toning hues (a scene from the Battle of Crimea, and swan-upping on the Thames), a vase of very dried flowers. No clutter: and all the surfaces were dustless, which indicated the services of a daily. The leather chair had *appeared* comfortable, like the others, but it didn't prove so; it was squeaky and cold and unsupporting, and Catherine wondered just how much time Adèle had actually spent here. She noticed how restless she was, that she didn't stay seated for longer than half a minute at a time, and that the swivel-spin nearly sent her flying as she got to her feet, which suggested she wasn't yet au fait with the quirks of her far-from-passive furniture. *Not*, Catherine decided, a house to grow old in: and then she felt guilty of uncharitableness, when she of all people – with the theoretical perspective her experiences ought to have given her – should certainly have judged better.

Adèle opened the doors of a suspiciously non-distressed mahogany 'Chippendale' cabinet. Inside was a battalion of bottles, neatly aligned in descending order of height.

'What's your poison, my dear?'

She poured them both whiskies, then she tugged at one of the over-gilded frames on the wall. The vista of swan-uppers and flapping fowl swung back to reveal the screen of a wall-mounted television set.

'*Voilà*!' Adèle said, waving her hand with a slightly lacklustre flourish.

A picture appeared on the screen.

'I never miss Guy, do you? But of course you've been away, out of it – '

' "Guy"?'

'*Parley with Pennicote*. Guy Pennicote. You remember? *The Cocktail Party* – he's got a – what are they called? A . . . a *talk* show. Of course, and it's all the rage.'

'How long has it been on?'

'A couple of years, I suppose. Last thing every Saturday night. It used to be quite – I always forget the word – satyric? No, "satirical", that's it. But now everyone's falling over themselves to get on to it. Who has he had recently?' She put a hand to her brow to indicate deep thought. 'Monica Vitti, David McCallum, Astrud Gilberto. Oh, and Rod Taylor. And I read that the Burtons are going to be on it some time, both of them.'

Tonight he was talking to Dirk Bogarde, and a leggy American actress called Tuesday Weld. Really they were present to assist in the massaging of the host's ego. His questions invariably referred back to himself, and if his 'guests' showed signs of wanting to promote their own personalities or their work he cut them short.

'I've noticed, he always sits on *their* right. That's his better side, you see. Every photograph you see of him.'

'Isn't that limiting?'

'Apparently not. He's such a hit, and he does it with only half his face. I never saw what was wrong with the other side, but Guy was – *is* – so particular.'

'Is he vain?'

Adèle gulped down her whisky.

'Was there ever vainer? Cocksure. I think that would be the word.'

He leaned forward repeatedly to touch Tuesday Weld's arm. At one point his fingers rested on her wrist.

Adèle let out a groan.

'Jesus wept – '

'She – she's very pretty,' Catherine said. 'Isn't she?'

'I suppose she is. But what's that got to do with the price of cheese, might I enquire?'

Catherine watched her watching. Her eyebrows were raised to denote her incredulity: either at the actress's attractiveness or Guy Pennicote's flirtatiousness. The camera moved in on their faces: clean-cut, modishly angular. They had both reached their apotheosis: persons wholly of their own times, with the looks that were a prerequisite, the 'now' of 'now'. Guy was already beyond considerations of background, or class, or even of talent. He was his own man and self-creation.

'Hmm' was Adèle's equivocal verdict as the appreciative audience launched into applause.

'Have *you* been on it?' Catherine asked.

'He *has* approached me.'

'Do you keep up with one another?'

'I don't know how it's happened, but yes, we do. Years of hoofing it round the shires, I suppose.'

'Not *so* long, though.'

'Quite long enough, my dear. While I was being pursued by Lionel Quynn, Guy met someone who knew someone who knew someone else. A man in a man's world, it's different for them, of course.'

Adèle eyed the offerings in the drinks cabinet.

'His chums and their chums were very helpful to him. Protective of one another, could I say?'

She made a chimp-face at the screen, at the photogenic talking head who had the audience eating out of the palm of his hand.

'And then Bob's your uncle – I'm sure Bob was his name; hardly his uncle, though, more of a father figure – Guy was on the panel of a quiz show where they have to guess a person's appearance from talking to them on the phone. Quite inane and embarrassing, but it was enough for his purpose, and in the next series he was introducing the show. Then he went on to another one with prizes where people had to answer questions jumping about a giant checkers-board, and he had a catch-phrase, "Claim your square" – bloody awful too – and he became, God wot how, a household name. Like Dettol or Fairy Liquid. Then *this* came into being, and Uncle Bob really *did* come up trumps, didn't he, the old sod.'

Was she jealous? Aggrieved? She was standing shaking her head: either because it was so unfair, or else so very, very ridiculous, the luck and the medium and the end-result and the gullibility of the public who lapped it up.

It was Adèle's idea. She might have been tipsy.

'We'll go round. See Guy. You'll be a surprise for him, I'm sure.'

' "Go round"? When?'

'Now, of course!'

'Where is he?'

'At the studio. The show's live. They know me, it's open sesame, couldn't be simpler.'

They jumped into the Jensen and, gears wrenching, they jerked and jolted their way the four miles there.

They were waved into the studio compound. Adèle was wearing her blue fox coat and a fuchsia satin turban à la Barbra Streisand and looked the sort of woman for whom barrier poles were raised and lowered without question.

'I can't remember – ' she ducked her head to read the signs ' – which studio they use.'

A gaggle of young women were standing under one of the illuminated signs.

'The fan club,' Adèle said.

They were all young, excited, long-legged, nubile.

'What do *they* do?' Catherine asked.

'That must remain a matter for conjecture.'

They were straining to see forward between one another's shoulders.

'I think,' Adèle said, 'they are about to have their girlish emotions cruelly teased.'

They drove – closer to 40 mph than the obligatory 4 – towards the spot. But with a dozen or twenty yards still to cover, two dark figures emerged at a sprint from a side-door and, confused by shadows, ran straight into the side of the car. The Jensen was rocked by the knocks and Catherine called out with shock. Adèle seemed to read the situation in an instant. She threw open her door and got out.

'Oh *Jesus*!'

'Not quite,' a voice said. 'But I'm getting there.'

'Guy darling, are you all right?'

'Damned stupid question, Adèle, if I may say so.'

He was slumped against the wall, being felt – for breakages presumably – by the young man he was with.

'I didn't *see* you. I wasn't expecting – '

'Thought we'd make a bolt for it.'

Adèle nodded towards the girls.

'Terrifying, aren't they?' Guy said.

'How's your – friend?'

'Okay, thanks.' The young man turned his model's face to them in the light from the door. 'But I think Guy needs some attention.'

'Oh Christ!' Adèle rushed over to him. 'Oh, darling – '

'Calm down,' Guy said. '*I*'m the casualty.'

'Don't say that. What's happened? Have you broken something?'

'If you promise you won't give us your Odette Hallowes – I shall let you drive me to hospital.'

'*Anywhere*, Guy – '

Adèle opened the passenger door and Catherine got out.

'A hospital will do very well, Adèle.'

By now the girls had spotted their idol. They started running across the compound, screaming.

'The curse of the banshees,' Guy said as they bundled him into the back of the car. 'I'll need *you* for protection, sweetheart,' he called out, grabbing the young man's hand and pulling him in after him.

'Oh, my frigging arm!'

Catherine got into the front and closed her door two or three seconds before the girls reached them. Adèle gave a blast of the horn but they were already pressing their hands and mouths against the glass. Those at the rear pushed forward and the ones in front used it as an excuse to rip open their blouses and thrust their pert, naked breasts flat on the side-windows.

'What a grisly sight,' Guy opined, smiling and blowing kisses. 'Put your foot down, Adèle. I think my arm must be broken.'

'I might knock someone down.'

'You've done that already. Another notch on your gearstick.'

'Don't say that, Guy. I'm very – volatile tonight.'

'Been drinking, have we?'

'Not much. Truly.'

'Much as I enjoy your company, Adèle dearest, I did have other plans for this particular evening.'

Catherine heard the sound from the back – a hand slapping a leg, a thigh – and she didn't look round.

'What if this gets into the newspapers?' Adèle said.

'Well, I don't think *any* of us would be best served by that, do you?'

'Do you remember Catherine?'

'Up in Mickletwistle,' Catherine said. '*The Cockt* – '

'Hello, Catherine.' The voice was most politely insincere. 'Adèle got herself a better half at last?'

'Certainly not,' Adèle responded. 'Shacking up was never my bag.'

The remark, startling in its trendiness, was met by silence.

'I needed a roof over my head – '

'Catherine was a very famous face for a while. But I don't expect you pay a lot of attention. To that sort of thing.'

'I might if the face is famous enough for my show. Is it, Catherine?'

'I've stopped all that now.'

'Seen the light?'

'She was in all the mags,' Adèle said, letting her concentration slip and driving through a red light. 'Now she's readjusting to the nineteen-sixties.'

'What happened? Did they deep-freeze you?'

'Something like that,' Catherine said.

'There is nothing refrigerated about Catherine,' Adèle said. 'She strikes me as being a very warm and mellow person.'

'Well, if anyone can get to the bottom of it – or the crux – I'm sure *you* can, Adèle.'

And so it continued, all the way to the hospital, as Adèle jumped traffic lights and drove against the tide on one-way streets. But so long as she thought she kept them from noticing what Catherine already had – that her hands were shaking very badly – perhaps she imagined it was excusable, as eccentric in her nicely mythical way as her head attire.

*

After a chaste night in the mews flat they returned to the hospital in the morning.

Guy, dressed and discharged, emerged downstairs carrying his arm in a sling, accompanied by a young male orderly who was guiding him by his other arm.

'Sprains,' he announced to them, 'nothing broken, quite.'

'But you look like the bloody war-wounded.'

'Better luck next time, Adèle.'

'I'm so sorry, Guy darling.'

The orderly held out a piece of paper and the patient, wobbling slightly, scribbled his autograph, then a succession of numerals: for the follow-up telephone call, Catherine supposed.

'Now whither, Adèle?'

'I don't know.'

'Oh, let's escape!'

'Escape? Where to?'

'Anywhere. For a few days.'

They both looked at Catherine.

'Come with us,' Guy said.

'I – I must go to Aquae-Regis,' she told them.

'*We*'ll go too.'

'Won't you want some privacy?' Adèle asked, construing the situation with a woman's eye. 'But *we* can take you there.'

'Of course we will.'

'Guy and I will go down to the coast.'

'That place we did the Rattigan – '

'Sandmouth – '

'We can pick you up again.'

So all was agreed.

'I'll drive,' Adèle said. 'It's the least – '

Guy winked to the departing orderly.

'What about Tuesday Weld, Guy?'

'There'll be other times – '

They made a couple of stops to pick up their two carry-alls. Catherine, luggageless, took a back seat while Guy gingerly eased himself into the front, beside Adèle.

'Catherine is travelling very light,' Adèle told her long-time, most unlikely foil. 'She is a free spirit. *Dégagée*.'

'Celebrity is a cussed awkward burden, Catherine.'

'It must be – '

'A bugger to shake off.'

'You needn't fear,' Adèle told him. 'You're not among fans now.'

'Weren't you impressed, Catherine? By my suavity, intelligence, sincerity? Didn't you spot the sexual chemistry between me and my guests? Didn't *you*, Adèle?'

'I was watching your guests, not you.'
'Watching Tuesday?'
'Off and on.'
'Ever thought of taking on a Girl Friday, Adèle? What about Catherine? Or is she not quite suitable?'
'Didn't you tell a journalist you were looking for one? A Girl Friday?'
'My knick-knacks get seen to every day. By Ma Harris.'
'A Boy Saturday, perhaps?'
'I'm only public property through the week.'
'Do the newspapers know that? You should watch yourself, Guy Pennicote.'
'My fame is but a bauble to this woman. Do you see, Catherine?'
'What Catherine sees is not what Mr and Mrs Public see. In their cosy little two-up, two-down, cat on the mat, china lady on top of the goggle-box – '
'They see the sexual chemistry.'
'They wouldn't have a clue what sexual chemistry was if they fell over it in the middle of the road.'
'How very patronising of you, Adèle. But I dare say you'll get busloads of that lot in to watch *your* nightly performance once the smart lot have moved on. And I don't suppose they would recognise a *thespian* if one dropped naked down their chimney.'
'Is that an instance of your "spontaneous, cosmopolitan wit", by any chance? Or an out-take from the script?'
'The critics say my esprit is much emulated but never equalled. Apparently I've reinstated epigrams on TV to an art form.'
'Just as I thought. A pith-artist. If ever there was.'
'Very droll, Adèle. You should sack that Quynn bloke. Thinking he's got to put the words into your mouth.'
'I presume yours are too?'
'What?'
'Put into your mouth.'
'Words, are you rabbiting on about?'
'If there's room. With everything else.'
'Whatever *can* you mean?'
'What do they use? Felt wadding? – to take away any last clue to an accent? I happen to know, Catherine – ' Adèle turned round in her seat ' – that Mr Pennicote is by and large an artificial construction.'
'Bi-? And large?'
'His accent – or, rather, the lack of same – being perhaps the most brazenly artificial thing about him.'

'I'm classless, Adèle. So I've read. I'm a man of the – more or less thinking – people.'

'His lips move, but the sound emerges from another part of his anatomy entirely.'

'Whoever told you *you* had a natural accent?'

'I was taught to speak by Dame Thelma Briscoe.'

'Never heard of her.'

'*That* doesn't surprise me. She knew Oscar Wilde very well. Latterly. She was a link – '

' – in the chain. And is now a name flushed down the lavatory bowl of history – '

'My diction has been oft-commented upon.'

'Yes, so I gather.'

'What d'you mean?'

He must have been thinking of her latest performance, with its garbled lines rendered in approximate order. But he held back from admitting as much, by some commendably prompted tact – or merely in recognition of how far they could take this slightly tired-sounding game. Maybe Adèle realised too, and that explained the determined set of her features and the sideways shift of her eyes through the side-window.

'*Oh*! to be *out* on the *road*!' she sang under her breath. She stretched her arms and placed them at ten-to-two on the generously sized steering wheel.

'This *is* a treat!' she said, and sounded as if she might actually mean it.

With his good arm Guy removed a pair of sunglasses from an inside pocket of his jacket and put them on.

'It gets a drag,' he said, 'being classless all the time.'

'Lionel Quynn thinks the play could be tightened up in a few places, but if it's not written by now it never will be.'

'I feel,' Guy said, 'I want to lie low. Somewhere very quiet, without a TV set.'

'I just want to take my face off.'

'I've brought swabs,' Guy said, 'from the make-up room.'

'How do *you* feel, Catherine?' Adèle asked.

'Quite – removed,' Catherine responded, wanting to articulate her feelings. 'Fairly – dreamy.'

'Are you "on" something?' Guy said. 'Or shouldn't I ask?'

'Of course you shouldn't,' Adèle told him. 'Lionel Quynn and his gels spend half *their* time in outer space. They travel faster than sound.'

'It's very pleasantly dreamy,' Catherine said. 'For the moment anyway – '

'This car cost more than most houses,' Adèle told them. 'Do you think that's immoral?'

'I can't see you domiciled in Dagenham,' Guy said. 'Or Surbiton. So stop worrying about it.'

'A man in the street told me I should give it away. To house the homeless.'

'No indoor sanitation. What use would that be to anyone in this day and age?'

'If I hadn't decided to do the rep, I wouldn't have gone to Sandmouth and Lionel Quynn would never have seen me.'

'I wouldn't have known Tuesday Weld from Mrs Mop. I get these notes pushed into my hand with two hours to go. And the running order, who's after who, that dribbles into my earpiece when we're live.'

'Isn't that a little queer?'

'Where?' Guy looked out of the side-window, towards the pedestrians. 'In the suede coat? In Kensington it's a likely bet – '

Already Catherine felt a little light-headed with the repartee: that and the low roof in the back. Her nostrils itched from the pile on the blue fox coat. Also, banter had never been one of her social accomplishments. For Adèle and Guy it was like the air they breathed, and she was in awe of their facility. But conversationally they were leading her out of her depth.

They had to stop twice for petrol, which entailed tyre marks burned on the tarmacadam as the other shoe jammed on the middle brake pedal. No one dared to suggest tea, but by one o'clock Guy announced he was bloody famished and Catherine herself felt – again – ergot-headed, so they went flying off the main road at a tangent and skidded across the gravel yard of a suspiciously trim pub called The Labourer's Arms. They ordered three 'Ploughboy's Lunches': dainty portions of cheese and salad were prettily augmented by a prawn, a slice of peach, a bayleaf, a nasturtium head, and a tiny folded eau-de-Cologne towelette. It turned out that Guy had encountered the owner before, in a previous incarnation – the friend of a fellow theatrical – and the lunch deteriorated into theatre chatter as Adèle expanded to fill the small parlour and Guy picked his moments to deliver his pinpricks at fame and reputation.

Adèle was a fast driver: or rather, her nervousness behind the wheel was such that it was easier for her to sit with her foot pressed hard down on the accelerator. In truth, she had great difficulty doing otherwise, since the angle of the pedal and the height of her heel forced the toe of her shoe into that position. Here and no mistaking was a return to the days of intrepid motoring, valiant and doubtless a little mad, when machine and driver vied to have command of the other. They raced, they sped, they hurtled, on hills they all but took flight as the radiator grille aimed high, for the wide wide blue.

76

Advent

And suddenly, there in front of them, framed by the windscreen, was Aquae-Regis, spread on its arena of low hills, raked in a semi-circle like an amphitheatre.

Seeing it again, Catherine gulped the saliva in her mouth. Not for pleasure, she was sure, not for any gladness of recognition and reminiscence.

The vista was subtly different. Much of the building stone had been cleaned, so that it had acquired the soft, lambent glow of mellite. There were far fewer smoking chimneys, and no hint left of that black, sooty pall which had darkened too many of their days. The result was that sunshine falling starkly between gunmetal rain-clouds lit an aureate city resplendent in its crystalline air.

Guy whistled through his teeth. Adèle nodded as she slowed to admire. Catherine wasn't at all sure what might be awaiting her at her journey's very end.

When they had covered the remaining two miles and reached the town itself, they drove about for a while, to get their bearings. The sun was now playing hard-to-find, and every so often the sky would take on a greenish tinge and the light would dramatically alter, thickening like water in a clouded aquarium tank. But the rain held off as they cruised along the crescents and terraces on Beaulieu and Paradise Hills. Guy propped his elbow up on the sill and supported his chin on two gesticulating fingers as they passed a grey-clad man of the cloth, and Adèle didn't realise Guy's window was still wound down when she shouted at a woman on a bicycle to move her big, fat, squashy bum out of the way.

In Eveleigh Crescent Catherine asked them to please stop outside her old home, and they did so. Adèle was going to switch off the engine, but Catherine asked her not to, please. So, as the engine ticked over, the three of them looked, and Catherine most keenly and reluctantly of all.

The house had been divided: a brass panel beside the front door was fitted with a number of bells. The first-floor rooms had gaily blooming window-boxes; on the second floor there were venetian blinds at the windows; and on the area railings a sign with a pointing arrow proclaimed the whereabouts of the 'Garden Flat'.

Catherine felt more ghostly than ever: dispossessed now, unhoused. Adèle seemed to perceive her confusion, and asked if she felt ready to move on. She nodded, and Guy turned round to tap her knee – but also, she realised, to catch another glimpse of a broad-shouldered, bare-armed butcher's boy cycling along the road in a bloodied apron. Adèle snatched at the handbrake, rammed the gearstick out of neutral into first, played footsy with each of the pedals until she remembered which was which, and off they lurched on their way. Guy leaned across to the steering wheel and blasted the horn at a delivery man carrying eggs into a private hotel: the man looked round in astonishment and a couple of the boxes tumbled out of his hands and crashed to the pavement.

'For God's sake, Guy,' Adèle told him. 'At *your* age – '

'By which logic *you* should have the wisdom of Solomon.'

'Why do I put up with it, my dear? Tell me that.'

But Catherine didn't wait to find out.

'Please,' she said, 'please let me out – I must get out – '

'What?' Adèle's eyes left the road. 'But I thought you were coming on with *us*?'

'Please, please – '

'For Christ's sake, Adèle, watch out – '

She turned round and pulled hard on the wheel to avoid another delivery boy on a bicycle.

'Aren't you coming – ?'

'Why, Cathy?' Guy asked.

'I don't know. I just have to – '

She didn't know, she couldn't have explained. Certainly it had nothing to do with joy. But with the voices maybe. *The* voice. On India Street she'd been sure that she heard it calling, then again on Moore of Corunna Street. A woman's voice.

'I just have to,' she told them. 'I'm so sorry. But – '

She could have said, I heard her, I heard my mother. But the two of them, Adèle and Guy, were locked in their own kind of ingenuousness and she saw from their faces that it preserved them from the very worst, most final truths about themselves. *Please*, they were begging her, whatever it is, please don't implicate *us* –

She loved-them-and-left-them, as Adèle would have had it; the powdery kiss on her cheek was lingering and genuinely regretful.

'Where will you stay?'
'It won't be for long.'
'Is there anyone who could put you up?'
'I'm not sure – if they're here or not, you see – '
Adèle looked at her with some concern.
' – if they've all come back. But I think they must have.'
'Is it a young person's town, though, Catherine?'
'I think I felt oldest when I *was* young,' she said. 'I think then I knew most of all.'
'The very best of luck, my dear.'
'Does she need luck?' Guy asked her.
'Oh yes. We all do.'
'What's this then?' He waved his bandaged arm.
'Well, you *could* have broken it, darling, couldn't you?'
Catherine waved goodbye to them. The car sputtered exhaust along the length of Tobago Street and their voices calling from the open windows grew fainter. The horn sounded three blasts of farewell on the far corner.
Then they were gone.

77

An Aerial Conversation

In the early winter of 1986 I took Roger Matheson to dinner at a rooftop restaurant in downtown Toronto.

Outside it was snowing. Inside the lights were kept very low, so we had the illusion of hovering over the city. The drapes of pale steel mesh were hauled up almost soundlessly on their hydraulics to allow us to see out, into the origins of what was later to become a blizzard.

Toronto was fast disappearing beneath us, smothering under polar snow.

I learned about his life. In London, being an office clerk in the Greater Metropolitan police force. His wife walking out with his son. Searching for them both everywhere, and finding not a clue as to how a young woman and child could simply disappear off the face of this earth. After that, becoming a private investigator in an agency in Holborn: just after the War there was almost too much work, looking for all those persons who had decided they didn't want their new lives to be anything like the old.

He had given up the investigator's life in 1954. Over coffee, while the Arctic romanced Canada, I asked him why.

'Too much coming to identify with my quarry perhaps.'

'How was that?'

'I got to think they had the right idea, like my wife, trying to get away. And anyway, it became much more trivial, the job. Later on the cases that landed on my desk had to do with husbands or wives cheating, and I was left having to "prove" infidelity. It was – I don't know – all too "suburban", I suppose. My clients came from comfortable homes, they had everything going for them, yet somehow the rest got all fouled up, they threw it away, and I could feel no pity for them. With their miserable little adventures.'

So, I asked, he'd thrown in the towel?

He crossed his hands on the tablecloth.

'There was something about you,' he said, 'when I saw you.'
'What?'
'When I received the information about you: the photographs, not the paperwork. I never forget a face. And I'd already seen your photographs.'
'How?'
He lit another cigarette from the one already burning between his fingers.
'It was my last case at the agency, as it turned out. It'll show you how far I'd fallen. I got a call, and the woman – she made it sound like a tea-party – she invited me round to a block of flats in Knightsbridge. She opened the door to me herself. Poor little rich girl, I guessed – well, fairly rich, "well-to-do". No mother. Lived there with "Daddy". She shooed away the maid and poured us drinks – I could tell she'd started already: to screw up her courage presumably. But she got to the point eventually, after she'd made sure she'd be paying for absolute discretion.
'She produced some photographs. A very striking woman they showed too. Then she asked if I would be averse to a little petty burglary. In Kensington. She opened a notecase and took out a wad of fivers. I had to think it over quickly, on the spot. I said "absolute discretion" came a little more expensive, but that didn't seem to deter her, she just drew out a couple of tens as well.
'It *was* very simple. She gave me a "shopping list": underwear, a few odds and ends of clothing – and later, some cosmetics. Nothing valuable. I appeased my conscience with that. I did a few assignments for her. I was to bring back details of her clothes, what the labels said. I was looking round when I found your photo.'
I stared at him.
'One afternoon the timing went haywire, you almost disturbed me, walking back home from school. I just got out and away and no more, at a sprint.'
I started to nod my head.
'Yes. Yes, I remember – '
'I had more or less everything she'd asked for by then.'
'Who was she?'
'Her name was Kilpatrick.'
'The model-man's daughter?'
'Harriet Kilpatrick.'
'But – what on earth did she want with the stuff?'
'She wasn't quite right in the head. No, that's not it. She was intelligent enough, sharp enough. But I suppose at some point her mind went way off at a tangent. Maybe she'd had some shock in her past.

And she just allowed this obsession about your mother to take over.'

'But why did she want the clothes?'

'At first she restricted herself to wearing them in the privacy of her own home – her father's home, that is – if she *did* wear them. But she couldn't drop the obsession. She had me find out about your mother's movements, where she shopped, where she got her hair done, ate out, had tea. As if she was a jealous wife and your mother was her husband's mistress and she couldn't think of anything else.'

'You followed her? My mother?'

'For a while. I had one last job in Kensington that I wasn't so keen on.'

'What was that?'

'My client in Knightsbridge had heard that fifty yellow roses had been delivered to the house. She had me go round and cut the head off every one.'

'I remember,' I said. 'I *do* remember.'

'Your mother thought it was you?'

'Yes, she did. Of course I denied it, naturally. And the more I denied it, the more positive she was that I *must* have done it. She got mad at me.'

'I'm sorry. I'm really sorry.'

'Probably it made up her mind.'

'What about?'

'Having me adopted.'

'Probably.'

'You think so?'

'I think she must have been getting very unsettled by then.'

I nodded.

'I found magazine photographs,' he said. 'Of New Zealand. Rotorua, the Cathedral Caves. A live volcano. Thermal pools. Waterfalls. Subterranean rivers, steaming cliffs. The lot, I used to stare at them.'

'New Zealand?' I repeated. 'Why – '

'She must have thought it would be the best place for you.'

'Not Canada?'

'I'm coming to that. Then it was New Zealand. Something about it must have appealed to her. That – that controlled violence of nature maybe. The photographer had written to her about the place – '

'It would have fitted,' I agreed. 'With how I was then.'

'That was the end of my assignment. Officially. But I was intrigued. When I had quiet days I used to drive over to Knightsbridge and tail Miss Kilpatrick. As I said, she'd had me look in your mother's wardrobe, take photographs and details of some of her clothes, and I recognised the things she was wearing some days. She went to the Helmsley salon a couple of times, and came away with purchases; and she went to a wig-maker in Margaret Street. She'd look at herself in shop windows and change her step, quicken it a little, because your mother had quite a fast stride.'

'*Why*, though?'

'Poor little rich kid. Like I said. Daddy's girl. Daddy's favourite. No room for anyone else as pretty as your mother. Her father was quite a handsome man still. And she was at a restless, very insecure age. Jealousy and physical desire got all muddled up.'

'And afterwards – ?' I enquired.

Before he answered he stared out of the window for half a minute or longer, into the snow. I thought he hadn't heard, or had forgotten, or was avoiding a reply. But he did speak at last, turning to face me.

'I got all worked up about Lois and our boy, it descended on me – when I couldn't deal with it. In the end I had a breakdown. Of sorts. Lay low in my lair. I decided I needed a complete change of scene, and I came out to Canada, because it was cheap to get here. I applied for several positions in the welfare services, without telling them my whole story – especially the recent part. But I was taken on, and I ended up dealing with the British kids being sent over. I was expected – irony of ironies – to understand some of the "difficulties" of adjustment they'd be going through.'

'And that's when *I* showed up?'

'I was lucky to get you at all, I suppose.'

'Why's that?'

'You were *meant* to be going to New Zealand.'

'You said that, but I don't see – '

'Your mother wanted it. But there was a hitch.'

'You know the story? Why she did it?'

'I know that – well, she couldn't cope with you. She said she didn't want you to have to risk meeting your father, but I guess that was an excuse. She was in a very seesaw state.'

'Why wasn't I put out for adoption at home? In Britain?'

'The panel thought you were better away. From *her*, maybe. You seemed to be like chalk and cheese, to their way of thinking anyway. The reports on your mother were pretty damning. I don't think they ever told her you weren't in New Zealand.'

'What?'

'She didn't hear officially – '

'You mean she didn't know I was in Canada?'

'By accident the New Zealand people heard later that she'd written letters to you. But the foster couple had moved and she got the address of their old house wrong. The Post Office would open the letters to return them, but your mother was cagey about using an exact address. It was just one of those things, lots of crossed and tangled wires.'

'But she wrote to me? Out there?'

'To New Zealand, yes.'

'They should've told her about Canada, though.'

'They did what they thought – rightly or wrongly – was best.'

'Best for whom?'

'As they saying goes – "for all concerned". Maybe they guessed your mother *wouldn't* get in touch, but that it was safest to keep the distance between you, just in case. To give you – give you both – a completely fresh start.'

'But the gifts I got. At the McLuskeys'. The packages.'

'Anonymous?'

'Yes. Yes, anonymous.'

'I heard about them.'

'Who else *could* they have been from?'

'You can't guess?'

'"Guess"?'

'Who might have been your benefactor?'

'You're going to tell me it wasn't my mother?'

'No, it wasn't your mother.'

'Who, then? Do you know? Please tell me –'

'A foreigner.'

'Who?'

'A woman who lived very far away. For most of the time, that is. In Rio de Janeiro.'

'*Who?*'

'Her name was Billington. Audrey Billington.'

I stared at him.

'Or Mrs Reginald Billington.'

I was completely mystified.

'She was a friend of your mother's. Long ago.'

'I thought – I presumed she'd have told you something – '

'No. Nothing at all. Who was she?'

'She married a racing driver, but an accident crippled him. Physically anyway, but mentally he was quite okay. He managed various équipe teams about the world, made a good living from it. They travelled about, but it was difficult, even with the money to transport themselves as comfortably as they could, and able to put themselves up in the best hotels.'

'But – but what does this have to do with me?' I was exasperated by ignorance. 'Any little bit of it?'

'She wrote to my old agency from Rio. She was trying to find your mother. She had no idea about her being a model. She could only give us the name – Catherine Hammond – and the history of their friendship in Aquae-Regis. Someone at the agency thought they recognised the face in the photo – it had come with the letter – and they tracked me down in Canada. The photo *was* of Catherine Fairweather, I was quite certain. Anyway – I was lured back into the business, against my better judgement: but it was as if it was fated to happen like that, I was being told – a "voice" was telling me – I shouldn't give up just yet.'

'And did she get in touch with my mother?'

'In the end, no, she didn't. I don't know what persuaded her not to.'

'And – so – that was that?' I asked, knowing it can't have been the case. 'She just paid her bill? End of story – ?'

'She paid her bill, yes. On the nail. But that certainly wasn't the end of the story. It was only the beginning.'

'How? How "the beginning"?'

'Well – *you*'d become the real object of fascination to her now.'

'But why was *I* of any interest to her? What possible –'

'I informed her – in the course of our exchanges – that Catherine Hammond had had a child. An unruly son. The circumstances, I told her, hadn't suited you –'

'Too true. That's an understatement –'

'And she just became fascinated, I suppose. Why your mother should have chosen to send you away. Your appearance, your character.'

'What was I to her, though?'

'She was a rich man's wife. A woman with no child of her own. At that juncture of her life the lack must have been a very serious one to her. I have to guess so. It began – her wanting to know – as a sort of dare to herself. Then she became lured too, by the details and by the mysteries – by the intrigue of having to keep herself anonymous –'

'You corresponded? About me?'

'I used to send her photographs. I wrote letters, of course. She came up from New York once, to Banff Springs –'

'To the hotel?'

'Yes. For a couple of nights. While we went through our paces for her. She knew all about your progress. Even your school reports, she liked to have a look at those.'

'Mrs Billington?'

'Yes. I know she thought of walking by the school once, incognito, to see if she could pick you out –'

'Where?'

'In England.'

'Dorset?'

'At the boarding school, yes. It was she who paid your fees –'

'*What?*'

'She may have gone – driven down to Dorset to have a look at you – but I think she would've told me in that case. She trusted me, which was the whole point.'

'I wish it made more sense to *me*.'

'Doesn't it?'

'Not really. I'm provided for – yes? – by a woman I never set eyes on, didn't know existed?'

'She loved her husband.'

'So . . .'

'He couldn't give her a child. I presume it was that way about. In those days, in the fifties, there was nothing that could be done about infertility.'

Now at the age of thirty-six the scales were falling from my eyes – almost casually, over the coffee and brandy liqueur, while Toronto spun somewhere beneath us.

'You didn't tell me, though?'

'I had instructions not to.'

'Why ever not? For God's sake. Shouldn't I have known?'

He shrugged.

Well, didn't I deserve to?' I asked him. 'Deserve to know?'

'Maybe she was frightened of gratitude. Or she didn't want to risk her husband discovering – he might've thought she was disappointed in her life –'

'It's too bizarre to –'

'It struck me, really, it was beside the point. That you should be made aware. You were getting a better start – a second start, and no expense spared. Away from your mother. If you imagined your mother was dispensing the largesse herself, probably it was no bad thing either –'

I sat with my elbows up on the table, holding my head in my hands.

'There's something,' I said, 'I still don't know. I need –'

He nodded, in anticipation of the question.

'Why don't I know that?' I asked him. 'Who he is? Who my father is?'

I watched as he shook a cigarette out of the packet and lit one.

'I've told you,' he said, 'what I was required to find out. Truly. All of it.'

He inhaled and exhaled. He was looking not at me but at the sprawling metropolis being smothered beneath us.

'The rest of it,' he said, 'what you have to discover – that's lying somewhere – out there –'

He nodded again, this time in the direction of the Atlantic, towards the old world, towards the city – Aquae-Regis – where my story had begun.

78

Exeunt

CATHERINE was not to be privy to the outcome of events, tragic in essence, which a wide selection of newspapers would publish a couple of days hence.

The subsequent news reports – and so many of them – were unable to agree on the nature of Miss Adaire's and Mr Pennicote's accommodation in the resort whither they had returned: shack, lean-to, fisherman's hut, prefab, seafront cottage, maisonette, lodge-house, sea-captain's residence, villa, (even) dower-house. In fact it was a white-painted, clapboard-fronted holiday bungalow of light construction and simple layout, with a front verandah and a generally sunny disposition, sited atop a line of dunes, only yards from the sandy shore. They selected it in a couple of minutes from a list handed to them at an estate agent's in the town. More anonymous than a hotel, the branch manager (misunderstanding the situation) agreed with them, more 'discreet': a local woman 'did' every day and, since (by their own admission) the visitors came quite unequipped, Mr Parrott telephoned the daily in question from his room (with the door closed) and arranged to have linen and towels provided, as soon as she could see to it.

'Like when?'

'Like now.'

'I'm havin' lunch.'

'It's for Guy Pennicote.'

'And I'm Dusty Springfield.'

They were in by three o'clock, stocked up from the grocer's and the fruiterer's and the off-licence. By four a strong wind had blown up and they closed the windows and french doors. The sky turned dab-grey, then steelier, and acquired bruises. The radio set happened to be faulty, and they weren't able to hear the weather forecast on the Home Service warning of the impending storm.

Adèle began preparing dinner – nothing so meagre as supper –

while Guy uncorked the bottles and set the table with his unique artistry, so that it wouldn't have looked out of place at Drury Lane, on an opera stage, or in a Harrods window at Christmas time. Minute by minute the wind was gaining in strength; the sea roared as it rushed for the shore; in an instant the clouds opened and dropped a deluge of golf balls on to the shallow roof.

The meal, cooked, was brought to the table and served. Guy had chosen which records from the owner's rack they would play – all, in their unwitting way, quite kitsch – and dashed between table and record player ensuring (with his one functioning arm) a clamour of sound to rival nature's battering. He turned the volume button higher and higher; they sang along to Gladys and Gertrude, to Vera and Dorothies Lamour and Squires, raising their voices to drown the gale, the lashing rain, the flying spray.

What they therefore failed to hear was the *closeness* of sea to the house, encroaching like a monster in the dark. They felt the house shaking, quaking, and mightn't the walls be starting to tilt, but by this point they had finished three bottles of wine between them. They were in no position, Guy with his able arm merrily around Adèle's bony shoulders, to appreciate that this was actually the area's worst flash-storm in two hundred years, that the dunes were crumbling as the breakers smashed into them. The soft ground was being eaten from under their rhythm-tapping feet, and while the stylus slithered across the records and brought such tears of laughter to their eyes that they could hardly keep up their vocal din, their fate was being sealed.

It was the floorboards splitting which did for Guy, a maverick one rearing up, slugging him on the jaw, and sending him sprawling. As the house tipped thirty, then forty degrees, and the joists cracked like matchwood, Adèle ran towards her bedroom, blindly, perhaps remembering her fox-fur coat. But she never reached either. Instead she slid on a dropped, wet lettuce leaf, lost her balance, and landed – spread-eagled – on top of the supine, unconscious Guy, as if she was taking his manhood, with that animal passion she had confined under lock and key all her life, because hers – unlike his – was a manner of love she had kept close-closeted, which she had not dared let speak its name.

But by then it was far, far too late to discover her body's potential for abandon. The house, folding around them, was now unmoored and on the move, sliding at a rate of knots down its sand-piste, hurling itself (as if passion were its object too) for the bewitching, philandering, faithless, devouring sea.

79

Furlough

SUDDENLY fatigue was creeping upwards, from her feet and ankles to her knees to the backs of her thighs.

She took a single room in the Buckingham Hotel, as it was now called. The Stimptons had gone, and the hotel was owned and managed by in-comers to Aquae-Regis. They had attempted to modernise, but in a misguided way. The green-painted panelling remained, but the upturned vintage soup-bowl silk shades had been replaced by Scandinavian teak-and-glass teardrops. The loose covers were now less 'loose' than wash-down stretch fabric and patterned not with a chintz rose-garden but bright tangerine and yellow daisies and sunflowers. The leather chairs survived, and the pembroke tables, and the velvet pelmets and curtains, worn quite thin in places by the contact of fingers; the parquet hadn't been lost beneath fitted carpet, the rugs were the ones she remembered, but the roses and ferns in the bowls were plastic and the napkins in the dining-room were paper and disposable.

Looking into all the corners of her room, because she had nothing to fill them with (which had caused some puzzlement downstairs, until she explained that she was being entertained in a private house nearby and only needed somewhere to sleep), she found herself among the newspapers lining a drawer. There she was, depicted as 'The Spirit of Endeavour', accoutred in a Helmsley faille evening A-line (it had been the colour of flame) and standing beside a Jaguar racing-car decked out in an équipe's strip. The turnover of ideas had been especially speedy that season and too fast for the manufacture of memories – with the location runs and her appearance being constantly fussed over by maker-up and back-comber and dresser. It certainly hadn't occurred to her that Audrey, say, might see and have the past revisited on her, to have to be raked over like hot scorching coals.

Already she thought she looked a little as some of the models then still in vogue had seemed to her: formal, over-presented, too made-up, hinting at privilege when of course the opposite had been the intention, that she should seem an independent modern woman dressing just as the whim took her, going where she wanted whenever she wanted, to Hurlingham or Billingsgate Market, any time from dawn till midnight. Now she thought she belonged wholly to 1957, to Millicent Helmsley and her brothers, to the vision of the advertising agency. She had been popular, a fashion, quite the rage even, and therein was the problem: she would always now exist in a bubble of time, because of the archaism of previous fashion which created her – the faddishness, *ne plus ultra*, of the Helmsley approach must have become blindingly apparent to others in the same line as the fifties wore on.

She returned the sepia'd page of newspaper to its resting-place, smoothed it flat, and closed the drawer. *Sic transit gloria mundi*. And so it was that she belonged to the world, confirmed in her brief fame and final ephemerality. She couldn't be offended, because it was only the manner of change, and there must be ultimate truthfulness in that. Through the disappointment of nostalgia she was approaching, haltingly but with candidly dry eyes, something like the deadly dull sobriety of wisdom.

Her bed at the hotel was narrow and (figuratively) a veritable depository of nails, so she managed little rest. The building went quite still on all sides of her, and in the dead silence she started to hear those voices which she'd too readily imagined the shadows had claimed for themselves.

She tried to sleep, but couldn't. She got up and walked over to the window and pulled the curtains back. Her eyes opened wide at the view. Moonlight had frosted everything in the street, so that in two or three hours winter seemed to have supplanted summer. The stone of the houses glowed eerily, and the road shimmered like a pilgrim's path. The area railings gleamed, as if they weren't merely iron but rare, precious, and of inestimable worth. Her mother used to drag her hands along them, to make them sing, and that was how she, as Catherine Marlott, had lost one of the diamonds out of her engagement ring, through what the man she had married before Alan told her was carelessness. But she had only shrugged at that, to let him know that it was as important to her to try to strike melodies from metal railings as it was to keep a cut jewel in place on her fourth finger. As usual, *she* had been sitting between her parents when the subject of her mother's behaviour in public came up, and it was she who'd seemed to have the mute power of defusing the situation. Her (nominal) father had begun shaking his head, sternly and hopelessly, and her mother had started to nod hers, too, but abstractedly, as if in time to a tune *she* could hear but which they could not, struck on an iron harp of the streets.

She returned to bed, in her room in the Duke-less Buckingham Hotel.

She lay on her side, with both hands clasped beneath her cheek, how she had always, unfailingly, been able to find sleep as a child. All she had needed to do then, as she was trying to do now, was to imagine the rug unfurled that could transport her over roofs and chimneypots, over towers and steeples and cupolas, beyond the encircling rampart of hills and the further hills beyond that, and thus and thus and so on, to carry her high above the seas and lands that lay between here and the destination in her mind's eye, where chiming trees granted wishes and slippers had the magical power of motion and horses flew, and where the dead returned as night stars – luminescent eyes – to gently guide and protect.

80

'Tis Thus One Journeys to the Stars

IN the depths of the temple, *in regno lymphae*, in the Kingdom of the Waters.

Tradition has it that the springs, maintaining a mean temperature of 117 degrees Fahrenheit at efflux, derive their heat from the workings of a submerged volcano. Among its various active chemical agents, the water is charged with magnesia, two carbonates, two muriates, sulphate of potassa or alumina, iron, and common salt. A Victorian guidebook enumerated the virtues of an 'external employment' of the Aquae-Regis water: 'it stimulates the skin and strengthens the muscles; furthermore it will render supple stiff joints, animate paralytic limbs, and quicken the circulation.'

Before the Romans crossed the Channel from Gaul, the site was already sacred: here lived the pagan gods of health and rejuvenation. While slaughter and pillage disposed of the idolatrous descendants of Bladud, son of Lud Hudibras, King of Britain (whose great-father was Aeneas himself), the 'immortals' fell: but Minerva's camerilla had their comeuppance in turn, and some (although far from all) of their graven images were toppled to make way for those of their successors, the hordes of Angles and Saxons.

The source itself was beyond all such historical considerations, and offered to the Romans the same constant supply as previously, issuing to the surface in rumbling hot plenitude (half a million gallons a day) and in a mellifluous torrent of sulphurous steam. An ornamental pavilion was erected to accommodate the spring, perhaps to secrete it. At a later point an outer hall was built and the beneficent waters – Aquae Minervae – were channelled into it, and thence in time to a succession of lesser chambers providing steam-rooms. Later still the outer hall was rebuilt, and the annexed accommodation subsequently upgraded. The aspect was decidedly more imposing, and those who came to take advantage of the facilities were correspondingly grander. Embellishments were continually being added over decades – the open-roofed baths were expanded upwards; an elevated terrace was provided for the favoured; and finally the effigies of emperors were raised on plinths in tribute to the town's well-established importance.

A century later that importance was waning, and another century after that the age of the Romans was effectively at an end: or, rather, it ran down and became something else – the hesitant dawning of a hybrid era – and the best that could be hoped for then was an easy interim period of transition with as little wanton destruction of the material past as was feasible.

Some portions of the baths suffered, a couple of emperors who had claimed eternal life for themselves became victims of gravity's pull, but the Roman deities were more tenacious than the ancient native ones and refused to wholly give up what had been theirs. Their grip was indisputably loosened, and they were obliged to blend into the background for several centuries, obscured by the nests of untold generations of coot and teal; when they resurfaced to the light they found themselves regarded as eccentric relics of an alien civilisation, yet they held on to their dignity, just, and still gave a very convincing display of their powers.

For Catherine it had so long been a twice-daily occurrence to pass the formerly hallowed spot that she'd often ceased to give it a thought. The weather-nibbled emperors in togas or military tunics were a no more special feature of the skyline than the Abbey's West Tower or the cupola of the Nonagon Room; the partakers of the waters in the Pump Room were simply slow-coach hazards to be negotiated on the way to and from school, usually when her own time was tight; the regenerative virtues of the spring had been unnecessary to girls of her station with their lives (although in unspecified terms) still ahead of them.

It was her mother who had first brought her, without even the pretence of a history lesson. They would have tea and a buttered scone or shortbread petticoat-tail in the Pump Room, listen to the string trio on the podium, then fill a couple of the tumblers that stood on trays to taste the tepid, gritty water. After that they would pay their admission money – 3d to admit adult and child – and venture downstairs into the belly of the building.

Now she retraced her steps: firstly in the airier Georgian section, down gracious flights of balustraded steps and along corridors of green-and-white-checked floors.

To left and right were the white-tiled treatment-rooms where attendants in white coats, used to receive patients for sessions by injection, douche and dry pumping on rheumatism, gout, sciatica, lumbago, dyspepsia. Nothing was to be glimpsed by the passing eye: although once a door had been left open by mistake – and a second behind it – and she had seen into a small room equipped like a scientist's laboratory with a tin bath and a full assemblage of flexes and plugs and crocodile-pincers. Her mother had been halted by the fearsome sight and had shivered, more than dramatic effect might have required. Catherine had never forgotten, the memory had always been confused with the nether life of the building – the infernal armoury, her mother's hand squeezing her own, the evidence of strain suddenly etched on her face, before she'd hied them both away.

The doors were now closed as she walked past, but perhaps the treatment was only a superseded detail of the past, like the condition of their lives then. The corridor was still curiously oppressive, although it had breadth and height and the advantage of skylights. Visible forty or fifty feet above her were the emaciated, leprous emperors, and the forbidding Abbey tower and the perpetually wheeling birds, and the sensation she had now as she'd had then, even with her mother's hand to hold on to, was that she was descending into the bowels of the earth. Or into purgatory. Aunt Dodie had never brought her here, not once – nor her father either – so she'd had no occasion to try to cure or disprove the feeling. Curiously, it was Jennifer Moncrieff-King who had corroborated her own impressions, telling her once that *her* mother had become disinclined to talk after the second flight of stairs, that the sight of the billowing steam seemed to leave her cold and that she would become silent and withdrawn the closer they got to the hot water of the baths and the source itself.

'What's the point, then?' had struck Catherine as being the sensible question to ask in those days when they did still talk.

'She just takes it into her head sometimes.'

'But *why* do you go?'

'Because she buys us hot chocolate afterwards, to cheer herself up.'

Ever-mercenary Jennifer, the Brigadier's only daughter, she had lived her life and lost it true to her form.

Why the hell should she start thinking about her now?

Then, through the hot mist, she sees her mother.

She's wearing a black woollen dress she has forgotten all about. In her latter days – how did she manage not to remember? – her mother always wore black. 'Very theatrical, Marguerite,' the man she had married would tell her, but she would only shake her head at him, as if it must be her part and not his to exercise compassion, to show a tender heart.

Her name is called. 'Catherine! Catherine!'

The voice is a synthesis of all her mother suffered, but it lacks self-pity.

'Caath-erine!'

Then the swirling mist comes between them again and the figure disappears. Catherine holds out her arms but her hands blur, they turn raggedly to cloud. Her loneliness is total and unbearable.

She calls after her.

'Mother – !'

But all she hears is water, boiling up through rock and spurting from its source. Water, and the constant, grave weight of sweating stone.

She starts to run in pursuit, feet treading on cloud.

'Mother – !'

For an instant merely she catches sight of the face. The distress which the word has caused is all too visible.

And then the steam begins to redouble, folding over on itself. The figure loses definition and melts back into the barm.

Catherine chases after it. She reaches out her hands, deep into cloud, but they make contact with nothing. She grasps at clammy, duplicitous air.

'*Mother* – !'

She listens for a reply but hears no more than she did before – the water and the stone.

In regno lymphae. She is at the heart of the temple.

She turns in several directions, but she has lost all her bearings. There are moments when the steam thins and through it she seems to be distinguishing shapes, but the resemblances are elusive, and perhaps illusory. The steam curdles again and as perspectives recede and disappear altogether she is left with the equivocalness of her hands waving in front of her face like sea fronds.

She cannot see further than three or four inches.

Beneath her feet the solidity of the stone flags is less than it was. The floor seems to be courting insubstance.

Nonetheless she continues in motion.

The heat clings to her like a second skin. She feels the breath being stifled inside a box in her chest.

For a couple of seconds she senses the presence of a shadow – a deeper gradation of grey – falling across her.

She stops and looks back over her shoulder. The mist eddies to reveal the shoulder of a man's dark overcoat, and she has the briefest of glimpses of a black homburg hat before the figure is consumed by another backwash of the humid rack.

Blood pummels inside her head and she stands listening for any sound outside herself. She cannot be certain, though, one way or the other. She opens her mouth and swallows down gulps of hot, dank, fenny air. She blinks into the nimbus but sees nothing.

She continues moving the other way. Perspiration oozes cold against her skin, while all the time the temperature of the space is increasing. The moisture starts to drizzle as spindrift on her face and she realises she is drawing closer and closer to the well-head.

She watches for her mother, her ears are primed to hear her. She travels on in a feverish swash. She has never properly imagined this tropical pluvial fire undermining all their days.

All she *can* be certain of is that her mother went here before her. Jericho, she understands now, was the final resting-place of not only those who couldn't afford otherwise, but the rare misfits of Beaulieu and Paradise Hills – the unbelievers, the villains, and the suicides.

The sorry last months and their tragic conclusion had been intentionally kept from her, but anyway obfuscation had only been the tenor of later events as they concerned her mother. Jennifer alone, the Brigadier's slain daughter, had let drop a clue, that her own mother had been frightened of descending too deep beneath the Pump Room, into the subjacent regions so far beneath respectable, balanced existence. In windswept Atlantic City the sneering accusation had been of immorality, but no other than her own brother came to her defence and denied it. In the Hollywood Hills she had read her mother's letter of twenty-five years before, articulating her confusion and predicting her despair, and there she had the evidence of her own eyes and memory: those days of frenetic tranquillity they'd spent together in Devon, in the cottage on the edge of the forest, sixty-six steps above the secret horseshoe cave, and the sessions in another little cottage, of bald red Scottish sandstone, where she was taken to be uncomplicated of her imagination, which was in truth her only defence against the callous business of the world. A life, after all, is lived at the mercy of others' pride and indomitable will, which may only be the external aspect of their fearfulness but which succeeds through intimidation. On the kitchen floor of Davaar, holding Doktor Mandelbaum in her arms, she had seen through the authority of her discipline as she wasn't meant to; the poor, unhappy woman's confidence collapsed and she herself was transposed further back than any of them could have had reason to suspect, to the wisdom she'd had lying in her mother's womb, taking form out of love and desire and recklessness, preserved in a bloody cocoon of dreaming and fear.

*

In the mist reality was falling away, and she realised it had never actually been sufficiently 'there' to count.

She turned a circle, with her arms stretched out and her hands open and her fingers reaching as far as they could: to the lengths and ends of herself.

Gradually, out of the mist she saw a fissure take shape. She moved towards it. The crevice appeared to widen. She still held her hands out in front of her. They seemed to fill the space, and the crack seemed to be opening to accommodate her.

Her hands, her wrists, her forearms, her elbows –

Heat blew up into her face. She closed her eyes and turned her cheek. She felt an almighty compelling strength pulling on her arms. She was unable to resist, and it was the last thing she knew.

In less than an instant she was stretched flat, to an endless thin shadow, she was being transported through a hot enveloping tube in a sourceless glow, lighter than air and faster than sound . . .

Now an eye – this eye of mine – watches her through a crack in the wall, in the dusty shuttered room.

She stares across at the gleaming pupil, like the brilliant point of a pin, on which the angels balance. My watching iris is brown, like those of the only love of her life, but a wall would not hold *them* apart now. She will find him.

But in the meantime she will leave a clue for the flesh of their flesh. She remembers something – anything – the silk scarf with the barouches, and it flutters to the floor. It lies there with – what else? –

– with the sliced heads of some yellow roses.

I shall remember, their son.

The eye – this eye of mine – is still here at the rift, it continues to watch her. In the eye's pupil, between the narrowing upper lid and the underlid, she sees the sinuous arabesque of the scarf and the drift of yellow rose petals. There is no sign of herself reflected back.

Now she is ready to panic, until she remembers – or, rather, until her child remembers for her.

So long as she is borne in mind, there is hope.

Then all is gossamer light again in the shuttered room in the old house in the western English city. She wonders, she wonders how long it will be – how long she will have to wait here until Maurice comes to find her and they can leave.

RONALD FRAME

PENELOPE'S HAT

'Sinuously clever'
The Sunday Times

'A very readable narrative by a considerable talent'
Evening Standard

'A dazzling, diverting read'
The Daily Telegraph

'Fascinating in a subtly observed way'
New Woman

'Frame has a conjuror's dexterity and a real gift for invention which make him a marvellous storyteller'
Literary Review

'This is by far Ronald Frame's best novel. It lifts him into the top flight of novelists of his generation'
Allan Massie in The Scotsman

SANDMOUTH PEOPLE

'A genuine piece of original writing . . . dealing with one day (St George's Day) in the life of a small but wealthy English seaside town in the 50s. This is a marvellous picture of England at a fixed point of time. Mr Frame has caught his characters in a sort of literary aspic. Ambitious as any literary effort so far this year and, what's more, a thoroughly good read'
Stanley Reynolds in Punch

'Ambitious . . . he writes stylishly and wittily and takes a great stride forward with this book. It's also cleverly plotted and builds up to an unexpected climax'
Susan Hill in Good Housekeeping

'A triumph'
William Leith in The Guardian

'A strange, haunting, evocative novel. A very unusual talent'
Margaret Drabble